To Dorothy & R
with

THE YOUNG COLONIALS

BARBARA ANSLOW

THE YOUNG COLONIALS
by
BARBARA ANSLOW

ISBN 1 897 66611 X

Printed in Great Britain by
Seddon Printers, Bolton BL1 4TH.

SYNOPSIS
of
THE YOUNG COLONIALS

A novel set in the Far East between 1929 and 1945

When in 1929 ten-year-old Pamela returns to Hong Kong with her parents and elder brother and sister after nine months' leave in England, she expects to resume her idyllic colonial life, but Portuguese and Eurasian companions introduce disturbing elements which result in her being sent to school in England the following year.

She rediscovers the joys of Hong Kong in 1937 when she rejoins her family and takes an office job, but always in the background of this luxurious life lurks the increasingly militant attitude of Japan. Pamela's choice of boyfriend brings her up against the social attitudes prevalent in the colony. She stays on in Hong Kong when her parents retire to England in 1938. When in 1940 a threat from Japan results in the sudden evacuation of British women and children to Australia, Pamela defies her parents' urgent cables to leave with the evacuees, and eventually has to face the Japanese attack and capture of Hong Kong and subsequent internment for three and a half years.

Some of Pamela's friends are with her in the camp, others (including her brother) are scattered throughout the Far East; how all these young colonials fare in their changed circumstances is the hub of this story.

THE YOUNG COLONIALS

AUTHOR'S NOTE

All the characters are fictitious; in particular, "Sandra" bears no relation whatsoever to the real-life nurse, Marie Paterson, who crept out of the Happy Valley Jockey Club Hospital under the noses of the Japanese guards and went for help to stop the atrocities there.

Original cover art by Maureen Rossi and Mabel Large

Dedicated to all those who perished during the Battle and Fall of Hong Kong in December 1941 and in the subsequent Occupation.

by Barbara Anslow

PART 1

1929 - 1930

JULY

Pamela twisted restlessly on the top bunk in the hot cabin. Though only wearing vest and knickers, she was damp with perspiration. No breeze came through the open porthole, and the tiny wall ventilator trained on to her face barely lifted her bobbed chestnut hair, for second class Cabin D261 was on the starboard side of RMS 'Rawalpindi' thrusting through the Indian Ocean taking her and her family back to their home in Hong Kong after nine months' leave in England.

"Is it time to go swimming yet?" she asked her eighteen-year-old sister Belle who was lying neatly on the lower bunk in her petticoat..

"That's the third time you've woken me to ask!" yawned Belle. "I'm sure I wasn't such a pest when I was ten." She squinted at her watch. "It's twenty past three so you might as well go now - I might get some peace then." She had been dancing until after midnight; had played deck tennis all the morning; and now, in mid-afternoon after a heavy curry lunch was recharging her batteries for the evening's frivolities.

Pamela slithered swiftly off the bunk and struggled into her orange swimming costume. Draped in a white towel with the red letters 'P & O' woven across one end, she shuffled into her rubber slippers and padded into the empty corridor, past her parents' cabin and the neighbouring one occupied by her brother Roddy and another boy - both fourteen years old they disdained the afternoon swimming session when the water in the pool was lowered for children.

Until the weather had become warm enough for swimming she had been very lonely, for all the children she met at Junior Meal times were far too young to be playmates during the rest of the day. Mothers of toddlers tried to appropriate her as assistant nursemaid; she became an unwanted hanger-on to Roddy or Belle until summarily dismissed; her mother suggested she read her school books, or even worse, practised her scales on the piano in the lounge. There was nothing to do between meals except wander into the writing-room and draw on the crested P & O note-paper until evicted by disapproving adults. Life changed when a canvas swimming-pool was erected at one end of the first class deck, and children from both classes invited to use it in midafternoon every day. Here, at last, she met some contemporaries - three firstclass passengers who, for a precious hour each day, provided the company she craved.

Once through the low gate separating the second class deck from the first, her heart began to flutter at the uncertainty of her reception by The Others, as she Mentally termed the first class children. Sometimes they were friendly, other times maddeningly superior ("What does your Father do in the Government? - He can't be very important as you're travelling second.") They were returning to

Shanghai which they continually boasted was vastly superior to Hong Kong.

They were already in the pool: John and Humphrey and the latter's young sister Fay. As soon as she climbed in they grinned and waved... everything was all right today! The slight motion of the liner, together with the artificial churning caused by threshing limbs, sent great gouts of water crashing over the rim of the pool and out on to the deck. Here was Heaven, Pamela thought - all too soon interrupted by the appearance at the top of the outside ladder of Ben, the grizzled old deck hand. This was the signal to leave. Usually the children could beg successfully for five minutes more, but today Ben shook his head.

"Out you get,"he grunted. "Got to get this lot stowed away by six; then get the hatches open ready for cargo work tomorrow. Not far off Bombay now... smell it already."

One by one they clambered out of the pool then deliberately slithered on the streaming deck, screaming and sky-larking.

"Cut out that noise!" This was Humphrey's father, dressed in white, his knee-length shorts almost meeting his long socks; he was calling from the deck above the pool. "Your mother and I are going to tea now - mind you and Fay get tidied up in time for your supper!"

Humphrey gave obedient acknowledgment, then added in a whisper to Pamela "While they're out of the way, you can come and see our cabin, if you like. I bet it's much bigger than yours."

Curiosity got the better of pride, especially as this invitation represented a step forward in the acquaintanceship for which Pamela thirsted. Eyes cast down, she followed The Others along the sacred accommodation corridors, praying that no adult would notice an alien entering a first class cabin.

"There!" Humphrey swished aside the curtain at the cabin's entrance. "John and I share this - what do you think of it?"

"It IS a little bigger than ours," Pamela allowed, "and you've got a window instead of a porthole: but I like portholes better, they're more ship-like."

"I like portholes best too," put in Fay eagerly, but Humphrey silenced her with a frown.

"We've got a little table too," John pointed out, "instead of just those pullout things in the dressing-table. Look!"

"I'd rather have a pull-out," said Pamela carefully. "You can have real tables any old time, when you're on dry land."

"But there's not enough room for four people to sit round a pull-out and play cards," Humphrey persisted. "Shall we have a game of Beat-Your-Neighbour-Out-of-Doors now?" He was dragging forward the two chairs. "John and I can sit on these because it's our cabin, and you and Fay can sit on my bunk."

Pamela hesitated - "But our costumes are wet."

"Sit on your towel, donkey!"

Her excitement at having been accepted further into The Others' circle was tempered by the anxiety of being discovered by Humphrey's parents making a damp patch on the bedclothes with her wet towel, and once into the game she was torn between hoping she would not win which would be a poor way of showing gratitude for having been included - and a fiendish desire to beat the other three.

The game was never finished. Humphrey suddenly snatched all the cards and crammed them back into the box. "Better go now," he told Pamela. "There'd be dreadful trouble if you were caught here."

As she leapt up he added "Now don't you admit this cabin is miles better than yours?"

"I like mine best," she picked her words with care. "I expect you like yours best, too." She longed to add "I don't really want to play with you again because you're so mean to me" but lacked the courage: besides, how could she exist for the remainder of the voyage without their company? She ducked her head and fled.

Her parents were adamant: they were not going ashore in Bombay; it was too hot; they had been to Bombay before and, in response to Pamela's final plea, they were not going because They Said So. When Belle and Roddy sought and obtained permission to go ashore with a chaperoned group of teenagers, Pamela begged unsuccessfully to accompany them. She had to resign herself to a day of utter boredom: no swimming, and no Others - she had already watched them file down the gangway behind their parents.

"Never mind Pam," Her mother patted her bare arm sympathetically. "You can have a nice lazy day reading, and you can have lunch with us as Rod and Belle won't be back until much later."

This concession helped the day along, but the afternoon dragged. Her parents retired for the inevitable rest. Pamela tried to do the same but the cabin was hotter than ever as the porthole was closed against would-be pilferers from the wharf only inches away. She got up and wandered aloft in search of some diversion. Alas, all the stationery had prudently been removed from the writing room. There was no one to talk to in the lounge, and no comfort in its stuffy upholstered sofas and armchairs; the decks, even on the shady side, were excruciatingly hot. Listlessly she leaned against the great ornate staircase that wound from the lounge down to the dining saloon and accommodation decks, then pressed her back against the mahogany rails and sidled crabwise down the stairs.

"Whatever are you doing Pam?" - Her parents, freshly clothed and on their way to afternoon tea, suddenly materialised at the foot of the staircase.

"Nothing," she shrugged. "There's nothing TO do. Can I come to tea with you?"

"You certainly can't - you know that," said her father.

"No one minded when I came to grownup lunch.."

"Give you an inch and you want a mile," her father growled.

"What about doing some piano practice?" smiled her mother. "You've done hardly any since we came on board. Now's an ideal time, with all the adults away or at tea. Off you go to the cabin and get your music!"

With the noisiest sigh she could muster, Pamela obeyed. She had no interest in music, and only tolerated the weekly lessons in Hong Kong from Mrs. Russell, a Portuguese widow, because her son Danny was always waiting outside to play afterwards, often with his cousins Marcus and Celeste. Once seated at the ship's piano, she found her fingers stiff from lack of practice; the theoretical daily half-hour's practice in her grandparents' home while on leave had been easy to dodge.

When the first adult sauntered into the lounge she quickly closed the piano lid and ambled on to the deck, watching for the return of Belle and Roddy, who surely would bring her a present to compensate for her boring day?

Two adults and three children were walking up the gangway - a uniformed stout soldier, a tall thin woman with a white broad-brimmed hat; two small girls whose faces were almost obliterated by their white toadstool topees, and an older boy in khaki shirt and shorts who wrenched off his topee the moment he reached the shaded deck; his hair was sandy, his eyes blue, and his thin freckled face was pink with the heat.

The soldier handed a document to the duty officer at the gangway and announced: "Mrs. Tait, wife of Sergeant Tait of R.A.O.C. Also Philip Tait, Teresa Tait and Mary Tait. Proceeding to Hong Kong. To be met there by Sergeant Tait. Little nipper here" - jerking a thumb at the younger girl - "got measles so this lot had to stay behind when Sergeant Tait's draft left for Hong Kong last month."

"Mrs. Tait and three children - Cabin 305 on D deck," nodded the officer.

"The same deck as us," thought Pamela happily.

She contrived to sit next to the boy at tea, saying boldly "My name's Pamela, I'm going to Hong Kong too. You're Philip, aren't you? I heard that soldier say your names."

"I saw you," he nodded, responding readily to her attempts at conversation. He was almost eleven; he'd lived longer in India than in England; he wanted to be a boxer when he grew up. After tea he disappeared for so long that she thought he must have gone to bed, but eventually he hailed her on the deck, explaining he had been minding the girls in the cabin while his mother dined.

Together they watched the last of the cargo being winched aboard, the final shift of laughing coolies riding ashore clinging to the great rope nets at the end of the crane on the wharf. When her mother sought her out at nine o'clock and decreed bedtime, Pamela pleaded in vain to be allowed to stay up until the ship sailed at midnight. The row of little black elephants on her dressing-table - a gift from Belle - was little consolation as she lay sleepless in the breathless cabin. The steward came in to open the porthole; she felt the first throb of the engines as they came to life; heard the distinctive croup-like P & O hooter; the splash as the released hawsers hit the water. Gradually a tiny breeze stole through the porthole, carrying with it a smell of putrid jetsam and over-ripe fruit. "I've got a friend, I've got a friend," she whispered to the rhythm of the engines.

Now the days were not long enough for all there was to do. She shared Philip's duties of looking after his sisters; when free, they ranged round the ship, exploring and chattering.

The first time she led him to the swimming pool The Others looked through him.

"Hullo Pam!" called Humphrey in a theatrically cheerful voice. "Thought you were never coming! Wondered if you'd been left behind in Bombay."

"I didn't go ashore. I say, you lot.." she began to introduce Philip, but Humphrey dived for her ankles and pulled her underwater. John hurled himself on top of them and Fay gleefully joined in. Philip stayed on the rope ladder, studiously looking away from them. He was still there when Pamela pulled away from the melee and realised that The Others intended treating him as the outsider she had once been.

"Philip is my friend," she announced firmly. "He got on at Bombay. He's going to Hong Kong."

"That dump!" Humphrey sneered.

"Can't he talk?" John's face was hostile. "Or swim?"

"Both!" Philip grinned, as he leapt in and executed a double somersault under water.

"I can do that too," John added, and the pool frothed as both of them tried over and over again to emulate Philip's demonstration. The resultant furore brought old Ben's concerned face in view over the rim of the pool.

"It's not a fight, Ben," spluttered Fay. "It's a game, we're just having fun."

That was the way it was from then on. Sometimes Philip just laughed when John and Humphrey boasted; other times he responded with ridiculously extravagant counterboasts. They argued endlessly but they became firm friends.

The pool was emptied after Singapore because of very heavy weather, but Pamela and Philip made the daily pilgrimage to the first class deck in case it had been refilled. By arrangement they met The Others there and stayed talking as long as they dared.

The morning Hong Kong came in sight the gate between the first and second class was opened to enable officials to pass freely. Pamela and Philip walked boldly across to join The Others at the ship's rail.

"Lovely, gorgeous Hong Kong again!" sighed Pamela as the morning mist dissolved around the humps of green mountains ahead. The ship dropped speed dramatically and nosed through Lye Mun, the narrow channel separating mainland Kowloon from the north-western tip of Hong Kong Island. She had forgotten the majesty of the soaring green peaks, the busyness of the harbour criss-crossed with ships small and large, sampans and junks. Importantly she pointed out landmarks to Philip. "See The Peak" indicating the great mountain in the centre of the island. "There's a cable tram to take you up it. Rich people have houses there.."

"That's where we're going today," put in John laconically. "My father's friends live there. We're invited to spend the day with them, and I've got to amuse their daughter - she's much younger than me... will want me to play with dolls, I expect.. ugh!"

"We live on the island," Pamela was continuing. "In Happy Valley; look, over there, where you can see the race-course."

"Where will you live, Phil?" Fay asked.

"Don't know. My Dad will tell us when he meets us."

Pamela said "You've still got my address, haven't you Phil?" To their disappointment they had discovered that he would not be joining her at the Central British School as there was an Army School in Hong Kong.

He pulled a crumpled sheet of P & O note-paper from his trouser pocket and read out "Number 28, Wong Nei Cheong Road; goodness knows how I'll ever find that!"

Holding her hands over her tell-tale amber curls, Sandra Smithson peered cautiously through the balustrade round the flat roof of her home on The Peak. She watched the family car turn on to the main road and out of sight and hugged herself with delight.

After breakfast that morning she had crept up the narrow staircase to the roof and crouched behind the store room, giggling to herself at the shouts of the servants below as they searched for her. She heard Ming the chauffeur start the car in the garage and drive it to the front of the house; heard her mother's terse instructions to the amah Ah Ling: "Ming will be back with the car in half an hour. Bring Missee Sandra to No. 8 Wharf by ten o'clock. Savvy? Ten o'clock!"

By then, Sandra thought happily, she would be with the Johnsons in their house nearby, ready to join their all-day launch picnic, the prospect of which had prompted her to evade the duty trip to Kowloon to meet business friends of her father's.

Now that her parents had left, she dared to leave the roof on her way to the Johnsons, confident that she could outrun the servants; there was no one in sight as she ran down the stairs, but as she reached the front door Ah Ling suddenly darted out of the lounge and seized her arm.

"Why so naughty girl?" she shouted. "I call, why you no come? Must get ready quickly go Kowloon-side!"

"I'm not going to Kowloon!" Sandra spoke in Cantonese because Ah Ling's knowledge of English was limited. "I'm going to the Johnsons' picnic. Don't you dare try to stop me!"

As she struggled to escape, she bit the amah's arm savagely. Ah Ling loosened her grip so suddenly that Sandra overbalanced and banged her forehead on the corner of the blackwood hall stand. Her screams of rage turned to yelps of pain, increasing dramatically when blood trickled down her forehead on to her cheeks and dress. She could fight no longer, and allowed herself to be helped to the bathroom to have the wound bathed and plastered, her face washed, dress changed and hair tidied. Uttering hopeless little sobs she was led to the car where, her white topee across her knees, she lay back during the drive down the winding mountain road to the city. She was silent when they reached the jetty and she was hurried on to the launch belonging to her father's firm for the short journey across the harbour. The clock on the tower above the Kowloon-Canton Railway showed half past ten and, remembering her mother's instructions, Sandra's heart quaked a little. On arrival at the wharf she was relieved to see that although the gangways were attached to the Rawalpindi a knot of people stood round the base of each, so boarding had not yet started.

"You're here at last!" her mother greeted her coldly. "Belong very late, Ah Ling! And Sandra, I'll speak to you later about this morning's behaviour."

"Never mind Gwen, they're in good time - lucky the ship was late getting clearance," said her father. "My Sandra, whatever have you done to yourself?"

"Missee fall and bump head," said Ah Ling quickly. "All right now."

"It was all her fault!" Sandra glared at Ah Ling.

"Do you feel all right now darling?" Her father tipped back her topee to see the extent of the plaster on her forehead; his face was so concerned that she saw a way to stave off her mother's fury. She burst into noisy sobs and threw herself about in a frenzy. Her father and Ah Ling cuddled and soothed her with such satisfying attention that she decided to prolong her sobs as long as she could.

The children on the upper deck viewed the scene on the wharf with curiosity.

"Whatever's wrong with that kid?" asked John.

"Just spoiled, I should think," sniffed Humphrey. "Do you know her, Pam?"

"No - and don't want to!"

"Phew ! " There was almost admiration in Philip's voice. "What a temper she has - she's trying to hit the amah helping her up the gangway!"

John's mother was hailing him from further along the deck: "Come with Dad and me to meet Mr. and Mrs. Smithson and their little girl Sandra who are just coming aboard."

Humphrey, Fay, Pamela and Philip watched with interest as John followed his parents to the head of the gangway where they met the couple with the bad-tempered little girl. The adults moved towards the lounge while John led the child and her amah over to his friends. His agonised expression clearly said 'Help me out!' as he politely introduced Sandra.

"How old are you?" Fay asked at once.

"Nine."

"You're only as big as me, and I'm eight.. Have you always lived in Hong Kong?"

"Except for Leaves."

"Humphrey and John and me all live in Shanghai. What happened to your head?"

"She" - with a glare at the amah - "pulled me over."

Ah Ling took off Sandra's topee, produced a comb and made to tidy the damp crushed curls..

"Oh stop it Ah Ling!" With a fierce movement Sandra pushed her away. "Leave me alone, I don't want you always hanging round me." She poured out a torrent of Cantonese, and the amah obediently padded to the far end of the deck and hovered there.

"Whatever did you say to the poor old thing?" Pamela asked.

"I told her things about her ancestors, like our Cook Boy does," Sandra giggled. "It's all her fault I had to come here this morning. I hid and my parents had to leave without me, then Ah Ling caught me and brought me."

"Why didn't you want to come to the ship?" Fay demanded.

"Because I'd been invited to a picnic with the Johnsons next door, an all day launch picnic, that's why. Anyway, I know the Johnsons, I don't know any of you!"

"What a charming child," drawled Humphrey. "Are there more like that in Hong Kong, Pam?"

"Don't know," shrugged Pamela, stifling a giggle.

Sandra turned to her and demanded "Do you live here too then? - Hong Kong side or Kowloon?"

"Happy Valley."

Which school do you go to?"

"Central British."

"I go to the Peak School, but I'm supposed to go to Central British next year - unless they force me to go to boarding-school in England."

"I should think they'd be glad to, if you always carry on like you did this morning," said Humphrey.

Sandra glared at him until Philip said sympathetically: "I'd be jolly fed up if I had to go and meet strangers instead of having a beach picnic." At once her face cleared and she became a different person. She beamed and chattered, and had the others laughing in fits when she impersonated Ah Ling remonstrating with her.

"Glad to see you're all getting on so well," smiled John's father as he ambled towards them. "It's time to be moving off - you too, Humphrey and Fay, Mr. and Mrs. Smithson have invited you and your parents to their house as well."

"Oh goody!" whooped Sandra. "And Philip and Pamela too?"

"I expect their parents have other plans," John's father said smoothly. The other adults appeared and Sandra dashed over to her father and begged "Can Pamela and Philip come too Daddy?"

"Not now I'm afraid," he smiled. "Very glad to meet you, Pamela and Philip. I hope you can visit us some other time."

"But I want them to come today, Daddy, they're my new friends!" cried Sandra, her voice rising as Pamela and Philip, faces the colour of beetroot, edged backwards towards the second class deck.

"Another day, darling; it's impossible now, you know," said her father gently.

"Really, I must go, my Dad will be on board by now," Philip muttered, moving away.

"Come with us, come with us!" Sandra tried to hold him back, but her father took her hand.

"Tell Daddy where you live, then!"

"I don't know yet..."

"Pamela, you tell Daddy where you live! Give him your address and then we can find you again. Daddy, write it down!"

"Of course." Her father pulled out diary and pen and Pamela, completely overcome with embarrassment,whispered her address. How relieved she was to hear Belle calling plaintively from the second class half of the deck that she was wanted immediately so they could disembark.

Squeezed between Chinese coolies on the lower deck of the cross-harbour ferry, the two dark-skinned children in European clothes were overwhelmed by the smells of crowded humanity, baskets full of fish, meat and vegetables, and acrid cigarette smoke..

"Sorry we have to travel second class, Celeste." Danny, the elder child, spoke in Portuguese; he had a protective arm round his small cousin; from the narrow bench her legs dangled one thinner than the other. "We'll come back first class, don't you worry."

"But how will we get home at all if you don't get any money on the ship?" Celeste's round face, framed with a short bob of glossy black hair, was creased with anxiety.

"I'll get plenty, you'll see!" - Thank goodness she had called on him that morning and boasted about the marvellous revolving pencil her brother Marcus had bought Pamela for a coming-home present! Such an idea had not occurred to him, and he couldn't have beared to greet Pamela empty-handed while Marcus handed over the pencil - yet where could he get money for a comparable gift? His twenty-five cents weekly pocket money was already spent, and he knew from experience it was no use asking his mother for more; he had to find a way of earning some. Meeting a liner at Kowloon Wharf and offering to carry luggage for passengers was all he could think of at short notice. The difficulty of the ferry fare to Kowloon was solved by taking Celeste with him; she gladly handed over the remains of her pocket money - a five-cent piece; luckily there was no charge for a child of her size.

-"But it's only a loan," he had insisted. "You'll get it back - doubled. It's an 'Empress' ship I'm going to - I'm sure to do well there because most of the passengers are Americans and they're all rich."

Once ashore, he rubbed his black shoes shiny with one corner of his handkerchief, smoothed down his short blue trousers and re-tucked his white short-sleeved shirt. "Got to look smart for the job," he grinned at Celeste's grave attention. He patted his hair firmly: both children were bare-headed - only pale-skinned Europeans wore topees. Because Celeste had to use one hand to brace her deformed leg progress from the ferry terminus to the docks was slow, until Danny motioned to her to get on to his back.

"I'll spoil your clothes," she sighed as she put her arms round his neck.

"I'll fix them again."

"Is this Pamela's ship?" Celeste laboriously spelt out the letters on the black prow of the Rawalpindi, dwarfed by the white Empress of Canada berthed further along the docks.

"Yes, it got in ages ago. Pam will be in her house already."

"Do you think she's gone to visit us?"

"Mother of God, I hope not!" It would be unbearable if he were not there with Marcus to greet her. "Look Celie, I won't be able to take you on the ship with me." There was no need to explain how she would impede his work. "You sit here, beside this bollard; it will be rather hot, so I'll make you a hat." Deftly he knotted the four corners of his handkerchief and pulled it over her hair; she laughed up at him with love in her eyes.

He walked purposefully towards the ship. It was easy to follow visitors up the gangway and through the labyrinth of corridors, always watching out for prospective customers. A plump middle-aged woman took his attention as she waved frantically at a coolie who was moving off with a large suitcase; perspiration oozed through her pink dress.

He said in his fluent English "Can I help you, ma'am - I can speak Chinese."

"Oh!" She looked down at him, obviously doubting the ability of one so young to be of assistance. "Well, little boy, how very kind of you!" With a podgy hand she pushed back masses of bright ginger hair from her florid face. "My steward has disappeared. I want to tell that man with my suitcase that there's another one in the cabin."

"Right, ma'am." In a few sentences, Danny transformed the puzzled coolie into a laughing, co-operative assistant, while the pink lady, whose luggage proclaimed her in white letters to be Kay Holtz, looked on in relieved admiration. How was she to know that Danny had suggested that the pink lady's luggage might include the sheets and blankets from her cabin?

They walked in procession towards the gangway deck, the coolie leading with the heaviest suitcase, Danny with a smaller one, and Kay Holtz with an enormous handbag and a portable typewriter.

"I'm sure I wrote the hotel to send someone to meet me.. " She was halted temporarily in the narrow corridor by a troupe of baggage coolies forging past in the opposite direction. "Hi, little boy!"she called agitatedly after Danny, who was eeling his way among the coolies, "Wait for me... I don't want to lose sight of my cases.. they have my valuable manuscripts."

She was breathless with anxiety and exhaustion when she caught up with Danny, the coolie and her luggage on the disembarkation deck. Danny pulled forward a deck chair into which she sank gratefully; she patted his head with a moist be-ringed hand and mopped her face with a large handkerchief, saying "You really are a most thoughtful little boy! What's your name?...... Daniel? You a passenger, Daniel? I didn't notice you on board before."

"No ma'am, I'm just here to help.. Which hotel are you going to stay at, Mrs. Holtz?"

"You noticed my ring!" She beamed broadly. "I've only been married a year, and what do you know, kind Mr. Holtz gave me a cheque to make this trip to the Orient! I been wanting to travel East all my life, because I'm a writer you see, and writers should go everywhere and do everything."

"The hotel," he prodded, "which hotel is it?"

"King Edward, Victoria. Do you know where it is?"

"It's on Hong Kong side, ma'am - on the island. Properly, the island's name is Victoria (after that Queen, you know); but here we always mean the island when we say Hong Kong. This side of the harbour, where we are now, is Kowloon - that's Chinese for Nine Dragons, for the nine hills in the mountains behind."

"That's very interesting Daniel," she said politely, but her eyes were darting everywhere as she continued to fret at the non-appearance of a representative from the hotel. Danny saw a chance to extend his role as porter: "Don't worry Mrs. Holtz, I can take you to the King Edward. If you're ready to leave, we'll take a wallah wallah across the harbour."

"Wallah.. what?"

"Wallah wallahs are little motor boats, much quicker than the ferries most people use; and they're just the other side of this wharf." It was imperative to him that they travel by wallah wallah for he would be unable to help Celeste all the way to the ferry terminus as well as carry the suitcase; he also calculated that Mrs. Holtz would be more likely to pay the demanded charge for the little party on the wallah wallah than hand him over his individual fare to go through the turnstyle at the ferry terminus..

"O.K. Daniel, lead the way, you're in charge," smiled Mrs. Holtz, allowing him to haul her to her feet.

"There's just one thing." Danny paused at the foot of the gangway. "Would you mind if my cousin came with us in the boat? She's that little girl waiting for me over there."

"Surely not. How cute she looks!"

"Oh no!" Mrs. Holtz was horrified when she saw the battered tiny motorboats below the wharf. "I couldn't travel in one of those! Isn't there something bigger?"

"They're quite safe," Danny assured her. "Quite a lot of people travel in them, especially late at night when the ferries have stopped running."

"Where's this ferry?"

He pointed to the green ferry, its upper deck be-ringed with life-belts, approaching the terminus.

"That's more like it" said Mrs. Holtz. "I'll wait for that."

"It doesn't come here," he explained. "The terminus is outside these docks.. a long walk."

"But I could never get on this tiny thing!" Mrs. Holtz stared unhappily down at the worn green-slimed steps from which she would have to board the swaying craft below. "I just couldn't do it. Anyway, I'd be afraid of tipping the boat over, with my weight."

"It's quite safe, really it is, Mrs. Holtz! And much more exciting than going on a ferry. Didn't you say writers should try everything so they can write about everything?"

"You're right, Daniel! O.K. then, here goes!" But she panicked at the last moment, moaning "No, no, I'll fall off the steps, I know it!"

She didn't though, thanks to the wallah wallah man whose bronze bare arms became like steel rods as he reached up to help her. Now she was proud and happy, laughing when the boat bucked its way across the harbour skirting the prows of anchored steamers and swerving round junks. Celeste became violently sick, and hung over the gunwale with Danny's arm tightly round her.

"She's too little for this," said Mrs. Holtz sympathetically.

"She's older than she looks - she's seven.. and she plays the piano marvellously, she's one of my mother's star pupils."

"Your mother teaches piano?"

"Yes Mrs. Holtz." He suddenly saw the lead he wanted and added quickly "She has to work because my father is dead. That's why.. why I do these small jobs like helping on ships, then I don't need to ask her for money." There, he had said it! Ever since he'd taken charge of Mrs. Holtz he had agonised that she might think he was doing so out of kindness and not offer him any reward.

I see," nodded Mrs. Holtz. "Well, Daniel, I think it's very noble of you to try to help your mother like this. You the only child?"

"Yes Mrs. Holtz, but Celeste's like a sister to me."

Celeste twisted round and smiled happy agreement.

"So you're a prize pianist!" said Mrs. Holtz. "I'd like to hear you play some day."

"Danny and me are going to play in a concert at Government House next month, Danny plays violin," Celeste volunteered in her careful English..

"Both of you, at the Governor's house - imagine that! Could I come and hear you there, do you suppose?"

"I don't think so, you have to have an invitation," Danny explained. "It's really a party for children."

"Oh well, maybe I can hear you some other time," she said equably.

They were nearing the landing pier. The dancing, sun-flecked wavelets of mid-harbour were behind them; before lay dark green treacly water in which jetsam of every description heaved gently up and down, wafting a nauseating stench.

Laughing little Chinese boys, clad only in short cotton trousers, were clambering among the pier supports. Others were splashing in the water, diving for coins which tourists were throwing from the sea wall.

"Oh, how can those boys swim in that filthy water?" shuddered Mrs. Holtz.

"Danny swam there once, and got twenty cents," said Celeste proudly.

"You're quite a boy, Daniel - you'll go far in this world, mark my words!"

Her fears and anxieties when she was helped off the wallah wallah on to the pier were quickly forgotten when she found herself immediately in the midst of the bustling life on the island. "Oh Daniel, not so fast! Those poor women, pulling that load of logs: how can men let them do it? And those babies, darling little pets strapped so tightly to their mammas' backs! Wait, wait, I must peek at that sweet little thing, it only looks about five minutes old! Oh, that old beggar.. some one ought to call a doctor to look at that dreadful sore on his leg. Look at those slim Chinese girls in their flowered pyjamas! So cute!"

She was fascinated by the sights beneath the wide-arched cloisters of the many-storeyed solid buildings making up the centre of the city. Round each concrete column squatted a bevy of coolies; some were resting, heads back, eyes closed, mouths open; others were smoking through crude pipes made of short bamboo poles; one little group crouched close together, smoking wispy cigarettes and playing with narrow cards; there were even families with tiny children plying chopsticks in small bowls of rice and vegetables.

"Imagine having your meal on the pavement, with all the dust and noise!"

"Some of them live on the pavement," Danny explained. "They even sleep here at nights, they're called street sleepers."

"That's terrible, terrible!" Her dismay mingled with ejaculations of alarm as they plunged across a road dense with cars, taxis, rickshaws and coolies carrying enormous loads of merchandise at either end of bamboo poles balanced across their shoulders. She gave a great whoop of relief when they reached the hotel. Uniformed attendants swooped on the luggage while she rummaged in her handbag and handed the coolie two small American coins.

Danny shuffled his feet. "Well, Mrs. Holtz, you'll be all right now, won't you?"

"Oh yes, Daniel! I'm so grateful to you. Now don't you go out of my life forever, you and Celeste! I want you to visit me sometimes. Will you do that?"

As she spoke, she pressed a crumpled note into his hand. A note.. he could hardly control his voice as he answered "Oh yes, Mrs. Holtz, of course Mrs. Holtz, and gee, thank you very much, Mrs. Holtz!"

Outside the hotel he opened his hot hand; a dollar, a whole dollar, she had given him; not a Hong Kong dollar, but an American dollar, worth twice as much and far exceeding the cost of Marcus' present for Pamela. He hoisted Celeste high on his shoulders and strode joyfully towards the money changer's shop in the next block.

A stray breeze blew the mosquito net against Pamela's face and roused her. A tram groaned past the house on protesting tracks. The wooden clip-clops of dawn workers clacked on the pavements. Cicadas in the trees behind the house screeched. From the nearby racecourse came the thud of galloping hooves.

She opened her eyes, stared for a moment, then remembered that she was home. She lay listening nostalgically to the familiar sounds, gazing round the room with its cream colourwashed walls, its severe government furniture and polished bare floor; savouring the aroma of the now-spent anti-mosquito coil that had been slowly smouldering on its stand beneath her bed. From the small back yard beneath her open window came the subdued voices of the servants from their quarters; from the dining-room below came the chink of dishes and the laboured push and pull of the heavy floor polisher on the wooden floors.

She held up one hand and gazed at the winking ring on her finger; turned and admired the red revolving pencil on her bedside table: Marcus and Danny had not forgotten her, had made a special visit to her yesterday afternoon to present the gifts. To add to her satisfaction, this was Saturday, her music lesson day, so she would be able to spend the afternoon with them. She wriggled over to the far side of the bed for a cooler spot, sighed in sheer contentment, and closed her eyes again.

She woke properly an hour later. By the time she had washed and dressed, her father had left for his office, Belle to resume her job in the English department store, and Roddy gone to look up old friends in the neighbourhood. While she had breakfast, her mother sat opposite enjoying another cup of tea, then announced suddenly that there would be no more piano lessons.

"No more piano lessons?" Pamela echoed in astonishment. "But why, I thought you wanted me to learn the piano!"

"You haven't shown much interest, have you?" Her mother mopped the perspiration pouring down her neck. "You've only scraped through your exams. Don't stop eating, I want to go shopping early before it's too hot."

"But I can't stop having lessons suddenly.. and do I have to go to town?"

"Of course, I need you with me: after we've bought the material for your school dresses, you have to get measured by the tailor. And I don't want to hear any more about the music lessons - Daddy and I made up our minds last night to stop them."

"But Mummy, Mrs. Russell's expecting me this afternoon, Danny said so yesterday."

"Your father said he'd call in on his way to the office this morning and tell her you won't be coming any more. Do hurry, Pam, I want to catch the next bus."

The lessons themselves she would not miss at all, but how could she face Mrs. Russell when she went to call on Danny?

As they seated themselves in the snorting bus, her mother exploded "Oh Pamela, take that great ring off! I won't have you wearing such a showy.. bauble while you're out with me. I don't know what that boy was thinking of to buy it for you."

"I told you," she tried to explain patiently , "it's a welcome-back present." Obediently she pulled the ring off, lovingly stroking the enormous purple stone set in a frame of yellow-gold filigree which had already bent out of shape.

"Nonsensical idea," sniffed her mother.

The savage snarls of the bus's engine made further conversation impossible. Pamela stared unhappily out of the window. Gradually, the blessedly familiar sights, so essentially the backdrop of her life and so missed in England, brought some balm to her troubled heart: the tenement houses whose ground floors were open-fronted shops, bamboo poles supporting washing, poking out of every upper window; pavements alive with chattering shoppers, and squatters cooking, eating or sewing; the professional bespectacled letter-writer at his ricketty portable table; itinerant hawkers, selling everything from sweets and peanuts to enamel mugs and bolts of material.

She was sufficiently heartened to re-open the subject of the music lessons when they left the bus in the city centre.

"I know I didn't practise very much in England, Mummy, but that room was so cold, and Granny and Grandad didn't like to be disturbed with my scales. I'll practise every single day now we're back here."

"It's too late now. Oh hello, Mrs. Bately" - Her mother greeted a friend who was approaching with her bean-pole daughter. "Yes, we got back yesterday."

Pamela stood glumly by as a lengthy excited conversation ensued; now and again she exchanged a few shy words with the daughter Hilary, two years older and not a close acquaintance.

The dreadful morning dragged on, with a visit to a furniture shop where her mother admired a nest of carved blackwood tea poys and unsuccessfully tried to get the price reduced to what she considered a reasonable amount.

"Far too expensive," she said in disgust, walking out of the shop.

Pamela seized the moment to say breathlessly "The Russells haven't much money. Danny's mother needs as many pupils as she can get."

"You wouldn't think so, with Danny spending all that money on your ring."

"But it was money he'd earned.."

"He could have put it to better use, then!" She propelled Pamela into the silk store, where the persuasive Indian assistants inveigled her into examining their latest stock. Bolt after bolt of shimmering rich silks cascaded over the counters; prices were quoted but 'special' reductions quickly offered. Pamela slouched on the tall chair beside the counter, her legs dangling bandily, and tried to think of another approach which might reinstate the music lessons; the silks were regretfully refused, the blue cotton for her school dresses bought, and they were on their way to the tailor's premises in a steep side street off Queen's Road before she found the courage to try again. "If I'm not having lessons any more, Mrs. Russell will think it's because you don't think she's a good teacher! I'll feel awful: I don't know how I can face her again."

"You don't need to. There's no reason for you to go there any more - in fact, your father and I would rather you didn't."

Pamela's world stood still. Taxis hooted, buses and lorries rattled past; inter-passing pedestrians jostled; urchins shouted for cumshaw: but all that registered was the shock of her mother's words.

"But Danny's my friend, and Marcus!" She tugged at her mother's arm to prevent her from going on until this matter was settled. "We've always played together, ever since I first went to piano lessons!"

"You've got plenty of other friends living nearer to us, and at school - friends of your own sort."

"Don't you like me playing with Danny and Marcus because they're not English?" Pamela breathed the words rather than uttered them,almost as though the two boys might be listening.

"Well.." The hesitation was unmistakable. "You really must mix more with children of your own nationality, that's all. Now, up the stairs here - the tailor's on the first floor, remember?"

On the journey home, Pamela fought against tears, not certain if she had been absolutely forbidden to play with Danny and Marcus again, or merely warned that her parents did not approve - to ask for elucidation might result in a direct ban on the friendship where perhaps this had not been entirely intended. She decided to leave things as they were for the present, and work the great question casually into the conversation at some propitious time.

"Have a lemonade," her mother invited unexpectedly as they walked into the house. "Ask Ah Tai to bring me one, too, with ice."

Pamela leapt towards the refrigerator before her mother changed her mind: minerals were not handed out freely as in the households of some of her school-friends.

"With a straw?" she dared to suggest, though knowing well that the box of straws was kept for parties and visitors.

"Yes, with a straw if you like. But you know, Pam, you're growing up fast, you'll have to drop these childish habits soon. Before we know where we are, you'll have left school and be earning like Belle, having the time of your life."

Yet when Belle came in to tiffin soon after, she looked anything but pleased with life. Her shingled hair dishevelled from the bus ride, forehead and arms damp with perspiration, she appeared briefly at the dining-room door and announced she was going straight upstairs: would they call her when the meal was on the table? There was an awful new sub-manager in the shop who had changed everything round while she'd been in England, and now she was in the glassware department instead of the jewellery and she was sure to drop things and break them; she'd had a ghastly morning and she was exhausted.

"Take her up a lemonade,Pam," directed her mother.

"I'm tired too.. can't Ah Tai..?"

"Certainly not, I don't want you getting back into your spoilt ways now we're back in Hong Kong!"

When Pamela arrived with Belle's drink as well as her own, her sister was lying face downwards on the bed in her petticoat, arms akimbo for coolness.

"You're not the only one who's fed up," Pamela grumbled, as she sprawled back over the rattan chair near the bed. "Look what's happened to me.. they've stopped my music lessons."

"And you mind?" Belle sounded amused. "I was pleased as punch when mine were stopped."

"It's not the music I'm fed up about: they don't want me to play with Danny and Marcus. Why, Belle? Do you know why?"

"Something to do with you getting older, I suppose."

"What's wrong with playing with them now I'm ten instead of nine like last year?"

"Fat lot of rest I'm getting, with you and your questions." Belle turned over and sat up against the head of the bed, sipping her drink slowly. "It's like this, Pam: looking a long way ahead, when you get to my age, among the friends you mix with is the person you're likely to marry, so it's no good you sticking just with people like the Russells and the Bellarios, because you could never marry any of them."

"Marry them? Danny? Marcus?" Pamela fell about the chair in paroxysms of giggles. "But why couldn't I if they asked me, and I wanted to, when I'm old enough?"

"You know, Pam.. you must know! It's because they're not English, that's why. Yes, I know Danny is half-English, but that's not enough?"

"Not enough for what?"

"Not enough to count. When it comes to earning a living, you see, Portuguese and Chinese and Eurasians can't earn as much money as us Europeans."

"But why ever not? Why can't they?"

"Just because.. they can't. Look how badly off Danny and his mother are - you've told me yourself that nearly all Danny's clothes belonged to Marcus first!"

"Marcus' parents are quite rich, they've got a whole house to themselves."

"They're exceptions."

Ah Tai called up the stairs "Tiffin ready!"

"Well, I think all this is silly!" Pamela got up and left the room. Her parents and Roddy were already round the table being served.

"Ah, the budding prodigy herself!" was the surprising greeting from her father. "Well, it seems that your talent has been recognised at last!"

Pamela screwed her head round and stared at him uncomprehendingly.

"We would never have talked of stopping your lessons if we'd known Mrs. Russell wanted you to play at Government House," added her mother.

"Better start eating if you're to be in time for your lesson!" Her father attacked his pork chop with great good humour. "So you're to play the piano for Danny's violin piece, Pam; he's a very honoured young man!"

"What young man?" demanded Belle, arriving downstairs doing up her dress buttons.

"Danny Russell. He and Pam are going to perform at the G.H. children's concert next month."

"So.. so my piano lessons aren't going to be stopped after all?" Pamela, trying to piece the puzzle together, dared to speak for the first time.

"You might as well carry on while you're doing well enough to play in a concert," her mother nodded. "But mind you, there's not to be so much time spent up at the Russells' terrace as in the past.. when you go there, it's for piano lessons and not for the whole afternoon."

Still bemused, she nodded obedience, and was careful not to cause any annoyance at the table. Like a model child, she packed her music books into her leather case, went upstairs to brush her hair without being so directed, and slipped out of the house in plenty of time for the lesson. Once out of sight of the house, she put on the glittering ring.

Danny's home was on the other side of Happy Valley. She took the rough path dividing the race-course from tennis courts and football pitches. It was a pleasant walk, shaded by huge Flame of the Forest trees whose bases were the haunts of hawkers of peanuts, olives and pungent-smelling delicacies. The small Chinese children with short haircuts and no hats laughed openly at Pamela's topee; she scowled at them: bad enough to have to wear the thing, without being jeered at as well.

Once across the Valley, there was a steep walk past Morrison Hill - a yellow, granite eyesore which was constantly being chipped away, and blasted twice a day; then a short journey along Kennedy Road above which stood Dragon Terrace where Danny lived. It was reached by a daunting flight of stone steps in sets of twelve. At the top a decorated concrete balustrade ran the whole length of the terrace. As always, Danny was sitting on the balustrade watching for her. He waved, and ran down the last set of steps to meet her.

"Wait a minute!" He held her arm as they reached the terrace. "I want to tell you something before you go indoors."

"About the concert? I know! I was awfully surprised!"

"Listen, Pam, do me a favour and don't say anything about the concert to my mother, until she mentions it to you."

"Whyever not?"

"Mumma's cross because I told her you must play for me at Government House instead of Celeste!"

"YOU said I had to?" Pamela repeated in bewilderment.

"Yes, because when your father came to stop your music lessons, my mother wasn't in: I had to think of something quickly to try to get him to change his mind, so I said you were going to play in the concert. Then I had to tell Mumma when she came home. She's so mad at me, but she says she'll just have to let you play now I've told your father; and she sent me to Confession this morning because of telling lies to your father.. because it was a lie then, though it isn't now; and I've got to practise scales all the afternoon as a punishment."

"But what about Celeste?"

"She understood when I explained - she's a wonderful kid, but her mother and Marcus are really furious."

"Oh Danny, what a mess!" She looked down at her sandals and sighed. "You know I can't play nearly as well as Celeste."

"I know that, stupid, but what else could I do? Don't you start getting cross with me too; I was only trying to help.. Mumma can't afford to lose a pupil, and it's such fun when you come up here for lessons. Now don't forget, not a word to Mumma until she mentions the concert."

With all this on her mind, the lack of regular practice, and the sound of Danny's plaintive scales in the next room, it was little wonder that Pamela found it difficult to concentrate at the piano. A rotating electric fan stirred the air, but her palms were hot and sticky and her face red with embarrassment at her performance by the end of the lesson.

Mrs. Russell, a short thin woman in black, only referred to the concert as Pamela rose to leave. "You know you will be accompanying Danny at Government House next month?"

"Yes, Mrs. Russell.. I'm sorry.."

"You are not to blame." The teacher hurriedly brushed aside further discussion on this difficult subject. "But you will have to practise really hard if you are to justify being chosen; if you're not up to standard in time, I must tell your parents so and Celeste will replace you."

"Mrs Russell, couldn't Celeste just do a little solo on the piano, as well as Danny and me doing our piece? She's so good, and it's such a shame for her to be left out."

A smile creased Mrs. Russell's sallow face. "You're a nice little girl, Pamela," she said, "but Government House have asked for just one item - there are other teachers sending performers, you see. Off you go now, and do as much practice every day as you possibly can."

Danny, violin in hand, appeared in the hall as Pamela closed the music room door behind her. "How was it?" he hissed.

"Your mother was very nice about everything.. except my playing. That was terrible - could you hear me?" - "I could - you really put me off. Wait while I put my violin away then we can go for a walk."

"Danny!" His mother called through the door, "I said you must practise all the afternoon and I mean it! Goodbye, Pamela." This last was said so firmly that Pamela, head down, slipped away from the flat as quickly as she could, and almost collided with the boy leaning against the balustrade.

"Goodness, Pam, you ARE in a hurry!" This was Danny's cousin Marcus, at twelve years old a head taller. She could think of nothing to say, still consumed with guilt at the enormity of Danny's deceit, and fearing Marcus' wrath on Celeste's behalf, she made to pass on, but he held her arm, saying "Don't go. No one's angry with you, silly, it's all Danny's fault."

"But I feel awful about it.."

"You mustn't any more. Come for a walk before you go home!" He was not so handsome as Danny, his complexion darker and his features heavier, and his serious manner was in great contrast to Danny's cheerful temperament, but she was flattered by his attention, especially when he insisted on carrying her music case.

"I can't stay long,"she said, "and Danny can't come, his mother says he has to do scales all the afternoon."

"Serve him right," Marcus grunted.

Together they clambered up the hillside behind the terrace until they reached a rough path high above the buildings. They looked for frogs behind stones, examining them gently when they found some, and keeping a cautious watch for snakes which could sometimes be found here. The path led to a muddy pool into which a hill-stream trickled. Three small Chinese children, stripped to the waist, were stamping happily in the water, enjoying the relief from the heat.

"I'm hot too," announced Marcus. "Let's rest a bit." With his handkerchief he dusted a boulder near the pool and motioned Pamela to sit down. He crouched beside her, took her hand and examined her ring with elaborate care.

"Which do you like the best, Danny's ring or my pencil? he asked.

"I love them both," Pamela said firmly. "And what a surprise they were! I never thought to bring you and Danny presents."

"Girls don't have to," Marcus explained. "Gloria's always getting presents from her boy-friends." Gloria was the eldest of his four sisters.

"Oh well, Gloria's old, even much older than Belle!"

"Age doesn't make any difference," said Marcus, looking down at his shoes and meticulously adjusting a near-perfectly tied shoe-lace. "You could be my girl-friend."

"Well, I am, aren't I? And Danny's too. I can't be your BOY friend, can I?" giggled Pamela, flicking an ant off her ankle. "Can we go on walking? There must be an ants' nest near here."

"All right." Marcus, quite unnecessarily, took her hands and pulled her to her feet. "When you're older, I'll talk to you again about this."

"About what?"

"Oh, never mind. You'll understand when you're my age," he said with a frown.

Perplexed at his manner, and fearing a return to the unhappy situation over the concert, Pamela said hastily "Tell me what happened here while I was in England! Did you get any prizes at school this year?" She knew this was a safe subject, Marcus being an industrious pupil, always being held up as a shining example to the slothful Danny, two classes lower at St. Joseph's Catholic College.

The little-used path narrowed as it wound round the hillside, past large brown earthenware jars which the children skirted knowing they contained the bones of deceased Chinese. Marcus went ahead and bent bushes and branches aside so Pamela should not get scratched. Now they were overlooking the race course, beyond which stood the row of houses where she lived. They stopped to watch the end of the race in progress.

"Goodness, look at the time - almost four o'clock! Pamela suddenly noticed the clock tower above the Jockey Club. "We'd best go back."

"Why so early? You used to stay all afternoon.."

"I know.. it's a new thing my parents have just started," Pamela floundered and coloured. "I don't want to do anything to make them change their minds about my lessons again."

"Of course not," Marcus agreed almost fervently.

Danny's mournful scales still sounded from the flat when they returned to the terrace, and they both giggled, although Pamela felt guilty doing so.

"I'll walk you home," said Marcus as she set off down the steps.

"No, don't bother," Pamela panicked, remembering her mother's warning. "Jolly nice of you, but it means you'll have to walk up all these steps afterwards, and.. it's so hot."

"I'm used to the heat - remember I was born here; it's just you foreigners from cold climates that suffer from the heat."

She hoped he would turn back before they reached her home, tense with anxiety lest her parents should see her with Marcus and issue more stringent edicts.

"Look Marcus, better not come any further.. in case my father rows me for not getting back earlier.. I'd be so embarrassed if you were there too.."

"All right then," he agreed reluctantly. "I can't help think you are exaggerating everything, though! See you soon!"

Because she dared not make any promises in the light of her parents' new rules, she ignored his last words and changed the subject. "I do love this beautiful pencil, I've never had such a lovely one," she called over her shoulder.

OCTOBER

"I don't want to.. I don't want to go!" shouted Sandra. "I won't go! Why should I?"

"It's all arranged, and you will go," said her mother evenly.

"Bath ready, Missee Sandra." Ah Ling called from the bathroom.

"Don't need a bath now, Ah Ling! No go party."

"Oh yes you ARE going!" Her mother propelled Sandra through the door. "Leave it to me, Ah Ling, I'll get Missee ready myself."

Ah Ling bustled about with the towels in one corner of the bathroom, but hastily escaped on meeting her mistress's forbidding glance. Sandra screamed and yelled but to no avail; without a word, her mother proceeded to bath and dress her.

Cowed and sullen, she was led out to the car and taken to Government House to join a hundred other children of highranking officials and businessmen.

In the large ballroom she found several of school acquaintances, and entertained them with a sotte voce impersonation of the Governor's wife's welcome speech. The stifled giggles at her cleverness helped to restore her good humour.

A concert by child performers was announced, and the audience hustled into chairs facing a dais containing a piano and music stands. This promised boredom, which proved the case at first, as halting pianists, tense violinists biting their lips at every false scrape of the bow, and breathless singers with agonised eyes succeeded each other on the dais.

"And now for our last item," began the Governor's wife in indulgent tones, "we have Daniel Russell, violin, accompanied by Pamela Doran on the piano."

Sandra recognised Pamela as soon as she sidled self-consciously over to the piano. The boy with the violin looked completely confident and threw Pamela a little smile as he nodded to her to strike the opening note. He smiled too as he played a lively dance; in comparison with his professional performance, Pamela's part was very minor. He grinned and made a great bow at the end, but Pamela, her face the colour of beetroot, crept off the stage with her head averted.

Now the guests were led into a long dining-room for tea. Sandra looked for Pamela but was shepherded to a seat before she could find her. After tea, every one was sent into the terraced garden overlooking the harbour for ten minutes' fresh air before a cinema show. Sandra searched among the milling children until she found Pamela standing in a quiet corner with her violinist.

"I didn't know you'd be here, Pam!" beamed Sandra. "I did like your bit in the concert! Wish I'd learned the piano, they tried to make me but I didn't want to. When can I come and visit you? I'd have come before but Daddy said he'd lost the address."

"It's 28 Wong Nei Cheong Road."

"Say it again!"

"Can I help?" The violinist quickly produced a tiny diary with pencil from the top pocket of his white jacket, tore out a page on which he wrote the address and handed it to her.

Before she could thank him Pamela said "This is Danny, Sandra. He's my friend. His mother is my music teacher."

Danny shook hands with a flourish. Sandra, tucking the folded paper between her wrist and her gold bracelet, was most impressed; here was a young boy, not much older than herself, with the ease and manner of a grown man; with him and Pamela a new life beckoned, a life away from the stultifying routine in her Peak home. A plan quickly formed in her mind.

"Do you think your mother would teach me to play the piano, Danny?"

"Sure she would." Out came the diary and pencil again. "Where do you live? And Sandra what?"

Happily she told him.

"We're Russell. I'll give you our address on another piece of paper and you can show it to your parents. And ask them to ask for lessons on Saturday afternoon, because that's when Pam comes to have hers."

"Oh yes, it must be when Pamela's there too," Sandra declared.

A voice on a loud hailer announced the beginning of the cinema show and there was a concerted rush for the ball room.

"Hold hands, then we won't get separated and can sit together," Danny hissed.

It was when the curtains were drawn at the deep windows and the chandelier lights began to dim that Sandra realised she had lost her valuable pieces of paper.

"They're gone, they're gone!" she cried, scrabbling on the floor in the darkness. "I can't find them anywhere. Ask the Boys to put the lights on again!"

"Don't fuss so Sandra!" Danny's voice was quite fierce. "If they're lost I'll write the addresses out again." He grabbed her arm and made her sit back in her chair.

The surge of panic subsided under his firm calmness. She felt as if she belonged with her two new friends, and stole a look at them as the Felix the Cat cartoon started: on her right Danny was re-arranging the white handkerchief in his breast pocket; he caught her eye and gave her an encouraging grin; on her left, Pamela was staring fixedly at the screen and looked rather cross; Sandra wondered why.

NOVEMBER

As he made a perfunctory sign of the cross at the entrance to the church, Danny saw that the row of penitents outside the confessional stretched halfway up the side aisle. He made a mental calculation: sixteen people waiting, each taking about three minutes - it would be at least three-quarters of an hour before his turn. It was now noon. Since he must be home by two o'clock when Sandra would arrive for her music lesson, and he must fit in a visit to Mrs. Holtz before tiffin, there would be no time for confession today.. the important thing was to make Confession before Christmas in two weeks' time.

It was almost a month since he had called on her. He could not explain to himself how essential he felt it was to keep in contact with her; it was not entirely (he told his irritating conscience) because she was usually generous with her dollar notes for the smallest service: he had a vague feeling of responsibility for her.

He sped down Garden Road from the church, past the lower terminus of the Peak Tram Station, through the Protestant Cathedral grounds, then down a flight of steep steps which plunged him into the city centre, known as Central. Dodging the buses, cars, lorries and trams, he reached the hotel almost breathless. The lift was out of order so he had to climb the three flights of stairs to Mrs. Holtz' room.

She was seated at a small table near the verandah, peering into her typewriter.

"Why Danny, where have you been all this time? I wondered what happened to you and your friends!" She got up and enveloped him with her voluminous, mauve cape which smelt of perspiration above her perfume.

"You look hot, fix yourself a drink!" She flopped into a rattan armchair and nodded towards a tray of bottles and glasses on the dressing-table. "And fix me a short, too, will you Danny? I been an hour trying to get that typewriter to work."

"O.K. Mrs. Holtz." Danny knew by now what she meant by a short, and was very proud of his knowledge. She accepted the gin and tonic gratefully and gave a great sigh after the first sip. Danny took his glass of lemonade to the table and examined the typewriter. She had previously shown him how to use it, and often allowed him to pick out sentences with one finger, but its internal arrangements were a complete mystery to him. Nevertheless, he obligingly lifted the shield protecting the type, prodded and peered, then gave a hoot of triumph.

"It's the ribbon, I think. It's got all twisted up on this side - see?"

She heaved herself up and loomed over him. "So it is, Danny - that's very smart of you. I think I better have a new ribbon, that one was getting faint anyway. Can you go along to the typewriter shop on Queen's Road, where we went to buy the oil last month, and get another ribbon?"

"Now?" He glanced anxiously at the travelling clock beside her bed.

"Well, I do want to get on with my article.. I've been held up all morning - and I just couldn't walk up and down all those stairs and I don't know when the lift will be fixed. Can you make it for me, Danny?" Already she was reaching for the enormous knitting bag in which she kept her money and her valuables, and fumbling in its depths.

"O.K. Mrs. Holtz - but I'll have to leave as soon as I've brought the ribbon to you."

"You only just came." Still delving for her money, she sounded resentful. "First time you've come to see me in weeks and you've hardly time to say hullo. What keeps you so busy these days? You and Pamela and Celeste used to come every Saturday afternoon: Marcus too. Don't you like coming any more?"

"Oh yes, Mrs. Holtz, of course we do! But now my mother has a new pupil on Saturday, she's called Sandra and lives on The Peak and comes by car, and we get a ride in her car afterwards before she has to go home.. so there isn't time."

"Is Sandra your new girl-friend?"

"Oh no, Mrs. Holtz! Pamela knew her first, she's great fun, Sandra is; we play dares all the time, and she always does the daringest things!"

"Why don't you bring her to see me next time you come? Ah, here's one of those Hong Kong dollar notes.. take care of the change, huh? I'm waiting for a letter from Mr. Holtz with my draft; it should come on the next boat, but until then I'm a bit short."

"O.K. Mrs. Holtz." Danny, folding the note carefully and putting it in his jacket pocket, hoped he'd hidden his disappointment at her parting remark which, he knew from previous experience, implied that there would be little or no reward for the current mission.

He made the trip to the shop and back in record time, handed her the change and said goodbye.

"You didn't stay long," sighed Mrs. Holtz, counting the coins carefully. "Never mind, maybe you'll come again soon, and don't forget, I want to see this wonderful Sandra.. here, take this, buy her some candy."

Because of his conscience he tried to refuse the 20 cent coin, but not very hard.

"Lollipops, Danny! Oh, peachey! Can I have the green one?"

"Whichever you like, Sandra - Pam doesn't mind which colour she has, do you Pam?"

"Nope." Not for one moment would Pamela let Danny see how hurt she was that Sandra was given preference in every way; even the time of Pamela's music lesson had had to be changed to fit in with Sandra's parents' wishes. Now, both lessons over, the two girls sat, legs dangling, on the broad balustrade bordering the terrace.

Sucking the spherical yellow lollipop patterned like a golf ball, Pamela marvelled that Danny should spend Mrs. Holtz' twenty cents on such delights for herself and Sandra, leaving nothing for himself: he even declined their offers of a lick.

Her pleasure was somewhat marred by the sight of Sandra's red head bent close to Danny's dark one as they whispered together. She felt particularly isolated today because Marcus was not present as Celeste was to make her First Communion in a few months' time and this afternoon there was to be the first special preparation class in St. Joseph's Church; Marcus was to take her and they were both getting ready. A little later they appeared, Celeste solemn in a trim navy blue dress with cream collar, Marcus in a crisp white long-sleeved shirt, red tie and grey trousers reaching his knees. Pamela looked down at her floral, drop-bodice dress, grubby as a result of climbing up the hillside behind the houses. It irked her that Sandra, who too had been up the hillside path, throwing stones in the muddy pool, still managed to look spic and span.

"You two look as if you're going to see the King," said Sandra. "We can give you a lift to the Church if you like, Ming will be here in a minute, and the others are coming for a ride."

Pamela always felt anxious climbing into the shining black Rolls Royce lest she or any of the other children should in any way sully its magnificence, and Mr. and Mrs. Smithson veto these treasured rides. Savouring the luxury of the experience, she sat in silence between Marcus and Celeste, while Danny and Sandra vied with each other in telling terrible jokes which grew more and more vulgar. Celeste stuck her fingers in her ears, and Pamela stared fixedly at her shoes.

'Cut it out, Danny," growled Marcus. "I thought you went to Confession this morning?"

"No, the queue was too long, but I'm going now."

"Well then.." said Marcus severely, and to Pamela's astonishment Danny sat back quietly in his seat for the rest of the journey.

After Sandra had waved vigorous farewells, and Marcus, Celeste and Danny walked towards the church porch, Pamela wished she had not come. She leaned against the railings enclosing the church enclave, and wondered what to do.

Danny turned back and called "You coming in to wait while I go to Confession?'

"Oh no!" A Catholic church was an alien place. "I'll wait outside if you like."

"It might take a long time - come in, Pam, it'll be all right."

"I couldn't!" Shyness, even a kind of secret fear, made her hang back. "If you're going to be ages, I won't wait - I'm supposed to be home by now."

A fresh group of children were turning in the church entrance, and suddenly Pamela was face to face with Philip Tait with his sister Teresa. He didn't seem at all surprised to see her, although his half-smile showed that he recognised her.

"Hullo Philip! Fancy meeting you here!" Pamela grinned.

"Why not? It's my church, not yours! What are you doing here?"

"My friends were coming to Confession and things, and they got a lift so I came as well."

"I'm going to Confession too," said Philip, "because I had to bring Teresa to her First Communion class."

"Just like my friend Marcus," Pamela beamed. "He's brought his sister Celeste."

"I'd better go in now, else Teresa will be late."

"I'll wait until you come out," Pamela decided suddenly.

"Will you? I might be ages if there's a long queue."

"Doesn't matter, I've nothing else to do." The possibility of trouble at home when she arrived late seemed worth risking now. She wandered round the outside of the grey church, wondering what could be going on within to attract so many children on a bright Saturday afternoon. Great palm trees surrounded the church, shrouding at the back a grotto dominated by a statue of Mary in white marble, beneath which was a marble prie dieu. She stared shyly at the statue. She knew from Danny and Marcus that Catholics set great store by Mary the Mother of God, and accepted this easily: Portuguese people and Catholicism seemed to go together, but it was difficult to relate someone as diffident and English as Philip to such a demonstrative religion.

She ambled back to the entrance and peered through the open doors. The layout did not look very different from that of the Anglican Cathedral she and her parents attended at Christmas and Easter and other special occasions. Rows of pews filled the body of the church. Two aisles, one on either side, formed short rows against each side wall. A raised pulpit protruded from the left wall beyond the last row of pews. The high windows were of stained glass depicting somewhat stilted pictures of saintly beings. A life size, coloured statue of Mary stood on one side of the altar, another of a brown-clad monk holding the Child Jesus on the other.

She had somehow expected to see rows of lit candles on the altar, but the only light there came from a small red flicker in a glass suspended from the ceiling.

She recognised Philip's back view in the straggling line of children standing in the aisle nearest the pulpit. Danny and Marcus were not in sight. On the other side of the church, the front pews were occupied by some twenty or thirty young children who were being addressed in a low, slow voice by a bearded priest.

Not daring to venture further into sacred territory (supposing some Catholic adult should appear and demand to know what she, a Protestant, was doing in their church?). She looked everywhere for Marcus and Danny. Suddenly Marcus emerged from behind the pulpit, walked halfway up the aisle, knelt down on one knee and made the sign of the cross, then slipped into a pew where he knelt with his hands together and his head bowed.

Four minutes later Danny too walked up the aisle, looking as devout and solemn as Marcus - until he raised his eyes and caught sight of her; then he winked, slowly and deliberately before joining Marcus in the pew. When Philip too returned from the Confessional, head down and hands clasped together, Pamela was even more amazed at the same devotion and solemnity. He looked up and his eyes caught Pamela's; he looked down again at once but his lips twitched slightly. She felt guilty, as if she was a distraction to the boys, and edged backwards out of the church.

When they came out, she introduced Marcus and Danny to Philip, who flushed rosily, accentuating the difference between his pigmentation and that of the other two, and for the first time Pamela realised how different the two races appeared.

"Why haven't you ever come to see me, Philip?" she asked. "You said you would."

"Lost your address."

"Well, I'll tell you again," she said, and did so.

Philip produced from his shorts pocket the chewed stub of an indelible pencil, licked the lead and carefully printed her address on his wrist. The fastidious Marcus was horrified, Danny frankly admiring.

"Come tomorrow," urged Pamela, "after tiffin."

"Depends. How do I get there?"

"Along Kennedy Road," she explained carefully, "cross Happy Valley by the short little road, and then you're in my road. It will take you about 20 minutes.. won't it, Danny?"

Danny had a better idea: he would meet Philip on Kennedy Road and conduct him personally to Pamela's house, a suggestion which troubled Pamela in view of her mother's edict against playing with Danny and Marcus. She could only stand and chew her lip, wondering what to say.

"Can't promise," Philip shrugged. "My parents sometimes won't let me out, so it's no good arranging to meet me, thanks, Danny." He turned to Pamela and added "I expect I'll get along to see you some time, Pam."

There were signs of an exodus from the church, and the little bevy of amahs chatting in the shade of the palm-trees made for the porch to collect their charges. Teresa sidled up to Philip and whispered something to him. His face went pink again. "Got to hurry" he nodded hastily and scuttled off with his sister.

Celeste was glowing with virtue when she appeared. "I'll be wearing a long, white dress, right down to my shoes," she said happily on the homeward walk. "Did you have a long dress, down to your shoes, Pam, when you made your First Communion?"

"Pam isn't a Roman Catholic, Celie," hissed Marcus.

"Are you a heathen, then, Pam?"

"Course not - I'm a Protestant."

"So don't Protestants make First Communions?"

"Yes, but not till they're real old - fourteen or something," Danny explained.

"And don't you have Mass, Pam?" Celeste went on with interest.

"No.. well, there are services on Sundays, and we go when we feel like it."

"Sounds like a good idea to me," said Danny in a low aside which made Pamela laugh, and Marcus scowl.

Kennedy Road hugged the hillside on one side and overlooked the harbour on the left. Immediately below stood rows of army barracks, their grounds sloping gradually down to the level which became Queen's Road, the main arterial way from one end of Central Hong Kong to the other; Kennedy Road ran roughly parallel to it.

Celeste soon needed a rest, so they all sat on the railings facing the harbour.

"That's where Philip lives," said Pamela, pointing towards the barracks.

"He didn't seem to want to be friends with us," said Marcus.

"Oh I wouldn't say that." Pamela sprang to Philip's defence, although she was disappointed at his lack of enthusiasm at their reunion. "He's the sort that never seems keen on anything.. he just waits for things to happen. He's great fun, really. He was my best friend on the ship."

"Well, he isn't now," said Marcus, surprising her by giving her bare elbow a squeeze.

"Goodness, it must be late." Pamela, glad of a watertight excuse to escape such strange attention, slipped from the railings and smoothed down her dress. "I'll have to hurry home, I'd better run on alone."

"We'll all go!" Danny announced. "We'll give Celeste a chair ride home, Marcus!"

Running, laughing, occasionally pausing for breath, they at last reached the foot of the steps to Dragon Terrace.

"See you tomorrow?" asked Marcus, as Pamela detached herself from the little group.

"Don't think so."

"But you told Philip.."

"Well," she floundered, "I know, but.. I can't come here again til my next music lesson; that's what my parents said. Got to go now, 'bye!"

She ran off quickly before there were any more questions, but she could hear them calling out loud farewells as they set off up the steps, again hoisting Celeste between their joined hands - long after they were hidden from view by the line of dhobi houses she had to pass on her way to Happy Valley.

DECEMBER

Lovingly, Marcus fingered the soft brown leather wallet; even two days after unpacking it on Christmas morning, his delight with it was undiminished, He wanted to take it to the party this afternoon but it was as yet too precious to be taken out of the home. Reverently, he placed it in the nest of blue tissue paper in its box, and locked it away in the small desk in his bedroom.

He reviewed his reflexion in the wardrobe mirror: sleek black hair combed back above his forehead to show a quiff; new grey suit, the trousers well below his knees; snake belt, white shirt and red and blue striped tie; long grey socks and black shoes. He tried to squeeze an incipient blackhead on his chin, but gave up when Celeste called up the stairs: "Danny says the car has come."

Shivering with excitement, he leapt down the stairs, marvelling again that he and Danny were to be Sandra's guests at her Christmas Party, seeing for the first time the inside of a house on The Peak where only rich white people lived. Pamela was also invited - another reason for his euphoria, for since she had returned from England five months ago, he had come to realise that having her around gave him a warm feeling, and he counted the days between each music lesson.

"'Bye, Marcus," Celeste sighed enviously as he passed her in the hall. "Goodness, you are lucky, Marcus!"

Danny was waiting on the terrace. Marcus noted he was wearing the dark blue corduroy trousers which had been his own until he'd outgrown them a year ago. Side by side, the cousins ran down the steps, keeping perfect time and chanting "Sandra's party, Sandra's party.."

Pamela was sitting in the front seat of the car, next to Ming. She looked a different person today; with heightened colour in her cheeks, and her hair bouncy and shiny parted on one side, the usual fringe held back by a pink celluloid hair slide. Marcus couldn't see her dress for she was wearing a plum-coloured brocade jacket. When Danny admired it she seemed rather disgruntled because it had been her main Christmas present.

"It's beautiful, though, Pam," Marcus said with feeling; he would have liked to add that she too looked beautiful today, but lacked the courage.

"But clothes for presents - I ask you!" groaned Pamela. "I was hoping for a miniature Singer sewing machine. I s'pose it will be clothes forever now."

Marcus told her about the wonderful wallet and promised to exhibit it after the next music lesson.

"I had this absolutely wonderful penknife with six gadgets," Danny said, pulling it out of his pocket and demonstrating all its functions.

None of the three passengers had ever before travelled by car to The Peak. When the Rolls started up the steep slopes, they stretched back in their seats, soon learning to brace themselves at every hair-pin bend.

"Reminds me of the scenic railway I went on in England," gasped Pamela, "only this is much more exciting."

Ming pointed to the white house on a knoll above them, outlined against a flawless blue sky and looking like a miniature palace The car turned abruptly into a narrow access road, so sharply angled that the children fell about, giggling and shrieking, but they were silenced in awe when deposited outside the splendid portico whose six steps were decorated at either side with green glazed pots of blooming red poinsettias.

The door opened and Sandra rushed out. She wore a pale green velvet dress with cream lace collar and cuffs, white socks and dancing pumps. "Come in, come in!" she beamed, grabbing Pamela's arm. "I made Ming bring you early so you'd be here before every one else. I want to show you all my things! Oh, where's Philip? Didn't he come with you? He was supposed to meet you at the terrace to get a lift with you."

"Haven't seen him for weeks," Pamela shrugged.

"Daddy said he didn't reply to the invitation, but I thought he would come anyway. Never mind, come and say hello to my parents."

"I remember you very well on the 'Rawalpindi' Pamela," said Mr. Smithson heartily. "And we have heard so much about you two boys that we are pleased to meet you at last."

Marcus liked his firm handshake, but felt less sure of his welcome by Sandra's mother, who extended a limp hand and looked past him rather than at him.

He followed Sandra and the others up the white staircase to her bedroom. It was fit for a princess! All the furniture was white, with handles and knobs painted gold. The light brown parquet flooring gleamed brightly, except where a pink thickpiled Tientsin carpet lay beside the bed. Taking in all this opulence, Marcus could only lend an ear to Sandra's staccato chatter as she displayed her Christmas presents - a printing set, several annuals, a stuffed life-like lion, games, jigsaw puzzles.. "But the best thing of all is just too peachey for words. It's in the garage - it's a canoe, all my own, with a paddle that's got an oar at each end. Come and see!"

Down the stairs they all trooped, and through to the garage.

"I can't WAIT to use it!" Sandra's words were tumbling over each other. "You can all come to my matshed at South Beach as soon as it's warm enough to swim ('cos we might fall in) and we can take turns in it. Daddy, Daddy! - She turned towards her father who was standing at the door smiling at her excitement. "Daddy, when will it be warm enough for swimming, so Danny and Pam and Marcus and me can go to the matshed, Daddy?"

"Not for a few months, darling."

"But when? March, maybe?"

"I doubt it - it's far too early to talk about swimming at Christmas. Now you really should be watching out for your other guests."

A dozen more children were welcomed. They all seemed to know each other, and eyed Marcus and Danny and Pamela curiously, almost with hostility. Games were organised, and the three outsiders hung back, conscious now of their fringe position at the party. At first Sandra pulled them in to take part, but as the afternoon wore on she became more and more excited, bossy and noisy, and made herself the centre of attention.

"No one is to take a cake until I say which one they can have!" she ordered, when they were all seated round the table. "I'm going to choose for you, because it's MY party."

Marcus was appalled at her manners; so, apparently was her mother, who called her name in a low but penetrating voice.

Sandra stood up on her chair and reached over to the plate of cakes and started to distribute them according to whim.

"Sit down!" ordered her mother, sweeping forward and forcing Sandra back into her chair. Sandra fought her savagely, shouting and crying. Her mother said nothing, but held her in a grip of steel until the struggling and shouting stopped; then Sandra stared at her mother and spat out vituperative curses in Cantonese. Marcus was shocked to the core. Pamela looked embarrassed too, head hung low over her plate, cheeks scarlet, and teeth dug into her lower lip. He felt a new surge of affection towards her; now here was an angel: modest, kind, quiet, charitably trying to ignore what had taken place instead of watching the two protagonists and giggling at the scene as some of the other children were doing! Looking across at her, he caught her glance as she cautiously raised her eyes, and smiled understandingly at her. She managed a faint smile back, but her eyes were bright with unshed tears. Marcus' heart swelled at her compassion. He wanted to reach out and comfort her, to take away her distress now and forever, All he could do was say a prayer to himself: "Through God's grace, may she be delivered one day into my care forever."

He was pleased with the prayer and repeated it to himself, deciding to write it down when he got home and preserve it in his new wallet.

He contrived to get near Pamela after tea when games were started. Side by side they sat cross-legged on the floor for 'Pass The Parcel', and he was thrilled by her brilliant excited smile every time he handed the package to her.

The game was just over when one of the house boys appeared in the doorway, saying loudly "One more people come party." Behind him stood Philip Tait, the Army boy, looking hot and dishevelled in a limp white shirt partly untucked at the waist, trousers too short for him, socks drooping over scuffed sandals.

"Philip, it's Philip!" Sandra ran across to the door and dragged him in. "Why are you so late? We've all had tea!"

"Hello Philip, I think we've met before," smiled Sandra's father. "On the 'Rawalpindi', wasn't it?"

"Yes, sir." Philip took the outstretched hand and shook it.

"Good gracious lad, you ARE hot! (Boy - a large glass of lemonade for the young master.) Have you walked all the way round from the tram?"

"Didn't come by tram."

"Oh, you got a lift up - that's good."

"No," said Philip. "I walked."

"Walked? All the way up the Peak? From.. where is it, Kennedy Road? All that way on foot?"

Philip nodded, his face still red from his exertions.

"Well, upon my word! Boy, let's have cakes, sandwiches, jellies, everything!" Mr. Smithson led Philip to the nearest armchair and made him sit down.

Marcus watched enviously as Philip continued to be the centre of attention, while Sandra crowed over and over again "And Philip did it all for me, just for me, to get to my party!"

Philip was given pride of place next to Sandra when photographs were taken; Sandra chose him as her partner to start off 'Oranges and Lemons'. The last straw was when Philip lost a seat in 'Musical Chairs' and Sandra turned Marcus off the chair he had won and insisted Philip should have it instead.

"She's impossible," he growled to Pamela as he joined her with the other losers.

"Oh, she's just excited," Pamela whispered.

The moment the game was over, Sandra shouted "Now let's watch Danny do his 'Felix The Cat'! Go on, Danny, do it like you did after our last music lesson."

"Felix The Cat! Do Felix!" chorussed the other children.

Marcus, all too familiar with his cousin's party pieces, cringed as Danny strutted up and down the room, singing and joking. The act was so vociferously applauded that it had to be repeated. Now Sandra, wound up to fever pitch, marched up and down beside him, joining in the song. The other children took their cue from her, and a hectic game of follow-my-leader developed, with Danny leading the way and Sandra immediately behind him. Marcus hung back at first, but when Pamela and Philip joined in joyfully, he felt he had to follow them rather than look disinterested.

"I'll be leader now!" Sandra shouted suddenly. She pulled Danny back and pushed him behind her then, leaping and strutting, led the children out of the lounge on to the wide verandah which ran the whole length of the house. She clambered over the bamboo and rattan reclining chairs and Danny followed suit, but the other children hesitated, then skirted the chairs.

"Not fair, not fair!" screamed Sandra. "You didn't follow the leader. You've got to do what I do! Come on!" She charged on, jumping on to a wicker table which rocked even with her light weight. By now the adults and servants were following the children to see what was happening, and shouted remonstrations; all the children except Sandra and Danny fell back.

"Scaredy cats!" she laughed scornfully. "You're all scared, except for Danny! Watch me!" Using a slender side-table, she scrambled on to the wide parapet of the balustrade, and stood astride it triumphantly. "Come on, Danny, you're not scared, are you? The ground isn't very far down." She looked out onto the bank ten feet below, and there were shouts from the amahs.

"No more of this!" Mr. Smithson pushed his way through the children. "Down at once, Sandra, at once!"

"No Daddy, it's a game, only a game."

"Get down, I say!"

Marcus caught his breath as Sandra inched backwards towards the outer edge of the parapet. There were gasps from the spectators.

In a second Danny had vaulted on to the parapet beside her and put his arm round her. A moment later Mr. Smithson was beside them. Danny held on to Sandra until her father lifted her down bodily. To Marcus' astonishment, there was no lecture or spanking - just a tight hug and a kiss.

"You've had enough party, Sandra," said her mother. "Most of the mothers and amahs are here to take your friends home, so let's find some presents for you to hand round to them before they leave."

She produced a box full of wrapped parcels, and Sandra was instantly diverted: "And can Danny have the best present? Can I choose it for him?"

"I think he deserves the first present," said Mr. Smithson, taking Danny's arm suddenly and gripping it.

"And Philip must have a special present too!" Sandra darted over to Philip, who was looking bashful, and dragged him forward. "For walking all the way up the Peak just to come to my party!"

"Really, Sandra, all the presents are much the same," laughed Mr. Smithson. "Come and take one, Philip - that really was a great effort on your part; and don't go running off home by yourself: Ming will drive you down when he takes Pamela and her friends."

At last it was over and all four were opening their presents in the car and talking at once. Everyone agreed it had been a wonderful party and that Sandra's house was beautiful.

"So are you," whispered Marcus in Pamela's ear.

She turned and stared at him, then burst out laughing.

"What's so funny?" demanded Danny.

Marcus held his breath and prayed inwardly, but in vain.

"Marcus says.. I'm... beautiful... too!" spluttered Pamela. "Me, beautiful! You're soppy, Marcus!"

"You're not bad," Philip ventured, "especially in that dress."

"You're as beautiful as a monkey," grinned Danny. He still wore the look of excitement brought on with his success as Felix the Cat.

'Show off' thought Marcus, and hated both boys. He felt denigrated: despite his new suit and his careful manners, he had not been a success. Philip, with his scruffy clothes and lack of grace, had been singled out and noticed; Danny in his secondhand trousers had achieved even greater notoriety; and Pamela had wounded him deeply with her lack of sensitivity for his feelings. He withdrew into his corner of the car and left them to their chatter.

"Oh, by the way, Pam," said Philip as they neared Kennedy Road, "I'm coming to your school next term."

"ARE you? Oh, peachey! Why's that?" "I passed some exam, they said."

"I'm so glad!" Pamela bounced up and down with pleasure. "We'll be in the same class, then we can go over on the ferry together, and come back together, and compare homework, and..."

Marcus tried not to listen. He sank back further into his corner, and wished there had never been a party.

FEBRUARY

The moment Pamela woke up and heard the crackers in the neighbouring streets, she remembered it was Chinese New Year.. and therefore a holiday. There was the chink of china downstairs as Ah Tai prepared the morning tea, but no sound of the heavy polisher on the wooden floors, for the amahs would do no work other than this first brew of tea.

When she brought in Pamela's tea, Ah Tai was already dressed in her best clothes - jacket and trousers of shiny blue brocade, protected by her workday white apron from neck to hips. Behind her came Ah Lee the teen-age 'makee-learn', bashfully exhibiting her new clothes - a jacket and trousers in plum coloured silk. Beaming happily, her hands behind her back, she stood looking at Pamela until Ah Tai grunted a command, then lunged forward and planted a loose brown paper parcel on the bed, singing "Kung hei fat choi!".

"Kung hei fat choi!" responded Pamela joyfully, pulling off the paper. Out fell a dress in the pinkest pink, with a high, smocked yoke, and long sleeves with smocking at the wrists. It looked rather short for her, and was undoubtedly a colour her mother would never dream of buying; fearing her mother would show her distaste when she saw it, Pamela put all her heart into her exclamations of delight and gratitude. She must try it on at once, the amahs insisted. She stood before the mirror, trying not to notice that her legs looked longer than usual, and that the dress made her look about six years old. Ah Tai hovered round, smoothing down the skirt, fingering the beautiful smocking with great satisfaction.

There was another present: a small bright red envelope containing a ten cent piece - 'lucky money', meant to assure the recipient of a safe passage through the coming year.

Pamela held her breath as she saw her mother appear behind her in the mirror. "Don't let her say anything awful!" she prayed.

"Wherever did you get that gorgeous dress, Pam?" Her mother was smiling beautifully.

"I buy, makee-learn buy, for Chinese New Year," Ah Tai beamed.

"It's really lovely! But you're both naughty to spend so much money. It must only be worn for special occasions, Pam."

There were hysterical paroxysms of laughter from Ah Lee, too bashful to face her mistress's pleasure.

"Can I wear it today, then?" Pamela asked.

"When we've finished all the things we have to do," promised her mother.

Here was the snag about Chinese New Year - having to help about the house. Her mother cooked breakfast, and Pamela and Belle had to wash and dry the dishes; Rodney escaped such duties because he was due to leave early for a camping holiday with the Scouts.

After breakfast, when the amahs came in to say goodbye, their faces were red with excitement, their eyes bright. They were handed the traditional employers' present - one month's wages each, and now it was their turn to express excessive gratitude.

"We'll have cold meat and salad for tiffin," Mrs. Doran decided. "So we just need a few potatoes peeled, Belle."

"Can't Pam do them? She's old enough." Belle was examining her face in the hall mirror. "Keith's coming for me at 2.. I've got things to do this morning."

"I'm going out after tiffin too," pouted Pamela, "AND I've got to do my piano practice this morning."

"Then get on with it at once," came the prompt order from her mother.

Pamela escaped to the lesser of the two evils, and settled herself before the piano on the carved blackwood stool. It was cold, so was the room, for the fireplace was empty, it was only used three or four times each winter, which made it seem unfair that most of the cold days came over Chinese New Year when the amahs were not available to deal with the fires, and no one else in the house would undertake the task. She took time to turn over the pages of her music to find her latest piece, and earned an aggrieved call from Belle: "I thought you'd gone in there to practise?"

She thumped out some scales as loudly as she dared, then tried out the new piece Mrs. Russell had set her to learn. Nothing about piano playing appealed to her - only the weekly meeting with Danny, Marcus and Sandra, and sometimes Philip, made the torment worth while. There had even been times lately when she didn't enjoy Saturday afternoons in the old way: Sandra and Danny were always whispering together and excluding her, while Marcus sulked shockingly whenever Philip turned up .

As for Philip, she wondered if he would call for her this afternoon as promised. He was the vaguest person she had ever known. Times and arrangements meant nothing to him - she was always astonished that he actually arrived at school each day, for he had as foreshadowed transferred to the Central British School after Christmas. They rarely met on the ferry in the morning because of his perpetual lateness, but travelled home together. Often she was late getting home because Philip had been 'kept in' for some reason or another - forgetting to give in his homework, or doing it badly.

"You're hopeless, Phil," she told him one afternoon when he couldn't find his ferry season ticket when he reached the turnstyle. She lent him five cents for the fare. He thanked her very casually, and never mentioned the matter again; even on a later occasion when he flourished a ten cent piece he had unexpectedly acquired, he didn't offer to repay her. She came to realise that he simply forgot about such things.

He was so often in trouble at school that she now as a matter of course reminded him to bring his sports equipment, and to take home the necessary books for homework. Sometimes his ineptitude irritated her, and for a day or two she would not bother to jog his memory; as a result he turned up to Art lesson without a rubber, his only pencil the inevitable indelible stub. The resultant effort was displayed to the class by the exasperated teacher, bringing forth giggles which did not seem to upset Philip in the least - he simply grinned cheerfully; nor did he mend his ways afterwards.. he really was hopeless...

"Pamela, Pamela!" Her mother's voice interrupted her reverie. "I don't hear much practising in there."

"She's just hiding to escape any housework!" Belle's resentful voice added.

Inevitably, Pamela was then summoned to help her mother in the kitchen to release Belle, who immediately dashed upstairs to her room. She emerged just before tiffin, smelling of bath essence, hair freshly shampooed, and dressed in a cream tussore low-waisted dress, and wearing a red bandana round her head, obliterating most of her hair.

"Tennis this afternoon, I see," remarked Mr. Doran with the indulgent smile he usually wore on his return from the Civil Service Club just across the Valley. "With the young man, no doubt?"

Belle crimsoned, and Pamela said cruelly "She took two hours to get ready this morning. I had to peel nearly all the potatoes because of that."

"And you didn't make a very good job of them, either," said her mother severely. "They're like marbles."

"I'll help with the dishes afterwards," came Belle's surprising offer. "I'm all ready to go out."

"Aha!" Mr. Doran pointed a finger at her. "We want to be looking really domesticated when the boy-friend calls, don't we? We want to show what a good little wife we would make, eh?"

Pamela giggled. Belle flushed again and bit her lip. Mrs. Doran heaped more potatoes on to her husband's plate, banging the serving spoon noisily.

"Surely a father can take a kindly interest in his daughter's goings-on? I wouldn't be a good father if I didn't, now, would I?"

"Get on, Adam." Mrs. Doran briskly guided the conversation to other channels, while Pamela studied Belle closely and considered this new development. The family had heard quite alot about this Keith, originally referred to as 'that awful new sub-manager', then 'Mr. Barrington' and now 'Keith', but this was the first time he was to call at the house. He turned up promptly at two, wearing long cream flannels and a white shirt and blue blazer; he was much taller than Belle, with a shock of stiff brown hair and a little moustache. He didn't look in the least romantic - not like Ramon Navarro or Rudolf Valentino. She liked him even less when her mother airily waved Belle's repeated offer to help with the tiffin dishes, with "Pam and I will see to them - off you two go and enjoy yourselves."

"But Philip's coming for me," she began in disgust.

"You can go as soon as he arrives," her mother interrupted, and with this concession she had to be content; but the work was finished and Philip hadn't come. An hour after the agreed time she decided not to wait any longer for him in case her mother found her another job, or suggested more piano practice.

"I think I'll go across to the Club, I might meet Rosie or Joan or someone there," she told her mother.

"Good idea! Soon I must fix up tennis lessons for you, Hilary Bateley's mother is starting her next month."

"Not lessons yet.. Hilary's much older than I am." All lessons were anathema to Pamela. "And Mum, can I sign for a sarsey at the club?"

"Sarsaparilla, not sarsey ...yes alright, but only one; I shall see the chit at the end of the month, so I shall know!"

The tree-shaded path across Happy Valley was thronged with Chinese families, the children stiffly dressed in their best padded garments. Everyone was buying peanuts and sugar cane and sweetmeats from hawkers operating from tiny portable stalls. Among the crowds Pamela suddenly spotted Philip.

"Thought you were never coming," she said.

"Well I did, but I've had to bring the girls." He indicated Mary and Teresa trailing slowly behind him. "My father's not very well, and my mother said I had to take them out so he could rest."

"What's wrong with him?"

"Pains in the stomach or something."

"Why did we have to walk all this way, Philip?" complained Teresa. "What are we going to do?"

"I don't know," he shrugged. "Mum said you had to come with me. I didn't want you to come."

"I want to go home," whined Mary, lifting up her left leg. "My foot hurts."

"Where? Let's have a look?"

Pamela was amazed at Philip's patience as he bent down, undid the button on her left shoe and removed it. There was blood on the white sock, and a tiny pebble fell out of the shoe.

"It's BLEEDING!" Mary's tears turned into a great howl which continued as Philip wiped the blood off her foot with his handkerchief and replaced sock and shoe.

"It's all right now," he patted her shoulder, "It won't hurt any more "

"It DOES!" Mary wailed, and the concerned crowd nearby thickened.

"Do shut up, Mary," Philip begged. "Everyone's looking at us!"

"I know!" cried Pamela suddenly, "Let's all have a sarsey, would you like that Mary?"

"Yes," she hiccoughed, tears staunched as if by magic. "Where is it?"

"In my club," said Pamela grandly. "Come on, Phil, it's just along at the end of the path. We'll share a bottle."

At the entrance to the single-storey club-house, opening on to its private tennis courts and bowling green, Philip hung back. "Isn't it only for members?" he whispered.

"I'm a member - at least, my parents are, so I am; and we're allowed to bring guests."

"You're sure?"

"Of course. My sister Belle is here today, playing tennis, and she's brought her friend, Keith. Come on!

She led the way through the bar to the open verandah and found an empty table, then called "Boy!" in her most important voice.

He was an old friend and didn't bat an eyelid when she ordered one bottle of sarsaparilla and four glasses and straws. Aware of the round-eyed wonder of Mary and Teresa, she signed the chit with her best hand-writing. The Boy poured the drink equally into the four glasses and flicked a straw into each.

"There's hardly any!" said Mary in disgust.

"Greedy pig," hissed Philip. "It's all Pamela's really - we're lucky to get any."

"What are you up to?" demanded an adult voice, and Pamela looked up to see her sister and Keith standing over them.

"Counting the bubbles, I'd say," laughed Keith. "Wouldn't you all like just a little bit more?"

"Yes, please," asked Mary promptly.

"Mummy said I was only to order one bottle," said Pamela. "Then I met Philip, and we had to bring his sisters."

"So now you need three more bottles. I'll stand you them," finished Keith, beckoning to the Boy.

Pamela's face shone with pleasure. "Oh, peachey! Oh thanks, Mr. Barrington!"

"Keith," he suggested, pulling up a wicker chair for Belle and one for himself. "Mind if we join you?"

He not only paid for their drinks, but also plied them with salted peanuts and potato crisps. The two small girls ate stolidly through everything, but Pamela and Philip, acutely conscious of their good fortune and not wishing to offend in any way, helped themselves more cautiously.

"There's a court free now, Belle," said Keith, getting up. "Let's go and grab it."

The children drained their glasses and finished off the last of the crisps and peanuts, then looked around for other amusements, but the ping-pong tables were monopolised by giant teenagers, and the dog-eared magazines from England were all for grownups. Pamela wanted to wait in the hope of a ping-pong table becoming free, but Philip insisted he must go home, obviously still feeling awkward as a non-member of the club.

"I'll come part of the way with you," Pamela said. "There's no one here for me to play with if I stay here on my own."

They made their way past Morrison Hill, for once bereft of its swarms of black-clad men and women coolies chipping away at the granite, and up to Kennedy Road.

"If it wasn't for having to get the girls to climb all those steps," said Philip as he glanced up at Dragon Terrace, "we could nip up and see Danny and Marcus."

"Any case, I'm not allowed, except for music lessons," Pamela began, when a loud "Hello!" drowned her words; then Marcus could be seen jumping off the balustrade and running down the steps towards them, followed closely by Danny.

A race developed. Marcus' longer legs gave him an initial advantage, but Danny's agility brought him nearer to Marcus at every stride. In a last desperate effort, Marcus took the last four steps with a flying leap and fell over at the feet of the others. Possessions shot out of his pockets on to the ground; Danny, arriving immediately after, helped pick up the scattered items, which included the coveted wallet. Marcus quickly snatched at it and a photograph fell out.

"Look, Pam," said Philip, "Your phizog!" He picked up the photograph and the others gathered round him.

"It's out of the photo of Sandra and me, at her party," said Pamela."You've cut Sandra off, you've spoilt it!"

"It's my copy, I can do what I like with it," cried Marcus, struggling to retrieve the photograph.

"What's that writing on the back?" demanded Danny, snatching at it.

"Give it to me, it's mine!" Marcus pushed at the children with one hand, and with the other, pulled the now-bent phogograph and thrust it into an inside jacket pocket.

"What IS written on the back, Marcus?" asked Philip.

"None of your business!"

"I expect it says Pamela is his sweetheart," laughed Danny. "Isn't that right, Marcus?"

There was no reply. Marcus, head down, was already running up the steps. Pamela stared after him in bewilderment. She should have been flattered that he kept her photograph in his wallet; instead, she felt strangely uneasy, the more so now that he was so obviously upset.

"Come back, man!" Danny called. "What's wrong with having a sweetheart? I've got one, haven't I? I've got Sandra for my sweetheart!"

Marcus went on running.

"Oh, you're all soppy," said Pamela crossly. "Come on Phil, let's go!"

"I'll come with you," said Danny.

"No thanks." Pamela's eyes were still on Marcus' fleeing figure. "We don't want you. You've spoilt everything."

Danny, his face instantly crestfallen, looked at her uncertainly. She turned her back on him and walked purposefully over to Philip and his sisters, saying "Let's get away from here."

"Pam.." Danny hurried after her, "Pam, why are you so serious about everything? We were only joking."

"Marcus wasn't."

"Well, you know Marcus - he's always serious."

"Oh, go home Danny!" she shouted crossly.

"Don't want to. I promised Mrs. Holtz I'd visit her this week, so I'm going now. Don't be so grumpy, Pam, it's not like you at all."

Tagging alongside the little party, he continued to try to wheedle Pamela into a good mood but she refused to speak to him. When she pointedly started to talk to Philip across him, Danny went to the other side of the road and walked level with the others, doing his clever impersonations which made everyone laugh except Pamela. She was paying him out, not only for highlighting the embarrassment over the wallet, but also because the whole episode reminded her of Marcus' unwanted attentions which made her feel uncomfortable. Also - and she could not say why this should matter now that she had Philip for a friend - she was paying him out for deserting her for Sandra as soon as the latter appeared on the scene.

When Philip and his sisters said goodbye at the entrance to their barracks, Pamela waved them off, then turned to retrace her steps towards Happy Yalley, but Danny held her arm and stood in front of her.

"I really didn't mean to upset you," he said, speaking urgently as she tried to pull away. "I'm sorry, truly sorry. I'll tell Marcus I'm sorry for what I said, too. Don't go on being angry, please, Pam!"

His abject apology was a great relief; she had been wondering for the past five minutes how she could ever return to Dragon Terrace for music lessons without talking to Danny.

"All right, I forgive you!" she said in an exaggerated voice, for it was easier that way, "but don't you ever dare to say anything like that again!"

"Oh, I won't, I promise! And Pam, maybe I won't call on Mrs. Holtz today after all. I'll walk back with you instead."

They talked earnestly on the way, Danny seeming to sense Pamela's disquiet at the discovery that Marcus kept her photograph in his wallet.

"People do things like that when they get older," he explained. "Anyway, if I had a wallet, I would have photos of all my best friends in it. Marcus is older than us p'raps that's why he does it."

"I'll feel so silly next time I see him," sighed Pamela.

"No you won't, because I'm going to explain it all to him - how you feel," he declared. "Now don't you worry about it any more, Pam. I'll tell you what's much more worrying - Mrs. Holtz."

"Why, is she ill?"

"No, not ill, but she hasn't had a letter from Mr. Holtz for a long time, and the poor old thing is really unhappy. I'm sure it isn't only because he hasn't sent her money; she's worried about him, and lonely for his letters. I think we ought to try to cheer her up.. take her for a picnic or something - you, me, Marcus, Philip, and Sandra if she can get permission.. let her see she has some friends who care about her: what do you say?"

"It's a lovely idea, Danny, but I'm not sure if I'd be allowed.."

"Oh, surely your parents wouldn't stop you from helping out Mrs. Holtz when she's unhappy? My mother always encourages me to go and see her."

Pamela remained silent. Although her parents had been less strict about how long she spent at Dragon Terrace since Sandra started music lessons the same day, she thought it most unlikely she would be allowed to join in a picnic which included Danny and Marcus.. but how could she say this to Danny?

APRIL

The great day had come and Sandra could still hardly believe her good fortune. Such a thing had never happened before. Perhaps it wouldn't happen even now - her parents might change their minds! In an effort to prevent this, she did what she thought would please them most: went to the piano and feverishly practised her scales. Even when her father came in to the room she kept her eyes on the keys.

"I'm trying to catch up with Pam," she explained. "We'll be able to play duets while she's here, Daddy. It was such a lovely idea to invite her!"

"Pamela's a nice little girl. Your mother and I both like her very much. I'm sure you'll both behave yourselves while we're away, and do what Ah Ling and Ming say."

"I'll be PERFECT with Pam - she always does what she's told."

"Darling, I really think you've done enough practice this morning, so could you do something else until Pamela gets here?"

But how could she settle to anything, with the glorious prospect of having Pamela to stay with her for nearly two whole days, while her parents went to Canton on business? All that time there would be no remonstrations or cold looks to fear from her mother, no need to dread the rising panic of another confrontation which would lead to an uncontrollable tantrum, no need to hide from the dread and anxiety in her beloved father's face whenever a tantrum developed.

For perhaps the first time in her life, Sandra made a conscious effort to conform. When Ming was sent to collect Pamela, she made to go with him, but her mother said No. Her first instinct was to argue and protest, but she swallowed the words and accepted the verdict without comment.

After Ming had left it became apparent why Sandra had not been allowed to accompany him: she had to endure a lengthy exhortation from her mother to behave well during the parental absence. The message was identical to her father's so why did she resent her mother's words so deeply? When Pamela arrived Mrs. Smith shot a warning glance at Sandra, and added a meaningful "Don't forget what I said" when she and her husband left for Canton.

"Isn't it simply wonderful you were asked to come, Pam? Weren't you surprised? I was!" Sandra danced about in delight. "We can do anything we want this morning. And guess what, this afternoon as it's warm enough to swim, Daddy's fixed up for Ming to take us to the beach with the canoe, because our neighbours the Johnsons are going too and they have a matshed next to ours at South Bay! They're all grownup but not a bit stuffy, you'll love them."

The April sun was hot that afternoon, but the water was not quite warm enough for prolonged swimming, so after a quick dip the friendly Johnsons carried the canoe down the beach, helped Sandra and Pamela into it, and showed them how to manoeuvre it.

The two girls paddled back and forth in the shallows until they felt proficient enough to venture further out into the bay. Most of the Johnsons had now disported themselves on the beach. Ah Ling, barefoot and with her black trousers rolled up to her knees, stood at the water's edge and shouted warnings to stay close to the shore.

Sandra ignored the repeated shouts. She was happier today than she had ever been, delighted with the company of an undemanding friend, away from restrictions; this was a different world, surrounded by a sparkling sea overhung with great green mountains.

"I could stay out here for ever," she sighed to Pamela.

The tide was going out and the canoe began to drift seawards. The amah renewed her shrieks; one of the Johnsons on the beach stood up and indicated very clearly that they should make for the shore.

"They can't make us come in," giggled Sandra.

"We'd better, though," advised Pamela.

"Goody goody! I told Daddy you always did what you were told! Perhaps you're right, though, we'd better get back."

They brought the canoe in to the beach, Ah Ling scolding loudly.

"We're not babies," said Sandra scornfully in Cantonese. "Anyway, we did come back, so don't go on about it."

Ming carried the canoe up the beach while Ah Ling draped a large towel round each girl and urged them to get dressed quickly. Sandra protested that they were not cold, their swimming costumes were no longer wet, and anyway, the Johnsons were calling them for a picnic tea so they could get dressed after tea. Ah Ling's voice immediately shot up into a higher register and she made a grab at Sandra.

"You come changee, Missie Pamela," she appealed in English, "then Missee Sandra come too!"

"Don't, Pam!" commanded Sandra.

"Well, my suit is rather damp," said Pamela. "It's thicker than yours, so I think I'll change now."

"Goody goody two-shoes!" yelled Sandra, seeing herself foiled. Still arguing angrily, she was forced to follow Pamela up the slatted steps and into the enclosed part of the matshed. Ah Ling tried to come in too, but Sandra slipped in quickly, slammed the thin bamboo door closed and twitched the wooden latch across. Ah Ling called in vain to be admitted, Sandra replying that they could dress themselves.

"Does she usually dress you?" asked Pamela as she struggled and wriggled to peel off her woollen suit.

"When I let her," grinned Sandra. "She thinks I'm a baby."

They ate a huge tea with the Johnsons, then joined in an hilarious game of cricket on the beach, the batsmen sending gouts of sand flying through the air as well as the ball; there was much outrageous cheating, and eventually every one was laughing so much that the game fizzled out. Sandra wanted it to go on for ever, this afternoon of unadulterated pleasure, and she pouted rudely when Mr. Johnson said Ming was waiting to drive her and Pamela back.

"Are you all going home now, too?" she demanded.

"Not quite yet - but it's time you two tiddlers left."

"But what are YOU going to do?"

"Oh, just sit about; play cards; John will play his ukelele and we'll sing." The Johnson teenagers and their friends smiled secretly among themselves, which Sandra found maddening. "We want to stay too!" she whined.

"You'll have a lovely evening at home with your little friend," said Mrs. Johnson firmly. "I expect Ah Ling will let you stay up a little later than usual as it's such a special occasion."

"You bet she will - I'll make her!" Sandra whispered to Pamela as the two girls followed Ah Ling to the car.

Despite the picnic tea they were expected to eat a large supper that evening.

"Leave it if you don't want it, Pam," advised Sandra. "I'm going to leave mine. They can't make us eat it."

"I'd better have some," said Pamela, her forehead creased with anxiety as Sandra laid down her knife and fork and pushed away her plate of steamed fish in white sauce.

"But do you want to? Don't tell me you like it!"

"Not very much, but.." Pamela hesitated, then rapidly cleared her plate.

"Traitor," hissed Sandra, waving aside Ah Ling's demands that she should behave as nicely as her friend and the threat that unless the fish was eaten she would have no pudding. She sat glaring at her fish, taking satisfaction in Pamela's embarrassment at having to eat her lemon mousse alone.

"Sorry," Pamela muttered when they left the table. "I didn't mean to show you up, but being a guest.."

"Doesn't matter," said Sandra huffily. "I'll get my mousse in the end - you'll see."

She was right. An hour later when both girls had bathed and getting ready for bed, Ah Ling brought in a tray with two dishes of lemon mousse and glasses of milk. "After finish, clean teeth," she said, "then go night-nights. I come back by-and-by to see you go sleep."

" 'Night-nights'?" repeated Pamela incredulously once Ah Ling had gone.

"She always says that. I told you, she treats me like a baby, they all do. That's why I like getting away from them as much as I can."

"But 'night-nights'!" repeated Pamela, collapsing on the bed in a gale of laughter.

"Don't you tell any of the others! Don't you dare!"

"I won't," Pamela gurgled,

"We're not going to sleep for hours," announced Sandra after they had cleaned their teeth. "There's lots I want to know."

She wanted to talk interminably about Philip, Danny and Marcus and all their activities, these people who seemed free in an adult world instead of captive like herself. Even Pamela's comparative freedom to come and go intrigued and frustrated her.

Ah Ling came in several times and urged them to stop talking. She put out the lights but still they whispered on. Lying there in the darkness with a willing and sympathetic listener, Sandra poured out all her unhappiness, her constant fear of her mother's disapproval, her distress at seeing her father's concern, and at the frustrations of her restricted life; finally, her dread of being sent to boarding school in England.

"But then you'd be away from your mother so you wouldn't have rows with her," Pamela's sleepy voice from the other bed pointed out. "I don't see why you'd mind going to school in England."

"It's because Hong Kong is my home, not England, not horrible cold, grey England, with houses with tiny little rooms, and toilets at the end of the garden.. ugh! No, I'm going to stay in Hong Kong, no matter what."

"Oh dear, you always seem to be having a fight about something."

"And I always win in the end!"

"Then you're jolly lucky. I have arguments too, at home, but I hardly ever win! I'm still trying to get round my mother to let me go to this picnic Danny's trying to fix up for Mrs. Holtz."

"I'm not asking about that," said Sandra. "They'll never say yes, but I'll get to it somehow when it happens."

"I do hope it's soon - it's getting hotter every day and Mrs. Holtz can't walk very far because she's so fat. Danny says she's down in the dumps too because her typewriter has broken down, he's had to take it to the shop to see if they can repair it." Pamela's voice trailed off in a great yawn. "You still awake Pam?" whispered Sandra. "Just about.."

"I know something else Danny said."

"What's that?"

"Promise you won't say I told you, 'cause he said I wasn't to."

"Um."

"You know Marcus's wallet? And that photo of you he keeps in it? Well, there's something holy about you on the back of it."

"Something HOLY?" repeated Pamela. "Something holy about me? Whatever is it?"

"I don't know, neither does Danny. Only Celeste knows, because Danny asked her to look in the wallet and find out what was on the back of your photo. And she did, but then she wouldn't tell Danny what it was - she just said it was something holy about you."

"Well, I think that's awful!" Pamela sat up in bed, wide awake now. "Fancy Danny making Celeste sneak Marcus' wallet like that!"

"You know Celeste will do anything for Danny, but she just wouldn't say what Marcus had written," repeated Sandra with relish. "What do you think it is?"

"I don't know! How could there be anything holy about ME? It's silly. Perhaps Celeste didn't read it properly, and got it all wrong. Oh, Marcus is so silly, anyway."

"Danny's stuck MY photo in his diary, because he hasn't got a wallet," giggled Sandra.

"Then you're ALL silly," said Pamela crossly, "and I'm tired and I'm going to sleep."

"So am I."

"And Sandra.. this has been the best day of my whole life!"

"For me too," said Sandra vehemently, relieved that Pamela's cross mood had passed. In Ah Ling's sing-song tones she added "Go night-nights now!"

"Night-nights!" Pamela sang back.

She woke first, crept out of bed and peeped through the curtains. Under a cloudless sky, green peaks dipped majestically down to gleaming inlets of water, and the sea itself beyond. In the distance tiny islands reared, and small craft crawled slow-motion across the shimmering sea. It was an entirely new experience for her to find sheer pleasure in scenery; she gazed and gazed, entranced.

"Boo!" Sandra suddenly appeared behind her. "What are you looking at?"

"Just the view. It doesn't look like Hong Kong at all - no streets or people or buses."

"That's why we live up here! Come and get dressed quickly, then we'll have an early breakfast and have a nice long morning to play before music lessons this afternoon."

As they washed and dressed, Sandra elaborated: "I'll make Ah Ling take us for a walk down to Aberdeen; then Ming can drive to Aberdeen and meet us and bring us back."

"Will he do that?" asked Pamela doubtfully. She couldn't imagine that adults would be readily satisfy a child's whim.

"Of course he will if I tell him to!"

Soon after breakfast, Sandra led the way to the path which ran steeply down the hillside. It was simply an earth track which had been battered into a regular route by generations of peasants and European hikers. Sandra, a long way ahead, sang at the top of her voice; leaping downwards, then standing, arms and legs akimbo, laughing up at Pamela's more cautious progress. Much further behind, Ah Ling could be seen picking her way, occasionally calling warnings.

"Isn't it lovely?" exulted Sandra, when Pamela caught her up. "I often do this, but it's much more fun with you than just with Ah Ling; I just love flying downhill! I wish this path would never end."

Pamela wasn't so sure; her calves were aching with the continuous flexing of the muscles to avoid slipping on the sharp incline, and her toes were stubbing painfully against the front of her shoes at every step. She was relieved when Sandra called a halt beside a small reservoir near the foot of the hill. They sat on the low parapet above the reservoir and waited for Ah Ling.

"You naughty girls.. go too muchee fast!" The amah was panting when she reached them. "Maybe you fall down.. or maybe stand on snake.. makee bite, makee die!"

"Well, we didn't do any of those things, so there," laughed Sandra, She started to swing on the railings above the parapet, but although the reservoir was almost empty, Ah Ling forbade this. Pamela was increasingly surprised at the limitations continually imposed on Sandra. She considered her own parents strict, but their rules were mild compared to Ah Ling's. She was beginning to understand why Sandra was in perpetual rebellion against authority.

When they emerged on to the main road which encircled the island, there was Ming with the car.

"There, I told you he'd do it," crowed Sandra as they scrambled in the back. "Lemonades, Ming, we're dying for a drink!"

Pamela watched in some astonishment as Ming produced two bottles of lemonade from a rattan picnic basket, opened them and handed each girl one with a straw.

"Ming knows what I like," confided Sandra. "These are straight from the ice-box, like I told him. But Ah Ling won't let him drive on until we've finished drinking, she thinks it's dangerous to drink while the car's going along. She nags him all the time, same as she nags me; she's his wife, you know."

Pamela gazed at the two servants curiously; there was no sign that they were related to each other in any way at all; they went about their business separately and solemnly, and seldom exchanged words - even now, when they were sitting next to each other in the front of the car.

Sucking appreciatively at her straw, happy in the knowledge that the bottle of lemonade was for her alone and not to be shared with Roddy as was always the case at home; lolling back in the comfortable car Pamela reflected that perhaps Sandra wasn't so badly off after all.

To save time, Danny ran up the hotel stairs instead of waiting for the laborious lift; he sped along the corridor and knocked urgently on Mrs. Holtz' door. There was a faint grunt from within. He knocked again, calling urgently, "Mrs. Holtz, it's Daniel! Can I come in?"

Hearing a wavering assent, he pushed open the door. Mrs. Holtz was lolling in a rattan lounge chair, her feet bare on the pull-out rest. An empty glass hung in the circle of rattan built into the armrest, and an exercise book was open across her stomach.

"Hi Danny," she said lazily. "I've been trying to write by hand, but it's so tiring. Will you go try to find out how much longer that guy on Queen's Road will take to fix the typewriter?"

"Yes, I will, Mrs. Holtz, but not just now, because we've got a great surprise for you!"

She lunged forward in the chair and held out a podgy hand. "You got a letter for me from Mr. Holtz?"

"Oh no, I'm sorry Mrs. Holtz, it's not that." To his dismay she started to cry and tears trickled down her powdered face. Awkwardly, he patted her arm and went on "We've planned a little surprise for you, Marcus and me, and Pam and Sandra. We're going to take you up to the Peak in a beautiful big car! Only you've got to come quickly, because the car's waiting outside the hotel right now."

"You fixed a trip for me? That's real nice of you and your little friends, Danny, but I'm rather tired today.."

"It's got to be today," declared Danny urgently. "Because of the car and everything.. and can you get ready ever so quickly, please?" (He dared not tell her that Ming was an unwilling party to the plan, and might grow impatient and drive off without them.) She decided to wear red shoes with spiky heels which she forced on over short white socks.

"Who's paying for the cab?" she asked suddenly as she peered at her reflection in the mirror and tied a green spotted bandana round her head to secure the avalanche of ginger curls.

"It's not a cab.. taxi," he explained. "It's Sandra's father's car. You see, Ming brought Sandra and Pam for their music lesson but my mother felt dizzy after tiffin and she told me to meet the car and tell Ming she couldn't have them.. but instead of Ming taking Pam and Sandra straight home, we decided to take you for a little picnic.. so they're all waiting outside in the car."

"That's so sweet of you all. I haven't been on a picnic for a long, long time." She made each 'long' sound like a hundred years.

Danny wondered anxiously if the flimsy pale green flowing dress with a loose cape, and high-heeled shoes, were the best things to wear on a picnic, but nothing could be done about it. It was an immense relief to see the car still waiting when he got Mrs. Holtz out of the hotel. Ming looked impassive, even when Mrs. Holtz was eased into the front seat beside him and she thanked him effusively for calling for her.

By the time the car was beyond the city centre and purring upwards towards the Peak, even Ming was softened in the light of Mrs. Holtz' wholehearted enjoyment of the occasion.

Squashed in the back between Sandra and the door, Danny hugged himself with pleasure at the success of his spur-of-the-moment plan: so much could have gone wrong, yet it had all worked out perfectly. His optimism half an hour ago in pocketing a packet of biscuits from the larder for the hoped-for picnic was completely justified. He remembered to send up a brief thank you to God for His part in the plan.

Of course Mrs. Holtz panicked when the car snarled up Garden Road and she was tipped back in her seat at a dentist's-chair angle, but soon recovered to exclaim ecstatically at the view below, marvelling at the myriad rooftops on the tenements in the town, and at the panorama of the harbour with its backdrop of the great humped hills of the mainland, and the toy-like ships in the harbour.

When the road narrowed and snaked round the western side of the island and the city was out of sight, she was enthralled by the new view of hills, greenery and sea, with little sign of habitation.

Her words tumbled over each other: she had never seen such beauty, such a contrast in scenes in so short a time; she would write about it the moment she got back to the hotel.. by hand because to delay, to await the return of the typewriter, would spoil the freshness of her first impressions.. nothing could compare with this first impact: and they were wonderful children to have arranged this wonderful experience for her.

Danny's heart swelled with affection for her. He pinched Sandra's arm and grinned delightedly at her to share the moment.

Now the road was too narrow for vehicular traffic. Ming parked, and agreed to wait in the car while they walked on to picnic at the foot of the great peak above them, known as High West. Watching Mrs. Holtz' stumbling progress on the uneven grass, and conscious of her laboured breathing, Danny settled for the first reasonable place. They found a suitable seat for her on a rounded boulder on which Marcus first draped his handkerchief, and sat down on the scrub grass beside her. The air was cool, for they were some 1,500 feet above sea level. A small wind tugged at the drapes of Mrs. Holtz' dress as they shared out the biscuits.

Marcus produced a rather crushed bag of pear drops, explaining he wouldn't have any because he was in the middle of a Novena and had vowed he wouldn't eat sweets until the end of it.

"What's a Novena?" asked Mrs. Holtz.

"It's where you say special prayers and make sacrifices for nine days in a row, because you want God to grant some special favour," explained Danny.

"That's most interesting; and what is your Novena for, Marcus?"

Marcus looked away and said nothing; Danny had a shrewd idea of the answer, but remembering his promise to Pamela, said nothing.

"Oh, I see - it's a secret," smiled Mrs. Holtz. "Well, I sure admire you for going through with your.. what was it, Novena?"

"Would you like Danny to sing for you, Mrs. Holtz?" Sandra was pushing him forward. "Go on, Danny: do Felix!"

He was used to an appreciative audience, but Mrs. Holtz was almost speechless with admiration, especially when Sandra joined him in the chorus, prancing and dancing she laughed so much that her dress split at one side, and she had to forage in her handbag for a safety pin to hold the separated pieces together.

"What next?" demanded Sandra. "I'd like to climb High West.. who's coming with me? Daddy always promised to take me one day but he never has. Let's do it now!"

"It's too steep," Pamela said at once.

"That's what makes it exciting! It will be gorgeous to run down afterwards - even better than the path to Aberdeen!"

"I can't.. in these shoes," Marcus was looking down at his neat black lace-ups. "I'll stay and keep Mrs. Holtz company."

Danny and Sandra were already racing up the beginning of the hill. Pamela started after them, but soon gave up and slithered back to join Marcus and Mrs. Holtz.

Sandra was so quick that Danny found it an effort to keep up with her. The slope became so steep that they had to grab the scrub and bushes in order to keep their balance. Shouting exultantly, they pressed higher and higher until an insistent tooting below drew their attention. Ming was standing by the car, one hand inside working the horn, and the other hand waving the unmistakable command to return to base immediately.

"Ming's always a spoil sport," Sandra panted. "We don't have to go back yet."

"We'd better." Danny was rather shocked to realise how far up the hill they had travelled, and how very sheer the downward slope appeared.

"You're afraid to go higher!"

"No I'm not, but Ming brought us.. we don't want to annoy him, do we? Tell you what - let's ROLL down.. we'll have a race."

To his relief she agreed at once. They hurtled down the hill, yelling with exuberance, sometimes with pain as their bodies hit sharp outcroppings of stones. The parched grass was hard and spikey too; when they picked themselves up at the foot of the hill they were scratched and their clothes grubby and untidy.

Mrs. Holtz stumbled over to them, all concern in case they had hurt themselves. Some of her curls had escaped imprisonment under her bandana, and dangled unevenly around her face. Her flowing cape had caught on a bush and torn. "I sure thought you were both going to be killed," she cried, taking a tiny flat silver flask from her handbag and drinking a quick mouthful from it. Mine was still hooting and gesticulating.

"I think we ought to get back to the car," said Pamela, "he looks a bit cross."

"Plenty of time," said Sandra easily. "I don't know why he's fussing so, my parents won't be home until late tonight."

"Still, we've been here quite a long time, Sandra," whispered Danny; even from this distance, Ming looked decidedly unfriendly. "And remember, we've got to get him to agree to take Mrs. Holtz back to the hotel when he drives Pam home.

"Oh all right," Sandra gave in, "but we'll all go to my house first and have some lemonade."

Ming refused to return Sandra's friendly greetings when they reached the car. Danny heard him scolding her in Cantonese in a low voice for the state of her dress and untidiness. For once Sandra appeared to accept his remonstrations humbly, then he heard her coaxing Ming to take the whole party to the house for drinks: he had to admire her powers of persuasion.

"He's not very keen," she whispered to Danny. "You'll have to have your drinks jolly quickly because he's fussing about having to take Mrs. H. home as well as Pamela."

The children scrambled out of the car the moment it stopped in the drive. Danny helped Mrs. Holtz out while Ming held her door open. The dogs in the walled yard beyond were barking; the front door was opened by the House Boy before Sandra could press her finger on the bell.

"Boy, bring lemonade for us all in the lounge," she ordered as she passed him. The Boy started to speak, but his words were drowned by Mrs. Holtz' booming voice as Danny and Marcus guided her through the door. "Well, this is some house! It's very kind of Mr. Ming to drive me here. Oh, those dogs, they sound so fierce - they aren't loose, are they? Because I read there's rabies in Hong Kong and I wouldn't like to get bitten. Oh, oh, that beautiful, gorgeous vase! It's just perfect!"

Danny became aware that something was wrong. The house Boy was running after Sandra, trying to convey some message; a frantic looking amah was padding rapidly down the staircase, gesticulating. Sandra took no notice, intent on leading her friends triumphantly into the lounge; threw open the door and bowed them in.

Danny, alerted to some kind of crisis, hung back; then every one ahead of him stopped in their tracks inside the open door, and he saw why: the lounge was already occupied by a group of people taking tea; among them he recognised Sandra's parents. In that split second before anything was said, Danny was sickeningly aware of the contrast between the immaculately dressed and groomed occupants, and the motley, dishevelled gang which had just entered. Every piece of dried grass on his shorts, every smudge on his hands, felt magnified; he was conscious of Mrs. Holtz' bandana drooping over one side of her face, the straggle of limp curls, the safety pin in her dress, her grotesque fat legs in white socks.

Sandra was gaping at her parents. "I thought you were still in Canton," she stammered.

The other adults were smiling, the Smithsons looked appalled. Ah Ling came running in and took Sandra by the arm. "Come wash," she hissed urgently.

"Not yet!" Sandra pulled away. "Daddy, we're all hot, can we have some lemonade please? "We'll go on the verandah so as not to disturb you and your friends." With a sudden return of manners, she ducked in the direction of the strangers and said "Good afternoon. These are my friends Pamela, Danny, Marcus - and Mrs. Holtz. She's a writer. We took Mrs. Holtz on a picnic, Mummy the music lesson was cancelled; it's the first picnic Mrs. Holtz has had for years."

"A picnic? Ah, that explains everything," laughed the man sitting next to Mrs. Smithson. "You've really been enjoying yourselves, haven't you?"

"Come and tell us about the picnic, Sandra," invited the woman opposite, patting the chair next to her. "Where did you go, and what did you do?"

"You can tell Mrs. Lindfield about it later," interposed Mrs. Smithson in a strained voice, only just audible above Mrs. Holtz' enthusiastic tribute to the kindness of the children to give her a picnic. "First, you would probably all like to go and freshen up, then have your lemonade."

Mrs. Holtz stayed where she had seated herself, adjusting her bandana and patting her hair; the children silently followed Ah Ling to the downstairs cloakroom to wash their hands. Pamela muttered that she didn't want any lemonade and would rather go home right away; Marcus echoed her words; Danny felt the same way, but he saw Sandra's anxious look and said it would be unfair to leave her to face an awkward situation without them, so they all trooped back to the lounge and sat awkwardly among the adults, drinking lemonade and nibbling biscuits. In their absence Mrs. Holtz had apparently been offered tea; now she took the flask from her handbag and poured the remaining contents into her cup. Danny saw the shock register on the other adults' faces, and suddenly realised why. Mrs. Holz' dependence on liquor had been growing so gradually that it was only now, in an unfamiliar setting, that he realised how great it was. She grew more and more voluble and less and less articulate. The adults were looking at each other uneasily. Danny jumped to his feet and said "Excuse me, please, Mr. and Mrs. Smithson, but I think we should leave now. Thank you very much for the lemonade and everything."

"Very well," said Mrs. Smithson, rising at once and pressing a button set in the wall. "Ming shall take you all home."

"Phew! Sandra's for it when those visitors leave," Danny muttered as the car moved off.

"Her mother was sure furious," agreed Marcus soberly. They spoke in undertones so that Mrs. Holtz in the front seat would not hear. "And I don't blame her: Pam and I looked quite respectable - but as for you, Danny, and Sandra, and you-know-who! - The Smithsons must have felt terribly ashamed."

"Don't rub it in," growled Danny.

"I don't expect I'll ever get invited there again," mourned Pamela.

"Now wasn't that a lovely afternoon?" beamed Mrs. Holtz, twisting round and regarding them all affectionately. Her face was damp, her dress dyed dark beneath the arms with perspiration, and clung in wrinkles across her bulging back. "You must all come to tea with me in the hotel one day soon. I don't know when I last had such a good time: wait till I write and tell Mr. Holtz about it!"

MAY

Celeste opened her eyes, saw daylight had come, and sighed with contentment; she had survived for this great day, had avoided the fate of the doomed children the First Communion class had been told about, who expired in their beds the night before, not having confessed some mortal sin beforehand.

Lying perfectly straight, on her back, she slowly made a perfect sign of the cross and whispered a prayer for help for the day. Outside, in the trees behind and below the terrace, the cicadas were rasping noisily; from the town rose the hum and buzz of domestic life, bus horns, dogs' barks, joyous gongs, wooden slip-slops.

She shared this small room with her fifteen-year-old sister Marie. She would have liked to get up and wash to make sure she was in plenty of time for this long-awaited First Communion Mass, but Marie as still asleep and it would be mean to wake her too early. She offered up her impatience to start the day as a special sacrifice. She said her morning prayers over and over again, chasing away any thought which savoured of the world.

She was still a little troubled about the matter of Marcus' wallet, although she had confessed having deliberately looked at some one's private possessions and telling others about them. The priest had seemed less worried about it than she was. In any case, absolution had been given and penance of five Hail Marys performed. Yet she felt that something more was required.. she should confess to

Marcus and ask his forgiveness. Oh, blessed thought.. to have this weight lifted from her heart, her guilt washed away by her humility in confessing to him! Then she had a vision of Marcus' dismay and embarrassment on learning that some one knew his secret and thought it better not to tell him: she would never reveal to any one - not even to Danny - the words on the back of Pamela's photograph, so at least that part of his secret was safe. No, she must not allow herself the relief of confessing to Marcus: that was her real punishment.

She gazed across to the shelf which held a small statue of Our Lady, a crucifix, and a tiny vase of nasturtiums. "Dear Mother of God," she whispered. "I want to feel perfect today. I want to tell Marcus what I did, but I mustn't, so I will offer it all up as a special sacrifice for the intentions of all us First Communicants today."

Marie slept on, looking as saintly as the nun she openly declared she wished to be. Again Celeste controlled her impatience to crawl out of bed and start the day. There was much more to pray for.

"Dear Lamb of God," she whispered earnestly, "please make Sandra's parents change their minds and let Sandra come back to Aunty May for piano lessons, because every one was only trying to make Mrs. Holtz happy by taking her on that picnic. Please, please don't let them send Sandra away to boarding-school in September because she would hate it. And please, make Pamela's parents let her go on having music lessons for years, instead of saying she's got to stop having them after she's taken Grade III exam. next month. And please make poor Danny happy again because he's so upset about Sandra not coming here any more."

There was still something more to be said. Sister had impressed on them at the last instruction session that God would never refuse anything a child asked on its First Communion Day. What Celeste longed for was the ability to walk properly; she even dreamed of a miracle by which her misshapen leg became normal overnight. This was to be her personal request - the Sister had suggested it - that she would some day be able to walk properly. But, her hands pressed tightly together and her eyes closed, she prayed instead: "Never mind about my leg, dear Jesus. there are so many other things I want.. for Sandra and for Danny, and please bless Marcus and let Pamela be delivered into his care forever when she is old enough. Amen."

"You'll feel like a fish out of water among all those Catholics and Portuguese," her mother had argued when Pamela's invitation to Celeste's First Communion party arrived.

"But it would be rude to refuse.. and Philip and Teresa are going and they're not Portuguese!"

Reluctantly, permission had been given, but now, looking at all the dark heads round the large table in the Bellario home, Pamela had to admit to feeling out of place; even the two pinkskinned Taits were Catholics, and she the only non-

Catholic present. Both Portuguese and English was being spoken. Among the iced buns and fancy jellies and cakes were glossy coloured Holy pictures for Celeste, Teresa and three other Portuguese girls from the neighbourhood, all still wearing their beautiful white dresses and veils. Like happy brides, their veils were now thrown back over their heads. Damp tendrils of hair clung to their foreheads, and their faces were flushed like crimson roses.

Celeste sat at the head of the table, her presents arrayed before her - a mother-of-pearl rosary, a statue of Jesus with the red heart showing through his clothes, a beautiful prayer book with its celluloid ivory covers emblazoned a gold cross, and exquisite little silver medals threaded through with narrow satin white ribbon. Pamela privately would have preferred more worldly presents, but Celeste was obviously delighted with them.

Gathered behind the children's chairs were Bellario brothers and sisters, parents, aunts and uncles and cousins, all entreating the First Communicants to remember them in their prayers. This repeated emphasis on prayer Pamela found embarrassing; at home, she was always reminded to say her morning and night prayers, and now and again she and her family attended Sunday service at St. John's Cathedral - otherwise prayer was not mentioned.

Now it seemed there would be even more prayers; the First Comunicants and other faithful were to attend a special Benediction Service at St. Joseph's after tea.

"I'd better be going home, then," Pamela said as chairs were pushed back from the table.

"Won't you come with us to the Church? Please do!" pleaded Marcus.

"But Pam isn't a Catholic like us," Philip said.

"Doesn't matter. God doesn't mind who comes - we're all His children."

"You can sit next to me, and I'll tell you what to do," added Philip.

Still she hesitated, only too well aware that her parents would not approve - but she had nothing more to lose, now that her music lessons were to cease next month; recklessly, she allowed the boys to take her with them.

In the church, she forgot her uneasiness at the sight of so many little girls beautifully dressed in white, and little boys with new haircuts and wearing miniature white suits. She was fascinated by the blaze of candles on the altar, and by the haunting music on the organ, and the hymns sung in a strange language.

"Aren't your parents coming?" she whispered to Philip.

"No, my Dad's ill again. But my Mum came to the special Mass this morning," he whispered back.

As soon as the short service was over, Philip drifted off with Teresa. The Bellarios stood around chatting with friends, Celeste leaning against her mother; there was a grubby patch on the front of her dress where her hot hand had braced against the crippled leg.

"Pam!" Danny suddenly appeared beside her. "Come down town with me? I ought to call in at the typewriter shop and see if Mrs. Holtz' machine is ready."

The alternative - to walk back with Marcus - was to be avoided at all costs, since Sandra's revelation of the undisclosed words on the photograph in his wallet.

"Yes, I'll come, but I mustn't be late home," she said.

Although it was Sunday, most of the shops were open.

"Wish I had ten cents for lollipops," sighed Danny as they passed the lollipop shop. "You know, there's a boy at school who makes money by having a raffle - sells tickets for five cents each, and when he's sold twenty, he buys twenty prizes; some cost ten cents or more, but most of them cost only two cents. Then he has a draw and every one gets a prize, even if it's only a cheap little one."

"So how does he make any money?"

"He doesn't spend ALL the ticket money on prizes, you silly! If he sells a dollar's worth of tickets, he only spends about seventy cents on prizes, so he makes thirty cents."

"Well," objected Pamela, "I wouldn't like to get only a two-cent pencil for a five-cent ticket."

"You'd be very pleased if you won a twenty-cent purse, though, wouldn't you? I think I'll run a raffle - will you buy a ticket?"

"Well," Pamela considered for a moment, "All right, I suppose so, I might just win something valuable."

"I'd see that you did," he laughed.

She turned and stared at him. "How could you? You wouldn't cheat, would you, Danny?"

"Course not," he said hastily. "Here's the shop, Pam."

The typewriter was still not ready. The Chinese foki took it out from beneath the glass counter and patiently explained that a part was missing and he was contacting other shops to find something that would fit. "Come back few days more," was the hopeful promise.

"Oh dear." Danny looked concerned as they left the shop. "I just can't go and see her today and tell her it still isn't ready, she'll get so upset."

"I couldn't go with you anyway," said Pamela. "I'm not supposed to go to the hotel any more."

"What's wrong with every one now?" exploded Danny. "Sandra's not allowed to come to music lessons any more; you're not allowed to come to the terrace except at lesson time, and you're not having lessons after the exam!" He thrust his hands into his pockets and walked on, head down. They became caught up in a water queue, which snaked along the main road and up to a side street where stand-pipes had been erected. No water was yet being drawn, for the pipes were only turned on at set hours. People waiting in the queue had empty oblong kerosene tins, but the latter end of the queue was mainly of cans only standing in neat lines while their owners went about their business in the hours which would intervene before the queue started to move.

"I know what the trouble is," Danny muttered angrily. "It's because Marcus is Portuguese and I'm only half-English! That's why Sandra doesn't come any more! That's why your parents are stopping your lessons!"

Pamela pretended not to hear: she followed humbly behind him, unable to offer the comfort of a denial, though wishing with all her heart to be able to utter the lie.

The voices came again, cutting across Philip's sleep until he opened his eyes and realised he wasn't dreaming. They came from the verandah which ran the whole length of the barracks flat. Through the open French windows of his room he could see the silhouettes of his parents.

".... must be a huge one - look at those flames!" That was his mother's awed voice.

"Must be one of the big buildings in Central," his father added.

Philip shook himself awake, leapt out of bed and pattered barefoot on to the stone verandah. It was still dark; to the extreme left could be seen the solid dark shapes of the built-up city centre - banks, offices and hotels. It was here that a great pink cloud billowed, fuelled by bursts of sparks and tongues of flame.

He craned to get a better view. More and more people in the barracks were appearing on their verandahs, and some in dressing-gowns were gathering outside the quarters for a wider aspect. Dogs, disturbed, barked and yapped. Small children woke and added their bawls to the commotion. The pink cloud rose higher, pursued by shooting gouts of flame.

"Let's hope it's one of the office blocks," said his father. "Not likely to be any one there at this time of night.. two o'clock.. they wouldn't stand a chance if they were."

Someone called up from the vantage point below. "I think it's one of the hotels," he said.

They had heard the servants saying there had been a big fire in Central during the night, but Danny and Marcus talked of other things as they walked along Kennedy Road to school the next morning. Fires were common-place, many caused through carelessness in fire-cracker shops, others through the custom of burning life-size flimsy paper models of luxury gifts to accompany the newly dead to paradise to keep them happy there.

"I bet I learned all the wrong history last night," said Danny gloomily. "There wasn't time to read the whole book."

"You had all the weekend," Marcus reminded him smugly.

"Except for Pamela on Saturday afternoon, and Celeste's party on Sunday." Danny could have added that he had also spent a considerable time persuading his mother to advance him some pocket money so he could buy some raffle prizes to exhibit to would-be ticket buyers as bait, plus a trip to the shops in Wanchai to buy the gifts, then the time taken to write out the tickets.

"And your raffle," said Marcus cruelly. He had expressed disapproval of the project as soon as he'd heard about it.

"There's nothing wrong in it," Danny protested. "Every one knows they're taking a chance on what sort of prize they get. You might at least buy one ticket, Marcus: Pam's going to."

"No thanks! I don't know how you can do it, Danny; it lets the family down - it's like begging."

Danny averted his face to hide the colour rushing into his cheeks. It was always there between them, the knowledge that the Russells were the poor relations of the Bellarios. "One day," thought Danny passionately, "I'll earn so much money that Marcus and his family will have to ask us for help, instead of Mumma having to ask them."

They turned into the school gates, and at once became aware of an air of excitement among the chattering students in the playground. Two dashed up to Danny and Marcus.

"Did you see the huge fire last night?" one asked. "In Central - it was still smouldering when we came by just now. You couldn't see any bodies though."

"What was it?"

"A hotel."

"A hotel? " Danny heard his own voice asking as at a great distance. "Which one?"

"Not the Gloucester, it's the one on the other side of the road."

"The King Edward," some one supplied.

"Heaps of people were killed, man!"

"Some jumped from the verandahs, but missed the jumping sheets."

"The fire engines and ambulances are still there, looking for bodies."

Danny thrust his schoolbag into Marcus' arms. "I've got to go," he choked, and ran of the gates, down the path to Garden Road and into the town: dodging cars, rickshaws and trams, colliding with pedestrians, his flying footsteps kept time with the prayer beating in his mind over and over again - "Please God, let Mrs. Holtz be all right."

The heart of the city was even more congested than usual, swollen with curious sightseers. The road by the hotel was blocked half-way down by the police, but he saw with a great pang of relief that the building was still standing, although two fire engines stood nearby, and an ambulance was parked on the opposite side of the road. Dribbling hoses lay along the gutters and the road was running with water. Pressed up against the road blocks, he could now see blackened verandahs, and gaps in the upper storeys, and his panic returned.

He asked the Chinese policemen about the extent of the fire; very bad, was the reply, many killed.

"But many saved, too?" Danny begged, and the answer was yes, many saved too.

"Where did they take the ones who were saved?"

The policeman said the injured were in hospital, the others in nearby hotels. He stood still for a few moments, trying to master his churning thoughts. Somewhere, in this town, was his friend Mrs. Holtz, frightened, maybe even injured, with no friends except himself; she needed him and he must find her and comfort her after the night's dreadful experience. He beat back into the farthest recesses of his mind the possibility that she might be dead; he knew he would be lost if he allowed himself to think that.

First he went to the adjacent hotels. He had never entered any of them before. Normally, their plush vestibules and exotic appointments would have awed him, but his singleness of purpose now gave him courage as he braved the stares of passing guests and hurried up to one reception desk after another and put his question. None of the receptionists could help: yes, survivors had been brought in but so far there were no lists. He tried to describe Mrs. Holtz but other anxious enquirers were crowding round and he was ignored. He wanted to cry. Instead, he ground his teeth and stopped a young English woman with a kindly face.

"Oh please, can you help me? I'm trying to find a friend of mine who was living in the King Edward Hotel, I don't know.. don't know where she is." His composure suddenly evaporated and he couldn't speak.

"Have you tried the police?" she asked. "I'm sure they will help. Go along to the main Police Station, do you know where it is?"

Yes, he knew, but although it was less than half a mile away, progress was slow: in addition to the traffic chaos, he had to thread his way past the water queue, doubly difficult because the water was then being drawn and he had to struggle past an unwieldy procession of people already served, jogging back along the line towards their homes, with paniers across their shoulders holding a slopping tin of water at each end.

He was overwhelmed with weariness and despair when he reached the Police Station and was directed to the enquiry office. Two English policeman stood behind a counter and looked at him questioningly.

"Please," he began, leaning against the counter to get his breath back, "please can you tell me about a friend of mine who lives in the King Edward Hotel? I'm trying to find out where she is now. I've been to all the other hotels in Central but I can't find her there."

"What's the little girl's name?"

"Oh, she's not a child, she's quite old. She's Mrs. Kay Holtz. She's American and lives by herself in the King Edward because she's a writer. Her husband lives in America. Someone in town told me you might have a list of where everyone from the hotel is."

"We're working on it," said one of the men, thumbing through some papers. "It's not complete, though, the hotel records haven't been found yet."

"Holtz, you said?" repeated the other, running his finger down a list. "No, we can't help you yet, sonny. Some are in hospital, you know.."

"Which one? Which one?" Panic was seizing him, he had to bite his trembling lip.

The elder of the policemen bent over the counter and put a friendly arm round Danny's shoulders. "Now don't you worry, sonny - leave it with us, and we'll find your friend for you."

"No use you dashing off to some hospital," said the other. "You wouldn't be allowed in, and anyway, they won't have all the names yet."

"Leave it to us," repeated the older man. "Leave your name and address, and we'll let you know as soon as we find out where she is."

While Danny, through stiff lips, supplied the information, the younger policeman disappeared, but soon returned, with an opened bottle of lemonade.

"Straight from the ice-box," he said, pouring it into a glass. "Drink up, it'll do you good."

Danny was too distraught to taste the drink, but its cold gassiness stimulated him, and he was able to answer the further questions put to him: how old did he think Mrs. Holtz was, and what did she look like?

"Now off you go to school - I'm sure that's where you ought to be. You've done us a good turn, telling us about your friend, it all helps to put our lists together. And don't worry, we'll let you know as soon as we have some news for you."

After he left the Police Station, he debated for a few moments whether to have another attempt to find Mrs. Holtz in one of the smaller hotels, but a great weariness had come over him. It was as if there was the whole island to search, and he couldn't face it. Instead, he walked slowly back to school, and then remembered the history examination; it seemed supremely unimportant now.

The history teacher would not accept his explanation for his late arrival, obviously regarding his story as an excuse to avoid the examination. Stony-faced and dazed, Danny let the mechanics of the rest of the school day manipulate him, but oh, it was impossible to avoid hearing the ghoulish rumours about the fire.

"Did any policemen come, Mumma?" he gasped as he rushed home, breathless after galloping up the terrace steps.

"Policemen?"

"They're finding out where Mrs. Holtz is for me, because her hotel was burned down last night," he hiccoughed. "They said they would come and tell me where she is."

"No one has come yet," she said, She tried to comfort him, but he could see she was as anxious as he was. After tea he went out on to the terrace to watch for the policemen, but after five minutes found he was unable to face what might prove to be a long period of inactivity. Instead, he went into his room and played his violin, sawing through his entire repertoire with meticulous care.

There came a tap on his door, and his mother came in swiftly and held him tight. Behind her were the two policemen.

"I don't believe it," was Sandra's first reaction when she heard about the King Edward Hotel fire in the Peak School playground the following day. "They'd have told me at home if it was true."

But when the ghoulish titbits were related, she slowly realised that indeed Mrs. Holtz' hotel had burned down, and then it made sense that the newspapers at home had been kept hidden and the subiect not mentioned. A great fear for Mrs. Holtz came over her. She quizzed the other children for details and they gladly supplied them: yes, some people had died, but lots more were saved. Mrs. Holtz? Well, yes, maybe a name like that was in the paper, but whether as a survivor or a victim the informant didn't know.

"The funerals are this afternoon," added one child. "I should think they would just about fill the cemetery up."

Back in the class-room, Sandra sat rigidly at her desk, glaring at anyone who spoke to her. One of the children whispered to the teacher that Sandra knew a lady who lived at the doomed hotel, and the teacher questioned her gently about it.

"I don't know anyone there," lied Sandra coldly, trying to pretend nothing she had heard was true.

Ah Ling met her at the school gate as usual. Sandra pushed her aside and raced on ahead. Her parents, she knew, were down in the city at this time on their business ploys. She tore through the house, yelling for the newspaper. The servants came running and she sobbed out her fears for Mrs. Holtz. They swore they had not seen newspapers in the house that day.. perhaps Master and Missee had taken them into town.

"But you must have heard about the fire! Tell me about it!"

It wasn't a very big fire, they said, nobody died.

"You're lying! The girls at school said lots died!" She hurled herself on to the settee, shaking with fear. The servants stood around, awed and solemn.

"Better have rest," said Ah Ling, then carried her upstairs and laid her on the bed. A glass of milk was brought, and she allowed herself to be helped to take a few sips, but when the amah made to take off the white school dress, Sandra wriggled petulantly and refused to turn over to make this possible, for a plan was forming in her mind, and being undressed and put to bed was not part of it. She closed her eyes and feigned sleep, then watched beneath her eyelashes as Ah Ling gently pulled down the venetian blinds and crept quietly out of the room.

She knew this was the time when the servants gathered together in the outer quarters, chatting and relaxing - so this would be the time to escape. She would call on Danny, for he would be sure to know about Mrs. Holtz. She considered taking Ming into her confidence and persuading him to drive her, but since the picnic at High West he had been less co-operative. Ah Ling told her Ming almost lost his job over his part in making such a picnic possible; and if Ming lost his job, so would Ah Ling, and Sandra, much as she resented being shadowed by the amah, dreaded life without her; without putting the thought into words, she knew Ah Ling supplied her with more maternal love than her mother did.

No, this visit to Dragon Terrace would have to be made on her own. Quietly, she got up, pulled on her sandals, and took the ten-cent pieces from her money-box and put them in the top pocket of her rumpled school dress.

At the top of the stairs, she listened for a moment. The servants' voices were just audible; that meant the kitchen door opening into the yard was open, with the risk of one of the servants ambling in at any moment, so she could not use the staircase. She decided to climb down the outside of the house from the verandah which ran the length of her parents' bedroom. It was more frightening than she had imagined, but her desperate need to escape overrode all other considerations. The dogs barked madly as she ran down the drive; she kept running until she reached the Peak Tram terminus. No car stood there, and she watched in anxious impatience as the giant reels paid out their greasy black cords of steel down the almost vertical track. At last the roof of the next car rose up into sight and homed in to its platform.

She had never before travelled anywhere by herself, and clung tightly to the rail on the back of the seat in front as she was borne down the terrifying track, for the sides of the car were doorless for ease of access at the various stops en route down the mountain.

She stood outside the lower terminus uncertainly, getting her bearings. Usually borne everywhere by car, always with some adult in charge, she felt the beginnings of panic, then spotted a row of sedan chairs on the pavement nearby. Here was something familiar, for she had often travelled home from school in such a chair on particularly wet or hot days, with Ah Ling trotting along beside the two chair coolies. She walked over to the nearest chair and asked to be taken to Dragon Terrace. The boys helped her in to the cane chair; then, with a mock heave as if at her immense weight, they trotted the short distance up the hill, past St. Joseph's Church and into Kennedy Road. The sun was very hot and she was thankful for the chair's canopy, for she had not thought to bring her topee. Usually she enjoyed travelling by chair, bouncing along with the pliancy of the bamboo poles, but now her mind was full of fear, which increased when she was set down at the bottom of the terrace. She flew up the steps, scanning the faces of the children playing there, but she saw no one she knew: supposing Danny wasn't at home? With rising panic, she ran along to the end house and knocked on the

Russells' door. The amah opened it and Mrs. Russell and Danny appeared.

"I had to come," Sandra gasped between panting breaths. "I must know if Mrs. Holtz is all right. They hid the papers at home, and no one will tell me."

"Come and sit down, dear." Mrs. Russell pulled her into a chair. "Danny, get some iced water! Now rest and get your breath back: is the car waiting for you?"

"No.. I came by myself.. no one knows I ran away, so tell me quickly before someone misses me and comes to take me back. She's all right, isn't she.. Mrs. Holtz?"

Danny handed her a glass of water. His face looked peculiar, set in strange, almost grown-up lines, and his eyes were red-rimmed; he was dressed in his best white clothes - short trousers, linen jacket, white shirt with black bow-tie.

"I'm afraid, my dear," Mrs. Russell said slowly, "that Mrs. Holtz was lost in the fire. She is in Heaven now, and much happier than any of us - she is with God."

"You mean... Mrs. Holtz.. she's dead?"

Danny nodded sadly; his eyes filled with tears and he looked away.

"Sandra dear," Mrs. Russell hovered anxiously over her, "I must take you home, before your family get worried. Danny, go to Aunty Angela's house and asked to use the telephone to send for a taxi."

"But can't Sandra come to the funeral first?" begged Danny.

"I don't think her parents would allow that," Mrs. Russell was beginning when Sandra cut in "I want to go to the funeral if Danny's going, I was Mrs. Holtz' friend too!" She began to cry, remembering how friendly Mrs. Holtz had been to her during the picnic.

"Please Mumma," Danny urged, "let Sandra come with the rest of us!"

Mrs. Russell went to her desk and took out a small notebook. "I will see what her parents say: I shall telephone Sandra's father at his office," she said. "Stay here quietly with Danny, Sandra, I won't be very long."

She was too awed by what was happening to protest when the amah took off the school dress, whisked out a flat-iron and pressed out the creases. By the time Mrs. Russell returned, she was dressed again, her tear-stained face washed, and her hair freshly brushed and combed.

"I'm so sorry," Mrs. Russell said. "I'm afraid your father won't allow you to go to the funeral. He is coming now to take you home."

"He can't, he can't! I must go with Danny!"

"Your father knows what's best for you, my dear." Mrs. Russell tried to imprison the flailing arms. "He doesn't want you upset any more."

She cried and stormed until she was sick, and was still vomiting when her father arrived.

"I want to go to the funeral!" she gulped. "I must, Daddy!"

"My darling girl!" He bent down and put his arms round her. "You must let Mummy and I judge what is best for you! Come along now, I'll take you home."

She wriggled away from him, but he took her firmly by the hand. "You don't understand, Daddy! Mrs. Holtz was my friend!"

"I understand how you feel, but.."

He went on talking as he led her to the door, but she closed her ears to his words. How could he understand, and still not allow her to go to the funeral? She felt hopeless and betrayed. When her father guided her reluctant feet along the terrace, her friends were assembled there: Marcus, Celeste, Danny, Pamela - even Philip had arrived. She would be the only one of Mrs. Holtz' friends missing. Her chest heaving with sobs, she stumbled after her father.

They stood at the side of the road, opposite the obelisk monument at the entrance to Happy Valley. By tradition wreaths were placed around its foot, to be added to the cortège on its way to the cemetery. The children held their little posies, fearing they would be lost and crushed among the large showy wreaths.

Although it was five o'clock in the afternoon, the air was still hot and muggy, the flowers already wilting. Danny's heart missed a beat when the first of the horse-drawn hearses appeared on the brow of the hill leading to the monument. Immediately behind it came another, then another - the procession seemed endless, travelling so slowly that it seemed an eternity before the first one drew level with him. He stared at the gleaming brown coffin through the glass, and tried in vain to imagine that it contained a body.

Celeste was crying quietly, Pamela and Marcus looked very serious and Philip calm, but Danny was in anguish: how, how, with all these identical coffins, could he tell which one held Mrs. Holtz?

The last of the hearses passed and some of the waiting crowd fell in behind it.

"Come on," whispered Marcus, urging his little group forward. Celeste, Pamela and Philip followed him, but Danny still stood on the pavement, staring after the hearses.

"Come on!" repeated Marcus.

"But we don't know which one is Mrs. Holtz!" Danny cried despairingly. "How can we go to her funeral?"

"We'll find out when we get to the cemetery."

Danny found himself being propelled along by Marcus, and they all joined the shambling followers along the tramlines round the race-course. The procession halted when the first of the hearses reached the Roman Catholic cemetery, and two coffins were carried out of their hearses and through the gate. Could one of them contain Mrs. Holtz? Danny felt quite helpless. He realised he didn't even know her religion. In normal times he could have forced his way through the mourners and asked someone about Mrs. Holtz, but all his common sense and initiative had deserted him. Utterly demoralised and lost, he threw out his hands helplessly to the other children.

"I don't expect she was a Catholic," whispered Marcus. "She never said so, did she? And she didn't know about Novenas, so she couldn't have been. We'll go on to the Protestant Cemetery."

So they followed the main procession to the adjacent larger cemetery. The mourners were guided through the open gates while the glass doors at the back of the hearses were unfastened and the coffins taken out. Marcus purposefully led the children after the knowledgeable adults who assembled beside a line of empty holes yawning side by side.

Danny's sense of hopelessness lifted as the coffins were borne towards the plots, for when the first was lowered on to the ground he could see a brass plaque on the lid bearing the name and age of the victim. Trying to find Mrs. Holtz' name temporarily took the horror out of the occasion. Yet when at last they found her coffin, all the children gaped at it with complete disbelief, unable to relate this simple, light-coloured box to the vibrant, colourful Kay Holtz they had known.

Throughout the service, the lowering of the coffins, the throwing of the first sods, the unreality persisted. Only Celeste wept, murmuring 'Hail Marys' through her tears. Marcus had his arm round her so she could lean against him. Philip stood very erect, staring straight ahead. Pamela was looking almost furtively at the coffin, then dropping her head. He had no tears himself then - they came later, when he was back in his room at home, practising his scales endlessly and loudly to try to blot out the memory, not of the spectacle of the funeral, but of the picture the newspaper reports had seared into his mind:

'We kept calling to her to jump,' one survivor recalled, 'but she wouldn't: she kept crying that she couldn't, she couldn't..'

He could hear her saying this, over and over again, just as she had declared herself unable to step off the jetty on to the wallah wallah the first day he had met her. 'I can't, I can't..' rang in his ears, until he threw down his violin and fell weeping on to his bed.

JUNE

Pamela leaned over the rail of the launch and anxiously scanned the pier. The Chinese seamen were already standing by the bollards ready to cast off. Her parents, who had been amazingly compliant about so many things since the hotel fire, had agreed that she could invite Philip to join them on the launch picnic this Sunday.. it would be so typical of him to forget to come.

But here he was, ambling along just as the first rope was released, as if he had all the time in the world.

"I thought you'd forgotten," she said reproachfully as he jumped aboard.

"Course not. Had a job to find my bathing costume." He followed her to the small forward deck to pay his respects to her parents. Protected against the sun by a canvas awning, this area was packed with rattan chairs, occupied mainly by parents with small children. Pamela dragged Philip away as soon as the cause of good manners had been served. Children of their age congregated amidships, lining the low rails as the launch backed away from the jetty and chugged througn the harbour. Although the engine housing immediately behind them emitted wafts of heat and a strong metal smell, the thrust of the little craft created a steady breeze which was continually refreshing.

"This is what I like best about Hong Kong - bathing trips," sighed Pamela, hanging her head over the ship's side and letting the wind blow her hair all over her face. "There's nothing like this in England."

Philip nodded agreement, adding "Poor old Sandra, having to go Home to boarding school!"

"Weren't her parents mean, making her miss the funeral? Mrs. Holtz has been dead a month now," mused Pamela. "Isn't it queer to think of that.. she's not in her room at the hotel, but lying in that coffin in the cemetery, all still. I can't really believe it even yet."

"Only her body is there," said Philip. "Her soul is in Heaven."

Pamela gazed up at the serene blue sky and tried in vain to imagine Mrs. Holtz resident in Heaven.

"Celeste is always saying prayers for Mrs. Holtz's soul," she said. "You're Catholic - do you do that too?"

"Only on Sundays, when I'm serving at Mass, when we pray for the souls of the faithful departed; she's the only person I know who's died, so I pray for her then."

"P'raps I ought to as well," said Pamela. "She hasn't got many people to pray for her, except Mr. Holtz."

Once out of the harbour the launch puttered across a wide expanse of shimmering blue sea, passing junks, sampans and a few weather-beaten merchant ships, then veered towards an island whose pale hills moulded an undulating outline against the clear sky.

It was time to change into swimming gear. There was a large cabin aft for the menfolk, and a larger cabin below decks for women and girls. Pamela handed Philip over to Roddy then scurried down to the ladies' cabin. As she wriggled into her swimming costume while modestly still wearing her dress, one of her school friends, Rosie, giggled "I think Philip is your sweetheart!"

"Don't be silly," frowned Pamela. "He's just my friend."

"But he's a boy!"

"I know that!" Pamela pulled her dress over her head to discourage further conversation, hurriedly buttoned her swimming costume at the shoulder, and quickly wormed her way out of the cabin.

The launch was approaching Silvermine Bay. A long sretch of white sand lay at the foot of green hills dotted with trees and foliage. Even before the anchor rattled out, several swimmers had dived off the side, Roddy and his friends among them. Non-swimmers climbed down the perpendicular iron ladder into the ship's dinghy to be rowed ashore by Chinese crewmen.

"Coming, Pam? called Philip, nodding towards the water, then diving competently off the side of the launch. The bay was very shallow and the launch anchored a long way from the beach: Pamela would have preferred to take the dinghy but was too proud to admit her timidity, so she held her nose and jumped into the green water after him. She had not realised, during the swimming sessions on the 'Rawalpindi' that he was a really strong swimmer. Her laborious side stroke left her far behind him, but he looked back for her, turned over and floated lazily until she caught him up. The beach still seemed very far away and she trod water to rest her aching arms.

"Want a lift?" asked Philip, presenting his freckled back. Thankfully, she put her arms on his shoulders and relaxed while he swam a leisurely, strong breast-stroke for the last fifty yards. They threw themselves full length on the white sand at the water's edge and let the wavelets break over them.

A group of children were cavorting nearby. "I saw you with your arms round your sweetheart, Pam," called Rosie. Her companions sniggered and stared. Pamela looked the other way.

"What did they say?" asked Philip.

"Oh, just something soppy." Pamela prayed that he hadn't heard, and got up. "Shall we look for shells? There are lovely ones here."

They ambled along the beach, stopping now and again to collect shells which they left with Pamela's mother who was seated on the beach with other mothers, under a large oiled sunshade.

Clear of Rosie and her friends, they plunged into the water again and wallowed happily in the tepid shallows; later, they became involved in beach ball game with Roddy and his companions.

When the launch's siren signalled it was time to leave the beach, Pamela swam happily back beside Philip, confident in his care.

"Hang onto me a bit," he offered from time to time, and she gratefully did so getting her breath back. Most boys she knew would have teased and boasted but not Philip and she warmed towards him.

The dinghy had landed its last passengers and was being hauled up into its davits; the ship's engines were beginning to throb but still the young lions were surging down the chute for a last plunge and diving once more from the board lashed to the rail - showing off in the water with furious bursts of swimming and calling to their friends determined to enjoy the pleasures of the inviting water to the very last.

Pamela got dressed as quickly as possible for Rosie started teasing her again about Philip. He was already waiting for her on the deck when she emerged; he looked rather strange as his usual springy sandy hair lay freshly combed flat wet and dark. His blue shirt was tucked somewhat untidily into his khaki trousers.

"Look what your brother gave me " he said exhibiting a cigarette card. It's the very one I need to complete my set of 'Ships and Shipping.'"

"Not fair " pouted Pamela. "I haven't got that one either. He might have asked me first if I wanted it."

"Hard luck " said Philip carefully pocketing the card.

They joined Pamela's parents on the bow deck for sandwiches, cakes, biscuits and lemonade. Rodney appeared briefly to claim a handful of sandwiches and a hunk of cake and to 'borrow' some money for lemonade.

"What happened to your pocket money?" demanded his mother as she opened her handbag.

"Spent it on the outward trip."

"I've told you before not to drink lemonade before you swim!"

"I didn't drown, did I?" grinned Roddy as he took the money.

Pamela remembering the new cigarette card in Philip's pocket looked up at her brother in surprise as he did not confess that his pocket money on the outward journey had been spent on cigarettes, not lemonade. His parents knew he had started smoking and attempted to prevent it. Pamela pondered on the realisation that some one as old as Roddy could be guilty of deception; this knowledge made her feel a little less guilty about her own prevarications over the time she spent at Dragon Terrace.

Deep in thought, she gradually became aware of Rosie and her friends at the launch's rail, beckoning to her. Rosie held up some cigarette cards.

"You and Philip go off with your pals," said her mother, so they followed the other children along the deck to the steps leading down to the ladies' changing room, which was used as a communal recreation room once everyone was dressed.

"Come down here, and we'll do some swaps with our new cards," invited Rosie, going down the steep companionway.

"I haven't got my cards on me," said Pamela, hanging back, "and it's so hot down there."

"My dad has just given me three more cards - bet you haven't got them," shouted one of the other girls. "Come and see!"

"I got a new one just this afternoon," volunteered Philip, taking a flying leap down the steps, so Pamela followed him. Rosie and her companions - boys as well as girls - were whispering in a huddle outside the tiny compartment at the bow which housed the anchor and chain and coils of rope.

"Come and sit in here and we'll show you our cards, you can have first pick," said Rosie, crawling through the open iron door.

"Why ever in there?" demanded Pamela, mystified.

"Just because."

"I don't think we're supposed to," she said doubtfully, but Philip got in and pulled Pamela after him, saying "It's quite fun.. never been in such a tiny place before."

Immediately the two were inside, Rosie squeezed out and the door was slammed shut by the other children.

"It's a trick, I knew it was a trick!" Pamela shouted. "Let us out!"

"Not until you've kissed Philip!" Rosie shouted back.

It was dreadfully stuffy, with a strong smell of lead paint, salt and hemp. Some light but little air came through the twin apertures above their heads through which the anchor chains ran out. Pamela's skin began to prickle with the heat; in a panic lest the children go away and leave them locked in forever, she pushed against the door, banging it frantically with her fists.

"I say, Pam, calm down," said Philip.

"But.. but they said we can't come out.. until.." hiccoughed Pamela, trying to gulp back her shaming tears.

"Well then, we might as well," muttered Philip, pecking her cheek quickly and moving away at once. "Let us out, you lot, we've done it."

"Do it again, we didn't hear anything!"

He bent forward again and she could smell his breath redolent of the mint humbug he had been sucking, as he puckered up his lips and pressed a noisy kiss on the other cheek.

The door was wrenched open, and Pamela, sniffing furiously, butted her way through the jeering children and raced up to the deck, hanging over the rail and breathing in great mouthfuls of salty air.

"You all right now?" asked Philip, joining her and looking rather pink-faced.

"Yes thanks." She gazed out to sea to avoid meeting his gaze.

"I've got something for you," he said, and pressed into her hand the cigarette card Rodney had given him. She tried to refuse such a handsome gift, but he seemed so anxious that she take it that she accepted and put it into her pocket. They leaned over the rail, side by side, as the launch nosed its way past the islands and turned towards the harbour. The warm wind blew into their faces and tore at their hair. Just behind them a gang of teenagers lounged with a mandolin and ukelele, strumming and singing "Ain't She Sweet?" over and over again. Pamela put her hand over the pocket with the cigarette card so that it wouldn't fall out, and felt a great wave of affection for Philip. No one had ever been so kind to her before. Of course, he was trying to make up for the horrid time in the anchor compartment. As to the kissing, she wondered why grown-ups seemed so interested in it.. smelling someone's breath and getting a patch of wetness on one's cheek.

JULY

Marcus leading, they walked in a solemn line through the cemetery, making what had become their weekly pilgrimage to the grave. Their speed was limited by Celeste's lumbering gait. The boys respectfully held their hands behind their backs; each of the girls carried a posy of morning glory picked on the way.

The heaps of thick yellow clay piled on the graves of the fire victims had settled down to smooth mounds. Mrs. Holtz' mound had a small vase, contributed by Danny's mother. Last week's flowers were brown and limp, the vase dry, Pamela took it over to the large fountain; no water had played from its elaborate centrepiece for nearly a year because of the drought, but a few inches lay in a barrel nearby, Reverently, she placed her flowers in the vase, then stood aside as Celeste added hers, and the boys did the same; they stood in silence for several minutes which Marcus terminated by making the sign of the cross and saying the first half of the 'Hail Mary"; they all chorussed the second half - even Pamela had learned it by now.

"May Mrs. Holtz's soul rest in peace with Jesus," said Celeste at the end, and every one made the sign of the cross again,

They always talked about her as they left the grave.

"Imagine, Mrs. Holtz not being able to talk any more, when she liked to talk all the time!"

"Two months she's been dead now."

"And two months since we've seen Sandra."

"Well," said Pamela, "At least Philip and I will see her next September when she starts at our school. They won't be able to stop us from seeing her then."

"Jolly rotten, having parents like that," said Philip.

"They're only trying to take care of her, she's been awfully ill," Marcus reminded them.

Quite suddenly, rain fell - huge drops, gaining momentum every second. It was so unexpected, after almost a year's drought, that the children stood still and put their heads back to savour the unfamiliar sensation of cool rain on their faces.

"Run! We'll get soaked!" cried Marcus, leading the way to a rough shelter at the far end of the cemetery. Danny heaved Celeste on to his shoulders and, panting, wet and laughing, they weaved their way among the paths between the graves to the open-ended hut which was obviously used for preparing tombstones. The rain continued to pour down with such frenzy that it bounced off the arid earth several inches into the air. It beat a deafening tattoo on the corrugated iron roof of the hut, ran into the yawning cracks in the parched ground, but simply could not be absorbed by the granite-like earth. Heavier and heavier it fell, crashing down with the sound of a gigantic crackling wood fire. Wherever there was a slope, there the rain swept down, swirling between the graves and carrying forward more yellow water as it cascaded on to the terraces below.

"We'll have to stay here till it eases off," shouted Marcus above the din.

"Unless this hut gets washed away first," yelled Philip.

At length the ferocity of the downpour lessened, the mad elemental noises weakened. Soon there was only the sound of the yellow water rushing past on its way to the lowest level, and the clattering drips from the nearby trees.

No longer liable to splashing from the rain, they moved to the front of the shelter.

"Goodness, look at that nullah!" Danny pointed to the hillside above them, where a great waterfall had appeared as if by the touch of a magic wand. The wide open drains built into the hillside all over the island were adequate enough during normal downpours, but now frothy, cream waterfalls were erupting and cascading their ever-increasing burden beyond the confines of the drains.

"Belle will be able to have all the baths she wants now, I should think," said Pamela. "She's always complaining that the water's turned off just when she decides to have a bath."

"I think we can move off now." Marcus left the shelter and the others followed. "Look, this must be the children's cemetery, all the graves have got angels and tiny crosses."

They had not explored this area before, and looked curiously around the little graves, stopping to read their inscriptions.

"This child has the same name as Sandra.. Smithson," Pamela called.

" 'Gary Smithson,'" read Marcus. " 'Beloved son of Gwen and Luke who left us so tragically November 6th, 1922, aged 4 years. Safe in God's keeping' ."

"Sandra's mother's name is Gwen, I heard Mr. Smithson call her that when I stayed with them," Pamela said slowly.

"And her father's initial is 'L'," added Danny. "I've seen it on the cheques he used to send for Sandra's music lessons."

They all exchanged glances in silence.

"So this poor little boy must be Sandra's brother," Pamela said at last. "But she's never said, has she, that she had a brother?"

"She might not remember, she would only have been about two or three in 1922."

" 'Tragic circumstances' " mused Danny. "I wonder what that means?"

Faced with the chilling reality of the little grave in front of them, they had little to say to one another as they left the cemetery.

Pamela continued to ponder over Gary Smithson's tragic death for the rest of the day. It was difficult to adjust to the idea that a brother of Sandra's lay beneath the marble angel. Too restless to stay indoors and read or paint, she called on Rosie, who had her uses as a neighbour, and they played noisy duets on the piano. That helped, but the uneasiness returned after dinner that evening. She wanted to ask her parents if they knew anything about the little boy who died, but dared not do so as it would mean revealing she had spent most of the afternoon with the boys from the terrace, and in the cemetery, both of which circumstances would be met with disapproval. But eventually her intense curiosity got the better of caution and she began to tell the family about the grave when Roddy interrupted to describe the overflowing nullah he and his friends had passed on their hike.

"We nearly got washed away, the force of the water was.. oh, astronomical! It was cascading across the road," he said.

"And do you know, they've still turned the water off this evening," Belle pouted in disgust. "Surely we've got enough in the reservoirs by now?"

"It will take a few more weeks of rain to do that." said her father.

"I'm fed up of never being able to bath when I want to," shouted Belle petulantly. She put her head in her hands, bent over the table and started to cry.

"Whatever's wrong?" every one asked.

"I don't know!" Belle gave a great wail, pushed back her chair and rushed upstairs to her room.

"She having boy-friend trouble again?" asked her father.

"Not that I know of" Her mother stood up uncertainly for a moment. "She's been out dancing often enough, but she's never seemed to be serious with any one since she fell out with Keith."

"Why did she finish with Keith?" Roddy asked.

"She never said."

"Better go up and talk to her."

"It beats me why Belle had to go off the deep end like that all of a sudden," said Roddy in his new gruff voice.

"Ah well, my boy," his father gave a knowing wink, "you'll soon be finding out for yourself just how difficult the ladies can be. And in another few years, we'll have Miss Pamela here a flapper too."

"Me a flapper!" giggled Pamela, seeing a vision of her eleven year old self in high heels and silk stockings, long beads and a dress with a fringed hem.

"Your mother was a flapper once," her father said. Trying to imagine her stern mother looking like Clara Bow or Pola Negri made Pamela giggle more than ever. In this atmosphere of frivolity, it felt unseemly to talk about graves, and she let the matter of the discovery in the cemetery go. Nevertheless, the subject was still uppermost in her mind when she settled down to sleep that night. Gary surely must have been Sandra's brother, and of course this would explain Mr. Smithson's indulgence towards his surviving child Sandra - but it didn't explain Mrs. Smithson's apparent lack of affection for her daughter.

Later on, there was something else that didn't make sense: through her open bedroom door, she overheard her mother telling her father that Belle was upset because Keith was going to be transferred to the Shanghai Office of his firm at the end of August - why on earth should Belle mind, when she had finished with Keith months ago?

"Go to school in England this year?" echoed Sandra. "THIS year? Next term, you mean?" "Yes, darling - next term,"

"But you said before it would be NEXT year!"

"That was before you were ill, wasn't it? Dr. Foley thinks it best for you to get out of this climate as soon as possible to get really well."

"I AM better! I AM well! I'm not ill any more." The ready tears gathered, always near the surface since the day of Mrs. Holtz' funeral, when she had suffered a nervous breakdown. Two months off school, with just Ah Ling for constant company, had left her petulant and lethargic. A few weeks back at school before the end of the summer term, so eagerly anticipated as an escape from isolation, had proved a dismal disappointment: she had missed so much that she was completely lost in class. The only sustaining thought was that after the summer holidays she would be going to the senior school in Kowloon and would meet up again with Pamela and Philip - but here was her father announcing she was to go to boarding school in England a year earlier than planned.

"Don't make me go yet, Daddy, don't, I can't bear it." racking hiccoughs and sobs engulfed her, and her father enveloped her in his arms.

"It has to be, darling," he soothed. "You know we don't want you to go away any more than you want to, but it's all for the best. I've managed to book passages for you and Mummy on the 'Rajputana' sailing the week after next."

"Aren't you coming too?"

"I can't darling, the office won't let me go until next year."

"Daddy, I'll do anything, anything, but please don't send me away this year! Please, please, let me wait until we can all go together. I'll die if you send me now, I'll die!"

"Of course you won't, sweetheart!" His arms tightened round her again. "You're turned ten.. beginning to grow up, so let's see more of a young lady, and less of a rather spoilt little girl."

She pressed her face against his cream linen jacket and pleaded and sobbed."It's all arranged, darling. The school in Worthing can take you in September." He pulled her away and held her shoulders so that their faces were level. "Now you've always had plenty of courage, Sandra, so be brave now, and face what simply must be."

She had always recognised the note of finality in his voice, and knew now there would be no reprieve. She hunched her thin shoulders and subsided into sad little sniffles.

"That's my girl! Now, Mummy and I have decided you deserve a very special treat before you leave Hong Kong; what would like to do most of all?"

"Can I choose anything?" her voice quavered.

He nodded, and she made her decision at once: "I'd like a party just for my music lesson friends - Pamela, Danny, Marcus, and Philip." They were the forbidden company, whom she had not been allowed to meet since Mrs. Holtz' funeral. She could see that her father was taken aback by her request. Before he could refuse it, she went on, "You said I could choose, Daddy, so that's what I'd like, please: a party, at the beach, and in the evening - a moonlight swimming party!"

"Oh darling.. you and your friends are really too young for moonlight parties," he protested. "They're for grownups."

"You said I was nearly grownup," she flashed. "Anyway, you said I could choose ANYTHING, and I want something I can always remember about Hong Kong, when I'm in England, far, away.. far away from you Daddy." Her voice broke, and self-control slipped away again.

"Don't cry, my pet," her father hugged her again. "You shall have your special never-to-be-forgotten evening swimming party with your music lesson friends."

Thought Pamela, surveying the scene at South Beach, "This can't be happening."

But it was: after two months of silence had come this invitation to an evening swimming picnic with Sandra and her parents. Now she, Marcus, Philip, Danny and Sandra were all together again, revelling in the delights of the beach at a time when they were usually leaving for home after an afternoon swim. they had hurtled in and out of the warm water over and over again; played ball games on the beach, and now lay on the sand talking happily.

"We've got a surprise for you, Sandra," announced Marcus, scrambling to his feet. "You wait here." The guests ran up to the matshed where they had left their rattan baskets, and returned one by one to hand over a parcel to Sandra as a keepsake. The gifts had been a talking point among them for days. Pamela's mother had given her the money to buy a little manicure set which Pamela herself had coveted in a ship window for a long time. Marcus produced an autograph book with multi-coloured pages; Philip a fancy pencil sharpener which Pamela thought looked suspiciously like the one she had bought him for his birthday. Danny's present was the grandest of all. He had been very mysterious about it, and told none of the others what it was, so when Sandra unwrapped it, the beautiful watch was as much a surprise to the other children as it was to the recipient. Marcus, Pamela and Philip were flabbergasted; Marcus couldn't resist wondering to Pamela under his breath how Danny had got hold of so much money to buy it. It was obvious to the children that even Sandra's parents were taken aback by the splendour of Danny's present.

Ming and Ah Ling cooked sausages over a small fire on the beach. The night air was so warm after the hot July day that there was no need for the children to dress before sitting in a circle on the sand to eat. Afterwards, Danny by popular request, entertained with his impersonations. Out in the bay, the small fishing boats gathered, their bright lights sending snakes of light wriggling across the still water. The sea looked like dark blue silk.

Mr. Smithson decreed it was time for the party to end. Mrs. Smithson called the children to the matshed to dress. Sandra's frantic protests that it was too early to go home were overridden.

There were two tiny changing rooms in the matshed. Pamela and Sandra went into one and wriggled out of their swimming costumes by the light of a torch, giggling and hunting for their clothes. Divided from the boys' room only by a partition wall of thin rattan matting, conversation was bandied back and forth.

"Isn't this lovely?" sighed Sandra, sitting on the wooden bench and pulling on her socks. "I've never had such a gorgeous party; and Pam, I wanted you to come and visit me when I was ill but it wasn't allowed; I was so upset they wouldn't let me go to Mrs. Holtz' funeral.. she'd have liked me to be there with you all, wouldn't she?"

"I should think so." Pamela's reply was vague because her thoughts had flown to the grave of the little boy with the same surname as Sandra, and she was wondering if she dared broach the subject.

"I'll remember this evening all the time I'm in horrible boarding school in freezing old England," declared Sandra. "Oh, that sock's on inside out; never mind, Ah Ling won't notice it in the dark." She groped under the bench for her sandals and went on fervently "Oh I just wish you were my sister Pam, then we would go to boarding school together, and it wouldn't be nearly so bad. It's rotten being an only one."

The question slipped out before Pamela could stop it: "Didn't you have a brother once?"

"A brother?" repeated Sandra, pausing as she struggled with the buckle of one sandal. "How could I? There's only me, you know that!"

Next door, the boys were singing a song about "Bye bye blackbird", Danny's unmistakable voice changing at the end of each line to imitate a banjo accompaniment.

"Oh never mind," Pamela muttered, pretending to have difficulty with the buttons on the back of her dress.

"Whatever do you mean?" Sandra persisted. "Why did you ask? Come on, you've got to tell me!"

There was no help for it now. Whispering in a halting voice, Pamela told her about the child's tombstone. In the torchlight Sandra's eyes grew round with astonishment. "He must be my brother," she stammered at last, "because those are my parents' names, but no one's ever said anything about him: why didn't they?"

To Pamela's horror, Sandra pushed her way out of the tiny compartment and confronted her parents who were lounging on the verandah with cigarettes and drinks.

"Daddy, daddy! Why didn't you tell me I once had a brother?" she demanded. "He's buried in Happy Valley, isn't he?"

Pamela, frozen in the doorway, saw Mrs. Smithson stiffen in her chair and put her hand to her mouth; her cigarette fell to the ground. Mr. Smithson leapt up and put his arms round his wife.

"Isn't he, Daddy?" repeated Sandra remorselessly.

"Yes darling, he is.. but he died a long time ago, when you were very small.."

"But why didn't you tell me?"

"Because it would have made you sad."

Mrs. Smithson was crying quietly, hiding her face in her hands.

"What happened to him? Why was it 'tragic'? What happened to him?"

"Darling, you're upsetting Mummy. Let's not talk about it now."

"I want to know, I want to know!"

"He fell off the verandah and was killed," said Mrs. Smithson in a strange muffled voice.

There was a very long silence, during which the boys, struck dumb by what they had overheard, slunk out of their changing room and stood uncertainly by the steps. Pamela stood perfectly still, unable to move.

"He had red hair like mine," said Sandra slowly, clasping and unclasping her hands. "And he took my teddy and climbed on the verandah with it so's I couldn't get it, so I pushed him over... I remember it now."

Now there were two graves to visit each week after Pamela's piano lesson. At Gary Smithson's they stood and mourned for Sandra, irrevocably out of contact on her way to school in England. By Mrs. Holtz' grave they fretted because there was no temporary wooden cross showing her name, whereas named crosses stood sentinel over the graves of all the other fire victims.

"It looks as if no one cares about her," said Danny as they walked out of the cemetery one afternoon. "You'd think Mr. Holtz would have written to arrange something."

"P'raps he hasn't enough money," Philip said.

"The Police told my mother that some of her jewellery was found so they sent it to him, he should have been able to sell it and send money for a cross, it's only wooden."

'Maybe he didn't like to sell her things," put in Celeste. "Maybe he wanted to keep them in memory of her, like we all gave Sandra keepsakes so she wouldn't forget us."

They walked on in silence, and Danny thought he knew why: the others had never seemed to get over their envy because the watch, his present to Sandra, was so much grander than any of theirs. It had cost him six dollars - and he knew none of the other presents had cost as much as fifty cents.

"What about Mrs. Holtz' typewriter?" asked Marcus suddenly. "It would be worth quite alot of money; was that saved?"

"I don't know." Danny bent down to lift Celeste on to his back. "Up you get Celie, I'm sure you're tired."

"Wasn't the typewriter still at the shop being mended then?" Pamela touched his arm. "Remember, we went to the shop the day before the fire, and the typewriter was waiting to be mended."

"Then it must still be there," said Marcus.

"So it ought to be sent to Mr. Holtz, then maybe he can sell it, and get more than a wooden cross.. a beautiful stone for Mrs. Holtz."

"Or," said Marcus, "we could write and tell him about it, and he might ask us to collect it from the shop and sell it for him.. that would save sending it all the way to the States, which would cost a heck of alot of money, then we could choose the stone."

"That's a real brainwave," said Philip.

"So," Marcus went on, "will you ask your mother, Danny, to write to Mr. Holtz, and tell him our suggestion about the typewriter?"

Danny had to try several times before he could stammer "The typewriter isn't at the shop any more."

"Isn't it?" Pamela stared at him in astonishment. "But we SAW it there, the day before the fire."

"It WAS there," admitted Danny, "but it isn't now." The confession had to come, there was no help for it. "I sold it to the shop. They gave me ten dollars for it, and I spent most of it on Sandra's present."

"But that's STEALING!" shouted Pamela. "You couldn't have done that!"

Danny lifted Celeste down and looked at them miserably. "I didn't have any money," he muttered, "and I couldn't not give Sandra a present... and Mrs. Holtz wouldn't have minded."

"I knew your mother wouldn't have given you enough money to buy that watch! You never even showed it to her, did you?" Marcus' tone was almost triumphant.

Only Celeste remained friendly, hugging, his arm and saying "Even though it wasn't Danny's typewriter to sell, I'm sure Mrs. Holtz doesn't mind that he did it, especially to give Sandra a present."

"Well, I think it's awful!" Danny cringed before Pamela's indignation. "I've never heard anything so dreadful in all my life, and I never want to talk to you again, Danny Russell."

They all rounded on him so much that he disentangled himself from Celeste's clutching arm and hurried home alone, wounded beyond belief.

He hoped and prayed Pamela would have forgotten about the matter by next Saturday afternoon, but no: she arrived just in time for the lesson, instead of half an hour early, and studiously avoided him after it was finished. He ran after her on the terrace, asking hopefully "Going to the cemetery now?"

"I shouldn't think you'd want to come, after stealing Mrs. Holtz' typewriter," she said coldly.

"It wasn't like that," he protested despairingly.

"Well, I think it was!" She turned her back on him and flew down the steps. Danny was too proud to follow. Looking over the balustrade, he saw Marcus and Philip waiting at the bottom flight of steps, obviously by pre-arrangement.

Celeste limped over to him. "I'm not going if you're not going," she said. "Don't be lonely, Danny."

He lifted her up on to the balustrade, holding his arms round her to keep her safe: but still he was lonely - lonely for Mrs. Holtz, lying cold in Happy Valley; lonely for Sandra, gone out of their lives forever; and lonely for Pamela's esteem which he was convinced now he had lost for ever.

"How would you like to be a bridesmaid, Pam?" asked her mother at breakfast the day the school summer holidays started.

"A bridesmaid, Mum? Me?" This was an honour accorded to dimpled, curly-headed friends, not to someone with a round face and short straight hair. "Who for?"

"For Belle, of course!"

"Oh, is Belle going to be married? Whoever to?"

"Surely you know - Keith?!"

"But I thought she didn't like him any more!" Pamela was really puzzled at the unaccountable behaviour of grownups.

"That was a long time ago. It's all changed now. They are to be married next month, and sailing on the 'Ranchi' to Shanghai, because Keith is being transferred there."

"Goodness!" Pamela slowly peeled the skin from a segment of pomelo while she absorbed this interesting development in the family.

"So we have to see the tailor about your dress," went on her mother, "I've got the material."

It was the loveliest dress Pamela had ever owned. Full length, of coral pink chiffon, it had frills at the neck and round the hem. A silver Juliet cap and Dorothy bag, and silver ankle-strap shoes completed an ensemble such as she had never expected to wear. There was to be a second bridesmaid, Yvonne Cromer, the daughter of Keith's employer, who was a little older than Pamela. they knew each other by sight from school, but the impending occasion brought them frequently together.

Yvonne's parents had a large white bungalow with a green roof above the beautiful beach of Shek O on the other side of Hong Kong island, and Pamela became a regular visitor there, collected by Mrs. Cromer on her shopping forays to Central. Pamela had never known such heavenly summer holidays, spending hours in the surf which thundered regularly on to the beach, and being plied with raspberryade afterwards. Piano lessons were a thing of the past now she had taken and passed her Grade II examination. With all the excitement of preparing for the wedding, she hardly missed the visits to Dragon Terrace.

On Pamela's return from Shek O one evening, her mother told her Philip had called. "He said he'll come again."

"When? I haven't seen him for ages!"

"He didn't say, but he saw your dress hanging up after Ah Tai had ironed it, and admired it very much.. I was quite surprised at his enthusiasm!"

Pamela, stretched out on a long cane chair, her bare legs supported on its pull-out extension, thrust out her jaw and blew her fringe, wondering how grownups could bear to drink steaming coffee in late August, especially just after a hot tiffin of chops and baked sweet potatoes, followed by banana fritters.

The ceiling fan was stirring up such air as came in through the open windows. A portable electric fan on the bookcase rotated and bowed its way round the room, giving a blissful breeze only for the brief moment it juddered in one's direction. Her father, his unfinished coffee beside him, had dropped off to sleep in the companion cane chair, and was snoring gently. Her mother was mopping at her streaming neck even as she sipped her coffee. Belle was resting upstairs before embarking on yet another shopping expedition, and Roddy was in the kitchen collecting a packed snack for a hike.

"Won't be back to dinner tonight," he told his mother when he re-appeared with his rattan picnic basket. "Going to the flicks directly after the hiking." As he went through the hall the door bell rang.

"Some friends of yours to see you Pam," he called back, "Dozens of them!"

"What?" Her mother looked up in surprise. "Whoever can they be?"

Pamela wriggled her feet into her slip-slops, tugged at the skirt of her brief cotton dress and padded to the front door, where Marcus, Celeste and Danny, and several of their young relations from Dragon Terrace, greeted her joyfully. They were all smartly dressed and well-groomed.

"I hope you won't mind us coming," said Marcus, "but.."

"Please, please, can we see your bridesmaid's dress?" cut in Celeste eagerly. "Philip told us about it, and we haven't seen you for such a long time."

Pamela stood in silence, biting her lip as she wondered how she could dispose of all these visitors before her parents saw them, fearing their reaction to the sight of a bevy of Portuguese children, mostly boys, on the doorstep.

"Please, Pam, do ask your mother if she will let us see your dress?" This was Danny, directing her an anxious pleading look, which she knew meant 'and won't you forgive me?'

Still she stood silent.

"Ai yah!" Ah Tai appeared. "Too muchee people!"

"Who have we here, Pamela?" Her mother's voice sounded behind her.

Marcus stepped forward and thrust out his hand, saying good afternoon in his most polite voice. "We came to ask if you would allow us to see Pamela's bridesmaid's dress," he explained. "Philip told us how beautiful it was, and we all would so much like to see it too. May we, please?"

Pamela, rigid with embarrassment, hardly dare breathe, until her mother said kindly "If you would like to." She motioned them into the house, adding "Pam, run upstairs and bring down the dress."

"Can we see Pamela wearing it?" begged Celeste.

"Oh no, not now!" Pamela was horrified at the thought of parading before so many boys, especially Marcus. "Any way, I'm all hot and sticky."

When she came downstairs, holding the dress on its hanger as high as possible to avoid the floor, the children were crammed together on the settee and easy chairs. Her father had hauled himself into a sitting position and was clearing his throat while struggling with a conversation with Marcus.

"Oooh!" She was aware of the whole-hearted admiration of every child. Marcus was leaning forward, gazing at her wraptly, his eyes never leaving her face above the dress. It was too much for her; she turned and scuttled up the stairs as fast as the dress on its hanger would allow, overcome with embarrassment. Dreading what her parents would say about the visitation, she lurked in her room so long that her mother eventually called her down, saying "Your friends are just leaving."

They were trooping through the front door as she came down the stairs.

"We're going to the cemetery now," Marcus told her. "Are you coming today?"

"You haven't been for weeks," Danny added carefully. "Do come!" His eyes pleaded again. "Philip said he'd come too; he was supposed to meet us here at your house this afternoon, but I expect we'll meet him on the way back."

It was a great relief when her mother quickly settled the matter. "It's too hot for Pamela to go to the cemetery this afternoon; and anyway, I'm taking her to have her hair cut later on, so you'd better go along without her."

"What about next week?" Marcus looked hopefully at Pamela. "Will you come with us then?"

"It's the wedding week!" laughed her mother. "We can't think about anything but the wedding now, I'm afraid."

After they had straggled out of earshot, Pamela went indoors and burst into hasty apologies: she hadn't known they were going to call on her - she hardly knew some of the relations Marcus and Danny had brought.

"It wasn't really Pam's fault all those children came," her mother soothed her ruffled father, who was again settling into a reclining position in his chair, Ah Tai having just brought him an iced beer. "And they were all well-behaved and charming about the dress."

Ten minutes later the door bell rang again.

"Some Saturday afternoon rest this is!" muttered her father. "Might as well have stayed in the office, for all the peace I'm getting."

This time it was Philip, his khaki topee tipped back off his head so that the green lining under the brim showed.

"Hullo!" Pamela was surprised at the pleasure she felt at seeing him again. "You've just missed the others; they've gone to the cemetery. I'm not allowed."

"Then I won't go either," said Philip. "Got something to tell you - can you come out for a while?"

Appealed to, her mother nodded permission, adding "Don't go far. Meet me at the tram stop at 4 o'clock, Pam, no later; and take your topee."

"Come on, tell me," urged Pamela, jamming it on her head as they left the house.

"In a minute." Philip fished in his shorts pocket and produced a ten cent piece. "I've got some money; let's go to the San San and have an ice-cream."

Pamela looked doubtful. The San San was a tiny shop-cum-restaurant in the parade of Chinese shops in nearby Wanchai, and strictly forbidden territory as its ice-cream and drinks were not guaranteed to be made with pre-boiled water.

"Their ice-cream is cheaper than anywhere else," Philip reminded her.

"Oh well, just this once, as there isn't time to go further today. Come on, Phil, I'm dying to know what your news is!"

A tram screeched past. "What I want to say is," Philip began when the noise diminished, "What are you doing on Tuesday morning at 11 o'clock?"

"Tuesday morning.. oh, I don't know! Why, what are you doing then?"

"I'm going to England!"

"Going Home? Next week? So soon?"

"Um, on the 'Dilwara' 'cause my Dad keeps getting ill and the doctors say he must get out of this climate at once."

"Oh Philip'" She thought of the close companionship at school, doing their homework together on the ferry, and comparing cigarette cards. Seeing him now, serious and troubled, pulled at her heart.

"I'm supposed to be helping with the packing," he said, "but Mum said I could come over to see you to say goodbye; she gave me the ten cents, too."

They came to the cafe - no more than a small cave of a shop selling brightly coloured sweetmeats. Almost on the pavement were two ricketty tables with chairs. As the two sat down, a friendly foki produced a grey damp cloth and wiped it across the table top.

"One vanilla ice-cream," said Philip, "with an extra dish and two piece spoon."

"Ai yah! Two piece dish, two piece spoon, one piece ice-cream!" laughed the foki indulgently as he went to the back of the shop to fill the order.

An older foki came over to the children. "You got money?" he asked suspiciously.

"Of course!" Philip produced the ten cent piece and proferred it.

"Good one?" demanded the man, ringing the coin on the table to test its genuineness.

"They don't do that with money in England, do they?" Pamela remembered.

"Don't know - I haven't been in England since I was about six." Philip carefully spooned half the ice-cream into the spare dish then pushed both portions in front of Pamela, saying "You choose!"

"No, you, because you're going away."

All right." Philip examined both portions carefully, then pushed one towards Pamela.

"You've taken the SMALLEST!" she pointed out in astonishment.

"I know," he grinned.

"I'll always remember that," she said solemnly. "I'll always remember that the last thing you did was to give me the biggest half of the last ice-cream we had together."

"So you'll get a worse tummy-ache than me if they really do make their stuff without boiling the water first," laughed Philip, earning a playful punch on his freckled arm.

"Hope no one my parents know sees me here." Pamela looked round anxiously. "We'd better eat quickly and get away, just in case."

They walked quickly to the tram stop near her house.

"Your Mum's not there yet," observed Philip. "Still, I'd better go, 'cos I promised I'd be quick. So long."

"Wait!" Pamela felt something more should be said. "Will you ever come back to Hong Kong, do you think?"

"Don't know," he shrugged.

"Where in England will you be?"

"Don't know."

"Well," she tried not to be exasperated at his characteristic vagueness, "where do your grandparents live?"

"Somewhere in Kent, and there's another lot somewhere else, I can't remember where."

"Will you write to me when you're in England?"

"Yes, all right - if I can find a pencil."

This made Pamela laugh, then she found she felt more like crying. "Oh Philip, who will lend you pens and pencils, and remind you to do your homework and things when you're at school in England?"

He refused to be serious. "Maybe you'll come to school in England one day, then you can look after me all over again!"

"My family would never, never send me Home to school like Sandra." Pamela shook her head. "Boarding school costs too much, and anyway, they don't believe in it."

"Isn't that your amah coming along?" Philip nodded towards a black-trousered figure weaving her way towards them.

Pamela turned. "So it is. Perhaps my mother's changed her mind about the haircut."

The amah reached them and said "Missee Pamela, you mammy talkee you come home now, no stay by tram stop, she no come."

"Then I'll be off," said Philip. "Good bye!" He crossed the tramlines and branched off on the short cut across Happy Valley, turning once for a final wave before he was lost among the avenue of Flame of the Forest trees. Pamela, lacking a hanky, wiped her mouth with her fingers in case any traces of the forbidden ice-cream remained, then followed the amah into the house.

"Philip's going to England next Tuesday," she began as she met her mother in the hall, "because his father's ill; isn't it a shame?"

"Never mind that now." Her mother's face was serious and stern as she pushed Pamela into the lounge. For a moment she wondered if she and Philip had been observed in the icecream shop, but in the next realised there would not have been time for the misdemeanour to be reported. Her father, his face red with unmistakable fury, was standing just inside the door, waving something in his hand: with horror she recognised the jagged photograph of herself which had been in Marcus' wallet.

PART 2

1935 - 1937

Returning to England for her schooling five years ago had seemed bad enough, but even that experience paled against the ordeal of Pamela's first week at work as a junior typist in the engineering firm of Holmes & Spire in Ipswich in December 1935.

Each day began with the relentless alarm clock, followed by anxious calls at the bedroom door from her grandparents. There was no incentive to get up, even though last night's china hot water bottle was now as cold as her feet. The soft and sagging bed with its looped brass ends and the bulbous eiderdown, the little room itself with its pale blue wallpaper embossed with white crowns, all represented a haven. Here, at least, she felt safe and secure from the outside world, and lingered until her grandfather's plaintive announcement that the jug of hot water he had placed outside her door for ablutions was rapidly cooling. As there was no heating in the room, she kept her dressing-gown draped round her shoulders as she achieved a sketchy wash in the decorated china basin on its marble-topped washstand.

Dressed in a navy blue skirt, and a red jumper she had herself knitted, she joined her grandparents for breakfast in the kitchen-cum-dining room dominated by a huge black kitchen range which was never allowed to go out during the winter. Here again there was no time to linger, but she had to force herself to brave the freezing back yard and mount the icecold bicycle for the two mile ride to Holmes & Spire.

Each morning she arrived with feet that were either frozen with cold or soaked with rain - sometimes both; glanced anxiously at her watch as she passed through the main door - a minute after 9 o'clock and the uniformed janitor in his glassed-in compartment would enter her name in his Late Book.

The first half-hour at the typewriter with almost numb fingers was sheer agony. Although she had passed an examination in typewriting at 35 words a minute, all her confidence vanished when faced with the unfamiliar invoices and statements; with credit notes which had to be typed with the red half of the ribbon and using red carbons: if she remembered to switch over to the red ribbon, she would forget to use red carbon paper; when she remembered both, the chances were that she would forget to switch the red ribbon back to black, and the next form she typed would start off in red and have to be heavily overtyped in black - a circumstance which rarely escaped the sarcastic notice of the accountant, Mr. Clarke.

Unfamiliar with the machinery terminology , she had never felt so ignorant in her life. She spent much time rubbing out, secreting spoiled sheets of paper in screwed-up balls into her handbag, too ashamed to advertise her mistakes by putting them in the waste-paper basket. Always anxious, she spent precious typing time checking and re-checking every finished sheet. She lived for the lunch break which, with several other girls, she spent in the cloak room, perched on a bench beneath their coats, munching her bacon sandwiches. The girls were friendly enough, but she was shy with them because they all seemed so worldly and efficient.

It was a real effort of will for her to return to her office at two o'clock, every nerve tense at the prospect of another session of trials, her faults and omissions and inadequacies revealed. Tea, brought round to each office in the middle of the afternoon, was doubly welcome: not only did it ease the tension for five minutes, but also marked the point from which the day's work was three-quarters over. By then it was dark outside; the office lights were on and the tempo of work increased as last-minute letters and invoices were rushed through. Working under such pressure, Pamela felt more vulnerable than ever; her nervousness increased her typing mistakes, and by the time the factory hooter sounded at half past five, her palms were damp, her hands shaking and her cheeks bright red.

Only the prospect of the blessed evening sustained her through each long difficult day. The morning mail arrived after she had left for work, so at the end of each day there was the hope of letters from the accumulation of the three deliveries: a letter from her parents or Roddy in Hong Kong; from Belle in Shanghai; more frequently, from members of the assortment of fan clubs to which she belonged - fellow fans of Harry Roy and his band, John Mills the young actor whose fascination was that he had once worked in a factory adjoining Holmes & Spire's premises, Leslie Howard, Charles Boyer.. fans whom she had never met, nor was likely to, but with whom compulsive pen friendships had developed. The fantasy world of films filled the vacuum in her life - the one good thing about her job was that she could now afford to go to the cinema twice a week after paying her grandparents a contribution towards her keep.

Now in her third week, she knew quite a number of girls by name and could exchange pleasantries with them. She intended, one day, to muster sufficient courage to walk into the Shipping Office across the corridor from Accounts, because she had noticed through the glass partition a wall calendar with a picture of what looked like a P. & O. line - any link with her idyllic childhood in Hong Kong gave her a thrill of nostalgia.

The opportunity came one morning when Mr. Clarke handed her a file to take to Lawrence, the junior clerk in the Shipping Office. She knew him by sight, a stocky youth of about nineteen, with chestnut brown curly hair, but she had never spoken to him. Now she plunged clumsily into the Shipping Office, determined before fulfilling her mission to examine the calendar. Her heart leapt as she stood before it - a painting of RMS 'Ranpura', the very ship on which she had travelled to England in 1930 in the care of the Bately family.

"Are you interested in ships, Miss Doran?' Mr. Rye, the shipping manager, suddenly materialised at her elbow.

"Oh yes, sir!" That reply didn't seem sufficient response to the kindly enquiry so she stammered that she had lived in the Far East as a child and frequently travelled on P. & O. ships.

"You can have that picture on January 1st, if you like," he said. "The calendar will be thrown out then."

She stuttered her thanks, then discovered she was gripping the file for Lawrence so tightly that her fingers were aching. Cheeks flaming, she went over to his desk and handed him the file.

"Thanks very much, Miss.. Doran, is it?" He stared at her so keenly that she was struck dumb and could only nod in reply.

"Why is it, do you think," he whispered (for private conversations were firmly discouraged during office hours) - "that every one here calls me Lawrence, not Mr. Smith, yet you girls are always Miss This or Miss That? Why can't I call you by your Christian name?"

"Don't know," she muttered, darting an anxious look behind her to see if Mr. Rye or any of his assistants were watching.

"Well, Miss Doran, from now on I'm going to call you whatever that 'P' on your case stands for."

She realised with huge amazement that Lawrence must have noticed her arriving with the old school attaché case in which she carried her sandwiches each day; that she, Pamela Doran, seventeen years old, who had never had a boy-friend, and knew no boys at all apart from relatives, had actually caught the attention of one.

"So what does the 'P' stand for?" he was whispering.

"Pamela. And I must go!" She came down to earth, suddenly remembering that she was Miss Doran, junior typist in Accounts, and that all her time between 9 a.m. and 5.30 p.m. belonged to Holmes & Spire because they paid her 17/6d. per week and she had not yet completed her month's probation.

It was three months before Lawrence suggested a date. The grandparents looked very troubled when she told them.

"But you don't know anything about him, Pammie dear, neither do we. I'm sure your parents wouldn't like you to go to the pictures with a strange young man."

"He's not a stranger to me," she patiently explained. "I see him every day at H. & S. and we often have little chats."

"You've only been at H. & S. for three months, so you can't know him all that well."

"But how can I ever get to know him better if I don't go out with him? I'm seventeen.. I'm sure you forget that sometimes."

"Perhaps we do." Her grandmother reached across the supper table and patted Pamela's hand. "But seventeen or not, we're still in charge of you."

"Belle went about with lots of young men when she was my age," Pamela pointed out. "She was only 19 when she married."

"That may be, but your parents know who she was with."

So the arguments went on, Pamela alternately frustrated then sympathetic to the bewilderment of the old couple, who, she realised, were trying to apply the standards and conditions of their own youth to those obtaining in England in 1936. Fortunately for her peace of mind, she had learned now that they were as anxious to keep her happy as they were to preserve her from harm, and that gentle persuasion would generally win her at least some degree of whatever freedom or favour she sought.

So it was that she waited for Lawrence outside the cinema the next Saturday evening, scarcely daring to believe that this, her first date, would actually happen - until she saw him striding towards her. He looked magnificently adult in a fawn belted double-breasted raincoat, and dark brown Trilby hat tilted forward. Immediately she was conscious of the schoolgirl style of her dark green best coat, chosen for her two years ago by her grandmother; of the plain green velour hat which hid most of her short straight hair, and of the sensible shoes with cuban heels.

"Good evening," he smiled, tipping his hat to her. "Been waiting long?"

"Not very." She would not admit the fifteen-minute wait in the cold March wind.

They tagged on to the queue which snaked round the foyer, and Pamela wondered desperately what she could think of to say while they edged forward slowly as seats in the cinema were vacated. The huge pictures on the foyer walls of film stars in all their glamour served to increase her feeling of inadequacy. Oh, for the perfect profile of Norma Shearer, the seductive sophistication of Marlene Dietrich, the soulfulness and beauty of Greta Garbo, the fresh chocolate-box prettiness of Ginger Rogers, the individuality of Katharine Hepburn.. Oh, to be any one but overweight, straight-haired, moon-faced Pamela Doran!

" 'Mutiny on the Bounty' doesn't start until 8 o'clock," Lawrence was saying. "We're bound to be in by then. Did you see that other Clark Gable picture 'It Happened One Night'?"

"No I didn't. I wanted to, but my grandparents said I wasn't old enough." The truth slipped out, and seeing his amused gaze, she blushed.

"Why your grandparents?"

"I live with them - have done for years, because my parents are abroad."

"Oh, of course - Hong Kong; I heard you telling old Rye you'd lived there. Did you like it?"

"Oh yes.. I hated leaving to come to school in England."

"Why did you? Aren't there any schools in Hong Kong?"

"Oh yes, heaps! But a lot of parents think the ones in England are better."

"When did you last see your parents, then?"

"Two and a half years ago, they were here on leave for seven months. And last year my married sister Belle and her husband and their little boy - they all live in

Shanghai - came on leave and I spent all the summer holidays with them in Wales. And I've got a brother too, Roddy, he's twenty one and works in Hong Kong: he was on leave the year before last and spent alot of time with me at our grandparents' place, so it hasn't been so bad."

"Did you go to boarding-school?"

"Oh no, that would have been too expensive. I went to day-school here - Eastgate High."

"Seems a funny kind of life to me ," said Lawrence. "How do you get on with the grandparents?" "They're jolly good to me, only they're rather ancient and don't like visitors to the house, and worry about everything I do."

"But you really know them better than you know your own parents?" suggested Lawrence, and Pamela looked up in surprise, because this was a traitor thought which she had never allowed herself to put into words.

The relentless questioning continued: "So when will you see your parents again?"

"Summer of next year. They're coming Home for good because Dad's retiring then, and they're going to buy a house in this area, a new, labour-saving one."

"Will you go and live with them, then?"

"Of course!"

"Why of course?"

"Well, they ARE my parents, aren't they?"

"But I bet you like your grandparents better!"

Was this so? Suddenly confronted with this dreadful statement, Pamela was horrified to admit to herself that this was true.

"How could I?" she mumbled in confusion. "It's just that I'm more used to my grandparents now. I'll get used to my mother and father once I'm living with them again."

"You mean you won't have any choice, I suppose," grunted Lawrence. "I've noticed how serious you always look, Pam, and now I know why! You've had a raw deal. Now it's time you had some fun." He didn't elaborate on how this was to be achieved, but pulled a packet of spearmint from his pocket and offered her some. Spearmint was on the grandparents' forbidden list, and out of habit she politely declined. He then produced a bar of Nestle's chocolate. "I'll have some when we're inside, thanks," she said, not wishing to add to anxiety about her appearance by getting chocolate marks round her mouth.. marks which wouldn't be seen in the darkness of the cinema.

"You're a funny girl," declared Lawrence, taking her arm as they were shown to their seats.

The film would normally have enthralled her, but for once in her life, reality was more exciting than the screen world, and she could not forget the handsome profile so near her own: savoured the smell of his mint-flavoured breath when he turned to her with some whispered comment about the film. Once his hand touched hers; convinced that this was an accident, and anxious not to appear forward, she quickly drew her hand away.

All too soon the lights went up, they were standing for the National Anthem, and she was brushing chocolate specks off her coat, mentally deciding that her grandmother must be persuaded that a modern one was essential. He took her arm again as they shuffled out of the auditorium. She tried to edge away - supposing some one should recognise her and tell her grandparents of this familiarity?

"What's the hurry?" grinned Lawrence, holding on firmly. "I'm seeing you home, you know."

This possibility had not occurred to her. Panic struck. How could she sustain yet another conversation with him on the ten-minute walk to Spring Avenue?

"There's no need, thanks," she said. "I always go home on my own from the pictures. I'll be all right."

"I'm taking you home," repeated Lawrence, carefully jamming on his hat at the favoured angle. "So where do we go?"

She told him, adding "I really don't mind going alone.."

"What are you frightened of, Pam?"

"Nothing! It's.. it's just that.."

"Just what?" he prompted, tightening his grip on her arm as they strode along quickly to combat the bitter wind.

"Well, I'm not used to boys. I don't know what to talk about."

"You managed very well while we were in the cinema queue!" he laughed. "Am I really the first boy you've been out with?"

"I should think you could tell that easily!" Her teeth were chattering with nervousness.

"I can tell you something else: you've got the mightiest inferiority complex of any one I've ever met. You think nothing of yourself, and it's got to stop at once - I'll see to that."

For some reason this made her laugh. "How?" she giggled.

"All sorts of ways." He waved a hand in the air. "You've got to break out of the cocoon your family keep you in, and be yourself. Surely you still see some of your school friends?"

"No.. I didn't have any special friends. You see, my grandparents didn't like me bringing people home, and well, most of the girls thought I was odd because I didn't live with my parents. Some used to say it was because my parents didn't like me and didn't want me with them.. and for a long time I wondered if that was true, because they didn't send Belle or Roddy to school in England.. but I knew the real reason why they sent me." She stopped suddenly, realising that she was talking to Lawrence as she had never talked to any one before.

"What WAS the real reason?"

She had never told anyone this; even now, she hesitated, but Lawrence persisted.

"It all sounds so silly now," she stammered.

"Tell me, anyway!"

"Well, there were these Portuguese boys I used to play with every week when I went to have my piano lesson. One was two years older than me, and oh, it sounds so stupid, but he used to keep a photograph of me in his wallet! All we children knew, but we didn't know what he'd written on the back, except that it was something.. something silly about me." She stopped suddenly, realising she had said far too much.

"What?" probed Lawrence. "What had he written?"

"Oh.. something like he wanted to look after me for ever," she stuttered. "One day Marcus called at my house and by mistake his wallet got left there and my parents saw the photo and everything. There was the most awful row! Next thing, I was told I was going to school in England.. to grow up properly or something."

"Well!" Lawrence was clearly impressed. "I never dreamed you had a past with a capital P! And what happened to Marcus after you left?"

"Haven't the faintest!"

"Didn't you ever write to any of your Hong Kong friends? Or hear from them?"

"No, I wasn't allowed to."

"So: no friends either here or left over from Hong Kong! What do you do with yourself in your spare time?"

"Read, go to the pictures." (She wouldn't tell him about the fan clubs, fearing his disdain) "Sew, draw."

"Is that all? How dull!"

"No it isn't, especially the drawing; it was my best subject at school. I really wanted to go on to Art College."

"So why didn't you?"

"It's hard to argue with people thousands of miles away, and letters take five weeks; my parents went on about supposing there was another Depression, and told me learning shorthand and typing would be the best way to get a job."

"What a damn shame! But Pam, it's your own fault, you've got to stick up for yourself, put your own opinions forward, instead of meekly doing as you're told all the time. Do you play any sport?"

"Not now, but I did hockey and tennis at school - wasn't much good at either."

"There you go again, pulling yourself down! Anyway, it doesn't matter if you're not a star performer; the firm's ladies' hockey team is crying out for members - even beginners, the notice said. People play for the fun of it, so why don't you join? I go to our sports ground every Saturday afternoon to play football - you could come with me. I'll call for you, will you come?"

Thrilled but flustered, she said "But I always go to the library on Saturday afternoons, to change my books and the grandparents'."

"Then do the library in the morning, for goodness' sake!"

"I go shopping then, and pay the rates, to save my grandparents having to walk too much.. Lawrence, we're almost there: the next house.." She pulled her arm away from his as they approached the tiny red-bricked semi-detached house with its yard strip of garden behind spear-headed iron railings. Lawrence stopped her as she opened the gate, and put a hand on each of her shoulders, forcing her to look at him.

"Listen to me, Pamela!" His voice was earnest and urgent. "You've got to live your own life, else your routine will be exactly the same in ten, twenty, thirty years' time. You're just marking time between visits from your family. If you're still keen on doing Art, why don't you take it up at night school? Look at me! Do you think I'm going to stay a junior shipping clerk at H. & S. all my life? Not me! I go to night school to learn shorthand and typing, because I'm going to be a top journalist one day. You must help yourself.. get out of the house and make more friends! Start by coming to the sports ground this Saturday. I'll speak to Miss Gordon about you joining the hockey club, and I'll call for you next Saturday after dinner, shall I?"

His face was so close that she could feel the warmth of his breath and see the pigmentation on his rosy cheeks. An old memory flashed through her mind, that of a hasty kiss from a small boy in an anchor locker smelling of salty rope.. perhaps Lawrence was going to kiss her! And if so, how did one kiss? Evasively, she dropped her head and mumbled "I'll try to come."

"You'd better - I'll remind you every day."

A light appeared behind the coloured glass at the upper half of the front door which was cautiously opened, and her grandmother peered out. "Is that you, Pammie?"

"Just coming, Granny." She gave Lawrence a relieved smile now that the crisis was over. "And thanks, Lawrence, for the pictures and everything."

"Thank you for coming," he said with mock gravity, and tipped his hat to her as he strode off.

Life had changed completely. Although she was still anxious about her work, she felt far more confident. Each morning heralded the possibility of chance meetings with Lawrence in the corridors. All day long, at her desk, she was alert every time the door opened, watching in case Lawrence should be the visitor. Every meeting with him set her heart racing and her cheeks aflame. He had taken her to the cinema a second time - and there was always the delicious possibility that he might ask her yet again. She knew he took other girls out too, but didn't find this surprising - the surprising fact was that he bothered to take HER out at all!

Through his insistence, she was now a member of the ladies' hockey team; had somehow overcome the difficulties of her Saturday chores. After dinner each

Saturday, she made for the firm's sports ground and played hockey with clerks and typists whose enthusiasm and energy made up for any lack of skill. Lawrence no longer called for her, but he was always around, either on the football pitch, or surrounded by a group of colleagues of both sexes in the pavilion. Sometimes he called Pamela over to join them, other times he didn't seem to notice her - a facet of his character which she humbly accepted.

When Spring came, tennis succeeded hockey and she happily spent two or three evenings a week on the courts, as well as Saturday afternoons. Sometimes Lawrence made a foursome with Pamela and two other girls, sending balls scudding among them and livening up the game. Now she had no time, or inclination, to write long letters to members of the fan clubs.

She had earned a week's holiday!

"Where are you going?" asked the girls in the cloakroom at lunch-time, hardly pausing for an answer as they expounded their own plans - London, Norwich, Scarborough, Skegness.

"Well, nowhere actually.." Pamela had learned to take it for granted that 'going away' holidays only occurred when some member of her immediate family happened to be on Home leave and could carry her off.

"But you can't just stay at home all week!" the girls declared.

She missed her new friends during that week. The weather was glorious - almost too hot to enjoy the luxury of lying in bed long after nine o'clock for seven days in a row. She spent the mornings in the garden beneath the laden apple trees, reading and dreaming, and most afternoons in the cinema. She went to the sports ground for tennis most evenings, but Lawrence was away on holiday and so the magic was missing.

In the autumn she became secretary of the hockey club and felt her self-confidence growing. Sometimes the girls tried to entice her to a dance but she dared not accept: the memory of the only dance she had ever attended still burned painfully. Her grandmother had chaperoned her to a dance at the local church hall the first Christmas after she left school. Boys hung about on one side of the room; girls, very much in the majority, sat on the other. No one had asked her to dance the entire evening. To this shaming experience was added her distress at the hurt expression on her grandmother's face at the end of the evening. No, she couldn't face such a thing again.

In the year she had spent at Holmes & Spire two girls left to be married - the firm was strictly against employing married women - and newcomers, much younger than herself, had taken their places. Their obvious rawness showed her how much her work had improved, but she noticed with a pang of envy that Lawrence soon got to know them and chatted with them.

The latest films and newest dance tunes were discussed endlessly in the cloakroom. Little else seemed important until one December morning when the newspapers astoundingly reported that the as yet uncrowned King Edward VII wanted to marry an American divorcee called Mrs. Simpson. All agreed it would be impossible to have a twice-divorced American as Queen of England. Ten days later, all the staff of Holmes & Spire, by invitation of the managing director, crammed into the canteen in the afternoon to listen to a broadcast by the King. They could hardly believe what they heard: they were to lose their new King they had so happily welcomed earlier that year. He had chosen Mrs. Simpson instead of his throne; in his place would reign his younger brother, the Duke of York, better known to the public as the father of the two little princesses, Elizabeth and Margaret Rose.

Within the week, the cloakroom discussions were again devoted to the latest Fred Astaire/Ginger Rogers film, and the rival merits of Ambrose's, Harry Roy's and Roy Fox's dance orchestra - and plans for Christmas.

Last Christmas, Pamela had known none of her colleagues by their Christian names; this year, she needed to buy a dozen cards to distribute, and was delighted with the number she herself received. She was invited to two parties, and despite the usual initial painful shyness, enjoyed them. In each, an incredible number of adults and children managed to sit round a table extended by the addition of other pieces of furniture to the full length of the parlour. Elbow to elbow, face to face, it was impossible to remain shy for long. Brothers and sisters, uncles and aunts, treated Pamela as one of themselves. After table and chairs had been stacked against the wall and dancing of sorts followed, she found herself partnered by cheery friendly adults; there was scarcely room to move so it didn't matter that she didn't know how to dance.

Despite a very hard winter at the beginning of 1937, life was so absorbing and full that she faced the rigors of early rising in a freezing bedroom and the bicycle ride in rain or sleet, with stoicism instead of with the misery of the previous winter. Her grandparents were less and less able to undertake the heavy housework. She had to keep the coal scuttles full from the coal shed in the back yard. When the snows came, she kept a path swept clear in the yard from back door to the outside lavatory and the coal shed, usually before she left for work in the morning. These hated jobs were amply rewarded by the loving care which she appreciated more and more as she grew older. Her grandfather built her a special wireless set for her bedroom, complete with earphones, so that she could listen-in to dance music at night in bed without disturbing anyone. Her grandmother continued to cook large evening meals to make up for the lunch-break sandwiches - delicious steak and kidney puddings, dumpling stews, rabbit casseroles, mouth-water roasts, date puddings and fruit cakes.

Suddenly it was Easter and everyone at Holmes & Spire began planning summer holidays again. To her surprise and delight, Pamela was invited to spend a week with Ella Gordon and her family on a farm in Norfolk.

When she announced this great news to her grandparents, they were less than enthusiastic. "Your parents will be here in September," her grandmother pointed out. "Wouldn't it be better to wait until they come, and have your holiday with them?"

"I can have another week off in September, remember: I get two weeks' holiday this year."

"But are you sure there will be enough room for you? You said the Gordons were such a big family when you went to their Christmas party."

"There's plenty of room," Pamela explained patiently. "It's a big old farmhouse and they go there every year. It will be such fun! The farm is near the sea, too, so it's got everything - country life and swimming.

"We'll have to write and see what your parents say," was the dampening comment.

"I can't see why they should mind!" exploded Pamela, unable to contain her disappointment. "I'm eighteen now. Anyway, it would take three months to get an answer from Mum and Dad and it will be August by then.. too late."

She could not imagine her parents refusing permission, so while dutifully writing to ask them about it, she accepted Ella's invitation and ringed the relevant week in August in her diary with an exclamation mark because of the thrills it promised.

Next week the cloakroom seethed with excitement: to mark the 100th anniversary of the founding of the firm, the directors had invited all the staff to a dinner dance in July. Furthermore, there was to be a competition for the best design submitted of a cover for the programme, with a prize of Ten Pounds.

Pamela experimented at home with drawings for the programme, but could find no inspiration and decided the competition was not for her. After tennis one evening Lawrence called her over and asked "Have you sent in your design yet?"

"Not me.. not a hope."

"Do you mean you're not going to have a shot at it? You, who said you wanted to go to Art College? This is just up your street."

Pamela had never mentioned her interest in Art to anyone except Lawrence, and now all eyes were on her and voices clamoured encouragement. "Lawrence says you can draw, so you must do a design," decided Ella. "And do it, quickly, the entries have to be in next week."

"I can't.. my ideas won't work.."

"Then dig out some more ideas, my dear girl," said Lawrence, patting her head gently with his racquet. "Win that prize, and bags I have first dance with you that night' Then Mr. Spire will ask 'Who is that handsome fellow dancing with our design winner?' And afterwards, he will remember me, and give me promotion right away! So is that a deal?"

"Big head!" laughed Ella. "How do you know Pam would want to dance with you?"

"I can't dance, anyway," muttered Pamela.

"That can be remedied," said Lawrence over his shoulder.

This conversation whirred round Pamela's mind all that evening, creating a confusion of emotions. She considered the chances of her producing the winning design very remote, but just supposing she did, and Lawrence demanded the first dance at the firm's centenary? To be in his arms was beyond her wildest dreams, but if this should come to pass, she could only shame both herself and him - and dared not take the risk. It would be better not to compete. That decided, she settled back against her pillows that night, put on her earphones and switched on the wireless to listen to Harry Roy and his Band.

Something strange happened: the music stayed in the back of her mind, while in the foreground grew ideas for a design. No matter how firmly she dismissed these ideas because she had no intention of taking part in the competition, they returned and developed of their own accord. In the end she had to get out of bed for pencil and pad. By midnight, when Harry Roy signed off his broadcast with the haunting tune of 'Sarawaki', her bed was littered with sketches from which had emerged a design - 'H. & S.' taking up the whole sheet and composed entirely of miniature excavators, concrete mixers and mobile cranes.

She worked on the final drawing over the weekend, using a magnifying glass to perfect the tiny machines which she painted in the colours of their prototypes. The grandparents were most enthusiastic, but still she had not decided whether to compete or not. Her colleagues wanted to know if she had sent in an entry.

"I'm thinking about it," was all she would say, until Lawrence sought her out in her office.

"Tomorrow's the last day for the design comp.," he hissed over her typewriter. "Finished it? Let's see it!"

"It isn't here, it's at home."

"Make sure you bring it tomorrow - and let me see it first!"

"I.. I might not give it in," she said honestly.

"You'd better!" He sounded as fierce as was possible in the undertone necessary because Mr. Clarke was busy at his desk a few yards away.

As she wheeled her bicycle through the side gate of the house next morning, she was flabbergasted to find Lawrence outside, seated on his motorbike.

"You've got the drawing? I just wanted to make sure. Show me!"

She untied the attaché case strapped to the bicycle carrier and took out the drawing. Lawrence was clearly impressed.

"You'll probably win," he nodded. "You really should be at Art College, you know. Have another go at your parents when they come.. this Autumn, isn't it?"

"September. But I don't want to go to College now and" - she had to say it - "I don't want to win that competition."

"Why ever not?"

"I don't want to go to Art College because I like it at H. & S. And I don't want to win the competition because I really can't dance, and you said.."

"Pam, you're the most serious person I've ever met and also the funniest!" Lawrence carefully laid the design back in the case which he secured to the carrier. "I shall teach you to dance - then there will be nothing to prevent you from taking the prize."

The lessons took place on the tiny verandah of the games pavilion at the recreation ground, in between tennis sessions. Pamela's initial awkwardness was quickly brushed aside by Lawrence, who first seized Ella and insisted she partner him in a demonstration. When it was Pamela's turn, she was overcome with the unfamiliar sensation of being held in a man's arms in general, and Lawrence's in particular. He gave earnest directions which she found difficult to follow because her attention was rivetted on his proximity.. his white aertex shirt and its salty masculine odour, and the warmth of his bare arms across her back. Tripping. jerking and apologising, she forced her thoughts on to his patient counting - there being no music - and at last managed to fall in with his steps after a fashion: no mean achievement as both were wearing tennis shoes, and the practice area measured no more than ten feet in length and four feet in width.

Afterwards, two older girls of great sophistication came off the tennis courts and invited Lawrence to dance with them in turn. Their steps with him were so accomplished that the verandah no longer seemed small as they dipped and turned.

Watching them, Pamela marvelled that Lawrence, who could dance with absolutely anyone, should take the trouble to teach such a clumsy person as herself.

Dancing lessons continued every tennis evening, and she began to improve. Other players took up the idea too and the verandah was always occupied by at least one couple trying out their steps.

Her grandparents remonstrated because on tennis evenings she did not get home until after dark. She explained about the dancing lessons about which they exchanged anxious looks.

"I'm sorry you're worried," she said. "But I just must learn to dance, you wouldn't like it if I went to the H. & S. do in July and couldn't dance, would you?"

A further delight loomed on the horizon. The forthcoming Coronation was to be a public holiday, and Pamela was invited to join a group from H. & S. planning to go to London to see the Royal Procession to Westminster Abbey.

"We'll have to travel to London the evening before," she explained excitedly to her grandparents, "so as to get a good place to view; thank goodness it's in the summer so it won't be cold at night.

"You mean, you have to wait on the pavement all night?"

Her grandfather was aghast.

"Yes, you take something to sit on, and sleep if you can! Lawrence and his father did that when they went to see Princess Marina's wedding. Lawrence said it was great fun, everyone was so friendly, and the waiting time didn't seem long at all. It's a chance in a million to see a King and Queen the day they are crowned, isn't it?"

"Well, yes, Pammie, but young girls staying up all night!"

"There will be some young men too, to look after us," she pointed out, and realised at once from her grandparents' faces that she had alarmed them even more.

"That doesn't seem quite the thing... I don't think your parents would like... we'll have to see what they say.."

This was the same situation that had arisen over Pamela's wish to join in Ella's farm holiday, for which permission from Hong Kong had not yet arrived. Trying to control her frustration, she gulped "I'm sure they would WANT me to see the Coronation, but I'll write to them this evening, and send the letter by air mail."

"That will be terribly expensive!"

"This means such alot to me, Granny, and so does the farm holiday, I'll remind them about that too. I don't mind paying air mail postage, it will be worth it! I can't miss the Coronation!"

"Don't count on it, Pammie dear," warned her grandmother.

But count on it she did, adding her name to the list of colleagues booking the trip to London. The details were excitedly discussed every day in the cloakroom - she just needed her parents' confirmation to dispel the grandparents' anxiety.

The time had arrived when an air mail reply from Hong Kong could be expected. She awoke one morning convinced that this was the day, but the only post that morning was a reproachful letter from one of her erstwhile fan correspondents asking why she had not written recently. She thought fleetingly of the months when such letters had been the centre of her life - in such contrast to the excitements and thrills of the present.

At eleven o'clock a typed statement was passed round all the offices announcing that the design competition had been won by a young trainee architect in the Drawing Office. Pamela was surprised at the extent of her disappointment, having allowed herself to dream of partnering Lawrence in the first dance at the firm's celebration. At noon Mr. Clarke took a telephone call from Mr. Spire: the whole office knew, because when someone important was on the telephone, Mr. Clarke always held up his hand for all typing to stop.

"Yes, Mr. Spire; of course, Mr. Spire. At once, sir." He put the receiver down reverently and told Pamela that Mr. Spire wished to see her in his office immediately.

She was appalled. Mr. Spire was so important that he conducted his business in a penthouse at the top of the office building. She had never seen him, and could only think she was about to be reprimanded, or even dismissed.

"So much for me thinking this was going to be my lucky day," she thought grimly as she climbed the three flights of stairs.

The door marked 'A.S. Spire' was slightly ajar and the occupant of the room visible through the crack, which made it doubly embarrassing to act as though one could not see him when knocking.

"Come in, Miss Doran!" The voice was booming, the shape rotund, the face kind and smiling. "Come and sit down. You'll have heard the result of the design competition; my partners and I would like you to know how much we liked your entry; although we had to give the prize to Mr. Glyn, your entry was a really close second."

All Pamela could feel at that moment was relief that she had not been summoned to be sacked.

"This artistic ability of yours," Mr. Spire was saying, "have you had any Art training?"

Only at school, she told him.

"But you're still very interested in drawing, obviously."

"Oh yes, sir. I wanted to go to Art College when I left school, but I had to learn shorthand and typing instead because of the Depression, my family said."

"A pity, because you have real talent waiting to be developed. I've discussed this with my Drawing Office Manager, and we both think you would be well advised to transfer to the Drawing Office next time there's a vacancy - which should be in about three months' time. Would that appeal to you?"

There was much more. Pamela had to strain to hear it above the thumping of her heart: Mr. Clarke could release her from the Accounts Office two afternoons a week which she would spend in the Drawing Office getting to know what went on there, and to discover if she would prefer that kind of work to secretarial work; if that proved to be the case, she was to take a course in technical drawing at night school, starting next September, the firm paying the fees; she must not feel anxious about the proposed change; if after all she decided to return to secretarial work, she could do so as Mr. Clarke had given her excellent reports and there would always be a place for her in the firm while she maintained this standard; Mr. Spire added that after six months' training in the Drawing Office, and provided she passed the examination at night school, her salary would be raised to a level considerably higher than she was receiving as a shorthand typist.

She didn't remember walking down the stairs; found herself back at her desk, looking blankly at a pile of invoices waiting to be typed.

Mr. Clarke came over to her. "Well done, Miss Doran. I don't want to lose you, but you deserve your chance." With astonishment she realised that he had known all along the reason for the interview. Somehow she managed to get her fingers to work on the typewriter, but her mind was full of Mr. Spire's words. At the first opportunity Ella slipped over to her and wanted to know what had happened.

"Mr. Spire liked my design, even though it didn't win," Pamela whispered guardedly; the rest she was saving for Lawrence, who waylaid her in the corridor half an hour later.

"Sorry you didn't get the prize," he said. "You should have won, it wasn't fair to give the prize to some one already in the artistic world, so I'm still claiming first dance on centenary night."

"If you like," agreed Pamela carefully, but she could not hide a grin of delight. "And Lawrence, Mr. Spire wants me to transfer to the Drawing Office when there's a vacancy." She giggled and added "He thinks I have talent!"

"Told you so! I'm not surprised," said Lawrence, although he looked it. "Tell me more!"

Senior clerks were striding purposefully past, files in hand; this was not the time for more conversation.

"I'll see you after 5.30 - wait outside for me," directed Lawrence.

Could this day hold yet more delight? Pamela felt as though her head was separated from her body for the rest of the working day. Mr. Clarke kept her for five minutes after the factory bull had sounded, and fearing Lawrence would not have waited for her, she raced to the cloakroom, grabbed coat and hat and tore to the bicycle stand. With great relief she saw him sitting astride his motor bike, reading the 'Melody Maker'. He waved aside her apologies, saying "Now tell me exactly what Mr. Spire said!"

Words falling over each other, she gave a full report.

"Aren't you glad I made you enter the competition?" he said proudly. "This is a chance in a million for you."

"I know, and it scares me in case I'm no good at doing the kind of drawing the firm wants."

"But you will try it," pronounced Lawrence. "You've proved you have talent, so let's have no more of this 'poor-little-me-I'm-no-good' talk! What about a celebration trip to the pictures this evening?"

"If anything else exciting happens today, I shall burst," thought Pamela dizzily as she cycled home as on winged wheels. Not waiting to put her cycle away in the shed, she propped it up against the wall and burst through the back door into the kitchen.

"I've got some simply terrific news!" she announced as she pulled off her hat and coat. "Although I haven't won the design prize, Mr. Spire sent for me and told me how much he liked my design, and.."

"That's lovely! We've got good news for you too," her grandmother interrupted. "Look!" She pointed to the unmistakable airmail letter propped up on the mantelpiece. Pamela's mind registered that the jagged edge meant the letter had been opened, so it could not be addressed to her.

"Your parents have had such a splendid idea," said her grandfather, reaching for the letter. "Your father's retirement has been put off for a year, so they won't be coming Home this September - and they've booked a passage for you to travel out to Hong Kong next month to stay with them until they do retire!"

"What?" gaped Pamela, unable to believe her ears.

"You're going out to Hong Kong next month, Pammie - sailing a week before the Coronation! Isn't that wonderful? It's what you've always dreamed of doing, isn't it? Your mother has given us all the details, but she's put in a little note for you too."

Pamela sat down and unfolded the flimsy sheet of paper. While the plan was only in the spoken word, it had been possible to think it wasn't real, but here, in her mother's firm hand were the concrete facts, and she had to believe them.

"I can't go," she said, shaking her head. "I don't want to go. I've got things planned: going to see the Coronation, the H. & S. celebration, the holiday in Norfolk with the Gordons and everything. And today, Mr. Spire, our director, says I've got artistic talent and he wants me to go to night school and study drawing, and transfer me to the Drawing Office later.. and I just can't leave everything to go to Hong Kong!"

For half an hour there was complete confusion, as the grandparents tried to allay Pamela's distress.

"We thought you'd be so pleased," they said. "It's costing your parents a great deal of money and it's so unlike you to be ungrateful."

They pointed out that she could return to Holmes & Spire next year and take up Mr. Spire's offer. Pamela almost choked on her efforts to explain that the offer might not still stand a year after it was made. She was quite unable to eat the cornish pasties put before her.

"You'll feel better in the morning," her grandmother tried to console her. "You've had such a lot of excitement today. Have an early night."

"I don't want an early night," she hiccoughed. "I'm going to the pictures with Lawrence."

There was more consternation: she was not in a fit state to go out, would be better to take an aspirin and go to bed.

Stony-faced, she went upstairs to freshen up; only when she was leaving the house and, through the layers of shock which had surrounded her since her arrival home, suddenly saw the anxiety in her grandparents' eyes, did she soften. "I'm sorry," she said,"but I can't stay in tonight, really I can't, but I promise not to be late."

They didn't go to the pictures after all. Lawrence changed the plans as soon as he heard her news. They spent the evening walking in the park, Pamela with her head down, answering his searching questions in short, broken, sentences, occasionally lapsing into silence while she fought to control the threatening tears.

Round and round they tramped, and round and round went the arguments.

"So you really don't want to go to Hong Kong?"

"No, no!"

"But you always sounded nostalgic when you told me about life there."

"I used to be.. but that's nothing compared with working at H. & S., especially with the chance of going into the Drawing Office. I don't want to change things now."

"I can understand that, but I should remind you that most people - including yours truly - would give their eye teeth to be invited to spend a year in Hong Kong, or anywhere abroad come to that. Tell me the honest truth: doesn't it attract you in the slightest to contemplate going back? All those lovely beaches you've raved about, and all that sunshine, and amahs to do all the housework ?"

She shook her head. "I don't need Hong Kong any more. My friends are all here. Oh Lawrence, I can't go and leave everything and everyone." She was too modest to explain how, for the first time in her life, she felt comfortable in the niche she had carved for herself. She had somehow accomplished something at H. & S., proved she was not the failure and misfit she had always felt at school in England. A fresh surge of self-pity engulfed her and she could not hold back the tears.

Firm arms enclosed her. "Cry, Pam, if you want to, get rid of your grief." He led her to the nearest bench and kept one arm tightly round her shoulders until she calmed down. Then he mopped her face with his handkerchief, asking "Better now?"

She nodded, not trusting her voice.

Stuffing the hanky into his pocket, he cupped her face in his hands. "Sometimes, Pam, I think you're the sweetest person I've ever met," he said, and gently kissed her lips.

Pamela stared at him, savouring the touch on her lips as of a fairy's paint brush, hardly able to believe what had happened or that such a delicious sensation was real. So it was true, she thought with wonder: the swooning look on the film stars' faces when their heroes kissed them! And it had happened to her.. was, in fact, happening again. She started to shiver.

"You're getting cold." Lawrence stood up, and she did not explain that the shivers came from emotion, not the cool May evening. "We'd better walk some more."

Slowly, they set off in the direction of Spring Avenue.

"Now, if you're quite certain you don't want to go to your parents," began Lawrence, "if you're quite, quite certain.."

"Absolutely certain," she broke in vehemently: those two simple kisses had shown her that life in England near Lawrence held even more promise.

"Then you must stand up for yourself. Simply refuse to go."

"I'm not twenty-one, I can't defy them!"

"That's what I mean by standing up for yourself. You wouldn't need to fight if you were of age, you could just do what you wanted to. Now you must explain to your parents what you've told me - they'll be bound to understand: up to now they've probably thought you were just dying to get back to Hong Kong."

"It's too late. My passage is booked, and they've arranged for me to travel with some family friends booked on the same boat."

"Passages can be cancelled."

"There isn't time -"

"Write by airmail. It's no good weeping about your lot unless you do something positive about it."

"Will you help me write the letter?"

"You bet I will. Come home with me now, and we'll do it together!"

Pamela's heart was thumping uncomfortably as they hurried along the quiet lamplit streets. Too much was happening. Every moment she expected to wake up and find she had been dreaming, from the interview with Mr. Spire onwards.

Lawrence took her into his house and introduced her to his parents, who were yawning over cocoa and obviously about to go to bed. They could not disguise their astonishment and irritation at this late visit, but became more friendly when Lawrence explained the reason. His mother even insisted on making cocoa for them.

The letter became a mixture of Pamela's specific reasons for wishing to stay in England phrased in Lawrence's forceful language. Lawrence then sat back and smoked as Pamela copied the final version on to a fresh sheet of note-paper. Despite the importance of her task, she found it hard to concentrate, for Lawrence had never looked more attractive. He had taken off his jacket, and his white shirt emphasised his vivid colouring. His curls were awry because he had been pushing his fingers through them while working out the draft - and his eyes were on her all the time she wrote.

Afterwards, they hurried to Spring Avenue, Pamela thinking guiltily of her parting promise to her grandparents.

"Now don't forget," Lawrence squeezed her hand as they reached the house. "Don't tell them about the letter until you've sent it, in case they try to persuade you to alter it, and post it at the G.P.O. on your way to work tomorrow morning."

PART 3

JUNE - NEW YEAR'S EVE 1937

JUNE

"Here she comes!" Mrs. Bately nodded in the direction of the dumpy girl with an anxious expression wearing a fawn belted macintosh and low-heeled shoes - one of the last passengers to leave the train.

"But it can't be! That frump can't be Pamela," said Hilary.

"She's the only youngish woman on this train, and her grandmother did say Pam would be wearing a fawn mac.. and look at the initials on her case!"

"But that's a schoogirl," began Hilary, but already her mother was walking towards the barrier, hand outstretched.

Once they had officially met, and Pamela's anxious look changed to one of relief, Hilary could recognise the neighbour she had last seen seven years ago: the same round face and questioning eyebrows - the same straight, short dark hair, and the same habit of looking down at her feet between conversations.

Having been warned beforehand that Pamela was only with great reluctance making this voyage to Hong Kong, Hilary was careful to talk only of trivialities during the journey to Tilbury. Pamela exchanged remarks courteously but her hands were tightly clenched and her lower jaw held rigid.

It was all Hilary could do to stop herself from whooping with delight at the first glimpse of the black funnel and fawn superstructure of the SS 'Corfu' rearing above the customs sheds at Tilbury, but nothing could stop her from kissing the rail of the gangway as she took her first step on it. Even Pamela's gravity gave way to laughter at that.

"Top bunk or bottom?" asked Hilary as she and Pamela walked into the tiny cabin they were to share.

"Top, please - unless you want it."

"No, you have it." Hilary was pleased to see the first real show of enthusiasm. "I'd rather not climb ladders when we're plunging through the Bay - or have you forgotten what that's like?"

"No I haven't." Pamela was re-discovering the chrome pull-down wash basin with concealed bucket beneath for waste water; the flap on the wall beside each bunk which could be propped up to take the morning tea; the built-in ventilator. "Everything's coming back to me; I never imagined I'd be travelling anywhere by sea again."

"And you're quite pleased, after all?" Hilary dared to ask.

"No." Pamela's voice went flat again, and she turned away quickly. It was inexplicable to Hilary that any one who had ever lived in Hong Kong should want to live anywhere else. The sight of a scattering of Chinese passengers, of the dusky Lascar crewmen in their loose blue tunics and red pill-box hats, the handsome and friendly Goanese stewards, thrilled her to the core.

After an hour on board she had assessed the European passengers and picked out several possible boy-friends. Without a glum Pamela in tow she could have been on speaking terms with them by the time the ship sailed.

Pamela's gloom persisted throughout dinner that evening, and she declined to join Hilary and her family in the coffee lounge afterwards, pleading tiredness.

"What am I going to do with her, Mother?" wailed Hilary after Pamela left them. "She's just like a suet pudding, I can't get through to her at all."

"Give her time, Hilary. Remember, she's left her first boy-friend behind."

"Goodness knows how she ever got a boy-friend in the first place!" Hilary made the most of her freedom for the rest of the evening, getting into conversation with contemporaries of both sexes. It was almost midnight when she tiptoed along the cabin door - but Pamela was not asleep; the light was on and she was huddled in the chair in her pyjamas, sobbing miserably.

"What on earth is wrong? You ill or something?" Hilary put a friendly arm across the heaving shoulders. Pamela shook her head and wept the more. Seeing that sympathy didn't help, Hilary tried another tack. "Don't tell me you're still in mourning for old England?" As there was only one chair, she sat down on the lower bunk, banging her head on the one above. "Ouch..no doubt this is the first of many encounters. No fool you, choosing the top bunk. "Come on Pam, just tell Auntie all about it, I'm really intrigued to know what good old U.K. can have to make you so attached to it."

In between tears and sniffs Pamela poured her heart out. Hilary became more sympathetic as she discovered that Pamela's distress was not caused simply by the parting from the young man - who didn't even seem to be exclusively her young man - but also for the sudden disruption of a whole way of life. She began to understand Pamela's bitterness against her parents for over-ruling her wishes about her future, and her concern for the grandparents left without her help with the daily chores which were too much for them.

She reached for Pamela's flannel, ran it under the tap and handed it to her. "Use this, you look like Dracula's wife," she said cheerfully. "And I know one thing that needn't worry you: explain to your parents exactly the situation about your grandparents, and I'm sure they will arrange for them to have some help in the house. I'll tell you this too: you've got every right to be fed up at having to come to Hong Kong when you didn't want to, but there's nothing you can do about it now because you're not twenty-one; anyway, it's not for ever! So why not make the best of it? You'll only feel worse if you don't forget your resentment.. and think of poor me, having to share a cabin with a constant misery! I promise I'll make allowances for the odd moan from time to time, if you'll promise to try to cheer up. Right?"

"All right." Pamela's voice shook a little, but she could almost smile. She brightened up even more when Hilary steered the conversation round to a gossip about mutual acquaintances of their childhood who were still living in Hong Kong. For no reason at all this developed into a giggling session, and Hilary congratulated herself that the worst was over.

There was no doubt about it: Pamela had to admit to herself after the first few days that she was beginning to enjoy the pleasures of shipboard life.

The morning cup of tea and fresh fruit, delivered to her while she was still in her bunk, was only the start of a luxurious existence. There was no rush to get up to enjoy the appetising breakfast. Afterwards, she could stride round the open decks, or play quoits or tennis with the Batelys, or lounge in a deck chair by the ship's rail with a book from the well-stocked library. At 11 o'clock stewards brought round beef tea and savoury biscuits. The four-course luncheon usually rendered Pamela so sleepy that she rested for an hour afterwards in the cabin: not so Hilary, who sought the company of her new friends on the games deck.

"Join us when you come to life again," she had often said, but this Pamela would not do. Without the backing of the familiarity of H. & S., she was again lacking in self confidence: whatever could she say to these new young men, so full of quips and banter? Instead, she took a sedate afternoon tea with Mr. and Mrs. Bately.

The evenings were more difficult. She dreaded the predinner drinks in the lounge. The cut and thrust conversation between Hilary and her parents amazed her; they spoke as equals; she could not imagine her own parents allowing her to retort and tease as Hilary did.

She would have preferred to retire to the cabin with a book after dinner, but Hilary insisted on a brisk walk round the decks first. Before long other passengers would appear and Hilary stopped to talk to the younger ones. This was the point at which Pamela always slipped away.

"Why won't you ever stay with us?" demanded Hilary late one evening when she joined Pamela in the cabin.

"I'd rather read," she shrugged.

"Honourable parents are complaining that I leave you alone too much," said Hilary lightly. "You're getting me into hot water."

"Oh dear!" Pamela could hardly imagine this was really true. In the few days she had known this adult Hilary, she couldn't imagine any one being angry with her: forthright, amusing, never hesitating to laugh at herself; knowledgeable and sophisticated - Pamela had never met anyone like her.

"Anyway," said Hilary indistinctly through her foaming toothbrush. "You'll come to the Book Evening, won't you?" She explained that this was a social occasion when passengers pinned cards to their persons depicting the title of a wellknown book, there being a prize for which passenger guessed the most titles.

"You like books, you'd be very good at it, so you'd better come - it will get me into good with my parents if I get you there, too."

Remembering the debt she owed Hilary for her understanding on the first night out, Pamela agreed. She glowed under Hilary's admiring comment "I say, you CAN draw!" at her picture of a sailing ship with torn sail, representing 'Gone With The Wind'. Four other passengers used the same basic theme, but her entry won first prize and brought her on speaking terms with several other passengers.

As lazy day succeeded lazy day while the 'Corfu' plied through the Mediterranean Sea, the busy exacting routine at H. & S. seemed less and less real, and her anguish at leaving England lessened.

When the availability of the swimming pool was announced, she went to see it, full of nostalgia for the voyages of childhood. What had seemed huge and deep then now looked like a small tarpaulin tank. A handful of teen-agers and young children cavorted in the water. She could see it was no place for her now, but stayed watching for a while, remembering the hilarious daily sessions with Philip, John, Humphrey and Fay. How uncomplicated life was in those far-off days! Hilary was badgering her daily to join in the dances held on the top deck most nights. Pamela's two evening dresses, chosen at the Co-op under the conservative guidance of her grandmother, were full-length versions of children's party dresses, one in blue taffeta, one in green, both with short puff sleeves and with a wide contrasting sash: how could she appear thus garbed among the shoulder-strapped, figure-hugging satins and silks?

"You've got a problem there," Hilary wryly agreed when Pamela exhibited the offending dresses. "Shall we take the sleeves out, for a start?"

The sashes were removed too, and replaced by a narrow silver belt borrowed from Hilary's mother; yet still Pamela hesitated.

"Now what?" demanded Hilary crossly, having spent all the afternoon in the hot cabin helping to unpick the wretched sleeves.

"I'm afraid.. I'm afraid no one will ask me to dance!"

"Dear God!" Hilary gazed at the ceiling in supplication. "Come along and find out - nothing ventured, nothing gained, and all that."

On the first occasion no one DID ask her - except Hilary's father when the situation became obvious.

In the cabin afterwards, Pamela hung up her dress and wept "It's no good. I'm too fat!"

"Then lose some weight, goose: four potatoes this evening, AND two rolls and butter - I ask you!"

A week of dieting plus the increasingly hot weather resulted in her losing two pounds.

"Keep at it," Hilary urged. "It really suits you to be slimmer. Now your hair - ever thought of having it set? It's nice and thick, it would take a deep wave. Have it done for the Coronation Ball; make an appointment right away because they were pretty booked up when I booked mine this morning."

"I shan't be going to the Ball," Pamela was climbing into her bunk, Her voice was shaking and she kept her face averted. "And I'm not going to the Barbers and I'm never going to a dance again!"

"What's this - a relapse?" Hilary's expression was challenging as she stood on the ladder and forced Pamela to face her.

"Coronation Day was something I was looking forward to so much at home" she mumbled.

"I know that - you told me five times first night out! Still, no need to go into purdah that day, is there? Or do you want to make yourself as miserable as possible as some kind of gesture? You're 18, not 8, Pam! And your parents aren't on board so there's no one here to see your gesture or care about it: only poor old me, having to explain to my parents once again that you don't enjoy our company enough to join us in the jollifications.."

"Oh Hilary, you know it isn't that."

"Prove it then! Come to the Ball - and get that hair appointment made tomorrow."

After the hair set, Pamela for once almost approved of her reflection in the mirror. The suggestion of waves gave her hair more body and made her face seem less round. The blue sleeveless dress with the silver belt contributed to her more grown-up appearance..

On Coronation night the dining-saloon was transformed with red, white and blue garlands and streamers. Crackers, paper hats and blowers added to the gala atmosphere, but at first it seemed that the new hair style had wrought no miracles, for she was asked to dance only by Hilary's father and his kindly friends since no other partners were forthcoming. As the evening progressed however, she became aware of constant glances from a slim, bronze-faced man every time he danced past, and the time came when he came and asked her to dance.

"I'm not very good," she warned as she stood up, and despite Lawrence's lessons, proceeded to justify her words by tripping before she could get into step, but soon she managed quite well, guided by the pressure of his finger on her back.

She guessed he was about thirty years old; his name, he told her, was Ray Scott and he was a rubber planter in Penang. In return she told him her name and that she was travelling to Hong Kong to join her parents.

"I've noticed you all the voyage," he smiled down at her. "You don't mix very much, do you? I bet this is your first trip out East?"

Almost apologetic for proving his assumption wrong, she explained that this was only one of many trips.

"Ah, so you've been salted away in a good old English boarding school to keep you out of harm's way," nodded Ray with a dazzling smile.

"Not boarding-school, just day-school," she corrected him again, missing a beat of music in her embarrassment.

"All right - day school," Ray laughed. "But now you're going back to Hong Kong to start earning your living?"

"I've been earning my living for two years in England!" This third contradiction made her giggle.

"Well, well! And I had you down in my book as a young lass just out of school! I would have spoken to you weeks ago if I hadn't thought it was cradle-snatching." He held her closer and claimed the remaining dances that evening.

"What have you got that I haven't - apart from a bust?" Hilary complained as they undressed after the Ball. "He's the best-looking unattached male in sight - makes all my boy-friends look like callow youths. Got a good bank balance, too, I should think, by the look of his clothes; it's a wonder he isn't travelling First."

Pamela's life was magically transformed. Ray waylaid her for deck games every morning, and drinks afterwards. ("Only lemonade again? Do I hear aright?") There was dancing most evenings and he danced only with her. She wore a constant smile, even when he was not around.

When the ship called at Colombo, he wanted to take her on a trip ashore, but Hilary's parents said No: they had already made arrangements for a family tour which included Pamela. That day without him seemed very dull, despite the sight-seeing. The ship sailed very early the next morning; he did not appear at breakfast, nor could she find him on deck afterwards. She slouched in a deck chair until Hilary came along and reported she had just seen him making for the saloon bar.

"Looks as though he had a thick night ashore," she added. "I expect he's been sleeping it off."

"Oh I'm sure he's not like that." Pamela adjusted herself more elegantly in the chair, but when Ray arrived soon after with a gin sling for himself and a lemonade for her, he did look somewhat jaded.

"'Fraid I'm not up to deck games today," he apologised. "I've got too many good friends in Colombo!" She held both glasses as he pulled up a deck chair; his fingers lingered round hers as she handed him back his glass, and the excitement of his touch sent shivers all over her. As he sipped his drink then placed it on the deck, she was thankful he was not looking at her as the shivers continued; in fact, he was not looking at anything now; he was lying back in his chair with his eyes closed; his mouth fell slightly open and he stayed that way until the lunch gong boomed. He awoke at once, bleary-eyed and apologetic.

"I'll make up for my lack of attention at the dance this evening," he promised.

There was certainly no sign of the morning's lethargy when, looking particularly magnificent in a cream tussore suit, he joined Pamela and the Batelys at the dance after dinner. He whirled her round the deck in a foxtrot, a waltz and a quickstep, then suggested they have a few minutes by the ship's rail to cool off. There, in a dark corner beneath one of the life-boats, he pulled her to him and kissed her, not gently as Lawrence had, but long and passionately. She caught his excitement, and clung happily to him, feeling senses responding which she had not guessed existed.

"I knew you were sweet from the first moment I saw you," murmured Ray between kisses, his arms tightening on her body.

In the distance, the band's trombone could be heard blaring out its solo of 'The Music Goes Round and Round.' They were pressed together against the rail, the keel of the beige lifeboat a few inches above their heads; below, the dark sea was flecked with white scudding spume. Ray pressed wet kisses into her neck, thrilling her so much that she only gradually became aware that he had undone the buttons at the back of her dress and seemed to be fiddling with the hook of her brassiere.

"Whatever are you doing?" Interest rapidly turned to indignation, then to panic. "I can't think why you're doing that!"

"I can teach you so much, little one," came Ray's muffled voice, for the kisses were now travelling over her taffeta bosom.

"You can't do this to me, you know," she said firmly, but the pressure of his lips was insistent and distracting. Trying to disengage herself from his grasp, she managed to put one hand behind her back, and grappled with his fingers which were still working on the brassiere hooks. She tried to twist away but was unable to free herself from his grip, so stabbed the deck wildly with one foot until her shoe found his ankles. Yelping with pain, Ray let her go, and she fled towards the nearest companionway, fastening her buttons as she went.

Hilary joined her in the cabin soon after. "Wherever did you get to? The parents were frantic when no one could find you. Are you all right, Pam, you're shaking like a jelly!"

"That Ray!" Pamela could hardly speak for shock, and it was some minutes before she could stammer out the story.

"Poor old Pam! Most men are like that, you know, given half a chance." Hilary's matter of fact attitude never failed to amaze Pamela. "Mean to say this is the first time you've come up against this sort of thing? What about Romeo at that firm of yours?"

"Lawrence wasn't a bit like that!" The memory of the comforting kisses in the Ipswich park brought a sudden yearning for the safe, familiar life she had left behind. She wept for the past, and for the humiliation of realising that all Ray's attentions had been based on the assumption that she would be easy game for him.

She refused to attend any more dances, or even to play deck games with Hilary lest she should meet Ray. When they passed each other in the dining saloon he gave her an uneasy smile but she could only stare sternly at him.

Life was better when he disembarked at Penang and she could walk freely about the ship without embarrassment, but the days dragged and she began to feel something of Hilary's mounting excitement as the ship neared Hong Kong.

Standing on deck early one morning she watched mist-shrouded islands gradually materialise into half-remembered, green shapes; great mountains rearing up against the pale blue sky as the ship breached the narrow Lyemun Pass between Hong Kong Island and the mainland. She had forgotten how enclosed the harbour was: forgotten the rows of grey tenements and shops lining the waterfront at the foot of the hills: forgotten the cluster of grey warships anchored near the Naval Dockyard: the expert way in which junks, sampans, launches and ferries wove their way among the ocean-going liners; yet, as she watched the panorama slowly unwinding before her eyes, all these scenes instantly slotted into place, and she knew she was coming home.

As the 'Corfu' edged alongside the wharf, she stared down at the little groups of Europeans waiting there and tried to identify her parents, but most of the men wore wide-brimmed topees which obscured their hair and shaded their faces, and the women held coloured oiled sunshades above their heads. She was looking for faces based on a three-year-old memory; Hilary, more familiar with the Dorans, spotted them first and pointed them out. Foreshortened by reason of their position twenty feet below, they seemed smaller than she remembered.

"I don't see Roddy, though," Pamela said.

"You shouldn't expect to, at this hour of the morning." Hilary's tone was sarcastic. "He's the world's worst at getting up early."

"I'm sure he's here somewhere," Pamela insisted, "Look, there he is, at the back of the crowd, beside the second crane."

"That's not Roddy," Hilary said. "Must be something wrong your eyesight; that person's a Portuguese.. Eurasian, anyway."

The long delay before landing formalities were concluded was almost over. Pamela, waiting beside the gangway with Hilary, found her palms damp. She recalled the acrimonious exchange of airmail letters with her parents just before she left England: they could hardly have forgotten her last anguished reproach: "You left me at Home when I was young and I hated it, but I made a life for myself and now you want me to leave that. Why not leave me here, where I'm happy? It always has to be what you want; I'm never considered. It's not fair and I'll never forgive you!" She tried to steel herself for the cold reception she expected.

The gangway was already rattling as the first passengers negotiated it - and suddenly, here were her parents, loving and welcoming as if those letters had never been written.

"Well, a real grown-up young lady!" Her father removed his topee to kiss her, and she saw with surprise that his head was almost bald. It was embarrassing to see him in short trousers; he was fatter than she remembered, and his hairy hand shook as he held her at arm's length to appraise her.

"You're as tall as I am, Pam!" said her mother, hugging her; here was another surprise, meeting her mother's face at her own level, and seeing for the first time, not the Mother figure, but a middle-aged puffy face, faintly made-up; dark eyes, short permed hair, graying in patches, and an air of uncertainty. Both parents seemed like distant relatives she had known long ago, and the strangeness persisted as they all left the ship and walked towards the dock gates.

"Excuse me," said a man's voice behind them.

Pamela turned to see a handsome, dark-skinned, dark-haired young man, immaculately dressed in a cream linen suit.

Excuse me," he repeated, inclining his head with the hint of a bow. "You are Miss Pamela Doran, aren't you?"

She nodded, recognising him as the figure on the wharf she had mistaken for Roddy; of course he was a Eurasian, she could see that now.

"I want to welcome you back to Hong Kong," he went on. "You may not remember me.. I live in Dragon Terrace.."

But she did! A head taller than her now, face long and angular, brown eyes bright and interested, she could recognise him more easily than her own parents.

"Danny! Daniel Russell!" She grasped the hand he had proffered with both hers. "I'm so glad to see you again!"

"I read in the paper you were due back today, so I took a chance you would remember me -"

"I'm so glad you did, Danny! I never dreamed I'd find an old friend actually waiting for me!"

Her parents were looking back, puzzled and impatient.

"It's Danny Russell," she announced happily. "Remember Mrs. Russell used to give me music lessons?"

Yes, they said, they remembered. They also managed to imply without actual words that they were in a hurry to cross the harbour; but so, apparently, was Danny, so all four surged through the throng of ex-passengers and coolies carrying luggage slung on bamboo poles towards the ferry concourse.

Time seemed to telescope. Pamela's eyes were drawn to the scenes about her - things forgotten for years but now suddenly familiar; she heard Danny's prattle and her own voice asking questions, yet all the time her eyes were darting everywhere, and she was only half-listening to the replies:

"..Sure I'm working! Insurance clerk at Ropers, ever since I left school. What do you do?"

"Office work.. shorthand and typing."

... So little had changed! The line of red rickshaws was waiting in exactly the same place beside the ferry terminal, the coolies patting the plump, immaculately white seats encouragingly. The orange single-decker buses still snorted at their terminus, ready to set off as soon as the waiting crowds had boarded.

The cross-talk was still in the background....

"Yes, Mrs. Doran," Danny was saying, "I still play the violin.. at concerts sometimes, and Celeste Bellario accompanies me."

"Oh, Celeste!" Pamela's attention returned again. "Can she walk better than she did as a child?"

"Much better now she wears an iron on her leg."

"And Marcus?" Pamela asked.

"He's in the States studying law - he's the brainbox of the family. Excuse me a moment" - Danny dived towards the magazine and sweet stall.

"Is that boy still with us?" Mr. Doran demanded as he squeezed through the ferry turnstile after his wife and Pamela.

"Yes, he'll catch us up," said Pamela. "Goodness, what a crowd!" They were absorbed into a mass of prospective passengers of all nationalities, separated from the landingstage by a roof-high folding iron gate. A ferry was just tying up and within seconds was disgorging its passengers who were siphoned out of the terminal without contact with the waiting hundreds. The iron gate was rattled open even as the last of the disembarkees passed through, and the new passengers surged forward.

"A small present for you, Pam!" Danny tapped her on the shoulder and thrust into her hand a box of sugared almonds. " A welcome-back present - remember I gave you a ten cent ring last time you came back from England?"

Until then she had forgotten the ring; now she recalled its glittering magnificence - and her mother's disapproval of it. As Danny seated himself beside her and her family on the ferry, she sensed disapproval of this new gift.

The looped hawsers slopped into the water and were rapidly drawn aboard by the crewmen; the propellers whirred and thumped the water. Danny was chattering respectfully to her father, who replied politely.

"..No, Daniel, we're not still in Wong Nei Chong Road; we've a house on Leighton Hill - a little higher up, above our old place.."

She wanted to listen, but she wanted to see everything as well: stately junks, tiny sampans; twin, light-grey warships moored neatly side by side; a Blue Funnel ship held at anchor; a Japanese liner with white-circed black funnel; trim launches, with a handful of passengers perched up front on rattan armchairs; wallah wallahs with their suicidal roll; small white river boats, decks scarcely clear of the water, tied up alongside the Naval Dockyard.

The ferry was coasting beside its island terminal; any minute, they would be ashore.

"Say, Pamela, there's so much more to talk about!" Danny's voice was urgent as the gangway was lowered. "If your parents will allow me, may I call on you one evening and take you out?"

"That would be lovely," Pamela began, but her mother interrupted with "Wait until Pamela has had time to settle here, Daniel. She's going to be very busy for quite a while."

There was no mistaking the caution and disapproval, reminding Pamela that her parents had always disliked her spending more time than necessary at Dragon Terrace; but here was a grownup Danny, a responsible young man earning his own living, thoughtful enough to come and meet her on her return which was more than her brother had done: how could they object to him? She knew she must establish right away that she was no longer a child and would choose her own friends. She turned to Danny and said "Ring me up next week - the number is in the book, isn't it, Mum?"

Roddy raised his head carefully from the damp pillow and eased his leaden limbs off the bed. For the past half hour Ah Tai had been calling up the stairs announcing the relentless passage of time. It was now or never, if he was to be up and dressed before the parents arrived with Pamela.

His head throbbed as he padded barefoot on the polished floor to the bathroom. Oh, for a life where he could sleep for ever - or at least, until the effects of a midnight launch picnic with too much gin had worn off! He came to life beneath the shower and began to feel guilty at not having got up in time to meet Pamela's ship. He also knew apprehension at the inevitable recriminations from his father on this account, for his father knew he had obtained two hours' leave from the office for this very reason.

Hearing a car grinding up the steep approach road, he hastily scattered talc over his damp body, pulled on underpants, white shorts and shirt, and wriggled his feet into open-toed sandals. He was just rubbing his thick brown hair when he heard Ah Tai's excited exclamations from the front door. His unbuttoned shirt flying about him, he raced down the stairs to add his welcome. He was taken aback to see that Pamela was no longer the plump schoolgirl he'd last seen two years ago. Now she was much slimmer and quite attractive despite being rather dowdily dressed in a loose blue frock with white collar and short sleeves. He felt ashamed, and totally undeserving of the enormous hug she gave him.

"Hallo stranger!" It seemed odd to realise she was now using perfume. "Sorry I didn't manage to meet the ship."

"It didn't matter!" She hugged him again. "It's so good to see you again."

She looked radiant, and he doubted if his parents had yet reproached her for the angry air letters she had written them before leaving England.

"I'll show you your room, he offered, seeing an opportunity to avoid his parents and put off the expected lecture.

She followed him gaily up the stairs, saying "It's a lovely house... oh, what a beautiful room! And the view is wonderful!"

He joined her on the broad tiled verandah with curved spaced balustrades. Watching her gazing so rapturously across the race course below, beyond the roofs of the Wanchai tenements to the harbour, he asked "How come you didn't want to come back here? You seem pleased enough now. I wasn't allowed to see those expensive air letters, (Dad exploded at the cost every time one arrived!) but you sure put the cat among the pigeons, I can tell you! I didn't get nagged about my bad habits for weeks while they were sorting you out."

Pamela leaned her elbows on the verandah parapet and cupped her chin in her hands. "I think now I wanted to stay in England because I felt sort of secure there," she said slowly. "Happy in my job, good prospects, plenty of friends.."

"Boy-friend?"

"Not really.. well, I was keen on Lawrence, but I was just one of his many girl-friends. He was so nice to me, he helped me to write those letters. It wasn't only that, though: I didn't like leaving Granny and Grandad without help for the things they're getting too old to do. Mum and Dad have just got to arrange some domestic help for them; I'll get on to them about that later."

"Good Lord, you HAVE grown up!" Roddy could hardly equate this responsible adult with the little girl he had hardly noticed before she went to school in England.

His mother was at the door. "Like your room, Pam?"

"Oh I do, Mum! It's so huge, and the view!!"

"Magnificent, isn't it? The promise of this house was the main bait when Dad was asked to stay on one more year. Rod, aren't you due at the office at eleven? You'd better do your hair, get some socks on and make tracks; you know you can't count on that car of yours to start right away."

"How dare you insult my own personal chariot?" Roddy grinned. "It does me right royally."

"More by good luck than good management," sniffed his mother, but she gave his hair a friendly pat.

"I won't come home for tiffin," Roddy called over his shoulder on the way to his room. "I skipped breakfast, and as it will be such a short morning I'll get something in town."

"Something solid, not all liquid, mind!" his mother called after him. He grimaced to himself, knowing all too well that her warning was justified.

He managed to leave the house without encountering his father, and leapt into his ancient black open-topped Morris. Once it had been coaxed into motion and the wind was on his face and coursing through his hair, he felt relaxed. He skirted the race course, deciding against the more direct route to Central through the congested Chinese residential area of Wanchai. The longer route along Kennedy Road, which hugged the hillside above Wanchai, took him past the fork which led to the road up the mountain to the Gap then down the other side of the island to Repulse Bay where he had spent the previous evening. He thought longingly of the beach and the sea as he drove on towards the town.

How he loathed his clerical job in the Government, the dreary files and the exactitude demanded in dealing with them! Five years of it he'd had, and was now on the permanent staff and expected to spend the rest of his working life doing similar boring work. The prospect appalled him so much that he had trained himself not to think of it; to muddle through each day and live for five o'clock and weekends. He had tried to explain to his father how he felt about his job, that he would rather do almost anything else for a living.

"You wouldn't get another job," his father had snorted. "You did absolutely no work at school. You're damn lucky I was able to persuade Gasson to take you into the Government. You stick where you are, my boy, and be grateful: plenty of people would go on their bended knees to have your job, and think of the pension at the end of it !"

Who cared about a pension at 23? He swung the car savagely round the curves of Kennedy Road, noticing from the clock on the tower of Gloucester Building that he was already late. His office on the fifth floor of an old building on the sea front was sub-divided by numerous wooden partitions with swing doors. He was relieved to be able to slip along to his desk without coming face to face with any of his superiors, and addressed himself to the batch of files in his In Tray - but not before he'd glanced at his watch and calculated that in five hours and fifty-two minutes he would be free again.

"I'd love to, but I'm too tired," said Pamela when Roddy phoned her at four o'clock that afternoon to say he would pick her up at 5.15 to take her to Deep Water Bay for a quick swim before dinner. It had been an exhausting day: rising so early on the 'Corfu', the excitement of landing and coming to her new home; a succession of calls both by telephone and in person from old family friends; and a shopping expedition in the afternoon with her mother to choose materials for summer dresses, followed by a visit to the Chinese tailor to select patterns and to be measured.

"A dip will do you a world of good," Roddy urged. "Be waiting outside the house, with my swimming togs, then we can drive straight to the beach." He added that he was bringing a colleague, Greg, and that he had also invited Hilary who'd said No. "Go and see if you can persuade her to come."

Pamela obediently rang Hilary and repeated Roddy's invitation. and was surprised at the vehemence of Hilary's response: "Not me! If he couldn't be bothered to come and meet us this morning, I can't be bothered to turn out this evening." When he turned up at 5.15, Roddy looked disappointed at Pamela's diplomatic explanation that Hilary was too tired to come, but in no time was singing at the top of his voice as he drove the car up the winding road to Wong Nei Chong Gap from where both sides of the island could be seen. Pamela had forgotten the tranquillity of the ocean coast: great richly wooded slopes running down to lovely bays.

They had the small beach to themselves - except for a few Chinese fishermen mending their nets. An astringent smell came from their catch, hung up to dry on primitive wooden props wedged into the sand.

They undressed beneath towels. Self-conscious, and wishing Hilary was with her, Pamela hung back as the two boys raced down the beach, their footsteps scattering sand, and plunged headlong into the sea. When they were swimming far out, she sidled into the water, and revelled in its warmth as she recalled shivering in the shallows at Clacton before plucking up courage to plunge into the cold North Sea.

Floating, sometimes lazily swimming, she felt completely relaxed, as her eyes feasted on the grandeur of the great mountains, pale green now in the sun against the light blue sky. If today was a good example of her life in Hong Kong, how thankful she was she had returned!

Later, all three stretched on the sand and chatted. The sun was going down, bringing the first breath of coolness of evening. The fishermen and their families were squatting in clusters, eating their evening meal, their sing-song voices the only sound.

"I wouldn't mind being a fisherman," said Roddy. "Lovely life, out in the open all day. Any one can have my job!"

"Have you got anything lined up yet, Pamela," asked Greg.

"Give me a chance," she protested. "I've only been here 10 hours!"

"Dad's got something organised for you," Roddy put in. "Hasn't he told you about it yet? He's fixed an interview for you with old Gasson in his department."

"No, he hasn't mentioned it." She felt annoyed and apprehensive: annoyed because a matter so important to her had been arranged without consultation; apprehensive lest the forthcoming interview would find her inadequate.

"He's keeping it for tonight I expect after giving me my lecture." Roddy sat up and felt for his watch among the heap of clothes on the sand. "It's quarter to seven.. just time for another quick dip before we have to leave. Who's coming?"

"I don't want to get wet again," said Pamela.

"I'll keep you company," said Greg.

The sea was turning paler and the hills beginning to darken. Pamela felt she was in a dream world, and only gradually became aware that little trickles of sand were falling over her arm. She turned and saw Greg was the perpetrator.

"You know," he said, "when Rod said his young sister was coming out from Home, I imagined a pig-tailed schoolgirl: I never expected someone like you!"

It was difficult to decide how to interpret this remark. Pamela could only croak "Like what?"

"Well, grown up." His hand closed over hers. "Attractive and all that - and old enough to take to the pictures."

The pressure on her hand increased. Embarrassed, yet flattered to be found worthy of interest after such a short acquaintance, she gazed firmly out to sea.

"Will you come to the flicks with Rod and me tomorrow evening?"

"All right." She tried to tone down the eagerness she felt. "Thank you very much." It was a relief when Roddy returned, dripping and demanding to know the time. When he learned it was already seven o'clock he gave a great yelp, seized his clothes and hastily pulled them on over his trunks.

"You're all wet," Pamela remonstrated.

"Better wet than slaughtered." Roddy stuffed his socks into a pocket of his shorts and carried his shoes to the car. "Dad sees red if anyone's late for dinner - you'll find out."

She did. Paternal displeasure lasted the whole meal, taking the form of heavy sarcasm through the soup course and gradually softening to a reluctant "Ah well, I suppose you're only young once, but don't let it happen again" by the time the fruit appeared. By now, Pamela was feeling decidedly sleepy. The voices round the table kept fading, and she found herself viewing the scene as though looking at a picture instead of being part of it.

Despite the hotel-like meals on the 'Corfu', the formality of this family dinner astonished her. The cook boy in his long white cotton gown served the main dishes, the amah following him with a frosted jug of water clinking with lumps of ice. Overhead, from the high, frescoed ceiling, a large 3-blade fan cranked slowly round, stirring just enough air for comfort. Cicadas shrieked in the trees outside, vying with the noise of passing trams and buses.

The French windows to the wide verandah were open and the curtains drawn back, giving as backdrop a panorama of black mountains humped against an indigo sky. Below the mountains stretched a pattern of pinpricks of light from the tenements of Happy Valley and Wanchai. Beyond, there was just a glimpse of black, treacly sea, and the dark outlines of ships' masts against the lights of Kowloon.

It was all so far removed from the tiny, cluttered dining-room in Ipswich, curtained off from the outside world, with only the ticking of the marble clock on the mantelpiece to fill the gaps in the conversation. How, she wondered, were her grandparents getting on without her? She jerked herself back to full consciousness to find her father's eyes on her.

"I don't think you were listening to me," he was saying reproachfully.

"She's tired out," put in her mother. "It's been a long day. Leave it to tomorrow."

"How can I leave it to tomorrow? It's tomorrow morning she has to see Gasson! I repeat, Pamela, you've an interview with him tomorrow at eleven. I've had a word with him and he knows about your office experience."

"I..I don't know if I'd be right for the job," Pamela dared to suggest. "I'd like to look at what else is advertised.."

"You can do that if Gasson turns you down," conceded her father. Obviously closing the matter, he then turned to Roddy: "Now, my boy, apart from your inherent laziness and general uselessness, what excuse can you produce for this morning's behaviour - asking for time off to meet your sister and then not getting up early enough to do it?"

Pamela sat silent through the ensuing lecture. Set against a desire to work out her own destiny was a certain relief that the path for this first interview had been smoothed for her. She realised her father was trying to help her, but a frisson of anxiety lingered: she hoped he didn't intend to monitor every aspect of her life in Hong Kong.

JULY

Standing at the entrance to the arcade which was part of the Gloucester Hotel, Danny took another nervous glance at his reflection in the huge glass windows. The shadowy figure was re-assuring: well-fitting light linen suit; white shirt with immaculate collar and cuffs; crimson tie centred and straight; hair sleek. He had brought his best clothes to his office and changed into them just before leaving ten minutes ago, so the suit was uncreased. He turned away from the windows and scanned the faces of passers-by.

People of all nationalities were pouring out of the city offices, mingling with the more leisurely American tourists from the President ship in the harbour, but there was no sign of Pamela. As the second hand on his watch moved relentlessly forward, he began to feel anxious: suppose he had missed her? Even worse, suppose she had forgotten, or changed her mind about coming?

This entrance opened on to Des Voeux Road, the tram-lined thoroughfare running through the city parallel to Queen's Road; perhaps she was waiting at the other entrance in Pedder Street? He stood uncertainly for a few moments, wondering what to do. An old Chinese woman nearby was selling the afternoon edition of the 'China Mail', dangling a placard which proclaimed in huge black letters 'Japanese attack Chinese at Marco Polo Bridge.' While he was wondering where Marco Polo Bridge could be, a voice behind him said "Hallo, Danny! Sorry I'm late, I got held up in the office at the last moment."

He was thankful he had decided to wear his best suit, for she looked excessively smart in a sleeveless white silk dress with green applique work round the neck and on the belt; white court shoes and white handbag. He was proud to walk into the hotel coffee lounge with her. There were many white customers, some Portuguese, Eurasians and Chinese, but racially each table was separate, except for one large group of Chinese businessmen presided over by a genial and stout European.

As they sat smiling at each other across the table, he felt lost for words. All day he had been bubbling inside with things to say to her, but those things related to the child Pamela he had known, not to the pensive adult opposite him. Clearing his throat, he asked "Would you rather have tea or a cold drink?"

"Something cold, please - I'm melting."

She chose an ice-cream soda.

"Then I'll have the same," said Danny with exaggerated heartiness. He would have preferred a lager, but any compromise was worth trying to get the conversation moving.

Yet silence fell again after the boy went off with their order. Pamela examined her pink-tinted nails and made great play of smoothing the table-cloth. Danny clenched his hands together beneath the table. He could not understand the stultifying effect this so-much-longed-for meeting was having on him; he never had any trouble in making conversation with the two Portuguese typists in his office, or with the many Eurasian girls living in his neighbourhood. Perhaps the reunion had been a mistake.

In desperation, he said, "You know, Pam, I just can't believe this is happening - us meeting again after all these years!"

"I've been feeling like this ever since I arrived back," she nodded. "I keep coming across things I remember, and people I used to know; it's weird."

"Thanks for calling meeting me again weird!" For a moment he forgot he was 19 years old and not the urchin who had exchanged insults with the child Pamela. She immediately looked anxious, as though she might just have offended him. She was always so serious. He recalled how hurt she had been when he'd turned all his attention to Sandra, who never wanted to be serious. He would like to apologise for this, but perhaps Pamela didn't even remember it.

The ice-cream sodas arrived, and Pamela sucked devotedly at her straw before spooning the ice-cream. "I never got anything in England like this," she explained when she stopped for breath.

England was the unknown to him, there was nothing he could build on there. Conversation was flagging once more. With an effort, he injected a note of mock reproval into his voice and tried again. "Hey, what have you been doing all this time, for goodness' sake? It's taken three weeks to find you free! Every time I phoned, either you were out, or just about to go out, or you'd just come back from going out, so couldn't go out again!"

"I've been everywhere." Pamela spread her hands. "Shopping; getting clothes made because I've lost weight and none of my English dresses fit any more; dinners and teas with my family's friends, who for some reason wanted to see me and couldn't get over the fact that I'd actually grown in the last seven years! I've been swimming most days with Roddy and his friends, and often we've gone to the pictures. And of course I'm working too."

"Where?"

"I'm now a stenographer, as they call it here, in the Colonial Government.. following in father's foosteps, and my brother's."

"That's good, Pam." His enthusiastic approval gave no hint of the hurt he had suffered when he had applied to join the Government when he left school, and because of his Eurasian background had been offered a subordinate post at a wage several grades below that paid to Europeans His dignity shattered, he had refused the offer.

"Do you prefer your new job to working in England?" he asked, conscious of the banality of the question.

"Well... I enjoyed my work in Ipswich, but they're not nearly so formal here. Do you like your job?"

They discussed their respective jobs until there was nothing more to say on the subject, then an embarrassing gap in the conversation opened up.

"Tell me more about the people we used to know!" Pamela suddenly demanded as if the matter was of the greatest importance.

"Well, the Bellarios live in Causeway Bay now." At least he was on familiar ground. "They moved three or four years ago. I told you about Marcus studying in the States. Marie was a postulant at the Convent, but she came out and is working in Lane Crawford's Silverware Department. Celeste is a brilliant pianist now, she's going to sit her L.R.A.M. soon, and teach piano when she leaves school. Do you still play?"

" 'Fraid not. I was never very good at it, was I? Sandra Smithson learned as much in a year as I did in three. I met some people last week who know Sandra's family, by the way. She's coming back here in a couple of years, she's at some finishing school in Switzerland, they said."

"Didn't you keep in touch with her?"

"No, I wasn't allowed to write to her, nor she to me. I never heard from Philip either - you remember him? I couldn't write to him because he didn't give me an address in England - but he could easily have written to me here, my parents would have sent it on to England."

"Philip was always hopeless," nodded Danny.

They both agreed, several times over, that Philip was always hopeless, then sank into silence again.

At the neighbouring table, the Chinese businessmen were getting up, beaming farewells and inclining their heads deferentially to the staid Englishman. After they had left, he called for another drink, and sat back mopping his brow.

This gave Danny an idea. "Would you like another ice-cream soda?" he asked Pamela brightly.

"I don't think so, thanks." She glanced at her watch. "I really ought to be going."

"Oh Pam, not yet!" He could not bear the meeting to end on such an unsatisfactory note; surely, if they talked longer, they would eventually overcome this initial awkwardness, and rediscover the selves they used to know? He felt a great chasm opening up between them; if he couldn't bridge it now, he knew they would remain as polite strangers, and though he had not known it would happen when curiosity had prompted him to meet the 'Corfu', he was even more drawn to this adult Pamela than he had been to her eleven-year old counterpart. He could not let her go like this. He said an inward prayer for help.

It had been a great relief to Pamela when he had asked if she would like another ice-cream soda because it gave her an excuse to look at her watch and herald leaving. The strained silences appalled her. Danny had changed so much: he used to be such a show-off and never at a loss for words, but now, once they had discussed the present whereabouts of their mutual childhood friends, there really seemed nothing else to say.

"I really ought to be going home," she repeated, fingering her white handbag.

"Maybe we can do this another day?" Danny's cheeks had become a deep, dark red. She couldn't help noticing his fingers shaking as he paid the bill. It was better for her to pretend not to have heard his suggestion for another date - surely he must see there was nothing left between them beyond the memory of a few years as occasional childhood playmates?

She noticed the stares of several European couples as Danny shepherded her out of the hotel, and this reminded her of her mother's disapproving silence when she had first learned of this date.

On the short bus journey to Happy Valley the noise of the engine made coherent conversation impossible, and for this she was grateful as she could think of nothing else to say.

At the stop before Wong Nei Chong Road, Danny said quickly "Can you spare a little more time? If we get out now, we could go to the cemetery - I want to show you something. It won't take long."

The bus was about to re-start so she had to make a snap decision. Because he looked so unhappy she leapt up and followed him out of the bus. Of course, she suddenly realised, he wanted to take her to Mrs. Holtz' grave.

"Here we are." He guided her towards a white marble tombstone topped by an angel which stood out sharply in a row of greying headstones with faded lettering. On the plinth beneath the angel's feet the lettering was fresh and clear: "IN LOVING MEMORY OF DEAR MRS. HOLTZ FROM HER FRIENDS DANNY, MARCUS, CELESTE, PAMELA, SANDRA AND PHILIP. R.I.P. 3.5.1929."

"Oh, poor Mrs Holtz!" The memory came back sharply. "I'm so glad she had a tombstone after all! And all our names are on it!"

"You like it, then?" Danny was watching her anxiously.

"Oh yes, I'm sure Mrs. Holtz would, too. It's really beautiful, and so clean compared with all the others in this row."

"Celeste and I come and clean it up quite often," he said, picking fallen leaves off the marble surround.

Something was puzzling Pamela. Something was missing from the wording on the stone: there was no mention of Mrs. Holtz' Christian name, and no mention of her status as the wife of Mr. Holtz.

"I got it done as soon as I'd earned enough money," Danny was mumbling. "It's only been up for a year. I hated myself when you all made me see how awful it was to sell that typewriter just to look big buying an expensive present for Sandra."

She saw the pain in his eyes and heard the pleading in his voice.

"You paid for all this? That's wonderful, Danny!" She put her hand on his shoulder. "We were all too hard on you over that old typewriter.. at least you hadn't spent the money on yourself. Surely you haven't been worrying about it all these years?"

"It was better once this was here." He stared at the surround and brushed a speck of red earth away with his handkerchief.

"I think it was a lovely thing to do." At last conversation flowed naturally. "It must have cost you so many dollars, and it was especially decent of you to put all our names on it. I'd like to make a contribution, as I'm part of it - "

"Nonsense, it's all paid for now. Apart from my job, I make quite good money on my evening work."

He explained, as they walked slowly out of the cemetery, that he sometimes played with the hotel bands. "Just odd evenings, if one of the violinists can't make it."

"You mean, you play jazz?"

"Sure! Why not? Jazz is music, and it's fun working out what you can make the fiddle do."

"I might see you perform some time! Friends of Roddy's are always trying to get me to go dancing with them, but so far I haven't been brave enough, I'm not much of a dancer, but Roddy says I'll have to take the plunge some time soon. Does your mother mind you playing jazz?"

"Not at all, she says as long as I don't forget how to play classical, it's O.K. And Pam, she was always so fond of you; she wants you to visit her; will you?"

"One day; she was very sweet to me, even though I hardly ever did any piano practice when she was teaching me."

"When?" he urged.

They settled on Thursday the following week after work, Danny should have branched off for Kennedy Terrace, but instead insisted on accompanying her past the Civil Service Club and along the path which cut through the Valley towards Leighton Hill. Workers and their families were out enjoying the warm evening, hawkers with their portable stalls doing a roaring trade. Pamela looked at the rows of gaudily coloured sweetmeats; the oily olives; the short lengths of succulent sugar cane, and paper pokes of local peanuts resembling bad teeth.

"Did we really eat all those things?" she shuddered.

"Look who's here!" Roddy caught them up, with several colleagues including Greg, all carrying tennis racquets, their white jackets slung over their shoulders. Tie-less, shirts soaked with perspiration and their shorts wrinkled, they had obviously gone to the Club straight from the office. There was a sweaty, beery smell about them.

"You remember Danny, don't you, Rod?" Pamela said. "Daniel Russell, up at Dragon Terrace, and Greg, this is.."

The introductions were effected and Pamela couldn't help contrasting Danny's gentlemanly appearance with the sloppiness of her brother and his companions.

"Danny plays with the hotel dance bands sometimes," she told Roddy. "I wonder you haven't seen him."

"I expect I have," nodded Roddy, "but I wouldn't have recognised you, Danny; anyway, we'll give you a wave next time!"

"As to which," put in Greg, falling into step beside Pamela "what about coming to the Gloucester this Saturday night? You promised you would some time."

"And when are you going to take us on at tennis?" demanded some one else.

Laughing and parrying with these jocular invitations, Pamela became aware that Danny had become morose and silent, obviously feeling completely out of the conversation.

He caught her eye and mumbled "I'll say goodbye now, Pamela, you seem to have plenty of escorts."

"I have, haven't I?" She thanked him with excessive warmth for the evening, trying to compensate for the exclusion she knew he felt.

"And I'll see you.. next Thursday?" His voice sounded uncertain, as though he expected a snub.

"Of course!" she assured him, and his face brightened. His brown eyes were really very like Lawrence's - but Lawrence was 10,000 miles away in England, and Danny was here in Hong Kong.

AUGUST

Hilary could scarcely hide her fury and disappointment. Pamela, seated next to her in the back of the Doran family car, was still apologising for Roddy's failure to join them for the evening launch picnic. Mr. Doran, polite but obviously annoyed at the role of chauffeur he had suddenly been called upon to play, put on a jocular act as the car honked its way through the busy streets of Wanchai.

This was only Hilary's second month at Bexton's, the shipping firm which ran monthly swimming picnics for its staff. Every member was allowed to bring one guest, but she had wangled permission for two - Pamela and Roddy - and now Roddy had not turned up.

Trams lurched past on groaning rails. Buses chuntered by, belching fumes. Bells rang. Gongs boomed. Street vendors shouted the virtues of their wares. Amidst laughter, chatter, banging and slamming of wooden slip-slops on pavement and road, all generations from shuffling grandparents to toddlers seemed to be out walking, some carrying bird-cages with occupants. Gorgeous Chinese girls in bright shimmering silk cheong-saam walked arm in arm with white uniformed sailors and khaki-clad soldiers.

Despite the heat and humidity, the car windows were almost closed to keep out the smells of food, drains and humanity.

"Damn!" yelled Mr. Doran, as a little family sauntered across the path of the car. "Why can't these people look where they're going?"

"It's very kind of you to give us a lift," Hilary ventured, leaning forward to cool her back which, with her flimsy dress, had stuck to the car's upholstery.

"Not at all. I was going to the Club anyway. Least I could do when you were left in the lurch by a pathetic little clerk exhausted after a hard day's pen-pushing and file-hunting."

Hilary felt Pamela wince. Why had Roddy not come? He had been so enthusiastic when she had first issued the invitation, and they had had such a good time the previous evening too, going to the cinema to see "One Hundred Men & A Girl", afterwards sitting in the Parisian Grill over gin tonics, while the pianist played soft romantic music. They'd talked for hours of their ambitions and ideals.

The opportunity to have a word alone with Pamela did not come until Mr. Doran had dropped them at the company jetty.

"Is Roddy ill? Or has he gone out?" Hilary asked quickly - for the launch, the 'Ariadne' was already tied up alongside and people were boarding her.

"Well.." Pamela's voice was hesitant, "he's at home, but he isn't up to a swimming picnic."

Figures were advancing, hands waving, so Hilary had to postpone further enquiries. She already knew most of the staff on board, and she and Pamela were quickly absorbed into a group of young men and women clustered in the stern of the launch. Drinks were bought and cigarettes lit as the 'Ariadne' pulled away. By the time the lights of the twin cities either side of the harbour had receded into the distance, and the launch nosed through Lye Mum Pass into the open sea, Hilary's hurt feelings were soothed by the balm of the warm evening. The mountains showed up dark and majestic against the moonlit sky. Mixed with the banter and laughter was the desultory twanging on a banjo and mandolin of 'When I'm Cleaning Windows'.

She noticed with some satisfaction that Pamela had lost much of the shyness that had inhibited her on the 'Corfu'; also, that she had continued to lose weight in the past months. She had let her hair grow, too, and had a permanent wave, and altogether looked very attractive in her pink sun-dress, with matching short-sleeved bolero hanging loosely over her shoulders.

"I bet you're glad now you came to Hong Kong," Hilary said when the men went off to get replacement drinks. "Nothing like this ever happened in Ipswich, did it?"

"True," nodded Pamela. "I'm too busy to have any regrets."

"So I've noticed - off to the flicks or the beach every day after office, and at weekends! We live almost next door to each other, but this is the first chance I've had to talk to you properly since we landed. How about your job- like it?"

"Everything about it. The work's interesting, and the girls are so friendly - especially Viola.. Viola Jackson, do you know her?"

"Slightly. I should have thought she was a bit too sophisticated for you, Pam!"

"You always said I could do with some sophistication; it was Viola who got me using make-up."

"Good for her. You've certainly come out of your shell." Hilary glanced about her to make sure no one else was near enough to hear, and went on "Do you ever hear from the favoured boy in Ipswich?"

"I've had letters from the two of the girls in the office, but not from Lawrence. He's a very busy person."

"Anyway," Hilary spoke carefully. "A litle bird told me you've got yourself a new boy-friend."

"I seem to have lots," Pamela laughed. "All Roddy's friends."

"I don't mean them - I mean the violinist."

"Oh, Danny! He's not a boy-friend, just an old childhood acquaintance. His mother taught me the piano - or tried to - years ago. He's a marvellous violinist - classical and all sorts. Sometimes he plays in the dance bands at the hotels."

"I know. Roddy pointed him out to me last week. "The band was good and he was so much part of it that I wouldn't have guessed he was really a classical musician."

"He is, though," Pamela said earnestly. "I'm sure he will be a world famous violinist one day."

"Then you'll be able to say you knew him when..." Hilary tried to inject a light note into her voice, for there was more to be said. "I hear you've been to the Hong Kong Hotel with this Danny, too."

"Goodness, can't you do anything in Hong Kong without being spied on? Is there anything wrong in having an icecream with a friend after work?"

"Not wrong," Hilary said gently, "but.. well, it might give the wrong impression, even though you say he isn't actually a boy-friend."

"I suppose," said Pamela slowly, "I suppose you mean because he's Eurasian."

"That's about it. Sorry Pam, I had to say it. Plenty of people have noticed, and Rod says your parents are put out, too."

"I know they are, but it shouldn't matter. Danny's one of my oldest friends. I don't see why the colour of his skin should come into it."

"Be your age, Pam! In case you've forgotten while you've been living in England, I'll remind you that colour does count here, socially and financially.

"It's all horrible!" Pamela's face went scarlet. "Danny's more serious and sincere than lots of the other boys I've met since I've been back. He's a good friend, and I'm not going to cut him out of my life because.. because of all you've been saying."

"No good talking to you then, is it? I admire your sentiments, but they won't get you anywhere.. any more than talking to your dear brother will make him change his way of life.

After a small silence, Pamela said "Roddy really did want to come tonight. It was just that awful row at tiffin."

"What happened?" Hilary allowed herself to ask.

"We'd just been listening to the radio World News about Spain, and Roddy said how awful it must be for the ordinary people there, with battles going on round them, and how he wished he could do something to help them."

That made sense: Hilary remembered the newsreel last night at the cinema of the attack on Bilbao, and the pathetic fleeing refugees.

"And Dad jeered at him," Pamela went on, "and said what good did he think he could do, when he could only just hold down an easy office job. Then they were both shouting, and Roddy said he'd throw it up and go to Spain to fight. And Dad went purple and yelled and said how could he when he hadn't a bean for his fare, and so on. Roddy got so upset he wouldn't stay to finish his tiffin and went to the Club and stayed there all the afternoon drinking instead of going back to the office. He staggered home about six o'clock and Ah Tai had to put him to bed."

Hilary bent forward to hide the tears starting in her eyes. "It's time he grew up," she said roughly. "Let's go and get undressed - we're almost there."

Repulse Bay was achingly beautiful in the moonlight. A cluster of lights picked out the hotel just above the avenue of trees lining the road below. Behind the hotel the shape of the hills loomed like protective shoulders.

Moving beams of light marked the progress of an ocasional car travelling down the road to the Bay, one end of which was bright with the garish lights of the modern Lido on the beach; at the other end stood the dark outline of 'Eucliffe', an imitation castle built into the hillside in recent years by a Chinese philanthropist. Small fishing boats across the Bay shone their probing lights which wriggled along the black sea like electric snakes.

Swimming ashore with the rest of the party, their threshing limbs creating phosphorescent patterns on the water, Hilary should have been blissfully happy. This was the sort of evening she had dreamed of while in England, and the date last evening had shown her a new, serious facet to Roddy's character and deepened her regard for him. His behaviour today had extinguished completely the flicker of love she'd begun to think might replace the bantering boy-girl friendship of the past three years. Now she put him out of her mind and threw herself wholeheartedly into enjoying the rest of the evening; hectic water polo; lazing in the shadows to recover; joining in a sing-song on the way back to the accompaniment of an amateur banjoist; and, because her heart was still sore, agreeing to a date next week with Douglas, Hugh and Pamela.

Sauntering down the drive from Leighton Hill on Saturday afternoon to catch a bus into Central, Pamela marvelled again at the change in her life since leaving England: no chores in the house (and freedom from guilt since domestic help had been arranged for her grand-parents); a job she enjoyed with friendly colleagues; wonderful weather, swimming most days and visits to the cinema; and the self-knowledge that since she had lost weight and had her hair styled she was reasonably attractive. She could think of Lawrence and the limited social life with H. & S. without regret. And tonight she was going to her first dinner-dance with Hilary, Hugh and Douglas and would wear the new evening dress she had designed, now to be collected from the tailor.

She wore a blue voile sleeveless dress, no stockings, peep-toe white shoes and no hat, having discovered that topees as regulation head-gear were a thing of the past, her only concession to the sun's rays being dark-tinted sun-glasses.

She was damp with perspiration by the time she reached the side street off Queen's Road where her tailor lived. A cluster of wooden notices, with crudely painted Chinese characters and English letters and sometimes drawings, hung from the upper floors of the tenement. A bulging blue eye set among red and black characters advertised an optician; a grinning set of false teeth the denture-maker; and her tailor's notice, in small uneven English letters:

"Mr Loong Kai, first-class tailor to movie stars. Step up to first floor please."

Carefully she mounted the wooden staircase without banisters, trying not to touch the leprous plaster walls. She wrinkled her nose at the mixture of smells - garlic, damp walls, pungent hair oil, cloyingly sweet scent and ancient drains. From upper storeys came the noise of many voices, Chinese music, the clatter of mah jongg tiles and unidentifiable home industries.

Half swing doors of splaying rattan, displaying the notice 'Loong Kai No.1 Tailor', led into a dingy room with peeling walls partly camouflaged by faded sepia photographs of aged ancestors. A small electric fan standing on the glass counter inside the door was switched on as soon as she appeared. Half a dozen Chinese men in white vests and trousers sat over trestle tables, busily cutting, pinning, sewing and machining; two more were pressing materials with hissing charcoal irons.

"Ah Missee, hullo! Dress all ready for you!" beamed Loong Kai; with a wave of his transparently thin hand, he motioned to a small boy to bring the evening dress from the glass-fronted case behind the counter. Trying it on in the tiny curtained-off cubicle Pamela admired the way the tailor had so perfectly interpreted her pencilled design. When she emerged to view herself in the pitted full-length mirror near the window, Loong Kai walked critically round her. "Missee look very nice," he said, "but dress little bit loose in back. My changee, my putee tuck."

He deftly slipped pins in the right places. "Can do very quickly. You come back tomorrow morning, dress ready."

"But I want to wear it tonight!" She could not bear to leave without it for the all-important date.

"You wanchee tonight - can do," said Loong Kai equably. "I bring dress to your house six o'clock."

"Can you do it by then?" Pamela was amazed at such an accommodating arrangement.

"Can," he nodded, checking that the points of the pins were on the outside of the material so as not to prick her when she took the dress off.

Emerging from the stuffy tenement into the equally trying glaring sun and heat, Pamela decided to drop into the nearby Bluebird Cafe for an iced drink. As she crossed Queen's Road a strident newspaper placard caught her eye: "Shanghai bombed - thousands killed.'

Shanghai, where Belle and Keith and their children lived, attacked! By the Japanese, her shocked mind reasoned, although the Japanese invasion of China which had begun with the Marco Polo Bridge incident had not so far affected the south. She forged through the crowds and bought a 'China Mail'. The news was in the Stop Press - just a brief report that bombs had ripped open the city centre that very day.

She took the first vacant taxi home and ran into the house waving the newspaper which her father immediately grabbed. The news had preceded her.

"Keith's Hong Kong Office phoned," mumbled her father. "They'll ring again the moment they get more details."

Roddy was kneeling beside his mother, holding out a cup of tea and trying to coax her to drink it. White-faced and weeping, she was unrecognisable as the authoritative parent she usually was. Pamela, herself shaking and tearful, put her arm round her. Ah Tai kept coming in to moan and commiserate until finally banished.

Anxious family friends telephoned as the news flashed round the Colony. The radio station constantly interrupted its programme to broadcast fresh flashes from Shanghai: the bombing had not been carried out by the Japanese but by Chinese planes aiming at Japanese warships in the harbour, hitting instead the crowded streets, shops and hotels. Ships were already filling up with women and children and would soon sail for sanctuary in Hong Kong, so offers of emergency accommodation were urgently required.

"There, Hen, they'll soon be here," said her father bracingly.

"If they're still alive," wept her mother.

"No need to assume the worst." Her father's tone was confident but Pamela noticed his hands shaking as he lit another cigarette. "We must make plans about where every one can sleep."

It helped to think positively. Even her mother perked up and worked out how many extra sheets, pillows and mosquito nets would be required. It was decided that Roddy would move to the Y.M.C.A. in Kowloon and free his room, and camp beds would be moved into Pamela's room.

In the midst of all this Loong Kai arrived, looking unfamiliar in a cotton smoky blue cheong sam and black cloth slippers. From a small cardboard attache case, battered and dark with age, he produced the lilac dress. It looked magnificent, and the sight of it was the last straw for Pamela; she burst into tears, crying "I won't need it now! I can't go out tonight!"

Astonishingly, her father put his arm round her and said heartily "Of course you're going out. Belle wouldn't expect you to stay in!"

Loong Kai indicated without words that Pamela must try the dress on before he would leave. She did so; it was a perfect fit, the colour was beautiful, the style flattering - but tears ran down her face and she could take no pleasure in it now, and had no wish to wear it - ever. As she fingered the taffeta folds, Keith's Hong Kong Office telephoned again: all the family were safe and well, and Belle and the children had already embarked and were due to sail for Hong Kong in a few hours.

"Made up your mind what to order yet, young Pam?" asked Douglas with the bright smile he bestowed on all females.

"Nearly." Pamela was pretending to study the menu, trying to disguise the awe she felt at finding herself in the Gripps on the first floor of the Hong Kong Hotel, in the company of two young men in impressive evening dress. Hilary had assured her beforehand that there was nothing to worry about, but she was petrified at the prospect of having eventually to take to the dance floor where all her imperfections in dancing would be revealed.

The five-piece Filipino band, its members resplendent in loose white blouses pouched over scarlet cummerbunds and narrow black trousers, was already playing softly.

Although she had no liking for the brash Douglas, she appreciated his elephantine attempts to help her feel at ease. He was sympathetic too about the news from Shanghai:

"Bad luck, your sister and her family going through al that lot,but at least you know they're all safe. Now Shanghai - there's a place for night life: makes Hong Kong seem like a convent!" He launched into a vivid description of his final night in Shanghai after a recent holiday there, the detail being rather remarkable since he declared he'd been drinking steadily all the time.

The quieter Hugh asked "Will you be able to put your sister and family all up in your house, Pam?"

She explained the emergency plans.

"And Pamela can come and stay with me if Belle's husband comes back to Hong Kong too," added Hilary.

"Not fair! Can't I come and stay with you, Hilary?" Douglas leered.

After the soup, Hugh asked Pamela "Would you care to dance? I'm no Fred Astaire, but I'll try if you're game."

"I'm not very good either." She was smiling in some relief as she got up from the table.

They danced quite well together, with only the occasional falter. He didn't talk much until the end of the dance, when he said with enthusiasm "I do like your dress!"

"So do I," she confided. "The tailor only finished it today." Modesty prevented her from adding she had designed it herself.

After the meat course Douglas tried to persuade her to dance with him but she refused firmly: had seen him swooping round the floor with Hilary, who was an excellent dancer. Even Hilary's laughing but reproachful "But Pam, we're supposed to swop partners!" would not move her. As Douglas stood up when she and Hugh rose to dance again, he said in a theatrical aside "You must tell me your secret sometime, Hugh!"

"We get on very well together, don't we?" smiled Hugh as they started to waltz, and he held her a little tighter. Pamela saw her mistake immediately: he'd construed her refusal to dance with Douglas as a desire to be only with him! It was easier to let him go on thinking this than to explain, but she tried to clarify the situation by saying "Yes, considering we've only had one dance together."

The room was now completely full, and noisy with clamorous voices and laughter and the occasional guffaw from some inebriated diner. The smoke-laden atmosphere and the heat of the sweltering night was only slightly palliated by the ceiling fans stirring such air as filtered through the large windows.

"I was wondering," began Hugh, but Pamela didn't listen to the rest of his sentence because she'd heard a new sound from the band - the sound of a violin. There had been no violinist earlier in the evening. She twisted her head until she had a view of the musicians, and saw Danny standing in front. His white blouse ballooned out as he plied the bow across his fiddle, his head down and his face in repose. He played a second chorus, this time bringing forth deep, double, haunting notes until the final bars, when they faded away completely. Then he took his seat among the other players and integrated his music with theirs.

"Some violinist, that," said Hugh.

"It's Danny Russell," nodded Pamela. "I know him. His mother was my piano teacher when I was small."

She caught Danny's eye and he nodded slightly. She was impressed with his seriousness, and with his disciplined playing, filling unobtrusively in with the rest of the band until, at a signal from the conductor, he rose and came again to the front to play one last chorus. Into this he put so much feeling that a burst of spontaneous applause broke out when he finished and the dancers left the floor.

Danny bowed, then went into a comedy number 'The Man on the Flying Trapeze.' A small plump Filipino saxophonist sang the lady's lament in a falsetto voice: Danny followed his words with short phrases in sympathetic vein; he swayed, he rolled his eyes, and grinned wickedly at the singer. He made his violin seduce, sigh, cry and yearn, and at the end received even more enthusiastic applause. Again his eyes sought Pamela's, and she laughed delightedly and clapped harder, and felt bursting with pride to know him.

"He really is jolly good," said Hilary.

"Marvellous!" Pamela couldn't hide her pleasure. "I've never heard him play in public before, except at a G.H. Party when we were kids and I had to accompany him on the piano. He's so professional now." "

"First class," agreed Douglas. "For 'one of dose local boys'."

Pamela knew the expression - forgotten during the years in England, but familiar enough since her return to Hong Kong: it was applied among Europeans to Portuguese and people of mixed race born in Hong Kong. Cheeks flaming, she demanded "So what's wrong with being Eurasian?"

Hilary sent her a warning glance; Douglas and Hugh both looked taken aback.

"Nothing wrong, Pam," Douglas shrugged, "just a fact, that's all."

"Danny's as good as any of us," Pamela stuttered. "He works hard, and supports his mother, and.."

"I didn't say he wasn't as good as us." Douglas wagged his hand playfully. "Now Pam, I'm sorry if I've offended you." He put his hands together and bowed his head in mock supplication. "Say you'll forgive me, or I shall instantly commit hari kari with the cutlery."

"Don't do it here, it would make such a mess," said Hilary lightly, but she frowned at Pamela and kicked her foot beneath the table. With a mighty effort, Pamela swallowed her indignation.

"I liked the way you stuck up for your friend," Hugh told her when next they danced. "I think you're about the most sincere person I've ever met."

He was holding her more closely now, and breathing deeply, his earnest face mirroring his admiration.

Pamela smiled rather absently. She had just discovered something interesting about herself; despite all Hugh's qualities, she would far rather be dancing with Danny.

Towards dawn, Roddy gave up all idea of sleep. He'd dozed fitfully until then, dropping into nightmares of the holocaust in Shanghai of which the Sunday papers had been full in sickening detail: hapless Chinese refugees trying to seek shelter in the international settlements; huge hotels devastated, the main department stores wrecked, the roads choked with bodies and rubble, and terror-stricken people, and burning cars with charred occupants.

Soaked in perspiration, he grabbed madly at the mosquito net to get his head outside its stifling canopy. Now he could endure the mangled sheets and wet, sweaty pillows no longer. He got up and walked on to the verandah, its tiles blessedly cool to his bare feet.

Dawn was breaking, yet already the city was stirring. The muted drone of early trams and buses floated up from the streets; a distant police whistle; the low hooter of a ship nosing into the harbour; the screech of cicadas in the trees surrounding the terrace. The outline of the mountains grew sharper as the sun came up, and the hum of civilisation increased steadily. He heard the lowered voices of the Boy and the amahs downstairs, and their soft footsteps as they started the day's work.

Below, Happy Valley race course materialised dimly from a swathe of mist. He could hear the thud of horses' hooves before his eyes could make out the galloping shapes at their daily exercise. He could just read the clock on top of the Jockey Club building - quarter to six. Ahead lay another dreary day at the hated office; how could he justify wasting his life on routine pen-pushing when people were dying violent deaths and there were so many more worthwhile jobs to be done?

The rhythmic clonk of the heavy polisher on the ground floor began; the street noises intruded; life was closing in on him again, and he had an urgent need to escape for a while. Turning into the room and throwing on his tussore dressing-gown, he fell over the stacked camp beds awaiting the arrival of Belle and her children, then padded along to Pamela's room and tapped on the open door. She was awake at once, looking tousled and alarmed beneath her net.

"Something wrong? Belle.." she began, but he smiled reassuringly and patted her arm through the net.

"Come for a swim before breakfast?" He whispered, so as not to disturb his parents, whose bedroom door was also open. "I've hardly slept all night, I need some air. Coming?"

"Sure we'll be back in time for breakfast, and work?"

"Got to, haven't we?" "Then I'll come."

"Good girl - perhaps Hilary will come too." He had not met her since the evening launch picnic he had missed, and there had been no reply to the apologetic note he had sent the day after. Now, hopefully, he dashed off another note before he dressed and gave it to Ah Tai to deliver right away. The scrawled reply "O.K. Ten minutes" cheered him.

By quarter past six he was driving off, Hilary insisting that she really wasn't awake and must finish off her night's sleep in the back seat.

"Big Wave Bay, huh?" he suggested. "I'll pick Greg up on the way - I phoned him while you two were taking hours to dress."

Greg was waiting outside the small boarding house in Causeway Bay where he lodged. He climbed over the side of the car and pushed Hilary's legs out of the way to make room for himself.

The car sped along King's Road, which curved with the sea-front, leading past the great buildings of the electricity company, sugar refinery, Taikoo dockyard and the oil installations; workers were pouring towards their gates in droves. Dodging trams, buses and pedestrians, Roddy rejoiced at the prospect of the quiet beach before he too was sucked into the daily grind. He began to sing at the top of his voice as he turned on to the winding road over the hills.

They were in a different world now, running between the slopes of green mountains, the only signs of civilisation the occasional wooden shanty near the roadside, with a Chinese family squatting beside it, pushing chopsticks at the rice in their small bowls.

Big Wave Bay was not accessible by car; they had to park at the head of a stony track which meandered down to the beach. The bay was enclosed on both sides by natural breakwaters of ragged rocks rearing out of the water so it always thundered with great rolling waves. A straggle of bushes and scrub, intermingled with wild purple clematis, fringed the white sand; behind were clusters of trees from which the mocking call of the ha-ha bird filled the air.

Kicking off sandals and slipping out of their outer clothes beneath which they wore their swimming trunks, Roddy and Greg sped down the sand to the water's edge.

"Ugh, cold!" Greg grimaced, hesitating, but Roddy ran on until the water was up to his waist, then plunged in. It really was very cold, but the shock was just what his system needed. Delighting in pitting his strength against the incoming rollers, he struck firmly out to the calmer water beyond, then turned on his back and thumbed his nose at Greg, who was still standing in the shallows. Hilary and Pamela were at the water's edge, their toes testing the temperature.

"Too cold for me," said Pamela, but Hilary ducked in quickly, came up catching her breath sharply, then struck out to join Roddy.

"All right when you get used to it, isn't it?" he grinned. "Race you to the farthest boulder!"

They reached it almost together and struggled out of the seething sea to sit on the barnacled rocks. The sun was up now, touching the sea with glinting diamonds.

"Aren't they a lazy lot?" Roddy looked back at Pamela and Greg who had abandoned the idea of swimming and were sitting side by side on the sand.

Hilary didn't reply, her eyes on the horizon. Roddy picked up a loose piece of rock and fingered it, watching her. "I'm jolly glad you came this morning," he said, carefully marking out squares for noughts and crosses on the rock. "I hope it means I'm pardoned over the Bexton picnic."

"Nothing to pardon," she shrugged. "It's up to you what you do with your evening."

"But I wanted to come, Hilary, you know I did! Pam told you what happened. I was really sorry to drop out."

"Your loss," she said coldly, still not looking him.

"So I'm not forgiven after all," he said, forcing the stone viciously into the squares he had drawn so that little scrapings of rock flew up. He started to fill in noughts and crosses at random. "I'm surprised you came with us today."

"I came because I thought I might get the chance to tell you something." Hilary turned to him for the first time. "It's this: until you can stand up to your father - or any one else - without becoming paralytically drunk, I don't think you're worth knowing. Maybe you don't care what I think - but there it is."

She slipped into the water and headed for the shore. Roddy sat staring at the incomplete squares until she reached the beach; then he scribbled ferociously across the game, and hurled the stone as far out to sea as he could before swimming ashore.

SEPTEMBER

"Te'phone, Miss Doran," said the white-uniformed messenger at the office door.

Pamela got up, peeling her dress from the leatherseated chair. There were knowing smiles and wagging fingers from the other three girls at their typewriters.

"That's the third time today," said Viola. "For a girl who says she's shy, you seem to do very well."

The telephone was in the mailing office a few yards along the corridor. Pamela's heart thudded on the way. Her first call had been from Hugh inviting her to the cinema; the second from Greg suggesting swimming after office; she had said No to both. There was just a chance this might be from Danny, but no, it was from Belle asking "Can you leave work on the dot? I'd promised to take the kids to the beach but I've just been summoned to a meeting about the future of us refugees. I'll pick you up at the office with the kids and run you all to the beach."

She had to agree, and swallowed her disappointment. She had not seen Danny or heard from him since the dinnerdance three weeks ago. Before that evening, she had only thought of him as a friend, but that had changed; dates with Gregg and Hugh were pleasant enough, but she would rather have been with Danny. And over this newly-discovered knowledge hovered the realisation that Danny had never shown any romantic affection for her - although she could recall certain looks which might mean he only needed a little encouragement.

"Wake up, Pam!" Gwen, the senior, was saying, obviously not for the first time. "Check this despatch with me, will you?"

She did so, and it was discovered that a word had been left out.

"Hell!" said Viola, who had typed the despatch. "Must be the heat - I'm sure there's a typhoon brewing. I'll take a break before I re-type.. recharge my batteries."

She lit a cigarette and sat back in her chair to enjoy it. How Pamela admired her elegance and confidence! In the months she'd been working in this office, she had formed a bond with these new colleagues far deeper than that with Ella and the others at H. & S. Yet she had not been able to tell them, in answer to their concerned questions, that she no longer wanted to accept invitations from Greg or Hugh, or any other of Roddy's friends; could not explain that those boys no longer interested her, and that she wanted to be available in case Danny rang her up to make a date.

It was now five minutes to five - there would be no phone call from him today. She wiped her carbon-grimed fingers on a tissue and covered her typewriter.

The young English clerk from the office next door called in that No. 3 typhoon signal had just gone up. Gwen, whose desk was nearest the window, looked out. "The Navy's pulling out," she reported. "All the destroyers are on the move."

Despite the typhoon signal, the sea at Repulse Bay was calm, but darting typhoon flies zig-zagged just above the water. Engrossed in controlling the antics of Jamie and Lisa, Pamela was taken by surprise when there was a shout from the beach, and the crash of bodies hurtling into the water nearby, then Roddy and Greg emerged spluttering beside her.

"So you came here after all," said Greg. "How come you refused when I phoned this morning?"

"Didn't know then what was going to happen.. about the children," she mumbled. "You can imagine what it's like with the two of them at home. I'm pretty busy."

"They're in bed by eight, though, aren't they? Come to the pictures with Rod and Derek and me tonight! Charles Boyer in 'History is made at night'."

Charles Boyer was one of her favourite stars, and she could think of no valid reason for refusing.

The evening proved a disaster. During the film Derek kept trying to hold her hand and wanted to talk all the way through. Afterwards, the men insisted on visiting the nearby Jimmy's Kitchen for club sandwiches and beer. Coming home just after midnight, squeezed in the back of the car between Greg and Derek, Pamela found their conversation, loosened by too many beers, irritating and futile. Both her companions wanted to put their arms round her, and she was hot and cross with the struggle to evade them when Roddy dropped her at Leighton Hill.

The house was in darkness when she rang the bell. A sleepy Boy, inelegant in white vest and loose cotton trousers, opened the door. She took a quick look at the telephone pad in the hall in case there were any messages for her, but the pad was blank. She slipped off her shoes, crept upstairs and undressed in the dark so as not to disturb Lisa who lay akimbo on top of her sheet wearing only knickers. For a long time she stood on the verandah in her nightgown, looking out at the lights of the city that never seemed to sleep, and at the dark hills beneath which Dragon Terrace lay.

"I've got the Boy to make you some sandwiches to take to the office," said her mother at breakfast next morning. "If the weather breaks, you won't want to be coming home to tiffin in a deluge."

There was, however, no rain at one o'clock, although the air was heavy and still, the sky steely and sullen. Not long after, the wind suddenly got up, and junks and sampans could be seen scurrying towards the typhoon shelters. Cargo ships and liners had steam up and were leaving wharves and anchorages, moving out of the harbour to the open sea for safety.

It was difficult to work with the wind making sport of the papers and files on the desks. Soon the windows had to be closed, despite the exhausting heat and stuffiness; the ceiling fan simply churned the hot air round and round. At half past three a message circulated the offices that ferries and Peak trams were likely to cease running, and all staff needing them to get home ordered to leave immediately. Only Viola and Pamela were left in the typists' room.

Reports from the clerks next door caused constant interruptions: this was to be the biggest typhoon ever; it was heading direct for the colony; no, it was changing direction and was going towards the Philippines instead; it had already caused havoc in the China Sea and a Dutch liner had been sunk.

At four o'clock it could be seen that the ferries were after all still plying between the island and Kowloon, but the harbour was empty of ships except for a thinning trail of junks tossing in the now turbulent water on their way to the typhoon shelter.

At a quarter to five Mr. Wade, the Assistant Chief Clerk, came in - the Colonial Secretary wished to dictate an urgent letter. Viola was typing a despatch, Pamela had just finished a draft report.

"You'd better go, Miss Doran," he said.

"Me, to the C.S.?" Pamela was petrified; Gwen, the senior, usually did his work.

"Hurry," Mr. Wade nodded.

She looked despairingly at Viola who said "C.S. won't eat you! He has daughters our age, he's quite human, you know."

This was far more daunting than the occasion earlier that year when she had answered the summons of the manager of H. & S. to learn the result of the design competition. Her clammy hands, her hair wet at the nape of her neck, and her dress creased and damp, added to her apprehension. She just did not feel fit in any way to appear before such an august personage as the Honourable Colonial Secretary, nor capable of taking his dictation and producing a perfect typescript of it in record time.

Her hesitant knock at his open door was not acknowledged. A second, bolder knock produced a gentle "Come in, Miss..er.. just want to get this letter away.. won't keep you long."

She sat rigid in the chair to which he waved her, leaning her note-book on the edge of his desk. He thought aloud while he decided what to dictate. Not sure when he was thinking and when he was actually dictating, she tried to record everything he said.

"Now let's hear what it sounds like," he said at last with a kindly smile.

Speaking jerkily, she picked her away among the false starts and amendments He nodded when everything was to his satisfaction.

Her office was empty when she returned, for the time was almost half past five. There was a note from Viola stuck in her typewriter:

'Daniel Russell phoned at 4.55p.m. Ring his office.'

Her heart lurched. She wanted to run to the telephone immediately, but dared not do so until the letter was finished. Taking out a piece of the pale blue paper with its impressive embossed red coat of arms at the top, she typed it without a fault, because instead of agonising about her work, her mind was on something else: 'Danny phoned, Danny phoned.'

As soon as the letter was handed to Mr.Wade and pronounced acceptable to lay before the C.S., Pamela tore down the corridor to the mailing room and dialled Danny's number. For a long time there was no reply, then a voice in Chinese bawled "Wei? Wei?" She asked for Mr. Russell. After another long pause the voice said laboriously "Alla go.. no body here.."

It was difficult to keep tears of frustration from starting in her eyes. Of course Danny would have left by now; it was almost an hour since he'd phoned. He would conclude that she hadn't wanted to return his call. As she walked dejectedly back to the office to collect handbag and raincoat Mr. Wade called her. "Would you like a lift to Happy Valley, Miss Doran? I could drop you there on my way home."

She would rather have been alone until she could recover from her disappointment and distress, but did not like to turn down the kind offer, especially as the weather seemed worse. Once out of the office, even the short walk to the car park convinced her she was right to accept; it was difficult to keep upright; broken branches and twigs hit her face, and the rain soaked her feet.

There were not many people about, although buses were still running. Mr. Wade drove up Garden Road and turned into Kennedy Road from where they had a panoramic view of the harbour.

"Ferries still running," said Mr. Wade. "A lot of lucky people got off work early under false pretences."

Pamela wasn't listening. Her heart was thumping uncomfortably as she toyed with an idea which had darted into her mind the moment Mr. Wade chose the Kennedy Road route: Danny would be home by now: should she ask Mr. Wade to drop her at the steps of Dragon Terrace? She could call on him and explain why she'd been unable to telephone. Of course, this was 'running after' him, and not the sort of thing she should be doing at all.. yet surely the train of events which was bringing her virtually past his door must in some way allow her to do this?

As the car rounded the last curve before Dragon Terrace, it was carried sideways by a huge gust of wind. Mr. Wade stood on the brakes and the tyres squealed. Had another car been approaching them at that moment there would have been a collision and both cars could well have crashed through the railings which carried the road above the tenements of Wanchai a hundred feet below. That realisation decided her.

"Would you mind dropping me by Dragon Terrace?" she ventured. "I'd like to call on a friend."

The warm wind tore at her hair and whipped up her raincoat as, head down, she started up the steps. Both excited and appalled at her decision, she wondered how she could explain her unexpected appearance without revealing the intensity of her feelings. She knew only too well that with the weather so foul and threatening, she should have gone straight home. She knew too that the eagerness which would be revealed by this extraordinary visit could leave her looking foolish and cheap if Danny's phone call had been for some trivial reason.

"But I've got to do this," she told herself, when timidity slowed her steps. "No matter what."

Then she heard a shout carried faintly on the wind, and looking up, saw a waving figure sitting astride the balustrade above. She couldn't believe it.. it was almost as though Danny was waiting for her! He vaulted on to the terrace, raced to the top of the steps and leapt down to meet her. His white shirt was flapping, his hair parted in tufts by the fierceness of the wind, his voice joyful and his face alight as he seized her arm and helped her up the last flight.

"I got kept late at the office," she gasped, "you'd left when I rang, so I thought.."

"I thought you didn't want to talk to me," Danny shouted back. "I felt too blue to stay indoors. I couldn't believe my eyes when I saw you coming. Oh, this is peachey!"

Peachey.. the old much-used adjective of their childhood; it added to her exhilaration. Then she and Danny, arms round each other for support, were struggling towards his home; sitting in the tiny flat, having biscuits and tea with his mother. It was unreal, an unreality increased by the strange circumstance of every window being closed, curtained and shuttered against the onslaught of the storm. Of course it was too hot and it was airless, but none of these discomforts troubled her now. She could almost be sure that Danny was as happy to see her as she was to see him.

Outside the wind worried the building and rattled the shutters. The local radio station provided weather news between programmes, and an announcement at seven o'clock that the typhoon had turned round and was heading direct for Hong Kong brought Pamela down to earth: she was now marooned in Dragon Terrace until the typhoon passed - and her family had not the remotest idea where she was.

"I hadn't realised how late it was," she fretted, "my parents will be so anxious; is there somewhere in the terrace I can phone from?"

"Sure; Leila and Joe in the flat upstairs have a phone," said Danny. "I'll take you up."

Leila and Joe, Portuguese newlyweds, welcomed Pamela in. She dialled the home number, bracing herself for the reception she knew she deserved.

"Pamela, at last! Where are you?" her father shouted.

She explained, and cringed at the inevitable explosion: "We've been out of our minds trying to find you! Phoning everywhere, your office, your friends, but most of the lines are down. Roddy has been driving all over town hunting for you! Your mother is distraught!"

He had to accept that she must stay at Dragon Terrace until the typhoon passed, after which Roddy, who had been unable to get back to the Y.M.C.A. in Kowloon, would come and fetch her. Chastened at the trouble she had caused, and dreading the dressing-down in person which would ensue when she got home, Pamela was comforted by Leila, who assured her "Your parents must love you, to be so concerned for you. Tomorrow they will be calmer."

The radio continued to report fresh disasters; cars were blown over inclines; sampans and junks sunk; trees falling; blocks of tenements collapsing. Even within the enclosed flat, the noise of the wind penetrated and blew with the fury of an express train, then sang like a high-pitched soprano. The volume of water in the nullah which ran down the side of the terrace increased until its roar could even be heard above the wind.

Above all this came a terrific commotion in the flat overhead - crashing glass, running footsteps, muffled shouts, thuds and bangs; then a hammering on the front door; the amah opened it and in flew Leila and Joe and their amah, all explaining incoherently that a broken shutter had smashed the glass of a window; the violent wind had rapidly filled the flat and blown out the other windows. Awesome crashes and bangs continued as furniture was shunted back and forth.

"All our wedding presents will be ruined," sobbed Leila. Tea was quickly served, and still the buffeting overhead went on.

"Let's have some music," suggested Danny. His mother went to the piano and he took his violin out of its case and tuned up. So that strange night progressed, Pamela reminding herself again and again that she really was sitting in the Russell flat beside a strange young Portuguese couple who were holding hands, and two amahs were standing by the door, too respectful to come in and sit down with their employers but too scared to stay in the kitchen; that Danny was standing next to the piano, playing his violin - all with a background of howling, tempestuous wind, the creaking of the old building with every fresh gust, and the rushing of water down the nullah outside.

When his mother tired, Danny played alone: some Chinese music which had the amahs in happy giggles; Mendelssohn's Spring Song, Traumerei, Stardust. By midnight it was decided that Leila and Joe should try to get some sleep in Danny's bedroom, their amah moving in with the Russell's.

"Pamela will share my room," said Mrs. Russell. "Danny can sleep on the settee in here." She went off to get more bedding, leaving Pamela and Danny alone. Pamela could not hide her happiness, and longed for a sign which would reveal his feelings for her, but he made no attempt to come and sit beside her on the settee. She wondered if she had misread the message of love in his gaze, until he picked up his violin again and very, very quietly, watching her all the time, he played little fragments of music. His handsome face was flushed and serious and he played so softly that the music was as faint as an echo.

"I thought maybe we could go to a show one evening this week," he said, still playing.

"That would be nice," she managed to reply through trembling lips. She marvelled at the way he played by touch, for his eyes were still on her as his left fingers moved from string to string and the other hand plied the bow.

"When, then?"

"I don't mind.. maybe Thursday or Friday.."

"Shall we make it Thursday?"

"Thursday," she nodded gravely. Then Mrs. Russell returned; and the wind howled and the shutters beat a tattoo against the windows; water thundered down the nullah, and the riotous crashing from the upstairs flat continued - and Pamela realised that this had been going on all the time, and it was only in her mind that the short conversation had taken place in a breathless hush save for Danny's plaintive music.

NOVEMBER

"Oh do stop it, you two! Can't you see I'm trying to read Daddy's letter?" Belle, just arrived back from a curry tiffin with other exiled Shanghai wives, perched tensely on the edge of a rattan chair on the verandah and waved the welcoming children away. Ah Tai's teen-age sister Fong, now employed to look after them, dabbed at them as they dodged round the chairs.

"Just behave!" roared Belle, the ferocity in her voice alarming even herself. These three months had been grim, living cheek by jowl with her parents and Pamela, conscious of the disturbance to their hitherto well-ordered lives, although she felt less of a financial burden since she'd started working half days in Lane Crawfords. There was the possibility that wives might be allowed to return to their husbands in Shanghai, but would it be safe to take the children? If not, she would have to remain indefinitely in this twilight existence.

Although she tried not to dwell on these uncertainties, this was one of the days when her patience snapped. "Oh darlings," she said, seeing the children's shocked faces as they stared open-mouthed at her, "I'll take you out just as soon as I've read Daddy's letter; be good for just a few more minutes."

Keith's precise prose explained that now Chinese resistance was at an end and the Japanese had taken over Shanghai completely, law and order had been reasonably restored, although life was still restricted and business difficult.

"The firm thinks we deserve a break," the letter continued. "Replacement staff is to take over here, my relief is due a week before Christmas, so I shall be in Hong Kong about the 23rd. Then - wait for it - we are to take our Home leave right away instead of waiting until August! We're booked on 'Patroclus' sailing from Hong Kong on 7th January."

Belle had to read that last sentence twice before she could take it in, then, for the second time that afternoon she uttered a great yell. Suddenly the verandah was full of people: the children, Fong, Ah Tai, Pamela, and her mother barefoot and dishevelled, straight from her afternoon rest and still fumbling with the sash of her kimono.

When she told them the news there was even more commotion. Her mother said "Thank God!" and Pamela shouted "Yippee!" Ah Tai rapidly explained in Chinese to Fong, who had no English, why everyone was so pleased.

"Going to England on the big ship!" sang the children, latching on to the fact which interested them most, and running round the chairs again.

"It will be a real family Christmas, with Keith coming," rejoiced her mother. "The first time we shall all be together at Christmas for I don't know how many years! Oh, we'll need your room, Pamela. You can stay with Hilary for those three weeks, Mrs. Bately offered to have you before."

"O.K. Pam?" Belle asked.

"If the offer's still open," said Pamela.

"Let's have a special celebration this afternoon tea at Repulse Bay Lido, my treat!" Belle cried. "You'll come, Pam, won't you.. and Mum?"

"I think I will," said her mother. "Dad won't mind - he's still snoozing."

"Not me, thanks," Pamela was shaking her head regretfully. "I'm just off out."

"Can't you put off whatever you were going to do?" her mother said. "It's such a lovely afternoon for the beach."

"Sorry, I can't. I promised to meet Danny at half past two; we're taking the tram to the top of the Peak for a walk."

There was a small silence; her mother started to say something, then changed her mind.

The children were building sandcastles in front of the Lido, with Fong helping them. A few people were swimming, beguiled by the warm sunshine. Belle, seated on the open verandah of the Lido with her mother, almost wished she had brought her swimming costume: it wasn't done for a married matron of 28 to leap into the air and turn somersaults, which was just what she felt like doing, although for some reason all sorts of cavortings were permissible in the sea.

"I don't know how you and Dad have put up with us so long," she told her mother. "We've been so lucky to be able to stay with you. Every time I meet Marie Horn she tells me dreadful tales of how difficult life is in those communal messes, with rosters for the bathrooms and no privacy. Well, we won't be bothering you for much longer now - and I think Pam's a real sport to agree to move out when Keith comes. She's really blossomed out here, hasn't she? I can't get used to her being so grownup."

Her mother burst out suddenly "She's such a worry to Dad and me these days!"

"Goodness, why ever? She's quiet and considerate, doesn't drink or smoke, or stay out late. I know you don't like her being so friendly with that Eurasian boy, but I told you before, Mum, leave her alone! That phase will pass much quicker if you ignore it."

"But it's been going on for so long! Dad should have put his foot down right away, after that night she had to stay at the Russells' flat, but we didn't like to snub nice Mrs. Russell by cutting Pam off from the family directly after that, when she'd been so kind."

"It will fizzle out," Belle insisted. "Remember you told me how wrapped up Pam was in some boy in Ipswich, that she actually tried to refuse to leave England because of him? Well, she soon got over that, didn't she? It's not as if she's exclusively with this Danny all the time, she's in daily contact with heaps of other fellows, playing tennis at the club, off to the beach with Roddy and his pals, and to the cinema a couple of times with that fellow she met at Gwen someone's wedding."

Her mother remained unconvinced. "But I've often heard her on the phone, turning down invitations from Hilary's friend Hugh and others. Do have a talk with her about it, Belle! Even if Danny isn't.. what he is, I don't like her being on her own with any youth.. out for walks... it's not right."

"But Mum, she's turned 18!" Belle had to laugh. "This is 1937, not 1917. Don't forget you used to let me go off on my own with Keith when I was younger than that."

"We knew Keith," her mother argued. "We don't know what Danny's really like - I mean, his morals.."

"Well, you didn't know all that much at Keith at first." Belle's eyes were dancing with reminiscence. "Remember that time months before we were married, when I broke off completely with Keith? We'd played tennis at the club that afternoon (and incidentally, met Pamela there grandly entertaining that little English army boy and his sisters, all sharing one bottle of sarsaparilla.) Keith and I went for a walk afterwards, along Bowen Road. Up to then, we hadn't as much as held hands. Suddenly, near the Military Hospital, when no one was in sight, he seized me and tried to kiss me. I'd been dreaming of him kissing me for ages, but I was petrified when he did! I thought for sure I was in for a fate worse than death - even though I didn't know then what form a fate worse than death would take. I wouldn't talk to him and insisted on going straight home. Poor Keith, it took him three months to ask me out again, he thought I'd damned him for life for one kiss, and all the time I was mad about him. Still am."

"Thank God you're one daughter I don't have to worry about," smiled her mother. "But what you've just told me doesn't make me feel any happier about Pam."

"She's no fool. And remember, Danny Russell is quite a local personality, well known through his violin playing; and he has an office career.. he wouldn't do anything stupid to jeopardise either."

DECEMBER

"It's an absolutely perfect day," said Danny, pausing to lean his elbows on the iron railings of the narrow road which, supported on concrete stilts, meandered round the Peak. The sky was like a sheet of bright blue porcelain: fierce sun-light burnished the bushes, trees and shrubs on the hillside below. It was warm enough to carry his jacket; the afternoon was only half over, and he had Pamela beside him.

He could still scarcely believe the way things had worked out after the typhoon: that she was content, even eager, to spend part of each weekend in his company. He watched her as she too gazed down on the green slopes, the distant rooftops of the tenements and commercial buildings of the city, and the still harbour beyond; one hand rested on the railings, near enough for him to cover it with his; yet, as always in these heavenly weeks, he held himself in check. He must do nothing, or say nothing, which might break the spell of this new and wonderful relationship.

"Best time of the year," Pamela said. "To think it's mid-December! In England now, it will be cold, wet, windy, and dark after half past three in the afternoon. I'd be wearing woollen stockings, woolly underwear, a jumper, cardigan, - and I'd need to put on a thick coat and hat and scarf when I left the office to go home."

"I wouldn't recognise you in all that." Despite his resolution, he could not hide the admiration in his eyes. The slender figure in a cream-coloured pinafore dress and pale green blouse, the tranquil face framed with lightly waved dark-brown hair, blotted out any other possible image of her.

"Excuse please!" said a strange voice behind them, and they turned quickly to see two young Japanese men, dressed in smart European suits.

"You make very nice picture," one of them explained, while the other pointed to the camera suspended round his neck. "You don't mind we take your photographs?"

"We don't mind, do we Pam?" Danny smiled. "Might get them to send us one if we give them an address."

While the Japanese with the camera made adjustments to lenses and flashes, the other darted about, deferentially moving Danny and Pamela this way and that against the railings - "so the background view should complete the artistic picture" as he put it. After taking several snaps, the two Japanese expressed profuse thanks, and one pocketed the address Danny had written out for him.

"I don't really expect we'll ever see anything of the photos," he shrugged as he guided Pamela past the group of walkers who had been held up while the photographers were at work, "but I sure would like to."

"So they will in Japan," came sardonically from an American at his shoulder, obviously a tourist, in immaculate fawn trousers, safari jacket and panama hat. "Those guys made sure they had the Naval Dockyard in the background of all their pictures, and they were using telescopic lens."

Danny, his face dark with humiliation, walked on in silence until they were clear of the other walkers. "That American spoke as if those Japs were spies," he said, "but there's no need for spies; everything in Hong Kong is so obvious and open. You can't hide the Naval Dockyard, or the barracks and the gun emplacements! Anyway, I just can't think the Japs would ever dream of attacking us while they're so busy in China; did you hear the radio news at tiffin-time, they're practically at the gates of Nanking."

"Roddy says they wouldn't dare to take us on here," said Pamela. "But he's so keen on his Battery in the Volunteers, you'd almost think he'd like them to try, just so as to have a crack at them."

"I'd join the Volunteers," Danny said slowly, "if I thought Hong Kong was really at risk."

"I think you'd enjoy it," Pamela went on. "They seem to have a lot of fun - weekly parades ending up in the Mess, and camp every year in the New Territories."

Danny knew this well, for some of his relatives and friends were active members of the Hong Kong Volunteer Defence Corps. He himself had not joined because of a fear that some accident might befall his hands during field activities, and hinder his violin playing. He quickly changed the subject. "Hey, I've got some news - Marie is getting engaged, Marie Bellario. She's invited us to her engagement party, two weeks today. You'll come, won't you?"

Pamela beamed immediate acceptance, and Danny hugged his happiness to his heart. They passed several couples walking arm in arm. If only he dared to take Pamela's arm...

Now the road curved round to the other side of the island, with High West rearing above them.

"Remember the day we climbed there with Sandra?" he grinned.

"You did, I didn't," Pamela corrected him. "I was too scared. Oh, do look at that gorgeous view!"

In the valley below nestled a reservoir, its waters penned in by a tiny dam at one end; through the arches of the dam miniature waterfalls trickled into a smaller reservoir. Further below lay the little fishing village of Aberdeen, its bay bristling with countless masts of sampans and junks.

"Oh Danny," Pamela shouted joyously, "there's the path that leads down to the reservoirs, Sandra and I ran down there once, with her amah chasing after us. Shall we take it? We can get the bus back from Aberdeen."

"Sure!" Anything that pleased her pleased him, but just before they branched off, they met the two Japanese men again - this time photographing each other. They gave Pamela and Danny an effusive greeting. One patted the pocket in which he had placed Danny's address, and wagged a finger reassuringly.

"See, no harm in them," said Danny, waving back.

The zig-zag path down the hillside was rocky and uneven. "It hasn't improved with years," Pamela commented. After she had slipped twice, Danny took her arm to steady her, and she did not object, but he was careful to release his hold as soon as they reached the concrete path across the top of the dam. When, soon after, they went into the tiny Dairy Farm ice-cream parlour at the foot of the hills and sat on opposite sides of the marble-topped table, he wondered how much longer he could restrain himself from revealing his feelings to her.

Cheeks pink with exertion, her hair damp at the temples, she smiled at him as she sipped iced coca-cola. When the glass was empty she gave a sigh of contentment and spread her arms before her on the cool table top. "That was lovely thanks, Danny," she said.

He wanted to say "You're lovely too." Somehow he held the words back, but could not resist laying his hands over hers, and she didn't draw away. Her fingers were warm and responsive.

The magic moment was suddenly spoilt by the entry of a group of European young people who distributed themselves among the tables and chairs and ordered ice-creams and drinks. Pamela quickly pulled her hands away, glanced over at the newcomers, and then waved enthusiastically at one of them.

"That's Viola, one of the girls in my office," she whispered. "She's the one who's always so nice to me."

Danny shot a quick look at the tall girl with short chestnut curly hair who wore shorts and a blouse; he envied her because she was in Pamela's company every day of the working week. The chatter and banter and whoops of laughter completely spoilt the period of the afternoon for him.

"We'd better leave and get the next bus to town," he muttered. "I'm playing at the Peninsula tonight."

At half past four the Assistant Colonial Secretary sent for a stenographer. Rachel, newly promoted to be the senior since Gwen's resignation on marriage, looked round the room. "Who's nearest to finishing?" she asked.

"Me, damn it," said Viola, "but I really want to get off on time today - I've got a date," and she grinned across at Pamela, who grinned happily back. "How about Josie, though?" she added with a wicked wink.

"Oh, not me," protested Josie, the newest member of the staff. "I couldn't possibly. Anyway, I'm in the middle of this endless draft."

She was just seventeen, and if it wasn't for her ginger hair, Pamela would not have recognised her as a pig-tailed schoolgirl on the 'Corfu'. The pig-tail was no more; her hair was a great halo of fluffy curls, her face made up, and her clothes strikingly smart. To date, her appearance seemed to be her only asset. Since the day of Josie's arrival, Pamela had begun to feel the same confidence in herself that she had painstakingly acquired at H. & S. Every task Josie undertook at the typewriter was an Event. She agonised out loud about getting the paper straight in the machine; each mis-typing was advertised with an anguished howl of "Look what I've put!" Sheet after sheet was ripped out, screwed up and pushed into her overflowing waste-paper basket.

"You can rub out on a draft, you know," Pamela had ventured once.

"But I always make a hole in the paper when I rub out," Josie explained. "I don't know why, it just happens."

No, there could be no question of Josie being up to taking dictation from the Assistant C.S. yet. Viola went off with her note-book and pencil. Pamela looked anxiously after her, and was most relieved to see her return five minutes later, with only a short letter to type. She had been looking forward all week to Viola's invitation to tea, with a modicum of awe and surprise that some one with such self-confidence and sophistication should seek her company.

"Ever been to Courtlands before?" asked Viola, referring to the guesthouse on Kennedy Road where she lived, as they trudged up Garden Road, past the lower terminus of the Peak Tram, and the small flower stall.

"No, I haven't," said Pamela, smiling at the flower stall foki, who obviously remembered handing her a buttonhole of carnations which Danny had bought there the previous evening.

"The food's good," Viola went on, "but it's expensive in a guesthouse; it would be much cheaper to share a flat with two or three other people."

Now they were passing St. Joseph's, the Catholic Church which she had once entered years ago while waiting for Danny and Philip and Marcus.

"You a church-goer?" asked Viola, following Pamela's glance.

"Not really. Now and again my father decides to go to the Cathedral, and we all have to go with him (except my brother, he won't.)"

"Do you believe in God?"

"Oh yes, of course! Don't you?"

"Not sure. He let a great friend of mine get run over and killed. I'd have believed in Him if she'd survived. I promised Him everything that night in the hospital while she was fighting for her life - but phut! She died, at sixteen, that was that for her."

"How dreadful," Pamela struggled to find the right words, having never before been faced with some one who doubted the presence of God. "But wasn't it really the fault of the person driving.. who knocked her down.. I mean, he must have been careless, or drunk.. You couldn't blame God for that, could you?"

"That's why I'm not sure about God," Viola nodded. "Life's really complicated, isn't it, when you come to think about it?"

At that moment what Pamela was thinking about was Danny, for across the road ran the boundary of the Botanic Gardens where they had spent an hour after the office closed the previous day. Together in the cool sunlight, their hands sometimes touching accidentally, they had walked among the ornamental shrubs and bushes, Danny talking earnestly of his plans to earn and save enough money to buy a new piano for his mother, and ultimately a better home; there was no limit to his ambitions as he prattled on, against a backdrop of deepest purple bauhinnias, flaming red hibiscus, giant ferns, beds of staring chrysanthemums and dahlias, and soaring palm trees...

Viola's room was on the third floor and had just enough space for a divan, small chest-of-drawers-cum-wardrobe, one chair and a tiny bedside table.

"Most of my belongings are in trunks in the store room," Viola explained. "One of these days I'll get a flat and have all my things round me."

She rang the bell in the wall, and when the young floor boy came in, ordered tea and sandwiches. "You have the chair, as you're the visitor," she told Pamela, kicking off her shoes and making herself comfortable sitting across the divan, her back leaning against the wall. "Now," she said, lighting a cigarette, "I want to know about you and Daniel Russell."

To every one else who had questioned her on this subject, Pamela had a stock answer - "He's just a good friend." But to Viola she found herself faltering "I think.. I think I'm falling in love with him."

"It certainly looked that way when I saw you on Saturday."

"We've never spoken about it," Pamela added hastily. "We just go for walks, or to films, or to the Gloucester, and talk and talk. In the Dairy Farm last week, when you saw us, that was the first time we'd actually held hands."

"Are you saying this is a truly platonic friendship? No kissing or cuddling?"

"Oh no! You see, I'm afraid to let him know how I feel, in case he doesn't feel the same way."

"Of course he's in love with you! Any one could see that. Oh, thanks Ah So" - as the boy returned with the tea tray. She went on slowly as she poured the tea, "What a pity, I feel so sorry for you both. You know it can't go any further, don't you?"

"We're happy as we are," Pamela said defensively.

"That young man didn't look at all platonic-minded to me," said Viola. "Apart from your feelings, for his sake you must drop him as soon as you decently can. It isn't fair to him, you could never seriously go out with him.. as you would with a European.. you could never marry him."

"No one's thinking about marriage!" Pamela's voice thickened. "It's just that I enjoy being with him more than with any one else. I don't think of him being Eurasian, he's just a kind, lovely person, fun to be with, and interesting. We understand each other, and I don't know why every one goes on about Europeans and Eurasians!"

"Yes you do," said Viola gently. "And I can't stand by and watch you heading for heartbreak. The prejudice here is so ingrained; it's all wrong, but it can't be ignored. Unless you make a clean break now, one of you - if not both - will suffer like hell when it comes after you've both become even more besotted with each other than you are now."

"It's all so horrible and snobbish." Pamela's teacup rattled in its saucer because her hand was shaking. "I know you're trying to help, and thank you for bothering so much about me, but I only want to go on enjoying things as they are now. You know I've only got another six months in Hong Kong."

"Do you really want to go Home with your parents in June?"

Faced with the question she had been considering inwardly for the past dream-like weeks, Pamela cupped her chin in her hands and said "There's no choice.. my parents wouldn't dream of leaving without me. They're frantic enough at leaving Roddy - and he's 24."

"But you'd rather stay?" probed Viola.

"I would, I would!"

"Because of Danny," said Viola.

"Partly, but for other reasons - the same reasons you chose to stay in Hong Kong when your parents left; I'm so happy here."

"Then keep it that way," Viola said bluntly. "Take my advice: break up this friendship with Danny."

"You're making too much of it," Pamela protested, "the Eurasian angle, I mean; every one is."

"So other people have spoken to you about it?" Viola lit another cigarette. "Your parents?"

"No, but they've been sort of guarded about showing disapproval. My neighbour, Hilary, was very critical once; and my sister Belle mentioned Danny casually the other day - but I knew what she was getting at. I know my family would far rather I only went out with English people, and I do, quite often, so" - her voice faltered - "why does every one keep minding that I go out with Danny sometimes?"

There was a silence as Pamela dabbed at her eyes.

"Look at it fair and square," said Viola at last, "it doesn't make sense for you to give up the company of someone you like so much, but let me tell you something. Look at young Josie: pleasant, good dress sense; inexperienced, minimal shorthand and typing speeds, very little topside - but she's English, so she's in. There were other applicants for the vacancy when Gwen left. I saw the file. One was a girl with an English surname, English father, Portuguese mother; marvellous school reports - she'd been to boarding school in England, as well as to secretarial college there; she'd even had some office experience in England, but she didn't set an interview because her application form showed she was Eurasian. Terribly unfair, of course, but that's how it is. Would you want that sort of humiliation for your children?"

Pamela shook her head dumbly.

There was a tap on the door and an amah came in carrying dresses on hangers in one hand and a pile of ironed underwear in the other. Quietly she put the clothes away and departed. Viola sat up, poured more tea and said "Having an amah on tap is one of the many reasons why I defied my folks when they wanted me to leave Hong Kong with them. If I'd gone with them, I'd have found myself doing their chores as well as my own - they're no more used to domestic work than I am. They're still waiting for me to give up living in this shoe-box and go to join them, but I won't; I have to live frugally, but one day I'll get a little flat; if you should decide, Pam, to stay on after June, maybe we could get a place together."

"Sounds lovely, but it'll never happen - they wouldn't let me." Pamela stood up. "I must be on my way if I'm to get home in time for dinner."

"It would be very nice if you didn't have to keep to someone else's timetable all the time, wouldn't it?" smiled Viola. "If we had a flat, for instance? Now you will think over all I've said this evening, and I mean ALL: won't you?"

Danny directed the taxi-driver to the steep slope leading to the square two-storeyed house. Pamela, sitting in the back with Mrs. Russell, could see at once the opulence of this new Bellario home; no wonder Danny yearned to get a better place for his mother!

The balustraded verandahs fringing each floor were lined with pots of flowers. At both sides of the stone steps leading to the great front door stood earthenware urns full of red poinsettias. Indoors, the ceilings were high and frescoed; the broad staircase and the floors shone, garlands of flowers and greenery hung on the pale distempered walls.

Pamela was overwhelmed by her welcome. Her hands were grasped by every member of the family and their friends; her cheeks kissed; enquiries made about her parents. Marie embraced her like a long-lost sister, and introduced her as 'my childhood friend' to Anthony, her doctor fiancé; two Bellario brothers, Ricky and Jack whom she barely remembered as older brothers of Marcus, reminded her they had met at Celeste's First Communion Party ten years ago.

The biggest welcome of all came from Celeste, now a plump schoolgirl, her hair caught in one long thick pigtail. Her left leg was encased in an unwieldy iron; she hugged Pamela tightly and looked searchingly in her face, declaring "I've never forgotten you, Pamela. You look just the same as before, but then I always had to look up to you and now we're level with each other!"

In this aura of goodwill and enthusiasm, Pamela followed Danny happily from one group to another, while amahs brought round trays of drinks and small chow.

"Time for a little dancing," announced Dr. Bellario, and Mrs. Russell sat down at the piano.

"You're dancing only with me," Danny whispered urgently to Pamela. He held her lightly, at a respectful distance, but she could feel his hands shaking. He didn't speak, and neither did she because she was afraid she would betray the fluttering of her heart. The rest of the dancers changed partners frequently, but Danny would not let her go. After the final dance Dr. Bellario led in Father Macardo, the parish priest, who said a short prayer and blessed the newly-engaged couple and the whole gathering.

"Before you leave," beamed the Doctor, "we want to take some photographs, so please don't rush off."

Two Chinese photographers darted about, snapping guests standing together in small groups as well as organising the whole party into one picture.

"Some of these should come out, at least," Danny told Pamela, after the battery of flashlights had subsided, "and we really will see them this time - not like those ones the Japs were going to send us, and didn't."

MONDAY - two days since Danny's arms had been round her at Marie's party; two days of remembering and dreaming, scarcely aware of the pattern of life around her. Even being sent to take dictation from the Honourable Colonial Secretary failed to shake her: it was as if the business side of her brain functioned separately, leaving the emotional side to sigh and dream as it would. But there were cracks in her efficiency.

"You won't mind my mentioning it, Pam, will you, but you're putting your carbons in back to front," Viola said. "What's the matter with you - did someone put you in a trance at the weekend?"

With an absent smile, Pamela relaid the carbons and shrugged her shoulders; sooner or later she would tell Viola how things were, but not yet, fearful of breaking the spell.

When the telephone call came late in the afternoon she tried to walk calmly out of the typists' room to the despatch department, but no one was deceived, her flaming cheeks when she returned bringing teasing remarks from her colleagues.

"Time for a drink at the Gloucester after office?" asked Viola. Pamela had to refuse. She didn't have to add "I'm going there anyway, with someone else," but the words spilled out because Viola was too valued a friend to be denied the truth.

TUESDAY. Fingers flying over the keys of her typewriter, she recalled the long talk over iced drinks in the hotel the previous day; the love she felt and read in Danny's eyes; the sudden realisation at seven o'clock that almost two hours had passed there, resulting in the necessity for a taxi home if she was not to be late for family dinner; the delicious memory of the swift ride in the back of the taxi, she sitting up primly, and shivering as his arms crept tentatively round her shoulders; his face turning to hers, his whispered "PLEASE may I kiss you?" and her willing lips meeting his.....

"That's fixed, then?" Rachel was saying. "Six thirty at Gwen's on the 23rd - I'll give her a ring this evening to say we'll all be coming."

Pamela's questioning look was all to apparent.

"You were dreaming again, weren't you?" Viola accused. "Gwen and John have invited us all to pre-Christmas drinks at their flat on the 23rd. Make a note of it in your diary, else you're sure to forget, in your present state."

"I don't think I can come, actually," Pamela said carefully. "I don't really know what I'll be doing then." It was perfectly true she didn't know what she would be doing at 6.30 pm on the 23rd, but what she hoped she would be doing as meeting Danny somewhere, like today after office hours when they planned to saunter through the Botanic Gardens again.

WEDNESDAY. This was a dead, blank day, because Danny had rehearsals at 5.30pm with a new band which had just arrived from Manila. There was no joyful feeling of anticipation as she typed her way towards 5pm and a date with him. She had no excuse when Belle telephoned to ask her to meet at the Club after work for tennis.

When she arrived, Belle was knocking up with Hilary and a tall young man who was introduced as Grant, a lieutenant in the Royal Navy. Jamie and Lisa, in Fong's charge, were happily seated at a table on the grass nearby, drinking lemonade and scrunching potato chips.

"Don't let them have anything more after that," Belle called, then having to mime her instructions because Fong knew no English.

How anxious Belle looked! Pamela, noting now the smudges beneath her sister's eyes and the creased brow, suddenly realised that for the past weeks she had not really looked at her. The papers were full of alarmist reports of a fierce Japanese onslaught on Nanking - a reminder of the potential power of the invaders.

Wrapped up in Danny she knew she had been entirely sef-centred recently. There had been earlier invitations for tennis and the seaside with the children, but she had made excuse after excuse because she wanted to be free for Danny. Now she made a mental resolve to give more time to Belle and the children.

Grant continually complained he hadn't played tennis since he'd left school, and constantly proved it, with hilarious results. Before long Belle was her usual buoyant self, lunging madly after impossible balls, and giggling like a schoolgirl when she missed an easy shot. By the time the light began to fade, all four were weak from exhaustion and laughter.

"My kingdom for a pink gin,' gasped Hilary, as they straggled off the court. Fong had long since taken the children home. Now Belle slipped on a jacket and said goodbye: "I'm off to see if there's any more news from up North," she explained as she hurried away.

Enjoying iced drinks, Pamela lingered in the clubhouse with Hilary and Grant; the latter, she discovered, was much younger than herself and Hilary; with his ready guffaw, he didn't seem Hilary's type at all.

"I say" - most of his speeches began that way - "I say, Hilary, do you think Pam would like to come to the Christmas dance on board next week?"

"Pluck up your courage and ask her," shrugged Hilary.

He did, looking so hopeful that Pamela felt embarrassed at refusing. He looked crestfallen but quickly recovered, saying it would be too good to be true if two young ladies he'd invited could both come.

Later, on the way home, Hilary observed to Pamela "Funny you refused Grant's invitation without knowing its date; I take it you're still exclusive to Danny Russell?"

"Yep." Pamela tried to keep the annoyance out of her voice.

"You're asking for trouble, you know."

"I'm not criticising your choice of companion, am I?"

"Oh, Grant! He's just a kid it's fun to be with now and again, and he happened to ring up today when I was at a loose end. I probably won't see him again after the dance. But don't be shirty with me, Pam, I'm really worried about you."

"You don't have to be - I'm happier than I've ever been in my life."

Hilary sighed and gave her a friendly pat on the back.

"Have it your own way, chum, but I do hope you will manage to be available on the 19th of next month; it's my twenty-first, and I'm having a party at the Gloucester.. and I shall take it as a personal insult if you're not there."

THURSDAY. With the prospect of meeting Danny after work to take in a film at the Queen's Theatre, this should have been a happy day in the office, but the political news pouring in hourly was too disturbing for Pamela to surround herself with a cocoon of private thoughts. There were rumours of dreadful carnage in

Nanking, the victorious Japanese entering the city and wreaking unheard of bestiality on the Chinese inhabitants.

"If a Jap came near me, I'd commit suicide," shuddered Rachel.

"I don't think I would," said Viola. "I wouldn't give the little swine the satisfaction of causing my death; life is more important that one particular incident in it. You have to take the long view." She looked across at Pamela and added

" I'm going to my tailor at 5 - how about coming with me?"

As earlier that week, Pamela mumbled a refusal.

"Another date?" Viola turned the moment into a joke, but her eyes were serious. "Some people have all the luck.

It was clear she was inviting a confidence, and Pamela ducked away quickly; she loathed snubbing her, but feared that to elaborate on her present happiness would lead to another disturbing heart-to-heart talk.

Later, at the cinema, Danny's arm crept round her shoulders, producing a maelstrom of exciting feelings which bore no relation whatsoever to the thrill of Lawrence's presence in Ipswich. The arm was quickly withdrawn before the lights went up. They blinked happily at each other as they stood while The King was played.

"No time for a drink, I'm afraid," said Danny. "I'm due to play with the Filipino band at the Roof Garden tonight."

They shuffled slowly out of the brightly-lit foyer which was crowded with people waiting for the next showing - mainly servicemen in uniform, some with exquisitely dressed, highly-scented and brightly-painted Chinese girls.

It was already dark, but the city centre was bright with great shop signs, and the placards the newspaper vendors held out were clearly visible: huge thick black letters proclaimed "RAPE AND CARNAGE IN NANKING".

"Poor Belle will be frantic," Pamela muttered as they sank back into a taxi. "She's terrified about this Nanking business in case it makes trouble in Shanghai and Keith doesn't get away."

"Nanking's 200 miles from Shanghai," said Danny comfortingly. He slipped his arm round her waist and put his other hand gently under her chin and guided her face towards his. There was no need to ask permission to kiss now, for she was as eager as he was.

"You know I'm crazy about you, don't you?" His voice in her ear was breathless and urgent.

"I think I love you, too."

"I want this to go on for ever!"

FRIDAY. They couldn't meet at all because at 5 o'clock Danny had to take his mother to a friend's funeral and subsequent mourning gathering. Eager and loving phone calls during the day sustained Pamela; in between, she dreamed of those exciting minutes in the taxi the previous evening, reliving the delight of his hungry kisses.

During dinner that evening, the radio was switched on for the news, and the astounding announcement was made that the Japanese had fired on and sunk an American gunboat on the Yangtse River some ten miles from Shanghai. Belle gave a great moan and flopped back in her chair, crying helplessly. Her father thumped his fists on the table, calling down curses on 'those Japanese upstarts'. Pamela could hardly believe the news - Japanese attacking the Americans? How dared they? How could that be? And if an American ship, why not a British ship? And indeed, why not Hong Kong?

"Keith will never get out now! It's bound to start a war and I'll never see him again," Belle was sobbing. "His ship won't get away, after all this."

SATURDAY. This should have been a wonderful day, for the office was to close at noon, and she was to meet Danny for a walk in the afternoon, but the house was full of gloom and anxiety at breakfast. When the South China Morning Post was delivered it carried details of the sinking of the US 'Panay'. There were also gruesome accounts of what was now termed 'the rape of Nanking'. All this sent Belle running from the table in tears, pursued by the bewildered children wanting to know why. Fong clattered upstairs after them and hauled them back, and this resulted in noisy protests, clearly available in the dining room.

"We haven't had a moment's peace in this house since those bombs on Shanghai!" roared her father, purple in the face. "What have I done to deserve all this commotion at my time of life?"

Pamela slipped away to catch the bus to work, thankful to escape the charged atmosphere, but things were not much better in the office. Routine work was disregarded. Emergency typing was needed as urgent reports and despatches about Nanking and the 'Panay' sinking demanded attention. The girls were told they would have to return to work after tiffin. Pamela, sick with disappointment at missing the afternoon meeting with Danny, dashed along to the mailing room to telephone him.

"Gee Pam, you must be important!" he said. "I'm rehearsing this evening and tomorrow morning I'm part of an orchestra playing at a special High Mass at St. Joseph's. I'll be free in the afternoon though, can you make it?"

"Oh yes," she said fervently, no longer caring that the clerks were only five yards away from the telephone. "I'll be counting the hours until then."

As she walked up to the drive to the house for tiffin, she noticed that her father's car was parked outside. This was unusual, as his custom on Saturdays was to stop at the Civil Service Club on the way home for a drink, and come in for tiffin about two o'clock. The reason for his early return soon became apparent.

"Here you are!" He burst out of the lounge to meet her, waving the mid-day edition of the 'China Mail' in his hand. His face was working as he punched at a picture in the photographic section. "This has got to stop, my girl! At once!"

He thrust the page at her bewildered face, and his podgy fingers stabbed at a photograph of herself, Danny, Maria Bellario and Antony Devala. The caption beneath read 'Miss Pamela Doran, younger daughter of Mr. and Mrs. A. Doran of Leighton Hill; Mr. Daniel Russell the violinist, with Miss Marie Bellario and her fiancé Dr. Antony Devala at a party last Saturday to mark the engagement of Miss Bellario and Dr. Devala.'

"No more sly trips out with this Eurasian," shouted her father. "Do you hear? You thought we didn't notice, didn't you? Well, now it's in the papers for all my friends to see, and it's got to stop."

His face as so near hers that she could smell his hot breath. Afraid he might strike her, she stepped backwards. He lunged forward and seized her shoulders and shook her. "Do you understand, girl? I won't have you having anything more to do with the Russell boy: that's an order, and by God, you'd better obey it!"

"Adam, Adam!" Her mother pleaded. "You've told her -now let her be. I'm sure she understands."

"Then let her say so!" he thundered, releasing her, and glaring into her face in a way which made him almost unrecognisable. No words would come, but suddenly her face crumpled and she started to cry hard, staccato sobs. Her mother cried too, and her father threw up his hands and swore. "Nothing but howling females in this house! I'm off to the Club. No, don't keep my tiffin, I'll have something in peace down there. And don't you forget what I said, Pamela: you'll not see Daniel Russell again; I've booked your passage Home with Belle and Keith on the 'Patroclus' in two weeks' time, to make sure."

Tossing the newspaper on to the floor, he lumbered out into the hall, mopping his brow and slamming the door behind him.

The office was so busy that afternoon that chatting was impossible, but with one brief question Viola discovered that a crisis over Danny accounted for Pamela's distress.

'So the crunch has come at last,' thought Viola, her sympathy tinged with irritation that whatever had happened had occurred on this particular day, when she was looking forward to a leisurely two hours at home after work, a lazy bath and hairwash before Raoul arrived for dinner and then to take her to see 'Ruddigore' performed by the local Philharmonic Society. Now, her conscience would compel her to spend some of that precious free time to try and help Pamela over her miseries. There was a vulnerability about Pamela's simplicity which asked to be protected; also, she had to admit to herself, she appreciated Pamela's obvious admiration - the perfect antidote to the wounding letters from her parents who still considered she was behaving in an undaughterly manner by refusing to live with them in England.

Just after five o'clock the girls were told they could leave. Pamela folded her arms across the typewriter, leant forward and wept.

"None of that here," said Viola firmly, taking her by the shoulders and motioning to the other two girls to go. "Buck up, Pam, keep going a little longer; come home with me for a while."

Pamela obeyed, walking like a robot down the corridor to the lift. Viola took her arm and guided her across Garden Road, talking brightly of trivialities and getting no response. When they arrived at Viola's room in the guesthouse, she collapsed into the chair and shook with sobs.

"Go ahead, get it out of your system," said Viola, rummaging in the wall cupboard above her head and taking out a half bottle of brandy she had bought for visitors over Christmas. "Have a shot of this first - it will do you good."

Pamela waved the drink away.

"Take it!" Viola commanded. "Even if you don't like it, it's what you need right now!"

Pamela drained the glass in one great gulp, grimaced and spluttered. Gradually the sobs subsided and she was able to tell her story.

"So," said Viola, at last lighting the cigarette she had been yearning for all the afternoon but not had time to have, "you're really faced with an ultimatum: give up Danny, or go to England next month."

"It's not a choice," moaned Pamela. "He's booked my passage. I don't want to go away! What can I do?"

What indeed? Viola could see no answer and suppressed a tiny sigh. She took a surreptitious glance at her watch, mentally adjusting her evening's timetable, then applied herself to the impasse. "Facing facts, you've got to count Daniel out of your life, because if you're sent Home soon you won't have him; and if you're allowed to stay longer it will only be because your folks are satisfied that you're through with him."

"My father didn't say that, he just said I had to leave with Belle and Keith." Pamela's tears started again.

"You need another shot of this." Viola reached for the brandy bottle. "I'll join you this time, as it's nearly Christmas."

Pamela despatched the second noggin with the same pained stoicism as the first, and sat back limply in the chair. "Why can't people leave Danny and me alone?" she said wearily.

"You know," shrugged Viola with some impatience. "No point in arguing about that again. Now let's get this straight, you definitely want to stay on in Hong Kong as long as possible, even with Danny verboten, don't you?"

"Even without Danny," Pamela gulped. "I've made a new life here.. friends like you, and the job. I'd be losing everything if I left now."

"I think your only hope is to convince your parents that you've given Danny up, and make them see how much staying in Hong Kong means to you. There's just a chance they'll give in and cancel the passage with Belle and Keith. But you've got to be strong and tell Danny right away that it's over."

"How can I tell him? What can I say without hurting him dreadfully? I can't bear to hurt him."

Viola looked at her watch again. Already an hour had flown by; she would have to telephone Raoul and tell him to come a little later. The telephone was at the end of the corridor where Ah So lolled over a tiny table, practising his English homework. He got up to let her sit down while she telephoned. His white loose trousers and high-necked jacket were crumpled, for he had been on duty there since 7 that morning. His open exercise book showed lines of simple sentences in careful writing.

"How many pages today, Ah So?" smiled Viola, as she dialled Raoul's number.

"One, two, three, missee," he replied, eagerly turning back the pages to show her.

"Very good." He went to night school several nights a week, and she always praised his industry.

Then Raoul came on the line. He sounded downhearted when she told him the change of plan.

"You perhaps don't wish to come to the theatre with me?" he suggested in his fascinating Swiss accent.

"Of course I want to come, Raoul, it's just that a friend has turned up so I'm not ready yet."

"A friend?" Suspicion was heavy in his voice.

"She wanted to discuss something with me." Viola could almost hear the sigh of satisfaction at the implied sex of the friend. "Come at 7.45; we'll still have time for dinner before the show."

"O.K." He still sounded rather rattled, as if he didn't quite believe her story, so she blew a kiss into the receiver as she said goodbye. When she returned to the room Pamela had nodded off. Viola crept quietly round her, getting out clothes for the evening. Still Pamela slept.

"Oh hell," thought Viola. "I can't wait any longer to get ready." She scrawled a note saying 'in bathroom, back soon' and laid it on the top of Pamela's empty glass, then dashed along to the bathroom. She washed her hair and showered at top speed, wrapped a towel turbanwise round her head, threw on her kimono and hurried back to the room. Pamela's eyes fluttered at the sound of the door closing.

"Goodness, I thought you were out for the night," said Viola, "I can see you're not used to brandy."

"Why, have I been asleep long?"

"Let's see, it's ten minutes to seven.."

"Ten to seven? Are you sure?" Pamela stood up, swayed, and sat down again quickly. "I must get home.. but I feel so peculiar."

"You can't go like that.. Oh Lord, I'd forgotten you said you didn't eat anything for tiffin; no wonder you're dizzy! You'll have to stay here a bit longer."

"But I've got to be home for dinner at half past seven."

"Tell you what," Viola improvised quickly, "you can have dinner here.. I'll telephone your parents and tell them not to wait for you. What's your phone number?"

"Um.. six three... no, three six one nine - or is it one three nine six.. something like that," said Pamela drowsily.

"I'll find out," said Viola hastily. "You stay in that chair till I come back." Out she went to the corridor once more, found the Doran number in the book and dialled it. Mrs. Doran answered. Carefully, Viola explained that Pamela had come to Courtlands with her after work - "and we've just realised how late it is; would you mind if she stayed to have dinner with me?"

There was a whispered conversation in the background. Viola could hear some of it: "..why doesn't she ring us herself?.." "..well you frightened her at tiffin, Adam.." "..I don't like the sound of it at all, there's something at the back of it, that boy I bet.." ".. she wouldn't do that Adam.. let her have dinner with Viola and come home straight afterwards.." "...to make sure, tell her Belle will come and pick her up outside Courtlands at half past eight sharp.." The gist of this was then politely conveyed to Viola, who pressed the cancel button and dialled Raoul again.

"Look, Raoul, I'm most terribly sorry, but I'm afraid we'll have to cancel dinner altogether tonight. Instead, can I meet you outside Courtlands at 8.35, we'll be in plenty of time for the show: O.K.?"

"What is happening?" came Raoul's plaintive voice. "How do I know you will stay with this plan?"

"It's a promise; see you later."

Pamela as still half asleep when Viola returned to the room.

"You've got to wake up!" Viola clattered about the room as noisily as she could, and turned the radio up loudly. "I've phoned your folks and told them you're dining here. Your sister is calling for you afterwards. Now I'm going to walk you along to the bathroom and douse your face in cold water to get you fit to be seen."

"Why, am I drunk?" Pamela looked stupidly amused.

"Just a bit." Viola helped her out of the chair. "My fault, I shouldn't have given you brandy on an empty stomach."

In the bathroom Pamela hung over the basin and submitted to several duckings. "If this is a hangover..never again," she groaned.

She was still unsteady on her feet on the way to the dining room fifteen minutes later, but Viola was relieved to see that she ate quite well; but with the return to sobriety came the misery again.

"I don't know what I'll do when I get home," she agonised as she and Viola stood outside the guesthouse. "You've been marvellous to me, but.. everything's so hopeless."

"Keep calm, and offer to strike a bargain like I told you," said Viola firmly, staring away into the darkness to ignore the crumpling face.

"But suppose they won't? I know they won't!"

"Then we'll talk about it again on Monday." Viola was already fidgetting. Raoul was due any minute, and she couldn't leave Pamela in her distressed state, standing at the roadside. In fact, Belle drove up just then and carried Pamela off with a friendly wave. When Raoul arrived to minutes later in his red MG, Viola felt she could now put Pamela and her troubles completely out of her mind for the weekend.

Raoul Tennien had troubles too which concerned her; he was, he constantly assured her, madly in love with her. He had a flat in a small block further along Kennedy Road, and was always asking her to share it with him ('You can have your own room, as you have in Courtlands.'). Much as he, and his work as a foreign newspaper correspondent, interested her, this was not the sort of commitment she wanted: nor would it be possible to undertake without reports filtering back to her family in England via her parents' many Hong Kong friends. She found Raoul attractive and informative, and she thrived on knowledge of every kind.

"So I get to see you at last," he grunted as she climbed in beside him. "This evening, I start to think you are perhaps stringing me along."

"Not you, Raoul," she assured him merrily, beginning to enjoy herself as the car sped down Garden Road. He turned to smile at her, and she was conscious of the charm of his sparkling blue eyes and near-white silky hair blowing across his forehead. She always made an inner judgment on every man she met as to his possibility as a permanent partner in life.

"Not you, Raoul," she said again, but this time to herself. He was far too charming: she would never be quite sure of him.

"Remember Dad said only ten minutes," murmured Belle as she let Pamela out of the car below Dragon Terrace the following afternoon. "I'll be back on time. And don't take it too hard, Pam, he'll understand."

Pamela managed a wan smile of thanks; it was Belle's intercession which had won this small concession of one final meeting with Danny. All last night and this morning Pamela had been trying to work out what to say to him; she was no nearer a solution when she saw him bounding down the terrace steps.

"Hello Pam, it seems ages since I saw you!" He took her hand and squeezed it. "I thought this afternoon would never come. Shall we take the bus to Repulse Bay?"

"I can't do that," she mumbled, pulling back from his embrace. "I can only stay a little while.. ten minutes."

"Ten minutes?" repeated Danny incredulously.

"I'm afraid so," she managed to say, although her voice was thick with emotion.

"But why only ten minutes?" He couldn't believe it.

"Just to say goodbye." The stark truth seemed the only thing to say.

"Goodbye? Goodbye!! Are you going some place?"

Still he didn't understand. For a moment she wondered if she could perhaps spare him the hurtful facts, so said painfully "My parents want me to go to England after Christmas, with Belle and Keith and the children.. sailing the first week in January.. so there's not much point in us.. in us going out any more."

She saw the mask come down over his face, and couldn't bear that he should think she cared so little for him. "Oh Danny, they don't want us to be together! So they're sending me to England as soon as possible, out of the way. I'm not allowed to see you any more after this afternoon."

Instantly his arms were round her, comforting and strong. They sat down on the bottom step while she sobbed out the whole story. There were tears standing in his eyes as he told her gently that he quite understood her parents' attitude.

"My mother warned me about this often," he said sadly, "she feared it would happen. I kept pretending everything would be all right, we've been so happy together."

Regardless of the proximity of several Chinese children playing nearby, throwing stones into the nullah, Danny cupped Pamela's wet face in his hands and kissed her very tenderly. "I know we can't go against your parents, dearest Pam, but I shall never forget the wonderful months we've had. I'm so grateful to you for all that."

"I don't want it to end, I hate them."

"Don't be bitter to your parents, it's not their fault." Danny was surprisingly calm. "It's just the way things are. It really isn't any good fighting it - remember all this misery wouldn't have come about if my mother hadn't married into a different race and produced a Eurasian like me."

"But I love you as you are.."

"And I'll treasure everything you've said, but you have to find some one else to love, try to see that, my lovely Pamela."

She began to realise, as he gently wiped her eyes with his handkerchief, that it was he who was consoling her, not the other way round: could it be that he didn't mind the breaking up as much as she did? He seemed to have accepted this new situation without question, without railing against fate; maybe she had been deluding herself all along, and his attentions had been little more than a passing fancy, despite protestations of love.

But when Belle's car appeared round the corner and the moment came for the final goodbye, Danny flung his arms round Pamela once again, and he couldn't speak the farewell words because great sobs were strangling them; and his shoulders were heaving and his head bent as he stumbled up the terrace steps without a backward look.

Looking round the festive table at Christmas lunch, Belle had to shake herself to accept that this was really happening. Keith sat next to her, delivered from all the fearsome dangers in China. The children were thrilled and contented. Roddy was home for the day, had even attended Morning Service at the Cathedral with all the family, and so far had not had a single argument with his father. Even Pamela, so quiet and sad these last days, looked reasonably cheerful today, and most attractive in a new crimson silk dress she had designed herself.

It was a pity the parents would not allow her to stay in Hong Kong until June, now she had completely dropped Danny Russell. The rest of the family, including Keith, had argued Pamela's case for her, but her father remained adamant: she must leave Hong Kong next week. Perhaps it was all for the best; there would be plenty of young men on the 'Patroclus' to take her mind of her broken heart.

CHRISTMAS

Danny broke the news to his mother immediately they arrived home after having Christmas dinner with the Bellarios.

"I didn't want to tell you too soon," he said gently, "but now I must. I'm leaving Hong Kong. I'm going to work in Manila."

She didn't ask questions, just sat waiting quietly for him to continue, but her slight chest began to rise and fall quickly.

"The boss of the band that's been at the Gloucester for the last months has often asked me to join up with them permanently, so now I shall. They're based in Manila, and going back there in three weeks time and I'll be sailing with them. I've already given in my notice at Ropers. You won't mind too much, being alone, will you mumma?"

"Not if that's what you want to do, Danny. How long will you be gone?"

"I can't say yet."

"But at least until next summer when Pamela has gone back to England with her parents?" she suggested.

"The arrangements have been changed; she has to leave next week, with her sister." He had not yet been able to speak to his mother of Pamela since the weekend, although he had read the compassion in her face as he had struggled miserably through each day this week. To say anything would be to tell her all, and her pain at the reason for his rejection would be as hurtful to him as his own; but they knew each other so well that there was, after all, no need for detailed explanations.

"I have to get away," he muttered, looking down so she should not see his mouth working.

"It's a good time to make a change," she said.

"I may not make so much money at first as I do here.. there won't be my office wage coming in every month, just what I get from the band." This prospect worried him most, but the wretchedness of the past week weighed more. "I'll send you money as often as I can."

She got up and hugged him. "I shall be all right Danny, don't worry about me. You've always been such a good boy."

He wanted, in the emotion of the moment, to pour out all his unhappiness, but resisted the temptation. Trying to make his voice businesslike, he said "I'll need a passport. I've been to the Passport Office, they want to see my birth certificate. I have to fill in no end of details..I'll show you the form."

His mother picked up her glasses from the top of the piano and adjusted them across her nose as Danny pulled a folded form from his jacket pocket and spread it out on the piano. She studied it carefully, then said "I'll get your certificate for you."

She was away in her bedroom for so long that he eventually tapped on the door and looked in, intending to tell her not to bother looking for the certificate tonight, but the words died on his lips; his mother was on her knees before the crucifix on her bedside table, and she was murmuring prayers in a broken voice. He stood in the doorway for a moment, uncertain what to do, until she turned and called him to come in and sit on the bed.

"God give me strength to tell you this," she said, sitting beside him. "and may God give you strength to accept it. Here is your birth certificate. I have never shown it to you before because, foolishly, I had hoped I could spare you this knowledge: your father and I were never married. He didn't even know you were to be born because he was only in Hong Kong for a short time."

Danny stared at her, shocked and unbelieving; then stared at the yellowing paper. There it was: 'Name of mother, Angela Margarita Bellario, spinster 'Name of father, Frederick John Russell, shipping agent.' There was so much to try to understand at once: his mother unmarried, he a bastard; no wonder he had always felt inferior to his relatives, wearing their outgrown clothes. His thoughts shied away from the realisation that she had committed what seemed to him the gravest of mortal sins.. of course she would have confessed it long since and surely been forgiven, but nothing could take away his illegitimacy.

"Your aunt wanted to take you into her family when you were born," his mother went on, "but how could I bear to let you go from me, even though I knew they would be able to do more for you than I could?"

"No one could do more than you have," he interrupted, giving her a savage hug, "no one, Mumma."

"They were all so kind - never forget that! When they saw how determined I was to keep you myself, it was agreed I would call myself Mrs. Russell, to make things easier for us both. Danny, your father was as handsome as you are; I thought we would be married. Oh, child, I'm so sorry to have had to tell you this, because I love you so much and I hate to see you hurt any more."

"I'm glad I know." His lips were stiff. "I had to know some time. It makes it even more important for me to leave Hong Kong. I shall make a fortune, so that I can give you everything you need to make you comfortable and happy. I'll make up to you for all your hard work, mumma, you see if I don't!"

Feeling somewhat fragile after a succession of Christmas parties, Viola didn't feel at all like work when the office re-opened after Boxing Day. To be summoned to the telephone at 10.00am was therefore a welcome diversion.

The voice on the phone was unfamiliar: "Please excuse me for troubling you; we have not been introduced; my name is Daniel Russell, and I know you are a friend of a friend of mine, Pamela Doran."

"Oh, you're Danny! Don't you want to speak to Pam?"

"Unfortunately I may not, but I should be most grateful if you would kindly give her a message from me."

"Of course I will - fire away."

"Tell her I'm leaving Hong Kong in three weeks' time. I'm joining a band in Manila."

"You mean permanently?"

"Sure. I've resigned my job here."

"Well, jolly good luck to you, Danny, I'll certainly tell Pam."

Viola chose to wait until the end of the afternoon to impart Danny's news. It was just as well, for the tears began to flow again.

"He's so thoughtful," she wept. "He vowed he wouldn't cause me any more trouble with my father - that's why he wouldn't give me his news direct. He's such a fine person, Viola."

"I'm very impressed," admitted Viola. "He will probably do very well in Manila - he might even end up in Hollywood! And" - seizing wildly to divert Pamela from her sorrows - "talking of films, I feel like a laugh. Let's go to the Queen's and see the Danny Kaye film, we can just make the 5.15 pm show if we hurry."

"But.."

"I know," Viola cut in; she rolled her eyes and mimicked Pamela's cautious voice "You've got to ask your parents first! Run along and phone them now: and don't ask them - tell them you're going to the flicks and you'll be late for dinner!"

It was good to hear Pamela laughing at the comic scenes, but as soon as they left the cinema, the misery returned. For once Viola could think of nothing of any comfort as she waved her off on the bus to Happy Valley, but on the way home afterwards, an idea came into her mind. Recognising her weakness for meddling, she resisted it at first, but by the time she reached Courtlands her mind was made up. She dislodged Ah So from his chair by the telephone before unlocking her room door, and dialled Raoul's number.

"Raoul, I'm so glad I caught you at home."

"Are you going to let me take you to the Gloucester tonight?"

"Hardly - I haven't recovered from Christmas yet. Raoul, I've got a little news item for you: exclusive. Aren't I kind?"

"It depends what it is, this news."

"You know Daniel Russell, the violinist - he was playing when we danced at the Roof Garden last week."

"Sure I know him."

"I heard today that he's just thrown up his job with Ropers and is going to join the band in the Philippines."

"So? That doesn't sound like big news to me, but thank you Viola, it will do for my weekly gossip column on Sunday."

"You mightn't be first with it if you delay," she pointed out. "Why don't you call him tomorrow at Ropers and get all the facts first hand: then you could put it in Thursday's paper."

After a short silence Raoul said "O.K. Viola, I'll do that, and maybe some time you will explain to me why you are so anxious that I do.. is Danny perhaps another of your friends?"

"No, but he's a friend of a friend of mine."

"Always you have so many friends," he sighed. "I never knew any one with so many friends as you have. No wonder you are always occupied when I want to take you out."

NEW YEAR'S EVE

Through a haze steadily built up by a succession of whiskies and gins, Roddy tried to focus on the large party at the far end of the ball room. This wasn't easy for other reasons - the place was crowded to capacity this New Year's Eve. The dance floor was barely visible, overflowing with would-be dancers who could only inch their way around. The band could be seen but not heard above the chatter and laughter.

"Is that Hilary over there?" Roddy managed to articulate to Greg.

"It is old boy, it is," nodded Greg.

"Think I'll go and say hello." Roddy slipped off the stool by the bar, but found he could scarcely walk without support.

"Skip it," advised Greg, grabbing his arm. "Stay here and look after me."

"I'll do that, Greg, because you're a real friend." It took Roddy several attempts to resume his perch on the stool. "Hilary doesn't mean anything to me any more, not any more."

"Let's have some sandwiches," urged Greg, seizing a menu. "Too late to order a meal,"

"Not hungry; another whisky, Boy!"

"And sandwiches," added Greg. "We need them, Rod, if we're to keep going tonight."

"P'raps you're right," sighed Roddy,.

After the sandwiches the haze bgan to clear a little. Hilary seemed to be the life and soul of the party at a table with a dozen or so other young people. He recognised several of them as staff of Hilary's firm, but the tall auburn-haired man seated next to her was a stranger to him. Even in the bustle of the occasion and his own shaky state, Roddy could recognise the proprietory manner with which the stranger treated Hilary. She looked splendid in an indigo blue dress which set off her pale gold hair. He could have been sitting beside her tonight, instead of propped up at the bar like an outcast. He started to call for another whisky, then recalled her scathing comments about his drinking; no, while she was around he would not become even more drunk than he already was. For a few moments, he put his head down on the bar and closed his eyes.

Suddenly the loud clanging of a gong cut across all the other noises.

"Ladies and gentlemen!" The words had to be repeated several times before the cacophony lessened. "In a few minutes it will be midnight, so please see that your glasses are fully charged to welcome in nineteen thirty-eight."

Roddy looked up. The speaker was Danny Russell, Pamela's forbidden boyfriend. Very elegant he looked in evening dress. He felt he had quite a lot in common with Danny, if the fellow was as unhappy about the compulsory breakup as Pamela seemed to be.

Danny began to hammer the strokes of the hour on the gong, the audience shouting the numbers as he did so. On the twelfth, balloons cascaded down from the ceiling; streamers snaked round the room, and the dance floor was invaded by tightly-squashed circles of dancers singing Auld Lang Syne. Roddy and Greg joined in, and once Roddy found himself quite near Hilary. She gave him a brilliant smile and mouthed "Happy New Year, Rod", and all the hurt and humility he had felt since their last conversation at Big Wave Bay so many months ago was obliterated. He was forgiven, and this was a new year, and he resolved to reform and control his drinking. Fired with this determination, when he returned to his seat at the bar he rejected his waiting drink and ordered black coffee.

The band was playing a slow waltz now, and Hilary was dancing with Auburn Hair. Roddy gulped down his coffee, hoping to claim the next dance with her, but she and Auburn Hair didn't leave the floor when the waltz ended; they stood together until the music started again, then danced very close together, their arms folded round each other, and Roddy realised that the brilliant smile she had given him had nothing to do with him at all, but everything to do with her auburn-haired partner.

Now, sobriety was no longer mattered. Back to the bar, he downed two double whiskies before Greg's bemused eyes. Staggering to the Gents, a third whisky in his hand, he passed Daniel Russell, who was leaning against a pillar beside the band's rostrum, drink in hand.

"A fellow sufferer," thought Roddy, still conscious of the wound in his heart despite the anaesthetic of alcohol. Daniel nodded politely at him. Roddy stopped, steadying himself against the pillar, and murmured "Jolly rotten, you and Pam having to.. you know. Sorry for you. Sorry for Pam too, she's very cut up. Know what it feels like.. damn sorry for you both.. bloody shame, I call it."

Daniel shrugged his shoulders. "Thank you for saying so," he said gravely. "I sure appreciate that."

"Well here's a happier new year for both of us," said Roddy, draining his glass, "and for jolly old Pam too."

"Is she.. out celebrating?"

"Don't think so. Greg and I invited her to join us, but she wouldn't. Said No to us, and No to honourable parents who've gone to pass the evening with some of their dreary friends; and No to Belle and old Keith. No to everything and everybody. Poor old Pam. Very cut up."

Even in his inebriation, Roddy could recognise the look of pain and desperation in Daniel's face. It was as intolerable to him as his own personal misery, and he turned away and stumbled off to the Gent's.

Pamela stood in her dressing-gown on the bedroom verandah and gazed at the warships in the harbour outlined in lights. Sirens and hooters continued to herald in the New Year. The verandahs of the neighbouring houses were lit, residents shouting good wishes to each other. The distant sounds of private parties, the clatter of dishes and cutlery, guffaws of laughter and snatches of music from gramophone records, reminded her of her personal isolation.

'But you don't have to be alone tonight,' she reminded herself bracingly. She had chosen to see the New Year in alone, nursing her sadness at the loss of Danny, and considering her future. The sharpness of the pain in her heart was slowly easing, but the feeling of emptiness and resignation was difficult to bear. She could find pleasure in nothing - even the happy atmosphere in the office failed to raise her from her melancholy. Nothing seemed worth while, even the simple acts of eating or talking. Perhaps life would always be like that now. Viola, to whom she had voiced these thoughts, had said very firmly "No; everything changes in time."

The telephone bell broke into her thoughts; she hurried downstairs in case the insistent shrilling should wake up Jamie and Lisa.

The caller's voice was guarded and muffled by a background of music and chatter: "Is it possible, please, to speak to Miss Doran?"

"Oh Danny, it's me!"

"O.K. to talk?"

"Yes, everyone's out except the children."

"Happy New Year, Pam! I took a chance on ringing you because Roddy just told me your parents were out. I just wanted to speak to you before you left."

"I'm so glad you did! But I'm not leaving next week after all! My parents are letting me stay until June when they go; they read in the paper about you going to Manila, and changed their minds."

"That's grand news, Pam! How are you making out?"

"I'm.." No more words would come then because of the great sob of yearning which rose in her throat.

"Cheer up" urged Danny. "Go about and enjoy yourself. Don't stay home and mope - I won't. But I'll never forget you, and thank you again for the happy times we had together. Got to go now, I'm on in the next number. Happy, happy New Year, dearest Pam."

Clinging to the sides of the rickshaw which seemed to be plunging about the road like a sampan in a typhoon, Roddy wondered vaguely if he was travelling in the right direction. If he was on his way home to the Y.M.C.A. from the Kowloon ferry terminus, why was the rickshaw bowling along between several-storeyed tenements, with the blurred shapes of street sleepers stretched out on the pavements beneath the verandahs? It was even more puzzling that the rickshaw journey seemed to be going on so long, because the Y.M.C.A. was a very short distance from the ferry. Oh well, the boy would get him home safely. He sank back into happy oblivion until suddenly jerked awake as the rickshaw made a sudden turn. He stared blearily into the darkness. Surely this low building he was now passing was the Civil Service Club in Happy Valley? He peered through the darkness; yes, there were the billowing screens behind the club's tennis courts, and the gleaming lines on the road ahead were tram lines. There were no trams in Kowloon, so he couldn't be there; this must be Happy Valley: he thought he was on his way home to the the Y.M.C.A. in Kowloon in these first hours of 1938 - so what was he doing in Happy Valley?

"Greg!" he called, turning round cautiously because of his aching head. "Greg, where are we?"

The only response was a grunt from the rickshaw coolie, and Roddy then recalled having lost Greg some time after they had left the hotel for Jimmy's Kitchen nearby. The coolie stopped, laid the shafts down on the ground, and asked where to go next. Roddy sat regarding him trying to collect his wandering thoughts. No clear idea emerged, and the coolie harangued him impatiently.

"No savvy," Roddy mumbled, starting to wag his head negatively - a mistake as it caused his head to spin. Then he remembered: he was on his way to Leighton Hill because he had to see Hilary. She would be home by now. Why he had to see her he had forgotten, but see her he must.

"Leighton Hill," he told the coolie, jingling the coins in his pocket.

"Leighton Hill," repeated the coolie, picking up the shafts and jogging on again. The jog gradually became a slow walk as he drew the rickshaw up the drive towards the terrace. At the final curve, he stopped, put down the shafts and muttered "No can."

Roddy felt sorry for the fellow. "You're tired, so I'll pull you, instead of you pulling me," he said in slurred Cantonese as he stumbled out of the rickshaw. The coolie rejected the suggestion with a laugh, standing stolidly at the roadside.

"No ride, no cash," threatened Roddy, and at length the coolie sat himself bolt upright in the seat while Roddy, after several attempts, positioned himself between the shafts and tugged at them. It took him some time to get started, but eventually, with the coolie grunting warnings to take care, he managed to haul the rickshaw up the last twenty yards of the slope. When he reached the terrace he let out a great whoop of triumph.

"Happy New Year, every one," he bellowed. "Happy New Year!"

Now the rickshaw ran easily. Stimulated by his success between the shafts, Roddy kept circling the perimeter of the terrace, carolling and whooping, drowning the anxious protests of the coolie rattling about in the swaying rickshaw.

Lights appeared in the houses. Doors and windows were thrown open. Voices sounded, but still Roddy yelled and pranced round with the rickshaw. His head was spinning, his legs weakening, yet he could not stop - until the voices grew nearer, and a dressing-gowned figure grabbed him by the arm and slapped him violently across the face. As he reeled and dropped in the shafts, faces crowded in on him, but the only one he recognised was his father's, red and contorted. Then he remembered: he'd meant to come and see Hilary to ask her if she had really forgiven him.. and now here he was, in the same drunken state she had so despised before. It was just no good. He was too weary and depressed now to worry about it; too weary even to try and help himself as his father and other dressing-gowned figures were trying to heave him up from the ground. Somehow, some time, he would turn over a new leaf.

PART 4

1938

JUNE

'Last day.. last day..' The words pounded endlessly through Pamela's mind. With the dazed detachment which had been with her throughout the past week, she followed her parents down the slippery steps of the pier on to the little white launch. A procession of her father's European colleagues, in uniform white jackets, shirts and shorts, and long white socks, trooped after her. Ah Tai the Boy, and the Chinese staff of her father's department beamed from the end of the pier as the mooring ropes were released and the engine barked.

The giant fire-cracker displays dangling from the canopy of the pier sprang to life. With spitting explosions, each fired cracker set off the one above it, all reaching a crashing crescendo as the launch backed away from the steps.

"Hard to believe this is the last time we'll hear that racket," her father murmured to her mother. Both looked grossly overdressed for eleven o'clock on a June morning; sweat was already darkening her father's light grey linen suit under the arms and across the back; her mother, duchesslike in a flowing georgette floral dress with cap sleeves, shaded by a wide-brimmed matching straw hat, fanned herself vigorously with a handkerchief. The canvas awning stretched taut across the deck space in the bows tempered the fierceness of the staring sun, yet even Pamela, wearing a sleeveless wide-necked mauve dress, felt the heat until the launch turned and sped across the harbour, creating its own blessed breeze.

"Goodness knows how we're going to get that lot aboard the 'Ranchi'," said her father, looking at the last-minute gifts which had been presented by the Chinese staff on the pier: a pair of huge china vases barely disguised by their wrapping paper; rattan carriers containing fruit; swathes of brightly coloured artificial flowers; a silver junk balanced precariously on a blackwood plinth within an oblong glass case; and an enormous framed photograph of the entire staff of her father's department.

The cross-talk and banter on the launch was so superficial that Pamela was not required to respond to any of the friendly remarks tossed to her, which was just as well since little of what was said was registering. The voices seemed to be at a great distance, a background to the only thought her mind would allow: "This is the last day.." - the last day of the countdown which had dominated life in the preceding fortnight. She had attended at Government House for the presentation of her father's retirement accolade - the O.B.E.; a succession of Chinese chows at garish exotic restaurants; dinner parties in private houses of her parents' friends. At home there had been daily deliveries of magnificent presents.

'More cloisonné vases, Adam!'

'Not another table cloth - that makes six!'

'One more camphorwood chest - that means ordering another packing case.'

The harbour had never looked more entrancing, the sun making diamond glints on the water. How she loved this place to which she had so reluctantly returned! With fierce determination, she repeated to herself the chosen mantra which excluded all other thoughts: 'Last day.. last day.'

Now the launch was nearing the bulbous black stern of the P. & O. alongside Kowloon Wharf; the white lettering 'Ranchi - London' reminded her that in four weeks' time the ship would be back in England, and... she tightened her grip on her white handbag and forced her mind back to the life-saving words, adding to them 'only two more hours.'

Now they were all on the wharf, picking their way across the crane rails towards the ship. Now they were aboard, Pamela and her parents inspecting the cabin where the advance luggage had already been stowed. Coolies trooped in with the hand luggage and unwieldy presents and dumped them on the floor.

"First class, eh Hen?" pronounced her father with great satisfaction, then exploded into laughter because that was exactly what the cabin was, his final promotion having earned him this privilege. The unfamiliar surroundings of this sumptuous accommodation added to Pamela's strange view of the occasion; surely she would wake up and find life normal again?

Now they were in the smoking saloon - a continually expanding group as more and more colleagues arrived to say goodbye. On her father's orders, the tables were kept supplied with long cold beers for all comers. Everyone seemed to be talking at once. Kindly faces mouthed remarks at Pamela, remarks she couldn't hear. She nodded smilingly, struggling with the beer she didn't like because it was impossible in all the confusion to ask for something more to her taste. The laughter grew more riotous, the conversations more staccato, and the air cloudier with smoke.

At half past eleven a great gong reverberated from the deck outside, followed by the call 'All visitors ashore!"

('Only half an hour more,' chanted Pamela's inward voice.)

Now the voices were reaching crescendo; glasses were rapidly drained, chairs scraped back, hands shaken, and the visitors making slow but inexorable progress towards the deck. Here, at last, was Roddy, turning up late as usual. He shook hands in his best manner with every one he passed as he squeezed through the throng to his parents.

"You live nearest the wharf and you're the last to arrive," his father reproved, but without the customary rancour.

"I knew I wouldn't be able to get near you for 'ho pang yaus' if I'd come any earlier." He leaned over the back of his mother's chair and gave her a hug. "Am I too late for a drink?"

His father pushed forward a wilting beer.

"Here's to the best of futures for us all," said Roddy, holding his glass high, then draining it in one long devoted guzzle .

"Pam dear" - Her mother was able to move over to her now that most of the visitors were shuffling down the gangway like a chain gang. "I do hope we're doing the right thing, and you'll be happy." The warning gong sounded again and drowned her next words; she was still agonising when audible again. "All this unrest in the world.. if only things were calm and secure, as they used to be, it wouldn't be so worrying."

They were out on the deck now, Roddy purposefully leading the way to the gangway. Pamela's heart was thudding painfully. Her mother clutched her with one hand and Roddy with the other. "I've a very heavy heart, leaving you two behind." Her voice was thick and tears streaked down her face. "Take care of yourselves, and look after each other."

"We will, we will," sang Roddy. "Letters Home by every P. & O. and all that! Cheer up, Mum, it's not forever! Pam'll be Home next year, and me in 1941."

Pamela turned to her father and received his unusually warm embrace. "Not quite what we had in mind when we brought you out last year, leaving you behind," he mumbled, his speech slurred by a plethora of morning drinks. "We'll miss you, you know, but if this is what you want to do, you deserve to have a shot at it. Been very pleased with the way you've behaved this year."

As she followed Roddy down the gangway, an exultant 'Now!" echoed through Pamela's brain.

Now that the gangways were drawn in to the ship: now that she and Roddy stood side by side on the wharf, staring upwards at the figures on the promenade deck, holding the coloured streamers thrown to them: now that the 'Ranchi's' deep-throated siren heralded her departure, and the great brown ropes were unleashed from the bollards on the wharf and hauled through the widening gap of green water, only now could she allow herself to believe this was all really happening.

"Goodbye, goodbye, God bless!" called her mother, crying still. Pamela called back, surprised to find her mouth wobbling.

Now the ship was backing slowly into the harbour, turning imperceptibly until she was facing the lane which would take her towards Lye Mun Pass and the China Sea. For some minutes she sat motionless in the water, a majestic black and fawn outline against the panorama of Hong Kong's green hills; then, with another grunt from her siren, she slid swiftly towards the Pass.

Now the figures on board were no longer decipherable: now they were beyond recall: now, at last, Pamela was free.

From the day three months earlier when Belle's letter had arrived with the astonishing suggestion, Pamela had never allowed herself to regard it as any more than a dreamlike possibility.

'Keith isn't being posted to Singapore after all,' Belle had written, "It's Hong Kong again! We're leaving England in September and the firm has already booked a flat for us in Macdonnell Road. Keith and I have a bright idea: it seems such a shame for Pam to leave Hong Kong when you go now she's so settled in her job, so why not let her stay on a bit longer? She can lodge with us, our flat is only a stone's throw from her office. Then she could sail Home next year, still before her 21st so she'd still qualify for her free passage."

At first her parents had not taken the proposal seriously. It was only when Pamela told her friends of the delicious possibility that they had to think again.

"Tell them how much you want that extra year," Viola ordered firmly. "Waste of time moaning to me about it: tell THEM!"

She did, but was met with counter arguments. It was the approval of Hilary's parents that did the trick; they had pointed out the advantages of leaving Pamela in Hong Kong while the Dorans hunted for their dream retirement house in Suffolk; they had also insisted that Pamela should stay with them in the gap between her parents' departure and Belle's return.

Her father was not easily persuaded, but eventually gave grudging consent. "Got to behave yourself, though," he warned. "Not the same as living at home, is living in lodgings. And no nonsense.. nothing like that business with the Russell boy."

Her passage on the 'Ranchi' had been cancelled, but her father continued to voice his unease from time to time, and she was quite sure he was capable of reversing his decision at the last moment. As the remaining months dwindled to weeks and then days, she had to balance the exhilarating prospect of staying in Hong Kong for another year with carefully avoiding giving her father any cause to change his mind. Her nerves suffered and so did her work. "There's only one way to play this," Viola had told her. "Concentrate on the present; don't think at all about the future until that ship clears Lye Mun."

And it was actually happening!

"Now for a taste of independence, eh Pam?" grinned Roddy as they straggled along the wharf to the dock gate.

"I still can't believe they're letting me do this!" Pamela felt light-headed, "I can't think why they did."

"Comes of being such a good child - such a contrast to me, they just had to give you a prize as a lesson to me."

"Oh come on!" She was embarrassed, though it was true that Roddy had been out of favour all this year because of the scene at Leighton Hill on New Year's Eve and because of his refusal to return to live at home on the departure of Belle and family for England in January.

"True!" Roddy insisted. "Anyway, now you can start indulging all your vices - you surely don't really like lemonade and ice-cream sodas, do you?"

"I'm afraid I do - I've tried gin slings and Pimms and things, but I just don't like them."

"Ah me, I didn't know such girls existed; you'll tell me next that you haven't started to smoke yet"'

"Tried it.. makes me feel grown up, but I'm not keen on it."

"You'll make someone an inexpensive wife one day." He pulled a packet of Players out of the breast pocket of his shirt, a lighter from his shorts and stopped to light a cigarette.

"Rod," called Hilary's mother, catching them up, "Would you care to come home and have tiffin with us today?" If Mrs. Bately was aware of last year's emotional turmoil between Hilary and Roddy, her manner made it apparent that she regarded it as ancient history.

"Thanks, Mrs. Bately, but I'm meeting Greg - giving him a curry tiffin at the Y. Nice of you to ask me, though."

"Come over and see Pam any time you like," she nodded. "She might get a bit lonely: Hilary's out so much these days; since she became engaged we hardly ever see her."

AUGUST

Jardine's gun fired its noon salvo. At once Hilary whisked the cover over her typewriter, grabbed her handbag and skittered along the corridor to the lift. Fanning herself with her hand as she emerged from its press of humanity, she pushed on her sunglasses and stepped out into the searing July heat. Voices of colleagues called after her.

"Must dash - can't wait," she threw over her shoulder. "Got to get my hair done before the Wilson wedding this aftenoon."

She hailed a rickshaw from the orderly line at the edge of the waterfront, and sank back thankfully beneath the raised green hood. As the coolie picked up the shafts and jogged steadily between hooting taxis and cars she saw the 'Corfu' backing out of Kowloon Wharf, homeward bound. She gave a fleeting thought to last year's journey, contrasting her unattached status then to the security of her present position as the fianceé of a young bank official whose future was committed to the Far East. She splayed out the fingers of her left hand and gazed lovingly at Ian's magnificent ring with its three diamonds.

The indulgence of the 3-minute ride to the Women's International Club where she was to have a snack was well worth the ten cents it cost; even walking slowly for five minutes in this heat created a lather of perspiration.

The club, which occupied a suite of rooms on the first floor of the Gloucester Hotel building, offered modest meals in an unpretentious restaurant; changing facilities and economic dormitory accommodation for working women. The restaurant was fairly crowded when she went in. Hilary slid into a chair at the first table she found empty and ordered coffee and a club sandwich. She was halfway through her meal when Pamela came in with Viola. To Hilary, they still seemed an unlikely pair of friends: Viola so sophisticated and Hong Kong-minded, with an endless supply of casual boy-friends; Pamela still gauche and immature, tending to keep to familiar groups, and content to spend several evenings a week at home.

"Sit here," invited Hilary. "I haven't time to finish this, I'm off to the hairdresser. What are you up to this afternoon, Pam?"

"It's our painting lesson at 3 o'clock," Pamela smiled happily, and Hilary remembered the Chinese painting class Pamela and Viola had recently joined.

"And you won't believe what we've decided to do after tiffin until it's time for our lesson," Pamela went on with a giggle. "What you and I always meant to do on the 'Corfu' last year but never did - practise shorthand."

"Good heavens, why ever? Aren't you both doing enough shorthand at work?"

"Anxious to improve ourselves," smiled Viola. "We're still career girls, Pam and I.. not like you bespoken woman, Hilary.. I love your ring, let me look closer."

Hilary held out her left hand; with her right she scrawled her signature on the meal chit, then picked up her possessions and rushed away.

The hairdresser's was in a side street just off the main road outside the hotel. It was below ground level, a-whirr with madly-spinning ceiling fans, and teeming with customers and assistants. The fans rendered the atmosphere just bearable until it was time to be imprisoned beneath the electric dryer, when perspiration dripped down her forehead, face, neck and arms. At the same time a very young Chinese girl assistant sat on a low stool beside her and manicured Hilary's fingernails. ("Ai yah," she sighed at the sight of the engagement ring.)

Free at last from the drier, she critically regarded her pink face in the mirror, wondering if the crimped waves made her look too formal. Yet the Wilson wedding was a formal occasion - the first she and Ian were to attend as an engaged couple; the bride was the daughter of Ian's boss at the Bank, the groom an Army Captain, so she knew she would be under scrutiny as a prospective Bank wife.

In the taxi home, she glanced at the headlines of the mid-day China Mail she had just bought. Hitler was ranting at Czechoslovakia again, complaining about the lot of the Germans in Sudetenland; Japanese troops were moving further south in China, causing more and more refugees to flee before them: disquietening news, but none of it seemed relevant to Hong Kong this bright Saturday afternoon; in any case, Ian maintained that Hitler knew he would never get away with an attack on Czechoslovakia as he had earlier in the year in Austria, for Britain was morally though not by treaty bound to protect Czechoslovakia - and the last thing Hitler wanted was war with Britain and France.

Ian was so positive about everything: this was one of the qualities about him which had first attracted her. How lucky she was to have met and fallen in love with him, and how lucky to be loved in return by such a fantastic person! There were times when she wondered how she could bear to wait two years before being married - Ian's Bank stipulated no marriage for its employees until they reached the age of 25 - but mainly life was so enjoyable with fiancée status, with both of them saving industriously towards furnishing a future flat on the Peak (in between splurges of instant extravagance) and collecting items for her bottom drawer.

'Gin sling, Boy," she called as soon as she reached home and flopped into the nearest chair. Her mother looked up from the book she was reading and remarked 'Oh, they've done your hair nicely."

"Do you think so? It's gone up so short. I wish I didn't have to wear a hat, there won't be any hair showing."

"It's not as short as all that," laughed her mother. "You must wear a hat - every other female will."

At Ian's side in the Cathedral an hour later, she saw that her mother was right Every one wore garden party clothes. There was a strong military presence in immaculate dress unifom. After the service, when the bells were pealing, bride and groom were borne away in a Rolls Royce drawn by groups of soldiers pullling on thick scarlet ropes - a spectacle watched in utter amazement by Chinese pedestrians who rarely saw white folk doing subservient manual tasks.

The magnificent reception in the Hong Kong Hotel lasted until 5 o'clock, by which time Hilary had been introduced to so many of Ian's colleages and their wives, and imbibed so much champagne, that her mind was in a whirl, and she hung tightly on to Ian's arm as they said their goodbyes.

"You didn't eat enough," Ian reproved. "Tell you what, let's go the Roof Garden and have some tea; afterwards we can dance. You look far too glamorous in that outfit to rush home and put it away."

That was another of Ian's delightful characteristics - sudden resolves, always interesting ones! The tea dance at the Roof Garden was already in progress when they arrived. A three-piece band played soft, unobtrusive music, and several couples drifted lazily round the small dance floor.

"Take that hat off," Ian commanded as they sat down and awaited their tea and toast. "I like to see more of your hair. Ah, that's better" - as she put the frothy hat on the table and shook her head to loosen her hair. "That's more like my girl! But don't get me wrong, you looked just perfect at the wedding; I'm sure you impressed J.B. no end. I was very proud of you."

He was so forthright, and said exactly what he thought; what had she done to deserve such good fortune?

Later, when they were dancing, she was aware of how well they looked together, catching sight of their reflection in the large mirror at one end of the room. He was a head taller than she; his white sharkskin suit outlined his well-built body. It was bliss to dance with him; he held her gently, his left hand curled lightly over her right. He didn't press her back as Roddy used to, nor did he progress round the floor in great swoops as did Douglas. She felt very cherished in his arms, content and happy too as he drove her home in his open-topped MG, the rushing air making havoc of her new waves.

She could only bear to part with him because they would be meeting that evening for a swimming picnic.

She asked the Boy to bring her slippers as he let her into the house.

"Have a good time?" her mother called from the verandah which had been converted into a temporary shop by Linen Boy who called regularly. His wares were spread out on the floor on a sheet of unbleached calico in which, twisted over his shoulder, he carried them from house to house.

"Lovely! We had tea at the Roof Garden afterwards." Hilary eased her feet out of her high-heeled shoes and into her slippers, gazing longingly at the embroidered linen napery and silk underwear. While her mother bargained over an elaborately cross-stitched table-cloth, Hilary fingered a night-gown of palest green, its shoulder straps and neck rich with open work embroidery. Linen Boy wanted $6 for it but eventually settled for $4, sighing it was "too muchee cheap" as he handed it to her, but there was a smile on his face as he refolded and packed his goods and departed.

"Pam home yet?" yawned Hilary, stretching out luxuriously in the chair.

"Yes, she came in about an hour ago. She's in her room. I called up and told her Linen Boy was here, but she wasn't interested."

"Tell me what does interest her," grunted Hilary.

"She's very interested in her job and that painting." Her mother's voice was faintly reproachful.

"But that's about all! Normal things don't seem to appeal to her. I'm not even sure if I've persuaded her to come swimming with us tonight."

"She's old enough to please herself," shrugged her mother.

Hilary told herself as she went upstairs that two months of Pamela as a paying-guest was enough. Though always content to listen she had little conversation. She refused most of Hilary's invitations - to the cinema, to make up a foursome at a dinner dance, or to the beach. Now Hilary had become impatient at these inevitable refusals: felt guilty leaving her at home night after night, yet irritated when Pamela was persuaded to come along because she contributed so little to the occasion. She shook herself mentally outside Pamela's room: secure in her love for Ian, she could surely afford to be charitable - the poor girl was very much on her own, with her parents gone and no close boy-friend. "Came I come in?" she called through the open door. "Got something to show you."

Pamela was sitting on the verandah at a small table, frowning over a painting of a bent twig.

"Don't know how you can keep working in this heat," Hilary said, "especially as you've been at it all the afternoon. "That's why." Pamela laid down her brush and sat back. "I like to work directly after the lesson while it's still fresh in my mind. Oh, is that a new nightie?"

"Linen Boy came down to $4.. I couldn't resist it."

"For your bottom drawer?"

"Of course."

"How was the wedding?"

"Like all weddings: crowds there; every one boiling in their best bibs and tuckers. All the men at the reception kept saying it will be Ian's and my turn next at the altar, and most of the women wanted to know if I've handed in our wedding present list to Lane Crawford's yet - can you imagine, with our wedding nearly two years away!"

"Embarrassing," nodded Pamela. "A funny idea, I think, giving a shop a list. I never heard of that in England; it's like asking for things."

"It's just plain sense; saves duplication of presents; who wants six toasters? Anyway, how did your afternoon go?"

"Doesn't sound exciting compared with yours!" Pamela gave her such a friendly grin that Hilary felt ashamed of her recent criticism. "I always love the painting classes. We got on well with our shorthand, Viola did one piece at 140, and I managed 120."

"You're putting us all to shame. I only ever managed 80 at shorthand school.. and I hardly ever do any at work now; my boss prefers to write out his drafts in his ghastly handwriting for me to type, says he gets better transcripts that way than via my shorthand! But why are you doing this, Pam? I know Viola's ambitious and wants a high-powered job somewhere else: you too?"

"No, I'm very content where I am, thank you! But it's sort of challenging to try and increase my speed, and it helps Viola."

"Oh well, it takes all sorts, I suppose.." shrugged Hilary with a laugh. "Now I've simply got to have a zizz before dinner if I'm to be any good for the swimming party tonight; you will come this time, won't you?"

"I'd like to, it's so hot, but.. do I know any of the other people, apart from you and Ian?"

"Of course you do: Hugh, he's bringing his new girlfriend Wanda someone, I haven't met her yet; and Josie from your office, it's her parents' matshed we're being allowed to use this evening. You probably don't know the other two lads, colleagues of Ian's, but I only met them this afternoon for the first time so they're practically strangers to me too."

"It doesn't seem fair, me sort of hanging on to you, just because I'm a lodger here."

"Nonsense! You'll come, then?" Watching Pamela struggling to find another excuse, she went on "You know what, you're slipping right back to the way you were when we left Tilbury last year.... downright anti-social and positively scared of men! If you're not careful you'll be like this for the rest of your life - and what sort of prospect is that?"

"You mean you think I'll never get another boy-friend?"

"Maybe! Don't you see, you don't have to regard every man you meet and go out with as a potential suitor - nothing has to be that serious. Oh, I know you had a tough time over Danny, but can't you try to be a little light-hearted about the opposite sex? Look on them as brothers, if you like.. or on an here-today-gone-tomorow basis. You make me feel positively mean every time I waltz off for a date with Ian, thinking of you here with just my parents for company - if they're in - so how's about giving me a break from guilt and coming along tonight.. please?"

They climbed out of the three cars parked beneath the avenue of Flame of the Forest trees above Repulse Bay beach, and meandered towards the line of flimsy rattan matsheds above the curve of the bay. Hugh carried an unwieldy portable gramophone, Ian a box of tinned beer, and the others had picnic baskets with food and swimming gear.

Hilary was relieved to see Pamela chatting amiably on the beach with the two new young Bank men; this meant she could cease feeling responsible for her, and abandon herself to the delights of the evening.

And what delights! Surely Heaven could be no better than this.. plunging into the balmy sea, lying stretched out on the warm sand afterwards, then into the sea again? Was there any sight more beautiful than the indigo sky pricked with stars and crowned with a full moon sending a shimmering path across the silken sea?

When a race to the raft moored in the bay was suggested, Hilary was too tired to join in. "You go," she urged Ian. "I'll drift back to shore and get the kettle on for coffee."

With a smart salute of obedience, Ian plunged after the others, but Hilary had scarcely filled the kettle and plugged it in than he suddenly appeared.

"They were all too far ahead of me," he explained, "so I decided to come and help you instead," but a moment later he abandoned pretence and hungrily enclosed her in his arms and muttered into her hair "Don't often get you to myself like this."

Hilary shivered with a mixture of delight and embarrassment: they had always both been fully dressed before when hugging and kissing; now his bare chest pressed against her thin swimsuit, and unmentionable parts of his lower body were hard against hers. His behaviour towards her had always been above reproach; she had not thought herself capable of provoking such wanton thoughts as he was now whispering in her ear.

"You don't know what you do to me, standing there in the moonlight in your swimsuit," Ian was breathing. "You drove me to distraction this afternoon... you looked so adorable in the church, and now.. how in God's name can I wait for two whole years to marry you?.. Oh hell, I can hear the others coming in!"

Later, as they all sat on the beach drinking coffee and beer and munching sandwiches, Hilary's mind kept returning to that brief sensual interlude. For some inexplicable reason, it troubled her a little. She remembered it still when, the snack finished, they lounged on the beach chatting, against a background of music from the gramophone. The conversation covered every subject, from the afternoon's wedding to the sinister threats to world peace.

"No need to worry," Ian insisted. "Intimidation just won't work this time and Hitler knows it. He'll climb down if we stand firm, as we must."

He looked his familiar confident self, his bare shoulders gleaming in the moonlight, the brightness of his bronze hair paled; he seemed a completely different person from the trembling suitor in the matshed kitchen an hour earlier.

They swam again later, lazily revelling in the calm, treacly water, then threw themselves on the sand once more to dry. The faint music from the nearby hotel had stopped. Only the swish of the occasional car along the coast road, and the sound of the sea lapping the sand like the rustlings of tinsel disturbed their solitude.

Ian had his arms round Hilary; Wanda and Hugh, the gramophone forgotten, were locked in close embrace; a little apart, Josie, Pamela and the other two men engaged in desultory conversation. One of the men moved nearer to Josie; the other young man and Pamela sat primly side by side, she throwing pebbles on to the sand as she hugged her knees and earnestly propounded the pro's and con's of whether to join the A.R.P. or one of the nursing services.. "because it seems only right to be ready to do something to help.. just in case. My friend Viola says..."

Overhearing, Hilary and Ian exchanged tiny grins and turned to each other for a hug of happiness.

"Two years," Ian whispered, smothering her with kisses. Hilary wondered what it felt like to be unengaged and uncommitted, like Josie and Pamela, with no settled future, no certainty of the right person telephoning you every day, calling for you in the car; however had she managed to live all those years without Ian at hand?

SEPTEMBER

Although he'd jumped at the offer of transferring from the Secretariat on the island to the Hawker Licensing Office in Kowloon three months ago, Roddy found there was one drawback, that of working in an office which was open to the public, which made him instantly accessible to the shroffs who sought out their employers' debtors at the beginning of every month.

This Saturday morning in September was one such occasion. By the side of his blotter, near enough to be slipped quickly out of sight if his senior officer appeared unexpectedly, was his list of debts compiled from the previous month's accounts which had been arriving during the last few days, accounts which enclosed an alarmingly large number of flimsy chits with his signature scribbled across them: from the Peninsula Hotel, the Hong Kong and the Gloucester; from the Parisienne Grill, Jimmy's Kitchen, the garage which kept his old car going, and Wong Lee his tailor.

It was this last account that gave the coup de grâce to his always precarious financial standing. All the time he had been living at home, his mother had supplemented his clothing expenses; he had forgotten how much summer jackets and shorts cost when he'd ordered a set at the start of the summer. His month's salary was halved the moment he received it, because his board and lodging at the Y.M.C.A. had to be paid in advance on pain of eviction. Both the garage and his tailor ran tiny family businesses and should morally be paid in full, but he had no such scruples about the hotels; his usual method of dealing with the latter bills was to divide his remaining money between them, scaling down each bill accordingly. Frowning at his calculations, he realised he would have to disregard the hotel bills completely this month.

It had been easy to evade the shroffs in the Secretariat, where they were not allowed in the private offices; then they had been obliged to watch outside the main building at the beginning and end of office hours, but were often thwarted by an early warning system triggered off by the first victim, which resulted in other debtors using unorthodox exits, or astonishing their superiors by offering to work late. No such escape was possible now.

Here was the suave shroff from the Hong Kong Hotel sidling round the public counter, holding Roddy with his eyes as he approached, denying evasion. "Good morning, Mr. Doran, sir. You well today?"

How could he feel well, with debts far in excess of his monthly salary!

"Maybe you forget pay bill last moon?"

"Did I?" He feigned surprise.

"More better pay few dollar now, few dollar next moon." The shroff extracted a well-thumbed note-book from an inside pocket of his grey jacket. "How much you pay now, Mr. Doran, please?"

" 'Fraid I'm a bit short again. I wasn't going to pay any, but just to make your visit worth while, I'll make it two dollars."

"Ah Mr, Doran, so little!" He beat the air with his thin hand, as if wiping out all memory of the paltry sum offered. "So big bill.. suppose pay ten dollar, chief say O.K., sign chits this moon; suppose not pay ten dollar, no more chits. So sorry."

With the greatest reluctance, Roddy had to pay up.

There was still half an hour to go before the office closed for the weekend - still time for other shroffs to appear with similar demands. He tried to attend to his work but his eyes kept flickering across to the counter. It was a relief when he was summoned to the telephone, which was in the inner office.

The caller was a friend at the Secretariat inviting him to make up a foursome at the Hong Kong Hotel that evening. Glibly, Roddy invented a previous commitment; he dared not add to his bill there so early in the month.

A further phone call followed, with a plea for him to even up the numbers at a party in the Peninsula Hotel that night. Again he fabricated an excuse, miserably conscious of the two Chinese clerks sitting nearby busy with their abacuses, their eyes sometimes flicking in his direction; he was under no illusions that they understood the situation.

By the time he returned to his desk it was noon, and he rapidly locked his drawers.

"Ah Mr. Doran, so pleased to see you." A long-gowned figure in blue-grey beamed across the counter, obviously having been lurking out of sight awaiting his return. This was the shroff from the Peninsula Hotel. Roddy's heart sank.

"Sorry Lai." He tucked a packet of cigarettes into his shirt pocket and strode across to the clothes stand to get his white jacket. "Too late for business now, I'm just leaving. You should have come earlier."

"I wait long time, Mr. Doran. Please you pay twelve dollar. O.K.?"

"Twelve dollars! You're joking.. my bill's not much more than that!"

"Account twenty-three dollar twentyfive cent. Last month not pay much money. Please you pay little today.. pay eight dollar, then can sign chits this month. If no pay, must write letter to office."

Sick with disappointment, Roddy pulled out his wallet and counted out eight dollars; the threat of no further credit was bad enough: even worse, the risk of his impecunious position being reported to the Government with catastrophic results.

To add to his gloom, he had to walk home because his car was in the garage under repair. His route took him through busy streets; along crowded pavements where, despite the overhead cover from the projection of the flats above the shops, the heat was relentless. Coolies, stripped to the waist, were propped up against the stone pillars, blissfully drawing on cheap malodorous cigarettes; unofficial hawkers were cooking lurid-coloured food on primitive charcoal apparatus, and selling portions on broad green leaves to squatting customers. His damp shirt clung to his skin; if his car was ready for collection, he decided to drive to Lai Chi Kok and wallow in the balmy sea and try to forget his troubles for a while. His spirits rose when he reached the garage and saw his car parked outside. Joyfully he leapt over the door and settled himself in the driving seat, then paid his August bill in full.

"T'ank you very muchee." Wai Kee hesitated as he pocketed the money, then added "Can pay leetle more, Master?"

"More? But I just paid the whole bill!"

"My changee wheel, old one no good. Very dear.. I buy new wheel yes'day."

"So it belongs on this month's bill, not last month's.." Even as he argued, Roddy could see Wai Kee's difficulty. With shaking hands, he paid over two precious dollars on account.

Wholly pre-occupied now with his financial affairs, he had little stomach for tiffin; he could not even summon enough mental energy to drive to the beach. Friendly fellow lodgers jollied him along to the recreation room to play billiards, and for half an hour the cut and thrust of the game aroused his interest; then his worries crowded in on him again. He went to his room, stripped off his shirt and sat at the dressing-table then pulled out from the top drawer the jumble of bills he had been tossing into it as they arrived. From his shorts pocket he drew out the list of proposed payments he had compiled in the office and tried to concentrate. The revolving fan on the chest of drawers gave only a few seconds' relief each time it swivelled past his sweating body. Papers stuck to his bare arms. Through the wide open window floated the sounds of slip-slops, Chinese voices; taxi horns and rickshaw coolies' warning shouts to pedestrians in their way. He could see across the road the terminus of the Kowloon to Canton Railway where a train was filling up with passengers. The half blue, half black funnel of a passenger ship at the wharf beyond showed above the shunting sheds. Across the harbour, a brassy sunshine illuminated the green mountains and the grey buildings huddled round its lower slopes.

Soaked in perspiration, lethargic with the lowering humidity, he faced his predicament. Living away from home for 9 months had given him independence, but at a price. He was ruined financially. The Y.W.C.A. charges were modest, but his parents had charged him immeasurably less, with hidden benefits such as toiletries and laundry. Now every drink had to be paid for - no more dipping into the family supplies of beer and minerals from the ice-box. He calculated that he owed nearly four months' salary. Appalled, he slumped forward on to the dressing-table, his head in his hands.

What he desperately needed was a new life. It was no good carrying on living unless he could see a way out of his present impasse. He needed help. He would ring Greg. Greg would help somehow, even if only by cheering him up.

He padded downstairs in his slip-slops to the public telephone on the reception counter. Greg was not at his lodgings; his landlady, a friendly Portuguese widow who was happy to chat, told him Greg was spending the weekend with some new friends in the New Territories - the Chesters.

Roddy had already heard about this family; Professor Chester had been at school with Greg's father and had recently been appointed to Hong Kong University; he and his wife and children had just moved into an old rambling bungalow in the New Territories, a bungalow which Roddy and Greg had often passed on one of their favourite hikes over the hills to Bride's Pool at Tai Po.

When he could get the landlady off the phone, he dialled the telephone exchange for the Chesters' number and eventually contacted Greg.

"I'm in a hell of a spot." He had to speak guardedly for two of the English officials of the Y.M.C.A. loitered.

"Didn't realise you'd be out of town this weekend: I need to see you."

Greg said he'd be back early on Monday morning; they could have tiffin together that day. Only able to hint at his problem in such a public area, Roddy resisted all Greg's attempts to terminate the call. His halting speech, half-finished sentences and despairing voice evidently at last conveyed his state of mind to Greg, who asked "Is it money?"

"Yep." He could hardly articulate.

"Come out to Fan Ling early tomorrow morning and we take a stroll to Bride's Pool, but it will have to be very early because my hosts have plans for the day: can you be at Fan Ling Station by 9.30am?"

"On the dot," Roddy gulped, looking at his watch: it was half past five; somehow he had to live with his miseries for another seventeen hours.

He had no heart to do anything but go upstairs, throw himself across his bed, and stare at the ceiling.

Soon after he was called to the telephone. "Listen Rodders," boomed Douglas, "I've just been told you can't join us tonight at the Pen. Well, you've damn well got to - we can't have one wench too many. Can't you cancel whatever else you're committed to?"

Roddy had already forgotten what excuse he'd given Douglas' friend earlier that day. In his utter dejection it was easier to tell the truth. "I can't go out tonight. Can't afford it."

"Who can?" roared Douglas. "Look, I'll stand you tonight - it's my party and I don't want to be responsible for two biddies.. want to concentrate on the one I'm taking along. O.K.?"

He didn't protest too much: an evening out was just the thing to take his mind off his anxieties. He shovelled the bills back into the drawer, called along the corridor for the Boy to run a bath, and quickly assembled his new cream linen suit.

It turned out to be an excellent evening. The girls were extrovert and good dancers; Douglas was generous with the drinks, too generous: the short walk home was amazingly difficult to negotiate: he seemed to recall falling into a rickshaw and being tipped out at the Y.M.C.A. entrance.

He was awakened the next morning by the whistle of the train to Canton as it shunted out of the station. He opened his eyes to look at his watch: ten minutes to ten - almost half an hour after the time he'd arranged to meet Greg at Fan Ling. He stumbled out of bed, holding his throbbing head, and fell over the alarm clock which he now remembered setting: he had a vague memory of knocking it on to the floor when he turned off the bell at 7.

There was no time for the shower he needed, a quick wash had to do, and a hurried drink of iced water begged from the Floor Boy for his bird-cage mouth. By 10.15 he was easing himself into the hot car seat and pushing on his sunglasses.

Fortunately, there was little traffic once he reached the outskirts of Kowloon. Despite the nagging knowledge of his lateness, his spirits gradually rose. He felt the tranquillity of the tiny villages he passed: ramshackle homes clinging higgledy-piggledy to the foothills; modest cottages with tiled roofs turned up at the eaves. He grinned at cheerful Chinese peasants shooing ducks towards a pond, others squatting beside a small rice grinder, slowly winding the handle. A small Chinese girl smiled shyly as she drove sway-backed pigs away from the road.

The mountain head of Tai Mo Shan reared 3,000 feet on the left, and more distant hills loomed ahead. On the right were the drowned valleys and long fiords beyond which gleamed the coves and channels which led to the China Sea.

On either side of the road, men and women in dark cotton clothes and broad sun hats were busy in the pale green ricefields, some leading slow-footed buffalo pulling primitive ploughs through the flooded lines. Roddy knew about the poverty of the peasants, but even though they had to work on Sundays he envied them their lot and their kinship with the soil, they could not possibly suffer the complications and miseries of his life.

Now the road became straight, lined with gum trees. For quite a distance he could push the car up to its limit. Hills and mountains encircled him; soon he would be clambering up them with Greg, breathing clean, fresh air, with Greg finding a solution to his problems.

"... over the hills and far away," he sang lustily as he breezed along.

Of course Greg was no longer at the railway station, so Roddy drove slowly down the drive leading to the Chesters' bungalow. It was built of stone, surrounded with barracklike wooden verandahs. In a roughly fenced garden enclosing the building, a wild game of football was in progress, the players all children, some European, some Chinese.

A voice called from the verandah "Hullo there!" A small frail woman appeared on the top step and waved. "Good morning! Are you Rod? Looking for Greg?"

"Yes and yes," he called back, vaulting out of the car and running up the wooden steps. "Good morning to you; it's Mrs. Chester, isn't it?"

"That's right; so glad you got here. Greg said you might call in if he missed you at the station." She had short, sandy-coloured curly hair and freckles. "He said he'd wait at the station until ten, and if you hadn't come then he'd set off for Bride's Pool. He suggested you drive that way as far as you can and catch him up. When you've had your walk, you can both drive back here in time for lunch or tiffin, or whatever you call it here in Hong Kong."

"Oh really... I don't want to barge in on your arrangements.."

"You're not: we're delighted to meet as many people as come our way, living out in the wilds. My husband has just gone off to collect some neighbours to come to tiffin."

"O.K. then, and thanks very much," Roddy turned to leave but a small girl ran up and took his arm. "Are you another uncle?" she asked.

"I suppose I am," he smiled.

"Come and play football with us!" A plump hot-faced blond boy was tugging at Roddy's shorts. "We're one less on my side, come on!"

"Not now John," said Mrs. Chester, shooing the children away. "Uncle Roddy has come to see Uncle Greg."

As he reversed the car along the drive, he calculated that Greg would by now have reached the ridge where the path into the hills grew too steep and boulder-strewn for motor traffic. Even this track towards the ridge was bumpy and narrow. The engine snarled and the chassis shook and groaned. Once he had to brake suddenly when three Chinese youths ran towards him down the path. His engine cut out and took much coaxing before it would re-start.

When he reached the ridge, Greg was nowhere in sight. Roddy hulloed through cupped hands, waved his arms like windmills and stared up at the steep hillside, scanning the tiny scars among the bushes which picked out the path. He could see no movement at all. He strode back to the car and pummelled the horn so that a peal of raucous laughter echoed round the hills.

Bride's Pool was on the other side of the nearest hill; even in the dry season there was usually enough fresh water for a welcome dip at the end of an exhausting climb. In the rainy season, white frothing streams of water looking like a bride's full-length wedding veil cascaded into the pool from the overhanging rocks. There were sometimes miniature pools above the ridge on this side of the hill too. As the echoes of the motor horn died away, he could hear the gentle trickle of water, then a different sound - an occasional rustling and threshing. He kept a wary eye open for snakes as he clambered above the ridge. Again he cupped his hands and called. There was no response, except the rustling.. or was it splashing? Warily, for some wild animals - even tigers - were known to exist in this area, he scrambled up further. Hanging on to the coarse tussocks of grass, he hauled himself up on to a tiny plateau, and immediately his blood froze: a body lay face downwards in a shallow pool of water: across the neck and shoulders a large boulder pinioned the body to the bed of the pool. That bright hair could only be Greg's. Shouting his name Roddy rushed forward, tugged the boulder away and dragged Greg out of the water. He was limp unconscious but alive, face contused. Water ran out of his nose. There was a jagged bleeding wound on the back of his head. Sobbing, and praying, Roddy frantically pumped Greg's chest until Greg gagged and spewed out gouts of water and blood. Somehow Roddy dragged him down the hillside to the motor track and heaved him across the back seat of the car, shouting continually for help in Cantonese in the hope that one of the tiny figures in the distant rice-fields below could hear. He was torn between driving quickly to get medical help, and driving carefully to prevent Greg from rolling off the seat and exacerbating his injuries.

He yelled for assistance as he pulled up at the bungalow. Mrs. Chester's face was horror-stricken as she ran down the verandah steps when he staggered towards her with Greg in his arms and gabbled out his story. There was the clamour of the frightened children, and an agonising hour until a doctor and ambulance came - a wait rendered more unbearable by the necessity of continually changing the blood-soaked bandages on Greg's head.

Afterwards, there were great blanks in his memory. How many hours had he and Mrs. Chester sat in the hospital waiting room after Greg had been wheeled out of sight along the corridor? How long before they were allowed to see him again, wan and bandaged, still unconscious from the anaesthetic, but alive?

How did he come to be sleeping at the Chesters' bungalow? How many mornings had he woken in tears, pressing his face into his pillow, trying to blot out the guilt that would never leave him, guilt for failing to meet Greg at the appointed time that Sunday? He didn't remember being introduced to Professor Chester, yet by the time the days had names to them again, this bearded middle-aged man with the soft voice and the gentle manner was an old friend.

Pamela appeared at his bedside one day. When she said she had just visited Greg in hospital, he wept unashamedly, muttering "My fault... my fault."

"That isn't true, you know," she said earnestly. "No one thinks so. We all think you're an absolute hero, you saved Greg's life!" Her sympathy disarmed him and he found himself telling her about the burden of debt.

"I can help you a bit," she said at once. "Why didn't you tell me before? Let me give you, say, $30 a month until you're clear."

"Only a loan, only a loan," he protested, shame-faced.

"A long term loan, then - I'll be saving money when Belle and Keith arrive and I move in with them, you know. That's settled then! Greg sent you a message, by the way; he says, when are you going to see him?"

The Chesters had said the same thing some days ago, but it was another week before he could bring himself to accompany Mrs Chester on her daily visit. Greg, propped up in bed, head no longer bandaged, hailed him with a mighty wave.

"Late as usual, Doran," he cried. "Better late than never, though." He seized Roddy's two hands in an iron grip as though he would never let them go, and exuded gratitude and affection as he chattered on. "By the way, I hope your pressing problems have sorted themselves out by now?"

"Past history," Roddy nodded. "Forget I ever mentioned them."

"Glad to hear that! I'm allowed home tomorrow, you know. Be sorry to leave here in some ways, I'm treated like royalty... my every whim granted, and a saucy nurse to tuck me up in bed each night."

"Don't expect that sort of treatment when you move in with us," laughed Mrs. Chester.

"I'm going to be a permanent lodger at the bungalow," Greg nodded happily told Roddy. "Who would have thought it, after all the years we've been passing it on our hikes? Oh, and did you hear the Police got those three jokers who beat me up? What a fool I was, not to realise what they were up to when they asked me the time! While I looked down at my watch, they flew at me and pulled it off my wrist. God, what a fight we had! Then I fell backwards and gashed my head and passed out. I guess they panicked when they saw all the blood and dumped the stone on me to finish me off. Look Rod, here comes that dishy nurse I told you about.."

It was almost possible for Roddy to believe that the ordeal on the ridge had never happened, until he realised that the lid of Greg's left eye was permanently half-lowered over an orb that never moved.

"It's time you went back to work," said Mrs. Chester on the way back to Fan Ling. "Why don't you go into the office tomorrow morning?"

"I suppose I should," he muttered. His thoughts were not on work, but on the prospect of leaving the Chesters' comforting hospitality: could he face life without it?

"Sam and I were wondering," Mrs. Chester was saying, "whether you'd like to leave the Y and lodge with us - if you wouldn't mind sharing a room with Greg.."

He didn't reply because he wanted to be sure he had understood her properly; she obviously mistook his silence for reluctance for she added in a rush "I'd be most awfully glad to have you both. I feel very cut off in the bungalow. I've never been abroad before. Sam is away so often, he hasn't a clue about the time of day, poor dear. I know the servants are in the back quarters all the time, but I'd feel much happier, more secure, with you two part of the household. I don't know what you pay for your lodgings, but I wouldn't need anything like the Y charges - I'm catering for a large family anyway, two more won't make much difference. Sam and I do hope you'll consider it."

He recalled the friendliness of the children; the compassion and support of his hosts during the last muddled fortnight. She was offering him the lifeline he needed; he knew he didn't deserve it, but he could not refuse it and stuttered out his thanks in a strangled voice.

Still guilt-ridden, he had dreaded the first day back at work, but every one from his European superior to the coolie messenger boy hailed his return with hearty pleasure. The senior Chinese clerk confided that two shroffs had called during his absence. "I tell them, please don't you fellows come to see Master until next month, because Master very ill - no can trouble him now."

He discovered that he could not drink anything stronger than lemonade or soda. Iced beer, looking so attractive in the frosted glass, tasted like vinegar; a gin sling like poison; whisky made him heave.

"Your taste buds are all to hell," a knowledgeable friend explained. "they'll come back to normal soon."

But he liked this clearer view of life which the lack of a regular infusion of alcohol gave him. Each day after the office closed he returned to Fan Ling, enjoying the placid countryside after the bustle of the city. The Chester children immediately claimed him for their games, for Greg though out of hospital was still convalescing. Dinner was served quite late as the Professor often roamed the countryside after his return from the University. The evenings were spent lounging on the verandah chatting - Mrs. Chester loved to hear the details of each person's day. They strained to listen to the indistinct radio news from London and discussed the latest world crisis, for Roddy was astonished to learn on his recovery that there was mounting war fever. Hitler's pressure on Czechoslovakia to relinquish the Sudetenlands had increased. Chamberlain had actually flown to Germany to try to avert the crisis, now the British and French seemed to be advising President Benes to let Germany take over all areas of Czechoslovakia containing over 50 German inhabitants, despite Winston Churchill's declaration that 'the belief that security can be obtained by throwing a small state to the wolves is a fatal delusion.'

Although this was very much a European crisis, Hong Kong was also beginning to show signs of uneasiness. Japan's troops were pushing the Chinese Army back towards Canton - only miles away from the British border with China. Supposing the Chinese Army fell back to the British border and the Japanese followed them? Surely the Japanese would not be so foolish as to provoke a scuffle with the British troops there - nevertheless the Hong Kong Defence Force was warned to prepare for mobilisation.

Mrs. Chester was jittery about living so close to the border while the situation seemed so volatile. The Professor had phoned to say he would not be home for dinner and she would not settle for the evening until he was safely back.

"Whatever happens in Europe, nothing will happen here, will it Rod?" Greg tried to reassure her. The hot, end-of-summer air was exceptionally heavy. Sheet lightning lit up the sky almost continuously. Glow-worms hung in the darkness outside the verandah, some homing in on the tall ornamental bushes growing in tubs on the steps. Cicadas screeched in the trees, and flying cockroaches blundered around the ceiling, crashing into the lights.

"Anyway, Mrs. Chester," added Roddy, "you have us to take care of you and the children, so what are you worrying about?"

"I just don't know what I'd do without you," she said simply. "I can't tell you how nervous I felt the first weeks we were here, and I didn't want to keep complaining to Sam, because this is exactly the sort of place he adores to live and work in.. all the new plants and flowers and seeds and creatures - they just enrich his life so. Did you know there are 27 species of land snakes in this part of the world? No, it wasn't Sam who gave me that interesting piece of information, it was young John, he's obviously going to take after him."

She looked so young and vulnerable in the muted light on the verandah that Roddy found it hard to accept she was the wife of the burly Professor; nor could he understand how any man could prefer to grub around in the countryside examining its flora and fauna when he could instead be sitting beside some one as appealing as Mrs. Chester.

When Sam finally came home that night, for once he didn't slouch up the verandah steps as if reluctant to leave his dream world; he strode quickly towards the loungers, his face worried. "Just met the D.O.," he said. "There's very serious news from London. Switch on the radio, Thea, we're due to get a special announcement over the air any time now."

The announcement soon came: the Admiralty had ordered the British Fleet to mobilise.

The Chief Clerk's head appeared above the swing door between his office and the typists' room. "There's a press notice in the pipe-line and two urgent dispatches coming up " he warned. "I'm afraid you girls won't get away at 5 today."

"So what's new?" muttered Viola.

Normal office hours had gone by the board this past week. Today Friday 30th September was worse; there were red files everywhere signalling their secret contents.

Though concentrating on accuracy Pamela was unable to disassociate her mind from the purpose of what she was typing: everything concerned the political crisis and preparations for war - in Europe at least, perhaps in the Far East too. Chamberlain after two abortive visits to Hitler in Germany to defuse the situation, was now making a third. If that failed Hitler's troops would march into Czechoslovakia and Britain would declare war on Germany: bombs would fall on England endangering her parents her grandparents; and ships at sea would be at risk including the RMS Chitral on which Belle Keith and the children were already journeying back to Hong Kong. As to what line Japan would take in the event of war in Europe, voiced local opinion was that the Japanese were too embroiled in their war with China to spare troops to attack Hong Kong - yet anything could happen. Roddy had phoned her that afternoon to say that the Volunteers were to be mobilised and he would be 'God knows where' until 'God knows when.'

It was half past six when the girls left the office; already the buildings in Central were ablaze with advertisement lights of all colours.

"Lovely target all that if the Japs decide to come and bomb us just for fun " Viola grimaced. "We wouldn't have a dog's chance.. no cellars, no air raid shelters.."

The A.R.P. Department formed only six months earlier was training air raid wardens and organising posts; there were plans to provide shelters but every one knew of the impossibility of providing safe shelter for a population of one and a half million.

The ubiquitous newspaper placards proclaimed the latest alarms: 'Chamberlain's flight: the world holds it breath.' 'Londoners dig trenches in Hyde Park.' 'Japanese closing in on Hankow.'

"Oh God," muttered Viola: Raoul was with the Chinese armies defending Hankow, and there had been no letters from him for weeks. "Let's go and have a drink - and see a show afterwards: it'll take our minds off all this hell."

They sat in the Gloucester Lounge, tired and depressed, toying with their drinks.

"You wouldn't think," said Viola, looking round the luxurious lounge with its smart patrons attended by smart Boys, "that a decision by one little man in Germany could put an end to life as we know it; the whole world could be involved - I'm sure the Japs would love to have a smack at us, no matter what it cost them afterwards."

Her pessimism - she called it realism - was well-known and usually discounted, but this evening Pamela could only say glumly "You really think things would happen here if it came to war in Europe? Hilary's Dad doesn't, neither does Ian."

"If most people here don't fear the Japanese, why start building expensive air raid shelters and tunnels.. pillboxes, barbed wire on all the beaches.. you know the sort of thing we're typing all day long. Sometimes I think we must all be mad, thinking only in terms of destruction." Uncharacteristically, she slouched in her chair and went on "Last weekend when I was at South Beach with the Rutherfords I borrowed their canoe and paddled way way out to sea. It was so heavenly, just me and the sea and the sky. It was so marvellous to be away from people going on about war. I felt quite possessed.. as if I wanted to go on paddling forever, in peace, with my back to the world, until I died from sheer exhaustion. Then a launch appeared in the distance, towing a girl on a surf board, and I jerked out of dream and paddled back to shore; now I almost wish I hadn't."

Pamela was appalled. She was used to Viola's individualistic ideas and statements - respected and admired them - but Viola had never before spoken like this. She could not repress a huge sigh of helplessness which brought Viola out of her personal abyss.

"Sorry Pam," she said briskly, signing the chit lying on the table. "No good dwelling on the worst. Time we made for the cinema."

On the walk across the road to the Queen's Theatre they again passed those frightening news placards. The foyer was noticeably without its bevy of uniformed servicemen who normally made up so much of the evening audiences. ("All on alert, I guess," murmured Viola.)

The newsreel at the beginning of the programme showed formations of British and American planes demonstrating their might and prowess: Hitler addressing cheering Germans in staccato sentences; laughing British men queuing to sign up at recruiting offices. The jokey commentary declared that England would not be intimidated by anything Hitler proposed to do; this should have been reassuring but Pamela found it alarming.

The bland Hollywood musical which followed distracted the mind for ninety minutes, then the tinselly world ended abruptly with a surge of triumphant music and the lights went up. A tinny recording of the National Anthem was played at break-neck speed. Most of the audience stood up until the record ran its course, the less respectful surging to the exits; then a party of attendants armed with disinfectant spray cans advanced towards the front, ready to freshen the air throughout for the next showing.

Stepping out of the brilliantly lit foyer into the busy street brought back reality, back to the heart-stopping newspaper placards; but the headlines had changed:

'Triumphant Chamberlain returns. Peace in our time." they read.

"You'd think they'd have given us this morning off," Viola grumbled as the Chief Clerk looked in for the third time to see if she'd finished typing a long despatch.

Nevertheless, there was a relaxed air throughout the office now that the threat of war in Europe had miraculously evaporated, taking with it the anxiety that Japan might have lent its military might to the Axis by attacking in the Far East.

Just before noon Roddy, jubilant that mobilisation of the Volunteers had been cancelled, telephoned Pamela. "Mrs. Chester has just rung to say they're throwing an impromptu party at the bungalow tonight and you're invited, and they want you to stay the whole weekend!"

"Just what I feel like, after all the overtime I've been doing this week," Pamela whooped.

The Chesters welcomed her heartily when she reached the bungalow that afternoon, so did Greg, whom she had not seen since she'd visited him in the hospital. He was very much thinner and seemed far quieter than the frivolous person he had been before. Tufts of blond hair were beginning to sprout from the bald patch on the back of his head where it had been shaved when his wound was stitched. The drooping lid and blank left eye gave him a vulnerable appearance which touched her. She felt for him the more when he sat on the grass watching the children playing mad games with Roddy.

When, that evening, callers from the district drifted in for the party, a gramophone was produced, the carpet rolled up, and desultory dancing ensued. Some one had brought streamers which were tossed around freely. The children crept out of their rooms and watched in delight until their mother tried to send them away.

"Let them stay awhile," Roddy pleaded. "It's not every day we celebrate peace breaking out."

So they were allowed to watch, tearing round the dancers to seize loops of streamers and drape themselves in them.

"Wonderful, isn't it, this euphoria?" Greg said to Pamela as they danced. He was so thin she could feel his ribs. "I'll never forget it... a fitting end to my convalescence - I'm going back to work on Monday."

"Take it easy, though, won't you?" Pamela thought he was still rather frail.

"I will," he said cheerfully. "I'm not yet quite up to ALL the razzmatazz of Hong Kong life.. got to start some time though."

When he had to relinquish her to the Professor, who was amazingly light on his great feet, she felt almost deprived.

The next morning after a late breakfast the Professor led a ramble round the countryside, pointing out the flora and fauna to the darting children. Roddy followed with Mrs. Chester, with Pamela and Greg a little way behind.

Greg had always been an easy friend to talk to, but she found herself thinking of him in a different light, remembering the warm feeling when dancing with him the previous evening.

('Don't be silly,' she told herself. 'It's just being here in this lovely place, this particular weekend, when everyone's so relieved that the war crisis is over - that's why I feel like this.')

Aloud she said, waving her arm around the peaceful scene, "No wonder you and Rod prefer living out here to being in the stuffy town."

"The quietness suits me fine." Greg turned to smile at her, and again that vulnerable face twisted her heart. There was such affection in his smile that her cheeks coloured.

"Mind if I tell you something?" he went on. "Rod was telling me how you're bailing him out of his money problems: I think that's bloody good of you, and you can take all the credit for the change in him. Look at him last night - every one (except you!) celebrating madly with the booze, and he stuck to tonics right through."

"He's shown terrific will power," she nodded, swallowing her disappointment at the realisation that what she'd interpreted as interest in herself was simply gratitude for her help to his best friend.

"We'd best catch the others up," she said coolly, "else we'll lose them."

Two cars carried the entire party to the beach in the afternoon. In the water, Pamela deliberately devoted herself to games with the children, disregarding Roddy and Greg's demands that she join them for a 'decent swim'. Afterwards there was a crazy game of cricket on the beach, then a picnic of sandwiches and lemonade when Pamela made sure she was among the children rather than with the adults.

As they walked back to the cars, Greg took her arm and said hesitantly "Pam.. have I said something to upset you? You haven't spoken to me since this morning."

She didn't know what to say, and walked on in silence.

"Whatever it was.. though I can't think what.. I'm sorry if I've upset you, truly I am."

"You haven't upset me," she stammered.

"So will you come to the flicks with me one evening next week? Please, Pam, it will be my first social engagement since Bride's Pool!"

She liked the feel of his arm guiding her along the path from the beach. "I'd like to come, thanks," she said.

"When? Not Monday because I've got an interview with my boss after work, but any other day of the week that you're free."

"Tuesday, please," she said as calmly as she could: Tuesday was sooner than all the other days of the week!

They had not been at their typewriters for half an hour on Monday morning before Viola noticed. "You look very dreamy today" she mouthed across the desk.

"Do I?" Pamela refused to be drawn, still treasuring the growing feeling of inner happiness, terrified of naming it in case she was mistaken. "If by dreamy you mean sleepy, I'm not surprised: we were on the go the whole weekend, it was really hectic."

Later, when Pamela's carbons were twice discovered to have been inserted the wrong way round, Viola looked at her speculatively and said "How about tiffin today at the Club?"

"Thanks, but I've got sandwiches. The Professor and the children and Greg and Rod all take a packed tiffin every day, and somehow the Boy automatically packed one for me too."

"They're spoiling you, those Chesters! Any one interesting at the party?"

"No one my age - except Rod and Greg," she said, burrowing in her lowest drawer to hide her pink cheeks.

Returning to the Batelys' home at the end of that day was an anti-climax after the weekend with the Chesters. No young children lived at Leighton Hill quarters which were occupied by older civil servants whose progeny were young adults. The concrete plateau on which these houses stood was empty except for a couple of cars which the owners had not yet garaged. The verandahs and windows were blank with green rattan blinds against the piercing sunlight of the late afternoon.

Compared to the perennial signs of life at the bungalow, the Bately house looked as tidy as a palace. Through the open lounge door Pamela could see Hilary's mother and three friends playing mah jongg, and waved to them.

"Have a good time Pam?" called Mrs. Bately. She didn't wait for a reply, adding "Hilary's upstairs, she's got some news for you." A great burst of knowing laughter from the other ladies followed Pamela as she ran up the stairs. Hilary came to meet her on the landing, brighteyed and red-cheeked.

"Here you are at last!" She seized Pamela's arms and pulled her into her room. "Got heaps to tell you - Mum didn't give it away just now, did she?"

"Give what away?"

"Ian and I are going to be married! I mean, SOON, not in two years' time like we'd planned. Because Ian wants to go to England to join the Army, so we'll get married before he goes, and sail home as Mr. and Mrs.!" She leapt on the bed and hugged her legs up to her chest. "Imagine, I'll be married in a few weeks' time!"

"Goodness, but what about the Bank?"

"He's already given in his notice - you don't know him: when he makes a decision he acts on it, fast!" On she prattled, bouncing on the bed, eyes huge, while Pamela tried to piece together the sequence of events. It seemed that he had decided to throw up his job and join the Army because of what the newspapers were now calling the betrayal of Czechoslovakia by the British Government's agreement with Hitler. Ian maintained there should be no more appeasement; England must openly prepare to stand up to Hitler in future; for this conviction he discounted the career for which he had trained and worked and which held such promise; he'd sent cables to friends and relatives in London and felt sure of being offered a commission.

"He doesn't think there will be war if Britain shows she's ready to fight if he steps out of line again, instead of all this appeasement." Hilary reached for the bell on the wall and pressed it. "Let's have tea up here - too many people downstairs! Ian's such a positive person, he'll never take the easy way. They nearly had a fit at the Bank when he said he wanted to resign. Every one he told sent him to some one higher up, until he ended up with the No.l, who shook him by the hand, wished him well, and promised to cable his Army contacts in U.K. to speed up the commission."

They drank their tea on Hilary's verandah. She constantly changed position on the rattan chair, and kept lighting cigarettes then stubbing them out, half-finished, as she listed details of the wedding preparations: she must finish collecting her trousseau (thank goodness Linen Boy was due again soon); see the printers about invitations, and get the wedding dress made: would Pam design one specially for her, and would she be bridesmaid - there was no time to arrange for more than one?

"We can't fix the date until Ian knows when he can join the Army, then it will have to tie in with the next P. & O. Home. We'll have a honeymoon at Repulse Bay, and go straight on board from there." She was on her feet again, ringing the bell to call the amah to run her bath. "I gave in my notice at Bexton's today - I don't know how I can bear to go on there, working out my notice, with all this excitement!"

"Raoul's back!" Viola beamed when she came into the office two days later. "Come home with me after office, I've got alot to tell you."

She would not divulge any of her news during the day, even when Pamela managed during less busy moments to impart the latest developments in Hilary's wedding plans. "Ian sounds a great guy," was Viola's comment, "giving up a career in the Bank just like that. Won't they both miss Hong Kong life, though! Wow!"

Later, in her tiny room, she sat across the bed, drawing on a cigarette. "I need some advice, Pam. Raoul is pressing me to move into his flat. I've always said No before, but I'm very tempted now.. it would be so much cheaper than Courtlands, I could save lots of money towards getting my own place.

"I'm asking you," she went on earnestly, "because you're innocent, and have an uncluttered mind. You'll see the picture clearer than I can. I've been mulling over the pro's and con's so long that I'm confused. I don't say I'll take your advice, mind you, but I'd like to hear it."

"I personally couldn't do.. what you're thinking about," Pamela ventured carefully.

"That's not the point - we're talking about ME."

There were some awkward questions to be asked. Pamela stammered "You'd be just a lodger..?"

"Just a lodger. Separate rooms. No commitment at all, although I'm very fond of Raoul; I was surprised how much I missed him while he was away this time. I practically fell into his arms when I met him again last night! But I'm afraid of getting too involved, too carried away; that could easily happen if I moved in with him - do you see?"

"But if he turns out to be the right person for you, then wouldn't you want to get engaged, and then married, to him?"

"That's the whole point. I don't want marriage for ages. I need time to be myself, in my own domain; that way I'll make sure that when I do marry - if I do - it's to the right person for the right reasons. Raoul's flat is lovely - large rooms, big windows and verandahs, two bathrooms. I'd be able to have my own bits and pieces around me there - the things I have to leave in the store-room here. I'd be very comfortable at Raoul's; it would be easy to kid myself that I was in love with someone who could provide me with lovely accommodation, so much better than this awful cubby-hole. What a pity you can't move with me into Raoul's flat! The room is big enough to share, and then we'd be respectable as far as the outside world was concerned - especially as he's away so much of the time."

The idea was too ludicrous even to be considered. "My parents would have me sent Home on the next boat - maybe even by air!" Pamela laughed.

Ah So brought tea. Five minutes later he returned with a message for Viola in his best English: "One friend come see Missee." Behind him stood Raoul, so tanned that his fair hair looked incongruously snow-white. Somehow he too fitted into the tiny room, concertina-ing his long body beside Viola on the bed. Ah So brought a third cup and saucer which he assiduously dusted on the side of his loose white trousers. At Viola's remonstrations, Raoul shrugged "After the way I have lived these past weeks, hygiene means nothing to me, but I thank you for your concern."

Pamela was quickly aware of the current of feeling between the couple. There was a sparkle in Viola's eyes, and a responding gleam in Raoul's. She felt in the way and rose to leave, but Raoul would not hear of this.

"I am the intruder," he said. "Please stay, Pamela."

His charm was irresistible. He leaned back against the wall and sighed "This time yesterday I was sitting on the floor of an old DC2, being jolted this way, that way, and dreaming of returning to civilisation. Now I am here I cannot quite believe it. I have showered: had my clothes washed and ironed, after living for weeks without running water. Today I have been watching the skies for Japanese planes and listening for bombs. Hong Kong seems so unconcerned.. if you knew what it is like up north.."

The words tumbled out, emphasised by his expressive hands. He had witnessed so much human tragedy that his tales would fill a book. He had travelled by whatever transport was available, sometimes by bicycle, riding over rough roads. Everywhere he was astonished and humbled by the stubborn resistance of the Chinese against the Japanese war machine. He'd learned that the horrors of the rape of Nanking the previous winter had hardened the Chinese will to fight. The incident which haunted him most was the breaching by the desperate Chinese army of dykes holding in the Yellow River, in a last attempt to stem the Japanese advance.

"Thousands.. probably two hundred thousand, were drowned - Chinese, not Japanese! Millions of peasants were made homeless, everything they possessed swept away. Oh yes, warnings were given of the plan to cut the dykes, but not every one heard in time; others wouldn't take the warnings seriously, or just plain refused to move from their homes. This had just happened before I arrived so I only saw the aftermath: bloated human corpses; bullocks, dogs, pigs; the debris of pathetic little homes.. and the faces, the gaunt bewildered faces of the survivors, sitting round patiently because there was nothing else they could do. And worst of all, the flooding didn't really stop the Japs - just delayed their progress for a few months. Now they're targetting Hankow, one day it will be Hong Kong."

"Do you really really believe that?" Viola probed.

"I do!" His words were passionate. "When the signs become clearer, you should get out of Hong Kong, all you women."

Pamela felt a great pang of panic. It was one thing to work in a constant atmosphere of defence measures to be taken in an emergency, another to hear such conviction that an emergency was certain to arise.

"We just can't get up and go," Viola reasoned. "This is my home! I don't consider U.K. my home now, and I certainly never want to live with my parents again. Anyway, it wouldn't be my decision: if a Japanese attack ever seemed likely, surely the Government would urge British women and children to get out in time?"

"And create a panic - especially among the Chinese here who have nowhere to go?"

"What about you yourself, Raoul? Are you sufficiently pessimistic to throw up your job here and leave?"

"Oh no Viola, I will take my chance; my work is where the action is, after all. But you ladies are so vulnerable. You should not have to face what happened in Nanking last year."

While in China he had heard first-hand accounts of the horrors in Nanking. Guarded reports of this had been published in the colony earlier in the year but now, in stark, simple terms, he told them the truth he had learned.

"But all that was vengeance on Chinese people, not British," Pamela said. "Surely they wouldn't treat us like that?"

"If the British were then the enemy, why not?"

Darkness had fallen. There was an air of unreality in the little room lit only by a bedside lamp. Raoul's words had opened the door to a terrifyingly new world, a world Pamela didn't want to think about at all.

The dinner gong sounded in the corridor; she could hear doors opening, voices and footsteps as boarders emerged from their rooms. This was normal life, not what Raoul had been describing. She gave a little shudder as she stood up to leave.

"I'll drive you." Raoul unfolded himself from the bed. "It's on my way. Viola and I are going to Repulse Bay for a snack, are we not?"

"Are we?" There was the suggestion of indignation in Viola's light words, but her eyes shone and a smile played around her lips.

"Oh-oh, some people jumped the gun," said Mr. Bately at breakfast, refolding the South China Morning Post the better to read the report which had caught his eye. "A plane load of kids from U.K. boarding-schools arrived yesterday. I suppose their parents sent for them during Munich, and couldn't cancel when everything blew over."

"Let's see." Hilary peered over his shoulder. "No one I know.. we're getting too old to know any one still at school!"

Pamela craned too and spotted a familiar name. "Sandra's come back, my old friend Sandra Smithson!"

Hilary read out "Miss Sandra Smithson, only daughter of Mr. and Mrs. L. Smithson of Rawlins & Dill also flew in yesterday. For the past year she has been attending finishing-school in Switzerland and this is her first visit to the colony since departing to boarding-school in England in 1930.' You'll have to give her a ring and say hello, Pam."

"She mightn't remember me."

"Why not? You remember her!"

In the office Pamela mentioned Sandra's return to Viola, and found that Viola too had known her as a child.

"Spoilt to glory by amahs.. even more than I was," grunted Viola. "A little horror to all us older children, she was - no one liked her; you say she was a friend of yours?"

"I didn't like her at first," said Pamela, carefully guarding her knowledge of the tragedy of the little dead brother. "But later we became great friends. I even stayed the night with her once."

"No accounting for tastes," Viola grinned, "but I bet she's a proper little madam now - finishing-school.. I mean!"

The voice on the phone, in response to Pamela's diffident call, was peremptory and affected, then became ecstatic when she gave her name.

"Pam, Pam! I never dreamed you'd be here too! Lovely, oh lovely! You're to come and see me right away, this evening: my parents are giving a welcome party for me, cocktails, 6.30pm. I just can't wait to see you! I'll send the car for you at six so we can have time to talk before other people arrive."

An ageless Ming was at the wheel when the shining Hispano called for her exactly at 6 o'clock, and he greeted her like an old friend. Pamela instantly recalled the excitement and reverence she had felt as a child when riding in the Smithsons' car.

They no longer lived on the Peak; now their home was a large flat-roofed bungalow overlooking Deep Water Bay. Its whiteness was dazzling against the surrounding greenery. Large glazed pots of carnations and daisies bordered the steps leading to the main entrance.

The slim 18-year-old in a white voile dress who met her at the door was a stunning grown-up version of the child Sandra, with lightly rouged high cheeks, pink lipstick, brilliant blue eyes, and thick auburn wavy hair almost to her shoulders, caught back behind her ears with ornate hair clips.

"So thrilled to see you again, Pam!" She hugged her warmly. "Not fair, you're still taller than I am! You've changed so much - I half expected to see you with short straight hair and a fringe."

In Sandra's luxurious bedroom overlooking the golf course above the Bay, they chattered in half-sentences.

"You never wrote to me in England, you rat.."

"Wasn't allowed to, none of us were - Marcus, Celeste, Danny, Philip..!"

"Tell me about them!"

"Don't know much,, I went Home to school soon after you.." Pamela quickly decided against explaining the circumstances. "Only Celeste is in Hong Kong.. Marcus studying Law in the States. I saw Danny last year but he's gone to Manila to make his fortune with a band. Don't know what happened to Philip after he left Hong Kong."

"He didn't write to you ever?"

"Never! And I couldn't write to him because he didn't know where he'd be living in England. He had my Hong Kong address but I expect he lost it, he always lost things, didn't he?"

"He had terrific character, though." Sandra moved over to the dressing-table to examine her make-up. 'My father still tells the tale of how he walked all the way up the Peak to my birthday party that time."

Sandra had obviously endured rather than enjoyed her schooling in England, always counting the days until she could return to Hong Kong.

"That man Hitler has done me a favour," she giggled. "He got me out of my last year at that ghastly school in Switerland. I'm never going away from Hong Kong again, no matter what happens. Oh bother, I can hear people arriving now..."

All the guests were strangers to Pamela - young people of both sexes, daughters and sons of the Smithsons' friends and colleagues so all known to each other. She felt an outsider, despite Mr. and Mrs. Smithsons' best efforts to make her feel welcome. By night o'clock Sandra's face was bright red with excitement, and her eyes sparkling. There was talk of some of the party going on to dinner at the nearby Repulse Bay Hotel.

"Super, super!" Sandra gurgled, "I'll get my handbag." On the way out of the lounge she passed Pamela and called "You'll come too, won't you Pam?"

Pamela, anxious to escape from all these extrovert strangers, quickly shook her head. "Got to get back home, they're expecting me." No one pressed her to change her mind, and she was taken home by Ming.

Over dinner at Leighton Hill she answered Hilary's interested questions with care: yes, it had been a good party; Sandra was good fun, and the bungalow was fantastic; yes, there had been heaps of other young people there but she hadn't met any of them before and couldn't remember any of their names. What she didn't disclose was her conviction that Sandra's interest in her had only been a passing curiosity, quickly satisfied, after which her attention had been directed to all the other guests.

"Is she going to get a job, or just be a lady of leisure?" Hilary wanted to know.

"She didn't say, she's just revelling in being back, free of school regulations. Says she intends to stay here for the rest of her life, by hook or by crook."

"Some one else I know used to say that, too," Mr. Bately said with a wink, "until another some one came along and changed her mind for her."

"And talking of Ian," smiled his wife, looking across at Hilary, "has he fixed up for his Best Man yet?"

"Oh mother, that was decided ages ago - Richard Brown.. I told you!"

"Well, dear, you've told us of so many plans, then reversed them - you can't blame me for getting mixed up. Oh girls, Dad and are having tiffin in Kowloon with the Neals tomorrow and staying there till evening; Boy wants to know if either if you will be in to tiffin."

"Not me," said Pamela. "It's our painting lesson, so I'm having tiffin with Viola at Courtlands first; then you and I are meeting at the tailor's at 3, aren't we Hilary?"

"That's right. Ian and I are having a quick snack first at the hotel."

"Is this the final fitting of THE DRESS?" Mr. Bately asked.

"Not yet," Pamela laughed, "there's a lot more to do yet."

"And if you keep on losing weight, Hilary," said her mother, "it will NEVER be the final fitting. You're not eating enough to make up for all your dashing about. I wish you'd take things easier".

"Raoul's off to China again," Viola confided the next morning. "He's leaving tomorrow. I'm terrified for his safety - and I just wish I knew what to do about his flat."

Pamela evaded the vexed question by asking "How long will he be away this time?"

"A couple of weeks, he thinks."

"So why not think about it until he comes back?'

"IF he comes back! The bombs won't pick and choose between Europeans and Chinese. It's such hell to make decisions these days, with the uncertainty of life where he's going."

This conversation took place in the privacy of the walk-in stationery cupboard, while they counted out sheets of Government House letter-head paper for their current tasks.

"What shall I do, Pam?" Viola sighed.

Pamela shrugged her shoulders and muttered "Don't know. It's as if our lives are getting mixed up with history in the making."

Viola apparently took this evasive reply to heart; at mid-day when the office closed, she said "You're right about our lives being entangled with history; what's happening in China is big history - Raoul has made me see that. Our little personal affairs are so trivial in comparison! What will it matter if I go to lodge with Raoul and get more involved with him than I want to? - Not a fig! How egotistical we are about our own emotions! I've made up my mind now: I'll give in my notice at Courtlands and tell Raoul I'll take over his spare room at the beginning of next month. Thanks Pam - you gave me just the spur I needed!"

Still somewhat bemused and worried at her unintentional responsibility in solving Viola's problem, Pamela trudged up the steps to the tailor's establishment after her painting lesson. There was no sign of Hilary. Loong Kai took the skeleton of the wedding dress out of the glass case opposite the counter and held it up for inspection. Pamela could see that the long bodice would look perfect on Hilary's pencil-slim body, and the lacy material hung well in the full skirt.

When Hilary had not arrived after ten minutes, Pamela could stand no longer the stuffy sewing room heavy with the acrid smell of heated irons on damp materials, and decided to wait downstairs in the street. Twenty minutes later she decided that Hilary must have forgotten the arrangement, so took the next bus home, cross at a wasted afternoon. This unreliability of Hilary's was entirely typical ever since she had become engaged.

" I could have gone to the beach with Greg and Rod after all," she thought irritably as she toiled up the slope to the house.

But there was no Hilary at home to reproach.

"Not come," said the Boy. "Plenty people telephone, askee talkee Missie Hilary."

Over a lonely tea, Pamela considered her last conversation with Viola. To a degree, Viola's decision to put herself in a position of possible deeper involvement with Raoul paralleled Pamela's situation with Greg. This Sunday the Moon Festival was celebrated, and she had accepted an invitation to an evening launch picnic which included Greg, Roddy and Josie. The time was coming, she realised, when Greg's persistent overtures must either be accepted or firmly rejected. She would prefer to let the matter drift, enjoying the frequent evenings at the cinema, occasional dining and dancing in the hotels, and the comforting companionship. He had kissed her when saying goodnight after their last date; she had surprised herself with her reaction and had wondered since if she dared run the risk of falling in love again. She was sure that Greg was only waiting for encouragement from her. Perhaps the time had come, when like Viola, she should stop being introspective and no longer hold back from what, after all, might only be a mild flirtation.

The phone rang and the amah called "B'long Master Ian, wanchee speak Missie Hilary."

Ian seemed surprised when Pamela told him Hilary was not there: then would she please ring him as soon as she returned? Chattily, Pamela expressed her puzzlement at Hilary's failure to keep the date at the tailor's. Ian made no comment, just repeated his request that Hilary telephone him as soon as possible.

At 7 o'clock he phoned again.

"I don't know where she can be!" Pamela was worried by now. "But she won't be much longer - she knows we eat at 7.30. When did you last see her, Ian?"

"About half past eleven this morning."

"But I thought she was having lunch with you."

"That was the idea." His voice was so strange that Pamela dared to ask "Is.. is something wrong, Ian? Have you.. quarrelled?"

"You could say that." His tone discouraged further questions. "If you're due to dine at half past, she's bound to be in soon. I'm going to drive down to your place now, to wait for her."

The phone was slammed down before she could say any more. Shocked and anxious, she was still sitting by the telephone when it rang again.

"Miss Doran? This is the Secretary of the Women's International Club speaking. You have a friend, Miss Bately, whose address is the same as yours. I am sorry to tell you that Miss Bately seems ill. She has been sitting in our restaurant for some hours.. perhaps you could come and help her?"

Panic-stricken, Pamela thought quickly: the Bately parents were unobtainable in Kowloon; Ian had already left the Mess. She telephoned for a taxi, grabbed jacket and handbag, and gabbled to the amah "Master Ian come soon; tell him Hilary come, I come home, twenty minute."

She leapt out of the taxi the moment it stopped outside the hotel arcade, and not waiting for the lift, ran up the stairs to the Club. As soon as she burst into the restaurant she could see Hilary's back view - a lone figure at the table farthest from the door. The secretary materialised from her alcove and put a hand on Pamela's arm, whispering "She's had some coffee, but that's all... just sits there, smoking and crying. Several people spoke to her and asked if she was all right but she waved them away."

Pamela ran the length of the room and sat down beside Hilary: "Here you are! We've been so worried about you!"

Hilary put her hands over her face, knocking to the floor an ashtray full of cigarette ends. Her shoulders shook.

"What's wrong, oh please tell me! Let me get a doctor!"

"I'm.. not.. ill." The words came slowly through stiff lips.

Clearly something was very wrong. "Let's go home," Pamela said gently. "Ian keeps 'phoning."

"I can't go home.. sorry, sorry, sorry."

"Of course you can, I'll help you." Pamela took her arm. "Ian's on his way to Leighton Hill now; he'll be there by the time we get home."

"NO!" With a great shuddering sigh, Hilary gripped the table tightly and muttered "I can't see Ian again... I can't marry him, Pam: I don't love him enough."

Now, Hilary realised that the first doubts had arisen during the moonlight picnic, when they had been alone in the matshed. She had been alarmed as well as thrilled at the depth of Ian's passion, reminding her that there would be a totally different life after marriage. Then there had been a feeling almost of panic when Ian first said he was leaving the Bank to join up in England, drastically bringing forward their wedding; but the excitement of the crowding, hectic preparations stifled the worry. It was only this morning, when he 'phoned her at the office and ordered her to meet him right away at the Gloucester where he announced yet another change of plan, that she realised she couldn't marry him.

He had just received a cable: London would take him into the Army as soon as he could get there - not as an officer initially, but a commission would almost certainly be forthcoming once he had done his basic training.

"I've been on to the R.A.F. at Kai Tak and wangled a seat on a plane leaving on Tuesday. You'll follow on the P. & O. we were both booked on before. I've phoned the Supreme Court and we can get married by special licence on Monday, this coming MONDAY, if we both get to the Registry right away and sign some papers. What do you say to that, Mrs. Lacey-to-be?"

"I can't believe it!" She was half-crying, her teeth chattering, hands shaking.

"You will!" Ian grasped her hands and squeezed them firmly. "Everything's working out splendidly." He rattled on with the plans; if he couldn't get away from his course to meet her at Tilbury, he would send his parents to collect her and take her to their home in the country near Oxford; he would come to see her as often as he could.

Watching his glowing face, she knew herself to be smiling in return, but the chaos in her mind mounted. Was this what she really wanted - a hasty ceremony bearing no resemblance at all to the originally planned wedding at the Cathedral and lavish reception at the Hong Kong Hotel, not wearing the dream-like lace gown, with no bridesmaid and no week's honeymoon at Repulse Bay? Then a trip back to England without Ian, living with unknown in-laws, and maybe never again returning to beloved Hong Kong?

She knew she didn't love him enough for that.

"Now off to the Registry we go!" He got up, wiping his damp face with his handkerchief and running his fingers through his tousled hair. Somehow Hilary found her voice. "I must dash along to the Ladies first," she muttered.

"Nerves! No wonder," grinned Ian. "Be quick.. I'll meet you at the door of the arcade."

In the Powder Room Hilary scrabbled in her handbag and tore a page from her diary; at great speed to sustain her courage, she scribbled "So sorry, dear Ian, but I can't go through with this because I don't love you enough to give up living in Hong Kong. Please forgive. So very sorry. Hilary."

Addressing the back of the folded sheet to Mr. I. Lacey, she slipped out of the Powder Room to Reception and arranged for Ian to be paged in five minutes' time, then, avoiding the main arcade entrance, took the lift to the Club two floors up and hid in the lavatory in the Ladies Room, crying quietly. Several times she noticed the black-slippered feet of the amah in charge pause outside the gap between door and floor and realised she couldn't stay there indefinitely without arousing attention; she walked out calmly, washed hands and face and went into one of the curtained-off rest cubicles where she lay stiffly, swallowing her tears, for as long as she dared. Twice she heard the amah's soft footsteps halt outside her curtain, and once caught the concerned old face peering in at her. She forced herself to get up and go into the restaurant and chose an empty table at the far end of the room, She sat with her back to the other patrons, withdrawn and stunned. A boy approached with the menu.

"Coffee," she mouthed lifelessly. When at last she bestirred herself to take the first sip, it had grown cold, but she gulped it down; only her churning thoughts registered.

How could she face Ian, her parents, her friends, people at the office?

Much later, the boy returned and asked if she would like more coffee, and she discovered the time was five o'clock, she had been in this state of turmoil for nearly six hours. She had half-smoked endless cigarettes on an empty stomach and began to feel nauseated. Reason told her she must go home but she could not move. She fought back the urge to heave to avoid leaving her refuge at the end table and perhaps passing people she knew on her way to the Ladies. It was easier to sit frozen in the now-familiar chair, staring at the yellow wall opposite, trying to let the subdued chatter of nearby voices drive away the turmoil in her mind.

"Excuse me, Miss Bately" The middle-aged club secretary was bending over her. "Are you feeling ill?"

"I'm quite all right, thank you," she managed to articulate. "I'm just a little tired."

"You don't look well.. you've been here so long."

"I'm O.K., really I am, and I'm leaving soon." Her empty stomach threatened to heave again. She tried to smile convincingly at the secretary, but instead her face crumpled and she put her hand over her mouth to hide its trembling.. surely all this was a nightmare?

It was true: every waking minute of every day of the following week reminded her of her folly in mistaking romance for love. There were anguished phone calls and letters from Ian, culminating in the meeting she had desperately wanted to avoid, when she tried to explain herself and wept, tortured by Ian's wounded face and her own self-knowledge. Her parents' bewilderment was hard to bear, the more because they tried to make excuses for her.

"You must do what you feel is right," said her father sadly. "Much better to say now if you have doubts - no good later."

"Of course, only you can decide." Her mother had to hold back tears every time the matter was discussed in those first days, "But I can't help thinking you're being far too conscientious.. no one really knows what marriage is going to be like - it's a leap in the dark to a new life. I'm sure you'd forget all about life in Hong Kong once you were caught up in your new life in England! I'd never been out of Yorkshire when Dad asked me to marry him and go out East. I was petrified.. I knew absolutely nothing about life abroad, but I loved and trusted your father so I took a chance, and life just couldn't have been more marvellous. You say you love Ian.."

"But not enough," Hilary interrupted.

"Oh well, dear, it's your decision, not ours," sighed her mother again.

Monday was a public holiday - the Double Tenth or the 10th day of October - so it didn't matter that Hilary stayed huddled in her bedroom, unable to face meals in the dining room. The amahs were in and out of her room about their duties, clucking and fussing, their mournful 'ai yahs' adding to every one's misery.

She could only suffer so much of her mother's solicitousness, overlaid as it was by distress and disappointment at the turn of affairs; yet she could not bear to be alone, and begged Pamela to stay with her. So Pamela sat at Hilary's bureau, doing her Chinese painting, while Hilary tossed on the bed or ranged restlessly about the room; leaving her painting when Hilary wanted to talk, and hugging her tightly during painful bouts of harsh sobbing which came without warning.

By Monday evening Pamela coaxed her downstairs to dinner, and through the haze of her own sufferings, Hilary could see her parents' faces lift a little at this first sign of recovery.

"Sorry, every one," she gratefully recognised the compassion and love they all felt for her. "I'll be better tomorrow at the office."

"Are you sure you're fit for work, dear?"

"Got to be Mum, if I want to keep my job."

But this jauntiness was gone when she walked into the cloak room at Bextons' the next morning. White-faced, she held out her left hand to her colleagues and said "Look, no engagement ring. I've changed my mind.. called off the wedding. It's al over, and I'm just going to ask Mr. Haig if I can withdraw my notice. Now you know."

Not even that honest approach could prevent the covert glances and whispered conversations; all the week, she was aware of them as she muddled somehow through her work.

"Maybe I ought to change my job," she told Pamela in despair one evening. "I was so pleased when Mr. Haig let me stay on, but now nobody talks naturally to me any more."

"It would be the same wherever you worked, I think; you know so many people..

and maybe, maybe some of it is your imagination. I think you're jolly brave to keep going so well at work."

It certainly took iron will-power to keep at her desk. Columns of figures, usually so quickly added up, had to be checked and re-checked because she could no longer trust her competence; her entries in the great record books were thickened where a sudden surge of misery had caused her to dig her pen deeply into the paper in an effort to regain self-control.

Things should have been easier after Ian had left, but no, a fresh wave of remorse engulfed her. She could not bear to be alone with her guilt, even pleading with Pamela to meet her immediately after work so she would have company on the bus journey home. When Pamela phoned her one afternoon to say she would be working late, Hilary had to grit her teeth to prevent tears; unable to face going home alone and her mother's distress without moral support, she rushed into the Queen's Theatre as soon as her office closed: stared at the screen numbly, grateful for the darkness which shielded her from the public gaze.

Without Pamela beside her in the bus, the journey seemed unbearably noisy and bumpy. She dawdled on the walk up the drive to the house, hopeful that Pamela would be home by now to help bridge the awful gaps in conversation between herself and her unhappy parents.

It was a vain hope: Pamela didn't arrive until dinner was over, kept working until eight o'clock because another political crisis loomed. Hilary had been vaguely aware during the past week of general uneasiness over the proximity of Japanese troops to the Colony's border with China, but her own overwhelming problems had obscured wider issues. Now she listened with alarm to the latest reports. The Japanese were thought to be massing near the border and the garrison had been alerted.

"Roddy phoned me this afternoon," said Pamela. "European families are evacuating the New Territories, just in case. The Chesters have moved across to Hong Kong to stay with some friends of the Professor; and Greg and Rod have booked in at the Y.M.C.A. until things blow over."

"And they will," nodded Hilary's father. "Those Japs aren't fools. They know they can't afford to take us on."

Nevertheless the crisis continued to worsen. Army trucks and lorries clogged the roads; the railway between Kowloon and Canton was closed.

The important city of Hankow fell to the Japanese, who were now constantly bombing Chungking which had become the Chinese capital.

Blackouts were practised in Hong Kong - no matter how illogical it seemed for the Japanese to attack a British possession, there was just the possibility that with the euphoria of its military successes in China, a part of the Japanese Army might be tempted to throw logic to the winds.

As she struggled through each day, trying to live with her shattered self-image, Hilary scanned the latest headlines but quickly disregarded them, confident that her father's opinion that there would be no trouble in Hong Kong was correct. Of more importance to her was the imminent arrival of Belle and family from England as a result of which Pamela would take up her abode with them.

"Don't go, don't go," Hilary begged. "You're the only one I can rely on: don't leave me yet!"

They talked long into every night, Hilary agonising over the past weeks, pouring out the slights of the day, taking some comfort from Pamela's uncomplicated attitude and consolation: "You did what you had to.. so no point in going on about it."

OCTOBER

Anxiety in the colony intensified when it became clear that a land and sea attack by the Japanese on Canton was imminent. A violent battle was expected as Canton was known to be full of some 200,000 Chinese troops.

A troopship arrived in Hong Kong from England, bringing military men and their families; instead of leaving the next day with troops who had completed their tour of duty, it lay berthed in the Naval Dockyard - ready, ran the rumour, to evacuate British civilians if a Japanese attack on Hong Kong threatened. Like most personnel in Government Departments, Pamela was again working longer hours.

"You don't have much of a life these days," Hilary said one evening after dinner as she and Pamela sat on the verandah enjoying the late autumn coolness. "You're working all day and half the evening; then you're sitting around with me. I'm a selfish pig. You ought to get out and about more. What's Greg doing these days? I thought you'd see alot more of him now he's in the Y.M."

"I do see him now and again.. at the launch picnic on Moon Festival evening the Sunday before last."

"I mean, you ought to be out on dates with him."

"Not any more." Pamela was carefully tracing with her fingers the pattern of the rattan weaving on her chair. "I like him as a friend but, well, he was beginning to get too keen; I thought it best to cool off."

"Could this have anything to do with.. with what happened to Ian and me?"

"Sort of.. I just didn't want to get so involved."

"Oh dear." Hilary couldn't stop the tears. "You're right to be cautious, but don't cut out every possible boyfriend because you're afraid. I don't think I could live with myself if I've caused you to creep back into your shell."

"But I'm grateful to you," Pamela insisted. "Anyway, Viola comes into it too: she and Raoul look so perfect together, as though they belong to each other; Greg and I aren't a bit like that."

"You've only been going out with him for about a month," Hilary pointed out. "I know you've known him for ages, but going out with him is different."

"Of course, but already I can see that how I feel about him doesn't stand comparison with how I felt about Danny last year! I'm over Danny now - it was a hopeless situation that I should never have let arise.. as you so often warned me! But with Danny, I felt in a dream world: there's nothing dream-like in being with Greg, although at first I thought there might be; now I just feel very comfortable with him, not thrilled. Viola might have been right when she said when I first started going out with Greg "Beware of pity." She thought I might be getting wrapped up in him because he was in such a bad state after that attack."

"And what does the great Viola say about me?"

"She said you have.. guts to pull out before it's too late. Honestly, Hilary, most people think that! You should stop slinking about as if you're in disgrace."

"I'm in disgrace with myself."

With the approach of the battle for Canton, Pamela's hours became so erratic that Belle begged her to move to the new flat in Macdonnell Road which was a very short walk from the Government Secretariat. This time Hilary had to let her go, knowing she must manage without her main prop.

Astonishing news broke: Chiang Kai Shek without warning withdrew his troops from Canton. Thousands of Cantonese volunteers, eager to fight for their city, were left without weapons. The bridge spanning the Pearl River into the city was bombed; Japanese warships steamed up Bocca Tigris; Japanese troops landed and the city quickly taken.

From Canton the Japanese advanced towards the Chinese border with the British at Shum Chun in the New Territories, while the colony held its breath. Shum Chun quickly fell to the Japanese who then turned their backs on the British, and the crisis was subsided.

The danger to Hong Kong might be over, but the aftermath of the Japanese latest conquest in China was only just beginning: thousands of Chinese refugees flocked to Kowloon and Hong Kong. Appeals were made for clothes, food and money to ease their lot in the wooden accommodation which was all that the Hong Kong Government could provide at short notice in this already over-populated colony. Bazaars and concerts were hastily organised to raise funds to improve life in the camps. It was at one of these concerts that Hilary heard a young American missionary describing the hardships of the refugees and passionately pleading for more help for them that something clicked in her mind - she felt miserable for circumstances caused by herself, whereas the refugees were victims of events in China which were beyond their control. Suddenly she had a reason for living again. All her spare time became devoted to welfare work for the refugees. In a stuffy wooden hut, she sorted through boxes and bales of used clothing, rejecting the rubbish, dividing the rest up into sex and sizes. The knowledge that such washed-out garments were so gladly received by the refugees in the adjoining huts tore at her heart and increased her zeal. Most of the other assistants were older, married women. When one expressed surprise that she should be doing this work "on a lovely Saturday afternoon when you could be out enjoying yourself", she felt a trace of inner peace for the first time since Ian left.

"You see, Ah So, twelve pieces to bring," said Viola in Cantonese, surveying her beloved furniture in the store room. "They are all marked. Tomorrow I bring a coolie and you check that he bring all these things to my new flat. Understand?"

"O.K. Missee." Ah So preferred to air his English in reply. "Tomorrow morning-time, I makee coolie take fur'ture from store room, take to you flat."

"YOUR flat," Viola corrected him as she edged out of the basement of the boarding-house.

"Very sorry you not stay Courtlands, Missee," Ah So said mournfully.

"You can come and seem me sometimes, I'll still look at your homework for you."

Viola laboured up the four flights of stairs to her room, reminding herself that living in a first floor flat would be yet another advantage to her move.

Her tiny room looked more crowded than ever, for her personal possessions and clothes were now stacked there in boxes and suitcases. There could be no comparison between this and the spacious room in Raoul's flat, where she would have her own bathroom, and the intriguing and amusing company of Raoul in between his absences. Recently he had started teaching her to drive his car, with the promise that when she had passed her test she could use it when he was out of the colony. He had been due back the previous evening but the amah said he had not yet returned. She had refrained from phoning this morning in case he'd arrived very late and was asleep. Now she phoned again, and this time he answered.

"Ah Viola! How are you?"

"Marvellous - all packed up and ready to move tomorrow. When did you get back?"

"Very late last night „.- I have only just got out of my bed."

"How was the trip?"

"Grim! Pathetic! I shall tell you about it in too much detail when we meet. When can that be?"

"I'm free now - "

"Then come now.. I shall be dressed by the time you arrive. We'll have some tea, and then maybe another driving lesson?"

Even that brief telephone contact transmitted his powerful personality. As she walked the short distance to his flat, carrying two small cases of breakables, she mentally looked over her shoulder at her orthodox parents, knowing they would never understand. She also reminded herself sternly that this move must not involve any commitments, but when he greeted her with his wide smile, she wondered how long she would remain uncommitted. He took her hands and pulled her towards him. She pressed his hands affectionately, but held herself back. He looked very tired, though immaculate as ever in starched long white slacks and a pale blue aertex shirt.

"And what have you been doing with yourself while I have been away? How many different beaux have escorted you?"

"I lost count," she retorted gaily, sitting opposite him on the verandah and helping herself to the tea the amah brought.

He recounted his experiences during the fall of Canton, his voice indignant and sad at the pathetic defence that never was, and the sufferings of the citizens.

"The trouble is, there are too many wars going on: the Nationalists against the Communists; and the Japanese against whatever faction of Chinese are in their way. Poor China! She is being rent to pieces, and no one outside of China seems to care." He gave a huge yawn. "Are you ready for your driving lesson?"

"Are you sure you're up to it today? Because it doesn't really matter, there's no hurry."

"My dear Viola, how do you know there is no hurry?

You wish to learn to drive so you can drive an ambulance in an emergency: an emergency is some unanticipated occurrence, is it not? Therefore an emergency can come at any time maybe next week, maybe next year, or maybe tomorrow." Draining his cup, he stood up. "I shall take you driving for one hour; then I must return and finish my report for the editor."

"Can I pop these things in my room?"

"Surely, I shall show you."

She followed him along the passage leading to both bedrooms.

"Have finish makee bed now, Master," said the amah, passing them on her way to the kitchen.

The largest bedroom, Raoul's, was on the front of the flat; Viola's was directly opposite. Both doors were open, showing everything fresh and tidy - except that at the foot of the coverlet on Raoul's bed three items lay neatly side by side: a folded pink silk night-gown, a hair clip and an open box of pink tissues.

She was a young French journalist called Délice, Raoul explained during the driving lesson. He had met her on the plane coming back from Canton. They had landed late, she knew no one in Hong Kong and had little money for accommodation, so naturally he had offered her hospitality for the night.

"Your room was already prepared for you and we didn't want to disturb it, so Délice shared my room." Raoul shrugged his shoulders this way and that. "She was fun, but a very bad journalist.. a dreadful memory, for facts, for everything..as you saw... you are driving too fast, Viola, take it more slowly."

"Where is Délice now?"

"On her way back to France if she was able to get her bank to advance her the fare this morning."

"I'm sure she managed that," Viola tried to laugh. There was no reason why she should mind that Délice had spent the night with Raoul; she had always known she was but one of his girl friends, recognised that his charm was his ability to convince the current one that she was the only one. Now she saw it would be less easy to ignore his way of life, living in his flat. For the past three months, he had been the only boy-friend constantly in her thoughts, and she had begun to allow herself to think it was the same for him.

The driving lessons used to be exciting. Today's seemed dull. Under the guise of feeling she was learning something worth while, the first lessons had after all been just a reason for an outing with Raoul at her side, putting his hand over hers to correct the wheel from time to time. She was astonished at herself for not realising this before.

He took over the driving seat as they began to drive back to the busy city.

"You need more practice before you can cope with half the population of Hong Kong trying to cross the road at once," he said. "It will be easier to arrange lessons at short notice from now on, won't it? You are a very sensible girl, Viola, to do as I have suggested for so long. I am sure we will both benefit."

He gave her his dazzling smile as he slowed down to turn the car into Kennedy Road, and put one hand on her knee and squeezed it. Her heart leapt but cold reason forced her to listen to her inner voice: 'No, Raoul, no, I couldn't share you.' She started to find the words to tell him that the move was off.

DECEMBER

Roddy sank into the long rattan chair on the verandah and lit a cigarette, too lazy even to read the Sunday newspaper: tiffin with Belle and her family in the Macdonnell Road flat always had a soporific effect on him, especially when, as today, curry had been served.

The others joined him on the verandah, Pamela settling down with the Sunday Herald, a cup of coffee on the small table at her side. The children could be heard protesting to the amah who was cajoling them into taking an afternoon rest. The lovely flat overlooking Kennedy Road gave a panoramic view of the harbour and the great Lion Rock at the back of Kowloon.

"So you and Greg will be moving back to the Territories now things have settled down?" Keith bent towards him to take a light from his cigarette.

"Next week," nodded Roddy.

"Are you sure it's really safe? asked Belle.

"Oh you women!" laughed Keith. "Would the Chesters, with all those young children, move back if it wasn't?"

"But isn't it a dreadful fag, journeying all that way to work every day?" Belle said. "I'd have thought the Y.M. was much more convenient."

"There's just no comparison," said Roddy simply. "I ride with the children early every morning - sometimes at the end of the day too! The air's marvellous; no noisy car hooters; and the Chesters are such a great family." He drew on his cigarette and stared at it fixedly, thinking of the most important reason why he wanted to live in Fan Ling, Mrs. Chester. It was during the four weeks he had been back in the Y.M.C.A. that he'd realised how much he depended on the family for contentment: and eventually he admitted to himself that life without Mrs. Chester in particular was no life at all.

Despite her constant care and consideration for her husband and children, he had come to see her as a person apart from her rôle as wife and mother; he fantasised about her constantly, her fragile beauty, her gentleness, and her loving smile. Four weeks without the blessed benediction of her presence had taught him to face the depth of his feelings for her. The frequent dates with Josie and other dancing partners, the flirtatious kisses and cuddles, were on a different plane.

Since leaving the Fan Ling bungalow, his only contact with the Chesters had been at weekends, when as a friend of the family he could reasonably visit them in the house near the Univeristy where they were lodging. Even then, he was forced to act out that rôle by carrying the children off for a trip in his car, denying himself her company for much of the visit.

"Don't think we'll have any more trouble from the Japs now." Keith was leaning over the verandah and spoke over his shoulder. "They've got what they wanted in the south. I'd say we're in for a bit of peace while they busy themselves chasing the Chinese Government, but I doubt if they'll ever take Chungking, it's 99% impregnable."

The Boy refilled the coffee cups. The children's plaintive voices could still be heard, arguing with the amah.

"Jamie is far too old for an afternoon nap," sighed Belle, "and Lisa doesn't see why she should have to rest if he doesn't."

"Tell you what!" Roddy heaved himself out of the chair. "Soon as I've finished this cup, I'll take the kids out for a run: want to come, Pam?"

"Suppose I might as well," was the surprisingly ungracious reply as Pamela tossed the newspaper on to the table.

Though the early December sunshine was warm, the swimming season was really over; yet the children begged to be taken to Repulse Bay. It was a beautiful afternoon as the car climbed the road twisting above the city to the gap in the peaks which led to the other side of the island. That first glimpse of the peaceful, uncluttered slopes never failed to thrill Roddy. Even the heartache for Mrs. Chester was temporarily forgotten. Lovingly, he manipulated the car round the road which ran down to Repulse Bay.

"Castle, Castle!" chorussed the children as they passed the turreted mock-castle overlooking the Bay; it was their signal that they were almost at the beach. The bluest, the clearest of skies canopied the steep, dark green mountains; the sea sparkled all shades of blue until it merged with the horizon.

The children joined in when Roddy started to sing his favourite song, yelling at the top of their voices in the final line "OVER the hills and FAR AWAY!"

"Ice creams first," decided Roddy when they left the car outside the Lido, "then we grownups might get some peace."

"They'll expect another lot later," muttered Pamela in his ear.

"So what?" He pushed the children ahead of him towards a marble-topped table on the open verandah, muttering "Don't be a sourpuss Pam, it's not like you."

His feeling of well-being continued: lazing on the sand before the Lido as the children ranged up and down the beach, he counted his blessings: his reformed way of life meant he was now managing to live on his income, at the same time steadily paying off his debt to Pamela; he had many friends of both sexes; Greg was much better - and next week he would have Mrs. Chester to give an aura of magic to every hour in her presence.

"Go away and play, do!" Pamela was shouting at Lisa. "I'm fed up with your moaning.. we DIDN'T bring your swimming costumes so there's an end to it. Buzz off and leave us in peace."

"Hey look, Lisa!" Roddy felt Pamela had been unnecessarily sharp. "I can see two canoe-ists having a race. I wonder which one will win?"

From the headland a quarter of a mile out sped two canoes, one paddled by a female, the other by a male, both in swimming gear. As they neared the beach, Roddy was able to recognise the girl as Sandra Smithson, Pamela's childhood friend, whom he had recently re-met at a dance in the hotel. She had greeted him initially with interest, but made no effort to introduce him to the party at her table. This he understood and accepted: what place had a humble Government junior clerk with a taipan's daughter and her set? Nevertheless, he now watched appreciatively as the trim figure in the leading canoe flashed her paddle furiously in an effort to keep ahead of her companion. Breathless and laughing hugely, she reached the beach just ahead of him and threw herself on to the sand. He, a blond giant twice her size, hauled both canoes out of the water, then flopped down beside her.

"I won, I won!" Sandra trumpeted.

"So you should.. you had two hundred yards start."

"Anyway, I won."

"Agreed. So you choose where we have dinner tonight." He turned towards her and attempted to slide an arm round her shoulders, but she rolled away on to her stomach - and was immediately in line with Pamela and Roddy several yards higher up the beach; she gave them a friendly wave.

"I'm not free this evening, Mike."

"But you said.."

"Oh dear, I must have forgotten: we have friends coming to dinner at home."

"Oh hell, Sandra! What about the cinema tickets you told me to get for the late show?"

"So terribly sorry." Sandra winked at Pamela. "Dreadful of me to forget. We'll sort something out some other time, yes? Ready now, I'll race you back!"

Brother and sister watched while Mike sulkily pulled the canoes back into the water, and helped Sandra into hers; just before she began to paddle away, she turned round and blew them an exaggerated kiss.

"What a girl!" Roddy laughed.

"That's all she is still, a spoilt little girl." Pamela grunted. "She's got a dreadful name already, and only been back here a couple of months. She was awful to that poor fellow."

"Oh come on, Pam, don't be such a prude. I feel sorry for that guy too, but she certainly makes the sparks fly when she's around."

"I think she's outrageous!"

Roddy was surprised at Pamela's vehemence, then suddenly realised that her demeanour all this afternoon had been rather strange: in between bouts of what he could only call sheer bad temper with the children, there had been long stretches of total silence between them as they had lounged on the beach.

"Anything wrong?" he asked.

"Course not." She jumped up, called the children over and organised games with them on the sand until it was time to leave. As the children struggled with shoes and socks, there was a shout from the road, and Sandra, now dressed, pelted towards them.

"So glad I caught you." She grabbed Pamela's arm. "I'm on my way to the Powder Room and I hoped I'd bump into you. Did you see Danny Russell's photo in today's paper?"

"Yes, I did."

"Did you meet him while he was here?"

"No."

"Danny back in Hong Kong?" Roddy interposed. "I didn't know."

"There's an article about him in the Herald; he came over during the week for some relative's wedding but went back to Manila yesterday. I do wish I'd met him; he looks terrific in the photograph! Must dash back to Mike - got to keep him sweet-tempered until he drops me at home.. then that's the end, he's the most disgusting groper, I can't wait to get rid of him."

She waved goodbye and ran back to the car waiting on the road.

"No wonder she snubbed him," Roddy turned to Pamela, then noticed her stricken face and tears standing in her eyes; a suspicion of the reason suddenly came to him. Hastily, he despatched the children to buy ice-creams.

"It's Danny, isn't it?" he said hesitantly. "Sorry I was so touchy with you earlier; in my dumb way, I didn't twig you were upset about something this afternoon."

"I've no reason to be upset." Pamela's voice was high. "I got over him ages ago, but it was just such a smack in the face to read he'd been back here and hadn't as much as telephoned.. I know I'm silly, though" - her voice shook - "He promised not to contact me when Dad let me stay on here last January. I'm just being stupid.. I suppose he's forgotten about me, and got a new life, and other friends."

"Of course he won't have forgotten you." He patted her hand. "He's just being realistic. Sure he's made a new life for himself, and so have you."

Still her face was working, so he stumbled on "Gosh, no one goes on mourning their old flames for ever! Bit like Hilary and me, really; I got over her, didn't I? (All the same, I'm glad she didn't marry that hearty Ian - never did like him.) But she and I always argued too much to get on together. And now, I couldn't be happier - except for my boring job: lovely digs with a lovely family; you and Belle and Keith and the kids behind me; my horse; outings with Greg and all my other friends..." ("And Mrs. Chester, and Mrs. Chester, and Mrs. Chester!" sang his heart.)

PART 5

New Year's Eve 1939

and 1940

New Year's Eve.. And, thought Roddy, little had changed in his life during the year just about to end, even though war had started in Europe, and Hong Kong paid lip-service to the situation by subscribing to Bomber Funds and knitting Balaclavas and scarves, and practising air raid precautions: the most important element for him had not altered since the day he had first met and fallen in love with Mrs. Chester.

His friends teased him about his devotion, but none seemed to guess the extent of his feelings - certainly not the succession of girls with whom he spent most of his spare time: dancing, swimming, playing badminton and tennis, and hiking over the hills; the kisses he yearned to rain on Mrs. Chester were reserved for them. He felt quite guilty about Josie, who was clearly misled by his attentions. She had hinted she would welcome an engagement announcement on New Year's Day - which was why he had bowed out of the New Year's Eve party at the Hong Kong Hotel, pleading a promise to spend the evening with the Chesters.

Now dinner was over and the younger children in bed. He had eaten too much and drunk some wine. Neighbours who had been guests at dinner had long since left. The two older children were busy with their new clockwork train set, the rails meandering over the floor and round the furniture. The Professor and Mrs. Chester sat in adjacent chairs opposite the settee where Roddy lolled. A standard lamp whose stand was in the form of a writhing blackwood dragon, and whose parchment shade was decorated wih delicate Chinese country scenes, threw a halo of brightness around Mrs. Chester's hair. She looked like an angel, and Roddy could not take his eyes off her.

"Time you two were in bed," she said to the children. "You've been awake since dawn."

They begged for extensions.. there were fervent pleas; it was New Year's Eve, they weren't a bit tired.

"Chase you there!" said Roddy, coming to life and making a ferocious face.

With much stifled giggling so as not to wake the younger children, the older two allowed themselves to be captured and settled in to bed.

When he returned to the lounge, the Chesters were listening to the oscillating radio news from London.

"All quiet?" Mrs. Chester's raised eyebrows asked.

"O.K." He sat down on the settee again, his eyes trained on the loved face beneath the lamp.

"Nothing new - long may it remain like that!" The Professor switched off the radio and pulled out his pipe.

The dreaded mass air raids on Britain had not materialised. The British Expeditionary Force was entrenched on the Continent, with no activity on the front since the declaration of war three months earlier. Only the losses at sea of the liner 'Athenia', and the naval ships 'Courageous' and 'Royal Oak' proved this really was war.

"I don't think I'm going to stay up to see the New Year in." The Professor prised himself out of his chair. "I'll just finish this pipe and get a breath of air, then I'm turning in."

"I'm ready for bed too," said Mrs. Chester, following him on to the verandah.

Roddy, looking at their companionable backs as they stood side by side looking out at the garden, felt a great loneliness. Irrevocably excluded, he had a sudden urge to be with crowds, away from their togetherness which emphasised the hopelessness of his love; if he left the bungalow now and drove to the ferry, he could be in the Hong Kong Hotel soon after midnight - in time for the last hour of the party. With the unaccustomed wine, he thought he probably wasn't fit to drive, but the roads should be fairly empty..

The sound of an approaching car broke the silence.

"Visitors!" called Mrs. Chester from the verandah. "Trying to first-foot us - the Stones."

Jim Stone was a young colleague of the Professor's who lived in the nearest bungalow two miles away. His wife Jess was so giggly that it was obvious this was not their first port of call this evening. The Professor was not pleased; he drifted off to bed and left the visitors to his wife and Roddy.

"Got to celebrate the New Year with all our friends," beamed Jim, bringing a half bottle of whisky from his jacket pocket. Perhaps in an attempt to atone for the abrupt departure of her husband, Mrs. Chester sparkled with friendliness.

"Put on the radio," suggested Jess. "ZBW's bound to provide us with some seasonal music we can dance to."

"Not too loud," cautioned Mrs. Chester. "The children are asleep."

The Stones had no children; they found it difficult to remember to keep their voices down. The Tientsin carpet was rolled back, and to the muted strains of 'Deep Purple', the four danced round the furniture - Jim with Jess, and Roddy with Mrs. Chester. Never before had Roddy had his arms round her, except in dreams. Fulfilment seemed unbelievable. With shaking hands, he held her very correctly and distantly.

"All change!" roared Jim at the end of the first dance, then cupped his hand over his mouth at Mrs. Chester's agonised "Shush!"

Obediently, Roddy danced with Jess, who giggled and encouraged him to hold her closer ("I don't bite, you know!") but his eyes were always on Mrs. Chester as she strove to keep the fawning Jim at arm's length.

Then it was midnight. Jim insisted on re-charging every one's glasses, and they mouthed 'Auld Lang Syne' at each other, shook hands and exchanged perfunctory kisses.

"Now we really must finish," whispered Mrs. Chester as Jim, his bottle empty, cast glances at the drinks cabinet. "Thanks so much for dropping in. We've enjoyed it, haven't we Roddy?"

He wanted to say "It's been heavenly" but nodded "Great fun."

The Stones were waved away and Mrs. Chester and Roddy returned to the lounge to close the French windows and lock up. The radio was still playing soft dance music - a waltz.

"One last dance?" he dared to ask.

"Oh, I don't think so.. it's so late.."

"Please, please!" He pulled her into his arms and held her urgently. She tried to struggle free, but he would not let her go, and pressed kisses on her arms, neck and throat.

"Rod!" Her shocked voice brought him to his senses. His hands dropped to his sides and he sank into the nearest chair; with great sobs he hid his face among the cushions, mumbling "Forgive.. forgive! I love you so, I always have."

"I know, I know." She sat on the side of his chair and held his shoulders bracingly until he was quiet. "And the Professor and I love you like one of our own."

"I've spoilt it.. I've spoilt everything!"

"No you haven't. It's best to talk about it, once and for all. I'm so touched by your care and concern for me; let's keep it like that."

"Care! Concern!" he echoed in despair. "It's love, Mrs. Chester, real love."

" 'It's love, Mrs. Chester', she mocked gently. "There you have it. The time will come when all you feel for me will be for some lucky young lady, and you will whisper her Christian name when you tell her about it."

"I'll never love anyone as I love you!"

"Wait and see." She gave him a final pat and rose. "You'll feel better in the morning."

"I'll move out after breakfast.."

"No need to do that, as long as we understand each other, but it's entirely up to you. Good night, dear Rod, don't be too upset. Let's pretend this evening never happened."

Staring into the quiet darkness, slowly smoking a last cigarette on the verandah, Roddy gradually calmed down. He knew he should leave the bungalow, but he also knew that he would stay as long as he was allowed to do so. The pain of the scene in the lounge was partly assuaged by the memory of the sheer paradise of dancing in her arms. It was the same hopeless situation he had faced for the past year. Perhaps he should, after all, have opted for the party at the hotel, where he would be dancing and wining with crowds of young people, forgetting his heartache.

'Run Rabbit Run!" sang the light-voiced vocalist of the hotel band. Words and music were barely audible among the clink of glasses, popping of champagne corks, laughter and conversation at the crowded tables.

"You're the only person I know who sees the New Year in on Coke!" groaned Greg, Pamela's immediate neighbour at the table hosted by Belle and Keith.

"Why not? It's what I like best."

"You're what I like best," Greg whispered, squeezing her hand. Pamela smiled then pulled away and turned to talk to Oliver, a young clerk from Keith's office. She was grateful to Keith and Belle for having added three colleagues to the party as their presence helped to lighten the burden of Greg's attentions - but he was whispering to her again: "Didn't expect to be still in Hong Kong in 1940, did you?"

"I certainly didn't; I haven't quite got used to the idea that I really belong here in Hong Kong now." Incredibly, reprieve from her return to England had happened yet again, earned nine months ago by the growing threat of the European war that had become reality in September. ('Daddy thinks you'll be safer in Hong Kong for the time being,' her mother had written after Hitler's intentions had been demonstrated by overrunning Czechoslovakia. 'The Japs seem to have quietened down.')

Her attention was drawn to Sandra Smithson at a table nearby which included several Naval Officers. Sandra's voice had been growing shriller as the evening progressed; how thankful Pamela was that she had rejected the half-hearted offer of renewing their childhood acquaintanceship - they had little in common now, if indeed they ever had.

Greg turned to Pamela to claim a dance, a polka, but Oliver was quicker. The floor shook to the rat-tat-tat of feet.

"Damn you, you've torn my dress, you bloody fool!" Sandra's voice sounded behind Pamela who turned to see an embarrassed young Naval Officer staring down at a trail of yellow chiffon on the floor.

"So sorry, caught my heel; honestly, I couldn't help it," he said.

"Of course you could help it! My dress is ruined!" Sandra's speech was slurred.

"I'll get it repaired tomorrow. I'm truly sorry, Sandra.."

"Leave me alone, for God's sake, and let me dance with someone who isn't such a clumsy oaf." She lunged back to her table and took the arm of the nearest officer who had sprung to his feet on her approach. "Come on Tim, see if you can do better."

Pamela watched Sandra take the floor again, her arms clasped tightly round Tim's neck as she sagged against him.

"Heavens, that girl's tight, isn't she?" whispered Oliver.

"She always drinks too much; she's known for it." Pamela couldn't hide her disgust.

It was obvious that Sandra was now in no state to dance. Tim was attempting to lead her off the floor but she tried to resist and fought him all the way before finally sinking into her chair and flopping forward on to the table scattering the cutlery. The other members of her party sat in silence and looked uncomfortable.

"Pam!" Belle, seven months' pregnant, levered herself out of her chair. "Come along, we must do something about her."

"She's with friends,.. she's nothing to do with us.."

"Come!" Belle, surprisingly pulling rank as elder sister, urged her. "Let's take her to the Powder Room before things get any worse."

Grimacing with distaste, Pamela followed at a distance as Belle persuaded Sandra to allow herself to be led into the Powder Room just in time, for she staggered into the nearest lavatory and was violently sick. Pamela stood by the cloakroom door, as far away as possible from the scene.

The amah in charge put her arms round Sandra and held her until the worst was over, while Belle hovered nearby. Afterwards, collapsing into a rattan chair, Sandra shivered and sobbed; tried to get up, then flopped back again, moaning. Belle sat beside her and laid a succession of wet cloths on her forehead.

Two girls from Sandra's party came in and stared anxiously at her.

"She'll be O.K. soon," Belle whispered.

"The fellows who brought us have to leave," one girl said. "They're due back on board in half an hour, so they need to take Sandra home right now."

"And goodness knows what her parents will say when she arrives home like this," added the other, surveying the limp figure in the chair.

"Don't worry, we'll look after her," said Belle. "when she's fit to leave my sister and I will take her home with us for the night. I can phone her parents and let them know."

Pamela wanted to escape from the whole affair, but she had to sit in the back of Keith's car and support a retching Sandra on the short ride to Macdonnell Road. Deprived of her comfortable bed, to which Keith carried Sandra, she had to make do with a narrow camp bed in the same room. She made no secret of her disgust, and Belle laughed at her downcast face as she whispered "Goodnight old thing! Don't be such a prude - we all make mistakes sometimes, and you couldn't leave an old friend in distress, could you?"

It was ten o'clock when she woke. Sandra was asleep; a trail of vomit from her bed to the bathroom told the tale of the night. Slipping on a dressing-gown, Pamela escaped quietly from the room.

"Happy New Year Auntie Pam!" sang the children from the breakfast table.

"How is she?" Belle cocked an enquiring glance in the direction of the bedroom.

"Still asleep," yawned Pamela, sinking into the chair the Boy had pulled forward, and reaching gratefully for the cup of coffee he handed her.

"Best take that to your room to drink," Belle said. "Sandra won't have a clue where she is when she surfaces."

"Oh really! Any one would think she was a princess or something! It's too smelly in there.. she's been sick again."

"Oh dear.. in that case, finish your coffee here, then I'll come in with you. Her father's just phoned - he wanted to come when I rang and fetched her last night but I said we'd invited her to tiffin, so he's coming for her about half past two - she should be respectable by then."

In the bedroom, Pamela stood beside the open window as Belle gave orders and the amah bustled about, cleaning the floor and removing the soiled top blanket. A few squirts of perfume sweetened the air. The spoiled evening dress which had been soaking in the bathroom was removed; the clanking of the pail handle roused Sandra; her eyes flew open wide, and Pamela, urged by a poke in the back from Belle, moved over to the bed.

"We brought you home with us from the hotel last night," said Belle. "You didn't seem very well; feeling better now?"

Deep colour spread over Sandra's face. "I still feel awful," she mumbled.

"You'll be better after you've had a bath - amah's already running it," said Belle cheerfully. "There's plenty of time. I've been on the phone to your father; he's coming to collect you after tiffin."

"Oh God!" Sandra, pulling herself up in bed, was staring at the stained slip she was still wearing. The pillow too was stained and sticky. She put her hands on her head and felt the matted curls, then stumbled out of bed across to the bathroom.

"I look-see Missie," the amah muttered, shuffling in after her.

Pamela dressed quickly; too nauseated to eat any breakfast, she sat on the verandah and drank more coffee, trying to put from her mind the unpleasant situation until Belle called her.

"Sandra's ready to dress - you'll need to lend her something to wear."

"Nothing will fit; she's shorter."

"Oh I'm sure you can find something just for now - a skirt and jumper I should think."

Sandra was standing by the bedroom window, clad in Belle's dressing-gown which came down to her ankles. Her damp hair formed a thick bright halo round her sullen face. The amah was stripping the bed; when she had finished and gone off with the bedding, Sandra demanded "I want to know what happened last night!"

Riffling through the wardrobe for a suitable skirt, Pamela muttered "You weren't very well.. my sister told you."

"She was just being tactful, wasn't she?"

"You really weren't well."

"I'm not a fool! I was taken to the party by three Naval Officers but they didn't take me home; instead, you bring me here. Obviously I got sloshed and I insist on knowing just what happened."

"All right, I'll tell you! You made a great scene on the dance floor when your partner stood on the hem of your dress and tore it. You wanted to keep on dancing though you were too drunk to stand up. Belle and I took you to the Powder Room and you were sick over and over again, and in too disgusting a state to go home at the time your friends had to leave. So Belle said we had to bring you here; and you were sick over me in the back of the car, and in my bed, and all over my bedroom floor!"

"Oh Lord!" Sandra turned towards the window, pressing her knuckles against her mouth,then she faced Pamela again, defiant and white-faced. "I apologise - but this must quite please you: you've always disapproved of me, haven't you?"

No honest denial was possible. Instead, Pamela held out a navy blue skirt and said "This might fit."

Sandra managed an ungracious murmur of thanks as she finished dressing. She stood regarding the effect in the mirror, then swayed and grabbed at the nearest chair, snapping "I'm starving.. I didn't eat anything in the hotel last night..I feel so ill." Her voice shook and tears ran down her cheeks.

"I'll ask Belle to give you something to settle your stomach, then you might be able to eat some toast," Pamela's voice was cold despite the kind words.

An Alka Seltzer and dry toast helped; though still looking very pale, Sandra was able to manage some soup at tiffin-time. Pamela was relieved that after the meal the children brought out their Christmas games and involved the adults, so it was easy for her to maintain civility towards Sandra without personal conversation.

When the Smithson car was noticed breasting the drive to the flats, Pamela saw the change in Sandra's face as she braced herself for the meeting. "Now I'm for it," she muttered. "They're bound to have heard from some of their dearly beloved friends what happened at the hotel. Still, thanks to that schmozzle in Europe, at least they can't ship me back to England."

JANUARY

A fortnight into January, Keith, Belle and Pamela received an invitation to dine with the Smithsons. Despite Pamela's reluctance, Belle insisted on blanket acceptance.

Over drinks and dinner in the Deep Water Bay bungalow, nothing was mentioned of the reason for the invitation, but Sandra's parents' gratitude for the care given to her on New Year's Eve was implicit in their demeanour.

At the first opportunity Sandra led Pamela off to her room, apologised sincerely for her behaviour, acknowledging the justice of Pamela's disgust and humbly tried to make amends. As an excuse she pleaded her frustrations at home and lack of purpose in life: "I'm so bored! When I first came back to Hong Kong all I wanted to do was enjoy myself after years of restriction at boarding-schools - and drive my gorgeous car the parents gave me for my 19th birthday."

Pamela knew about the car, as did most Europeans in the colony. The white MG sports model, usually open-hooded, was notorious for the number of traffic offences committed by its driver - and, it was whispered, the number which never came to court.

"Since the war started," Sandra continued, "lots of girls in my circle have gone all patriotic and started working as censors, or training to be nurses in case there's fighting here, and it's no fun driving around on my own every day.. I want to get a job, a real post, so I can be self-sufficient, and have a flat of my own, and run my own life without being answerable to anyone for where I'm going and when I'm going to come back. Of course, THEY won't hear of it.. say it's not necessary for me to earn my living, it would be degrading for my father if I had a job!"

"But your mother has had a job for as long as I can remember!"

"You know why, don't you?" Sandra's voice was harsh. "I only found out recently: when my brother died, she got my father to set her up in her own business, to give her an interest.. I suppose she couldn't stand the sight of me at home! Cigarette?"

"No thanks, don't smoke."

"You wouldn't! Little Miss Perfect, as usual!" Sandra's voice was kinder than her words. "My parents always used to hold you up to me as a good example when we were kids: they still do! Every time I try to get them to agree to let me have my own flat they cite you, how you live with your sister and brother-in-law 'in a proper family circle' as they put it."

"They won't be able to say that much longer! When Belle's baby arrives I'll be moving out - they'll need my room."

"Where will you live then?"

"In a flat in Kennedy Close, with two other girls."

"You lucky devil! You lucky, lucky devil! Who are the others?"

"Viola - my friend at the office, and someone else.. we're still working out who."

"Let it be me! Oh do let it be me"

Horrified, Pamela floundered "You said your parents wouldn't hear of you.."

"They wouldn't let me go into a flat on my own," Sandra cut in, "but I just KNOW they'd say yes if I was sharing with you. Please, Pam!"

"We've got someone in mind already.."

"Who?"

"I can't tell you." Negotiations betwen Hilary, the third possibility, and her parents were at a delicate stage; Mr. and Mrs. Bately were retiring to England and trying to persuade Hilary to leave with them. "Anyway, Viola would be the one to decide because we're taking over the flat from a friend of hers.."

"You don't want me!" The old petulant look returned. "Can't say I blame you, though honestly, I'm turning over a new leaf. Promise me, Pam, that if your third someone doesn't materialise you'll beg Viola to let me come?"

"It really isn't likely." Pamela shook her head. "Look, why don't you do some business training - shorthand and typing - NOW, so that when you're 21 you'd be competent enough to take a good job and become independent of your parents."

"It's no good, I've pleaded for training; they offered me a course of bridge lessons - and I can't stand cards! Apparently my rôle in life is to learn how to be a Hong Kong hostess and circulate among eligible males to find a suitable husband. I actually got myself a clerical position despite having no experience, with Taggs & Boon, all ready to start this month. I didn't want the parents to know until I'd begun working, but some one told them on New Year's Eve and they rang Mr. Boon and cancelled everything - that was why I was in such a foul mood at the hotel that night."

"How rotten!" Pamela began to feel a twinge of sympathy. "I can see your problem, but why not join your friends who are training to be auxiliary nurses.. more volunteers are always being asked for, and what you'd learn would be useful, even if there's never a war here."

"Nursing's not my forte. And don't talk about war here, it couldn't happen; the Japs wouldn't dare."

"Let's hope not! There's St. John Ambulance Brigade then.. that functions all the time, war or no war. Viola belongs to the driving section.. you say you love driving."

"But doesn't that mean I'd have to go to boring parades, and do drill and displays, and stand by to pick up people who faint?"

"Oh you're quite impossible! You're so spoilt, there's no pleasing you! You'll just have to go on being bored, I'm afraid."

Instead of showing anger, Sandra burst into laughter. "You're so good for me, Pam! I'd be a different person if you'd let me come and share your flat. You're such a goody-goody, some of it would just HAVE to rub off on me!"

On the Continent, German and Allied armies continued to face each other without doing battle, but the menace remained. There were shocking losses at sea, brought home to Pamela when the 'Rawalpindi' - converted into an armed cruiser - was sunk with guns defiantly firing.

Letters from England had ominous news. Ella wrote that all the young men at H. & S. were in the services and she had taken over from Lawrence who had joined the Navy. Pamela's parents wrote of the dangers of walking in blackouts, and the prospective installation of an air raid shelter deep in the back garden "though how we shall ever persuade Granny and Grandad to set foot in it, I don't know!"

It seemed quite wrong to Pamela that at a time of such hardship in Europe, she should be happier than she had ever been: about to realise a long-cherished wish to share a home with Viola and Hilary. It was sheer luck that Raoul had decided to give up his flat at a time when she and Hilary were looking for lodgings, and offered Viola first refusal of the lease.

"He spends so much time in China now that it's not worth him keeping the flat on," Viola had confided. "When he comes back from Chungking next month, he's going to move into the Y.M. Strictly between us, he'd have kept the flat on if I'd agreed to move in and pay a small contribution to his rent - no commitment etc.. but I said No the last time he suggested it, and I said No again."

"You still care for him, though, don't you?" Pamela suggested.

"Of course, trouble is, so do half the females in Hong Kong," Viola laughed. "I'm much happier playing the field."

Chinese New Year, with its two days' holiday, offered her time to sort out her possessions in readiness for the move, but the envisaged leisure didn't materialise. With the servants away and Belle's baby several days' overdue, Pamela and Keith bore the brunt of the housework and cooking. The weather was cold and wet, the washing wouldn't dry, and the children were crotchetty because they had to stay indoors.

By the last evening of the holiday, all three adults were exhausted, and sighed with relief when the children were in bed.

"Thank goodness for amahs!" Keith had just sat down for a quiet cigarette when the telephone rang and he had to get up again to answer it.

Belle and Pamela looked up in alarm as he said sharply "Calm down, Rod: tell me again, slowly, what happened." Then: "Oh my God! Is there anything we can do?"

"What is it, what is it?" begged the girls.

"Professor Chester," mouthed Keith, still listening intently to the voice on the line. "Snake bite. He's dead."

Sitting in the Sha Tin bungalow later that night with Roddy and Greg, Pamela could imagine the joyous holiday ramble over the hills, the Chester family strung out in a line: the picnic despite the bad weather because the Professor never noticed climatic conditions; the searching among the sodden shrubbery for the new specimens of plants and flowers: the moment of horror when the Professor stumbled back from the adder he had surprised in the bushes, and ordered the rest of the family to back off. The children had sobbingly supplied the details over and over again. "Daddy made sure we were all well away from him before he did anything else, then he cut his leg and Mummy sucked it, then Mummy sent us back home for help, but the amahs were still away and Roddy and Greg were out riding, so we phoned the Stones and they carried Daddy home because he was unconscious, and Mummy was crying and crying.."

Mr. Stone had driven the Professor and his wife to the hospital while Mrs. Stone stayed with the children until Roddy and Greg returned; by that time the hospital had telephoned to say the Professor was dead, and Mrs. Chester would be kept there under sedation. "I wanted so much to see her, to try and comfort her," moaned Roddy to Pamela, "but they said no visitors."

From the bedrooms came a wail which was soon echoed from every bed, and all the little Chesters came padding out to the lounge to be consoled, and so the dreadful night continued.

At the graveside the next day, Roddy stared stony-faced at the coffin as it was lowered, unable to accept what he was seeing; the servants from the bungalow and the children were crying loudly. Mrs. Chester, in a black and white dress and black jacket, was dry-eyed, but her face was gaunt, her features taut. How could he ever have thought her youthful and fragile? The image he had held of her in his heart was shattered forever: in its place, a grieving widow, girding herself to face a harsh future which, he knew, had already been decided. As was usual on the death of an expatriate breadwinner in the colony, the Professor's employers were discharging their responsibilities by paying for passages to England for her and the children on the next P. & O. liner which was due to leave Hong Kong in a week's time.

When finally the tearful family was waved off on the 'Narkunda' in her wartime grey overcoat, Roddy knew he was waving goodbye to a fantasy.

FEBRUARY

Belle's baby was born on St. Valentine's Day, and captivated Pamela who had not seen the two older children in their earliest days as both had been born in Shanghai. She was quite jealous when Sandra took to calling in and insisted on holding Tina.

("She just wants to keep in touch in the hope of worming her way into our flat," was Pamela's opinion.

"You're very hard on her," Belle reproved. "She knows Hilary's definitely booked for the flat now and there's no room for a fourth. She's genuinely fond of Tina.")

Two weeks before the prospective move Sandra asked if there was to be a housewarming.

"Splendid idea!" Belle beamed before Pamela could answer. "Keith and I will stand the drinks."

"And I'll lend you Ah Ling," added Sandra.

That was how she came to be present at the party held in the flat a week after the girls had moved in. Even among the twenty-odd guests, her voice could be heard continually as she darted from group to group.

Pamela resented everything about her: the vivid green dress with pleated skirt; the freshly coiffured red hair now cut short; the excitable voice dominating every conversation; the attention she drew from all the menfolk present - with the exception of Roddy, a fact which gave Pamela some satisfaction. This was the first social occasion when Roddy and Hilary had met since their break-up three years ago, and Pamela had secret hopes that they might eventually get together again.

The party was still in full swing when Belle and Keith and Hilary's parents drifted off. The remaining men insisted that the girls join them at the Hong Kong Hotel for dinner - here again Roddy was an exception. Pamela saw his hesitation and watched him fumbling for excuses; she knew his problem - there would be an expensive hotel bill to share at the end of the evening, and he had only just cleared his loan from her. On the pavement outside the flat, as the cars filled up; he still demurred until Sandra pouted "Why are you such a sourpuss? Don't you like us?"

Roddy had no choice but to go to the hotel with the others. His reluctance was not only because of the cost: seeing Hilary again at close quarters had greatly disturbed him. Now that his heart was free of Mrs. Chester, he began to recognise a revival of his old yearning for her. Despite the good times he'd had with a succession of girls in the past three years, none had ever stirred him as Hilary had, but although she was friendly enough at the party in the flat, her attention was focussed on lively men from her office. Now he had no stomach to watch her laughing and dancing with them at the hotel - but Sandra had forced him into this situation and he hated her for it and could barely be civil to her. When he managed to claim a dance with Hilary, she held her body aloof and spoke only in generalities. Painfully, he realised that she would have heard of his long-standing devotion to Mrs. Chester and no doubt despised him for it. After the dance was over he sat morosely at the table, trying to think of an excuse to leave early.

"Roddy! You haven't had a twirl with me yet!" Sandra swooped on him. "It's your turn, come on!"

"I'm just leaving," he protested, but she pulled his arm and he was forced to follow her on to the floor. He put all his anger and frustration into holding her tightly and dancing in the wildest possible way, to the music of 'In The Mood.'

"You're hot stuff," Sandra panted, anticipating his every move, her green skirt swirling; she jigged tirelessly, her steps growing more adventurous every moment. The other dancers cleared the floor to give them more room. Light and lithe, she twisted and side-stepped. The band came to the end of the number, but the conductor indicated reprise after reprise before signing off. Roddy and Sandra were both red in the face with exertion, yet within ten minutes they were in each other's arms again, stamping and singing "Roll Out The Barrel."

Dancing with Sandra had somehow released him from his depression. He felt renewed, emancipated. When the other girls were taken home at half past eleven, he and Sandra could not draw themselves away from the floor, locked together and moving slowly to the music of 'Mood Indigo.'

SPRING

The flat proved ideal in every way; it was only a 5-minute walk from Central; the shared expenses were within the limits of the girls' salaries, and they all got on well together. They took it in turns to organise the daily menus, Ah Lum (inherited from Raoul) doing the shopping and cooking as well as the housework and laundry.

Apart from her annoyance at the continuing affair between Roddy and Sandra, Pamela had never been happier. She felt almost guilty at her good fortune at a time when there were daily reports of the war in Europe: Finland invaded by Russia; Denmark and Norway by Germany; dreadful losses of British ships through enemy action. Letters from England, though cheerful, were shot through with references to the war.

At this distance, all this seemed unrealistic compared with the normal circumstances of life in Hong Kong, where the only tangible reminder was the appearance in town of groups of pink-faced, newly-arrived conscripts to the Army, sent to release more seasoned troops for service in Europe. True, there were occasional practice blackouts and A.R.P. and defence exercises, and she knew from her daily acquaintance with the red-jacketed files in the office that detailed plans were afoot to meet an attack on Hong Kong.

Having Viola and Hilary as flat-mates radically extended Pamela's circle of friends and resulted in a busy social life. Weekends, formerly spent with Belle and her family, were fully occupied with tennis, hiking and picnics. She could hardly imagine a better life - until a phone call at the office from an unfamiliar voice:

"Am I speaking to Miss Pamela Doran?"

"Pamela Doran speaking," she confirmed.

"This is Lawrence.. Lawrence from H. & S. in Ipswich; do you remember me?"

They met after five o'clock at the tiny Canadian Cafe near the office. She was stunned to see he was even more attractive than in her memory. It amazed her that he had remembered her, for he had never answered the letter she'd written on arrival in Hong Kong in 1937.

"I didn't know my destination was Hong Kong when I was pushed on a troopship in January," he said, "else I could have got your address from Ella; but I recalled she'd once said you worked for the Hong Kong Government.. that sounds important, IS it?"

Over drinks, she told him about the job, and the new flat. He told her he was a Writer in the Navy. "Sounds good, doesn't it?" he grinned. "Doesn't mean what I'd like it to mean, though - I'm just a clerk as I was at H. & S., but I shan't remain one - I'm doing private study to get higher up; eventually, after the war I'll get into journalism."

He had been drafted to a small destroyer with the China Fleet. "Great experience, living with so many different kinds of people at close quarters - very different from you living with only two others, I can tell you! You look a different person - make-up, a perm, smart clothes: you've certainly done well for yourself, Pam!"

"I've learned a lot since I left England. What an ignoramus I was then!"

"You were just young," said Lawrence kindly. "I'm delighted to see you so self-confident now. In fact, I'm delighted to see you Full Stop."

Before she had time to make some modest rejoinder he went on "You'll be able to show me round Hong Kong, take me to all the most interesting places."

"I'd really enjoy that. I love it here."

He gave a great laugh. "Do you remember weeping on my shoulder in Christchurch Park because you didn't want to be sent back to Hong Kong?"

"Oh I do!" She also remembered his gentle but wonderful kiss, and now her heart warmed at the nearness of this present-day Lawrence.

She learned more about Hong Kong in the ensuing weeks than in all the years she had lived there. Lawrence's questing nature led him to investigate everything. They took the train from Kowloon, through the New Territories, to the border with China which Japanese troops had left a few months earlier.

On the island they explored the Tiger Balm Gardens where the millionaire inventors of the pungent Tiger Balm ointment had built massive highly-coloured gargoyles and statues; visited Chinese temples and markets, and took jolting tram rides from one end of the route to the other, Lawrence absorbing all he saw. He wrote short articles on his observations and sent them off confidently to newspapers in England.

Pamela only realised how much she had come to depend on his presence when his destroyer left harbour for two weeks' exercises, leaving her with a heart that yearned for more than the platonic friendship Lawrence offered.

Their outings were always purposeful, Lawrence's pursuit of local knowledge relentless, especially when he heard that one of his articles was to be published in England. One Saturday afternoon they took the bus to Happy Valley to explore the old part of the Colonial cemetery. There was a race meeting; trams, buses, taxis and cars were converging on Happy Valley. It was a struggle, once off the bus, for Pamela and Lawrence to elbow their way through the excited crowds - mainly Chinese - bound for the Jockey Club ticket office, and make for the cemetery entrance opposite.

They came upon the pioneers' graves, clustered near a huge circular fountain on the first level. The great granite headstones told their own history: nearly one hundred years ago the first British settlers had reached Hong Kong; whole families had died within a few years of each other - young children within days - victims of cholera or some other plague. As Pamela and Lawrence walked along the narrow concrete paths, immersed in the past, the present occasionally intruded as a low roar came up from the race-course, grew steadily, culminating in a great cacophony of cheering and exhortation, then dropped suddenly to a steady buzz of consternation or congratulation when the race was over.

On an impulse Pamela led Lawrence to the graves of the King Edward Hotel fire victims. Some were unmarked, the others neglected - except for Mrs. Holtz's, where a wreath of china flowers beneath a glass dome lay in front of the clean white tombstone, its inscription bold and clear.

Lawrence was intrigued to see Pamela's name there, even more so when she told him about Mrs. Holtz.

His memory was prodigious. "And this Marcus," he said, pointing to the other names on the stone, "he's the one who had your photo in his wallet, yes? What happened to him, and the others? Are they still here?"

"Only Celeste. Marcus is studying law in the States. Philip - we lost track of him when he went to England. And Danny is in Manila, playing with a band, as far as I know." She purposely didn't elaborate, but Lawrence would not let the matter drop. "So it's Celeste who looks after the grave?" he probed.

"I suppose so.. but Danny had the stone put up when he first went to work and earned enough money." An explanation was necessary to explain how she knew this, so she added lightly "I saw him when I first came back - just before he went to Manila."

"Do you write to him?"

"Oh no!"

"And what about Celeste, do you see much of her?"

"I've met her once - she's much younger than me. She's Portuguese. Our paths don't cross."

"Because she's Portuguese, d'you mean?"

"No.. well, yes, we move in different circles."

"How strange! Is that usual in Hong Kong?"

"More or less," Pamela said, uncomfortably aware of Lawrence's astonishment.

"It's a racial difference, is it? And is it the same with the Chinese - have you any Chinese friends?"

"No, I haven't, as a matter of fact.. I wouldn't know what to talk to them about."

"All this would make an engrossing article," mused Lawrence. "We must discuss it again." For the time being his interest was concentrated on the cemetery. He made copious notes and took photographs.

They were both scarlet-faced by the time they had climbed the last flight of steps to the top plateau of graves, and stood there recovering their breath and looking down on the race course in the valley below.

"All those thousands of people, just watching horses run!" exploded Lawrence. "You wouldn't think there was a bloody war on in Europe." He had recently had a letter from his mother listing the latest food rationing in England - two ounces of butter and a shilling's worth of meat per person per week. "I bet everyone down there on the race course had a jolly good meal around mid-day....the British at least should be ashamed of themselves."

"We're not at war here.. we're not short of anything so we don't have to be rationed," Pamela pointed out.

He was critical of everything about life in Hong Kong. Even Belle, who had often welcomed him in her flat, came under fire for the easy life she led.

"Easy!" snorted Pamela. "Do you call it easy, having to get up at two in the morning to feed a hungry baby?"

"But that's about all she does do! The amah baths the baby and looks after the other kids; the other amahs do the cleaning and laundry, and the cookboy does the cooking. Your sister has time for gossip sessions over coffee with friends, and afternoon mah jong; she's free to go out in the evenings with Keith because the amahs are always there to babysit. No doubt about it, European women here have the life of Riley."

"Well, think of the climate: you haven't had a summer here yet; it gets too hot to do housework.."

"But not too hot for the Chinese amahs to do it."

Therein lay the difference between Lawrence and the other young men of Pamela's acquaintance: a date with Gregg or Hugh brought friendly bandinage and entertainment; Lawrence was serious and challenging. His eagerness to talk, to draw out her opinions, improved her self-confidence, but she couldn't help wishing he would be a little affectionate. So far there had been no attempt to hold her hand in the darkness of the cinema, no goodnight kiss at the end of the evening although this put her in a very good position to reply when Viola quizzed her about him at breakfast one morning.

"An interesting young man, Lawrence," Viola began as she cut the top off her boiled egg. "Most interesting, but you're being rather exclusive with him, aren't you?"

"That's because he IS interesting."

"Not getting too serious, are we?"

"Not!"

"Don't get shirty, Pam: you know my meddling's well-intentioned. Don't want to see you hurt again, so I just have to remind you to keep it low key. You always take everything so seriously."

"We haven't even held hands!" Pamela scraped butter furiously on to her toast. "We have a great friendship, and I'm thoroughly enjoying it."

That was the truth, but not the whole truth. Sometimes, when she and Lawrence sat opposite each other in the Canadian Café - his pay would not run to drinks in costly hotels - there was a look in his eyes which set her heart pounding.

"My God, look at that!" shouted Lawrence as they came out of the cinema on Whit Friday. He pointed to the newspaper placards:

"GERMANY INVADES HOLLAND, BELGIUM AND LUXEMBURG"

They bought a paper and studied it in the café. The Low Countries had been attacked by air and land. In Britain A.R.P. services were warned to be on alert, and the general public told to carry gas masks.

"How I wish I could be in there, fighting those Germans!" Lawrence clenched his fists. "What good am I doing here?"

He grew even more bitter that weekend as each succeeding report was worse than the last. Swimming that Sunday afternoon at Repulse Bay was completely spoilt because he railed continually at his situation.. "Lying here on a beach, idling away the hours, while in England people are worrying about air raids, and checking their children's gas masks!"

Later, spooning ice-cream sundaes in the Lido, they watched a red and gold sunset above the darkening sea. Lawrence had calmed down now but his mind was still on the momentous news from Europe. He looked so despondent that she put her hand over his and said daringly "YOU may be sorry you had to come to Hong Kong - but I'm jolly glad you're here."

There was a long silence, then his hand gripped hers. "I was afraid of that; for me as well as for you." He looked into her face very intently. "You mean a great deal to me, but I'm determined we stay just friends. It isn't fair to begin to be serious when I've nothing to offer you and life is so uncertain anyway. There's such a lot I want to achieve before I can get serious with anyone; you see that, don't you?"

"Yes of course." Pamela tried to withdraw her hand to maintain her dignity, but Lawrence pressed it again. "I shall be as jealous as hell if you have dates with other people," he said, "but I don't have any rights over you, and I have to feel free myself."

This new understanding, however unromantic, gave Pamela a certain contentment. During Lawrence's frequent absences at sea, she accepted invitations from her other friends, partly because this avoided giving the impression that she was committed to Lawrence, and partly because the news from Europe continued to be so appalling that she didn't want to spend evenings alone. The Low Countries fell quickly to the Germans who then rapidly pushed the British Expeditionary Force to the French coast. Though bombed and machine-gunned from the air, miraculously 300,000 survivors were safely evacuated to England by ships of all sizes. Reports of great gallantry poured in, but nothing could soften the truth that this was defeat, not victory.

In desperation Churchill offered France union with Britain in an attempt to prevent wholesale surrender and the complete capitulation of France, but in vain: France signed a peace treaty with Germany. Britain stood alone against the enemy.

"This will make no difference; we will fight on!" growled Churchill's stirring voice on the radio.

JULY

With German air raids starting over England, the British in Hong Kong became uneasy on their own behalf. If the unimaginable could happen in England, could it not happen in Hong Kong too? Germany's rapid victories on the Continent might well fan the ambitions of her Axis ally Japan.

When Japanese troops were seen returning to the Chinese border with the British in the New Territories, the Governor issued a shock announcement: all European women and children were to be compulsorily removed from the colony to a temporary place of safety.

There was consternation and disbelief as this edict was quickly put into effect. Within 72 hours the wives and children of service personnel were shipped away on the 'Empress of Japan', and civilian families instructed to prepare to sail within the week. During that time, when no enemy actively threatened the colony, many residents declared the evacuation unnecessary, but the Governor remained adamant: only women belonging to essential services would be allowed to remain - an exception which applied to Hilary as a V.A.D., Viola with the St. John Ambulance, and Pamela because of her work with the Government.

"Rubbish, of course you must leave," Belle said when told of Pamela's exemption. "It won't be safe to stay here."

"As safe for me as it is for Keith and the men."

"It won't really be safe for anyone, if the Japs come - but the men aren't getting the chance to go."

"My boss says I'm needed in the office."

"He can't make you stay. Anyway, Pam, I won't be able to manage the children without your help."

There were so many imponderables. The 'Empress of Japan' had offloaded the first draught of evacuees in Manila, but would they be moved on, and if so where? Surely not England, now vulnerable to invasion and only approachable through hostile submarine-patrolled seas? Australia then, or New Zealand, both two or three week's journey away? Should summer clothes be taken, or winter? How long would they be away from Hong Kong?

"Wherever you go, it will be safer than staying here if the Japs come," Keith declared, reminding them of the horrific details of the Japanese occupation of Nanking three years earlier. "There's just no two ways about it, Pam, you have to leave."

"I'm staying," she declared, but felt guilty on two counts: not only because she realised how desperately Belle would need her help, but also because the real reason for her stubbornness was not that of loyalty to her job: she simply could not bear to abandon the wholly delightful life in the flat, punctuated with wonderful times with Lawrence.

All that week she was subjected to pressure. There was no Lawrence as his destroyer was on escort duty with the 'Empress of Japan.' Every evening Keith called for her and drove her to Macdonnell Road for dinner. Ostensibly this was so she could spend as much time with the family before sailing day, but she knew the real purpose was to wear down her resistance to leaving. As a last resort Belle cabled her parents, and on Wednesday evening produced a reply:-

'IMPERATIVE PAMELA GO WITH BELLE STOP AM CABLING GASSON INSISTING SHE LEAVES.'

"Dad can't interfere with my life," Pamela shouted with tears of frustration. "I'm 21 and I can make my own decisions. He has no right to bring Mr. Gasson into it!"

She had to spend a miserable hour, trying to listen patiently to Keith's carefully reasoned arguments: Belle and he would never forgive themselves if there was fighting in Hong Kong and she should be injured or killed - or worse: it was quite probable that this rush evacuation was simply a precaution, and that in a very short time the evacuees would be brought back to their homes. Still she stuck to her guns.

She sat dumbly beside Keith as he drove her home. "I can see your mind is made up," he said when she got out of the car, "but promise me one thing: at least, get a suitcase packed; you never know how the situation might deteriorate in the next two days; you might want to change your mind at the last moment, and I'd feel happier if you were prepared."

Here was one way she could please him, and she gladly agreed.

"Tonight," urged Keith, "as soon as you get indoors."

Both Hilary and Viola were in when she arrived. They too had been cabled by their parents in England with orders to join the evacuation, so were wholly sympathetic when Pamela wept about her traumatic evening.

"Do what I'm doing: ignore the cable, pretend it never came," advised Viola, creaming her face. "And don't worry about Mr. Gasson: your father might have been his superior in the past but he isn't now."

Just before retiring, the three girls stood on the tiny verandah to breathe some fresh air. gazing at the dark harbour and the Kowloon hills beyond; groups of pinpricks of light outlined ships and roads; over the high buildings in Central hung a pinkish-yellow glow from myriads of coloured shop signs. From the town below sounded hooters, screaming brakes and engine roars; the grating of trams on their rails; the continuous hum and buzz which was a mix of all sounds of humanity.

"Raoul phoned me today," said Viola. "He's such a pessimist! He thinks ALL women and children should leave, Asiatic as well as British."

"That's ridiculous," laughed Hilary. "What country would - or could - take three million Chinese? No good them going to other parts of China, the Japs are almost everywhere."

"True." Viola pulled out another cigarette from the tin on the verandah table and lit it. "Hell, I didn't mean to have another tonight, I'm trying to cut down, but what the heck.. goodness knows what the future holds! Raoul says we three are mad not to take the chance to get out while we can. I was surprised at his concern - haven't seen him for weeks; but I suppose he's ringing round all the girls in his address book and telling them the same thing."

The cable to Mr. Gasson had no serious result: the Chief Clerk looked into the girls' office at nine the next morning and made a diffident announcement. "You girls are really needed here, but if any of you wish to leave tomorrow, I can't stop you; you all understand that, don't you?"

Young Josie was the only one who would be leaving, not only because her parents insisted, but also because as she explained "It will be a cumshaw holiday! I wouldn't miss it for anything."

All day long Pamela agonised over her position. Roddy telephoned, so did Belle, and later Keith, all still urging departure. She longed for Lawrence's support to withstand the concerted pressure which was beginning to undermine her will. Was she perhaps putting her life in jeopardy uselessly, trying to hold on to the contentment of her present way of life - a contentment which could vanish instantly if war came to Hong Kong? And was it really fair to abandon Belle when she needed her help?

Harrassed by more pleading phone calls that last evening, she was morose and tearful.

"Cheer up old thing," said Viola. "This was how I was when I first defied my family and refused to go to UK with them. You've always been such a goody-goody that you've never had the courage to stand up to your family before. It's tough, but you only have to hang on one more day."

But what a day! A typhoon was hovering nearby; even the harbour water was choppy, the sky ominous, and the air full of a warm wind among which twirled heavy typhoon flies.

That afternoon every European in Hong Kong seemed to be on the dock-side. Only fathers and husbands were permitted to board the ship when their families embarked, so Pamela's farewells to Belle and the children were said at the foot of the gangway. Belle, wan and anxious, had Tina in her arms as she gave Pamela a last hug and said brokenly "I do wish you were coming."

"Sorry, sorry," Pamela wept.

"You can still go," Keith urged. "I've got your suitcase here." He had apparently called at the flat while Pamela was in the office that morning and collected it, in the hope of a last minute change of mind. For a few moments she wavered. There was undeniably a feeling of panic now that the evacuation was in progress: a liner had been diverted from war duty to carry several thousand women and children away from the colony, people forced to leave their comfortable homes and loved menfolk for some uncertain destination for some indefinite time: the Government must genuinely feel the place was under threat of attack

"Do go, Pam!" begged Roddy. "The office will manage without you."

Hating herself for her hypocrisy as well as for deserting Belle, she shook her head, but tears ran down her cheeks as she watched the family disappear into the body of the ship.

There was a long wait on the wharf before the husbands returned dejectedly down the gangway. When Keith rejoined Pamela and Roddy his face was taut and grey.

"It's hell on board," he said, staring at Pamela with cold anger in his eyes. "The accommodation is appalling. I just don't know how Belle will manage. My God, Pam, I hope you know what you're doing.. I'll never forgive you for letting us down like this."

"We can't be expected to sleep in here!" wailed Sandra when she and her mother were directed to their accommodation. Her father, following behind with hand luggage, halted at the open door for the simple reason that there was no room for him to advance. What had originally been a 3 berth cabin had been adapted to take four more people by the addition of a set of rough wooden bunks and two fully made up camp beds.

Three women were already sitting possessively on the original berths. Although the porthole was open the air was hot and humid.

"There's no room for those." Mrs. Smithson nodded towards the camp beds. "They'll have to go."

Mr. Smithson folded them up and stowed the bedding on top of the wardrobe. It was then possible for Sandra and her mother to reach the wooden bunks, at the head of which was the door to a tiny shower room.

"This is dreadful!" shuddered her mother. "There must be somewhere better. Let's get out of this shambles and book passages on a civilian ship!"

"Not a hope at short notice.. and we don't know how much time we have."

"If time is short, what chance have so many of us, crammed in here, if we're attacked?"

Through the open cabin door came an anxious Government official, the back of his cream linen jacket soaked with perspiration. "Here you are," he called to the two young women behind him, "B71, this is your cabin."

"Surely not?" Mr. Smithson said. "This is full up."

The official consulted his list. "B71 7 beds; there are camp beds for these new ladies."

"But there's no room to put them up!"

"Sorry, sir.. it will be a bit squashed, but it's all we can do."

The newcomers were as appalled as the other occupants, but the official shrugged his shoulders helplessly and left them.

"Luke, there must be somewhere else!" Mrs, Smithson picked up her handbag, took her husband's arm and propelled him out of the cabin. "It's out of the question to stay here."

"We'll try." He looked hunted, and waved to Sandra to stay where she was "just in case."

The new women stood uncertainly by. "No point in going to all the trouble of getting the camp beds made up if the bunks are going to be free," said one.

Sandra glared at them as they eyed her mother's bunk. It was humiliating to have to stay on the top bunk while the other five passengers exchanged remarks about 'people who thought they ought to have preferential treatment.' The whole experience was rapidly becoming more nightmarish, with heat building up in the cabin, and noisy activity in the corridor where babies cried, parents shouted, and excited children screamed.

Her mother returned alone. "We'll stay here for the present," she told Sandra. "Daddy is doing what he can to arrange something better."

Obviously in a chastened mood, she helped to re-erect and make up the camp beds, and the two young women unfroze a little. The three in the best accommodation sat firmly on their beds as if afraid some one would take them over if they moved.

"It's a tight fit," said Mrs. Smithson, throwing pillows on to the camp beds, "but believe me, we're fortunate compared to some - I've just come through the public rooms and they are being used as dormitories!"

It was no surprise when Mr. Smithson returned, admitting defeat. "You'll just have to make the best of it," he sighed, as the 'all visitors ashore' gong reverberated through the corridors.

Standing next to her mother on the crowded deck as the ship's hawsers were loosed from the bollards on the wharf, Sandra saw Roddy standing beside Pamela. He had kissed her soundly before she boarded, and now waved enthusiastically. In a way, this evacuation had solved the growing problem of Roddy. He had been fun to be with at first, and he was the best dancing partner she had ever had; but he would insist on using his old car to take her out, and it was really uncomfortable after her marvellous MG. He couldn't afford to take her to tea and dinner dances as often as she would like, nor would he allow her to sign the hotel chits in his stead. She had been wondering for some time how she could gently drop him. Whatever the future held - either trouble in Hong Kong, or return of the evacuees after the current crises had receded - the Roddy problem could now be put aside for a while.

When the ship in her war-time coat of grey edged away from the quay, the faces of passengers and spectators alike reflected despair, frustration and helplessness: this could be a journey to disaster en route, or a journey to safety - in the latter case those left behind could be staying to face air attack and bombardment.

Perhaps the only really happy people aboard were the school children, who gleefully congratulated themselves on having escaped from the end of term exams which had been due to start the following week.

Out in the open sea, the ship developed a great, lazy roll. The portholes had to be closed, and the air in the cabins became unbearable. As one by one her travelling companions succumbed to sea-sickness, Sandra decided to escape to an open deck. "I'll come down for you when it's time for dinner," she told her mother.

"Count me out," was the faint reply from the lower bunk.

The decks were empty save for a group of teenage boys and girls, who had found the ideal rendezvous where they could congregate without their mothers' supervision. Far away in the distance, on either side of the ship a small destroyer rolled and plunged, sometimes disappearing completely from view. For the first time Sandra began to realise the threat this stormy night might hold. If a Japanese torpedo found the Empress's hull, there could surely be no survivors. How could her luxury-filled life have changed so quickly? She thought longingly of her comfortable room at home, and resentfully of the big party she should have been attending that evening; her closest friends would be there, their membership of essential services exempting them from evacuation.

The sea air made her hungry so she went to find the dining saloon; here a notice announced that passengers would be admitted as seats became vacated. There was a long queue, and here she came across Belle and her children. The baby was roaring and Belle looked desperate.

"Oh Sandra!" She grasped her arm, "can you possibly help me? Tina's due to be fed: would you take Jamie and Lisa into dinner with you, and I can go off and feed the baby?"

Taking charge of two weepy children was the last thing Sandra wanted to do, but there was no way of refusing.

"Bless you, you're an angel!" - Belle's face was radiant with relief.

As they waited, gripping the handrails on the bulkhead to maintain balance, some of those in the queue ahead were overcome, and abandoned the idea of eating, so Sandra was soon able to lead the children into the saloon. The magnificence of its frescoed ceiling, pillars and panelled walls contrasted with the troopship-like furniture - plain deal tables without linen; benches instead of chairs; utility cutlery and crockery. The tables had not been cleared of the remains of the previous occupants' meals, thus undermining most appetites.

After the meal Jamie led the way to what had been the ball-room in happier times; now, it was home to hundreds of women and children, whose camp beds were jammed so close together there was scarcely room to move between them. Belle was tucking the baby into the bed she would have to share with her.

"I hate to bother you again Sandra," she said hesitantly, "but I just must go to the toilet. Could you hang on here with the children for a few minutes?"

How could she refuse such a request? She found herself adding "Go and have some dinner too, before you come back."

Circumstances were taking her over; she didn't want to become involved in such responsibilities, but could find no way out. All round her, frantic mothers were scrabbling through suitcases beneath the beds for night-wear, and trying to undress their babies. Older children who were not protesting in these unfamiliar surroundings were bouncing up and down on their beds, excited and noisy. Belle had already put out the children's pyjamas, so Sandra had Jamie and Lisa in their beds by the time she returned.

"You've been so good to us," said Belle huskily. Sandra shrugged her shoulders, said goodnight and forged her way out of the ball room.

Back in her cabin, she found everyone asleep. The now blacked-out port-holes increased the claustrophobic effect. It was only 8 o'clock and she could not face settling down for the night in such an unpleasant atmosphere, so made for the promenade deck again. Heavy rain was sweeping across the rails; the wind tugged at her hair and her clothes. The escorting destroyers were invisible in the black night.. she hoped they were still there. The teenagers had disappeared, the deck was empty, and she quickly discovered it was too wet and slippery for safety. Against the billowing, howling wind, it took all her strength to force open the door into the body of the ship - there were no men around to help, and how she missed them: men to fulfil her every wish, and cosset her!

Inside, she could find nowhere to sit or relax.. and how could she bear to return to the foul cabin? Overcome with self-pity, she slumped against the carved wooden stairhead and wallowed in her misery.

Children's cries and babies' squalls sounded from the ballroom nearby. She put her hands over her ears and started down the stairs, then paused, struck by a sudden pang of compassion for Belle in the midst of all that noise and discomfort. Against her will, she found herself making her way into the dimly-lit room whose drawn curtains added to the stuffiness.

Belle, still dressed, was sitting on her bed, patting Tina to sleep. "I'll never dare to sleep beside her in case I roll on top of her," she sighed. "And Lisa's been sick twice in her potty, but I daren't leave Tina to go and empty it. Could you.."

Aghast, Sandra looked quickly away, and Belle actually laughed. "I'm not asking you to empty the potty! But I'd be so grateful if you'd hold the fort while I do."

To Sandra's relief, the three children were sleepy. The difficulty was finding herself face to face with the distress of weary and sea-sick mothers trying to cope with upset and seasick children. At one end of the room was a queue of mothers waiting with tins of baby milk powder and bottles while stewards dispensed hot water to make up the feeds - to the tune of the screams of outraged babies waiting for their meals.

By the time Belle returned, Sandra had made a decision. "I'm going to change places with you.. yes I am, don't argue! I'll take you and Tina to my cabin - the bunk is wider than your camp bed and it will be more peaceful there. No arguments.. just get your things and Tina's and let's go!"

She was past caring how the other occupants of the cabin would react to the arrival of a small baby with its mother. Mrs. Smithson woke, and though astonished at the transfer, welcomed Belle and approved of Sandra's initiative; she also insisted on moving to the upper bunk and settling Belle and Tina in her own.

That night in the ballroom seemed endless; there was always some child crying or vomiting or calling out; some mother pushed beyond endurance and shouting at her children to be quiet. There was no queue for breakfast, so many passengers too ill to think of food.

When Sandra returned to her cabin, Belle was awake, feeding the baby. Her mother was in the bathroom washing napkins - which Sandra would never have believed had she not witnessed it. The other occupants of the cabin were obviously not pleased to have a baby in their midst, but there was no one they could complain to, so had to content themselves with resentful glances and whispered comments to each other.

Grateful as she was to Sandra for changing beds with her, Belle insisted on spending the daylight hours in her original billet, but it was taken for granted that Sandra would take the two elder children to their meals, and babysit while Belle had hers.

At lunch Sandra was delighted to be hailed by several friends; they were billeted in makeshift accommodation in the bowels of the ship and until now had been laid low with sea-sickness. She spent the afternoon with them, overjoyed to have some one of her own age to talk to again. They compared rumours and experiences; linked arms and walked round the still heaving decks, singing popular songs at the tops of their voices. They eventually met up with more acquaintances;one had heard there was on an upper deck a small lounge which had not been converted into sleeping accommodation. They scoured the ship until they found it - a room with comfortable sofas and armchairs, deep pile carpeting, and gracefully looped brocade curtains. A handful of other passengers had already laid claim to two chairs and one sofa and declared their intention of sleeping there that night. The girls decided to do the same; they would take it in turns to go off for meals, leaving the others to spread themselves to keep the accommodation occupied.

After her checkered night, Sandra was beguiled by the heavenly softness of her armchair - no children here to punctuate the long hours with yells and moans and demands! Perhaps Belle would be able to manage in the ball-room tonight.. but when she rejoined the little family to take Jamie and Lisa to dinner, Belle was looking so exhausted after hours of amusing the children in the noise and discomfort of the dormitory that she knew she could not desert her now.

There was a problem with Tina's napkins. Temporary drying lines were strung up in the corridors, but even getting the use of a basin in the washroom to do the washing was difficult. Some women formed groups and took it in turns to watch over a party of small children while their mothers dashed off to the washroom. Chaos reigned during their absence. Few mothers were used to dealing with their own children for twenty four hours a day, let alone with other people's. There were tantrums and continual wails for the missing amahs.

After dinner, as Sandra shepherded the children back to the ball-room and resigned herself to another uncomfortable night there, she grimaced to herself at her situation. The only good thing about it was the effusiveness of Belle's gratitude, and a certain grim satisfaction that this was the job goody-goody Pamela should have been doing.

"I must be mad," she thought during the night when Lisa was sick and her clothes had to be changed in the feeble light.

When daylight came the ship was in calm water, nudging into Manila harbour. Land had never looked so desirable. A neat line of American destroyers at anchor gave added assurance.

Under an overcast sky the ship docked. Officialdom announced that after passport examination passengers would be disembarked in small batches and driven to a United States Army camp called Fort Mackinley, a few miles from the centre of Manila. Mothers and children were dealt with first, and Sandra basely felt relief as she waved Belle and the children down the gangway where uniformed American Marines were on hand to carry luggage.

For the rest there was nothing to do but sit on their suitcases on the outer decks waiting their turn to move on. A furious rainstorm blew up, deluging luggage and passengers. Rain was still cascading down when Sandra and her mother disembarked, and their hair, clothes and shoes were quickly sodden. In this bedraggled state they had to seek out their heavy luggage in an adjoining shed, after which marines ushered luggage and passengers to small canvas-covered trucks.

As the benches in each truck filled up, a flap was tied down over the back to prevent rain beating in. The discomfort of wet clothes was intensified by a fierce prickling on the skin brought about by the steaming atmosphere beneath the tarpaulin. Even when the trucks moved off and some air blew between the gaps in the sheeting, the situation was not much better as the passengers were bounced this way and that against each other and their possessions.

Travelling blind in such conditions, Sandra found there was only one attitude to adopt - that of resignation. She and her mother sat in silence, their feet wedged against luggage to help them keep their balance; those passengers who never stopped complaining simply worked themselves up into a fury which made them hotter and more uncomfortable. When the truck gave a mighty lurch, sending Sandra plunging forward onto the suitcases face-first, her mother hauled her up and gave a wry smile saying "O.K.? - Well, as O.K. as any one can be here at the moment?" Sandra felt a rare surge of companionship towards her.

When the truck finally stopped, the passengers were helped out by kindly servicemen who called everyone "ma'am". It was still raining, but no one could get any wetter than they already were, so there was no point in waiting for a break in the weather before moving on.

"Welcome to Fort Mackinley," said a tall marine who jumped Sandra out of her truck. "Our camp is at your disposal, ma'am."

The camp consisted of groups of two-storeyed wooden buildings with wide verandahs, on stiltlike foundations as the ground was very marshy. It was set among large tracts of grassland. The surrounding countryside reminded Sandra of England - there were even black and white cows in a distant field.

Every little group was led across water-logged grass by a waiting serviceman, to an allotted hut.

"Here we are, ladies, Hut Number 10," said Sandra's marine. "Remember your number. You ladies are to be on the top floor."

This was a relief as the ground floor rooms and verandahs were full of women with children. Sandra took off her wet and muddy shoes and walked barefoot upstairs into a large and well-windowed room. There were about 80 camp beds, well spaced out, already made up and each topped with a low frame which held a mosquito net. Friendly marines waited round the room to help where required, even holding babies while mothers unpacked.

An announcement was made that supper would be served in the dining hall two blocks away, but the priority in most adults' minds was to peel off wet clothes and wash themselves. Their first view of the communal ablutions room provided on the ground floor of each hut flabbergasted them. Though spotlessly clean, the sight of a row of lavatories, unscreened, on one side, and of unscreened washbasins on the opposite side, produced tears and indignation. There were no baths, just communal showers dripping into a draining trough, divided from the lavatories and washbasins by a half-wall. Many children at first refused to use the lavatories in full view of every one else.

Soon, at every washbasin a mother was frantically washing her baby's napkins and clothes. Diffidently at first, a handful of adults ventured into the shower bay, wrapped in towels; one blocked the open entrance to shield the others from the public gaze; soon came giggles and squeals of merriment, and gradually more women joined the showering group.

Sandra decided to do the same, but her mother shook her head in distaste and waited in the queue for a free washbasin. Embarrassment of standing naked among seven other women was soon forgotten in the sheer joy of showering and washing her hair. Afterwards, wearing clean dry clothes, she felt human again, as she and her mother followed the signposted route to the dining hut. At last the rain had stopped, but the grass was like a bog.

"We might as well have kept our wet shoes on, instead of getting another pair wet," said Sandra.

"I don't believe this!" Her mother halted outside the dining hut, staring at a long queue of evacuees inching past a line of great food vats presided over by Army cooks.

"If you want to eat, you've got to queue," said the woman behind crossly, "and if you don't want to - let me!"

Waiting children whined; fraught mothers snapped, some had babies straddled across the hip, and were weighed down still further by handbags bulging with important papers and passports which they had dared not leave in their accommodation.

En route to the serving tables, each person was handed a tin drinking mug with collapsible handle; knife, fork and spoon; and a tin dixie can as a receptacle for food, its lid serving as a second plate. The meal smelt marvellous - hot potatoes, cabbage, stew, gravy, bread and tinned fruit. Everyone took their food into the hall, seating themselves on benches at wooden tables wherever they saw a vacancy.

While waiting for a seat Sandra spotted Belle and the children already eating. She shrank from getting involved with them again, but Lisa noticed her and nudged her mother who waved energetically with her fork as she was holding Tina with her other hand.

"We're Hut No.6," called Belle, "Where are you?"

"No. 10, top floor."

"Oh dear, I had so hoped you'd be with us!"

"I'll come across later on, and give you a hand for a while," Sandra had to say.

"I'd be so grateful! My milk seems to be failing.. I'm going to have to ask for milk powder.. no wonder Tina's been crying so much, poor little soul. "

Later that evening Sandra took Lisa and Jamie to the ablutions room at Hut 6. A school teacher evacuee was directing, in turns, groups of small girls and then of small boys, into the showers; she had also sought sheets and ropes from the marines and curtained off the end toilet to provide privacy for the more sensitive. Now the first shock of communal ablutions was wearing off, however, good-natured banter prevailed. Lisa and Jamie were red-cheeked and bright-eyed when Sandra took them back to their hut, where Belle was struggling to give a suspicious and disapproving Tina a bottle of Cow & Gate milk obtained from the obliging U.S. Army.

"She knows it isn't the real thing," sighed Belle. Her face was damp with perspiration, despite whirring ceiling fans throughout the hut, and she looked completely drained. Beside her on the floor was a pile of wet and smelly napkins.

"What happens about those?" asked Sandra, "Is there a laundry where they can be sent?"

"I don't think so.. I'll see to them later when the children are all settled for the night."

Sandra eyed the unsavoury bundle, and said quickly before she could change her mind "Goodness knows when that will be, Belle! I'll do them.. but how do I go about it?"

Washing napkins was a task which Belle herself had never undertaken until she'd boarded the 'Empress of Japan.' "You sort of wiggle them about under the tap, rinse them and wash them," she said vaguely. Their eyes met, and they both broke into peals of laughter.

Treating the unpleasant job as a joke helped Sandra to get through it. At the washbasins she found mothers tackling the same task with the same lack of experience. They pooled hints, whooping triumphantly when the washed napkins were pinned on the lines on the verandah. There was only one problem: how to distinguish Tina's nappies from all the other identical ones hanging beside them?

"Who cares if we get each other's, as long as they're clean and dry?" was Belle's response when Sandra reported back to the dormitory. Tina had taken every drop in the bottle and was now asleep, having a camp bed to herself wedged between

Lisa's and Belle's. "You're simply wonderful, Sandra! I can't thank you enough; Keith will be so grateful too when I tell him, I'm going to write to him tonight."

"First go and shower!" Sandra knew Belle had had no opportunity to wash since leaving the ship. "I'll watch the kiddies."

When she trudged back to Hut No.10 she was drooping with tiredness. Her mother was sitting up in bed, creaming her face and putting curlers in her hair.

"What have you been up to this time?" She turned an amused gaze at Sandra who kicked off her shoes with a great sigh.

"I've been baby-amah again, and wash-amah, and my fingers have gone all crinkly, and I never want to have a baby as long as I live!"

AUGUST

Although there was no sign of aggression on Japan's part against Hong Kong, those first few weeks there after the evacuation were anxious ones. Nevertheless, grass widowers continually wrote complaining letters to the newspapers, demanding the immediate return of their families who had now been sent from Manila to Australia. The evacuees wrote pleading letters home; none of them wanted to stay in Australia - their temporary accommodation was uncomfortable and they missed the luxuries of Hong Kong life.

Meanwhile, each new day brought worrying news from Europe. The Germans were shelling the eastern coast of England and invasion was feared imminent; British industrial cities were devastated one by one by Nazi bombs. The daily count of enemy planes brought down on British soil could only hint at the horrors of the air raids there; children were sent away from vulnerable areas to the countryside, and many were drowned when a ship taking them to safety in the United States was torpedoed.

All this seemed quite unimaginable when the dreadful headlines were read in newspapers in Hong Kong over a leisurely breakfast served by docile servants, for in Hong Kong social life, business and sport carried on normally, although recent legislation had conscripted all British men of fighting age into the local Volunteer Force or other essential services. British girls responded to appeals for their presence at Army and Navy dances to partner great numbers of servicemen. Viola, Pamela and Hilary often attended these dances as a duty, which it certainly was, as they were kept on their feet non-stop.

"I don't think I can take much more of this, even for good old England," puffed Hilary as the three girls sank into the back of a taxi bearing them home after a dance at the China Fleet Club. "I shall have corns before long."

Hot and sticky with the exertions of the evening, Viola sighed "What would be perfect now would be a drive to Deep Water for a lazy swim. If only I had my car!"

She had been saving hard for this ever since she'd passed her driving test. The fund progressed in fits and starts; all week she would forego the luxury of a rickshaw ride through Central to shop, only to succumb to a gin sling in the Gloucester Hotel after working late. A cheque from her parents for her birthday had recently turned the far-distant goal into something almost attainable.

"If I can save just a little more than usual at the end of this month and next," she mused over her accounts, "I'll be able to think about buying in November. Tell you what, Pam: once I've got my car, I can give you driving lessons - at half the going rate."

"No point - I'm never likely to own a car!"

"So what are all your savings for - bottom drawer?"

Pamela shrugged her shoulders, and Viola let the matter drop. It was only too obvious that Pamela was far more involved with the young petty officer from Ipswich than she would admit. When Lawrence's ship was in port, she was in a state of perpetual expectation, always washing her hair, experimenting with make-up and fussing about her clothes; when he was at sea, she was dreamy and lethargic. Yet to the outward observer, when together they seemed more like brother and sister than boyfriend and girlfriend. Even Raoul had commented on the pair. He had called to collect Viola for a farewell date before flying to Chungking on a 3-months' assignment, just as Pamela and Lawrence were leaving for the cinema.

"If you care to wait a few minutes, I will give you a lift downtown," he offered.

They refused politely, saying they preferred to walk the short distance, and set off side by side at a brisk pace; Lawrence did not even take Pamela's arm when they crossed the road.

"So cute, those two: so English," smiled Raoul.

Viola, checking that her key was in her handbag, knew exactly what he meant; an evening with him always included manoeuvrings to keep his attentions and caresses within the bounds of propriety. However, she could not resist saying "I'm English too."

"No," he pressed her arm, "you are a colonial. You were not brought up in the restrictive English atmosphere."

"My parents tried," she grinned, "but they were up against the questionable company I kept.. you, for instance."

His response was a deprecating smile as he said "Perhaps you shouldn't then come with me to Repulse Bay for dinner tonight? It would be a shame though, as the table is already booked, and I thought you might like to drive us there."

For answer she took his proffered arm as they walked to the car. This was the first time she had driven his car as a qualified driver, for she had never accepted his offer to use it while he was out of the colony. Supported by his confidence in her abilities, she steered carefully along the winding mountain road to Repulse Bay.

"Very good," he said as she parked outside the hotel. "Very good indeed; you could go a little faster, but it is not compulsory."

They dined on the open verandah, its balustrades lined with large green porcelain pots bursting with bright flowers. They danced to the music of a small orchestra, but the late August heat was too oppressive for much exertion. Lingering over coffee, they smoked and chatted. Although it was well past ten o'clock, snatches of the voices of late swimmers could be heard from the bay below; far out, the sea was pricked with the lights of fishing boats.

"This picture of tranquillity will remain in my mind for the next three months," sighed Raoul. "You wouldn't believe what balm it gives, in the midst of war."

"Then why go back to China?"

"It is my job.. it is reality. Life here in Hong Kong is make-believe, "but it won't last! Viola, I want to ask you something very important." He took her hand and held it tightly. "I want you to think again about the future - your future; to be sure of having a future, you must leave here as soon as you can arrange it. Go to Australia, you'd be taken care of under the evacuation scheme, even now."

"You're as bad as my parents! They're always writing to urge me to go. But how can I, Raoul? This is my home now. I'm thrilled with the flat, I have a super job.. I almost have a car!"

"Listen to me! There are no guarantees that all these assets will remain! You are an intelligent girl, but you are not facing facts. You realise, don't you, what will happen if the Germans invade Britain? Hong Kong will be completely isolated, cut off from Allied help. Even now the colony isn't defensible, with most of naval ships on their way to British waters. If the Germans overrun Britain.. yes, my dear, it could happen.. and Hong Kong was attacked by Japan, who could send reinforcements here?"

"Wouldn't Australia help, or Canada?"

"Why should they involve themselves over one tiny island - they must look after their own lands."

"But surely the Japs would fear American intervention if they became aggressive - there's that huge fleet in the Philippines and Hawaii."

"U.S.A. is desperately trying not to become involved in any war."

"Oh Raoul, you know too much about politics!" Viola shrugged as if to try to banish his gloomy prognostications. "I just can't agree that things will come to such a pass. Anyway, Singapore could help us, with their enormous air force - "

"Which will be needed to defend Singapore if an attack ever came there!"

"I'm sure the Government would get us all out if the Japs became really threatening."

"There might not be time. I would say you can count on about two months in which to get away. Does your education extend to knowing about the Burma Road?"

"Vaguely - it's the road through Burma to China: we've closed it, haven't we?"

"Closed the only practical route by which the Chinese can get war supplies to defend themselves against the Japanese," nodded Raoul. "Why was it closed? I'll tell you. Since France fell, Britain is so vulnerable to invasion that she couldn't help any of her colonies if they were attacked. The closing of the road was a conciliatory gesture towards Japan in an attempt to split Japan from her Axis friends. But now it is rumoured that the road is to be re-opened in October because of pressure from China. At the very least this will annoy the Japanese; at the most.. anything could happen here - even what happened in Nanking when the Japanese army went in there."

Remembering Raoul's vivid account of the rape of Nanking, Viola looked away.

"Forgive me," Raoul was saying, "Forgive me, but am I right in thinking you are a virgin?" At her embarrassed nod, he went on, "A peasant soldier flushed with victory would not be as gentle with you as.." He left the sentence unfinished, and his serious expression showed her that this conversation was not an attempt to seduce her, but a final attempt to convince her of the consequences of staying on in Hong Kong.

"Forgive my bluntness," he was repeating, "but I had to make you understand the situation clearly. I think you do, so I shall say no more."

He called for the bill with a snap of his fingers and they left the hotel. Instead of driving back to town, he diverted to nearby Deep Water Bay. The tiny beach, nestling below the golf course and sheltered by rearing thickly wooded hills, was empty. About a mile out a small white launch gleamed at anchor in the dark sea. A few swimmers betrayed their presence by the glinting phosphorescence of their movements in the water.

"Shall we swim?" Raoul parked the car above the beach and reached in the back seat for a small rattan basket.

"I don't carry a costume in my handbag," laughed Viola.

"Who says you need a costume?" He leapt down the short bank of grass and spread a towel on the sand.

It was necessary to deal with the matter firmly, yet with a light touch. "Mrs. Grundy?" she said.

"And who is this Mrs. Grundy?" he teased. "Do I know her?" He put one arm about her shoulders and pulled her face towards his.

"Now Raoul.." Her protests were smothered with a long, long kiss. No kiss was ever as thrilling and tender as his. The tensions of these anxious days fell away as she relaxed in his arms... what did it matter if he had a host of other girlfriends? Tonight she was the only one who mattered.

"Ouch!" A small shell beneath the towel pushed against her back and she sat up quickly, in the same moment shaking off Raoul's arms. He immediately dug the shell out of the sand and patted the towel encouragingly, but she shook her head and stood up, saying "Time we were leaving. It's almost midnight."

"So what? Who knows when we shall see each other again? You - I trust - will soon be on your way to Australia, and anything can happen to me in China."

He looked like a Greek god, his fairness silhouetted against the black hills, his hands warm and pressing hers urgently. The temptation to respond was compelling, with the war going so badly in Europe, and the lurking enemy in Japan.

What if there was very little future for them except now? Yet she twisted away from him, and when he realised her determination he let her go and followed her up the bank towards the car.

"You must forgive my over-enthusiasm," he apologised as they got in. "You are such an attractive young woman, and I fear I am seriously in love with you."

This was so exactly how Viola would describe her feelings for him that she told him so. He put his hands on her shoulders and spoke with great intensity. "I must be honest with you. I value my independence greatly. I believe it is the same with you, so we understand each other. As you know, my chosen life involves moving around and taking risks.. it has to be that way if I am to report the truth. If.. if we were to find ourselves truly in love, and consider marriage, I would still need to live the life I do now...could you accept that?"

"If I were sure about our love for each other.. I think I could.. yes, I know I could."

"Let us talk about this next time we meet - wherever and whenever that is." Raoul opened his wallet and handed her a folded slip of paper carrying the printed letterhead of his employers. On it he had typed his full name, his parents' address in Switzerland, and the name of his bank in Hong Kong and Switzerland. Viola read all this with growing wonder at the realisation that he had made such detailed plans, and that his declaration this evening was no spur of the moment impulse.

"When you get to Australia, write to me through the news agency, and if you need money write to my bank.. I have left instructions there about that. Now confirm to me the name of your sister's husband's firm so I can make contact with you that way if all else fails, then everything is tied up, and we can proceed to enjoy what is left of this lovely evening."

They had been serious for too long; by mutual consent, the conversation was flippant on the drive back to town. It was only when they said goodbye outside the flat that the reality of Raoul's departure to danger returned.

"I am the world's greatest fool to choose to leave you," he whispered, holding her tightly and kissing her neck, her lips and her closed eyes.

"Come back safely, fool!" She drew away from him at last and, in a daze, felt for her key.

SEPTEMBER/OCTOBER

A cholera epidemic hit the colony at the end of the summer, and appeals were made for volunteer nurses to man the emergency cholera wards.

Hilary's flat-mates were astonished when she announced she had offered her services.

"What about your job?" demanded Viola.

"I've asked for leave, and got it!"

"But cholera patients.." Pamela looked most concerned.

"We've all been inoculated regularly, haven't we? And there are heaps of precautions at the hospital; I've been told we leave our uniforms there every day after duty, to be laundered and sterilised; and we have to keep one pair of shoes at the hospital to wear in the wards. There's no more risk than riding on a bus of ferry and maybe sitting next to someone who's incubating cholera."

Nevertheless, there WAS a risk, and that was why she had volunteered. Through one of Ian's former bank colleagues she'd learned that Ian was now a prisoner of war in Germany. She could not help agonising over him, knowing how his vibrant energy would be stifled and frustrated in a prison camp. She tortured her conscience with the memory of his set face at their final meeting, and deliberately filled all her spare time with tennis, dancing, film shows - whatever offered after office hours. This nursing appeal was a heaven-sent opportunity for her to expiate her lingering guilt.

Not only Pamela and Viola disapproved: Pamela's brother-in-law Keith, and Roddy and Greg who were now lodging with him while his family was in Australia, called at the flat with their advice on the matter.

"It's not a job for young girls," Keith said. He reminded them of some of the stomach-turning sights he had seen in makeshift hospitals when Shanghai was bombed in 1937. "You've no idea what you're letting yourself in for - apart from the risk of infection."

After they had gone home, Roddy telephoned Hilary. "Just wanted to say how much I admire you over this nursing," he mumbled. "I wish you wouldn't do it, but.. well, you make me feel very humble."

That was all, but the gruffness of his voice revealed a depth of concern which stirred her heart.

She, who had never made her own bed except when on leave in England, found herself thrust into a life so totally engrossing that there was no room in her mind for anything but the job in hand.

The isolation hospital, an old-fashioned building with wide verandahs, was being used just for convalescent cases, and it was here that the volunteer nurses spent their first days. Although their patients were over the worst of the illness, they were very emaciated and weak and suffered from perpetual thirst which the nurses had constantly to satisfy with barley-water or tea. Previously entirely unfamiliar with male anatomy, Hilary quickly adapted to tending to their bodily needs with bedpan and bottle; harder to accept was the patients' constant noisy use of spittoons.

On the third day Hilary was transferred to a reception hut where the cholera cases were first taken on admittance. Here, doors and windows were insect-proofed with meshed wire. A huge coir mat, soaked in strong disinfectant, was placed at each entrance for cleansing shoes. The hut had concrete floors to minimise the danger of infection.

This was nursing in the raw for which the girls had to wear all-enveloping overalls and masks. New cases were arriving every hour, most dirty and smelly; in their spartan surroundings , they looked pathetic and hopeless. A doctor would immediately administer an intravenous injection of saline, and often it was difficult because of severe dehydration to find a suitable vein. A saline container on a bamboo frame hung beside each bed and had to be kept refilled until the prescribed amount had been absorbed; this job was allocated to the volunteers, and Hilary felt a wave of panic when realising that such a grave responsibility rested on her.

Conscious patients were distressed at the chronic diarrhoea which affected them. The smell of excrement hung in the air despite the liberal use of disinfectants.

Hilary inwardly cringed over and over again that first morning in this hut. The fetid smell was still with her at one o'clock when the nurses were served with tiffin in the hospital proper, and she could not eat. At the end of that day, as she stepped out of her uniform and tossed it into the laundry basket, she thought "I can never come back here..Keith's right, I'm not up to this sort of thing."

The charnel-house atmosphere and the human misery in the hut remained with her as the rattling bus - snorting diesel fumes which further assaulted her uneasy stomach - bore her homewards. Tired, and dispirited at her failure to meet the challenge she had set herself, she got wearily off the bus. Sedan chairs were lined up opposite the bus stop; their owners beckoned to her hopefully, and for once she was too shattered to resist the indulgence. The cheerful chair-boys helped her to settle in the upright rattan chair before they stationed themselves one at either end, and with a concerted guttural whoop, heaved the shafts on to their shoulders and set off. Both men were well-muscled and their bodies contrasted sharply with those of the cholera patients. Their loping walk slowed during the sharp ascent, and by the time the chair was lowered to the ground outside the flat, the men were panting and their cotton vests dark with perspiration. After Hilary paid them, they squatted down over the shafts and lit wispy home-made cigarettes.

Perhaps for the first time in her life, Hilary saw the coolies as people, individual and vulnerable as the patients she had tended that day. Remembering them again, she shuddered as she walked up the stairs. "I can't go back to all that," she whimpered to herself.

But she did, despite the efforts of Pamela and Viola to stop her as they listened to her experiences. Even the amah, bathing Hilary's swollen feet, said "No good you go that place, get sore feet, Missie."

It was tempting to agree. This was Hilary against Hilary: the self-indulgent, fun-loving girl of the past against the young woman whose guilty conscience over her treatment of Ian had awakened a debt to society as a whole. There was nothing she could do to make it up to Ian for what had happened, but no limit to what she could do for others.

Soon there seemed no other life outside the walls of the hospital compound. The busy hours flew by and when she got home each evening she was too tired for any social life. The conversations in the flat seemed irrelevant. Viola was still agonising whether to spend her savings on a little secondhand car a friend wanted to sell: would this be a wise step in view of the increasing uncertainty of Japan's intentions towards Hong Kong? - Hilary thought of her patients and wondered how they would fare if the Japanese attacked.

"If we were all suddenly pushed off to Australia," Viola was going on, "I'd need all my money to set myself up there. I don't expect we'd be able to take very much with us." Hilary remembered the pathetic little belongings from which her patients refused to be parted - an old sepia photograph carefully kept in a much-used brown paper bag: a small red 'lucky' envelope saved from Chinese New Year: a safety pin, a needle with a length of thread in it: a coil of used string.

Again there was talk of more compulsory evacuation, because Japan had summarily occupied French Indo China, without opposition: how could there be, with France now neutralised by Germany? This was another reminder that Britain was also virtually neutralised and in no position to help Hong Kong if attacked.

Germany, Italy and Japan signed a pact which put Japan firmly against Britain and France. The U.S. Consulate advised all American citizens in Hong Kong to leave. Viola received a cable from Raoul in Chungking with the same advice.

Some Americans left, and a few more Europeans, but the majority of foreigners in the colony carried on hopefully with their jobs and pursuits: but for the fact that the local Defence Forces were accelerating their training, and tunnels being built into the hillsides near populated areas, a visitor would not have guessed that Hong Kong was more vulnerable now to enemy attack than at any other time in her history.

Viola and her friends were most impressed by Raoul's cable, but preferred to take a chance and stay in Hong Kong rather than face the upheaval of leaving jobs and homes to go to an unknown country.

A late-season typhoon threatened. Pamela looked worried because Lawrence's ship was sent to sea to ride out the blow. Hilary fretted in case weather conditions the next day would prevent her from getting to the hospital, but the typhoon veered away during the night and the only effect the next day was a blustery wind.

"Thank goodness," said Viola. "When this lot passes, we might get a good day for the Double Tenth." - A friend's firm was providing a launch that day for a staff outing to Castle Peak Bay, and Viola, Hilary and Pamela invited; but this had been arranged some weeks ago, and now, because of the nursing, Hilary had to refuse.

"But surely you can have a day off," protested Viola. "You said yesterday the epidemic is running down."

"We're still needed though," Hilary said. "You'd be surprised what those patients get up to when they're feeling better." She related the difficulty of persuading some of them to continue taking their medication once they were over the worst; even when a nurse placed a particular pill inside the patient's mouth to ensure it was swallowed, he kept the pill there until the nurse had moved on, then spat it into his chamber-pot - a deception revealed when the pot was emptied as the pill contained permanganate of potash.

Some patients objected to having their temperatures taken, and convalescent cases tried to evade the nurse by visiting other patients in the ward, or pretending to attend to a call of nature at temperature-time.

Those were lighter moments, but the sadder ones gnawed at her heart. There was the dying man who repeatedly plucked her hand in such distress that she called a Ward Boy to translate his agitated mutterings. It emerged that he was a baker's assistant and belonged to the Bakers' Union; he was now desperate that the hospital record his union membership number and ensure that his death was reported to the Union, as he had already paid for his coffin. When Hilary arranged for this information to be written in Chinese and signed, she folded the precious record, put it into the top pocket of her uniform and patted it reassuringly. The poor man managed a half smile, and touched his forehead several times with his spindly hand in a gesture of heartfelt gratitude.

Spending all day working in such harrowing circumstances reduced the importance of what was happening in the outside world, yet she could not but be aware of more tension building up in the colony. The British were about to implement their decision to re-open the road through Burma to Chungking to provide China with a supply route to the capital, despite the risk that this could provoke retaliation from Japan.

Lawrence called on Pamela unexpectedly in her office to say farewell: his ship had sudden orders to leave Hong Kong that day.

"He hasn't been told where they're going," Pamela said tearfully that evening, "but he's pretty sure they're bound for Home - says it's been on the cards ever since France fell."

She seemed to take his departure very hard - which surprised Hilary and Viola because of the apparent platonic nature of the relationship.

In the third week at the hospital the number of new cases fell dramatically. There were empty beds on the reception ward and Hilary was transferred to the convalescent wards. Here, all the nurses made a favourite of an ancient lady who had made a remarkable recovery. She had been the perfect patient, always smiling and grateful, but the morning she was told she was to be discharged, her demeanour altered: she wept, shouted, beat the wall with her head, ranted and tore her clothes in wild distress.

"Whatever's wrong?" Hilary beseeched the Ward Boy.

"She not want leave hospital. She like stay here all time. She street sleeper."

As a child, Hilary had often stared curiously at the rows of shivering bodies on the colonnaded pavements in Central, and accepted her parents' explanation that these people simply had no homes so were forced to sleep wherever they could find room. Now, face to face with one of that number as an individual, she was appalled.

The Ward Boy went on "She ask you to beg doctor not to send her away. She very comfortable here."

The old lady grasped Hilary's hand and held it tightly, nodding confirmation, and smiling again, full of hope now she felt sure she was understood. Hilary had to use every vestige of willpower to keep tears from her eyes: how could any one call this spartan and cheerless accommodation 'comfortable'? Squeezing the old hand comfortingly, she promised to try to persuade the doctor to keep her in hospital longer, knowing that nothing but death would prevent this patient from having to rejoin her relatives on their chosen patch of pavement. The wrinkled face, with its trusting smile, haunted her long afterwards.

The day the Burma Road re-opened passed without any untoward incident in Burma or Hong Kong. The optimists said they always knew Japan would not dare to make any trouble; the pessimists said "wait and see."

This was Hilary's final day at the hospital. It was only as she passed through the iron gates for the last time that she realised what an enormous strain those weeks had been. She had never felt so tired in her life.

There was to be a prestigious charity ball at the Peninsula Hotel the next evening.

"Just right to celebrate your emergence into public life again," said Viola. "You'd better wear a label round your neck - most people will have forgotten your existence!"

"They seemed to remember me when I turned up at the office this morning," yawned Hilary. It would have been wonderful to have spent that first free Saturday morning in bed, but Bextons had been very generous in allowing her time off for the nursing.

Trying on evening dresses that afternoon to decide which to wear, Hilary began to realise how wrapped up in that other life she had been. Her hair had grown longer than she usually wore it, and it needed another perm; she had lost quite a lot of weight; her closely cut fingernails (against infection-carrying) needed manicuring and painting, and her eyebrows needed plucking. She was too heavy with weariness to consider a trek into town to the hair-dressers. She wondered too if she could summon enough energy for an evening's dancing; nor had she much heart for it. The nursing was over, and she was free to enjoy herself, but Ian was just as much a prisoner as before, and there was nothing she could do about it. She sprawled on the bed, hid her face and wept herself to sleep.

"Wake up, Hil - it's five o'clock!" Pamela was shouting. "You've been asleep for hours, and there's a letter for you."

It was from her parents, and she tore the envelope open quickly, as always these days when there was nothing but bad news from Britain; but this time her mother sounded cheerful, no raids had come their way and the three girl evacuees newly arrived in the house were settling down well. The final paragraph had the best news of all; they had had a 'kind letter from Ian's mother, who wanted them to know that Ian had written quite cheerfully from his prisoner of war camp in Germany, and that he had married a lovely girl from Oxford just two months before he was captured.'

Sitting with Pamela, Roddy and Greg on the Star Ferry that evening, a silver silk jacket over her bright blue gown, Hilary felt an excitement at the forthcoming ball she had not known for the past two years. The harbour looked beautiful, dark hulls of ships blotting out the sea and carrying brilliant lights on their superstructure. The coloured bulbs of the huge advertisement signs on the tall buildings bordering the island's shore threw wiggling reflections on the water's edge. There was a gentle wind, and scudding clouds revealed glimpses of a new moon.

At the hotel, every one in the party danced with everyone else in between the courses of the sumptuous banquet. Free of the burden of guilt about Ian at last, Hilary drank more than was good for her in her tired state. She found herself dancing more often with Roddy as the evening wore on. He was very comfortable as a partner; she knew his style so well. Now they were drifting slowly on the floor to the haunting tune 'Somewhere Over the Rainbow..' His arm tightened as he whispered "You look so marvellous tonight, Hilary."

Embarrassed, because in the old days they had never paid each other compliments, she said "Must be all that hard work at the hospital I wonder you can't smell the lysol."

The ferries had stopped running by the time the ball finished, so home-goers bound for the island piled into wallah wallah, Hilary was very content that Roddy sat next to her as the prancing craft crossed the harbour. The city lights rose and dipped so alarmingly that it was necessary for the passengers to cling to one another to keep their balance. She huddled happily in Roddy's encircling arms, re-discovering the old attraction with wonder and repose.

Only half-awake, Viola luxuriated in bed the next morning, beautifully tired after the ball. She had become very friendly with an attractive Royal Scots officer, and (she dimly remembered) accepted an invitation to the premiere of 'Gone With The Wind' the following week. He was not the first new admirer she had acquired since Raoul's departure, but so far the most interesting. Raoul wrote rarely and seemed a million miles away, and she was beginning to doubt if they had a future together.

Through her open door she could hear the rustle of newspapers and the murmur of conversation. She rolled over and looked at the bedside clock: eleven thirty. She got up, put on kimono and brocade mules and pulled a comb through her hair before sauntering into the lounge. The other two girls, already dressed, were halfway through breakfast.

"Thought you were never going to surface," said Hilary.

"What you like breakfast, missee?" asked the amah.

"Just tea and toast." She had eaten enough last night to last the whole day. "What's the news?"

With daily German air raids on Britain, this was now the first question every one asked each morning.

"No paper yet." - Hilary studiously addressed her fried egg.

"But I thought.." Viola began, remembering the rustles, then saw yesterday's 'China Mail' lying on a side table. She sat back in her chair and lit a cigarette - the most cherished one, the first of the day.

There was something new in the room: a great vase of pink gladioli stood on the sideboard. "Golly!" she said, "What gives?"

"Came this morning.. for Hilary," said Pamela.

"Roddy?"

Hilary nodded. "Goodness knows what got into him," she muttered.

"I'm jealous! No one ever sends me flowers before breakfast. Mmm, that toast smells good!"

The others, breakfast eaten, wandered on to the verandah.

"Any sign of the paper boy?" Viola called.

"Can't see him."

"He must have forgotten us again. Amah, you go newstand and ask for our 'Sunday Herald.'

"No can," the amah mumbled.

Viola stared at her in surprise, then gaped in huge astonishment as Hilary came in from the verandah holding out the missing newspaper. "It did come," she said, "but we didn't want you to see it until you'd had something to eat."

"There's bad news I'm afraid," added Pamela. "It's Raoul, he's been hurt."

There, on the front page, in letters as large as those of the headlines about air raids on England, was the statement 'HONG KONG WAR CORRESPONDENT BADLY INJURED ON BURMA ROAD'

The story followed. Raoul was driving a truck from Chungking to Rangoon to find out how the newly re-opened Burma Road functioned. The convoy had been bombed by the Japanese, Raoul's truck was hit and crashed down the steep mountainside. It had taken many hours to bring him and the other wounded back to the road, he was now in hospital in Chungking with multiple injuries, and his chances of survival said to be slight.

For two minutes Viola stood re-reading the report, then flew to the telephone, riffled through the directory, dialled the Chinese airline and demanded an immediate flight to Chungking.

"Sorry, no seats available until mid-week," chanted the clerk.

"That's ridiculous. I must get to Chungking before then!"

"Sorry, madam, but can take your name in case of cancellation.."

"That's no good. I want to leave today, tomorrow morning at the latest."

The clerk repeated his regrets. She banged the receiver down and clenched her hands.

"Viola," Hilary was bending over her, "relax: have another cup of tea."

"There's no time to lose, you saw what the paper said!" She was already re-dialling the airline number.

"But the plane fare.. your job.."

"My car money will pay the fare, and I'll take a chance on my job.. I've some leave due."

When the airline clerk came on the line she mentioned Raoul's name and the need for an early departure.

"I try," he sighed. "Please telephone later."

Pamela brought a fresh cup of tea. Sentences were started and left unfinished:

"Wouldn't it be best to wait until you hear more.."

"Perhaps Raoul's newspaper can give you the latest.."

"This might all be a great exaggeration..all that money on the fare might be a terrible waste.."

The telephone rang: C.N.A.C. had secured her a seat on the next morning's plane.

"I do hope you're doing the right thing" Pamela fussed.

"Of course I am," Viola snapped. Hadn't she and Raoul agreed that as soon either of them was sure about their feelings for the other, they should say so? Well, she was sure.

These early November days were pleasantly cool. The ceiling fans in Pamela's offlce no longer whirred, her hands were no longer so damp that the purple carbons smeared them. This made working easier, but the room seemed very dull without Viola. The two married women, Lois and Norah, who had replaced the stenographers evacuated to Australia were friendly enough but she had little in common with them. To cover Viola's temporary absence a 17-year-old Eurasian girl, Jenny, fresh out of shorthand school, joined the staff. She was so eager to succeed in the job that the married women teased her endlessly and Pamela found herself taking the newcomer under her wing and was rewarded with touching gratitude.

The flat was a lonely place for Hilary was out with Roddy most evenings. They frequently invited her along but they were so obviously completely wrapped up in each other that she refused to play gooseberry. She continually worried about Lawrence. The only letter she had received from him since he'd reached England had been strictly factual: he had visited H. & S. and found the offices staffed by strangers - elderly men and women and school-leavers as the regular staff had joined the Services; he was still studying for promotion and expected to be drafted to an aircraft carrier before long. She was a little surprised that he had not thought to call on her parents to give them up-to-date news of her - but she recognised this was in line with his stated policy of non-commitment.

Alarm bells were ringing all over the world. There seemed no limit to Britain's catastrophes. The fear of invasion from the Nazis still lurked. The Luftwaffe continued to bomb London and the great ports. Now Greece was at risk from Germany and calling on Britain for help. Pamela dreaded listening to the BBC News yet could not turn the radio off.

Viola's letters were her only solace: 'Raoul is improving fast; gets out of bed to view the air raids, then dictates his reports to yours truly.' Once on her way back to her lodgings, she'd been caught in a raid and sheltered in a tunnel 'scooped out of rock; ghastly inside, no ventilation, a wooden bucket for sanitation. I was almost shot when I came out of to get some air and wiped perspiration off my neck with my hanky.. immediately there were shouts, barked orders, and pointed rifles!!! Apparently there had been rumours that spies had been caught signalling to the bombers with white handkerchiefs. By the way, two other journalists are getting me to type their reports - I've already recouped the cost of my air fare.'

Re-reading this letter, Pamela felt more discontented than ever; her life seemed so dreary and uneventful. She knew she was partly to blame for turning down so many invitations to parties, dances and the cinema - still mourning Lawrence.

In this dejected mood, for once she did not give a prompt refusal when Hilary asked her to join in a Sunday picnic at Big Wave Bay.. "Keith's coming too," Hilary urged, "and some people from his firm, and Rod's bringing a friend," she said.

"Does that mean Greg?" Pamela dared to ask.

"Probably.. don't let that put you off, though; he knows the score. Do come, we're really worried about you spending all your spare time in this flat."

They travelled in two cars. Keith took Pamela and three of his grass-widower colleagues; Roddy took Hilary, Greg and Keith's secretary Jill.

"Warm enough for a quick dip," said Keith as they sprawled on the soft, silver sand of the almost deserted Big Wave Bay. In the trees at the foot of the great green mountains the ha-ha bird called constantly, mocking and echoing.

"Who's for the briny then? I'm all set!" Roddy wriggled out of his white shorts revealing his swimming trunks and performed a clumsy cartwheel on the sand. While the other men changed on the beach, Hilary and Jill went behind nearby rocks to do the same but Pamela remained sitting on the sand; she had seen Greg's hopeful expression at the beginning of the expedition and decided to keep apart as much as possible. She sighed inwardly as she watched the others cavorting in the water, diving into the great billowing waves,then striking out beyond them. Everything around her was so beautiful - the sea sparkling, and the distant hills across the Bay shouldering one behind the other in ever-decreasing paler shades of mauive and grey; the air was like wine. This peace and tranquillity was almost painful because of her unhappiness. It was difficult now to believe that Laurence had ever been with her in Hong Kong, and she was beginning to wonder if she would ever see him again, not only because of the hazards of war but also because theirs had been such an undefined relationship. Life seemed to be passing her by: she closed her eyes and lay back on the sand.

"Mind if I join you?" Greg, dripping with water, was standing before her.

"Free country." She sat up, resting on her elbows and looked away from his earnest smiling face. He sat down beside her in complete silence for five minutes, then his hand touched hers tentatively. "Look Pam," he began, "I know it wouldn't mean anything to you, because of your friend Lawrence, but couldn't we have the occasional date together, strictly platonic of course? Flicks this evening, for instance?"

She gazed fixedly out to sea. Perhaps, after all, the time had come to put the memory of Lawrence to one side, and begin to live a normal life again. Greg was a good sort, he knew her circumstances; it would be comforting to have a pleasant companion.

Out in the Bay, the swimmers separated; some were racing back to the beach; two were sitting side by side on the outer rocks.

"Do you remember this place, Hil?" Roddy was pointing to the barnacled boulder beside him where, three years earlier, he had scratched noughts and crosses: only because he had made those marks himself could he recognise their weather-beaten remains.

Tracing the faint grid with her finger, Hilary nodded.

"I deserved everything you said to me that day." Roddy hesitated, then went on "I'm almost afraid to say this to you, in case you dive off and leave me again. But can we... would you consider... I don't mean yet, but maybe the year after next when my leave is due.. could we.."

"Are you asking me to marry you?"

"Oh Hilary. Would you? Will you?"

"Can we have a respectable engagement first?"

"Right away! "He hugged her and kissed her wet face. "You're freezing and shivering! Race you back to the beach!"

Pamela watched the two figures fused together for a moment before they sprang into the water. A great sadness came over her, and a great yearning for Lawrence; she knew she was not, after all, ready to relinquish his memory.

"What do you say, Pam?" Greg was patiently repeating.

"Sorry Greg." She turned away from his pleading eye.

Thank goodness for the continuing letters from Viola, to cheer her days! 'There's so much to tell you about life here. Very few cars, just impossibly ricketty buses, and these only on the main roads that run round the cliffs Chungking stands on. There are 480 steps (I counted 'em!) up from the river to the city streets. The rich take sedan chairs, the coolies are in dreadful shape - eyes bulging, clothes in shreds, broken teeth, bandy legs. Raoul says most of them smoke opium.. no wonder, the wretched lives they live. Multiply by infinity the number of beggars in Hong Kong and you'll know what they're like here.. children picking lice off their clothes. When foreign visitors arrive, the police cordon off the poorest streets to keep the beggars out of sight. Can't get used to seeing coolies actually carrying Chinese officials on their shoulders, up these perpendicular streets! Some of them have got great callouses on each shoulder, and ghastly hernias, bound with straw - you can see this through the great holes in their trousers. Much of Chungking's water is brought by coolies lugging bucketfuls from the mains (which have been bombed many times) - or else from the Yangtse 200 feet below. Most places have no mod cons.. just great clay jars in their rooms which they have to empty daily in the nearest public privy. I can't wait to get back and wallow in a bath with as much water as I like.'

Pamela too was counting the days until her return when Keith telephoned with the astonishing news that Sandra Smithson and her mother had arrived back from Australia.

"However did they wangle that?" was Pamela' s reaction.

"It seems that Mr. Smithson is to be transferred to Canada early next year and they all wanted to travel there together - a bit of wire pulling there as well, I should think. Anyway, Sandra wants to visit us - she's brought back snaps of Belle and the kids: I've asked her to dinner on Sunday - O.K. for you?"

"Oh dear," Pamela could not hide her dismay.

"Why? Got a date?"

"No, but you know Sandra isn't my favourite person."

"Come on Pam.. she's past that rebel stage now; she was a lifesaver for Belle on that ship."

"But what about Roddy? Will he be there too?"

"Haven't seen him yet to ask him, but I expect so; Hilary too."

"That's the point," she wailed. "Sandra will for sure want to break them up the moment she knows they're engaged; she considered Rod her property at the time of the evacuation."

"What a devious mind you have! Sandra gets through more young men than any one else I know. In fact, she' s bringing with her on Sunday one of the officers from the ship she travelled up on; does that set your mind at rest?"

When they met in Keith's flat Sandra's greeting was so effusive that Pamela felt almost ashamed of her own unfriendly feelings. Roddy and Hilary -on their way to a party - briefly paid their respects then left. Pamela watched closely for signs of any revival of Sandra's former interest in Roddy, but none was apparent.

During dinner she prattled on about life in Sydney, where few people had ever heard of Hong Kong and most were very critical of the evacuees and their colonial ways.

"Can't say I blame them," Sandra said candidly. "We were always yearning for our amahs and cookboys, we couldn't get used to having to do our own washing and ironing and cooking and cleaning. It was the laundry that got me down most of all. Best moment of my life was when I got back to my room at home and tipped a suitcase full of dirty clothes on to the floor for the wash amah."

She produced a sheaf of photographs of Belle and the children, taken a few days before she left Australia. They were all sitting, smiling, on the steps leading up to the open verandah of a small weatherboard bungalow.

"It's a delightful home in a tiny town," Sandra assured Keith, "So different from the awful communal accommodation we all had when we first got to Sydney."

She and her mother had taken a small flat in the centre of Sydney. "I got myself an office job to pass the time until I could get back here. Now I can work a switchboard, and type with two fingers, so I'm going to take a job. My parents can't stop me now I'm almost 21. Any one know any well paid posts going?"

"There are vacancies galore, if you're serious," Keith looked up from the photographs. "In our filing department, for instance."

"Filing!" Sandra made a face. "I want to be someone's personal private secretary."

"You can't expect that kind of job until you've had plenty of experience," said Pamela primly.

"I have had plenty of experience," giggled Sandra, grinning at her escort whose face turned red. "I want to get work quickly, so as to be well dug in by the time the rest of the evacuees get back and start wanting their old jobs."

"That's not likely to happen for a very long time," sighed Keith. "The whole world is too unsettled."

"You're as bad as my father! He says both Mother and I must join some defence organisation if we don't want to be re-evacuated next time there's a scare. Think I'll join St. John Ambulance - I really fancy driving an ambulance, and the uniform is quite snazzy, especially the hat."

"You once told me you'd hate the marching, and having to swot first aid and take exams," Pamela reminded her.

"That still goes, but I can put up with all that if it's a guarantee against being sent away from Hong Kong again."

"Anyway, you'll be leaving soon, when your father's transfer comes through!" Pamela was thoroughly exasperated by Sandra's flippant attitude towards war work.

"I'll face that when it happens." Sandra's voice was curt as she got up to leave. "I'll drive you home, Pam, if you don't mind a trip to the Ferry first to drop Derek."

"It's hardly worth it.. such a short walk," Pamela tried to protest, but Sandra insisted. In the car Sandra had an inane conversation with Derek, but once he was left at the ferry she became serious.

"I do envy you and Hilary and Viola your flat; I'd still love to come and live with you girls," she said. "I wouldn't mind sharing a room with you - it would lessen your share of the rent, wouldn't it?"

"I suppose so." Pamela frantically searched her mind for excuses. "But four would be too many." She tried to hide her abhorrence of the proposal in a torrent of words. "You're used to your own room, even your own bathroom! You wouldn't enjoy sharing at all."

Sandra went quiet at the dismissive tone, but as she stopped the car outside the Kennedy Close flat, she pulled Pamela's arm and said urgently "I need your help for.. for what I have in mind. Do please, please, let me move in! I promise you'll never regret having me!"

"What's the point?" demanded Pamela in exasperation. "Even if we three agreed, it wouldn't be worth all that upheaval for you when you're due to leave for Canada soon."

"But don't you see, Pam, that's why I want to live with you.. I don't intend to go to Canada! My parents don't know it yet of course, but I'm determined to stay here. And it will be much easier for them to accept that if they see me settled in a flat with three respectable citizens. After all, I'm only trying to do what you, and Viola and Hilary too, did.. trying to organise my own life instead of having it organised for me. Is there anything wrong in that?"

"No of course not." Pamela remembered her own delight when she had achieved this same goal. She also remembered Sandra's wild behaviour, her petulance, her ruthlessness in getting her own way, and hurried on "You must have other friends living in flats, bigger than ours, who could take you in. Sorry, we just can't have a fourth person. I hope you find a job and a place to live somewhere soon...and thanks for the lift."

"I was counting on you, Pam." Sandra's face was hard as Pamela stepped quickly out of the car before any more argument was possible. Her voice shook a little. "I told you my secret."

"Oh I'll keep your secret," said Pamela wearily. She hunched her shoulders in a gesture of apology. "I'm sorry I can't help."

Later that evening Keith telephoned, saying Sandra had just called him and reported her plans for the future and the abortive conversation with Pamela.

"Couldn't you unbend a little, Pam, and forget about her past?" Keith pleaded. "She's a great kid really - has hidden depths. Belle is still singing her praises. It would be nice to be able to help her after all she did for us."

Pamela felt a wave of fury. Why should she be made to feel in the wrong? It was most unfair of Keith to put pressure on her, a tacit reminder that she had abandoned Belle at the time of the evacuation. Gritting her teeth and trying not to cry she said "We couldn't take her unless she shares my room, and I just don't want that!"

"I don't know what's got into you Pam," Keith barked. "You used to be such a timid, biddable child; now you're thoroughly stubborn and selfcentred."

"Thanks!" Pamela smashed the receiver down and wept.

Of course Keith phoned again and apologised, pleading as excuse Sandra's tearful request for his intercession.

"Well, I'm tearful too," Pamela shouted, "and life wouldn't be worth living if I had to share my room with her."

Keith bellowed with laughter and said "There are times when you remind me of your big sister, telling me off like that. I deserved it, too."

Despite the apology she remained disturbed. When Hilary came home and asked how the evening had gone, she was hard put to refrain from pouring out the whole story, realising she could not do so without revealing Sandra's private intentions. Instead, she answered Hilary's friendly questions so briefly and guardedly that Hilary misunderstood and went to bed in a huff.

This coolness was completely forgotten the next morning when the newspaper arrived, for the main story was of devastating air raids on Coventry causing hundreds, and maybe thousands, of casualties.

"And our families worry about us here in Hong Kong!" said Hilary, tucking into breakfast as she read of the problems of re-housing the homeless and feeding the dazed survivors in Coventry.

Pamela whooped when the postman brought a letter from Viola. There was only one page, headed VERY CONFIDENTIAL in fat capitals: "I am considering (just considering, mind you) staying on here. Tell Hilary, but don't whisper it anywhere else until I confirm. I've been invited to join the staff of the British Liaison Group here, at a fantastic salary! Must decide quickly because if I don't accept I'll have to be on the plane for Hong Kong on Saturday."

"Read that!" Pamela pushed the flimsy sheet across the table to Hilary. "She can't do it! After being so pleased with this flat, and having her own pieces of furniture! She can't just throw up her security here, with Home Leave! She can't be thinking straight! She's told us what a dreadful place Chungking is, and now she's planning to live there.. she's just carried away by the novelty of everything."

"And Raoul!" Hilary added. "Calm down! Can't you see, it's because of Raoul, that's why she wants to stay."

"But she knows he isn't reliable. He has girl-friends everywhere. Surely she can't be fooled by him.. she's always advising me, and now.."

"You need never worry about Viola," laughed Hilary. "She's a survivor. I bet she stays on in Chungking. I would, in her shoes."

Yet not even Hilary was prepared for the cable which arrived two days later: 'MARRIED TODAY: WISH YOU HAD BEEN WITH US. LOVE VIOLA AND RAOUL.'

PART 6

1941

MAY

Pleased as Sandra was with her post as secretary to the No. 2 at Hendon Shipping, it seemed a shame to have to work on Saturday mornings. The dinner party at the Gloucester the previous evening had proved more riotous than usual and she had slept heavily; her flatmates had already left for work by the time Ah Ling managed to rouse her.

She was an hour late as she parked her car in Statue Square - just three minutes' walk from Hendon's grey three-storeyed building on the sea front.

The initial jerk of the lift as the boy in his white uniform and pill-box hat slammed the door closed sent a throb of pain through her head. She was still wincing when she walked into the large office.

"Good.. er.. morning, Miss Smithson." Her boss, Guy Bridger, poked his head over the top of the swing half-doors which separated his sanctum from the rest of the office. In his forties, tall and dapper, his thin moustache added to his supercilious manner. "I was beginning to wonder.."

His wife, like hundreds of others, was still banished in Australia, and Sandra excused his sarcasm because she knew how he resented the presence of other British women in the colony.

"I'm sorry, Mr. Bridger. I'm afraid I overslept. I'll be with you in a moment."

She sat at her desk and flipped open the diary to Saturday 3rd May 1941. The office boy set her desk fan in motion, for the slow-moving ceiling-fans only stirred the upper air in the tall old-fashioned room.

The session with Mr. Bridger was brief: a few letters to compose and dictate to Gloria, the young Portuguese stenographer; a statement of comparative cargoes to make up from sheafs of records and type; several telephone calls to make.

Calling Gloria over, Sandra lit a cigarette and leaned back in her chair. Gloria, her round face haloed with a frizzy perm, sat at the side of the desk, legs tucked neatly together, and pulled her white cotton skirt down over her knees. Conscientious and hard-working, she was too immature to be able to conceal her chagrin at Sandra's appointment; Sandra knew that until her arrival Gloria had been acting as Mr. Bridger's secretary since his English original had been evacuated. Observing Gloria's shaking hand while taking dictation, Sandra soothed her prick of conscience with the conviction that Gloria lacked the confidence to be a personal secretary; besides, a real English accent and a certain poise were essential on the telephone.

While Gloria was typing the letters, Sandra drafted the cargo statement; made and answered phone calls. The hand-written draft statement looked such a muddle where she had altered and re-altered figures that she decided against typing it herself, so handed it to Gloria saying "You can do this sort of thing so much better than I."

"Yes, Miss Smithson." There was a glint in Gloria's eye which hinted at a rebellious spirit behind the submissive manner.

Mr. Bridger had gone to keep an appointment, so Sandra lit another cigarette and telephoned several friends to check on the weekend's programme.

There was to be swimming at Shek O in the afternoon; a tea-dance at Repulse Bay Hotel, and a dinner dance at the Hong Kong Hotel - each function with a different set of friends. At intervals during the morning the young English sub-managers called in to exchange banter and suggest dates. That was one of the many advantages of working with a large firm - the ready company of a host of young and personable colleagues.

Gloria placed the typed cargo statement with its copies on Sandra's desk ten minutes before Mr. Bridger returned. "I like to do the hardest job first," she explained, "The letters won't take long."

When Sandra handed Mr. Bridger the cargo statement he gave her a rare smile, saying "This looks very neat."

"I'm improving, aren't I?" Sandra said.

"I believe you are," he agreed gravely, "but please ask Gloria to put a fresh ribbon in her typewriter."

Scarlet-faced at her bluff being called, Sandra ignored Mr. Bridger for the rest of the morning. She hoped he would not call her in again, but just as the office was about to close, he did so.

She looked pointedly at her watch as she faced him. "Sorry to keep you," he said, "but Mr. Lamb is on the phone and he would like a word with you in private."

She panicked inwardly: surely this morning's deception had not been reported to Mr. Lamb, the No. 1? He was a widower in his fifties; intensely reticent, so she always pretended to flirt with him at the firm's periodic cocktail parties. She would much rather be his secretary than the sarcastic Mr. Bridger's, but Mr. Lamb had a Eurasian secretary even older than himself who was obviously an institution in the firm. Now Mr. Lamb, stammering, was inviting her to join him at a business tiffin in an hour's time because the new English clerk who should be accompanying him had had to go home with a sudden attack of malaria.

It was Mr. Lamb's custom, she knew, to take a member of the staff with him on such occasions, partly to lead them into the workings of the firm, and partly to listen in to the conversations and refresh his memory later on as to what was said. It was a daunting prospect for Sandra, but she accepted at once, realising the value of such a date with the taipan: it would impress her parents, and help support her case when the time came to tell them of her intention to stay in Hong Kong instead of accompanying them to Canada. She looked down with satisfaction at her pink voile dress with matching bolero; her friends told her pink clashed with her red hair, but she thought the effect eye-catching.

"Very good of you to come at such short notice, Miss Smithson," Mr. Lamb murmured as they walked into the Hong Kong Hotel.

It was something of an international gathering: three Chinese men who quickly discovered from Sandra's asides to the table boys that she spoke Cantonese, and could not conceal their admiration; two Americans; one French and one Swiss executive, and two elderly British businessmen. Soon realising that she could not contribute in any way to the business side of the conversation, Sandra concentrated on charm, and a studied attention to everything every one said even though she understood little of it.

"It was very, very boring," she related to her flat-mates the next morning, "but old Lammikins is quite sweet. He wanted to drive me home in his car, and leave his chauffeur to bring mine."

"How come you've only been working for four months and you get to have a date with the taipan?" yawned Hilary, still in her dressing-gown. "Pam and I have been slaving away at our typewriters for years, and we never achieved anything like that!"

There was no rancour in Hilary's words, and even Pamela seemed amused. Sandra secretly exulted in the gradual improvement in her relationship with them since she had come to live with them. When she first came, she knew perfectly well she was not really welcome except as a third person to fill Viola's vacancy and help share the expenses. Her parents had of course been against Sandra leaving the parental home, especially as the transfer to Canada was so near; but in the end it was this same circumstance which earned their permission: they decided to indulge her whim for the remainder of her time in Hong Kong, with more than a hint that the experience would soon convince her that living away from home wasn't as paradisal as she had always imagined.

With financial backing, she was able to contribute generously to the upkeep of the flat: made herculean efforts to control her ebullient personality, and to keep reasonable hours. Even so, Pamela's hostility in particular had lasted for some weeks; she especially objected to Ah Ling taking up residence as well, though Sandra could not see why, if Ah Lum did not object to sharing her tiny room out back. So Ah Ling came and fussed and look after her clothes, brushed her hair and scolded her as in childhood days, while Pamela and Hilary mocked and criticised.

Her parents' brilliant ideas at Christmas had begun the thaw. Two days before, a large new refrigerator, enveloped in red paper, was delivered to the flat to replace the tiny one left by Raoul. Then a gala dinner was given at Deep Water Bay on

Christmas Day for some twenty people, including Pamela, Hilary, Roddy, Keith and Greg, and a handsome gift for every guest hung on the magnificent Christmas tree.

Even after Christmas her parents continued to extend hospitality. There was so much they could offer - the company launch for picnics, for instance, although because of the increasingly hostile attitude of Japan, the more distant beaches were no longer accessible. Even the beaches they did visit were now ugly with great rolls of barbed wire across them, with gaps for swimmers. Concrete pill boxes were being constructed above the beaches, and at key points on the roads.

Thank goodness her training with St. John's was over! She hated the discipline of attending lectures, and mugging up for examinations which she had somehow passed. All the same, she felt quite proud at her first parade, marching with hundreds of others - mainly Chinese and Portuguese - to the military band of the Royal Scots. This earned her a close-up photograph in the 'Sunday Herald' as a result of which there was another outcry about the continued absence in Australia of British wives and children. The unhappy husbands made repeated representations to the Government and wrote vituperative letters to the newspapers: why had so many women been allowed to avoid evacuation by hastily joining defence organisations? Why had a select few from those evacuated been allowed to slip back into Hong Kong in recent months? If the place was safe for these few, surely it was safe for all! Either bring back all the evacuees at once, or send away the British women and children still in the colony!

Whatever disruption the evacuation had caused in the lives of so many, the past few months had been the best of Sandra's life, with parties and dates galore, and no parental restrictions. Sometimes she felt a pang of guilt that she should be so happy when there was so much misery in the world. Britain's ports and cities were being systematically bombed by the Luftwaffe; on the African continent the British Army had been driven back into Egypt and the Suez Canal was at risk; Greece and Yugoslavia had been lost to the Germans. Food in Britain was getting scarce due to shipping losses - poor Pamela suffered dreadfully every time a new naval loss was announced, in case it was her boy-friend Lawrence's ship.

If there were food shortages in Hong Kong through freight losses, Sandra had not noticed them, except for British chocolate which had been replaced by what she considered an inferior substitute from Australia. True, local prices were rising, and Pamela was counting on the Government giving in to public demand and paying its employees an extra allowance to meet the cost of living. It was obviously a sore point with her that despite all her years of office experience, she earned considerably less than the amateur Sandra - a fact which gave Sandra secret satisfaction.

Life would be perfect if one could forget about the Japanese troops stationed on the border in the New Territories, and if Mr. Bridger would treat her with respect instead of disdain.

Pamela went to pieces at breakfast one morning on reading a newspaper report of the collapse of an air raid tunnel in Chungking with huge loss of life, so Sandra took charge and rang the Hong Kong office of Raoul's agency for details; it was a great relief when the agency reported Raoul had telephoned his story of the disaster and he and Viola had not been involved, although hundreds of Chinese had perished in the incident.

Mr. Lamb began to seek Sandra's company, and the time came when she deemed it politic to accept a dinner date with him at the Peninsula Hotel. To her surprise, she was the only guest. He was almost inarticulate with shyness, and she was forced to chatter the whole boring evening. She was dying to dance, but it transpired that he had an old war wound in one leg which prevented dancing. Ever since that dinner, although friendly and pleasant when their paths crossed in the office, she had deliberately acted coolly: better to discourage a taipan from issuing invitations than to refuse them.

'Gammy Lammy' she secretly called him, and once referred to him as such to Pamela when relating how she had dodged his circle at the last firm's cocktail party. Of course stuffy Pamela disapproved the irreverence, however private, but then Pamela disapproved of practically everything.

The morning her father telephoned her at her office to say "We're sailing on the 'President McKinley' in ten days' time: give in your notice today", she braced herself for the confrontation which had to come. Instead of giving in her notice to Mr. Bridger, she went to see Mr. Lamb, told him her parents were leaving without her and asked him for a 3-year contract with the firm. Armed with this, she drove to Deep Water Bay that evening and put her case for remaining in Hong Kong as calmly and persuasively as possible.

Her parents were dumbfounded. Of course it was out of the question: how could she ever have imagined they would leave her behind at such a delicate political time: she had made a complete fool of herself, of them and of Mr. Lamb with her absurd contract!

Now there was no pretence at arguing reasonably. She reminded them she was legally old enough to make her own decisions - she had a job and a home. She was sarcastically reminded by her mother that her salary at Hendons had never covered her expenses at the flat. Sandra had expected a battle, but nothing as bitter and determined as this.

"You planned all this, didn't you, when you insisted on moving to Kennedy

Close?" Her mother's livid anger at this level was something Sandra hadn't seen for years: it provoked the uncontrollable rage of childhood.

" I want to live my own life!" she screamed. "It's up to me where I live and what I do."

"We understand that, sweetie." Her father spoke in the compassionate tone he had used years ago when she was in a tantrum. "So you shall live your own life, but not here in Hong Kong, on the edge of a volcano which could erupt at moment."

Sandra struggled to keep her voice from wobbling. "People have been saying that for years. It's ten months since the evacuation, and nothing's happened. Lots of people have come back from Australia, even some with small kids. Perhaps nothing will happen here, perhaps it will, but I'm old enough to make my own decision and I want to stay."

"You're still our daughter, even though you're 21, and you're very precious to us. Do, do calm down and be sensible! There's really no alternative but for you to come to Canada with us." Her father's hand, she noticed, was trembling as he laid it gently on her shoulder. "Go back to your flat tonight and tell the girls we will go on paying your expenses there until they can get a replacement. Ask Ah Ling to pack up your things and have them ready for collection by tomorrow afternoon, then come and stay here until we sail - there's so much to organise and it would be easier if we are all here on the spot. I'll ring Lamb and explain why you won't be in the office any more."

Although touched by his distress, Sandra was appalled at his suggestions. She waved a hand round the sumptuously furnished room opening on to the wide verandah; everything here was uniquely oriental - the deep-piled Tientsin carpets across the gleaming parquet flooring, the carved blackwood furniture, the parchment lampshades with delicate Chinese paintings.

"But I belong here! I was born here! I'm used to Hong Kong. I hated being at school in England, even more in Switzerland. I don't want to go to Canada, it will be even colder than England. It's just not fair to expect me to leave my real home, when I'm beginning to lead an independent life."

"What makes you think you're independent?" her mother sneered. "You know quite well that without our cheque book you couldn't exist on your own here."

"I thought you'd want to help," mumbled Sandra.

"Not to enable you to put yourself in danger!"

"No more in danger than all the other people who are here! As for managing to keep myself, I'll soon learn to do that - Pamela does, Hilary does. Cut me off if you want to, but I'm staying here."

"You wouldn't have your car," her mother reminded her. "That's being shipped to Canada whether you go or not."

"You can't do that - you gave it to me! It was a present!" "A present you won't have any longer unless you come to Canada," said her mother evenly. "It's in Daddy's name, remember."

So that was the trump card. Shocked and bitter, she grabbed her handbag and ran out of the room, her face working with anger and fury. Her father put out a placating arm but she shook it off and stumbled down the entrance steps to the drive.

"Drive carefully darling," he pleaded helplessly from the verandah as she jerkily started up the car. She could hardly see through her tears as she steered down the drive to the main road. Her throat ached from the recent shouting, and she was crying still with frustration and desperation at the prospect of leaving the place she loved, By the time she reached the summit of the road over the hills and braked to begin the descent towards the town, her mind was made up. Despite the loss of the car, she would not give in to her parents' blackmail: there must be a way she could live in Hong Kong without their financial support! It would be very difficult; she would not be able to afford to employ Ah Ling or use the telephone endlessly, or buy new clothes to satisfy every whim, and it would be dreadful to have no car...

Once over Wong Nei Cheong Gap, ever before her lay the harbour twinkling with lights of many ships: two Star ferries were crossing each other; coloured neon signs decorated the seafronts on both sides, a sight so familiar now but soon to remain only in her mind. She stopped the car in Kennedy Road, got out and gripped the iron railings at the side of the road until her hands stung. Tears ran down her cheeks, for she knew only too well that her parents were right - she would never be able to live in Hong Kong without their support; she had no option but to leave for Canada with them and stay with them until she was married.

... There was, she suddenly saw with great clarity, another alternative: she could get married in Hong Kong.

JULY

Called to the telephone in the office one afternoon in July, Pamela was astounded to hear Viola's unmistakable "Hi!" She and Raoul had just flown in to Hong Kong for a few days. "Can we come and see you this evening?"

Both were very pale because the daily air raids in Chungking kept them indoors so much. They were in transit for Singapore where Raoul was to take up a new job.

He explained "I had to leave China. For months I have been disturbed by the attitude of the Kuomintang. Seeing Chiang Kai Shek and his mob at close quarters has shown me he is far more interested in defeating the Chinese Communists than in fighting the Japanese."

"I thought the KMT and the Commos were now a united front against the Japs," said Hilary.

'Theoretically," nodded Raoul. "But the Reds have been too successful against the Japs for Chiang. Did you know that early this year Chiang organised a massacre of thousands of Red troops, many of them medical men? Such events have happened before, but never on such a blatantly horrific scale as this. Neutral observers in Chungking are appalled and disillusioned. All the apparent patriotic fervour whipped up through the world by Chiang is false.. if you knew the bribery and corruption...! Chiang wants to beat the Reds and become head of China before he chases the Japs out. Mao knows this, and only puts up with it because he sees China's internal struggle as secondary to the conflict with Japan."

He looked round at Hilary and Pamela's bewildered faces and sighed. "You girls know nothing of what I have just said, do you? It is too sad for me to stay working in China and watch her being torn apart from her own people as well as by the Japanese. So I must move on."

What he did not say was that as his disillusionment with the KMT had developed, so his sympathies with Mao Tse Tung's party increased. A hint of his change of heart was beginning to colour his news dispatches; there had been veiled criticism from Head Office and suggestions that he alter his slant, but he knew if he was to remain true to himself he could not write against his personal interpretation of events in China.

"We'll be based in Singapore," Viola elaborated, "but Raoul has to cover all Malaya as well, while I live in the lap of luxury in a bungalow with all mod cons and plenty of running water, and no air raids."

"No raids at the moment," corrected Raoul. "Maybe, in the future - a Japanese attack is as possible there as it is here.. The likelihood grows greater now Japan has signed her non-aggression pact with Russia and doesn't have to worry about her rear flank if she extends the war in Asia. You girls should not be here, you know."

"We're taking a chance; so many people in high places think there won't be trouble here and have even got their wives and children with them," shrugged Hilary. "I'm surprised, Viola, that that strong-minded husband of yours allowed you to stay in Chungking with all the bombing going on there."

"It was against my wishes, believe me," Raoul said.

"I simply refused to marry him unless he agreed I could stay," Viola smirked. "Now tell us all about Sandra's marriage.. that really was a turnup for the book!"

"She took us all by surprise," said Hilary. "She just up and got married by special licence at the Registry two days before she was due to leave for Canada with her parents: married the taipan of Hendons, no less!"

"He's all of fifty. And she'd been making fun of him ever since she joined Hendons." Pamela made no secret of her disgust. "She only married him to be able to stay in Hong Kong in luxury."

"Did you go to the wedding?"

"No, she didn't tell us about it until that very morning! She was flying around everywhere shopping for days before, but we all thought she was getting ready for Canada."

"How did the Smithson parents take it?"

"Shocked silly!" laughed Hilary. "She hadn't wanted to tell them until after the ceremony when they could do nothing about it, but apparently Mr. Lamb (I still can't call him Sandra's husband!) insisted that everything must be above board. Though he's always been represented as timid and reserved, he showed them how tough he could be when the Smithsons tried to persuade him to call off the wedding."

"Did they turn up?"

"Yes, but in high dudgeon, Sandra told us; her mother wouldn't even speak to her."

"Sandra didn't care - she got her way as usual," said Pamela.

"Now the Smithsons are on their way to Canada, and Mr. and Mrs. Lamb honeymooning in Manila!" Hilary still found the situation hilarious.

"So we're looking out for another lodger - this time, someone who'll stay, instead of rushing off to get married as the last two did," said Pamela ruefully.

The next afternoon Viola and Pamela had tea together at the Women's Club. "I did so want to see you on your own," said Viola. "How's the morale these days?"

"So-so." Pamela could never be other than honest with Viola.

"You look rather down. It can't be much fun to see people all round you getting engaged or married! Do you still hear from Lawrence?"

"Last time was four months ago. He's on an aircraft carrier, but not allowed to say which. Of course, he might have written again and the letters lost -I know some of my parents' letters have been lost because they number them. Anyway, Lawrence is so busy trying to get ahead that there isn't any place for me in his life. I'm trying to forget him."

"Never do that!" Viola said sternly. "All experience counts, you know, to form the mature you. Remember Lawrence and all you gained through knowing him - but leave your heart open for someone else." She laughed suddenly and added "Oh hell, who am I to try to dictate to you? Haven't I disregarded all my own advice to act cautiously?"

"You don't look as though you regret it!"

"I don't, not for a moment. Mind you, I've had to get used to Raoul's way of charming every woman he meets, even now we're married; he always was like that, but I've come to see that he just has to give his whole personality to every one he talks to - no more than that."

"I always thought of him as the perennial bachelor," mused Pamela, "and I'm beginning to think I'm the perennial spinster."

"What rot! There's plenty of time for you to meet the right man."

"I wonder... All my love affairs seem fated. I'm almost scared to go out with any one person too often in case it developes into another disaster."

"Oh dear, Pam, you still need Aunty Vi around to keep your confidence up." Viola sighed as she poured a second cup of tea for both of them. "I promise I won't nag and preach again, but hang on to this: remember how for ages I was uncertain about whether Raoul was right for me, but there came a time when I had no doubts at all - nothing could have stopped me from going to him in Chungking. It will be the same for you - you'll recognise the right man when he turns up. Now are you going to have this last éclair, or shall I eat it?"

It was hard to remain buoyed up by Viola's words, especially the following weekend when a defence exercise which included the voluntary services occupied most of Pamela's acquaintances. She had had to spend Saturday afternoon in her office as a token of her war-time position. Now she faced a lonely evening in the flat, made gloomier because a practice blackout was in force.

The catalogue of disasters in Europe nagged at her conscience. She felt she should be training for some war-time service other than mundane typing, had in fact discussed this with the Chief Clerk: he insisted she would be needed in the office in an emergency as much as nurses in the hospitals. Tonight she resolved to tackle him again.

Though always dreading bad news, she turned on the radio for the bulletin from England. This time her worst fears were realised: H.M.S. Hood had been sunk, with few survivors. Even though this might not be Lawrence's ship, she shivered, staring at floor, kneading her hands together, and jumped violently when the telephone rang.

"Pam? - Sandra! I've just heard about the 'Hood' - was it..?"

"I don't know, I don't know!"

"Are you alone? Can I come right now? I'll be with you as soon as I can get there."

By the time Sandra arrived Pamela was huddled in the corner of the sofa, weeping over a cup of coffee.

"What can I do to help?" she asked at once.

Pamela shrugged hopelessly. "I don't even know if it's his ship."

"Perhaps it isn't," said Sandra bracingly, sitting down beside her and taking her arm. Even through her misery, Pamela was surprised at the compassion. "Why not come and spend the evening with Miles and me? It was his suggestion that I come and get you."

"I can't," Pamela wailed.

"Yes you can. Nothing easier. Tell the amah to tell Hilary where you are when she comes home."

"I don't want to go anywhere," moaned Pamela, "I feel awful, I look awful."

"Make your face up then!" Sandra propelled her into the bedroom.

"Don't be surprised if Miles doesn't talk much," Sandra warned as she drove expertly up the hairpin bends to the Peak. "He's incredibly shy, but a dear when you get to know him."

The whole situation, with Sandra taking complete charge and rushing her away like this was so extraordinary that Pamela began to emerge from her state of shock.

Miles welcomed her with an embarrassed smile and made no reference to the reason for this visit at half past nine at night. Sandra soon realised that however unsuitable she had thought this marriage Miles was deeply in love.

After the long-gowned Boy had served drinks, Miles only stayed long enough to finish his, then excused himself to make telephone calls "I told him he had to leave us to talk," Sandra confided as she moved her cane chair nearer to Pamela's. "He's an absolute darling; he does everything I ask. I can't believe I'm so lucky, the way things have turned out."

She rushed on to detail her new life. She was now an officer in St. John Ambulance Brigade and spent much time at Headquarters, which was much more interesting than when she was just an ordinary member. Miles hadn't wanted her to continue working at Hendons, and she didn't mind leaving in the least: now she could lie in after a late night! There was plenty to do because Miles had explained she should give her services to voluntary and charitable organisations. It was bliss to be so loved and approved: she attended important social tiffins and dinners, and opened bazaars.

Of course, Miles was fussy about her driving herself around so much, so to please him she sometimes allowed herself to be driven by his chauffeur. Yes, she missed the night-after-night dancing of her single days, but when she and Miles attended dinner dances, he never minded her dancing with other men.

"You certainly seem to have landed on your feet!" Pamela, more relaxed after the small brandy Miles had pressed on her, felt her disapproval of Sandra melting away; at the same time, she thought wistfully that other people's private lives always seemed much more satisfactory than hers.

"There's only one thing we argue about." Sandra dropped her voice and fingered the arm of her chair. "Miles wants a child, and I don't."

Pamela stayed silent, her mind shying away from such a personal subject.

"I don't mean I never want children," Sandra went on defensively, "I just don't want a family for ages. A baby now would put a stop to all the best things in life."

"Most mothers don't seem to mind when they've actually got their children," Pamela said. "Belle, for instance, she's always happy with hers."

"Except on an evacuation ship in a typhoon, on camp beds in a room with hundreds of others," giggled Sandra. "That's another thing: if I got pregnant while this Jap threat is still hanging over Hong Kong, Miles would immediately send me to Australia. So I just dare not."

"I can see that's a bit of a worry for you." Pamela spoke guardedly, uncomfortable at discussing such a private matter while her host was in the next room.

"Miles won't take any precautions." To Pamela's increasing embarrassment, Sandra was whispering on: "He feels he's getting old and shouldn't postpone fatherhood. But I've got my life to lead as well, so it's up to me to see to things, and so far I've been clever."

Pamela sat up straight in her chair. "You mean.. Miles doesn't know?"

"Course not! No point in upsetting him, is there? Ah Ling told me what to do.. what to take. Do you want to know?"

"Oh no! I think all this is awful..." Her voice trailed away in dismay and disgust.

"I was only trying to distract you from your worries by telling you mine." Sandra's hiss was reproachful. "Now you've gone all goody-goody on me! You never change!"

"Neither do you!" Pamela stood up, "If you don't mind, I'll phone for a taxi and go home now."

"You can't do that! You can't! If you must go now, I'll drive you."

"I don't want you to. I'm.. I'm really grateful to you for bothering about me tonight, I truly am, but - "

"You still dislike me so much?" Sandra cut in. "You've always disapproved of me, haven't you?"

"We're so different." Pamela shrank from explaining her abhorrence of Sandra's deception. "We've nothing in common."

"And you'd rather not continue our acquaintanceship? O.K. Pam, I'll get Chan to drive you home and I won't inflict my company on you again."

NOVEMBER

Danny ran down the gangway on to Kowloon wharf into Celeste's waiting arms.

"Gee, it's good to see you!" He searched her beaming face. "You're all grown up!" She wore her curly hair about her shoulders, and despite the iron on her left leg, looked very smart in a navy blue suit with white trimmings.

On the ferry to the island they spoke about his mother, whose failing health was the reason for his return from Manila.

"I have taken over her piano pupils for the time being," Celeste said. "It has given me a good start as a teacher. I do hope you can stay a long time, Danny, Auntie has been a different person since she knew you were coming."

"Two weeks, my boss says. They want me back in the band so they're giving me an unpaid holiday."

Celeste chattered on: "Marie is expecting her third baby in February.. they're hoping for a boy as they already have two girls." Two of her brothers had joined the Volunteer Defence Force. Marcus was still in the States where he had a wonderful position, having recently qualified as a barrister; at this news, Danny felt a pang of the old cousinly rivalry. It was sobering to realise how much more successful Marcus' career was than his own.

"I belong to St. John Ambulance Brigade," Celeste went on. "There's all this talk that there might be an emergency here so I thought I should train for something. It's actually very interesting - and you would never guess who is my commanding officer!"

He couldn't, and she announced with a wide smile "Sandra Smithson, who used to be one of your mother's pupils! She's married now, and we have to try to remember to call her 'Mrs. Lamb'."

"Course I remember Sandra! Imagine her being married! I bet she was surprised to see you in her group or whatever it is."

"I shouldn't think she remembers me."

"Didn't you remind her?"

"Oh no Danny, she's very important! Anyway, I don't expect she noticed a little kid like me when she used to come to music lessons. She's married to the taipan of Hendons. He's very old."

"Trust Sandra to marry someone high up!"

"Pamela is still here," Celeste went on. "Her parents retired to England ages ago. I pass her in Central sometimes."

"And is she married?" He tried to make his voice sound natural.

"I don't think so - I would have noticed it in the paper for sure."

On the bus ride through the town to Happy Valley he became aware of defence works. A tunnel was being built into the hillside opposite his old office in Queen's Road. The entrances to the main Government buildings had protective walls of gray concrete blocks, sandbagged against blast. He was used to signs of preparations against war in Manila, where planes from the U.S. war bases swarmed in the skies, and lorry-loads of G.I.'s clogged the roads on manoeuvres, but here in tiny Hong Kong the preparations somehow seemed more alarming as they involved the protection of civilians. In the middle of the residential streets between Central and Happy Valley stood one-storeyed erections which Celeste told him were called pen shelters; it was obvious that only a small percentage of those living nearby could be accommodated in these shelters.

There were neither pen shelters nor tunnels anywhere near Dragon Terrace. He found himself appraising the old block of flats for their durability against air raids. No wonder the prosperous Bellarios had moved elsewhere - the place looked old and dilapidated.

As soon as he saw his mother, he knew he must stay in Hong Kong for as long as she survived. Shrunken, grey in the face, she lay in her rattan chair beside the piano, and cried when she kissed him; he hated himself for not having realised how ill she was when the first guarded letters from Celeste had arrived. In the evening she asked him to play the violin, and insisted on being helped up to the piano to accompany him.

Next day he went to see her doctor, who diagnosed advanced pernicious anaemia which just might respond to expensive new treatment. He discovered that she had carefully saved all the money he had sent regularly from Manila, and immediately arranged for the hoped-for cure.

He needed a job, so visited his former office to see if there was a vacancy. There was not: the war in Europe was affecting imports radically, and such firms needed less staff now. For two weeks he applied for every clerical post advertised, and eventually was taken on by a small Chinese bank; he was poorly paid, but augmented his wages with occasional bookings with hotel bands.

He had never noticed before that the Dragon Terrace flat was damp; now the dark bulging patches on the walls horrified him and he searched for a healthier home, and found a second floor flat in Kowloon with a verandah overlooking the harbour. It was obvious she would not be teaching music again, but the piano moved as well.

The work at the bank was a challenge but he learned quickly. His Portuguese colleagues soon accepted him into their circle; they urged him to join the Portuguese Company of the Defence Corps. ("It's great fun, man, especially when we go to camp!")

Years ago, he had hesitated to join in case his precious hands should be damaged; he accepted now, in the atmosphere of political uncertainty, that the old excuse could no longer apply. He found the foot-slogging and the lectures on machine guns and search-lights no hardship because of the comradeship of his fellow-volunteers - and it all helped to take his mind off his anxieties for his mother.

He knew it was only a matter of time before he would bump into Pamela. He had long ago come to terms with the inevitability of the end of their association, so there was no point in renewing their acquaintanceship. Nevertheless, it was a shock when, dashing in to the Hong Kong Bank to cash his mother's cheque one day, he heard her name called as he approached the counter.

"Miss Doran," the teller repeated and the girl ahead of him, with long dark brown hair in page-bob style, wearing a floral dress and white linen jacket, walked over to the teller. He watched her as she took her money, counted the notes and turned away from the counter. She had changed very much, seemed taller because of the high wedge heels; her long hair made her face look thinner..

"HULLO Danny!" She smiled at once. "I heard you were back - Rod told me he saw you in the Pen last week. How are you?"

"I'm O.K. thanks." He had not expected such a warm and enthusiastic welcome, and could only add "And you?"

"Grand! Are you back for long?"

"I don't know yet.. a while, anyway." His words were jerky because his heart was pounding; this older, modern Pamela was even more attractive than the person he had fallen in love with four years ago; painfully, he reminded himself again that she was completely unattainable, and always would be.

There was an awkward silence, then she glanced up at the clock and said "Got to go, this is supposed to be my tiffin hour. Goodbye Danny, give my regards to your mother."

He wanted to call her back; to tell her about his mother's illness; to ask about Sandra's marriage; and how her parents were faring in bomb-ridden England. She was disappearing between the glass revolving doors and he had to turn his back on her and let her go.

There was a new awareness of Japan's aggressive attitude. Two battalions of Canadian troops arrived in the colony to augment the armed forces; defence exercises increased, and Pamela had never before worked so many extra hours each week.

"We'll need cover this afternoon and Sunday, I'm afraid," said the Chief Clerk one Saturday morning. "Work it out between you, and let me have a roster."

"This is getting too much," complained Lois. "Another weekend ruined."

"I can come in tomorrow after Mass," said Jenny eagerly. I don't mind working all day."

"You do it then, ducky," nodded Norah , "My keen days are over. You'll do this afternoon, won't you Pamela?"

"Might as well," she shrugged. It was difficult to relax at home these days, her mind full of the emergency arrangements which formed a large part of her typing.

Towards the end of the morning she was called to the telephone and was astonished to hear Sandra's voice - there had been no word from her since the unhappy conversation five months ago.

"I know I should have asked you this before," - Sandra sounded very subdued - "but you were so cross last time we met. Did you ever get news of Lawrence?"

"No I didn't."

"Oh dear.. and another carrier's gone down: you must be going through hell."

"Oh well, maybe he wasn't on either." The unexpected concern made her lips tremble.

"I hope not, I really do. Pam, can I see you? I so badly need to talk to someone!"

"Why me?" Pamela's voice hardened as she realised the basic reason for the sympathy.

"You're my oldest friend! Can I come and see you this afternoon?"

"I've just been told I have to work." How glad she was to have a valid excuse!

"Oh God, Pam, I MUST see you! Look, you're going home for tiffin, aren't you? I can come and see you then - I'll bring some sandwiches from the hotel. Please, please, can I come?"

"If you like." A mixture of humanity and curiosity made her agree.

"Will any one else be there?" Sandra persisted. "I don't want any one else to hear."

"NO." Pamela tried to keep the note of exasperation out of her voice. "Gail's away, and Hilary and Rod always eat at the P.G. on Saturdays.

Sandra began to pour out her woes the moment she arrived. The marriage was a dreadful mistake! At first everything seemed fine, with Miles granting her every wish; but it had become boring, she wanted more freedom to come and go, more company with people of her own age.

"So I thought it might help if I had a baby after all, it would make life more interesting. Well, now I'm pregnant, and I know it isn't what I want at all! I feel dreadful, and I'm going to get fatter and fatter; and as soon as Miles knows he will insist on me getting out of Hong Kong. I was crazy to let this happen, but I kept hoping the evacuation would be over soon. I can't possibly have this baby, but Ah Ling won't help me to get rid of it although I'm only two months on, and she's put the fear of death in me about even trying to abort. Pam, Pam, what can I do?"

"You've seen a doctor?"

"No fear - Miles would soon know if I did. Ah Ling says I'm pregnant, and I know it myself."

Pamela sat in silence, trying to absorb the torrent of facts. Sandra looked far too young to be married as she leaned back on the sofa and twisted her handkerchief into a ball.

"What CAN I do?" Sandra repeated miserably.

"Nothing, as far as I can see. When is the baby due?" "Early June."

"Then just think: this time next year it will be almost six months old and sitting up and you'll be proud as punch."

"But I won't be HERE!" Sandra wailed. "I'll be in Australia, or Canada, or wherever Miles sends me. Pam, never get married - or at least, not until you've KNOWN the person for ages beforehand. It's like being imprisoned with a stranger, and you have to think of what they want to do all the time. Oh, I know I sound disloyal to Miles: he's marvellous to me, the first person I've met who never criticises me or tells me off. He gives me everything I want - except freedom. It's all my fault for engineering the marriage, and now the two worst things imaginable are going to happen - I'm going to have a child and I'm going to be sent away from my home - and I just can't bear it!"

"Australia might not be so bad," Pamela said bracingly. "Did you know Keith's just come back from spending his leave there with Belle? He says it's a lovely country. I'm going there on leave next summer - don't fancy a trip to England while the war's on." Sandra was beginning to show a little interest, so she gabbled on: "Hilary and Roddy are getting married next February, then they're going on leave - very overdue because of the war. They're braver than me, they're going to England, despite the bombs." In full flow, she had to stop herself from disclosing the family secret that Roddy intended to join the British Army, and Hilary to train as a full-time nurse.Instead, she said "I'm afraid I'll have to be getting back to the office now, it's almost two."

Sandra's face crumpled again. "I'm terrified of having a baby," she whimpered.

"Nothing's as bad when it happens as you imagine beforehand," Pamela tried to offer some comfort. "Lots of people have babies! If you'll just relax a bit, and stick out the uncomfortable period.."

"I'll stick out, that's for sure." There was a faint giggle in Sandra's broken voice, so Pamela hurried on "You won't have to do a thing for the baby - you can afford to pay for help, and you can just lord it in the nursery and take all the credit when visitors come and admire it. It won't be a bit like that ghastly time you had on the ship, helping Belle and the kids."

She had said the wrong thing. "Don't remind me of that!" Sandra was weeping again. "Babies everywhere, all yelling. I can't bear to think of it."

"You must stop feeling everything's a great tragedy for you!" Pamela shouted in exasperation. "Just remember you've always been able to work things to your own advantage - I've often been quite jealous of your ability to do that."

"You, jealous of me? I've always resented the way your life goes along so calmly and properly, never offending any one, and secretly admired you ."

"Good heavens!" Pamela hooted. "I'd never have known it! In that case, do please take my advice and tell Miles soon about the baby."

"I'm not going to until I can't hide it any longer! I wouldn't be allowed to dance, or play tennis, and I know he'd send me away, oh life is so bloody!"

"You won't always feel like this," Pamela suggested wearily, reaching for her handbag.

"God, I hope not!" For the first time Sandra laughed outright. "Thanks a million for listening to me, Pam - you're the best medicine I've got."

"Come back for another dose if you feel like it," she said impulsively.

DECEMBER

The Christmas festivities had started. Even the tiniest Chinese shops were bright with coloured lights. Patriotic fervour was reflected in personal announcements in the South China Morning Post whereby Mr. and Mrs. So-and-So informed their friends that they were making a donation to the Bomber Fund this year in lieu of sending Christmas cards. A seasonal bazaar was held at Flagstaff House in aid of the British War Fund, and for the same purpose a dinner-dance - nicknamed the Tin Hat Ball - was scheduled for the first Saturday in December.

"The tickets are jolly expensive - but it is for the war effort," said Hilary when she and Roddy decided to join Keith's party of lonely grass-widowers, as well as Pamela and Greg and his friends.

As always since the evacuation, there was a preponderance of males, and Pamela was in constant demand on the floor. Once she danced with Roddy's old friend Douglas, whose arrogance had so annoyed her on one of her first party dates in Hong Kong. She smiled inwardly at her early inexperience and narrow-mindedness, now at ease with his outsize personality, matching smart remark with smart retort. He pressed her for a date, and she accepted -his extrovert approach would make a change from Greg's wistfulness.

A rumour went round the tables in the second half of the evening - a late arrival had heard a Far Eastern B.B.C. radio broadcast which reported that large Japanese convoys had been sighted in the Gulf of Siam. Reaction was varied.

"So what? They've been around for months."

"Then why report it so specifically now?"

"Do you suppose they're coming here, or to Southern China, or to reinforce Indo-China?"

"Whichever - it won't be tonight! So why don't we enjoy ourselves while we can? We've had crises before, heaps of 'em."

Just before midnight the band stopped playing in mid-number, and on a balcony above the dance floor appeared a middle-aged European man in lounge suit, waving a megaphone.

"Drunk?" whispered Hilary. "Or is it an act of some sort?"

The man continued to wave the megaphone until the mutter of voices began to subside. "Attention, attention!" he entreated. "Listen to me: any men connected with ships in the harbour - report aboard for duty - AT ONCE!"

They discussed the announcement uneasily on the wallah wallah taking them back to Hong Kong. A summons to return to ship was common enough in the typhoon season, but not at this time of the year.

The harbour was exceptionally busy. Several steamers and merchant ships were already under way. Floodlights illuminated others at anchor; smoke plumed from their funnels; motor boats and wallah wallahs plied between shore and shipping.

"At least there's no blackout," said Roddy, tightening his arm round Hilary. "If it is an emergency, it can't be that serious."

But when they landed on the island, there were more signs of unusual activity: it was almost two in the morning, yet they were held up on the short drive to Kennedy Road by lines of fully loaded Army trucks.

"I don't like the look of this." Hilary shivered when she and Roddy said goodnight outside the flat. "I can't see us making that picnic at Big Wave Bay tomorrow.. no, today!"

"Don't worry: I'll phone you after breakfast - we'll know what's going on then, and can decide what to do," said Roddy.

The decision was taken out of their hands: the Volunteers were mobilised before noon; Roddy, already in uniform, called in at the flat on his way to report for duty.

Hilary had hysterics.

"For God's sake sister, cut it out!" begged Gail "I haven't been called out yet, neither have you - they can't have a war without us nurses, can they?"

"It's not likely to be the real thing," Roddy tried to comfort her. "And even if it is, I'll be back and forth to see you."

"If it is the real thing, can we get married right away?" She clung to him, feeling he was already a stranger in his khaki uniform and clanking accoutrements. "Can we?"

"Yes, yes! As soon as we know for certain what all this is about."

The local radio station had grave national news: Japan and the United States were locked in talks in Washington to try to ease the political tension between them; an American senator had voiced the opinion that hope was almost abandoned of reaching a peaceful conclusion.

Keith, also uniformed, called just after Roddy left, and gave his assessment of the situation. "We're nearer to war with Japan than we've ever been. Mobilisation here is very wise, whichever way the cat jumps; good practice if it's peace, readiness if it's war."

Too apprehensive to sit around in the flat, Pamela and Hilary took the bus to Repulse Bay and tried to relax on the beach in the sun. A few people were swimming, and several Chinese children played on the sand. From the Lido behind them floated the strains of a small band providing music for customers having tea. A tiny yacht was anchored in the Bay and a handful of swimmers frolicked round it. It was almost possible to think that life was normal until you heard the drone of lorries and trucks on the road above the beach, and saw the ominous rolls of barbed wire across the sand. Suddenly they felt cut off from what was happening, and took the next bus home.

There was no word from Roddy or Keith that evening, and the late radio news had nothing new to report. After they went to bed, Pamela could hear Hilary's stifled sobs, and yearned for normality. War here was completely unimaginable, but she could not forget Keith's grave words.

"Missee Pamela, Missee, te'phone!" The amah was shaking her urgently. "Must wake up, office te'phone you, wanchee speak!"

"The office? What time is it?" Still drunk with sleep, Pamela rolled out of bed and pushed her feet into her slippers.

"Ha' past six - too early," muttered Ah Lum throwing a dressing-gown across Pamela's shoulders as she lurched towards the telephone.

The Chief Clerk's voice came tersely over the line, instructing her to get to the office as soon as possible.

"Is it.. is it war?" she ventured fearfully.

"An emergency: everything has been alerted," was the guarded reply.

Hilary and Gail, awakened by the commotion, pressed for details as Pamela hurriedly dressed.

"It can't be the real thing" said Gail, "else we'd be having air raids; must be just another precautionary alarm."

"But to call at this hour.." Hilary plucked at her nightgown.

"Trying to simulate a genuine attack, testing the defences probably," said Gail. "I'll ring the Night Desk: Tim will know what's going on." She dialled the number and started to speak, then stopped, listening intently, her eyes widening. "It's started!" she yelled. "The Japs have attacked the U.S. fleet in Hawaii, and all the volunteer services here are being called out."

Any hopes that this astounding news was exaggerated were dispelled as soon as Pamela arrived at the office. Without doubt, a state of war now existed between Japan, and the U.S.A. and British Empire. Simultaneously, Japan had attacked Hawaii, Manila, Malaya and had already crossed the British border beyond Kowloon. If further confirmation were needed, it came an hour later when 36 Japanese planes appeared over Kowloon and bombed the airport and surrounding residential area.

The Secretariat staff was considerably depleted as most of the young clerks - British, Chinese and Portuguese - belonged to the Defence Force, and Pamela's colleagues Norah and Lois had gone to their nursing posts. Jenny didn't appear until half-way through the morning, the air raid having delayed her departure from home. She brought a pamphlet she had picked up after the raid; it was printed on cheap paper in poor English with amateur illustrations, urging British soldiers not to fight the Japanese, but to think of their families and lay down their arms.

In anticipation of food shortage and shopping difficulties, essential services personnel were hurriedly issued with passes entitling them to eat at a specified restaurant in town; Pamela and Jenny were allocated to the Parisienne Grille. At one o'clock they made the brief journey down Battery Path into Central. Both girls had been given red steel helmets which they self-consciously carried with them.

"Wait till my little brothers see this!" laughed Jenny, swinging hers. "They will be so jealous." The roads were full of lorries and vans en route to various depots with people and equipment, adding to the usual traffic congestion of buses, trams and cars. At key-points were posted anti-aircaft units and armed sentries. Air Raid Wardens of all nationalities were prominent in their green uniforms.

The atmosphere in the P.G. was not a bit warlike; here was the same dimly-lit room where Pamela had so often dined with friends; the same pianist playing unobtrusive music in the corner; the same cosmopolitan clientele, with just a few tables occupied by uniformed customers.

The siren screamed just as they finished their meal. In the tunnel the sound had been muted; here it was loud and terrifying. Planes droned, and distant anti-aircraft fire stuttered, but they heard no explosions. Jenny made a hurried sign of the cross.

When the all clear signal sounded, they hurried up Battery Path. A stream of chattering Chinese poured out of the tunnel beneath. The entrances to the international banks opposite were clogged with waiting customers, and long queues snaked round the buildings.

Work came in flurries in the afternoon. The men were constantly in anxious consultation as each new development was reported. There were plenty of rumours but little real news, and no more air raids. Perhaps, Pamela thought hopefully, these two earlier raids were all the Japanese had been able to manage.

"Leave at 5, you two girls," said Mr. Gasson. "I think you should stagger your hours from now on. Miss Doran, if you could be here by 7 in the morning and stay till 3, Miss Bennett could come at 9 and leave at 5."

Watching the sky apprehensively, Pamela walked quickly home. Already there were changes since the morning. Uniformed figures passed constantly, some on foot, others in official transport; the Peak Tram terminus appeared to be an army post, its entrance heavily sandbagged and guarded by steel-helmeted sentries.

Only the amah was in the flat; she was pale with fear. "My plenty frightened, plenty boomboom when Japanese airplanes come. No like go market buy food." She usually bought fresh vegetables and meat daily at the market in Central; other groceries the girls ordered by phone from the Asia Company. Pamela rang the shop at once and ordered food for the next few days.

"No can send tonight," sang the compradore, who usually delivered an order within the hour. "All boys go home, no like bombs."

Ah Lum, a widow, was anxious about her three small children who lived with her parents in Kowloon; she had been trying all day to contact them via friends with telephones, but without success.

"You t'ink more bombs come, Missee?" she asked fearfully.

The comforting answer should have been a confident 'No' but Pamela was no longer sure of anything after this peculiar day; everyone in the office had seemed apprehensive about the coming night, despite the popular theory that the Japanese were night-blind, which would preclude night bombing.

"No savvy," she said slowly. "More better you go Kowloon, see your family. Go now! Tonight blackout - no lights in streets or house."

"I makee supper first."

"Maskee supper. I can do."

When Hilary came in, Pamela was heating baked beans and cutting bread for toast. Over the snack they exchanged experiences of the day. Hilary had been helping prepare the wards for military casualties, but none had arrived. "There's a dormitory for us nurses in a house opposite the hospital, but I'd rather come home each night, in case Roddy calls in or phones. I wonder what's going on over there?"

'Over there' was the British line of defence in the New Territories, some 22 miles away. No sounds of battle were audible in Hong Kong, and so far no reports of action had been issued.

When darkness fell they stood on the verandah and stared out at this strange world of darkness, the normal night hum of traffic and active humanity muted. Two Chinese Air Raid Wardens could be seen patrolling the area, sometimes shouting at some tenant to complain about a chink in a curtain. Occasionally, cars and lorries drove slowly past, dark shapes with bluish blinkered headlights. There were no blackout curtains at the large French windows in the lounge, so they trundled the sofa into the enclosed hall; here, with the lounge door shut, they could sit with a shrouded light. By common consent, Hilary's bed and Gail's were jammed into Pamela's room: they felt safer altogether. "It's really happening," muttered Hilary when they tried to settle down for the night. "I just can't believe it." But the wail of air raid sirens twice before dawn left no doubt. Air raids started soon after Pamela reached the office the next day, and continued intermittently all morning. As the Secretariat was a very old building, without protection from bombs, it was decided to move to the recently-constructed tunnel across the road. Built into the hillside beneath the grounds of Government House and not fully completed, it smelt of clay and newly-sawn wood. The floor was formed of planks, and a rough framework of wooden struts lined walls and ceiling. From the entrance, branches of working bays zigzagged, There were no refinements; even the cubicles allotted for toilets were empty, necessitating trips to the ablutions in the Secretariat.

Pamela helped transport papers and files. Telephones were rapidly connected, spaces allocated, desks positioned against the walls.

When she returned to the tunnel after tiffin, reports of air raid casualties were trickling in; ricketty tenement homes in the thickly-populated districts had collapsed or caught fire; people were trapped, many killed.

She was not prepared for the pang of fear which engulfed her when she first emerged into the sunlight at the end of her shift. Despite its oppressiveness, the tunnel was a cocoon against danger. Her heart jumped when the air raid siren wailed as she walked home; she was too far from the tunnel to run back to it; the nearest haven was the Peak Tram terminus.

"Is it all right if I wait in here while the raid is on?" she asked the sentries outside.

"Get in," one said, and pushed her towards the sandbagged entrance leading to a basement room occupied by several soldiers. She recognised as ammunition boxes the green cases lining one wall, and thankfully fled the moment the all clear siren blared. Back home the amah's absence was making itself felt. In the remaining hour of daylight, she washed the breakfast dishes, peeled potatoes and put them on to boil; opened a tin of corned beef and washed her underwear. The situation was completely unreal, with all routine disrupted. There was a sensation of the suspension of everyday life while this intrusion, the war, was attended to.

"Only malaria patients, so far, thank the Lord," Hilary reported when she came in. "I can see Matron starting lectures soon to keep us busy."

The radio news that night was cheering: some Japanese troops were ambushed and most annihilated on the Castle Peak Road - Roddy's area.

"No wonder he hasn't been able to phone." Hilary's voice was determinedly bright. "Those Japs are finding they've bitten off more than they can chew."

Later, Gail arrived with more news. Despite the destruction of the few R.A.F. planes and most of the airfield the previous day, civilian aircraft - British, American and Chinese - were running a night shuttle service inland to well behind the Japanese lines; enemy planes were dropping more propaganda pamphlets urging surrender. No help could be expected from the R.A.F. in Singapore which the Japanese were bombing heavily.

"You've got to hand it to the Japs, getting all this organised while we were all sitting around thinking they'd never dare," Gail yawned.

Alarming news was circulating in the tunnel when Pamela arrived the next morning: the British defence line in the New Territories had been overrun by Japanese troops who were now advancing steadily towards the second line on the outskirts of Kowloon. The grim implications of this stunning disaster showed in many of the directives Pamela typed. Jenny didn't appear at all, but at noon she telephoned that she would get to the office as soon as she had finished helping her family to pack up essential belongings and move from Kowloon to stay with relatives on the island until the situation improved.

Later came reports of growing panic in Kowloon, where people were queuing and jostling on the ferry concourse, desperate to cross to the island, away from the approaching Japanese army.

Government departments, already thinly staffed through deployment of younger members in the Defence Force, were now urged to release more clerks to take their place in the field.

"Just off to get uniform and draw our weapons," said one of Pamela's Secretariat colleagues. "Can't wait to have a go at the bastards."

"I'll tell Rod when I see him you're propping up the tunnel here, Pam," added the other.

Because Jenny still hadn't arrived, Pamela extended her shift to 5 p.m, and when she finally left, it took a conscious effort to forsake the security of the tunnel and the company of authoritative officers. She heard the distant whoosh of a shell and jammed on her red helmet. The sentries outside the Peak Tram post gave her a wolf whistle as she sped past.

A loud toot on a car horn and the squealing of tyres drew her attention to an ambulance drawing into the kerb ahead.

"Hi Pam!" Sandra's face, framed with the St. John's jaunty blue hat, appeared at the open window. "How are things? Know what, I'm having a great time! Not many casualties here, thank goodness; it's much worse in Kowloon I hear. If it wasn't for people getting hurt, I'd say war is very interesting; everyone's so friendly and I never have time to be bored. What about you?"

"I don't see much that's going on, working in the tunnel."

"In a tunnel - how ghastly! I couldn't stand that. No wonder you look so pale. What news of Rod and Keith?"

"None. Rod is somewhere in the Kowloon area." She decided against mentioning the retreat from the New Territories in case it was not yet common knowledge. "Keith is out Lye Mun way, on searchlights."

"I bet they're enjoying doing something worthwhile," Sandra grinned. "I'd best be off - on duty again later tonight; I'm just going home to see Miles, he's been sleeping all afternoon, he was at the Power Station last night; you know he has a gammy leg.. he's part of the old boys' force, the Hughesiliers, guarding the Power Station against sabotage."

"Have you told him about the baby yet?"

"Have I hell! I wouldn't be allowed out of the house if he knew."

"But surely you shouldn't be rushing around the way you are.. ow, that sounds like another shell."

It was; a dull thud sounded from the hillside above them.

"A dud, like so many of their silly little fireworks!" Sandra revved up the engine. "I must go, and Pam, I'm O.K.! I've hardly felt sick at all since the war started, I've been too busy."

Pamela ran the remaining short distance to Kennedy Road. Her feeling of relief when she reached the shelter of the porch to the flat turned to dismay at a shouted greeting from the landing above: "Missee, missee, I come back, bring my family! We come look after you and other missees!"

Outside the flat door Ah Lum squatted, with her aged parents, her children and other relatives. The staircase was littered with assorted bundles of possessions.

"Ah Lum, there isn't room for so many people!" She spread her arms helplessly at the cheerful company.

"Maskee not much room," said the amah happily. "No good stay Kowloon-side. Too muchee boom-boom, and by n'by Japanese come."

In each of the two tiny rooms comprising the servants' quarters were double bunks. The ten arrivals crowded in and clucked their satisfaction.

"Now I cook supper," announced Ah Lum.. "I bring plenty rice from my friend's shop."

At least it was a relief to have help in the flat again, but there was a price; the new arrivals quickly established contact with the servants in adjacent flats, and excitedly and endlessly related their experiences in Kowloon.

"Too many people wait for ferry, Missee," Ah Lum told Pamela. "All wanchee come Hong Kong-side. Plenty bad men come take thing from shops and flats. Policemen shoot bad men."

There was more bad news when Hilary came home and reported that wounded from the battle front were now in the hospital. "It's awful, Pam! Lots of them are Royal Scots, they were terribly shot up at Shing Mun, and there's a Volunteer from the Armoured Cars - he's lost a leg. These things are really happening, and Rod is in the thick of it."

She broke down and sobbed, then wiped her sleeve across her eyes and went on "We've been told to bring an overnight suitcase tomorrow because Matron wants us to sleep near the hospital in case it's difficult to get there with all the shelling......Whatever's all that racket?"

A week ago Hilary would have exploded on hearing that the amah had brought her family to live in, but the reality of her day's experience had given her a totally new view on life. "I suppose we'll have to let them stay until they can get somewhere else. Don't let them overrun the whole flat though - I'll want my room back one day soon."

When Gail came in she immediately set about packing a small suitcase as she too had had instructions to live at her hospital until further notice. "Just as well you've got Ah Lum and her folks to keep you company, Pam," she said.

Settling down for the night was difficult, with the expectation of more shelling. Just before they put out the light they tuned in to the late radio news. It was comforting to hear the measured familiar voice announcing "This is the B.B.C. News from London" - but the words that followed paralysed them: "The Admiralty regrets to announce that the British battleship 'Prince of Wales' and the battle cruiser 'Repulse' have been sunk by Japanese bombers off the east coast of Malaya."

Stunned by the realisation that the main naval presence in the Far East was lost, no one slept much that night. Confidence in British ability to hold back the Japanese from the city of Kowloon was shaken.. of course the island was impregnable, but if the enemy got as far as the shores of Kowloon, merciless shelling at point-blank range was inevitable.

Desultory shelling was in progress when Pamela left the flat next morning. In the dawn gloom the harbour looked strangely empty; then she noticed masts sticking up out of the water, and she realised with dismay that the few remaining ships must have been scuttled.

Deep depression pervaded the tunnel over the loss of the great British ships off Malaya and the local news grew more ominous. Oil installations on the outskirts of Kowloon were on fire, sending a heavy pall of smoke drifting over the peninsula. Vital points which could be of value to the enemy were being blown up by the retreating British - the electricity station, the cement works and the docks. Fifth columnists mingled with the panicking crowds, creating more disorder. Shops and homes blasted open by enemy action were rapidly stripped of anything of value, even the floorboards ripped up for firewood. Official transport struggled to carry out emergency work in bombed streets. Uncontrollable crowds swarmed on to the wharves, fighting for places on perilously overfilled ferries.

Late that afternoon, an elderly Portuguese clerk from one of the Kowloon Government offices reached the tunnel and offered his services. Dishevelled and shaking, he told his story. The Japanese army was fighting its way into the outskirts of Kowloon. With his wife, and a suitcase of possessions, he'd managed to get aboard the last ferry. Under shellfire, the overloaded craft tipped dangerously as passengers scrambled to find the safest shelter. A nurse was hit by shrapnel and bled to death. He had intended to take his wife to relatives at North Point, but transport was almost non-existent, and walking that distance amid the increasing shelling was out of the question. In the end he had left his wife in a friend's office in Queen's Road.

Pamela asked if he knew Jenny's family: he didn't, but added "I expect they are in the Peninsula Hotel if they didn't get across the harbour; many Europeans and Portuguese are sheltering there." Alone in her bedroom that night, she tried to block out thoughts of these distressing reports. The presence of the tearful amah and her family nearby provided little comfort when shells whined and whooshed overhead.

Hurrying to work in the morning, she found Garden Road had suffered during the night's shelling; it was spattered with red clay from numerous craters, and littered with broken branches from the nearby Botanic Gardens: among all this, water from broken mains was rushing down the hill. Across the harbour the docks and godowns on Kowloon seafront were on fire; fearfully, she wondered what fresh disaster could befall the colony..

The answer to her thoughts came two hours later when it was reported that Kowloon was officially being abandoned, all defending troops withdrawing to the island to consolidate the protection of Fortress Hong Kong. Retreating? After only four days' fighting? The question was in everyone's mind but no dismay was voiced in the tunnel; the atmosphere was of brisk preparation for the pending siege, to keep the defences secure, and law and order until help arrived from outside the colony. Where the help would come from could not be hazarded, now that the United States was struggling with her own disasters, and Malay and Singapore equally occupied in defending themselves against the Japanese. With battles on all fronts in Europe and in Africa, nor could Britain easily spare troops for the Far East.

The air raid siren wailed incessantly. Even from inside the tunnel, bombing was audible - sometimes near enough to vibrate the walls and ceiling and send blast waves.

To minimise journeys to and from the tunnel, the staff was offered billets nearby in Central. Pamela gladly accepted this, and ran all the way to her flat that afternoon to collect some clothes. She found the amah anxious and unnerved by the day's bombing and shelling.

"I no can go market today." She spoke as though expecting reproof. "No get milk for you.. only very little left."

"It doesn't matter." Pamela explained that she would no longer be sleeping at the flat.

"When come back, Missee? " - Ah Lum looked alarmed.

"I don't know." It was only as she said the words that she realised how uncertain the future was. "You and your family stay here, eat all there is, and take care of flat."

"Oh Missee!" The amah's voice went suddenly high and uncontrolled. "You think Japanese come Hong Kong side?"

"No, of course not! Here have plenty big guns - we can stop the Japs getting ashore here, don't you worry." She handed the amah half of her remaining cash and picked up her suitcase.

"I carry," Ah Lum swooped forward.

"It's not heavy, I can manage it. More better you stay here.. else you must walk back in the dark."

"I come!" insisted Ah Lum, and Pamela could not stop her from accompanying her to the appointed billet, Dina House - a small block of sturdily-built flats off Queen's Road. Between Dina House and the sea front ran two parallel roads each lined with huge old colonial office buildings providing a shield against gunfire.

Pamela was allotted a camp bed in a room with three stenographers from other Government departments. She only knew them casually, but by bedtime that evening they were all exchanging gossip and giggling like schoolgirls in a dormitory. The new camaraderie helped to cover the strangeness of lying in the darkness on a flimsy canvas bed with minimal bedding and no pillow, listening to the threatening shells, and knowing too well that the bombardment would intensify.

Hilary scanned the sky, stained with billowing smoke from the oil fires in Kowloon: listened intently, waited as a shell shuttled over Central until she heard its explosion, then ran across the road to the hospital. Although the V.A.D.'s sleeping quarters were directly opposite, it took courage to make that brief dash, for the hospital on the mountainside was very vulnerable to the guns on Kowloon seafront.

At this moment the hospital area looked an even more enticing target, for several military ambulances were parked near the entrance as wounded were unloaded.

"Here, nurse!" She was commandeered at once, and helped to make the patients waiting on stretchers comfortable until they could be carried indoors. She was not yet used to seeing British bodies broken and bleeding. Nothing in her experiences in the Cholera Hospital had prepared for this: those Chinese patients had been victims of disease, not of deliberate, bloody violence; easing off blood-stained trousers and jackets - often having to cut them - took all her willpower. Her fellow V.A.D.'s were the same. At first most wept with their patients as they tried to wash the dirt of the battlefields from lacerated and shattered limbs. And all the time, whenever a new batch of casualties arrived, Hilary searched the faces with thumping heart lest Roddy should be among them.

He was certainly not among this morning's arrivals, who had crossed the harbour overnight after the military decision to retreat from Kowloon. Though shocked and weary, they wanted to talk, not sleep. They found the retreat from the mainland unbelievable.

"Four days! Just four bloody days! We only held them back for FOUR DAYS!" one kept repeating.

"While we guarded the roads, they came over the hills, wearing rubber shoes.. and us in our noisy Army boots.."

"They just never stopped coming, more and more of them. They knew exactly where to go, where our defences were! There were fifth columnists everywhere, signalling with mirrors to the Japs." There was no end to the bitterness.

When free to report to her ward, Hilary risked censure by diverting to the office, hoping to see the list of patients brought in overnight. A hasty glance while the Records Sister's back was turned showed no familiar names and she sped along the corridor to the ground floor ward reserved for the most seriously wounded cases; as most of these patients could not be moved to safety during air raids, the ward had been rendered as secure as possible; it was gas-proofed too, so the windows could never be opened, and the reek of damp plaster mingled with the sickly smell of pus always hung in the air. This always bothered her when she first entered the ward every day, but was soon forgotten in the busy and demanding work; there were revolting dressings to change, incontinent patients to tend, and constant orders from the curt but noble Ward Sister to obey.

The youngest V.A.D. on the ward was a totally inexperienced Canadian teenager named Rosemary Horne, who sidled through the door five minutes after Hilary.

"You're late, Nurse Horne," snapped Sister. "Over here at once; hold this basin."

"Sorry, Sister." Rosemary was still fastening her white head veil over her long dark hair, and hurried over to obey. Both Sister and Hilary knew why Rosemary was late; she had joined the V.A.D.'s two days ago when her boyfriend Johnnie of the Winnipeg Grenadiers was admitted to hospital with a bullet wound in his arm. She had no nursing qualifications, but her energy and competence were soon evident. At every opportunity she dashed along to the adjoining ward to see Johnnie - an activity at which her fellow V.A.D.'s connived to make possible. A brief visit to Johnnie this morning explained her late arrival.

"How is he?" Hilary mouthed at her when Sister's back was turned.

"Fine! Up in a couple of days, I should think."

At mid-day the air raid siren howled, and the nurses immediately set about protecting their patients; under each bed was an extra mattress which was heaved on to the bed over the patient, one end propped up against the bed head to leave breathing space. The nurses themselves huddled beneath the beds. It was little comfort that the bombs were small: the damage even a small bomb could do in a ward of helpless men was terrible to contemplate.

Mobile patients from the other wards were moved to the cramped storage basement where spare mattresses were kept on the concrete floor.

No bombs dropped nearby this time, but alarms interspersed the busy day and played havoc with mealtimes and the general routine. Gulping down a cup of tea in the dining-room, Hilary peered through the paper criss-crossings on the window facing the harbour, and saw that the godowns on the wharves in Kowloon were still burning fiercely.

"Hard to believe all this, isn't it?" She nodded to a colleague at her side. "Look at the Peninsula, with the Jap flag flying! This time last week we were getting ready to go to the Tin Hat Ball there!"

"I keep thinking I'm dreaming all this,", the other girl murmured.

When she returned to the ward, news was circulating that the Japanese had demanded the surrender of the colony, with the threat that refusal would bring even more severe artillery bombardment. Soon after, a copy of the Governor's response was passed round: "Not only is this colony strong enough to resist all attempts at invasion, but it has the backing of the people of the British Empire, of the U.S.A. and of the Republic of China. British subjects and all who have sought the protection of the British Empire can rest assured that there will never be any surrender to the Japanese."

"Now we'll be shelled to pieces, there's only a mile of water between us and the Jap guns," was the pessimistic opinion in the wards.

"What about the Chinese Seventh Army coming up behind the Japs?" asked one of the nurses bracingly. "We can hold out until they get here."

During her tea-break, Rosemary disappeared to see Johnnie and was away so long that her absence was noticed.

"You obviously haven't enough to do to keep you busy here," Sister observed. "From tomorrow you can transfer to the laundry."

That evening Rosemary wailed "I'll have to wash sheets and blankets and bandages for 44 people! AND their pillow slips and pyjamas. I don't know how to wash clothes, I've never done it before; don't they have to be boiled or something?"

"Not now, the boilers are out of action; and the orderlies who look after them have been put on combat duty," Hilary said. "Never mind! In the laundry you won't be under Sister's eagle eye all the time - it will be easier to get off to see your Johnnie."

One comfort in this spartan new life was the close companionship of fellow V.A.D.'s when off duty. Their leisure time together was limited because their onerous duties left them ready to drop into their beds and sleep soon after supper, but these interludes were full of overlapping conversations and shrieks of laughter, as the mistakes and reproofs of the day were recounted. There were giggles and hoots of laughter in the dormitory until the senior nurse called a halt. Only when all was quiet in the blacked-out room did they take account of the colony's big guns booming away into the mainland, and the Japanese shelling in return, and thoughts centred on family and friends in other parts of the colony. Hilary and most of the other nurses had had no word of their menfolk since the start of the war. "All the wires are needed for essential operational calls," was the official reason, which explained but did not comfort.

Hilary was dismayed when she learned she was to be in a party of nurses soon to be transferred to St. Stephen's Hospital at Stanley seven miles away. Apart from apprehension at such a long journey during bombing and shelling, she shrank from leaving the one place where Roddy would be likely to contact her.

With the prospect of the unwelcome move on her mind, she found it difficult to sleep that night and was still wide awake when the telephone in the corridor shrilled. She stumbled out in the dark to answer it, and the call was for her! Over a very indistinct field line, she heard Roddy whooping ecstatically at having located her. He was alive, he was safe, he wasn't even wounded! He was supposed to be resting for 24 hours after crossing the harbour, but so many of the Chinese drivers in his unit had stayed in Kowloon to look after their families that he had chosen to spend his rest time at the wheel. He was now in the Aberdeen area.

"And I'm going to Stanley in a day or two - St. Stephen's!" She had to shout it three times before he could catch her words.

"Right! I'll get to you there when I have leave - that's a date!" he yelled. "Got to go now, there's a queue for the phone behind me. Oh, I saw Keith just after we got back to the island, he's all in one piece."

"Thank God! Roddy, take care, take care!"

Sandra no longer found her duties a game. There were constant calls for ambulances to take the wounded and dead to hospital; and to stand by while rescue squads dug out those trapped in collapsed buildings. She had become expert at guiding her battered ambulance through narrow streets littered with debris and broken water and gas mains. The added hazards of being hit by a bomb or shell, or sniped at by roof-top fifth columnists, increased the sense of achievement when each mission was safely accomplished. Never in her life had she felt such fulfilment, proud to be helping to keep life going in the chaos which was present-day Hong Kong.

Most of the shelling was directed to the north shore, where Miles and his fellow Hughesiliers guarded the Power Station and where they had to stay day and night because of transport problems. Despite the dangers of travelling the two miles along King's Road, the wide main seafront thoroughfare to the Power Station, Sandra decided to visit him there and take him more clothes. She had to manoeuvre over shell holes, concertinaed tram lines, and burnt-out cars and lorries. Dominating the Kowloon waterfront was a gigantic yellow "Victory Balloon" which although tethered, floated gently to and fro. Spasmodically, as the wind blew in her direction, she could hear distorted snatches of Japanese marching songs blaring through huge open-air speakers.

"Don't you dare come again until the situation is safer," Miles ordered when she appeared. He was sufficiently uninhibited by the present unusual circumstances to give her a tight hug in front of his colleagues. He begged her to give up her dangerous work, leave the Peak house and move into one of the hotels in Central for the duration. Sandra argued that the house was out of range of the shelling, being on the other side of the island away from the mainland artillery.

"But we could be shelled from the open sea at any time," Miles said. "I shan't sleep easy unless I know you are safe. Go to the Gloucester, please, darling."

Because she could not agree to his other plea that she abandon her work, she promised to move into the hotel.

At the end of her next shift she drove the ambulance up the rutted Peak Road where her relief Margaret Hurst lived; here Margaret took over Sandra's seat and drove her home before reporting for duty.

Thank goodness the house was still unscarred! She walked through the front door which the watchful Boy had opened, and revelled in the order and cleanliness after the chaotic day in town. She stepped out of her shoes and padded into the lounge, throwing herself on the sofa. As usual the Boy brought her a pink gin and she took that first deeply pleasurable sip and closed her eyes.

"Missee!" Ah Ling was standing nearby, anxiety and alarm in her voice. In jerky Cantonese, she revealed that the basement of the house was filled with a dozen Portuguese refugees from Kowloon. Tearfully, she explained that she and the Boy had been unable to prevent the Billeting Officer who brought them from entering the house.

Miles had told Sandra some weeks earlier that his house and others on the Peak had been earmarked as havens for the dependants of local fighting forces in the event of war, but she had never imagined such a situation could arise. One half of her mind was outraged at having strangers in the house; the other half saw clearly that nothing that happened during these catastrophic days could be precluded on the grounds that it just wasn't done.

"We'll have to let them stay," she told Ah Ling slowly. "They must be very squashed in the basement; they can use the two spare bedrooms upstairs too."

Ah Ling, aghast, protested: whatever would Master say when he came home?

"When Master comes home, they will go home too," Sandra retorted. "Help me pack now - tomorrow I go stay hotel."

There were more anguished protests.

"Master says I have to go hotel," Sandra shrugged. "Must do what Master says."

"I come too,"

"Better you stay here and look after the house."

"Boy look after house."

"What about Ming?" - Ah Ling's husband was employed in a nearby house on the Peak. "Won't he want you to stay near him?"

"Maskee Ming!" Ever since Sandra could remember, Ah Ling had always acted as an individual, never showing publicly that she was related to Ming in the days when they had worked together in Sandra's parents' home.

They were packed and waiting in the hall by seven o'clock the next morning. By half past Margaret had not arrived with the ambulance. Sandra made repeated attempts to telephone the Hurst home and eventually made contact and was told that Margaret was in hospital, having been injured when a shell jerked the ambulance off the Peak Road and down the hillside. She then rang her Headquarters and was told no spare transport was available.

"I'll use my car meanwhile," she decided. No longer gleaming white, the body of the car was smeared with dull, black emulsion. Miles had insisted on this after the first few days of war when it was realised that the sun glinting on shiny metal provided an easy target for the enemy. The hood, so rarely used normally, was up and looked very fragile a protection against falling shrapnel.

Shells could be heard now, crumping and thudding.

Ah Ling panicked and pleaded with Sandra to stay at home.

"You stay if you want to, Ah Ling," Sandra got into the car and started the engine.

"You go, I go." The amah climbed in beside her.

The narrow road winding down to the town had been hit so badly that only one-way traffic was possible. Long delays at hairpin bends where the shattered road reduced the space for turning, caused a queue of vehicles. Before the queue could move at the last of the bends, a flight of Japanese bombers soared over the island and bombs slanted towards the Central District below. There had been no air raid warning because the electricity had failed. Praying that the bombers were flying too high to notice the snake of transport round the bend, Sandra huddled down in her seat, and urged the amah to do the same, but Ah Ling preferred to sit up rigidly, her terrified eyes never leaving the sky.

The cars jerked forward as soon as the planes disappeared. Acrid dust hung over Central. Chunks of masonry from the great buildings littered the roads. Sandra parked near the Gloucester and quickly made a booking, then sent Ah Ling to the room with the luggage.

It was only when she reached her Headquarters for duty and got out of the car that she became aware of an unnatural silence - no bombs, no shells, no booming from the huge British guns defending the island. In the office she learned that the Japanese had sent a second truce delegation to the Governor, stating that hostilities would be suspended until 4 p.m. and threatening that unless the surrender demand was accepted by then, future bombardments would be more severe than heretofore.

"Surrender? Not bloody likely!" was the chief reaction, but all essential services took advantage of every hour of the truce period to effect repairs, restore communications and move stores.

During this lull, Sandra called at the tunnel to see Pamela, whose appearance shocked her; she was pasty-faced, her hair lank, and she wore a much sat-in tartan skirt and grubby jumper. They stood outside the entrance in the brilliant sunshine for five minutes, revelling in the quietness.

"I don't know how you can bear to be stuck underground all day long," Sandra said.

"And I can't imagine how you can stay out in the open, with bombs and shells and snipers around," Pamela admitted. "You know, I don't feel I'm doing anything worth while at all, just sitting at a desk ready to type the odd thing."

"You must be needed, Pam, else they wouldn't keep you here. Anyway, ask them! If they'll let you go, why not join the Brigade? We're so short of people to help in the ambulances - so many regulars can't get to their posts to work."

"I wouldn't be any good." Pamela twiddled the pencil hung on a cord round her neck. "I can't drive, and I'm not trained for nursing or first aid.."

"No, you're not, are you?" It was strange for Sandra to feel superior and she couldn't help relishing the thought. "If you change your mind, come and see me - I'm staying in the Gloucester until the worst is over, Room 568."

Of course the surrender offer was summarily rejected, and after 4 o'clock heavy bombardment and air raids began again. Sandra was called to the scene of a street food kitchen where the waiting queue had been machine-gunned from the air. Such carnage she could never have imagined. She retched over the bloody moaning victims she helped her Chinese assistant to load into the car, and anguished at having room for no more. On the way to the hospital she called out to a passing Stores Department van and directed the driver to the scene so he could collect more of the casualties. When she had handed her patients over to the hospital she had a sudden attack of nausea and swayed against the door.

"You shouldn't be doing this kind of work," said the mature nurse who came to her aid. "You're pregnant, aren't you - three months?"

"About that," muttered Sandra. "It was so awful in that street, so many killed.."

"No point in thinking about it." The nurse's steadying arms were about Sandra's shoulders. "Where are you living? Is someone looking after you?"

Reassured on both points, the nurse allowed Sandra to leave. Darkness had fallen. It was difficult, by the feeble light of the shaded headlamps, to find a place in Central to park which wasn't blocked by craters and debris.

The great arcades on the ground floor of the hotel were full of frightened Chinese seeking more shelter than their flimsy tenements could provide. Precarious candles, hurricane lamps and torch beams provided the only light. She had to pick her way over people and bags and parcels of possessions in order to reach the staircase - with the electricity failure the lifts were out of action.

The moment she got to her room, Ah Ling took over; insisted that she rest, helped her undress, brought her food. "No good you go outside again," she reiterated in Cantonese, "Too dangerous for you, and bad for little baby. Master very angry if you go on doing this work."

Later, lying on the bed in the dark, listening to the battle noises, she felt unutterably weary; for the first time she thought about the coming baby with concern for it rather than for herself. Maybe Ah Ling was right and she should stop her work and rest until the war situation had become less hazardous?

All Hong Kong was shaken awake that night by an earsplitting explosion of unimaginable magnitude which reverberated round the hills, followed by the shattering of thousands of window panes.

Imminent invasion? Bombardment by Japanese battleships? There was terror in every heart for some time, but nothing more happened beyond the desultory shelling.

Pamela turned over on her narrow camp bed and clapped her hands over her ears and tried to sleep; she was terrified and painfully aware of her growing addiction to the tunnel; what had begun as a feeling of relief when she went in every morning, and apprehension when she left at 5 o'clock, had now developed into a fear that one day she would simply be unable to quit the tunnel at the end of her shift.

"Whatever was that?" In the nurses' quarters on Bowen Road, the girls peered behind the blackout curtains and stared at the harbour whence the explosion had come. A pink and black cloud of smoke billowed above the Hong Kong seafront beyond the Star Ferry concourse.

"It's something in the harbour," someone said fearfully "Perhaps the Japs are trying to get across here."

A doctor rushed over from the hospital and ordered all the nurses to get to the basement shelter. "As a precaution," he explained. "That bang was probably a one-off, but just in case.."

The hospital basement was already crowded with ambulant patients who sat up giving wolf-whistles as the girls scrambled in and huddled together on the mattresses.

"You been in the wars too?" One sympathetic patient nodded towards Hilary's bandaged fingers.

"Too much lysol in the water when I was washing the sheets," she explained.

"My fault really," said Rosemary. "Hil was doing my job for me while I went to see Johnnie off to the front."

Sandra pulled the pillow over her head to shut out the horrifying bang and Ah Ling's terrified cries. She longed to have Miles next to her - the one person who cared for her through all her wilfulness and selfishness. That boom, so near, like a million cannon, shattering nearby windows, meant that nowhere in Hong Kong was safer than any other. She resolved to join Miles at his wartime post the next day, and stay there as long as he did.

The small military lorry, covered with camouflaged canvas, stopped at a pillbox at the side of the road. There was a brief exchange of conversation between the officer sitting next to the driver and the officer who materialised from the pillbox; then four uniformed figures, bent double with rifles and equipment, emerged and climbed into the back of the lorry. There were good-natured grumbles as the others squashed up to make room in the complete darkness.

"Where are we going?" asked one of the newcomers.

"Your guess is as good as mine, man," came a weary reply. "God, what a shambles."

Since the totally unexpected speed with which the Japanese had captured Kowloon and the British Forces had poured back on to the island, all pre-arranged defence plans had been thrown into confusion. Many combatants had become separated from their units; ad hoc decisions were taken at low level to use whatever troops were available in a given vicinity - this was why the ten Volunteers in the lorry were a mix of machine gunners, riflemen and artillerymen.

The overworked vehicle groaned uphill and bumped over boulder-strewn roads, sometimes lurching dangerously near the granite hillside escarpments.

"'Over the hills and far away'," sang the driver softly.

"That the best you can do, Rod?" quipped some one as the van rocked crazily from one crater to another like a ship in a gale. "What about 'Life on the Ocean Wave'?"

"O.K." Roddy started a rollicking chorus at the end of which one of the newcomers called out: "Hey, Rod.. it IS Roddy Doran, isn't it? I'm Daniel Russell."

Their companions moved this way and that to enable Danny to get nearer to the driver.

"Good to see you Danny.. at least, I can almost see you!" Roddy told him Pamela was working in the Government Tunnel and Hilary at the Military Hospital; Danny said his mother was sheltering in the building of the bank where he usually worked, adding "My cousin Celeste is with St. John Ambulance Brigade in Happy Valley... Holy Mother of God, what was that?"

The massive explosion echoed round the hills; Roddy stopped the lorry until the reverberations subsided.

"Sounded like all Green Island blowing up," someone muttered.

On the seafront at Central, two jubilant soldiers emerged from the pillbox through whose slits they had fired on the unlit vessel approaching the jetty. The whole ship and its cccupants had been blown to smithereens. It was an hour later before they learned they had blown up a British launch ferrying dynamite from the ammunition store on Green Island to the island - the launch had arrived earlier than scheduled.

The launch disaster dominated all conversation in the tunnel in the morning. At last Pamela felt able to put her fears for her own personal safety into perspective, and looked for an opportunity to ask Mr. Gasson to allow her to join a nursing organisation. Ironically, her typewriter had never been busier: reports poured in that oil tanks at North Point on the island were on fire, and the loss of so much essential fuel meant making rapid new plans.. less fuel dramatically reduced the length of time Hong Kong could hold out.

A heavy air raid took place so near the tunnel that everything on the desks shook and rattled. Outside, vehicles were on fire; a number of Indian policemen on guard were badly injured and were carried into the tunnel until an ambulance could get through to take them to hospital.

"Any one who can help, come at once!" went the call. Desks were hurriedly cleared, and the men who usually sat at them laid the injured across them. Pamela joined other girls, trying to give first aid to these huge, khaki-uniformed Indians who were groaning with bleeding wounds and broken limbs.

"They need splints; see if you can find something suitable," someone directed - and Pamela hurried away to see what she could find, thankful for a job which did not involve attending the injured. When she returned with pieces of wooden struts, girls were tearing up their petticoats to bind round splints; others were supporting broken bones until they could be splinted. Pamela stood dumbly by, stricken by the sweating, suffering brown faces. By the time ambulances arrived one of the men had bled to death.

Back at her desk, she hammered away at her typewriter, facing the fact that she was physically and emotionally unfitted to be a nurse. She felt even more useless when three of the secretaries, shaken by their first encounter with wounded, sought and obtained permission to join the hospitals - but this solved her problem after all. "Now don't you go leaving us Pamela," said Mr. Gasson at the end of her shift. "We can't spare you as well, especially as Miss Bennett isn't likely to turn up again."

Sleep was impossible after the explosion. In the morning Sandra was too weary to get out of bed. The continued shelling hurt her ears. She was tired of this exhausting, uneasy life, and at last accepted Ah Ling's strictures that her St. John's activities would put her baby's life in jeopardy. A phone call to her Headquarters explaining she was unfit for duty was sympathetically received. It was a relief to be cossetted again, and to be brought breakfast (albeit meagre) in bed.

Of course Ah Ling protested when in the afternoon she insisted on getting up and dressing; she would obviously protest even more if she knew of Sandra's plan to go to Miles at the Power Station, so she lounged in the arm-chair watching for an opportunity to leave undetected. In the end she had to send Ah Ling to get a pot of tea, then grabbed her secretly-packed suitcase and slipped out of the room.

The corridors outside were narrowed by lines of refugees of all nationalities sitting against the walls. She took five minutes to reach the staircase, and even here weary people lolled on every step.

Her car was still intact where she had left it, although bonnet and roof were spattered with dirt and dust, and pitted with marks from flying debris. She drove carefully through the messy cluttered streets, past the Naval Dockyard from where great guns thundered their shells across the harbour to the enemy in Kowloon. She chose the back streets of Wanchai rather than the wider but vulnerable open road on the waterfront; perhaps this was a mistake because the side streets were almost blocked in places by collapsed tenements. A rescue party was tugging aside the remains of a block of flats and hauling out screaming children. On the pavement lay a heap of dead bodies awaiting removal.

"No, I can't do any more," she said out loud, unaccustomed after nearly two weeks of ambulance work to pass by any one in need. She dared not risk being delayed, for darkness was falling, making the journey to North Point doubly difficult over the shattered roads.

Through Wanchai at last, she could smell the acrid smoke from the blazing oil tanks ahead. On the seafront side of the wide Kings Road factory buildings were blazing. She had to guide the car on to the pavement to escape flaming fragments blown across the road. A gutted tram lay on its side; lamp standards leaned drunkenly; overhead cables and telephone wires dangled in mangled loops, some melted, some scorched black.

Suddenly a great barrage of gunfire erupted from Kowloon. She wanted to turn back, but shells were falling in the road behind her as well as ahead; if only she could keep going for another half mile she would reach the cover of the Power Station. Regardless of the obstructions in the road, she put her foot on the accelerator, sobbing and cursing. The hood of the car was rent apart by flying shrapnel; she was driving through heavy smoke now; she couldn't see properly, but it seemed imperative to keep going. Her sobs became little animal cries as she gasped for breath. She heard the detonation of the shell in front of the car, felt the glass from the shattered windscreen on her face.

"Poor little baby," she heard her own voice croak as blackness engulfed her.

Pamela's in-tray was piled with papers when she reached her desk the next morning.

"Just as well you didn't go off nursing, Miss Doran" said Mr. Gasson. He hesitated a moment, then added "You've heard the latest news, I suppose?"

"Well, someone at breakfast said there's a rumour that the Japs have made a landing - but no one believed him; he was told off for spreading false rumours."

"It's true I'm afraid. A party got ashore last night at Lye Mun.. they had heavy losses, but some of them got up into the hills. You'll find the story here."

He ducked away in embarrassment at Pamela's horrified expression. Lye Mun was Keith's operational area. Her fingers were trembling so much that typing was difficult. Each fresh sheet told of a new disaster. It was only when she forced herself to concentrate on the physical act of typing rather than on the words that she achieved a calm of sorts.

No wonder gunfire had been noisier than ever last night! She learned now that the Japanese had been concentrating their fire on the northern seafront which faced the narrowest passage between island and mainland. British pillboxes were pounded, the Power Station put out of service. Sampans and motor boats full of Japanese troops plied continuously across the harbour, undeterred by losses inflicted by the British defending forces. Even as she typed, further messages poured in - brief reports via telephonists at the little A.R.P. posts throughout the island; some of the messages from places under direct attack left off in mid-sentence when the line was destroyed.

Throughout the day the grim news mounted; more Japanese were landing; bitter bloody battles were taking place, and a considerable enemy force was gradually but steadily pushing up into the high ground at the northern end of the island. Torn with anxiety about Roddy and Keith and fear for her own safety with this new menace, Pamela was thankful to be kept busy. Shift times were becoming blurred, with the mounting difficulty of getting from one place to another on time. She worked until after six o'clock, when an American shorthand typist arrived with a note from the Police Department accrediting her and she was immediately conscripted to relieve Pamela.

Once more, that frightening moment, walking out of the tunnel into the line of fire, this time with the terrible knowledge that Japanese soldiers were only a few miles away, actually on the island.

She puffed out her cheeks in relief as she reached the sandbagged entrance of the P.G. and sat at an empty table. There was now little variety in the rationed meal - rissoles, fried leftover potatoes and peas; tinned fruit and cream. She lingered over the meal and the cup of tea, dreading even the short journey to Dina House. A group of European men in rescue service uniform at the next table were talking about the Power Station. She leaned nearer to listen.

"... under fierce attack. Those old boys - the Hughesiliers - held out, fighting side by side with the younger lot."

".. Cut off by the Japs, who tossed grenades through the windows.."

"Two of the Hughesiliers were killed.. Miles Lamb and one other - maybe more."

Pamela's ears rang with shock for a moment then she pulled at the arm of the last speaker: "Please, are you sure, about Mr. Lamb?"

"Well," the man hesitated, "don't quote me, but that's what I was told by someone who'd had a phone call from someone else."

"He's my friend's husband!" She left the unfinished tea and ran across the road to the Gloucester Hotel. Technically there was a blackout, but a spectacular fire at the western end of Queen's Road illuminated the buildings nearby and threw tongues of flickering light on Central. In the arcade, the lingering smell of disinfectant could not wholly disguise the body and urine odour of crowds living, eating and cooking there.

On her way to Sandra's room, she was astounded by the sight of women and children, European and Chinese, camped in the corridor.

Ah Ling was the only occupant of the candlelit room; she didn't know where Sandra was: "Go out long time, I so worry, not see for three, four hour. Not see Master long time.. two days, three days."

Pamela kept her alarming story to herself, and wrote a note for Sandra giving her room and telephone number at Dina House. Ah Ling begged her to stay and wept when she left.

"Is this your room? How many are in it?" asked a Scottish voice and Pamela found her arm held by a tall fireman carrying a Eurasian toddler.

"No, it's not mine," she said. "I'm just visiting."

"How many in there?" he asked again.

"Two."

"They're big rooms, won't they let my wife and kiddies come in till I can find somewhere else?" He nodded towards his Chinese wife and boy of about five who were slumped against the wall. "We came in from Causeway Bay this morning when we heard about the landings, we were awake all last night with the racket; I have to go on duty soon, I haven't much time to get them settled: ask your friend if they can come in this room at least for a while."

Pamela hesitated; in Sandra's absence it was hardly her place to let in extra lodgers, but the man's concerned face and the drooping children were irresistible. "I'll try," she said, and went back into the room and closed the door while she explained the situation to Ah Ling. The amah could not accept that the war had changed everything; that it was only right to give complete strangers a haven in Sandra's room.

"Who pay?" she wanted to know. "And only got two bed."

"Government pay," Pamela guessed wildly. "Maskee not enough beds, no got beds in corridor! Can sleep in chairs. Only for tonight."

When the family was settled in the room, the father, who introduced himself as Tony Graham, took Pamela's arm and together they forged their way through the corridors and arcades. He then insisted on escorting her to the door of Dina House, his cheerful company an immense comfort in the shadowed streets, with their hidden perils of robbers and snipers as well as the omnipresent risk of shells.

Her room-mates at Dina House welcomed her with relief, since she had been due back two hours earlier. There were visitors from other rooms relating the latest rumours and news. Japanese troops were said to be well entrenched in the hills, and pushing towards Causeway Bay and Happy Valley. No one could believe this: how could the enemy make such progress, now that all the military - including two Canadian and two Indian Battalions, the Royal Scots and Middlesex Regiments, as well as the H.K.V.D.C., were pitted against them? Again she heard of the heroic stand at the Power Station, but no confirmation of the names of fatalities there.

Later that evening she felt her way down the staircase to the telephone queue in the hall and eventually managed to get through to Room 568 at the Gloucester. Ah Ling answered, but had no news of Sandra. She then dialled the Peak house, but that line was dead.

It was a harrowing night. Two more camp beds had been squeezed into her room, and the new occupants were tearful and restless as they anguished about their husbands who were fighting with the Volunteers in the hills.

There were terrible notes to type the next day. A battery of Volunteers near Lye Mun had been overrun by the enemy and some bayonetted to death. No victims were named, and Pamela tried to convince herself that Keith was probably no longer in that area. A medical post had also been captured, and wounded Canadian soldiers, R.A.M.C. men, and members of St. John Ambulance Brigade bayonetted and shot. The Repulse Bay Hotel was surrounded by Japanese troops and anxiety felt for the large numbers of British women and children who had flocked there for shelter.

The men in the tunnel treated the devastating reports with a calm efficiency.

"Just do this one first, if you will, Miss Doran, " was the nearest the Chief Clerk got to panic when the advance of enemy forces towards Wong Nei Cheong Gap was reported. The Gap in the hills was between the main road down to Repulse Bay on one side, and that to Happy Valley and on to Central on the other; the principal lines of communication between British forces east and west ran through it - whoever held Wong Nei Cheong Gap held Hong Kong. .

Her mouth dry, Pamela typed the bald words as the horrifying implications began to creep into her mind.. perhaps the Japanese could not after all be thrown back off the island.

That evening she went again to Sandra's room in the hotel. Mrs. Graham opened the door.

"The lady not come at all," she said. "Amah very worried. She go to lady's HQ. - St. John's isn't it? They say she stop working day before yesterday because she ill. So this afternoon that crazy amah, she say she go walk to house on Peak, maybe her missee there. She only get killed, suppose she can walk so far."

Pamela stood motionless, trying to contain her fear.

Twenty-four hours Sandra had been missing; surely if she had decided to stay elsewhere she would have let Ah Ling know? Again she tried telephoning the Peak house, but the line still wasn't working. Racking her brains for inspiration, she suddenly thought of ringing Miles' firm, Hendons - someone there might be able to help. It was half past 5 on Saturday afternoon; in normal times no office would be open, but now weekends were no different from weekdays; it was worth a try.

At least this line was still working; a tremulous Portuguese girl's voice said "Hullo?"

"Is that Hendons please?"

"Yes, I am Mr. Bridger's secretary, Gloria Sevallo.. but Mr. Bridger is not here, he is working with Food Control. Sometimes he comes into the office, can I take a message?"

"I'm a friend of Mr. Lamb's wife," Pamela explained carefully, "and I wonder if any one in the office knows where she is living now?"

An agonised sob on the other end of the line sent Pamela's heart pounding so loudly she could only just hear the mangled words that followed. "Mrs. Lamb... somebody found her car on King's Road, wrecked and burnt, but Mrs. Lamb.. she could not be seen anywhere. And.. and poor Mr. Lamb was killed yesterday at the Power Station."

Even in the dark and misty night, Roddy knew every hill and mound; every tiny footpath and nullah; the bend of every road, the shape of every cove on the coast below. How often during his grown years, had he plunged exultantly down every hillside, racing his friends, singing at the top of his voice! Now, leading a small group of his newly-allocated platoon, it was necessary to maintain complete silence, for although the nearest Japanese front was thought to be two miles away, costly bloody experience had shown that enemy forward runners lurked in all directions.

Though treading as carefully as they could, it was impossible to walk with stealth in Army boots. Bracken crackled, parted branches creaked, and leaves damp underfoot from the night's rain squeaked. He only hoped that the rush of water coursing down the nearby nullah was loud enough to blanket their presence. In the near distance rifle and mortar fire sounded spasmodically.

It was difficult to keep contact with his men; the three immediately following him had to be close enough to see his hand signals, yet far enough apart that if one walked into an ambush the others would have a chance to escape. Every so often Verey lights soared into the sky, hinting that the enemy was getting nearer.

"The object is to get to Repulse Bay before the Japs can reinforce their troops who took the hotel," the temporary C.O. had said. "Each group to set off separately and by slightly varying routes." He had pointed out these on the map with fingers that shook. "Meet here, where the roads join. Off you go, lads, as fast as you can - but for God's sake be quiet."

The need for speed was no secret: a large number of women and children, as well as wounded soldiers, were stranded in the hotel. The need for quietness had become terrifyingly obvious - the Japanese were taking no combatant prisoners, bayonetting, beheading or at best shooting all who fell into their hands.

Peering down through shrubs and bushes, Roddy could see the glint of a road; this meant the agreed rendezvous had been reached. He signalled to the men to halt, and sank wearily back on his heels to await the arrival of the others. The sky was beginning to lighten. He prayed that the rest would turn up while there was still a modicum of darkness.

Crouched among the bracken, he became conscious of the weight of his boots, the heat of his dirty uniform, the hardness of his tin hat and the burden of his rifle and ammunition and other accoutrements. He was also wistfully aware of hunger and thirst. Like his comrades, he had been without proper rest and regular meals for two weeks. Every inch of ground gained by the enemy had been hotly contested. There was plenty of food on the island, but the logistics of getting it to the battle-grounds dreadfully difficult. Since the enemy had captured the reservoirs and turned off the supply taps, water was the most precious commodity of all. It was bad enough for the civilians who had to rely on the residue lying in the tanks of whatever building they occupied; baths were a luxury of the past; lavatories could not be flushed; lacking water for tea or coffee, even teetotallers drank bottled beer when lemonade ran out. For the soldiers in the field, dependent on tanks of water being brought to them, every drop was doubly precious; personal washing except in nullahs went by the board.

The first birds chirruped gently in the trees around him. He looked up and saw the sky's greyness turning to mauve, lighter and lighter. How often in the past had he sat at the opening of his tent among the hills with Greg and others, watching just such a sky, and looking forward to yet another exhilarating day of hiking, leaping across narrow ravines and bathing, nude, in fresh water pools!

With dawn came the planes, dropping their bombs in the hills now, directed to their targets of pockets of British soldiers by the ubiquitous fifth columnists who repeatedly flashed mirrors from their hideouts.

The rustle and commotion caused by the arrival of the second group was masked by the rumble of the bombers.

"Can't wait much longer for the last lot," Roddy whispered to the man behind him; it would be broad daylight soon, yet the numbers for the foray would be pitifully few without a full muster.

There was a sudden scrambling above them, and slithering of boots, and the remnants of the last group arrived panting and dishevelled, helmets awry and perspiration on their blackened faces making light streaks on their cheeks. Their route high in the hills had come too near to Japanese scouts; two of their number had been killed; two others were wounded and not fit to take part in the present action but insisted on doing so - no one left wounded behind now if there was any alternative.

The nearest route to the hotel was the road beneath them, but was too obvious a target. Instead, they crawled through barbed wire entanglements on a winding route among the cover of trees and bushes, along the lower slopes of the hills which brought them immediately above the back of the hotel. They saw at once they had arrived too late - the Japanese had already consolidated around the hotel. Their horses, tanks and mechanical transport lined the periphery, guarded by dozens of fully-armed soldiers; more lorry-loads arrived as they watched.

Roddy had a momentary mad desire to tell his men to hurl their hand grenades over the hotel to try to destroy the enemy transport; reason reminded him that the grenades might miss their target and cause injury to women and children and wounded in the hotel, as well as reveal their own weak presence. Also, the C.O. had given them a second objective if the first proved impractical - to try to make for Wong Nei Cheong Gap which had changed hands several times; it was again in enemy hands, and the British were attempting to launch another counter attack there and in need of reinforcements.

Again they arranged to travel in small parties, starting one after the other with a five minute gap between each. The terrain was more difficult now they were climbing, They could see the road below; it was straddled with bomb and shell craters and broken boulders from the hillside; in places part of the tarmac had vanished completely.

They were surprised by the sudden crack of rifle shots all round them, followed by the padding of fast approaching footsteps.

"Run! hissed Roddy, signalling to the men helping the two casualties. "We'll cover you. Make for 'Eucliffe.'"

Unable to see their targets, the cover party could only toss hand grenades in the direction of the firing, which gradually grew so spasmodic that the party cautiously crept forward again, hoping that this pocket of the enemy had retreated. A fusillade of bullets exploding among them, and the trampling of shrubs and twigs confirmed that the posse of Japanese had been considerably reinforced. There was no point now in trying to make contact and give battle. Roddy waved towards 'Eucliffe' and they all sped down the hillside. Silence was no longer a priority - all that mattered was escaping from the hail of bullets. Their clothes and limbs were torn on the barbed wire they had so carefully wriggled through half an hour earlier. Rifle fire followed relentlessly.

They had to break cover to drop down on to the main road leading to the large Chinese mansion above Repulse Bay beach. Heads down, they streamed across and caught up the two wounded and their helpers. They stumbled through the imposing entrance whose ornate iron gates hung off their hinges.

From the outside there was no sign of enemy occupation. They flung themselves against the main door; it didn't yield, but movement could be heard inside, then the door opened a crack and a Canadian voice yelled "They're British, they're not Japs!"

Inside were combatants of all sorts who had been cut off from their respective units - Canadians, Middlesex troops, and Chinese, Eurasian, Portuguese and British Volunteers. Few had weapons.

No sooner had the latest arrivals poured through the door than dozens of Japanese soldiers erupted from the hillside, leapt on to the road and, firing furiously, raced through the castle gates. Hand grenades followed; windows shattered; the massive front door blew open The defenders with weapons were quickly overpowered by the superior numbers of enemy soldiers pouring in.

Stunned, and choked with dust, the men on the ground floor were beaten by rifle butts and pushed out on to the terrace which faced across the bay. Everything happened so quickly that there was no chance of self-defence. From the basement echoed great thumps; the defenders there had locked the doors and piled heavy items of furniture against them. Hand grenades were lobbed through the windows, and presently a sorry straggle of battered troops, hands tied behind them, was bundled on to the terrace to join the others.

They were dragged, prodded and kicked to the low wall above the cliff,made to sit, legs dangling, facing the sea. Some were crying, some cursing, others dumb with disbelief - all in no doubt about what was to come. Roddy stared with detachment at the crutch of his trousers darkening as, without control, he passed water. He heard the cocking of the guns, the guttural commands, and looked wildly about for some hope of escape but there was none. This, then, was the end; he fixed his eyes on the wide sweep of the bay he knew so well, the great green hills soaring around it, the higher more distant hills paling beyond, beneath a sky porcelain blue and flawless. This could be any bright winter's morning with its promise of another beautiful day.. another beautiful day.. another beautiful day.. He was repeating these words to himself when the first shots rang out.

There was momentary pain, and a snarling darkness.. then he heard his voice saying those words again and opened his eyes. A hand was clapped over his mouth and there came a whispered warning "Shush.. there are Japs just above us."

He became aware that he was lying on his back in a rough cave with two other men crouched nearby. They gave him encouraging thumbs-up signs. He could hear water lapping His hands were no longer bound. His body felt bruised and battered, but why was he still alive, remembering the impact on his neck in his last moment of consciousness on the terrace? He felt his neck and fingered a wad of sticky damp cloth held there by a twisted handkerchief.

"You were lucky, pal." The accent was Canadian. "Your bullet didn't finish you off.. went through your neck."

Raising himself painfully on his elbows, he asked "Did you get hit too?"

"No, we nipped down here just before the buggars got through the castle door."

"What about the others.. who were with me?"

"All goners.. on the rocks outside here. My buddies and I had a look - saw you were still alive so dragged you in here."

"Dead? All of them?"

" 'Fraid so. Keep your voice down, else we'll be next."

"You're sure they're all..?" Roddy's voice choked.

"Too sure. Look, forget them, if you want to survive. The Japs will find us sooner or later if we stay here - we must get away tonight; we're strangers here, do you know these parts?" "I ought to.. lived here all my life. Name's Rod Doran." "Hank Leander from Winnipeg," grinned the other, "and Jed and Arnie."

"We'll have to swim for it," Roddy said. "Make for Stanley, it's well defended - and my girl's a nurse there."

"How far is it?"

"A few miles;" Roddy decided not to be too precise, "but we can take it easy once we're out of the bay. We should leave as soon as it's dark."

The long intervening hours had to be endured first. Most of the time they dared not even whisper, for from time time there were burst of activity on the terrace overhead - firing, shouts, screams, the staccato rattle of shots followed by the thud of bodies landing on to the rocks. Whenever there was a lull one of the Canadians crept cautiously round the mouth of the cave, then crawled back with a hopeless shake of the head; there were no more survivors.

When it was almost dark they shed their outer clothes and boots. Each man had his folded shirt and trousers tied round his waist. They worked out an uneven formation in an attempt to avoid detection, and crawled out of the cave. It was as well the gloom partially obscured the harsh details of the broken bloody bodies lying at all angles at the foot of the cliff; Roddy tried not to look at the distorted faces.

"Strike out for the sea, away from the castle, not straight across the bay," he advised, and all three followed him with small quiet strokes. There was no sound of following fire, and Roddy thought it safe to lengthen his strokes. The others copied him. Too late he saw the phosphorescent glow in the water created by the faster movements. Machine gun fire from the castle swept the sea around them. They immediately dived and swam on. There was no sign of Arnie when the other three surfaced.

"Just keep going," Roddy called grimly. "We're out of range now."

He kept his ear cocked for the sound of a pursuing boat, but none came. When they were far out beyond the bay, they floated together on their backs to recover breath.

"How much farther?" asked Hank.

"About another five miles.. but we can take it easy."

"Five miles!" echoed Jed. "It's O.K. for you Rod, the farthest I've ever swum is two lengths of the school baths."

"Want to know something?" grinned Roddy. "I've never done this distance before either - but by God I'm going to do it now!"

"Another trayful for you, Pamela."

"O.K. Mr. Gasson."

It was no longer 'Miss Doran' and 'Sir'. The intimacies of tunnel life had long dispensed with such formalities. Every one had their personal anxieties for family or friends, many in areas cut off by the fighting. Communications were chaotic, telephones constantly disrupted by war damage. No official casualty lists appeared - such news came by word of mouth.

One day seemed just like another; there were no longer days of the week, and no weekends. By now it was obvious even to the most optimistic that the enemy was building up to a huge offensive to take over Central. Leighton Hill only a mile and a half away was under attack, British troops and volunteers holding out under withering fire. Wong Nei Cheong Gap was finally lost, and the survivors of the British and Canadian troops who had tried to recapture it were being pushed relentlessly back to the lower slopes of the hills above the city.

Nursing her anguish at confirmation that Miles had been killed, and at the frightening lack of news of Sandra's whereabouts, Pamela found herself typing like an automaton as disaster followed disaster. The defenders on Leighton Hill were forced to withdraw towards Wanchai, and in order to deny the enemy the cover of the large houses on the terrace, had set them on fire as they retreated. Knowing that her old home was going up in flames added to Pamela's distress, no matter how firmly she reminded herself, "It's only a house, it's not people."

All day long the gunfire grew nearer and louder as the Japanese continued to attack the centre of the town from its environs.

"You'd better leave when you've done this little lot, Pamela," said Mr. Gasson, handing her a sheaf of papers.

She glanced at the top report as she rolled the paper into the typewriter; she couldn't believe her eyes: picked up the sheet with both trembling hands and read it again: 'Last night Mrs. Sandra Lamb brought to Jockey Club Hospital, Happy Valley. Injured in King's Road last week, cared for by Chinese family living near until fit to be taken to hospital. Not badly injured but is in early pregnancy and should be removed to better conditions a.s.a.p.'

"Oh thank you, God, thank you God!" The words echoed in her mind over and over again as her fingers raced over the keys. This time she forgot her fear as she left the tunnel, conscious only of the wonderful fact that Sandra was alive. At the top of Battery Path stood the square redbrick building known as the French Mission. She scurried past it because at this point there was a gap between the banks and offices below, a gap which gave a view of the harbour and the guns on Kowloon waterfront. A young white priest wth red hair, wearing a black cassock, stood on the path talking to passersby. He called out to Pamela in a soft Irish voice: "Excuse me, madam: are you a Catholic by any chance?"

"No, I'm C. of E. Why?"

"A priest is on hand inside to hear Confessions," he explained. "These are dangerous days. It's best to be prepared to meet one's Maker."

She stood still for a moment, silenced by the implications of these words; an old memory darted into her mind.. of the young Philip and Danny in the Confession line in St. Joseph's Church: a desire for comfort overwhelmed her. "Can I go in.. just for a minute?" she found herself asking.

"Of course, my child." He led her through the great door into a tiny open courtyard surrounded by three storeys of rooms. She had expected to find herself in a chapel, but no: a priest, head bent, was sitting on a chair just inside the cloistered periphery of the courtyard; beside him knelt a Chinese schoolgirl, and behind her at a respectful distance stood a queue of waiting penitents of various nationalities. She would have liked to join them, but what could she say? All she could think of was gratitude for Sandra's safety. She backed towards the door.

"Let me give you a blessing." The red-headed priest gently took her arm. "You are sorry for all your sins against Our Lord, aren't you?"

She had never thought very much about sins, but supposed she must have committed some. "Yes, Father, I am. And I wish I were a better person, I'm not brave.."

"God loves you as you are, because He made you like that," said the priest, making the sign of the cross on her forehead. "Go in peace, and pray for me."

That strange encounter remained with her as she ate a hurried meal in the P.G. and gave her the courage afterwards to make her way through the shellfire to Hendons to pass on the good news of Sandra. The office was in Des Voeux Road, parallel to Queen's Road on one side and on the other parallel to the seafront which was under guard by the military and out of bounds to civilians. Under every sheltered pavement beneath the solid city buildings huddled hundreds of Chinese - evidence of the flight of frightened people from outlying districts now in the hands of the enemy.

Hendons' entrance was guarded by two large, turbanned Indians who opened only one half of the door to let her in - a precaution against unwanted intruders trying to gain entry. The entire ground floor was occupied by Portuguese and Chinese, mainly women and children. Sleeping accommodation had been formed by pushing desks and chairs together. Filing cabinet drawers served as cots for babies. Despite the cramped conditions, there was an air of orderliness. A middle-aged Eurasian woman came over to Pamela and asked if she could help.

"I'm Pamela Doran, I'm looking for Gloria, Mr. Lamb's secretary; I spoke to her on the phone the other day."

"Here I am, Miss Doran!" Gloria scrambled up from the floor where she had been amusing a group of children, and hurried over.

"Have you heard? - Mrs. Lamb is safe!" Pamela cried. "A Chinese family rescued her and nursed her; now she's in the hospital at Happy Valley waiting to be transferred to the Queen Mary."

"Thanks be to God!" Tears streamed down Gloria's face as she seized Sandra's hands. "Are you sure? Is it certain?"

"I typed the report myself."

A buzz of excited conversation exploded; people from the upper floors came down to find the reason for the commotion and joined in the celebration.

"Stay and have a meal with us, Miss Doran," Gloria begged. "The stew is just ready."

"I've just eaten, thanks." Pamela shook her head. Some of the women round her had husbands in the Volunteers, and plied her for the latest war news. She replied guardedly, trying to conceal her apprehension.

It was time to pull the blackout curtains across the windows; candles were lit on top of the filing cabinets. There were whispers in one corner as Pamela said goodbye, then Gloria asked "Can you wait just one minute, please, Miss Doran? The children would like to sing for you."

She stood by the door, touched by the childish trebles coming from all parts of the huge room; some sang off key, some couldn't pronounce the English words properly; there was no accompanying music, but the message was unmistakable.. they were singing a carol.. 'Away in a Manger'.

Until then, she had quite forgotten it was Christmas Eve.

The ferocity of the shelling in Central was so alarming when she left Hendons that she decided to take shelter in the Gloucester and call on the Grahams in Sandra's room.

"Why don't you stay here tonight, Pam?" Tony too had slipped into using the friendly diminutive. "This racket isn't going to get any better. I'm going on duty soon, so there's room for you."

"I ought to get back to Dina House, the others will be anxious."

"Try phoning them.. they'd be even more worried if you went out in this; if you can't get through I'll drop in and tell them."

Still she hesitated.

"Better you stay here," Mrs. Graham called from the bathroom, where she was trying to wash the children with a towel dabbed with bottled soda water.

"Pam!" Tony pulled her over to the door out of his wife's hearing. "Do stay here! Keep it under your hat, but there's a strong rumour that the Japs will try to land in Central from across the harbour tonight. You'll be better off here, the hotel is so much bigger than Dina House, and there are far more people around to protect you. Besides, you'll be company for Lily and the children."

She needed no more persuading, and managed to get through on the phone to Dina House to explain her absence.

"Good job you rang," her room-mate said, "A message came for you from Keith someone - your brother-in-law? He's in the convalescent hospital in the Gloucester, wants you to visit him when you can."

This was surely the strangest Christmas Eve she had ever spent, sitting on the floor next to Keith in the former Grill Room which, lit by candles, was now spread with Army biscuit mattresses occupied by convalescent troops tended by European women wearing slacks and jumpers.

Keith, in pyjamas and blue hospital dressing-gown, was able to sit up - in fact he preferred to because his back had been lacerated by shrapnel three days earlier. His face was pale and haggard but lit with smiles as Pamela, without any self-consciousness, held his hand tightly.

"I've been so worried about you," he told her, "and here you are, fit as a fiddle. What have you been doing all the time?"

Ruefully, she told him of her uneventful contribution to the war effort.

"Some one has to do the routine jobs.. you do the typing and that frees someone else to do some other job they can do better," he assured her.

She told him about Sandra and Miles.

"And she's pregnant? Poor little girl." He gave a great sigh. "If only all you girls had had the sense to leave when you had the chance!"

The men on neighbouring mattresses wanted to talk to her too. Most were regular soldiers from the Middlesex and Royal Scots regiments, without visitors because their families were in Australia. Bitter about the loss of their many comrades in the battle they craved the chance of conversation with a female, especially a young civilian with no connection with the carnage they had known. Seeing their need, Pamela found it easy to chat and join in their banter, until the latest news bulletin was passed round: a huge fire in Wanchai was hampering the defence line there; the approaching Chinese Army could soon make contact with the Japanese forces; the latter item raised an ironic cheer as it had been reported too frequently to be believed.

Reading between the lines, Keith told Pamela quietly "The Japs are in charge of two-thirds of the island.. we hold just the chunk between Wanchai and Aberdeen - and Stanley peninsula."

"Will they get any further?"

Keith hesitated, then said "Frankly, I don't see how we can stop them. You can't argue with hard steel and unlimited reserve troops. One by one our big guns are being knocked out. All of us here have been told that as soon as we're on our feet again we'll be kitted out and back in service - that's how bad it is."

It was now late in the evening. Promising to come again the next day, Pamela said goodnight and left the Grill Room. Most of the refugees in the arcades were asleep as she worked her way round their recumbent bodies towards the staircase. Strange noises were coming from the road outside: the continual smashing of glass and occasional bursts of hilarious laughter. Curiosity overcame caution, and she forged a passage to the road. Here a chain of policemen passed bottles of liquor from piles of crates, smashing the bottles open on the pavement then pouring the contents into the gutter. The men joked as they worked, some kissed the bottles goodbye before smashing them. The road was running with booze. The refugees nearest the scene ayahed with disbelief - as much at the astonishingly cheerful attitude of the destroyers as at the wanton waste.

"But why?" Pamela asked herself as she watched.

"Best get inside, ma'am," said a lurking Air Raid Warden. "You know why they're doing this, don't you? It's so the Japs won't have the liquor to make them too irresponsible when they get here."

"You really must stop walking about Mrs. Lamb - you know what Dr. Gordon said."

"But I'm perfectly well now, Matron, it's almost a week.."

"I'm aware of that." Matron propelled Sandra back to her bed. "You were very lucky not to lose your baby, but it's imperative that you rest until the ambulance comes."

"When is it coming?" Sandra muttered as she leaned back against the iron bed-head and surveyed the ward despondently.

It was two days since the Chaus had brought her to the hospital. They had pulled her out of the car before it caught fire, carried her to their tenement flat nearby, and nursed and fed her until she was fit to walk. She had expected the war-time hospital set up in the Jockey Club building in Happy Valley to be a blessed haven after the Chau's cramped home; instead, it could hardly have been worse. The telephone only functioned spasmodically, and Happy Valley was cut off from Central by blasted roads, constant shell fire and air raids. There was no water in the taps so no one could wash, lavatories could not be flushed, bedpans and urinals could not be cleansed; at least there was a small supply of drinking water in a galvanised tank but this had to be carefully conserved for that purpose only. Despite lavish use of disinfectants, the stench of urine and excreta could not be quelled. Now another smell seeped into the ward - that of unburied corpses which had to be stacked in garages outside because the Sanitary Department lorries could no longer get through to remove them.

Weakly, Sandra cried into her hands. She should have been collected from this awful place immediately her presence was reported! She should not have been left in what was meant to be a temporary war hospital for Chinese convalescents, tended mainly by auxiliary nurses under the supervision of two regular nurses and a matron, none of whom had any patience with her and her complaints. The only person who was sympathetic was the eldest of a group of St John Ambulance girls who introduced herself as Celeste Bellario, cousin of Daniel Russell whose mother used to teach her the piano. Sandra only remembered Celeste because she had a crippled leg. It was clear however that Sandra had made a great impression on the child Celeste, who was eager to chatter forever about those far-off days.

She fretted at having no news of Miles or how the war was going. The only clue as to what was happening in the rest of the colony lay in the constant reverberation of gunfire around and above them. Every new Chinese patient brought into the hospital voiced the same fear: "Japanese come, Japanese soon come."

Until bomb-damaged, upper floors of the Jockey Club building had been used as wards and also sleeping accommodation for the nurses; now all the patients were concentrated into the ground floor ward - in peacetime the betting hall - and the nurses' camp beds were wedged behind the line of betting booths on one side. To afford Sandra as much privacy as possible, she had been put in the bed nearest to the nurses' dormitory, but there was no way of blotting out the piteous moans and cries of the wounded, or the incessant hawking as they spat into the spittoons. Wearing a nightgown lent by one of the nurses - she possessed nothing beyond the clothes she had been wearing when her car was hit - she sat up in bed as Mrs. Burwood, a middle-aged and bulky Auxiliary Nurse, approached with a plate containing a dollop of burnt rice and a sliver of corned beef.

"I can't eat that." Sandra pushed the plate away and sank down in the bed again.

"You'll have to eat what there is, like the rest of us," said Mrs. Burwood tartly; shortage of food and water limited the quality and quantity of food; also the kitchen on the first floor was open to the sky through enemy action, and none of the nurses who took turns doing the cooking spent more time there than was necessary.

Oh, she was tired of this war! The early days of exhilaration and power, dressed in her impressive uniform, driving her ambulance, taking thrilling risks and basking in the praise and gratitude of those she helped, were over. She yearned for her own home, her own bed - or at least the comfortable room in the Gloucester. She could smell her own unwashed body. Tears running down her cheeks, she stuck her fingers in her ears to muffle the screams of the little Chinese boy brought in an hour ago, one arm shot away at the elbow.

"There, there, Mrs. Lamb!" Mrs. Burwood reappeared and patted her hand. "My friend Docky has found a couple of biscuits in her bag; see if you can manage them. One of the other patients will be pleased to have your rice, it won't be wasted."

As Sandra accepted the biscuits with a shamed face, Mrs. Burwood added "Later on, I'll bring you something so you can have a little wash - Docky's got a bottle of eau de cologne, so we're each having a few drops of it on a blob of cotton wool to give ourselves a lick and a promise. But we're waiting until the patients are asleep, because it wouldn't go anywhere among all those poor souls."

"Hullo Mrs. Lamb!" - Celeste appeared by her bed, earnest and beaming. "I just came to say goodnight. It doesn't seem at all like Christmas Eve, does it?"

"You can say that again," nodded Sandra.

"No Midnight Mass this year! - Matron won't allow us out; I don't suppose it will be any better tomorrow - imagine missing Mass on Christmas Day, and me going to be a Nun!"

"Are you really? I had no idea."

"It's been my ambition for a long time," Celeste confided. "I've been accepted to become a postulant next April."

"But Celeste, you've hardly lived yet! How old are you? Eighteen, nineteen? How can you give up everything in life before you've experienced it?"

"For God."

"But your music.. your teaching.."

"I shall still teach - but not for a living; for God."

Sandra wanted to ask so many questions, unable to accept the renunciation of such a young life, but Celeste's tranquil face made her hold back. Instead, she said "How I admire your strong faith and your tenacity of purpose! You make me feel very inadequate."

"Oh no Mrs. Lamb!" The admiration was returned one hundredfold. "We are so honoured to have you in the Brigade."

"I'm not much good at the moment."

Matron interrupted: "Time for bed. The night shift is just taking over."

The day nurses went through the half-swing door into the sleeping area, chatting quietly and laughing as they undressed in the darkness. One voice a little louder than the rest demanded plaintively "Where are we going to hang our Christmas stockings tonight, girls?"

Sandra marvelled at the banter under the present circumstances, and made a mental resolve to try to be as resilient as her companions. She had barely closed her eyes when machine-gun fire echoed round the Valley. The nurses sat up and listened tensely as the sound grew rapidly nearer. Flashes could be seen through the blackout curtains against the betting hall windows. Without doubt the action was moving closer to the hospital, circling the road round the race course. The hope that the guns were British was quickly dashed as answering fire could be heard from the direction of the town.

"The Japs are pushing our boys back into Central," said Mrs. Burwood. "We're right in the middle, God help us." She got up and went over to Sandra and pulled back her blankets. "Up! I'm going to push your bed in to the booth with ours."

When the firing sounded just outside the Club, the nurses were afraid to speak. Imagination ran riot. Sandra put her hands protectively over her womb. Gradually the furore outside diminished. Whatever was happening was no longer in the immediate vicinity of the hospital.

"We've been by-passed, girls," Matron told the nurses quietly. "We won't be harmed - they will have seen our Red Cross flag. Settle down and try to get some sleep."

How could any one sleep, with apprehension of the future behind enemy lines, and constant gunfire in the distance? Yet Sandra must have dozed off several times, remembering the shock of the situation every time she was jerked awake by a burst of firing. She realised morning had come when the creaking of camp bed struts signalled that the day shift nurses were getting up.

"Merry Christmas, Sandra!" Mrs. Burford called.

"Oh, he didn't come!" Docky pretended to feel for a bulging stocking at the end of her bed. "Maybe Father Christmas didn't like the look of the Japs."

Matron's head appeared above the swing doors. "Good morning all! It seems reasonably quiet outside; I suggest you all go and stand at the back entrance for a few minutes and get some fresh air before breakfast."

Longing for release from the stuffy atmosphere in the ward, Sandra exchanged her night-gown for her dark blouse and slacks, now carefully washed and mended by the Chaus.

"You're not supposed to get up," Mrs. Burfield said.

"I AM up, I need air too." She followed the nurses through the ward to the back door which led to the paddock, garages and spectators' area in front of the race course.

A heavy mist paled the hills and hung over the whole Valley. On the plateau opposite the gaunt remains of the burnt-out Leighton Hill houses were just visible, looking like ancient ruins. There was dew on the grass which was pitted and churned by falling shrapnel. The keen air was tainted by the malodorous whiff of ordure from the clogged lavatories and the mortuary nearby, but it was good to be out of the claustrophobic ward. Sandra saw her companions in broad daylight for the first time, and wondered if she looked as woebegone as they did. Most had lost weight so that their grey cotton uniforms - dirty because no laundering had been possible for some time - drooped sadly. Confinement in the gloomy ward, lack of air and sleep, shortage of food, and continuous anxiety for themselves and their relatives and friends, had made them pale-faced and heavy-eyed.

"Well, girls!" The young Scottish doctor suddenly materialised from behind the garages. "I've just given you your Christmas present - an empty morgue." He had rounded up some Chinese stretcher bearers to help him dig shallow graves on the racecourse to dispose of the putrefying corpses.

"Bet that's the only Christmas present we'll get," grunted Docky as the gunfire gained momentum with the day,and the nurses trooped back to the ward.

As they came through the back entrance, a commotion erupted at the main entrance: an elderly Indian stumbled in, his hands roped together, propelled forward by a posse of Japanese soldiers. Their unkempt uniforms were draped in green netting with branches of leaves stuck in the mesh; bayonets and rifles were at the ready. Beside them a sergeant held a cocked revolver.

Dr. Gordon walked towards them with purposeful strides, putting himself between the Matron and the soldiers. The sergeant covered him with his revolver and said in halting English "This.. hospital?"

"Yes, hospital. I am the doctor, these ladies the nurses."

"Show papers!" With his revolver, the sergeant nudged the doctor towards the table which contained the hospital records; he scrutinised the papers, flinging them to the floor as he finished, then conversed with the doctor while the other soldiers stood around regarding the nurses with open curiosity.

Dr. Gordon, still covered by the revolver, turned to the nurses and spoke calmly and meaningfully. "We are all now prisoners of the Japanese. We are to remain in the hospital and look after the sick people, and do what the Japanese tell us. They are leaving sentries posted at the entrances. I'm afraid I'm not allowed to stay with you, they want me to go with them - I don't know where. Chins up!"

The nurses exchanged looks of consternation at the departure of the only British man in their midst. Matron stepped forward, explained there was no water to wash the patients and asked if the nurses could collect some from the fountain in the cemetery across the road. Permission was given, and the sergeant, soldiers, and the Indian and Dr. Gordon left.

Matron gathered the shaken nurses round her and exhorted them to stay calm, then detailed a group to collect water from the fountain.

"Mrs. Lamb," she said to Sandra, "I think you should act as if you are a nurse." She produced a spare veil from her desk and pinned it over Sandra's head so that most of her hair was covered. "Put an apron over your clothes, we haven't any more uniforms."

Sandra was relieved at Matron's forethought: she had not missed the soldiers pointing at her ginger curls.

"I don't want you to do any really hard work," added Matron. "Just make yourself look busy if the Japanese come back."

"Jack and Jill went up the hill to fetch a pail of water," sang Docky as the deputed nurses walked through the ward to the front entrance, swinging their utensils.

Three minutes later they were back, their faces blanched, their containers empty.

"Those sentries took our watches and rings!" gasped Docky.

" 'Gold for Japan', they kept saying," panted another.

"They even took my wedding ring," sobbed Mrs. Burwood. "I pretended I couldn't get it off, then the brute threatened to cut my finger off with his bayonet so I had to hand it over."

Worse had followed after the soldiers motioned the nurses towards the cemetery. As the gate was locked they had to climb over the wall; when they hitched up their dresses to do so, bullets suddenly flew all round them from the upper terraces of the cemetery. No one was hit, but they all raced back to the hospital, to the blatant amusement of the sentries.

There was no question of risking lives by making further attempts to get to the fountain: every one was too shaken by the incident, and confidence was further undermined when foreign voices and approaching footsteps were heard outside.

"Keep together as much as possible," Matron whispered. Sandra joined the nurses not attending to patients round the table in the centre of the ward.

A large contingent of armed Japanese soldiers trooped in. They surveyed the nurses and chattered to each other. Sandra copied her colleagues and kept her head bent over the table until they shambled out, weapons clanking.

"Now they've gone we'll get breakfast for the patients," decided Matron. "After that, we can take it in turns to eat."

This plan was immediately scotched, for a second group of soldiers wandered in, looked round then ambled out; so it continued throughout the morning.

"They're just curious," Matron whispered bracingly. "They probably haven't seen white women working before. Don't show any concern - but I think we'll postpone breakfast a little longer."

During a lull, a young Chinese girl in St. John's uniform ran into the ward, wild-eyed and crying. Japanese soldiers had found her group hiding in an upstairs room and dragged them away to their own quarters; she herself had managed to get in a cupboard and escape their attentions.

Helpless to intervene with what was going on, Matron could only send the distraught girl to rest in the nurses' alcove. Presently the young victims themselves came in, shocked and crying their hearts out, their clothes dishevelled. Celeste was among them, her shamed distraught face bent low and her hands pressed tightly together. Sandra tried to comfort her but Celeste would not speak or raise her downcast eyes.

None of the night shift nurses had dared leave their colleagues round the table in the ward, but at noon Matron insisted they should try to get some sleep; they retired behind the betting booths but no one undressed - they simply crawled beneath the blankets in their uniforms. The day nurses busied themselves with bandage rolling, only leaving the table when a patient requested a bedpan which after use had to be emptied in the sluice beyond the back entrance - a trial because of the stench from the overflowing W.C.'s and because the route involved passing the sentries.

Patients well enough to eat began pleading for food. Matron dared not allow her staff to leave the ward for long periods so there was no question of cooking in the kitchen upstairs; a hurried visit there yielded some cold cooked rice which was distributed sparingly with tinned cold beans.

The sounds of war seemed much further away, the commotion caused by the proximity of large numbers of enemy troops and transport more and more intrusive.

For the nurses the bandage rolling had become a mechanical action, the cloth available for making these long since exhausted; it was simply a matter of rolling and re-rolling the same bandages in order to appear occupied every time soldiers tramped in to the ward.

Docky was making and re-making swabs out of the remains of a roll of cotton wool. "If I roll these things much more, they'll be hard enough to use as hand grenades," she said, and raised a few wan smiles.

A thunderous roll rent the air, followed by lesser rumbles; there was no lightning to suggest a storm, and the nurses feared a new attack was imminent.

Five o'clock, six o'clock - and still the situation was the same, the nurses continually the object of close scrutiny of the visiting soldiers. When it was time to change shifts, the night nurses emerged from behind the booths, their dresses rumpled and their faces haggard for they had been unable to sleep at all.

The St. John's girls crawled beneath the nurses' beds for added safety, fearful of what the night might bring. Some of the younger nurses of the day shift decided to do the same.

"What about you, Sandra?" Mrs. Burwood had stopped calling her 'Mrs. Lamb' during this fraught day.

"I think I'll take a blanket and sleep under my bed," she said. No one had put into words the reason for hiding, but the stark fear of rape was foremost in every mind.

For additional protection, all the camp beds were jammed side by side hard against each other.

Sandra's bed was on the end. "Get under mine, if you like," offered Mrs. Burwood, "then when the beds on either side of me are occupied, you'll be perfectly all right."

'All right' proved to be something of an overstatement. After half an hour Sandra's bones were aching from pressure on the unyielding concrete and she began to feel cold and wondered how much longer she could endure such airless discomfort.

Presently, the unusual quietness of the night, with no background gunfire, was disturbed by ribald, discordant singing from the other side of the building; by loud voices and the shuffle of approaching footsteps. The powerful beam of a torch swivelled round the hall, showing through the swing doors to the betting booths. These doors were pushed aside, revealing two soldiers with bayonets and rifles; behind them stood unarmed comrades. The torch, as strong as a car headlight, was flashed along the row of beds.

"Get up all!" came the command.

Above Sandra, the bed creaked and shook as Mrs. Burwood crawled awkwardly to the end and stood on the floor. The soldiers walked past all the beds, scrutinising every nurse in turn, shining the torch full on their white faces. They pulled four of the youngest nurses out of the line; protests and pitiful cries were met with a chilling "Go Jap! No go, kill all!"

As the weeping girls were taken away, the English-speaking soldier turned to the others and roared "Sleep!"

This must surely be a nightmare, Sandra shivered, but the agonised sounds of misery coming from the remaining occupants of the beds were real enough; even more so, the heart-breaking distress of the four victims when they returned.

Half an hour later more soldiers slouched in, laughing and swaying; roughly they selected fresh victims.

"It will be us oldies next when they run out of youngsters," whispered Docky to Mrs. Burwood.

"They'll have to go to sleep some time.. perhaps they'll give up soon," Mrs. Burwood said shakily. "There's not so much singing now."

"Do you think it's safe for me to get into my bed now?" Sandra whispered. "I'm simply frozen down here, and so stiff I can hardly move."

"Poor girl! Why not crawl in with me? There's nothing of you, even with the baby, and if they come back again you can just snuggle down between the blankets close to me."

Lying against Mrs. Burwood's ample soft body soon restored life to Sandra's limbs. Compared to the hard floor, even sharing a narrow camp bed with a 13-stone companion was heaven. She stiffened as the torch beam flashed into the hall again.

"Down!" hissed Mrs. Burwood.

With only a tiny channel of air between the blanket loosely around Mrs. Burwood's neck, Sandra could hardly breathe. Nerves a-jangle, she dared not move a muscle as the soldiers came in, chose three more nurses and went off with them. Emerging and taking great gulps of air after silence fell again, Sandra found that Mrs. Burwood was crying soundlessly.

"I keep thinking of my two girls, and wondering if they're going through this too.. They're at the Queen Mary Hospital. I should have taken them away from Hong Kong last year when we had the chance! My husband would never forgive me if he'd been alive."

"We couldn't have guessed this would happen." Sandra tried to console her, shocked at the distress of such a competent assured person.

After the third victims came back to their beds there was a lull. Matron crept round the booth in the darkness, trying to bolster morale. "I am very proud of you all. Keep your spirits up. Someone will come to our rescue. The Japanese will all be asleep soon, they smell of saki, and the poor girls said even the sentries are drinking at their posts. Just keep calm, things will be better when it's daylight. I shall demand to see a senior officer and seek reassurance that all this stops."

The firm compassionate voice calmed; the raggedy singing thinned and finally subsided completely and the exhausted nurses drifted into troubled sleep.

An idea had been germinating in Sandra's mind since the singing stopped. Matron had said that someone would come to the rescue - but how would succour come unless someone in authority knew what was happening at the Jockey Club? If she could somehow get away, under cover of darkness, and contact some one in authority, perhaps the raping could be stopped; if her turn came she doubted if she could accept her fate with the self-control shown by her colleagues, and couldn't imagine anything worse for herself or her baby. Her plan would entail crossing the Japanese lines to the British, and would have to depend on the situation as she found it, but she decided to aim for Central, not directly via Kennedy Road or Wanchai for the last gunfire had come from that area, but by a safer, though longer route higher up the hillside which she could reach through the terraced cemetery.

She wriggled out of bed, trying not to disturb her sleeping companion who, however, roused instantly in alarm and held on to her protectively.

"Shush.. I'm going back to my own bed," Sandra whispered. "All's quiet now."

Waiting until she was sure none of the other nurses in the booth were awake, Sandra picked up her shoes and crept under the swing door. She had to choose her moment to make for the exit to the main road to avoid the notice of the night nurses who sat close together round the table. At last she was able to steal across the shadowy ward undetected and over to the main entrance. The sentries' clearly audible snores gave her the courage to go on. Sitting on stools, their backs leaning against the sandbags and their legs splayed out in front of them, they appeared to be dead drunk. She stepped carefully over their feet and on to the empty open road.

She crossed quickly to the cemetery wall and climbed over it, then began the rigorous ascent from terrace to terrace. The eeriness of being surrounded by countless graves was diminished by the daunting task that lay ahead. At the very top of the cemetery a gate opened on to the main road which led to Central; what was uncertain was whether that road was in Japanese or British hands. She crept through the gate and peered along the road in both directions: empty, though signs of recent warfare were visible in the gradually receding gloom - craters, broken rocks and boulders, shattered steel helmets.

Panting after the exhausting climb, she crouched under cover of a tree at the side of the road and considered the situation. She realised now she was not very far from Dragon Terrace. In music lesson days, Danny and Marcus had often led her and Pamela along a path in the hillside above the Terrace to hunt for frogs and examine earthenware pots containing Chinese bones. She recalled that at one point the path overlooked the cemetery, but where was it? The light she needed to find her way was slowly beginning to emerge, but with it came the dangers of being seen and caught in what might be an enemy-controlled area.

Morning sounds were starting, birds waking up and frogs burping; the occasional distant snort of cars and lorries. She dared stay no longer on the road searching for clues to the path. One of the concrete nullahs which carried storm water down the hillside and beneath the roads to the filter beds materialised in the half-light. Thank goodness it was dry! She climbed into it and using her hands on either side to keep her balance, clambered up and up. Once a tiny green snake slithered in front of her right hand and she almost lost her balance in avoiding it.

Daylight came, gray and misty. Down in Happy Valley she could see rows of horses and army vehicles congregated on the race-course - a whole army of them. In sick wonderment, she realised that the soldiers who had taken over the hospital were not an isolated group, but a great part of the Japanese army. Again she puzzled over the lack of battle noises. With all the horror taking place in the betting hall in the night, the silence of guns and shells had not fully registered in the bewildered minds of the beleagured nurses. She looked across at the harbour. Between the masts of sunken ships ferries and motor boats were plying. A large gray warship was travelling slowly in the fairway towards the Naval Dockyard, a ship at whose stern flew the unmistakable flag of the Rising Sun. No guns were firing at it nor from it. She pushed away a dread thought which kept nagging at her befuddled mind.

From the road a long way below she could hear the clumping of boots, dragging footsteps and shrill shouts. Peering down through the bushes, she watched in disbelief as a straggling column of unarmed British soldiers marched disconsolately along, guarded by shouting Japanese soldiers. Thoroughly frightened, she pulled back in to the bushes. Now, in broad daylight, she was able to identify her position when she came upon the tiny muddy pool where as children she and Danny, Marcus and Pamela had often paddled; from here it was easy to find the path leading to the back of Dragon Terrace.

Within minutes she was high above the roof of the terrace and could see Kennedy Road below. Japanese soldiers stood by a road block opposite the terrace steps; this confirmed her original conviction that the safest route towards Central would be along the upper slopes of the hills above it, but her mind shied away from the persistent thought that no route was safe now.

The journey was laborious and tiring. Her hands and face were scored and scratched by branches and bracken as she tried to keep under cover. She was forced to rest frequently, not only to regulate her painful breathing but also to re-assess her position. Gradually she worked her way westward and stared down at the city buildings.. stared and stared, for the Hong Kong & Shanghai Bank and most of the tall buildings were hung with great white sheets suspended from the windows. She looked across the slopes to Government House and saw the Japanese flag flying there. Only then did she admit to herself the fears she had been refusing to accept for hours: the unspeakable, the unbelievable, had happened - Hong Kong had surrendered.

She sat down, put her face in her hands and cried, not knowing what to do, or where to go. "I shouldn't be here all by myself," she whimpered. "Miles should be looking after me."

Faint with hunger and completely demoralised, she slumped back in the bracken and moaned and raged. After a while she became aware of sounds of civilisation above her - a window being opened, a door slammed, the clanging of utensils, a tap running - and best of all, English voices. Leaping up, she scrambled towards the voices, heedless of stinging nettles and thorny bushes; suddenly her head was level with a road, and on the other side of it was the British Military Hospital.

"Hold on a bit longer Hank." Roddy's voice was hoarse as he tightened his grip on the Canadian's arm. "Not much further now."

"Let me go," murmured Hank.

They were the only survivors of the swimmers from 'Eucliffe'and Roddy was not going to give in now. "We'll be ashore in no time - you can keep going! See that bay ahead - we can land there and then it's only about half a mile to Stanley."

Two Japanese planes were high in the sky but there was no sound of British anti-aircraft fire. This was not surprising; during the past weeks he had seen too many posts destroyed and silent.

There was no sign of activity on the narrow rocky beach ahead. With Roddy's help, Hank managed to haul himself out of the water. The two men lay face downward, side by side, breathing noisily, their numbed bodies hardly aware of the crags and stones beneath them.

"What day is it?" asked Hank drowsily.

"Boxing Day, I think. Hey, don't go to sleep, we've got to get under cover." Roddy sat up and looked round. The coastline was edged with coils of barbed wire, broken in places. "We'll be able to get through," he said, untying the wet wad of clothes strapped about his chest. It was a struggle to put on the wet garments, and painful to walk bootless on the rocky foreshore.

Hank found new strength as they crawled through a gap in the wire and climbed on to the low plateau. Roddy knew well the hiker's path through the small woodland copse to Stanley. Now empty cartridge cases, broken bottles and crushed empty food tins hung on the bushes and shrubs; with alarm, he recognised the smell of decaying corpses; he hadn't expected the battle action so near Stanley, but kept his fears to himself.

As they neared the little village on the narrowing neck of Stanley isthmus, a flurry of activity erupted nearby - footsteps, shouts, moving vehicles. They exchanged looks of alarm and held back, hoping to hear something which would confirm whether the movement came from friend or foe. Suddenly from the bushes and undergrowth around them burst Japanese soldiers, waving rifles and bayonets. Surrounded and stunned, the two could do nothing but allow themselves to be propelled forward into the village street. Here, large numbers of British soldiers were roped together, trudging in the direction of Stanley Fort. Roddy and Hank were quickly roped to the last men in the column.

"Bad luck, cock," murmured a Middlesex private beside them, nodding towards their wet clothes. "Tried to swim for it, did you?"

"Yep.. where's our line?" whispered Roddy.

"What line? Don't you know it's all over?"

"You mean.."

"We've bloody surrendered."

They were hissed into silence by the nearest guard.

Roddy's heartbeats thudded in his ears as he tried to absorb this news. Many of the little shops on either side of the road were shattered or burnt. Timid but curious

Chinese faces peered out of broken windows and doorless houses. The prisoners were mainly silent; their open jackets hung from their shoulders; most were bareheaded; there were dirty and bloodstained bandages round heads and hands; some had great bandages about their legs which showed where the trousers had been cut away. Few carried any possessions. They were unshaven, dirty, their eyes shamed and angry. They had had no respite and practically no sleep for three weeks; they were sullen and without hope.

The rockface on either side of the road to the Fort was jagged and scarred; spent bullets lay everywhere; bloodstains smeared the pavements. The remains of a British machine gun lay on its side. A great fear leapt into Roddy's mind: Hilary! How had the nurses in St. Stephen's Hospital, right in this battle area, fared?

"Where d'you come from mate?" asked his neighbour as the guard moved on.

"Repulse Bay."

"You swam from there?" The voice squeaked in amazement, and the guard ran back and struck the speaker across the shoulders with his rifle butt.

The hospital was in sight above the tennis courts they were approaching which appeared to be an assembly point for British prisoners. Roddy followed his column past the guarded entrance to the courts, his eyes fixed upward on the hospital. It did not seem to be damaged. The remains of a huge fire was still smoking on ground outside the building. He tried to assess his chances of contacting Hilary there.

The talk all round him was full of bitterness and disgust at surrender.

"It was all for nothing, then, Stan and Nobby copping it.."

"Should have done it earlier if there was no chance.. hundreds of our lot slaughtered here last night. We didn't even know until this morning about the surrender.. and the white flag went up in town 4 o'clock yesterday afternoon!"

"Are they all O.K. up at the hospital?" - Roddy quickly latched on to the last speaker who had obviously been some time in Stanley.

"Some of them."

"TELL ME!" he yelled.

"Japs went in with bayonets. Killed two doctors. Murdered patients, bayonetted them in bed, right through the mattresses. Killed some of the nurses."

Too late Hank mouthed "His girl's a nurse there."

"I don't believe it," Roddy shivered, searching the rugged faces round him.

"Course it's true. We were there."

-"I was lucky, hid in a locker.."

-"Poor buggers too ill to get out of bed, never had a chance."

-"Hell on earth, the screaming.."

-"See that bonfire up there? Japs made us burn the corpses, and all the evidence.. the mattresses and bedding."

-"Those poor girls.."

Their flushed, wild-eyed faces as they relived these horrors magnified in Roddy's sight, their voices echoing and re-echoing. Hank made him sit on the ground and said "Stay here, old man, I'm going to find a guy in authority, who really knows.."

Roddy's head slumped forward on to his bent knees, his hands hanging loosely, his face dazed, mouth open. At the back of his mind he saw himself racing away from the armed guards, up the sloping path to the hospital calling Hilary's name, searching for her, but his limbs would not move.

Hank's concerned face appeared again. "I've found a couple of your buddies, Volunteers." He had to shout to get the words through. The two Volunteers were not of Roddy's Battery but he knew them by sight.

"Hilary? Hilary Bately? No, her name wasn't among the nurses who were killed - 3 British women and four Chinese."

"Are the other nurses still up there?" asked Hank.

"Hell no! The Japs let one of our fellows drive them all to Bowen Road Hospital - they were raped, you see."

Three men had to hold Roddy down.

Although it was 4 days since the surrender, the Allied civilians were still living in their war-time billets awaiting instructions from their captors.

At least the Japanese Army had occupied the city with surprising discipline; took over such buildings as they required and posted guards outside them who stared impassively at those civilians who ventured on to the streets in search of food. There was still no electricity, but water now ran in the taps.

In Dina House the meagre food supplies were pooled and cooked communally - in fact, taking a turn in the kitchen provided the only alternative to sitting around in the crowded rooms, endlessly discussing the battle and the future, trying to fill the great vacuum in their lives created immediately hostilities ceased.

Money for such food as could be bought was running out, and no banks were open. There were stories of wholesale looting of damaged and abandoned shops and houses. Make-shift stalls were set up on the pavements displaying a miscellany of stolen goods. Even refrigerators, radiograms and carpets were transported by rickshaw, clutched by scruffy unlikely owners.

"There'll be nothing left by the time we get back to our homes," fretted Mrs. Barrington, one of Pamela's older companions who cried every night because she had no news of her Volunteer husband.

"IF we ever get back to them," added Rachel Cane, a beautiful Eurasian school teacher; her pessimism was hard to bear during these difficult days: on Christmas night she had told all the women to prepare to be raped when the victorious

Japanese soldiers entered the city, nor was her forecast far wrong they had later learned that but for the provision of 500 Chinese girls from the Red Light district, this might have happened.

In company with Jack Roffey, a middle-aged Air Raid Warden, and two girl telephonists, Pamela made several trips into town, but was always glad to return: it was unnerving to walk past stony-faced guards whose eyes swivelled from side to side, missing nothing. Having heard that the convalescent hospital in The Gripps had been emptied and the men sent to Murray Barracks, she got Jack Roffey to take her there in the hope of seeing Keith, but the entire barrack area was cordoned off and well-guarded - it was impossible to get near enough to identify any one among the hundreds of uniformed prisoners.

She also made an attempt to visit her flat with Jack, but had to give up half-way when he suddenly shouted "Don't look up!" He was too late; already she was staring at the trees beside the Peak Tram Station where bodies of Chinese in dark cotton clothes hung. As well as being tied to the branches, the men were looped to each other with ropes round neck and hands. Those higher up were still alive, crying and pleading, trying to save themselves from being dragged down and throttled by the weaker who had already hung themselves.

"Looters, most of them," muttered a passing European. "Mostly they're shooting them on the spot; these ones are unlucky."

She didn't argue when Jack quickly led her back to Dina House.

Without any newspapers or official reports, rumours abounded. By roundabout means, Pamela heard of Roddy's survival; of Sandra's bravery in escaping from the Jockey Club to summon help for the nurses there; and that Hilary was safe and well at the Bowen Road Hospital, having been spared the horrors at the Stanley hospital because illness had prevented her being sent there.

There were no casualty lists so many wives and parents were in torment about their menfolk in the Volunteers or other services. Added to all this, the civilians still had no idea of their own future life under Japanese occupation.

"In Shanghai" said the confident wife of an old China hand,"when the Japs took over in '37 we were allowed to stay on in our own homes."

"The British weren't the people who were defeated there," Rachel pointed out in her husky drawl.

Pamela kept out of this conversation, her heart fluttering because her mind was full of a whisper she'd heard that morning: the Japs were said to be considering paying a secret Chinese group to undertake wholesale and simultaneous assassination of all civilian Europeans.

PART 7

Early 1942

JANUARY/FEBRUARY

The numbness of shock carried Roddy through the ignominy of defeat - the sight of heaps of surrendered helmets, gas-masks and firearms, the bitterness and dejection of everyone confined in the Fort under guard.

Dull-eyed, he took his turn at the daily task of burying British dead under Japanese supervision, while others retched at the stink of the bloated, maggot ridden bodies, and wept at the sight of bludgeoned comrades.

A rumour that they would be sent to a camp near the city became fact when one morning they were ordered to parade for departure. Their Brigadier addressed them cheerfully, reminding them that a soldier was at his best when faced with adverse conditions. The column, almost a mile long and including sick and wounded, was led out of the Fort and through the village, where Japanese flags fluttered from the windows of shops and homes, and Chinese bystanders jeered.

They were marched across the island, past battle areas, past rough graves of their fellows - just heaps of earth marked with drooping branches tied in the shape of a cross; past shattered pill boxes, burnt out transport; even worse, they saw swollen purple bodies of Indian troops with their hands tied, some with bayonets still wedged in their stomachs.

They had covered almost twelve miles when halted at North Point. The camp, one boundary of which was formed by the sea wall, had originally been built for and occupied by Chinese war refugees who had fled to Hong Kong in 1937 from Japanese occupied areas in China. More recently, Japanese troops had used the camp as stables for their mules and horses.

Herded through the barbed wire entrance into huts, many of which were war-damaged and bereft of doors and floor-boards, the more energetic prisoners shifted debris and manure out of the huts and tried to patch roofs and walls with whatever came to hand. There were no lights and no latrines; the prisoners had to balance on the sea wall to evacuate into the harbour. In such insanitary conditions, with the poorest of food, many became ill. Natural leaders emerged and improvised debates, lectures and classes in an attempt to bolster morale.

When Roddy met up with some of his fellow-volunteers who had been injured during the fighting and spent some time in the Military Hospital, he learned that Hilary had been spared the ordeal at St. Stephen's College. In his heartfelt relief, he promised himself he would never again complain at any setback in life: stopped moping and energetically supported all the camp activities. His health improved and he escaped the dysentery epidemic which was sweeping through the camp. Soon the Japanese in charge saw the disease as a threat to themselves: they began sending the most severe cases to the Military Hospital. When one of his sick hutmates was about to be sent there, Roddy gave him a message for Hilary pencilled on the margin of an old Chinese newspaper. Every few days a canvas-covered lorry brought into camp several recovered patients from the hospital and took away a fresh group of sick men; its arrival was a great event in a life where there was little to do except pace round the limited periphery of the camp to try to keep warm.

One afternoon Roddy followed the lorry as usual to the administration hut, watched the new arrivals climb out, then turned away when he saw his friend was not among them.

"Doran!" hissed a voice behind him.

He turned, and one of the convalescents whispered "Your girl's inside the lorry.."

There was no time to say more, for the guards chivvied the speaker with the other men towards the administration hut to be officially registered.

The lorry driver leant against the front wheel, smoking. Roddy edged towards the tailboard, and lifted the loose tarpaulin screen. Hilary and another V.A.D. in their white uniforms and veils, sat just inside. To the ragged, starved men, used to drabness, dirt and masculine company for so long, the girls looked like angels. A concerted and heartfelt wolf whistle brought the driver swiftly to the rear of the lorry. He pushed Roddy back, snapped the tarpaulin curtain across and hissed to the girls "No talk!"

"Please!" Hilary's voice was thick with emotion. "Please.. my friend outside, please."

The driver looked about him; the prisoners were silent now, almost menacing; the guards were out of sight. He held up two stubby fingers and grunted "Two minute!", and the watching soldiers breathed an audible sigh of satisfaction.

Holding back the tarpaulin, Hilary bent over the tailboard; Roddy, regardless of the audience, reached up and kissed her. The softness of her skin, the love in her eyes, and her ethereal appearance with tendrils of fair hair escaping from the veil, brought a surge of longing which left him weak.

"Never thought I'd see you again," he mumbled brokenly. "Can hardly believe this is real after all that happened.. Are you all right? At first I thought I'd lost you at Stanley.."

"I never got there.. I had an infected hand.. I was so lucky." She wept into his chest. "But my friend, only seventeen, went there instead of me... she survived, but..."

"It's over now. You're safe, I'm safe.. all our family have come through. Darlingest Hil, as soon as we get the chance, we'll get married."

"Oh yes!" Tears were running down her cheeks. "As soon as we possibly can."

She pulled a small cloth package from her nursing satchel and gave it to him. "Some odds and ends I managed to scrounge for you! I'll come again if I can wangle it.. they've started sending us nurses for the trip because one of the men died on the way to the hospital last week and they don't like handling infection."

"I'll always be looking out for you." He hugged her as best he could from the ground. "God, this is so wonderful, Hil! Why didn't we get married years ago? Why?"

"We didn't have the money." Hilary laughed through her tears. "As if money matters! We know that now."

Movement among the crowd signalled the return of the guards escorting Canadian stretcher parties bringing new patients, and the driver quickly pushed Roddy away.

After the van had gone, he walked back to his hut on air, to lie on his bunk and relive the short encounter over and over again. Then he sat up and opened the parcel; there was a poke of newspaper containing a few ounces of sugar; a small tin of evaporated milk; a paper screw of tea leaves; a little bottle containing half a dozen aspirin, and a handmade needle case on which were sewn his initials; inside were two needles, a safety pin, and several lengths of white and black thread. Also a scrap of paper on which she had written "Every stitch with love for you, Rod." He pressed the case against his heart as if it was made of gold.

The stencilled handwritten statement from the Japanese Administration headed 'Foreign Internists Regulations' which arrived in Dina House was read with consternation:

Civilian 'internists' were to live communally, different nationalities in separate quarters, and men separated from women. The actual quarters were not specified, but the rules were: inmates would be allowed out once a week, and then under supervision; every one would be required to take an oath to have no more connection with 'enemy activity'; cameras, books and maps were forbidden; infringements would be 'strongly punished according to Japanese military law.' Basic food and fuel for communal cooking would be supplied; other foodstuffs 'and sundries' would be paid for by the civilians themselves.

"But where will we get the money from?" every one wondered.

Gone were the dreams of returning to their own homes to resume some semblance of normal life. Worst of all, there was no authority to contact to try to find the answers to all their questions.

"Go hotel today," announced the Japanese officer whose sword was almost as big as he was. " 'Leven clock."

"Hotel!" Mrs. Barrington smiled for the first time since indisputable confirmation of her husband's death. "That sounds wonderful!"

Laden with their possessions, they were counted out of Dina House and led into Queen's Road where they were joined by a crocodile of compatriots also carrying their all, children padded out with several layers of clothes to minimise luggage. Some of the Chinese onlookers laughed at the sight of the heretofore superior whites so humbled; others looked anxious: if life could change so radically for the British now that the Japanese were in charge, could it not perhaps also change for the Chinese?

"Well, it's not the Gloucester or the Hong Kong," Jack Roffey murmured as they turned down Pedder Street and passed these august buildings into Des Voeux Road. "I thought that would be too good to be true." He insisted on carrying Pamela's suitcase as well as his own, leaving her two hands for the rolled blanket and sheet she'd brought from Dina House.

Along the empty tram lines, past the main Central shopping area, the large Chinese department stores, they went; still on, into the slum quarter, past block after block of tenement buildings. They were halted outside a dilapidated three-storeyed building with a painted notice hanging from the first floor proclaiming it to be 'Kai Toon Hotel' beneath large Chinese characters.

"Here!" announced the Japanese officer, banging on the brown grilled door emblazoned with a large white cotton banner with inked Chinese characters and a red chop recognisable as that of Japanese authority. A timid Chinese man emerged and bowed to the officer, who turned to the dismayed queue behind him and ordered "GO! Fill top floor first. Every room - four peoples."

Up the echoing wooden stairs they climbed, appalled at the grimy walls, the smell of decay and the complete lack of any feature of a hotel as they knew the term: no lift, no dining room, no lounge. Each floor had simply two rows of small cubicles running back to back the length of the building, the front row opening on to a tiled balcony overlooking Queens Road, the other facing a narrow corridor with tiny windows looking on to a small yard and the leprous backs of more tenements. Wooden partitions not quite reaching the ceiling separated the cubicles in which a double bed athwart the back wall took up the entire width. A wooden chair and a tiny washbasin were the only concessions to comfort.

"They can't mean four of us to share one room!" exploded the first arrivals on the top floor.

- "We MUST protest!"
- "It's inhuman!"
- "Just impossible.. one bed for four!"

There was utter confusion as more and more were urged up the stairs with no time to arrange accommodation with friends; it was just a case of filling the rooms as they came to them.

Pamela found herself with Rachel Cane, Mrs. Barrington and Miss Lewis, an elderly Air Raid Warden of tubby proportions who alone would take up more than half of the double bed. When they were all in the room the only place for the luggage was under the bed.

"We were better off in Dina House." Miss Lewis eyed the grimy washbasin in disgust.

"This must be just a temporary stop," Pamela pointed out. "We're all nationalities and sexes in here.. that paper said we'd all be divided up into separate quarters."

"You know what this is, don't you?" Rachel was standing in front of the spotted mirror above the washbasin, repairing her makeup. "It's a brothel."

Pamela, now used to Rachel's gloomy statements, thought this was a joke, but voices from adjoining cubicles shouted "Yes, that's what it is! How dare they house us in a brothel?"

However irrational it seemed, she was so terrified of catching some dread disease in such surroundings that she could not bring herself to undress that night, thus enduring even more discomfort than that occasioned by four adults sharing one bed; the only way was to lie across the width, supplementing the two small pillows with rolled bundles of clothes; protruding feet had to be supported by precariously-piled luggage.

There were no bathrooms, and the lavatories were the Asiatic squatting type - drains with a concrete indented foot mark on either side. Each floor had a charcoal stove where the occupants strove to concoct communal meals with the meagre rations sent by the Japanese each morning.

No one was allowed out of the bolted front door which was manned by a young Japanese guard. The only diversion between meals was to gaze down on Queens Road, watching out for friends in the occasional procession of internees under guard; every one in the Kai Toon had the same thought: "Hope they won't be pushed in here with us" - and waved more vigorously in relief as the procession passed by.

In the evenings they huddled together in their cold cubicles and conjectured about their future: Shanghai, Hainan Island, and Tsingtao were thought to be possible destinations by those who claimed to know.

The boredom in the hotel was somewhat allayed when the hesitant Chinese caretaker was bribed to unlock the small staircase leading to the flat roof; then the occupants of each floor took it in turns to go up there; during the best hours of sunshine it was warm enough to sit on the flag stones; when the January wind was keen and the sun hidden, it was necessary to pace up and down to keep warm. Before long, their Chinese neighbours found that these people wanted food at any price and proceeded to supply it to any one who could pay. On adjacent roofs they brought portable cooking pots fuelled with twigs and charcoal, and sold hot milkless tea, soup, fried vegetables and unidentifiable meat and fish - all handed carefully across the narrow gaps between the buildings. Both Mr. Gasson and Jack Roffey insisted on buying food for Pamela when it became obvious that her purse was empty.

One afternoon she spotted Sandra among a party being led along the road. She was wearing her wedding hat at a jaunty angle, and waved cheerily in response to Pamela's arresting yell. She carried a large handbag and a small rattan suitcase. Keeping pace with her on the pavement was Ah Ling who carried a long blanket roll; following was a coolie in black cotton Chinese suit, from a bamboo pole across his shoulders were suspended two suitcases.

"Are you O.K.?" Pamela shouted as the group passed immediately beneath the hotel.

"You bet!" Sandra held up one thumb and indicated Ah Ling and the coolie. "Look who I've got to help me - Ah Ling and good old Ming!"

Yes, on closer view, the coolie was just recognisable as the formerly immaculately-uniformed chauffeur to Sandra's parents. Touched by their loyalty, there was a lump in Pamela's throat as she watched the procession wind its way further west.

She was alarmed to be summoned to the ground floor of the hotel one morning. "I'll come with you," said Jack Roffey who, at more than twice her age seemed to have appointed himself an honorary uncle. The front door was held ajar by the caretaker, watched by the guard outside; peering through the gap was Ah Lum, who seized Pamela's hands and began to cry.

"Oh missee, you O.K.? So sorry, flat door broken, bad people come, take plenty thing. I say No can, but they push me and take.."

"Never mind Ah Lum. Are all your family safe?"

"O.K. but no got food. Plenty more bad people come every night, pull up floor boards, take chairs for burn. Tomorrow we go Kowloonside, stay with friend. See, missee, I bring clothes for you! Bad men take nearly all but I find few things." She hauled from the ground a bundle tied in a sheet, and the caretaker opened the door a little wider to let her pass it through. Pamela tried to thank the amah adequately. "I'll make all this up to you one day," she promised, "I really will! However did you know I was here?"

"I go that Dina House, Chinese man say English people go Kai Toon Hotel. I find," was the simple answer.

The guard suddenly terminated the visit by pushing the amah away and slamming the door.

The bundle contained underwear, an old jumper and a pair of plimsolls - apparently the only clothes not worthy of the looters' attention. Wrapped up in the jumper were photographs torn out their frames: of Roddy, Keith, Belle and the children; her parents outside their new bungalow in Ipswich; Viola and Raoul after their wedding; a blurred close-up snapshot of herself and Lawrence taken by themselves on a Peak walk. These reminders of the old life broke her as nothing else in these last weeks had done. She had never felt so alone, without family, home, money or possessions. Completely demoralised, she gave up trying to work out what lay ahead.. too fearful to contemplate an indefinite life of imprisonment - and the worst thing was the realisation that there was absolutely nothing she could do to influence the future.

They had been in the hotel for two weeks when they heard they were to be moved again: not over perilous battle-ridden seas to some strange Chinese port, but to Stanley, 7 miles away, the peninsula renowned for its fresh sea breezes which housed the new modern jail: even that would be preferable to living in their present conditions!

The arrival of a Japanese doctor who administered typhoid injections all round raised hopes of an imminent move.

That night they were awakened by shouts and clanging gongs. From the balconies they could see smoke and flying sparks erupting from the upper floors of the tenements opposite. Screaming inhabitants poured out on to the pavements; a fire engine arrived but a fierce wind blew the water from its hoses in all directions. Hot air and showers of sparks blew across to the Kai Toon. Grimly aware that they could not escape if their building caught fire, the internees made hasty emergency plans. They filled every available utensil with water, and it was tacitly agreed that if evacuation became necessary and the guard refused to open the front door, the strongest men would charge the door and take a chance on being shot at when they broke through.

Fortunately the wind dropped, the flames were gradually doused and the danger over, but the fire hazard added to the general apprehension and it was with whoops of relief and delight that orders were received the next morning to prepare to leave for Stanley that very day.

Two hours later they were led to the waterfront where they merged with internees brought from other accommodation; there was a gala atmosphere as friends greeted each other on a wharf where a large river steamer was berthed. Earlier arrivals were already streaming up the narrow gangway with their ungainly possessions. Pamela heard her name called, looked up and saw Sandra waving from the top deck. She was propelled up the gangway by the people behind her, then picked her way between passengers sitting on the decks to where Sandra was perched on a suitcase against the rail.

"Oh Pam, am I glad to see you here!" Sandra hugged her fiercely. "You know about Miles?" Her face crumpled and tears came to her eyes but she quickly brushed them aside. "I've just got to be glad the baby and I are still O.K." She said the words as though she had repeated them often.

Sometimes they both talked at once, words tumbling over each other.

- "Oh Pam, I don't know where Miles is buried, or if...."

- "Don't worry about it now, San. - I thought you were still at Bowen Road Hospital after that amazing journey -"

- "Only stayed there two days, they wanted me keep me longer, but Ah Ling and Ming came and took me to the Gloucester. There was a Eurasian family in my room.."

- "The Grahams! I took them in after you'd gone.."

- "I had to let them stay because it was the husband Tony who told Ah Ling what had happened to me and where she could find me."

- "Look at all your luggage - and your wedding hat!"

- "Ming got lots of my things from the house - I don't know how many times he walked up the Peak and back. Oh, I've got a note for you from Hilary.. she thinks the V.A.D.'s will be kept at the hospital for a while."

A burst of cheering heralded the ship's departure. Every one looked happy and optimistic except Sandra's immediate neighbour, a sandy-haired policeman, who grunted "Lucky the sea's calm! This ship's top-heavy; the least bit of rough weather and she'll be over."

"Shut up moaner!" His companion, a younger policeman, gave a great sigh of contentment: after the weeks of incarceration in unsavoury conditions, deprived of air and light, this journey in the January sunshine and invigorating fresh air seemed like heaven - whatever it led to. "Just close your eyes, think of a whisky soda at your elbow, and imagine you're off on a launch picnic as in days of yore!"

"But where IS the whisky soda?" chimed in another in mock complaint.

"And the cucumber sandwiches?"

"And a rattan lounge chair instead of this hard deck!"

As the ship chugged out of the harbour and round the coast, it was hard to realise that these green soaring hills had been the scene of battle such a short time ago. The tiny fishing hamlets looked as peaceful as ever as the fishermen mended their nets at the water's edge.

The ship anchored in Stanley Bay, the water by the tiny jetty too shallow for its draught. A large junk came alongside to disembark the passengers; it was simply a high-sided shell with no gangway or ladder. Already the men were leaping into it and holding out their arms to help others.

"I can't do that!" Sandra held back, hands across her middle.

"Don't worry, we'll get you safely down there," said the ginger-haired policeman, and he and his companion swung her over the gunwhale between them and lowered her gently by her outstretched arms until the men already in the junk reached up to receive her.

"Now what?" Some one voiced the thought of all when they clambered on to the jetty. Soldiers pointed towards a steep path leading from the beach to rough ground beside the gleaming white civilian jail.

"I can't move all my stuff by myself," Sandra panted as she struggled with two suitcases and her blanket roll. There was no one to help, every one being concerned with their own problems.

"Give me this." Pamela took one of the suitcases and put her blanket roll round her neck.

Even so Sandra was still complaining as they reached the top of the path; from here they could see the internees being directed past the jail towards a long flight of steps leading up to blocks of cream-coloured buildings.

"It's not the jail, anyway," said Pamela bracingly. "It won't be so bad if we're in the staff quarters."

Earlier arrivals lined the railings surrounding the plateau, joyfully calling out as they recognised friends.

"What do we do now?" called a woman behind Pamela.

"Find somewhere to sleep, wherever you can! Bag the first vacant room you come to, and hang on to it. They're filling up fast. There are people coming in by lorry too - better hurry!"

It was out of the question for Sandra to hurry. By the time she and Pamela reached the buildings every room they tried was occupied. There was no organisation, no one to ask for help. They could only wander through the 2-storeyed block, knocking on every door.

On the concrete landing between the staircases they came upon a mother and three small children.

"Are we going to sleep here, Mummy?" one child was asking.

"Just for tonight, if Daddy can't find a better place." The mother, holding a fat baby, sat down on one of her bundles.

"This is hopeless!" Sandra began to whimper.

"We'll find somewhere, don't you worry," said Pamela with a confidence she didn't feel. "Look, you stay here with our things while I keep hunting."

She sped up to the top floor, hoping accommodation here might have been overlooked by other seekers. Three women were just emerging from the last room at the end of the corridor

"Any space in there?" she asked.

"It's empty," one woman called over her shoulder. "Our friend has found a much larger room so we're moving."

Pamela swooped in. The room was about ten feet square and bare except for a tiny bookcase and one wooden kitchen chair - but it was a haven; leaving her coat as a marker she rushed back in triumph for Sandra.

"But this is awful!" Sandra stared in disgust. "No beds, no curtains, bare boards.."

"At least it's a roof over our heads," Pamela snapped. "Now I'm going to find out where we can get camp beds - I've seen people carrying them in. You stay put, and be sure to say we're keeping a place for Hilary if any one else tries to come in here."

It was easy to find the source of the beds; a steady line of people shouldering them wound down the slope from the bungalow which housed the Japanese camp authorities. With great difficulty she managed to half-carry, half-drag two beds to the room.

"You shouldn't have carried two," Sandra said, looking at the red weals on Pamela's hands. "I could have got mine myself."

"Not while you're.."

"Oh God, I hope you're not going to nag me all the time about what I must and mustn't do!"

"I will if I think I should," said Pamela seriously. "If you want me to help you, that is."

"Oh I do, Pam, I couldn't manage without you, you know that," Sandra assured her. "Goodness, I'm hungry! I wonder when we'll get a meal?" She opened the window which overlooked the grassed courtyard between the blocks. "Can't see any sign of food, but something must be served somewhere."

They dared not leave the room together while the hunt for accommodation was still in progress, so took it in turns to go out and investigate. It soon became evident that there were no working kitchens, no dining rooms and no one in charge of anything at all. They made their beds, unpacked Sandra's meagre food supplies and shared half a tin of corned beef. Darkness was approaching. Pamela flicked the light switch but no light appeared. Looking out of the window she realised there were no lights anywhere: obviously electric power had not yet been restored in Stanley.

"No lights! It's dreadful!" Sandra sat on her bed and wept. "We can't live like this."

"It can only get better. I'm sure something will be sorted out about food by tomorrow." Pamela was hopeful rather than certain. "Give it time. At least the lav. here is the real thing - not like in my hotel."

To wash themselves they had to queue in the corridor for the bathroom with the other occupants of the flat - some 25 men and women distributed among four rooms. The Japanese edict that the sexes were to be segregated had not been afforced. There was no hot water, and the cold wash had to be accomplished at speed in consideration of those waiting outside.

"Wish I'd been blown up completely at North Point," moaned Sandra as they tried to settle down for the night. "No point in living at all, like this."

"Don't be so silly! It's a darned sight better here than the hotel I was in, at any rate."

"But we thought Stanley would be so marvellous! It's such a let-down, coming to a bare room. I don't know what my parents would see if they could see me now!" Sandra's tears started again.

"I know what Ah Ling would say," said Pamela suddenly, "Now you be good girlies and go night-nights!"

The sobs became giggles and they drifted off to sleep.

Optimism proved partly justified. Every day a lorry brought in sacks of dry rice, wilting vegetables and sometimes raw fish. Volunteers cooked communal meals in makeshift kitchens built inside old garages. Rough firewood was provided to fuel the stoves. The rations were only sufficient to provide two meals a day, and doctors estimated that each internee only received only 900 calories a day - less than half needed for survival.

Several small domestic boilers had escaped the looting at the end of the fighting and these provided hot drinking water once electricity was restored. It was a shock to find that water was the only drink available - no tea, coffee, sugar or milk were supplied.

To form the camp the Japanese had enclosed by barbed wire an area of the Stanley isthmus which included British and Indian staff quarters and club, St. Stephen's College and ancillary buildings; the sea formed two of the boundaries.

When it became clear that it was up to the internees themselves to run the internal life of the camp, leaders emerged from each block and committees were formed so that a cohesion of sorts evolved. As the senior Government Servant interned, Mr. Gimson the Colonial Secretary was designated Representative of Internees for dealing with the Japanese authorities.

That February was very cold. There was no heating and few people had been able to bring sufficient bedding. There being no dining rooms, meals were usually cold by the time the internees had brought them from serving table to billet. No crockery or cutlery was provided - people used whatever utensils they had brought into camp. No towels, soap or toothpaste were supplied. Morale sank lower each day, further worsened by the lack of news from relatives and friends in the military camps as no communication was permitted.

Pamela had to suffer Sandra's depression as well as her own; night after night Sandra wept for Miles, repeating her self-recriminations: she hadn't loved him;

hadn't done enough to make him happy; she'd been selfish and demanding; he'd never complained, he'd always been marvellous to her.. and he would have been so thrilled to know there was to be a baby and she'd never told him. Some mornings she would not get out of bed: "What is there to get up for?"

"You'll want some hot water to drink, won't you? Why should I have to be up first every morning to get it?" Pamela's voice was as petulant as Sandra's.

"Don't care if I have it or not."

"I'll just get enough for myself, then," Pamela retorted - but of course she brought Sandra's share, and they sat on their beds sipping it, warming their hands on the mugs.

"I'll get up first tomorrow, truly I will, Pam. It's just so hard for me to get started in the morning. My lump may not look very big, but it feels like a football: acts like one sometimes, too."

Like every one else, she had lost weight in the past weeks. Her skinny neck and arms and leg accentuated the pregnancy bump. Her hair had grown almost to her shoulders, emphasising the thinness of her face. She looked like a woebegone schoolgirl huddled in the bed. "I'll collect both meals today - you've done it all for long enough," she said.

There were over 700 souls to be fed in the Married Quarters which they had discovered was their official address, these particular blocks of flats having in peacetime housed married Prison Officers and their families. A zinc bath containing cooked rice, and an iron cauldron full of watery stew, were lugged from the nearby garage to a makeshift table (an old broken door balanced across rough wooden trestles) set up in the inner courtyard. Trusted internees (trusted, that is, to serve an equal share to all comers and not to favour their friends) ladled out helpings into cracked bowls, tin plates and old tins.

The sun was out this morning and there was no hardship in waiting in the slow-moving queue. But by five o'clock when the second meal was served the warmth had gone and a keen wind blew. When rain started Pamela sought Sandra in the queue and offered to take her place.

"I've said I'll do it today!" Sandra wouldn't be moved. "go back and don't fuss so."

When she returned to the room she thrust the two dishes of food at Pamela and collapsed, wet and shaking, on to her bed.

"You should have let me take over." Pamela knelt beside her and rubbed her cold wet hands. "Get this hot food inside you as soon as you can."

It wasn't hot at all, but it was food and they quickly devoured it.

"Worst yet," said Sandra, licking her plate to get the dregs of the lettuce stew.

The flat had a tiny kitchen, its only contents a deep sink and ridged draining board. Here the occupants queued to wash their dishes.

Most evenings the two girls walked round their block for half an hour before bed-time, but tonight it was too cold and wet and they were weak with hunger. Sandra looked so ill that Pamela suggested they open the last tin of sausages.

"You said we had to keep this for emergencies." Sandra pulled the tin out of her case and licked her lips at the garish picture of plump pink sausages on the outside.

"Let's pretend this is an emergency." Pamela did not want to reveal how much Sandra's appearance alarmed her.

Carefully, Sandra peeled the tin open with its fragile key, knowing too well the difficulty of trying to get the food out if the key broke. There was no way of heating the sausages: they dug out half of them, shared them and ate them with their fingers.

"Who would have thought," said Sandra slowly, "that two cold sausages could be such bliss to eat?"

Next morning the Japanese ordered all internees to assemble on the level ground near the jetty; guesses both hopeful and sinister were voiced as they obeyed were they to be sent into the jail after all? Were they to be transported to some other camp, without any of their possessions? Or were they to be told to prepare to return to their homes? When a squad of armed soldiers motioned them into orderly lines, the dread thought in most minds was that they were about to be massacred where they stood.

"Wish we'd eaten the rest of those sausages last night," whispered Sandra.

After an hour the internees were suddenly dismissed and told to return to their quarters. As they trooped back, groups of soldiers could be seen running out of the blocks.

"Search parties," someone suggested. "That's why they wanted us out of the way."

"Looking for radios and weapons, maybe.."

"I bet they pinched anything they liked the look of, too."

"Our sausages!" wailed Sandra. "We should have eaten them all while we had the chance."

The sausages were still there - but not for long: in complete agreement, they ate the lot there and then.

Mr. Bridger visited them one day. He had grown a beard which had flecks of grey. His suit hung on him as if on a clothes hanger.

"I heard you lived here, Mrs. Lamb," he began awkwardly, half-sitting on the narrow window-sill (these days no one stood when they could sit down, to conserve energy) "so I thought I'd come along and see how you are faring."

"I'm very well looked after, thanks," Sandra nodded across to Pamela. "Where are you living?"

"The bungalow next to the cemetery, sharing a room with six others; two are from the firm - you remember Marpett and Gough? They send their regards, and we want you to.. er.. accept this.." From his jacket pocket he produced a small round shoe polish tin, twisted it open and revealed a thick blob of Marmite. "Thought it would be good for you," he added in the silence that followed.

"Oh Mr. Bridger, what a wonderful present!" Sandra's voice was thick. "Do please thank the others - but how can you spare this?"

"We wanted to," he shrugged, rising and hitching up his drooping trousers. "We're so very sorry about Miles.. Mr. Lamb. If there's anything we can do, just let us know." He cleared his throat and backed towards the door as Sandra's face crumpled.

Pamela called him back as he reached the door. "Would you like me to take a tuck in the waist of your trousers? It wouldn't take long."

"Could you.. Miss Doran isn't it? I'd be so grateful! I have my best pair, I could wear them for a day or two while you work on these."

That was the beginning of Pamela's rôle in camp as seamstress. Work was limited by shortage of needles and thread but she was pleased she had packed a few such necessities in her bag before leaving the Kennedy Road flat. She rated her small pair of scissors her most treasured possession; neighbours sometimes borrowed them but she insisted they use them in her room - even people wanting their hair cut had to come to her room and bring their hairdresser with them!

"Singapore's fallen!"

For days this had been claimed in the the skimpy English-language newspaper the Japanese sometimes sold in the camp; now it was confirmed by the sympathetic Chinese driver of the ration lorry.

Stanley was stunned. The fall of Singapore signalled the end of any hopes of Allied help from there to help dislodge the Japanese from Hong Kong. In their magnaminity at their success, the Japanese gave a film show in St. Stephen's Hall. Here Pamela and Sandra sat side by side on the wooden steps in the small gallery and watched newsreels showing Japanese troops working their way down the Malayan peninsula, their triumphant entry into Singapore city and the signing of the surrender. There followed glimpses of Japan's busy industrial workers smiling over their tasks, and a factory engaged in bottling beer. When thousands of bottles of beer jerked along a conveyor belt, throats which had been denied any alcohol for two months cheered ironically.

"What hope did we have here, if Singapore couldn't hold out?" muttered Sandra on the way back to the Married Quarters.

"I do so hope Viola got away before the Japs got there," Pamela anguished.

"I'm sure Raoul would have sent her off to Australia long ago, when the Japs first attacked," Sandra said. "You know how bossy he is: I fancied him myself once but he was too bossy for me!"

Raoul had tried over and over again during the relentless progress of the Japanese down the Malayan peninsula: pleaded, argued, reasoned, ordered, but Viola was adamant, insisting "We agreed ages ago you'd never make me leave you."

"We couldn't guess then how things would turn out," he said. His journalistic work was now allotted half an hour at the end of each day; the rest of his time spent with the Rescue and Demolition Squad, digging out bodies and casualties from beneath bombed buildings. Viola continued her work in the Cipher Office, which had changed premises three times in as many weeks because of air raid damage. Their lovely bungalow on the Bukit Timah Road was in ruins. Now they occupied a tiny room in the Adelphi Hotel in the city centre.

It was only when the Japanese army was crossing the causeway to Singapore Island that Viola began to take account of Raoul's blunt expectations of what the future held: she needed no reminding of the horrific stories trickling from Hong Kong of atrocities on Europeans - women and nurses as well as soldiers. When the nurses in Singapore were urged to leave, she could withstand his pleas no longer and applied for a passage, but it was no longer a matter of ringing the P. & O. agents and booking: she had to join a long queue of women and children outside the shipping office, enduring the searing heat and sudden air raids rather than run for cover and risk losing her place in the line. It was six hours before she emerged with a ticket.

Four ships were due to sail that night; 'hand luggage only' was the strict instruction. On the way back to the Adelphi the placards of the latest issue of the one sheet Straits Times shrieked 'GOVERNOR SAYS SINGAPORE MUST STAND. IT SHALL STAND!'.

As she packed, Raoul prowled and snapped, convinced she had left it too late to escape in safety

"Don't make me go Raoul.. we'll face it together," she wept into his sweaty shirt.

"You must, my dear one.. for your own safety, and because then I can go where I shall be more use."

He explained that he had that day been asked to join a group of guerillas which would escape by sea and return behind the Japanese lines to harrass and monitor their movements, and provide intelligence for the Allies in preparation for future counter-attacks. Even in her misery, Viola could see the light of adventure and commitment in Raoul's eyes, and knew nothing would deflect him from his chosen role.

"How will we contact each other?" she asked, tearfully sewing bank notes and papers into a belt to wear round her waist.

"If you get to India, contact my bank in Colombo; if it's Australia, the main branch in Sydney. I shall keep in touch with both; be sure I shall find you, my dearest!"

That last drive through the city surpassed in horror anything she had experienced in the Chungking bombings. Military vehicles and civilian cars clogged the roads, further impeded by temporary gun emplacements. Every kind of debris had to be circumvented - rubble, bomb craters, shattered palm trees, tangled overhead cables and wires, uprooted lamp posts. Piles of corpses littered the pavements because no one had time to bury them, the stench so overpowering that the car windows had to be kept closed despite the blistering heat.

Overhead, Zero fighters zoomed low, machine-gunning vehicles and pedestrians. Car horns brayed and tooted, bombs crumped, and anti-aircraft fire pounded. The approaching twilight was turned into a red daylight by flames outlining rows of burning godowns; the air was foul with smoke from their contents - rubber, oil, copra and latex.

Now the road was completely blocked by cars and possessions abandoned by those who had driven as near the wharves as conditions allowed. On top of the cars were tied items which their owners had apparently hoped to take aboard with them - trunks, carpets, bedding even chairs.

Locking the car, Raoul held Viola's hand as they clambered over debris, cars and furniture - it was impossible to walk side by side among the congestion of people and luggage - adults with suitcases, children with bulging schoolbags on their backs. Above in the twilight billowed a huge cloud of dark smoke, spreading oily black smuts which settled on skin and clothes.

"From the tanks at the naval Base," Raoul muttered. "Fired so the Japs won't get them."

The four ships lay in the harbour, not far out. "They're not much bigger than Star Ferries," Viola said.

"Pretty sturdy, though. They've been up and down the China coast these many years past, weathering typhoons. I shall expect a fully detailed report of your trip in due course - for the book I shall write after the war."

Salvoes of artillery fire exploded all round the queue waiting to board the launches to the ship.

"Don't wait here," Viola urged. "It might be ages before my turn.. I'd rather you got back to shelter."

"And miss all this?" Raoul pointed to an incredible spectacle further down the quay where beautiful new cars and vans were being pushed into the sea to deny the Japanese their use.

As she stepped into the launch he gripped her arm and whispered "Take care of yourself for me, my Viola.. and don't do anything your friend Mrs. Grundy wouldn't like."

The single-funnelled 'Liang So' of two thousand tons normally had berths for twenty-four passengers. Now ten times that number swarmed on board, crammed into the cabins, the small dining saloon and bar and the corridors; some were even climbing down the perpendicular iron ladders into the hold - an option Viola did not care to take. The alternatives - tiny decks at bow and stern - were rapidly filling up, despite the clutter of working deck gear. She managed to squeeze in beside a derrick on the stern deck, and had to sit on her suitcase to accommodate it.

As the vessel moved slowly away from its anchorage, the passengers had a panoramic view of the line of burning dock buildings, and of the city beyond encircled with a glow of red from burning blocks. High up hung the hideous black smoke. Japanese artillery was still pounding away, puffs of grey erupting from its targets.

Viola glimpsed several familiar faces among the passengers but was not near enough to talk to them; her immediate neighbours were extrovert Australian nurses still in uniform, voicing their indignation at having to leave their patients against all their instincts and training.

"None of that!" warned their stern-faced Matron. "Orders are orders. Make yourselves useful here." They did: helping mothers with children, disoriented old women and many cases of plain hysteria. So many of the passengers were leaving behind menfolk and faithful servants as well as their homes: leaving the secure life they had known for years for a dangerous journey to an unknown destination. The risks were all too evident as the ship manoeuvred past hulks and masts of sunken vessels, and skirted minefields. The issue of bulky life-jackets was a further reminder of what might lie ahead.

Despite the hard deck and cramped limbs, Viola slept.

When she awoke very early in the morning, the air was fresh, the sea calm and sparkling, the sky an empty pale blue vault. The nightmare that had been Singapore for the past weeks seemed unbelievable now, the only noises the voices of waking children and the steady chug-chug of the ship's engines. There was no sign of the other evacuation ships, although a complete panorama of the surrounding ocean was obscured by distant small islands of the Malayan archipelago.

Gradually, the ship's company - a polygot of nationalities who were survivors of sunken vessels - created organisation out of chaos. Tarpaulins were strung above the open decks as protection against the sun; passengers were sent in groups to the bathrooms for ablutions; mugs of tea and handfuls of biscuits and cheese were distributed.

Most of the refugees had had so little sleep in recent weeks that they were content to rest, however uncomfortable the conditions and in spite of children's plaintive voices. Viola felt herself drifting off and was content to do so. She was jerked awake by shouts of "Planes! Jap planes!"

There were six of them, high in the sky but coming closer and lower every second. Every one struggled into their life-jackets and rushed for cover; some forced their way into overcrowded corridors between-decks; the rest huddled together beneath the fragile shelter of the sun tarpaulins.

The first bombs missed the ship but rocked it violently and sent plumes of water cascading over the decks. By the time the planes returned again the four-inch gun on the fo'c'stle was firing, its feeble pop-pop soon inaudible above the roar of the attackers. The next bomb fell through the forward hatch and exploded inside; another blew the bottoms out of all the lifeboats on the starboard side. The ship began to list at once - soon after, fire poured from what had been the bows; frantic passengers struggled on to the stern deck from the corridors below, where they had thought to find safety.

There was no need for the order to abandon ship. People clawed their way to the rails, grabbing any fitment to keep them from slithering down the fast-tilting deck into the maelstrom of the fast-submerging bows. Somehow in the pandemonium the three serviceable lifeboats were launched and small life-rafts tossed overboard. Watching the lifeboats rapidly filling up as people scrambled down swaying rope ladders, Viola jumped over the rail and made for the nearest raft. Just as she reached it two nurses boarded it from the other side. Women and children were calling for help all round them, hanging on to life-jackets they hadn't managed to put on in their panic. The nurses on the raft dragged up a badly-man burned Chinese seaman; Viola rescued a tiny elderly English lady who, instead of expressing gratitude, moaned that she had lost her bag with her passport, her pills and her spectacles, and "couldn't see a thing." A small girl - her blond head only just visible above her life jacket - floated by, screaming; Viola dropped into the sea and brought her on board. Now the raft was perilously low in the water, and still terrified people drifted by, piteously crying for help.

"We can't take any more," said the old lady, "we're almost sinking as it is."

But the cries were too heartrending to ignore; Viola slipped into the water again and helped aboard a young girl in her teens, deciding herself to swim alongside holding on to the looped ropes round the raft.

The surviving seamen were trying valiantly to get lifeboats, rafts and swimmers away from the dying ship which was creaking and gurgling, her tanks spewing oil into the sea and emitting choking fumes. There was a terrible risk of the oil igniting; the two nurses joined Viola in the sea, all three trying to push the raft beyond the treacly water.

Figures on the freighter's stern, which was almost perpendicular, were still leaping into the sea and grabbing at wreckage to keep afloat, even as the ship finally slipped out of sight.

So many of the survivors who watched knew that relatives and friends had gone down with the ship. Viola had never heard such anguished cries.

"We three will take it in turns to swim alongside," said the elder of the nurses to Viola. "My name's Pat, this" - nodding to her youthful ginger-haired colleague - "is Liz. And you're?"

"Viola."

"Right, Vi: you and Liz get aboard now. and if I were you I'd take off your oily dresses. I'll stay out for a while."

"Is it safe to have so many on here?" fretted the old lady as the two girls, impeded by their life jackets, heaved themselves on to the raft.

"If we all keep still ma'am." said Pat bluntly. "What's your name then?"

"Mrs John Lorder, my husband.."

"Was he on the ship?"

"No, he wouldn't leave Singapore, even though he's too old to fight." She started to cry.

"Don't worry about him, he's better off than we are," Liz said roughly.

The teenager was sunk in despair, her head in her arms. Under protest she had shed her oil-soaked dress but obviously suffered agonies of embarrassment at revealing her burgeoning figure in its skimpy underwear. She managed to gulp that her name was Janet and that she had lost sight of her mother and brother.

At first all the rescue craft and swimmers were close enough together in the calm sea to keep in verbal contact. It was gradually established that Janet's brother was in one of the lifeboats but there was no sign of her mother; nor did any one lay claim to the small girl on the raft. She was about two years old and couldn't give her name.

"Then we shall call you Girlie," announced Pat.

"The nearest island is about ten miles due east," shouted the seaman at the oars of the life boat which was passing most of the rafts. "You probably can't see it yet, but I can. The current's running that way, you should get there in a few hours."

Viola was in the water again when a small wind blew up; little waves slapped against her face. Whereas all the rafts had been floating gently in the same direction, now vicious currents separated them; some were being carried gently towards the island; others were completely out of sight.

"We're no nearer," Viola whispered up to Pat as darkness fell.

"I know." Pat spoke guardedly so that Mrs. Lorder and Janet shouldn't hear. "We'll just have to see what the morning brings. Get on board now, your teeth are chattering."

It was impossible to get comfortable; all except the seaman were encumbered with life jackets they dared not discard; the seaman lay athwart the raft and the child whimpered in Mrs. Lorder's arms; the others lolled up against each other. Viola and the nurses took it in turns to stay awake and keep watch - not that there was anything to watch but the black sky pricked with stars and the dark sea rising and falling.

The child cried out that she had wet her knickers.

"I've wet my knicks too, Girlie," laughed Pat. "We all have, haven't we? Never mind, we'll be able to hang them out tomorrow on a palm tree."

When dawn broke there was no island in sight. Appalled, exhausted, starving and thirsty, they tried to come to terms with their situation.

"Best to relax.. try not to talk.. conserve our strength," advised Pat. "Another evacuation ship will surely come this way."

"No ships can get through," sobbed Mrs. Horder, "The Japs are everywhere. We're doomed."

The sun was rising; soon it was beating mercilessly down on them. They snatched chunks of floating seaweed and drooped it over their heads, past worrying about its sliminess and strong smell. They put on their oil-stiff dresses as added protection.

"I must have a drink, I must have something to drink!" Janet kept moaning; suddenly she snatched the seaweed from her head and sucked savagely at it before the nurses could stop her.

"We'll have coconut milk as soon as we get ashore," Pat tried to soothe her.

"Isn't that what desert islands always have, coconuts?"

'It had better be soon," thought Viola - then she wondered if she had actually spoken the words. The fierce sun was playing tricks with her eyes as she trailed her hands in the water and splashed some over herself and Mrs. Lorder and the child who seemed almost comatose. The two nurses were bent over the seaman, trying to provide him with shade as they comforted him.

When the sun went down the nurses confirmed that he was dead and gently rolled his body into the sea. Mrs. Lorder had a seizure at the sight and died twenty minutes later. Janet, stony-faced, said through stiff lips "At least we can all lie down properly now."

Rain fell that night. The three adults opened their mouths and sucked in as much as they could. Pat had managed to retain her white shoes and tried to collect rain in them, but the shower didn't last long enough to provide any reserves.

When daylight came and they could see nothing but water around them, Janet rolled back her eyes and died. The others were so weak that it took them a long time to push her body off the raft.

"We can only pray," murmured Liz, her fair skin scorched by the sun.

"And try to keep awake," Pat said sternly. "Let's take it in turns to sing." She began with a hoarse chorus of 'Waltzing Matilda' but soon had to stop as her voice gave out. Liz took over with 'Hush A Bye Baby' because Girlie had awakened and was giving sad little cries through blackened swollen lips.

When it was Viola's turn she sang 'A Tisket A Tasket, a little yellow basket..' and saw herself dancing at Raffles with Raoul; that old life, with plenty of food and comfort, seemed centuries away. She closed her salt encrusted eyes to shut out the present; Raoul was right all the time: she should have left Singapore weeks ago; what a waste, to die like this...

SPRING

By morning Pamela was shivering so much that her teeth were chattering. The knife-like pains she had suffered all night were no better.

"What's the matter?" came Sandra's plaintive voice. "You've been waking me up on and off all night."

"Tummy.. diarrhoea.. can't stop shivering.." She winced when Sandra's cool hand touched her forehead.

"You're burning! You're ill!" Sandra heaved her ungainly body out of bed. "I'll get someone."

"Enteritis or dysentery," sighed the overworked doctor who lived in the block, the stethoscope round his neck the only indication of his calling. "You're the tenth case I've seen in the Married Quarters since midnight."

In a haze of griping pain, sickness and light-headedness, she groaned as the wheeled stretcher was trundled over the sandy path to the camp hospital. Through a blur she was aware of kindly arms placing here in a real bed, on sheets so cool that they hurt her burning body. Her insides seemed to be pouring out of her, but she was past agonising about the indignities of soiling the bed. The pills she was given made her sleepy and weak. She thought, in a detached way, she would probably die; it seemed the easiest thing to do.

"So you've decided to wake up, Miss Doran!" She lifted heavy eyelids and saw the white-veiled head of a young nurse. "What about a cup of tea?"

It was real tea, with milk and sugar, in a cup, not the raw liquid in the enamel mug she was used to in her billet. The nurse helped her to sit up in bed.

'Acute gastro-enteritis' proclaimed the chart on which her temperature was recorded in dizzying zig-zags. She was astounded to learn she had been in hospital for two days.

Everyone of the twenty beds lining either side of the oblong ward was occupied. Some women were sitting up, some lay comatose, two were writhing - obviously in the same state as she herself had been when she'd been admitted. Still on a liquid diet, she qualified for a tiny bottle of fresh milk from the miniscule ration the Japanese provided daily for young children and the sick. It was so long since she had tasted milk that she found it rather rich.

She learned that stomach troubles were endemic in the camp, and remembered the day preceding her illness, when working with the vegetable squad: the Chinese cabbage leaves had felt hot and slimy and some were thrown away, but most was cooked and eaten as there was no other food to go with the rice.

After the noisy Married Quarters, there was a welcome serene and ordered atmosphere in the ward, despite its stark appearance - grey stone floors, no curtains at the windows and no chairs; instead of bedside lockers, by each iron bedstead stood an oblong rough concrete block (removed from the anti-blast walls built at the entrance the year before in preparation for the building's use as an emergency hospital.) On the floor above lived the sixty civilian nurses who staffed the hospital, squashed into large dormitories. Pamela knew this because one of the nurses, while making the bed, asked her about her living quarters.

"What, only two of you in one room?" The nurse was most envious. "You should see us upstairs - twenty in one room, fifteen in the others, and not an inch to turn round in any of them."

"When Mrs. Lamb's baby arrives, and our friend from the Military Hospital, we'll be pretty crowded too."

"Even then, you'll be well off compared to us; we've forgotten what privacy is. Now - Pamela isn't it - you should be able to walk to the bathroom today. I'll give you an arm, you'll feel a bit shaky at first."

Her legs felt like rubber, and the short walk along the corridor to the ablutions was tiring. There were no baths, just wash-basins, and a row of low-walled cubicles with Asiatic squatting lavatories, now constantly in use by both sexes.

"You'll get used to it." The nurse laughed at Pamela's embarrassment. "No room for inhibitions here! Now, can I leave you to get back to the ward on your own?"

She began the return trip by steadying herself against the wall, and almost overbalanced when another nurse hurried in calling "Mr. Bennett, Mr. Bennett! Are you alright? You've been in there a long time."

"Perfectly all right, thank you nurse," came a polite voice from the end cubicle. "I won't be long."

It took Pamela several moments to associate the name Bennett with Jenny from the office; she had never met any one in camp who knew Jenny's whereabouts, and had assumed she had somehow avoided internment. Now she wondered if this Mr. Bennett could be Jenny's father, and delayed returning to the ward until he emerged from his cubicle. Tall, middle-aged and sandy-haired, she could see nothing of Jenny's dark vivid looks in his broad kindly face: Bennett was a common enough name, after all.

Visitors were allowed in the afternoon, but no-one had come to see her - not even Sandra. Already feeling more confident after her trip to the ablutions, she wandered on to the narrow verandah shared by the line of wards which overlooked the sea - just twenty yards away, a rocky shore barred with barbed-wire fencing. The March sun was pleasant enough to entice several walking patients on to the verandah. Just eight feet along stood Mr. Bennett in his dressing-gown, by his side two young dark-skinned boys with black hair and a look of Jenny.

"Mr. Bennett, please.." She hardly knew how to begin the conversation. "Please.. are you Jenny's father?"

"I most certainly am.."

"Then.. where is she? We worked in the same office in the Secretariat but I haven't seen her here."

"She is safe and sound with her mother and the little ones, living with Portuguese friends in Kowloon! Now you must be Pamela?"

"Oh yes! I've worried about her, because she never came back to the tunnel after the first two days. I'm so relieved to hear about her."

Mr. Bennett explained that Jenny and the family had tried to cross to Hong Kong when the Japanese were moving into Kowloon; there was no transport, they were carrying as much luggage as they could, and were slowed down by the pace of the younger children. "My wife sent the two bigger boys - Gerald and Maurice here - ahead in the hope that they at least would get the last ferry across the harbour and join me - which they did. The rest of the family was stranded in Kowloon, and went back to the house and some Portuguese friends moved in with them. I'd expected Nita and the others to be sent to Stanley when we were, but she has dual nationality and must have decided it would be better for the children to avoid internment. Now I hear rumours that most Portuguese people are going to Macao for the duration... I don't want my family to be so far away, so I keep badgering the Jap authorities to bring them to Stanley. One day, please God, they will."

After the cossetted life in the hospital, it was a great shock to be thrown back into the life of self-preservation. Sandra had missed the epidemic but was full of grouses.

"I daren't come and visit you, in case I caught your bug. It's been awful here without you, I've had to do all the queuing. Yesterday I was late and there wasn't enough fish to go round, all I got was a dollop of vile fish soup over my rice. And

I'm right out of cigarettes, I'll die if more don't come in soon."

It was a sore point with Pamela that Sandra spent her dwindling hoard of money on cigarettes, when there were rumours that food extras would also soon be on sale.

"I need cigarettes," Sandra muttered. "You don't know how I need them."

When next a supply arrived in camp, she bought her limit of four packets, and Pamela's allotment as well. Both Jack Roffey and Mr. Gasson always offered to buy Pamela's ration, knowing she was a non-smoker and were prepared to pay twice the price, which would have given her profits to spend at the promised food canteen, but Sandra insisted that her need was greater. It was a waste of time to argue with her and only caused exhausting rows which Pamela, still weak after her illness, could not face. In fact, almost every one in Stanley was beginning to look ill and starved. She supposed she did too, but there were no mirrors and she could only peer at her face in the tiny glass in her compact and note the beginning of anxiety lines on her forehead, and shadows on her hollowing cheeks.

Now few people had the energy for brisk evening perambulations round the blocks. Movements were lethargic; walking up a flight of stairs wearing, and the smallest cuts and sores usually turned septic and healed very slowly.

One night in desperation a small group of men escaped from the camp, but the elation this news brought was quickly dampened by stricter vigilance on the part of the Japanese; roll calls were increased, and the obvious fury of the Japanese authorities led to anxiety that there could be more unpredictable reprisals. A little later, four policemen escaped, only to be caught a week later; they were seen being bundled into the jail and their fate only guessed at. An atmosphere of listlessness and helplessness was spreading throughout the camp.

Pamela was lying on her bed one afternoon, trying to summon enough energy to get up and repair a friend's jacket, when she heard Sandra calling out urgently as she came along the corridor.

"There's a new notice!" Sandra burst into the room, her face transformed with excitement and hope. "It's about repatriation! We're going to be exchanged for Japanese prisoners from England and America! We're going to get out of here!"

The notice only mentioned the possibility of repatriation in very general terms, but that was enough to create euphoria. The balloon of hope was pricked a few days later when it was announced that plans were afoot for repatriation of Americans only.

"I should go with the Americans!" wept Sandra. "My parents are in Canada, and that's in the Americas. I should be allowed to go anyway, because of the baby!"

Her belligerent representations to the British authorities in the camp were gently but firmly rejected. "Even if you had a case, Mrs. Lamb," it was explained to her, "you would be too far on in your pregnancy for any ship to risk having you on board."

She raged for days, working herself into such a state that she could not take her turn in the food queues, yet querulous and upset every time Pamela left the room to do some chore. Her cries and shouts could be heard all over the flat; the word spread; Mrs. Burford called several times, still grateful for Sandra's part during the war in summoning help to the Jockey Club, but Sandra would not listen to her bracing advice. Her St. John's colleagues came and tried to placate her; she turned her face to the wall, stopped crying, stopped talking and sank into sullen silence. She only sat up when Pamela brought her food, wolfing it greedily. She cried for cigarettes but there was none.

The Block Doctor called. It was obvious from his manner that her reputation had gone before her. He had little patience but spent some time talking firmly in an attempt to get through to her. He gave her one dose of precious sedative, confiding to Pamela on the way out that this was as much for her as for the patient, because "you need help too."

For several blessed hours Sandra slept. Friendly callers were shooed away - except for one who came in like Father Christmas - Tony Grahame with an old sack containing tins of meat, soup and fruit.

"We only heard yesterday about the tough time you were having with Mrs. Lamb," Tony whispered. "You were both very good to us in the hotel, and we'd like to repay you ."

"But your family -"

"We have enough to keep us going for a while, Pam, and there's more where that came from. No, don't ask any questions, and keep it quiet."

When she awoke and saw the food, Sandra rubbed her eyes unbelievingly.

"No, you're not dreaming," said Pamela gaily, "These tins are real." Sandra gradually perked up, as every day for the next week Tony brought tins of food which provided real feasts.

It became obvious that other internees were also benefitting from this unexplained largesse, for the communal dustbins were crammed with empty food tins. The source was not universally revealed until the Japanese authorities discovered that the large food godowns just outside the camp boundary - stocked by the British against a siege - had been looted. The much-trodden path from the godown door led to the fence behind the quarters occupied mainly by the Police, and the Japanese guards swooped and searched them. Those looters who had time hid their remaining tins in water cisterns, at the back of food boilers.. wherever space afforded. Some hastily buried tins in the garden plots outside their blocks. The Japanese found some of the food but quickly tired of the running up and down the staircases, knowing they were being outwitted, and abandoned the search when they had found a few tins; but they cleared out what was left in the godowns and the bonanza was over.

Easter was at hand. It was easy to accept the mood of Good Friday, but difficult to take part in the rejoicing of the Resurrection. Pamela had always attended church at Easter in the past, and felt compelled to join the faithful who congregated in St. Stephen's Hall that Sunday morning. There was so little to rejoice about in Stanley, yet she found herself stirred by the service, thanking God for her own survival, and joining in the alleluias with a fresh sense of hope.

For hope it was which kept every one going from one day to the next. You could listen eagerly to the latest rumours, discount the more outrageous, and just hope that some of the others would come true. No one seriously believed any more the one about the Chinese Army advancing on Kowloon, for had it not been in that situation since before Christmas? Nor was the tale that a tiger was roaming about the camp at night taken seriously - until its spoors were found on the path leading to the hospital, and Japanese soldiers were seen scouring the scrub and bushes outside the camp boundary. The final proof came when a British butcher from the Married Quarters was taken to town to carve up the tiger's carcase, and a photograph appeared in the Hong Kong Daily News showing him standing by the beast's body with his knife in his hand.

At last the repeated requests of Mr. Gimson and the Director of Medical Services to the Japanese to provide better food bore fruit. Flour was supplied; it was full of weevils and had to be well sifted, but the bread the camp bakers made with it tasted heavenly, even though there was little to spread on it beyond such luxuries as those with money could sometimes buy in the canteen. More varieties of vegetables arrived - sweet potatoes, egg-plants, carrots, tomatoes, in place of the dreary spinach and lettuce and cabbage of the first few months.

Things were improving in other ways. Although the approach of the warmer weather at first posed problems because few people had been wearing summer clothes when they came into camp, some fairy godmother sent in unisex khaki shorts, and brightly-coloured T-shirts. Pamela and others clever with their needles were kept busy with essential alterations to make these garments fit - but there was no way the shorts could be adapted to Sandra's present shape - her summer wear consisted of dresses made out of her night-gowns, the long hem being cut off and inserted as a wide gusset down the front.

'Internees may now receive parcels from friends in town' read a new notice.

" 'may' is the operative word" was someone's cynical view. "Pigs might fly, too!"

Yet a few small parcels began to arrive from Chinese and Third National friends. One morning Sandra's name was on the list. Parcels had to be collected from the Japanese administration bungalow and opened there for inspection. Pamela went with her, and shared the thrill of seeing a small sacking bag with Sandra's name painted in thick black ink on the outside; it was from the Chinese senior clerk in Miles' firm, and contained a small tin of jam, one of sardines, slabs of Chinese brown sugar called wong tong, and a cake of crude soap. Every three or four weeks, another little parcel came for Sandra, yet nothing could distract her for long from her condition.

When kind friends brought makeshift baby clothes made from part of their own garments, she grew even more depressed.. the gifts were just more reminders of what lay ahead of her.

"I can't stand it much longer!" she ranted. "I can hardly move, I can never get comfortable. I'm dreading the birth.. it should never have happened. And I know I'll never be able to look after the baby when it comes. What can I do, what can I do, Pam?"

"Just take one day at a time," Pamela said wearily; she had run out of cheerful rejoinders long ago.

In the middle of June the 'Asama Maru' anchored in the bay and was boarded by some two hundred American internees to begin their journey back to the States. With overwhelming envy, the British and other nationals watched the ship leave, their only consolation the largesse freely distributed when the travellers had vacated their billets. Pamela and Sandra inherited from Gail her bed and bedding ("That will do for Hilary when she comes!"), several tins of food and half a tube of toothpaste.

"What bliss!" Pamela giggled that night as she put paste on her tired toothbrush for the first time in months - but nothing could assuage Sandra's black despair.

"It's not fair that we're still stuck here, why doesn't something happen to get us all away?" she moaned. "Why only the Americans? I want Ah Ling, I want Ah Ling! I just can't bear it here any more."

Tired of the endless battle against a wall of determined misery, Pamela stuck her fingers in her ears and tried to sleep.

SUMMER

The Japanese had decided to send the V.A.D.'s to Stanley. Three battered orange buses stood outside the Military Hospital, the July sun showing up their dustiness, their dents and scratches. Rosemary clung to Hilary's arm when the nurses were ordered aboard. "Sit with me," she whimpered.

"Where else?" Hilary rolled her eyes to the sky and grinned affectionately. Over the past months she had come to accept Rosemary's dependence on her; now initial sympathy had given place to wry banter, interspersed with the occasional brisk reproof.

Despite the excitement of the move to Stanley, there were tears in many eyes as the buses moved off. The girls had become attached to their patients; had become a cohesive group, working together, sleeping side by side in dormitories, spending their off-duty time together; organising concerts which even the Japanese medical staff and guards enjoyed, though they sternly banned any act in which they considered the performers inadequately dressed.

Hilary knew she was losing the chance of a meeting with Roddy: at the hospital the trucks transporting sick men from the military camps sometimes brought an additional, unauthorised orderly - the husband or fiancé of one of the nurses. Once Roddy had managed a visit this way, coming from Shamshuipo Camp in Kowloon to which he had been transferred; they had only been able to manage a five-minute meeting, but the possibility that it might happen again had given her hope every day.

"I can't go back to that place," Rosemary was muttering, her knuckles white as she gripped the top of the seat in front of her.

"No choice, dearie; none of us have!" Hilary, desperately sorry that Rosemary should have to return to the scene of her brutal experience in Stanley, dared not show sympathy now. "Aren't we the lucky ones, getting a Cook's tour of the island, after we've been cooped up all these months?"

It was surprising to pass through half-empty streets which had always been teeming with people. No trams were running and they saw very few cars. Road names had been changed: the newly-painted signs were in Japanese characters with English translations which bore no relation to the original names. War damage was still in evidence: windowless tenements with broken verandahs yet still obviously in occupation because washing strung on bamboo poles protruded from the structure. A few tiny shops were open but most were boarded up.

The winding road over the hills also bore signs of the recent battle. In some places landslips made passage difficult and dangerous. Rusted remains of burnt out vehicles poked out from the burgeoning undergrowth.

As Stanley came in sight, Rosemary bent her head and rocked in distress. Hilary put an arm round the shaking shoulders. "We're here, kid, you've got to face it. I know you'll be all right, you'll have your Mother.."

"She'll want to know all about it.."

"You don't have to tell her everything - she'll understand."

It seemed as if all two thousand internees were waiting to greet them, clustered round the accommodation blocks above the road where the buses stopped.

When she heard her name joyfully called, Hilary did not at first recognise Pamela with her bare feet, short straight hair, pointed face, and wearing men's khaki shorts and a T shirt. Hilary felt overdressed in her floral cotton skirt, pink blouse and white sandals.

"Good heavens, Pam! You're slimmer than I ever was!"

"I'm so GLAD to see you at last!" Pamela hugged her fiercely. "We've kept a place for you in our room."

Others were pushing forward, claiming relatives and friends. Matron was booming away in the background: "Now, girls, I've just been told there are rooms in the Science Block for those whose people haven't got billets for them."

Their luggage had come in a lorry and was strewn on the grass nearby.

"Come and find your things," Pamela was tugging at her arm.

"Just a sec." Hilary pulled Rosemary forward and introduced her. "I just want to see her settled first, her mother's here somewhere."

"I want to stay with you, Hilary!"

"I won't be far away Rosie, and I'll come and see you when we've found our way around."

"Rosemary!" A tall attractive women with fair hair pinned on top of her head pushed her way through the crowds. Rosemary shrank behind Hilary, who squeezed her hand tightly and propelled her forward. In her mother's close embrance, Rosemary hid her head and sobbed, while Hilary waited uncertainly.

"Get your luggage" - Pamela was urging.

As Mrs. Horne put her arm round Rosemary's shoulders and led her away, Hilary called "Where are you living?"

"Indian Quarters, second block on the right, ground floor." Mrs. Horne said.

"Second block on right, ground floor," Hilary repeated. "I'll come and see you soon." Even in her affection for Rosemary, she felt a great surge of relief now that her self-imposed responsibility was over..

"What's wrong with your friend?" Pamela asked, guiding the way to the cream-coloured blocks above the road.

"She's been very ill - had a nervous breakdown. Oh Pam, where did you get those shorts? Are they a kind of uniform? Every one seems to be wearing them!"

"We were told they were made for the African market, but we were lucky to get given any summer clothes at all! Forget shorts, I want to know all you've been doing, and what you've seen from the hospital, and have you had any news of Roddy or Keith, or any of our friends? Oh, it is so good to see you again!"

"I saw Rod about two months ago, he's skinny but fine.. well, fine for a prisoner of war; said to give you his chin-chins if I saw you. No news of Keith though, he's in a different camp from Rod. How's it been here? You look pretty run down yourself."

"We don't get much sleep at night, and are on the go all day; (up these stairs Hil, our room's on the top floor). Melly's a screamer.. oh, fancy me forgetting the great news - Sandra had a daughter on the 15th of last month, her real name's Melissa!"

"Don't tell me they're billetted near you?"

"In the same room."

"What, you and I, and Sandra and her kid, all in together?" Hilary was thunderstruck.

"Not your idea of heaven is it, sharing digs with me and my offspring?" said Sandra engagingly as they arrived. She had the same drawn exhausted appearance as Pamela, her hair tied back with a piece of tape; she wore a faded cream petticoat as a dress. The baby, naked except for a napkin, was asleep in a tiny cot; she had a feathering of red hair.

Looking round the small room, Hilary tried to hide her dismay. There had been a certain cosiness in the hospital dormitory: this curtainless room with bare floorboards was stark and comfortless; suitcases and brown paper bags were stuffed in one corner; cartons bulging with clothes and other possessions spilled out under the camp beds. Sandra sat in the only chair. Napkins fluttered from a piece of string tied from one window catch to the other. A faint smell of urine persisted. A dented kerosene tin was full to the brim with soaking napkins. Dirty clothes were piled on the floor against the window. Two unwashed enamel plates and spoons stood on the window sill. Unless she had seen it, she could never have believed that these two girls could allow themselves to live in such squalor - and to be so oblivious to it.

"We're so much better off here in the Married Quarters than the people in the Indian Quarters." Pamela was actually gloating about the dismal billet. "They're dark inside and out, with tiny rooms, stone floors, and Asiatic lavs."

Hilary's private opinion was that nothing could be as sordid as this room, and she resolved to move out as soon as she could. This was not immediately possible because a gong in the yard sounded and Pamela explained "Supper's up: we have to line up and collect it. We've got a spare plate, thanks to Gail - your bed came from her too." She rushed next door to the kitchen to wash the two dirty dishes. Melly woke and started to bellow, and Hilary put her fingers in her ears and offered to collect the food for all.

In the long queue she was quickly recognised as one of the new arrivals; complete strangers begged for news from the town..

"I don't know any," she explained over and over again. "We weren't allowed out of the hospital grounds."

- "You must have heard rumours!"

- "What's the latest from Europe?"

- "Have the Japs really been sinking all the American fleet, like they're always claiming in their newspaper?"

There was something pathetic about the eagerness of the scantily-dressed people who crowded round her. Many of the men had grown beards because, she learned later, few had arrived in camp with spare blades for their razors; some women had let their hair grow long; others, like Pamela, had it cropped short; perms of course were a thing of the past.

Most of the men were bare to the waist, just wearing slacks or shorts. The women mainly sported the dreadful khaki shorts, and uniform T shirts. Few people had footwear.

"It's not that we haven't got shoes," Pamela later explained. "We all arrived here properly shod, but we don't know how long our shoes have to last, so we keep them for wet and cold days."

The food appalled her - a dollop of rice and a cupful of stewed soya beans and marrow: a poor substitute for the meals at the hospital where the basic rations the Japanese sent were rendered tasty with flavourings and additions from the store larder.

"What do we drink?" she asked after she had eaten her meagre meal.

"Just hot water, I'm afraid." Pamela said. "We get an issue of tea now and again, but we're out at the moment." She leaned out of the window and added "The hot water queue is beginning to move. I'll go and get some as soon as I've finished eating."

"Hang on, I've brought some tea." Hilary rummaged in her satchel and produced a small paper poke of tea leaves.

"Go now, Pam," Sandra urged. "If you wait too long the boiler will run out, like yesterday, and we'll have to wait another two hours."

Hilary watched in amazement as Pamela leapt up at once, abandoning her meal, and shot out of the room with a chipped enamel jug and a small tin can which she carried by a loop of string threaded through a hole on either side.

"Is there something we can cover Pam's food with?" she asked.

"We've only got one plate each." Sandra's voice was indifferent as she slowly ate her food. "Doesn't matter if it gets cold - it tastes the same muck."

The baby's cries began again. "You can wait till I've had my meal, Melly." Sandra patted the child with her spare hand. "If I don't get to eat, there'll be nothing for you."

Shovelling the last spoonful of rice into her mouth, Sandra pulled up her shirt and tried to feed her. Hilary watched uncomfortably as time and again the baby failed to latch on to the nipple.

"I wish to God Pam would hurry up!" Tears of pain were streaming down Sandra's face. "She knows what to do. This hurts like hell."

But even when Pamela returned it was five minutes before the feeding was properly established, then Pamela slumped on to her camp bed, her back against the wall, ate the remains of her food and slowly sipped the mug of milkless tea Hilary had poured for her. "So THRILLED you're here at last!" she beamed at Hilary.

"You wind her, Pam, I'm exhausted." Sandra handed back the satiated infant "Ugh... she's wet again, my dress is damp." She turned away in distaste as Pamela laid Melly in the cot and removed a well-filled napkin.

Later, when Melly was winded and almost asleep, Sandra flopped back on to her bed with a great sigh.

"Go out and get some air," Pamela urged. "By the time you come back I'll have all the nappies on the line."

"Sure you don't mind? I do need a break." Sandra was already at the door.

"My God Pam, don't YOU ever get a break?" exploded Hilary the moment Sandra disappeared. "You're working harder than she is at being a mother!"

"Well.. she went through having the baby, and Miles being killed.. and anyway, she did all this for Belle during the evacuation." The kerosene tin had no handle, and Pamela had to clutch it to her chest to carry it to the bathroom. "When she gets back I'll show you round the camp before curfew."

"When's that?"

"Eight o'clock. We all have to be in the vicinity of our blocks by then, and in our rooms by eleven."

"Camp rules, or the Japs?"

"Japs. They're strict about it, too. Several men have been beaten up, caught out of their own blocks after hours, visiting their girl-friends."

It was twenty minutes to eight before Sandra returned.

"We won't be able to go far tonight," said Pamela as she and Hilary hurried off.

"Just take me to the Indian Quarters, I want to see how Rosemary's getting on. You know, she went to St. Stephen's during the war in my place, and was raped, and saw that dreadful massacre. She's only seventeen.. and afterwards, she heard that her boyfriend had been killed at Wongneichong Gap. I'd like to keep an eye on her."

There was just time, in the twilight, to run down the path to the two-storeyed red brick blocks clustered round a green which led to a tiny rocky inlet with barbed wire fencing. Sunburnt children chased each other noisily; people strolled in little groups; couples lolled on the worn grass; some, knees up, sat back to back for support.

As they entered the Hornes' block, Hilary saw at once that Pamela's assessment of the Indian Quarters was only too true; these flats each had two tiny rooms and a miniscule kitchen and sluice; the floors were stone and the walls gray.

Rosemary was sitting on her camp bed staring blankly at the opposite wall when Hilary and Pamela arrived. Her mother was squatting beside a smoky chatty on the verandah, fanning the lick of fire beneath an old herring tin in which she was frying cooked rice.

"So here you are!" Hilary spoke heartily. "Settled in?"

"Look at it! It's like a prison."

"So what?" This was no time for sympathy. "At least you're lucky, you and your Mother, to have a room to yourselves. Pam and I share a room with a mother and a new baby; and there are twenty-three more people in our flat, all sharing the bathroom!"

"It's not just Mummy and me; there's an old woman as well - this is her bed, next to mine. Mummy's bed has to be kept folded on the verandah in the daytime, to make room. Why, oh why, did we have to come here? I just hate it."

"It was fun in Bowen Road, but that's over now!" Hilary gave her a mock punch. "We V.A.D.s will get together and have fun here, too, once we're organised. Pam has been telling me there are concerts, and we can even go swimming sometimes - there are heaps of things to do until we're free again."

"But there'll be no Johnny, no Johnny!" Rosemary's sobs brought her mother from her task on the verandah. Hugging her daughter tightly, she mouthed desperately to Hilary "I just don't know what to do with her."

"It's almost five to eight!" Pamela thrust her watch before Hilary's face. "We have to go."

"Don't leave me!" Rosemary pulled away from her mother and clung to Hilary. "You mustn't leave me!" "Don't be silly; we've got to go - Jap orders." Hilary firmly pushed the grasping arms away.

"Come tomorrow, then. You must come tomorrow!"

"Not if you're going to act up like this." Hilary winced as she saw Rosemary's eyes waver at the stern rebuke. "So what about it? Here's your mother, slaving away in the heat to make your food more appetising, and you making all this fuss." She held her breath, uncertain whether her words would cause more hysteria, then relaxed as Rosemary clenched her hands together and spoke more normally. "See you tomorrow, won't I, Hilary? Thanks for coming."

That first night in Stanley confirmed Hilary's determination to find another billet. The great heat made it necessary to keep door and windows open: but every time the baby cried there were vociferous demands from the occupants of the adjoining rooms for them to be shut. It seemed as if the light was being switched on and off all through the night, with Sandra sitting up feeding the child, or Pamela bumbling about reaching for dry napkins. Added to this was the spartan camp bed after the comparative comfort of the army bedstead at the military hospital.

In the morning, she found herself the only person in the room free to go to the hot water queue after the clanging of an iron railing on a bin lid in the courtyard below proclaimed the night's curfew over. Her plan to visit the V.A.D s to try to arrange to move in with them was shelved when she reluctantly decided to tackle the washing of the night's yield of used napkins - for Sandra was again feeding Melly, and Pamela looked completely drained: Hilary had no idea that babies needed so many meals and at such inconvenient times.

"Hasn't Sandra any other friends who can help?" she asked Pamela whom she had enticed to the bathroom on the pretence of showing her the nappy washing routine. "Why are you expected to do so much?"

"Some do sometimes," Pamela shrugged, "but I'm on the spot, I suppose.. and she does share all the food parcels she gets from town."

"I should jolly well think so! She's treating you like an amah."

She could not escape until after the eleven o'clock meal was over, then trudged up the slope to the Science Block near the College and tracked down her colleagues. They were crammed into several adjoining rooms, with little space between their beds; they were trying to re-arrange their possessions to make more room, with cheerful acceptance of their inadequate accommodation. Even before she spoke, she was invited to join them.

"We missed you last night, Hilary!"

"It isn't the same without you!"

"Wouldn't you rather be here with us?"

"I'd love to, but there really isn't room.."

"We'll MAKE room!"

She arranged to move in that afternoon. On the walk back to the Married Quarters she noticed small groups of people assembling in various places: in an old garage; beneath the shade of a tree; even on the landing by the stairs up to her room.

"They're classes," Pamela explained when asked. "There are no end of professors and teachers here, you can study almost anything." She held an open safetypin between her teeth as she struggled to arrange a clean napkin on Melly while Sandra rested on her bed, wearing just bra and pants.

"Have you taken up anything exciting?"

"Not me - no time!" Pamela gave a hoot of triumph as she managed to secure the napkin. "Though now you're here things will be easier; I might try a language to keep my old brain ticking over."

Disarmed by Pamela's affectionate beam and assumption that her chores would now be shared, Hilary decided this was not the moment to announce her move; she would need to choose a politic time to do so.

"I'm going to see the doc tomorrow," Sandra said. "I'm sure Melly's not getting enough milk from me, and it's such agony.. as soon as he agrees to put her on the list for dried milk, I'm weaning her."

"Don't think of it!" wailed Pamela. "You MUST keep your milk as long as possible! You know how unpredictable the Japs are about sending supplies! You'll get used to the feeding, it will get easier, I know it will. Belle used to say.."

"All very well for you, Nanny!" Sandra cut in. "You don't know what it's like, always smelling of stale milk, and dreading the next feed. And I'm absolutely hamstrung.. can't go out for an afternoon, or have a decent night's sleep!" She started to cry, and Pamela immediately put an arm round her sympathetically.

Hilary could no longer hold back her anger and disgust. "I think it's time you stopped feeling sorry for yourself, Sandra!" she said. "You seem to think no one has worries and discomforts but yourself - and you're putting too much on to Pam."

"I suppose she's been complaining to you!" Sandra shouted through her tears.

"Of course she hasn't, but I've got eyes in my head, and I see you're using her as your whipping boy because you don't know how else to cope without amahs running round you as they used to. Pam looks really ill."

"And it's my fault, is it? She doesn't have to help if she doesn't want to!"

"You're a spoilt little madam!" Hilary stared coldly at her. "You always were, and you always will be. And I'm not staying in this room to see you making a lackey of Pam: I'm moving out of here."

"Moving out?" Pamela's jaw dropped.

"Going to live in the Science Block, with the V.A.D.s."

"But we kept this space for you! I just longed, prayed, for you to come. You can't go.. you can't! "Pamela collapsed on her bed in helpless tears.

"Sorry Pam, I don't like leaving you, but I can't put up with Lady Bloody Sandra here and her squealing infant." She was already pulling her suitcase out from beneath the bed, and reaching for her possessions on the window sill.

"I can't bear for you to go," Pamela moaned.

"Listen!" Sandra banged the door closed and stood in front of it. "Listen Hilary, I know I'm a trial, and so is the baby: Pam has been absolutely wonderful, looking after us, and I won't have you upsetting her like this! Yes, I'm all the things you called me, but she's always been loyal. You can see how devastated she would be if you left, so let's admit - you and I - that we're not each other's kind of people, and, God help us, try to get on for Pam's sake. Please, please, stay!"

The sight of the dawning of hope on Pamela's tearstained face was too much for Hilary. She pushed the suitcase back under the bed with her foot.

Within twenty-four hours she was regretting her compassion. Despite Sandra's obvious efforts to please, the atmosphere became explosive. There seemed no way of preventing Pamela from bearing the brunt of the chores except by undertaking them herself - and this she had no intention of doing on a long-term basis. She could only accept her living situation by spending as little time as possible in the room, yet Pamela's worn face was a constant reproach every time she returned.

"Don't you ever get time to yourself?" she asked in exasperation on coming home after a glorious afternoon at the beach with her fellow nurses, and finding Pamela watching over the sleeping child while Sandra was out visiting. "We've never had a chance for a proper conversation since I came."

"As soon as Melly's more settled, things will be easier," Pamela assured her. "Guess what, we've been promised a pram! Someone's child has grown out of it so it's going to be passed to us."

"To Sandra, not to you!"

"She's the nearest family connection I've had in Stanley until you came, Hil. We've stuck together, we're like sisters really; we don't have to be polite to each other all the time."

Seeing how her indignation had hurt Pamela, Hilary went on more gently "What worries me is how much more of this you can take without having a breakdown, when you'd be no use to anyone. I can help you with the queuing, but I'm damned if I'm going to babysit! You should be out in the fresh air, relaxing and mixing with other people, making the most of this enforced break from the office. Who knows, it may not last much longer, and then you'll be back at work again in Hong Kong - and you certainly won't be fit to hold down a job in your present state."

Pamela was not Hilary's only worry. She frequently called on Rosemary, who had become more and more taciturn and now barely acknowledged her appearance. Attempts by other nursing colleagues to coax her out of her room for picnics met with no success.

Hilary found it increasingly embarrassing, trying to make conversation day after day under the eye of an irritable and worried Mrs. Horne. Three days of heavy rain gave her the excuse to stay away from the Indian Quarters. Although it was a relief to stand in the rain and feel its coolness after the oppressive heat, wet clothes soon became a problem. Few internees had macintoshes. Precious shoes became too sodden to wear; it was easier to walk barefoot, despite the unpleasant squelching of mud between the toes.

On the fourth morning the rain petered out, the sun shone, and window sills and verandahs were lined with misshapen shoes laid out to dry. Limp wet garments which had been draped about the rooms for the past few days were hung out of the windows.

"I'd give anything for a swim this afternoon," moaned Sandra. "We could take Melly with us."

"She'd get sunstroke," said Hilary bluntly.

"We could take it in turns holding something over her to shade her!" Pamela's face lit up with delight at the prospect of an afternoon's swimming.

"It doesn't sound at all practical to me," Hilary said as tactfully as she could. "The path down to the beach is steep and rocky and twisty, hard enough on one's own, without carrying a little baby.

"We'll manage somehow, between us," Sandra maintained.

"I'm afraid Hilary's right," Pamela looked quite deflated. "It wouldn't be safe to take Melly there. Look Sandra, why don't you and Hilary go for a short swim and I'll stay here with Melly."

Sandra's face shone, but Hilary was guiltily aware of Pamela's great disappointment; her conscience told her she should be the one to stay with the child and release Pamela, but she could not face spending a hot afternoon in the room with a fretful baby."

Half an hour later the long-promised pram arrived and she made a quick decision. "Why don't you leave Melly with me this afternoon, you two? I'll take her for a walk round the block in the pram for an hour."

"Would you really do that?" Sandra's expression was a mixture of hope, disbelief, and a little shame.

"I will today; won't make a habit of it, mind you!"

This sacrifice of her time and principles was amply repaid by the euphoria in the room as Melly was prepared for her outing, and Pamela and Sandra set off for the beach.

"Keep your fingers crossed that the Japs won't suddenly call off swimming for today!" Pamela called gaily over her shoulder.

"Mind you're back well before the infant's next feed is due, Sandra - there's nothing I can do for her," Hilary grinned, carried away by her own gesture of goodwill.

She had intended to limit her walk to the level perimeter of the Married Quarters, but found herself deriving unexpected satisfaction from the outing. Complete strangers stopped to look the baby, wanted to know her name and age and cooed over her. Casual acquaintances joked about the suddenness of her motherhood. Encouraged by Melly's ready acceptance of this new experience, she pushed the pram down the path to the Indian Quarters, where she spotted Mrs. Horne on the verandah, arms folded on the parapet.

"Do please come in!" Mrs. Horne beckoned urgently, leaning over the parapet to whisper as Hilary approached: "I can't do anything at all with Rosemary. She won't even eat now. Oh.. who's this in the pram, what a lovely baby!"

"My friend's child." Hilary manoeuvred the pram up the step and into the flat. Melly registered her objection to the change of motion by whimpering. Joggling the pram up and down to pacify her, Hilary poked her head into the room where Rosemary sat on her bed, her back slouched against the wall, shoulders hunched up to her ears.

"Hi there Rosie! Glad to see you weren't washed away in all that rain!"

"Say hello to Hilary," her mother urged. "She's bothered to come to see you.. and look what's she's brought!"

"My friend Sandra's baby!" Hilary spoke loudly to try to get through the dull-eyed stare. "You remember Sandra Lamb who came to our hospital at the end of the war? The baby's called Melissa, Melly for short."

The whimpers turned to full-scale yells.

"You haven't touched your food!" Mrs. Horne's voice was a mixture of despair and anger. "You can't keep on like this. Hilary, tell her she must eat!"

"What's wrong with the baby?" Rosemary's light voice interrupted as she got up and peered into the pram.

"She's just upset. She's got prickly heat."

"Can I pick her up? I'm used to babies, aren't I, Mummy?"

"She certainly is," Mrs. Horne said eagerly. "Back in Toronto she always looked after our neighbours' kids in the school holidays. She's very good with babies."

"I can see that." Hilary stood quite still and watched Rosemary's face become human and animated again as she carefully lifted Melly out of the pram, folded her gently against her own body so that the child's head lay across her shoulder; then she swayed almost imperceptibly back and forth, humming softly and patting the baby's back until the staccato cries diminished to whimpers, and the whimpers stopped altogether as the eyelids drooped.

The summer was beginning to wane, the days hot and glorious and the early mornings and evenings pleasantly cool. Hilary's days were as full as when she had been working in the Military Hospital, with queuing, clothes washing and socialising, as well as doing two voluntary shifts a week in the camp hospital.

Conditions in the room were vastly improved, for Sandra had weaned the baby and Rosemary had appointed herself full-time nursemaid. She arrived from the Indian Quarters every morning after the curfew was lifted and took complete charge of Melly. When the baby was asleep, she busied herself in the bathroom with the current load of napkins, trilling 'Umbrella Man' and other popular songs. Only at night was Sandra reminded of her motherhood, when Melly awoke and missed Rosemary's cooing ministrations and yelled crossly.

With time to enter more into what social life the camp offered, Pamela was a different person - even more so when her office colleague Jenny Bennett arrived in Stanley with her mother and younger brothers. Privately, Hilary considered Jenny too young and frivolous a friend for Pamela and found her rather a pest, forever appearing in the room with some new outrageous rumour; but Pamela seemed to enjoy the obvious respect Jenny had for her - and every little pleasure in camp life was a bonus.

PART 8

Late 1942 - Mid 1943

OCTOBER

Despite constant reports of Japan's victories wherever her armies attacked, optimism for release was continually voiced in Stanley. Every one lived in hopes of speedy liberation.

"It won't be long now!"

"We'll be out by Christmas!"

"Churchill said it will be over soon!"

They were too cut off from the outside world to guess how this could be accomplished, but it was essential to survival to hope.

This complete lack of communication - even with relatives and friends in the men's prisoner of war camps only twenty miles away - was one of the worst hardships. Six weeks after the V.A.D.s came to Stanley, this situation suddenly changed: a number of women received money from prisoners of war in Kowloon. There were no accompanying letters, and the amounts sent were very small, but the principal pleasure came from seeing one's man's name on an official sheet as sender, thus knowing he was still alive; and the knowledge that one's signature of receipt would be a comfort to the man when it was sent back to Kowloon. Hilary received five yen from Roddy and Pamela five yen from Keith; they were touched and grateful, knowing that the men could ill afford to part with any of the tiny allowance the Japanese allowed to military prisoners.

Soon after came a further concession - a blank post card was issued to every internee to send to a chosen relative or friend. As messages were restricted to twenty-five words, there was much pencil chewing about what to put, especially as criticism of camp life was out of the question.

"We'll all be free by the time my parents get this," said Pamela, trying to fit in news of Hilary for transmission to HER parents since Hilary was sending her card to Roddy.

The euphoria of these concessions did not last long; two women were notified that their husbands in Shamshuipo Camp had died of diphtheria; it was whispered that an epidemic of the disease was sweeping through all the men's camps. Now the occasional remittances took on even greater significance as proof that the senders were still alive - especially as no replies came to the post cards sent to Kowloon.

"Can we borrow Melly for our Nativity Play?" asked Jenny, bursting into the room one morning.

"Nativity Play! We won't be here at Christmas!" Sandra laughed scornfully.

"The Fathers think so," said Jenny. Two American Maryknoll priests had chosen to refuse repatriation to stay in camp to minister to their flock. "They're starting rehearsals next week. I'm going to be the inn-keeper's wife. Melly would be perfect for the Baby, can we have her?"

"She'll be six months old by Christmas," Pamela smiled. "She'll be too old."

"It won't matter, you do agree, don't you Mrs. Lamb?"

"I suppose so," Sandra shrugged. "If we're still here by Christmas I won't care what happens."

"Thanks a million, I'll go and tell Father." Jenny reached the door then turned back. "Oh, have you heard the latest? The Japs are sending the men from Shamshuipo to Japan." Seeing Hilary's face, she added quickly, "It's only a rumour - there may be nothing in it."

Hilary, usually so stoical, broke down. "Off to the unknown," she wept. "We'll never see them again."

Sandra wept too. "It must mean the war's going to last for years and years!"

The long working day was over. Roddy tipped his closely-shaven head back to feel the benefit of the cool trickle of water from the Heath-Robinson shower on the whole of his naked sunburnt body, then dried himself on a small threadbare piece of towel, anticipating the moment he had looked forward to all day - the evening meal and a few hours of rest and tranquillity. Only the prospect of what was to come kept him and his fellow prisoners going during the hours of hard manual labour under the Japanese, digging and shovelling earth to extend the airfield at Kai Tak Airport.

He wrung out his tattered shorts on which he had been standing in the shower, then smoothed them into shape and folded them neatly. From a nail outside the shower stall he took his gray fandooshi and tied it on. Now standard uniform in the camp, this was the only clothing provided by the Japanese - an oblong napkin secured round the waist with ties which served as both underwear and shorts.

He walked barefoot across the broad parade ground to his barracks which were occupied by some eight hundred Volunteers and several small regular fighting units. Two adjoining barracks, home to three thousand British Army prisoners of war, and a smaller block which now served as a hospital, made up Shamshuipo Camp. These buildings had been looted at the end of the fighting: the new occupants had had to replace doors and repair roofs and walls with whatever debris was available.

He waved to Ricky and Jack Bellario, who were squatting on the steps outside their block, patiently debugging the straw paliasse they shared. The common experience in Shamshuipo had renewed his boyhood acquaintance with them and they often reminisced about escapades on the hillside above Dragon Terrace.

The members of his own little gang sat outside their barracks, bare legs stretched in front of them, backs supported by the wall: Greg, wearing a home-made eyeshade; Douglas and Hugh. Most of the prisoners belonged to some gang within which fierce loyalty obtained; loners were more likely to drift into apathy, cease the struggle for existence and die.

"Friday special tonight!" Greg squinted up at Roddy. whose meal he had collected earlier. "Guess what? Rice and slops!"

"What's new?" Roddy lowered himself on to the hard ground, wincing as he tried to make his bony frame comfortable, and took his enamel plate of rice and stew. He tried to eat slowly because someone had said it was more beneficial that way; with more signs of malnutrition developing every week, it was best to adopt any advice which might help.

"Three more went today," said Douglas moodily; his old bounce had long since vanished.

"Any one we know?"

"A Royal Scot, a Middlesex and one of the old boys from the Naval Dockyard."

"All dip. cases?"

Greg nodded. Dysentery had been taking its toll since the early days, but the diphtheria epidemic was far more extensive, and few victims survived because so little serum was available. It was common knowledge that only those rated strong enough to have a chance of survival would receive the precious serum. This was one of the reasons why those sent on work parties accepted the hard work with equanimity - they could spend long hours out of the disease-ridden camp.

Later, they sat watching the last of the day's funerals pass by, the rough coffin bumping on the two-wheeled hand-cart which usually carried the daily food rations - and the brimming latrine buckets. Friends and colleagues followed in silence. In earlier months, the remnants of one of the regimental bands used to play at each funeral; but when the death rate accelerated and the plaintive bugles were heard so often each day, the British officers stopped the practice which was emphasising mortality and lowering morale.

"Look at that s...!" Douglas pointed to a Japanese soldier following respectfully in the procession bearing a small bunch of nasturtiums. "You'd never believe he's the same who beat up John Carron this morning for signalling to his wife! - Kicked him, butted him with his rifle.. only stopped short of finishing him off because one of his officers came round the corner."

John Carron, like a number of other prisoners, was married to a Chinese girl who was not interned. On certain days the Japanese allowed friends and relations to stand within fifty yards of the camp boundary, and the men searched for familiar faces. The waiting women took advantage of any momentary distraction to run closer to the wire and toss over a parcel of food. Some guards turned a blind eye to this; others picked on a particular woman and clubbed her.

"Dusty Philo's girl-friend got it today too," Hugh reported. "Was pushed over and pummelled. Dusty went mad.. we had to sit on him to keep him under control."

"She's got guts, that girl!" Douglas added. "Crawled away from the guard, kow-towing madly; she was back an hour later, further along the fence, beaming and waving, and managed to throw Dusty a small parcel!"

"Times like these, I wish I had a Chinese girl-friend," sighed Greg.

That night, as he and Roddy sat side by side on the long sleeping platform taking it in turns to puff at a skinny cigarette made of butt ends, he said "Didn't mean that.. about wishing I had a Chinese popsy.. I'd give anything.. everything.. if your sister was my girl-friend."

"Thought that was all over long ago."

"It had to be, she wouldn't be serious. She'd be even less interested now."

The poor diet had affected his good eye, which had lost vision in a way that obliterated the view immediately in front of him, although he had sight on either side of the centre point. There were several such cases, the doctors called it "central blindness" and were working hard to find treatment.

"It won't last," Roddy said as heartily as he could, for none of the victims believed the doctors' assurances that the condition was only temporary. He knew Greg's days were much more burdensome than his; bad sight kept him from the outside work so he was given the worst chore of all - membership of a gang which collected the full latrine buckets and trundled them, splashing and odorous, daily through the camp to the pier beyond the wire where they emptied them into the sea.

"What wouldn't I give for half an hour's swim at Big Wave!" sighed Greg. "Imagine pelting down the beach, and plunging into that fresh sparkling water.. seems like a dream when you smell that green scum by the pier."

"I'm thinking about a pint of iced lager," sighed Hugh. "I'd give my all for just one pint of iced lager!"

For the rest of the evening they fantasised about simple delights of the past. Strangely, sex didn't come into this; here, all energies were devoted to the business of survival, in comparison with which the urges of the flesh were minimal.

Lying hot and sleepless on the hard bed at night, scratching bug and mosquito bites and waving away flies, Roddy's thoughts, as usual, turned to Hilary. In his mind's eye he always saw her in her nurse's uniform, its very whiteness a balm to the dreary life in camp, the veil giving her loved features a sanctity which comforted him. During the battle he had not expected to survive. Now she was safe in Stanley and he had seen her familiar signature on the pay-sheet acknowledging receipt of the money he'd sent her, he felt confident they would meet again soon and start life together.

In the meantime the present had to be endured, and within the limits imposed by the Japanese - limits which they had however learned were open to variation without notice - a bearable routine had emerged. Despite the hard labour on the airfield, he welcomed the break from the monotony of camp life. There was no possibility of escaping on the way to Kai Tak - they were closely guarded by Japanese with rifles and bayonets at the ready. Occasionally one of the Chinese coolies working alongside the prisoners gave them a cigarette or morsel of food. Those men with Chinese or Portuguese wives or girl-friends had the bonus of seeing them at closer quarters than the guards in the camp allowed: these ladies showed stoical patience and devotion, lurking all day near the work site in the hope that their men would be able to come within speaking distance.

The men left in camp cut and cleaned vegetables, cooked rice and the communal stew in makeshift kitchens; swept and cleaned gutters and water channels to prevent them from becoming mosquito breeding areas. Also, much time was devoted to collating information from every one who could contribute in order to compile lists of the battle casualties. Even now the fate of hundreds were in doubt. Known military deaths totalled over one thousand out of a garrison of ten thousand five hundred; some British and Allied civilians had also been killed, and unknown hundreds of Chinese civilians in the bombing and shelling.

Despite the great odds against success, there had been several attempts to escape from the camp. With the aid of Chinese guerillas, two groups succeeded in getting to Chungking, others to India, their achievements causing the Japanese to withhold "privileges" in the camp for months thereafter. Yet, despite the shock and rigours of incarceration following bloody fighting, and the hardships deliberately laid upon them, most men settled down to a bearable life. Classes on a wide variety of subjects were set up; concerts and other entertainments organised.

All this was suddenly threatened when it was announced that one thousand prisoners were to be sent to Japan to work in coal mines and factories. There was dismay and despair; no one wanted to be transported to a strange enemy country, perhaps to be lost, never to return or be accounted for. But there was never a choice; one thousand troops were selected, medically examined, photographed, inoculated and provided with essentials they had lacked since imprisonment - boots, canvas shoes, new clothes and mess tin. They were marched out of the camp early one morning to the music of the combined regimental bands.

"Lucky devils, off on a cruise!" called those watching them go by.

"Think of us when you're lying back in your deck chairs, drinking whisky sodas!" someone yelled.

Roddy watched them file through the camp gates with guilty relief that he was not amongst them; he dreaded having to leave Hong Kong because he would be so far from Hilary. The departees included several of his office colleagues and fellow Volunteers all young and among the healthiest; he had feared he would be added to the draft, for substitutes were being arranged up to the last moment when some of those detailed fell ill with malaria.

A few weeks later a rumour circulated that a further draft to Japan was being compiled. Roddy made sure he worked well enough on his labour party to be kept there, not only on his own account but also for Greg's sake: it was unlikely that Greg would be sent on a work draft and he depended so much on Roddy. It was a great effort to get up at half past four every morning when the Japanese corporal clumped through the barracks calling for the workers. At the end of the day he had no energy left for the camp entertainments.

His added endeavours were all in vain: one evening he returned from work to find the camp buzzing with the news that the list of the next draft for Japan was posted: not only was his name on it, but also Hugh's, Doug's and Greg's: poor health was no longer a reason for exclusion.

"Prisoners of war going to Japan!" Through a timid interpreter, the Japanese Commandant addressed the eighteen hundred men lined up before him on the parade ground. "His August Majesty the Emperor has spared your miserable lives, for which in return you must work hard for the benefit of the South East Asia Co-Prosperity Sphere!"

"Not bloody likely," went a whispered comment from the ranks wearing their newly-issued clothes. To cheers and waves from those left behind, they marched out of the camp gates towards the pier.

Embarkation on to lighters was slow because first each prisoner had to be sprayed with disinfectant by Japanese orderlies wearing white smocks and cloth masks. This indignity was met with much swearing, protest, and a chorus of imitations of bleating sheep.

"If that's the ship, she's not very big, is she?" Roddy was inspecting the weary-looking vessel of some seven thousand tons they were approaching; its dark hull had few portholes and little superstructure; fore and aft protruded a four inch gun.

" 'Lisbon Maru'" Hugh read out. "Where the hell are they going to put us all in that tub?"

They soon found out. The three holds had been very roughly converted into layered troop decks, with cubicles about twelve feet square. Twenty men were allotted to each cubicle which contained nothing but a raised planked platform to serve as a communal bed. Roddy, Greg, Hugh and Douglas contrived to keep together and ended up in on the second level of the middle hold, their companions mainly Royal Scots.

There was a barrel of drinking water on each level. Ablutions were on the main deck of the ship, reached by a perpendicular ladder up the side of the hold; they consisted of a single water tap and makeshift latrines suspended over the sides of the ship.

A group of late arrivals in the hold reported the embarkation of about six hundred Japanese troops on to the upper decks. "They look as jam-packed as we are," some one observed.

The ship sailed later that afternoon. The senior officer in the middle hold, Captain Rayne, worked his way through all the cubicles, talking to the men and encouraging them to make the best of their difficult conditions. "The Japs have promised we'll all be allowed on the upper deck in groups for exercise in rotation," he said.

Rice and mush was handed out - at least stomachs were full as the men tried to settle down for the night. Those suffering from electric feet and beri-beri could find little comfort from the communal beds, where no one had room to turn over without butting his neighbour. Diarrhoea which afflicted almost everyone, caused frequent disturbances as the victim hurried up the vertical ladder to plead permission from the guards at the top to visit the latrines - and didn't always get there in time.

Yet within forty-eight hours many of the men began to benefit from the journey; the food was better than camp rations; they were not required to work, and the regular exercise sessions on deck in the fresh sea breeze brought colour to their cheeks. These breaks sometimes provided an opportunity for men to speak to friends from the other holds; once Roddy's time on deck coincided with that of the Bellario boys from the stern hold, and they spent an hilarious half-hour recalling frog-races behind Dragon Terrace. In the evenings some men played cards beneath the dim lights in bulkhead mountings, others visited acquaintances on other levels, or took part in snap oral quizzes and sing-songs.

It was while the prisoners stood in line in their cubicles for roll call on the third morning that a muffled explosion shook the ship; the lights flickered then went out. "Torpedo!" yelled appalled voices. The ship's guns began firing. Daylight was suddenly extinquished as the Japanese on deck pulled heavy tarpaulins across the hatches. Every man made for the stairways.

"Keep with me!" Roddy grabbed Greg's arm. "Never mind if we don't get out with the first lot." Men tried to push past them, some with life-jackets which effectively blocked the way for all. Overhead, running feet and frenzied commands barked in staccato Japanese increased the panic below.

"ORDER!" The roar came from Captain Rayne. His voice, hoarse as he strove to be heard, gave brief reasoned instructions: he did not think the ship likely to sink; every one must stay calm and avoid panic and conjecture and await orders. He then climbed to the top step of the ladder and called repeatedly for ventilation.

The ship began to list slightly, but the men sat obediently on their sleeping places. Some burrowed in their knapsacks, turning out items not essential to survival. Roddy took out his most treasured possession the little sewing-case Hilary had given him - and, using the safetypin, secured it to the inside of his underpants.

The 'Lisbon Maru's' engines had stopped, and the noise of a ship approaching could be heard; from the increased concentration of footsteps and buzz of Japanese voices, it was deduced that the Japanese troops were being transferred to the other ship. The prisoners readied themselves for their turn, but when it was heard moving off, a wave of panic swept the hold. Horror, fear and fury that they were to be left to their fate in the listing ship threatened the tight discipline which had so far held. When they heard wooden hatch covers being battened down over the tarpaulin, howls of naked terror rent the air; only the authoritative and calm voice of Captain Rayne maintained order.

It was early evening, twelve hours since the ship had been hit. The list had very gradually increased, the air was foetid, the heat stifling, and the men breathing raspily. Every time one of the officers climbed to the top of the ladder and pleaded for help, the guards shouted warnings.

"Any hope of trying to break out, do you think?" murmured Douglas. "Can't stand this much longer."

"They'd shoot.. but some would survive." Roddy shrugged. "But anything would be worth trying.. better than dying like this."

Outside, something was happening: there was a violent jerk, then the sound of water lapping against the ship's sides.

"We're moving, we're under tow!" said Captain Rayne.

Very slowly, the ship crept along, but not for long: there was a sudden crack - unmistakeably the parting of the tow-line, then a whine and a ping as the broken cable whipped back across the hull.

The ship had stopped again, but the list was more marked. There were fearful mutterings among the men, while a padre moved quietly among them, trying to calm them.

Roddy had found his own way to hold on to his sanity: he was writing a letter to Hilary in his head: 'You wouldn't believe it if you could see Greg, and Hugh and Doug and yours truly, lying side by side on boards with sixteen others. We're boiling hot because there's no ventilation. We've not had a thing to eat since last night; the Japs did send us down some water this afternoon but now the casks are empty.. well no, not exactly: you see, we're not allowed out of the hold now so can't use the latrines on deck. (After all your nursing experience, I can talk to you about these things.) So we are using the water barrels instead. It's unbelievably squalid, and yet somehow we are accepting our lot as something we just have to put up with to show those Japs they can't get us down. Dearest Hilary, how much time we've wasted in the past three years! How I long to turn the clock back! My darling, I pray you are living in better conditions than I am at the moment - this is one time when I won't say "Wish you were here!" 'Something wonderful happened just now. We were all lying quietly like we've been advised to, listening to every creak and slosh of water, when some one began to play a mouth organ; hearing 'Old Folks at Home' gave us a real dose of nostalgia, I can tell you. It made me sad yet I wanted to listen; it was somehow heartening.. reminding us that there IS another kind of life than the one we're living on this tub. The player was soon stopped though, because too many men were getting upset.

'Here I am again, darling. Actually I must have slept a bit - no idea how long because I can't read my watch in this blackness. Some of my neighbours are moaning and calling for the padre. The M.O. is doing what he can to help some men who seem to be having heart attacks. Every one is awake now, gasping for air and water. Food doesn't matter; I'm too het up about how we are going to get out of this hell to think of eating. Most of us are stripped down to underpants, and this so-called bed is slimy with our sweat. The smell from our waste matter is everywhere. People are getting more desperate and agitated. I'm only sustained by what really seem impossible hopes and wishful thinking. Captain Rayne has just told us to keep totally quiet because he can hear tapping on the bulkhead between our hold and the stern one; apparently they are getting water in there, and have been pumping but can't make much headway because the men on the pumps keep fainting through lack of air. He is now contacting the bow hold the same way. (All the holds are enclosed just as we are.) We keep slipping to the end of our bed because of the list.

Fantastic fellow, our Captain. He's up that vertical ladder again, still trying to persuade the guards to open up the hatches. The air here is so foul that I wonder we're not all gassed. Now two more officers have gone up the ladder, and we can hear them banging away with bars and bits of wood, trying to force the hatches open. Hugh says one of them has a knife.'

Even Hilary was forgotten when the officers finally managed to cut through the tarpaulin and force up one of the hatch timbers, so throwing a shaft of sunlight into the hold. They struggled through the gap on to the deck and were met by machine-gun fire; one of the officers was killed but this didn't stop other men scrambling out after them.

Captain Rayne called down "We've silenced the guards: every one out! The ship's on a sandbank but her back is broken and she'll go down any minute. There's land about four miles away; keep calm: steady does it!"

Roddy pushed Greg in front of him as they reached the ladder; they were halfway up when the ship gave a tremendous lurch, and water began to pour through the hatch. Some men were washed off the ladder and could be heard struggling in the bottom of the rapidly filling hold. It was a great struggle to hang on to the rungs with gouts of sea water pouring over them.

"Nearly there" grunted Greg, and then they were both sprawled on the sharp-angled deck, blinded at first in the brilliant sunshine. The only Japanese in sight were lying about the deck, bloodied and still. The ship's stern was completely submerged, the bows still clear of the water.

Some men were rapidly tying together pieces of timber to form make-shift rafts, but Greg and Roddy decided to jump from the ship immediately; just as they did so some one above tossed out a wooden locker which caught Roddy's back, knocking the wind out of his body; he managed to grasp the box while he gradually got his breath back.

"You O.K.?" Greg surfaced nearby.

"Back's numb.. and my legs. That bloody locker... anyway, I'm keeping it now, don't know what's happened to the blighter who threw it over."

Hundreds of men were dropping into the water; some had life-jackets, others held on to debris and tried to propel themselves away from the dying ship. A few minutes later the bow arched towards the sky and sank quickly.

"God!" Roddy quickly steered his mind away from the fate of the Bellario boys and hundreds of others trapped in the stern hold, and concentrated on survival. He could see high land in the distance. Several small Japanese naval ships were moving slowly round the disaster area, and the heads of swimmers were bobbing towards them.

"Let's go!" called Greg, striking out strongly towards the ships.

"I can't Greg, my legs won't work properly: I can't kick."

Greg turned back at once and grabbed the box. "Then we'll both hold on," he said, "and I'll do all the kicking; we must keep going though, this current's fierce."

There were some two hundred yards away from the nearest boat when the first prisoners reached it - and were met with deliberate small arms fire.

"They're picking everyone off!" yelled Roddy. Greg swiftly changed direction to escape the continuing rifle fire. All round them other survivors clung to planks, baskets, broken deck rails - any kind of debris that provided a hand-hold; among them was an officer who called out encouragement: "We should fetch up on the island you can see due west. I think it's Sing Pang, off the coast of Chekiang - it's a rocky coastline, so mind how you land. See you there!"

"How are we doing now, Rod?" Because of his poor eyesight, Greg had to rely on Roddy for directions. "Must be getting fairly near, I think I can hear breakers."

"About another mile." Roddy looked anxiously at the sky; sunset was beginning to form, soon darkness would engulf them. He could just see figures dragging themselves up the rocky incline at the water's edge. He cursed his useless legs as Greg panted with the continual kicking.

They were still some way from the shore when darkness fell, the current continually impeding progress. Even when they could feel land beneath their feet, they were thrown backwards and forwards on the rocks before they managed to haul themselves out of the water. Bruised and bleeding, they lay panting against the cliffs with dozens of others, wondering how they could ever climb these sheer heights.

Life was beginning to return to Roddy's back and legs, but with excruciating pain. When the survivors around him talked about climbing up the cliffs in the morning he knew he would be unable to go with them.

"Look, lights! Coming round the headland!" some one shouted. "Lots of them.. coming this way!"

For twenty minutes they watched the little lights coming nearer; any rescuers were welcome, even Japanese ships; they almost wept with joy when they saw the little Chinese fishing fleet approaching.

'You won't believe where I am now, darling: in Shanghai! After getting off the ship alive, and being rescued by Chinese fishermen, we thought it was too good to be true! They were so marvellous to us. When they saw I couldn't walk they carried me from the sampan to their village on an old door. The villagers gave us hot soup and rice and some of their clothes - remember most of us were only clad in our underpants. We slept on the ground beneath trees and bushes, about a hundred of us, covered by tattered covers lent by our generous rescuers. Even with all my aches and pains, I felt I was in Heaven. What a sight we all looked when we saw each other in daylight next morning, decked out in Chinese black loose trousers and thin jackets; we were dirty and red-eyed, and scratched and bruised. Kept seeing more and more familiar faces, incredible that so many were saved. Met up with Hugh, but I'm afraid Doug is lost, Hugh saw him cop it when the Japs fired on them swimming up to the patrol boats when the L.M. went down. Ironic thing is that, according to some of the other blokes I've spoken to, later on that day these same boats went round and picked up men and looked after them really well. 'After an alfresco breakfast of rice, dried fish and berries, the women cleaned us up and generally spoiled us .. then alas, later that day a Jap launch appeared in the bay; their men came and rounded us all up, and there we were, prisoners again! They made us give back the Chinese clothes and took us on board. Strange people, they were gentle with me and I was taken below to a tiny sick bay and well looked after. Every prisoner was given a mug of hot cocoa with milk powder, boy it tasted like nectar! We were even given some cigarettes, and our nakedness covered by odds and ends of Japanese uniforms. I inherited a thin pair of white naval trousers and a warm sailor top. I was jolly grateful for them because it was damn cold when we were off-loaded here and handed over to the Military on the docks. No one offered to carry me now - I had to get along as best I could with Greg on one side and Hugh on the other. It was right back to the old routine at Shamshuipo - face-slapping, barked orders etc. Some of our men brought in on other boats arrived starkers! We clothed guys have parted with anything we can spare - my white slacks now adorn an Artillery Officer. None of us had shoes or socks. All our lovely new gear went down with the L.M. (but I still have your sewing kit, safety-pinned to my undies.) We are guarded by a cordon of Japs with fixed bayonets... what threat they think we could be to them in our parlous state, God only knows. When they had kicked and slapped us into line to their satisfaction, we marched... correction, shambled, out of the dockyard gates, along a street lined by staring Chinese. A few jeered but most kept their faces blank; we felt they were sympathetic but dared not show it. We eventually fetched up at another dock where, glory be, lots more of our men from the L.M. were penned.. people I'd thought had gone down with her: Jack Bellario was there, but not his brother or his brother-in-law Antony.

'We've been kept beside this dock, without cover, for two days now, waiting for a ship to take us to Japan. This morning one of our surgeons argued with the Japs to allow the sick and unfit to be taken to some shelter for treatment; again and again he was slapped down and humiliated, but persevered with such patience and politeness.. we all wanted to clap him, but of course dared not in case it prejudiced the Japs against him while he was still trying to get something out of them. Don't know what the date is, we've completely lost count of the days in all the confusion and trauma. I don't even know the time, the hands of my watch are frozen at twenty past nine, when I hit the China Sea. Some of the men still have watches that are working, though - remember that famous ad. in the jeweller's window in the Gloucester Arcade with a Rolex Oyster sitting in a glass of water ticking away? Well, that ad. told no lie. We got one really good meal today, soup thick with onions and potatoes and turnips.. needed it, too, it's windy and so cold.

Luckily there's quite a lot of rubbish lying around on the dockside (it's out of bounds to the Chinese population else it would have been looted months ago), old crates - boxes and cartons, and we guys have improvised little dens and sleep in them, bundled together for warmth. Reminds me of the street sleepers we used to step over (and take so much for granted) in Hong Kong - a thousand years ago, it seems. 'Now I must try to get some sleep in the bit of cardboard carton I'm sharing with Greg and two other men.. I wish we had the other half, then my feet wouldn't be so freezing. Goodnight, dearest; telling you all this helps to keep my mind on the future: makes me realise I can put up with anything as long as you and I have each other.'

DECEMBER

Danny patted his bow tie into place and took one last look in the mirror. The electricity had failed again; this was Macau, the only neutral territory in the Far East - theoretically free, but blockaded by the Japanese on sea and land, its utilities limping along with broken-down and irreplaceable plant. In the candle light, he could see his shadowy reflection: the borrowed dress suit, the jacket shorter than he would have liked; in the background, the conglomeration of furniture, boxes and suitcases crowded in the gloom. Only his mother's white face showed clearly, as she sat in a rattan chair behind him.

"You look fine, son," she said, as he tugged at the jacket hem. "You should be leaving, it's almost half-past." She gave a shiver, and he brought the crochetted cover from the large bed in the corner and draped it across her shoulders. The electricity had been off for half an hour now, and the December cold was seeping into the high-ceilinged room.

The old marble clock on the mantelpiece struck a sepulchral note, muffled by age.

"Best go," his mother urged.

Slowly he pushed the catches home on his violin case, then shouldered into an ancient navy blue overcoat.

"I shall be all right, you know," she gently reproved his obvious reluctance to leave. "There are seventeen other people in this house, not counting the servants. I still have a tongue in my head."

He shrugged his shoulders, acknowledging his overanxiety, and bent to kiss her. A light tap on the door chased the frown from his forehead.

"I'm so sorry I'm late." Celeste, in a dark cotton skirt and woollen jumper, looked flustered. "Those imps of Marie's, they just wanted to play in the bath for ever; the amahs couldn't get them out. Off you go, Danny!"

He gave Celeste a quick hug, still hurt by the sad eyes and the thin haggard face. She had never recovered from her dreadful experience at the hands of the Japanese; it had been a nightmare for her family too, as she had steadfastly refused emergency treatment to prevent conception, insisting that birth prevention was against God's law. It was a mercy no pregnancy resulted, but her spirit was so crushed that she had abandoned any idea of becoming a nun because she felt unworthy, and no priest could convince her otherwise.

He called out his goodbyes to other members of the Bellario family as he went down the staircase through the spacious hall which had become the dining-room since the number of occupants had swelled to more than four times above normal occupation. After the surrender of Hong Kong, Portuguese, Chinese and Eurasian members of the local Defence Force had the option of returning to their homes and families, or becoming prisoners of war with the British. Jack and Ricky and Antony decided to remain prisoners, thinking they would be regularly fed in camp so would not be a burden on the rest of the family. Danny however chose to throw away his uniform and go home to care for his mother. After the three men were sent to Japan the Bellario family, including Danny and his mother, moved en masse to Macau, where life was less circumscribed than in Japanese administered Hong Kong. The villa had now reached saturation point: Danny had a camp bed in a small basement room with an uncle; Celeste shared his mother's room and bed.

Running down the stone steps flanked on either side by large green glazed pots of white marguerites, he buttoned up his coat against the chill wind. The narrow path leading to the main road was overhung with shrubs and bushes. He pulled his coat tightly round him to avoid thorns or sharp twigs: clothes and material were becoming scarce, and it was important that he kept his garments in good condition, for without a smart appearance he knew he would lose this very part-time job at the hotel which provided his only source of income in Macau.

Despite its neutrality, the Portuguese colony was as affected by the war as if it was a participant. A Japanese gunboat lay out in the bay. The Japanese Consul had a large staff far beyond what was necessary to serve the Japanese residents. Japanese troops and Kempetai (Secret Police) openly paraded the streets, whereas the British official presence was limited to a Consul General and two assistants. Business life was at almost at a standstill, so there was little work for the thousands of refugees from Hong Kong - Portuguese, Eurasians, Indians, Russians and Chinese. Lisbon transmitted money to help support their own nationals, but this was never enough in families such as the Bellarios where numbers had increased so dramatically.

Even if one had the money, the food was not always there to buy because of the blockade. Luxuries and medicines were in shortest supply. The special tablets his mother needed were expensive and hard to find. With them she kept a tenuous hold on life; without them and he lived in fear of the inevitable periods when he could not get them - she drifted into a semi-coma. In two days' time the present supply would run out; tonight's fee would just pay for a fresh lot.

He quickened his pace as he turned on to the main road; here beggars abounded - harmless during the day but a menace at night, especially in the total darkness of a power failure. They brushed against him, chanting their hard-luck stories. Probably most of them were genuinely starving, but he dared not stop to give them a couple of small coins for fear of many more of their kind clustering round him with perhaps sinister intentions.

The hotel was built on a rise overlooking the sea. As he strode up the steps the power supply suddenly returned. A network of feeble lights outlined the narrow streets below, while the hotel glowed, its old-colonial façade irregularly illuminated by the surviving bulbs

Inside, the candles on the dining-room tables were being doused to preserve them for a future emergency. Dinner was already being served to a modest number of cosmopolitan customers, all well-dressed. A mixture of languages echoed - English, Chinese, Russian, Portuguese, French.

Taking his place beside the five-piece orchestra on the rostrum, he felt himself coming to life again. The hours in the Bellario villa were full of anxiety, boredom and uneasiness; anxiety for his mother's health and for Celeste; uneasiness because he could contribute so little to the family coffers, and also because he sensed the Bellarios' resentment that he was free and Jack and Ricky and Antony prisoners. He was even more obsessed with this feeling after the sinking of the 'Lisbon Maru' on which it was believed Ricky and Jack and Antony were passengers.

With his violin firmly under his chin, his bow delicately held in his right hand, Danny could for the evening forget the unhappy daytime existence. As the few couples moved round the dance floor flanked by dimly-lit tables, the old magic of the music took hold of him. He was not required regularly - the Portuguese band was tuneful and adequate, but the occasional addition of a talented young solo violinist made the hotel more competitive with its rivals.

When the dancing was over for the night, he was often too wound up to leave at once, reluctant to leave the make-believe atmosphere for the gloomy reality of his home. With Lexie Savora, the pianist, he played on long after dancers and diners had left. They improvised softly, conveying to each other by a flick of the wrist or a raised eyebrow what to play next. Sometimes their cigarettes burned away in the ash tray on top of the piano when they were carried away by a particular theme.

Afterwards, Lexie always made for the gambling hall attached to the hotel. Sometimes Danny stood beside him in the crowded, smoke-filled room, peering over at the large table, fascinated at witnessing a gambler's run of luck, and wishing he dared risk taking a chance with the money he had just pocketed. Lexie, a widower in his forties seldom won but always hoped. The fever was in his blood, and vicariously Danny was caught up in the thrill.

This was one of Lexie's lucky nights. "Why don't you have a go, Dan?" he urged, shovelling his winnings. "The gods are on our side tonight."

It was very tempting to try and double or quadruple his pay, especially as Christmas was only two weeks away and he had no money to spare for presents.

"Tell you what, I'll stand you a bet!" Lexie was drunk with his success. "Go on, man!" He pushed Danny forward to the table, propelled him into position and made him choose his numbers. "Hurry up, while my luck lasts."

But it didn't last. With a sick heart Danny watched his chips raked away. His self-respect forced him to hand the precious patacas expended to Lexie, who refused them, saying "Use the money to try again, one more time!"

Shamed at the charitable gesture, Danny forced the money on Lexie and quickly shouldered his way out of the room, sick with the knowledge that he had lost half of the fee he had earned that night.

"Why did you let me do it, God?" he muttered to himself as he hurried through the now unlighted streets, past street sleepers, blowing newspapers, dogs scavenging in the gutters; but he knew it wasn't God's fault.

Pamela squatted before the fireplace, heating sausages two at a time in a blackened tin over the tiny fire enclosed in bricks in the grate. A tin of sausages was the choice item in the Red Cross parcels which had arrived in the autumn, and they had saved this especially for breakfast on Christmas Day - a double treat as there was normally no breakfast at all.

Sandra was dressing a squirming Melly; she did up the button on the back of the blue silk dress Pamela had made out of a petticoat just as Hilary returned from the hot water queue.

"There you are madam, all ready for your first Christmas Day!" Sandra sat Melly in her cot. "Now the rest of us can have breakfast and open our presents."

" 'Open' !" Pamela mocked, turning out the last of the sausages. "I can tell you, none of mine are wrapped up . "

They had long since agreed a roster for the use of the only chair; this morning it was Hilary's turn; she sat in state to eat her share of the scorched and broken sausages while the others sat on their beds. There was still tea, sugar and condensed milk from the Red Cross shipment which had saved them from despair and starvation.

Every internee - even babies - had received an identical small carton of goodies: a tin of corned beef, sausages, meat and vegetable stew, margerine, creamed rice, condensed milk; a few sweets, a bar of chocolate and a small bar of soap. A limited amount of bulk food had also come - dried fruit, sugar and tea, which was distributed regularly in small quantities. Even clothes were sent - thick khaki sleeveless jerkins which were converted into skirts, trousers, jackets or slacks according to taste and ability. Pamela had never been busier; her fame as an expert needlewoman spread, as people admired the gored skirt she made for herself, slacks for Sandra and a loose jacket for Hilary; sewing cotton and needles were supplied sparingly by the Camp Welfare Office, the cotton measured out in yards appropriate to the specific job proposed.

This sunny Christmas Day was not really cold enough for thick clothes, but the girls wore their new garments because they WERE new and smart and every one wanted to make the day special. Pamela's present to each of the girls was a set of three hanging pockets made of offcuts of the khaki material. Sandra presented Pamela and Hilary each with a handkerchief - not new, but washed and pressed as flat as possible in perfect folds. Hilary had made tiny calendars carefully printed in pencil on pages torn from her old pocket diary.

A succession of visitors called in with Christmas wishes, the first Rosemary who presented Melly with a rag doll made of bits of old towelling. She was thrilled with Melly's new dress. "The carol singers are going to sing outside the hospital in half an hour," she said, "I'll take her there, the patients on the verandahs will love to see her! I just hope the Japs don't ban the singing at the last minute."

A case of diphtheria in the camp had already frightened the Japanese authorities into postponing all indoor gatherings, church services and concerts.

"Now we can really enjoy Christmas!" Sandra, as usual relaxed once Melly was in some one else's care. "Oh no! Rosie's forgotten to do the nappies.. I hope she remembers when she comes back."

"Maybe she'd like a day off as it's Christmas," said Hilary drily.

Pamela didn't want a row today. "You'd better do them, Sandra," she said persuasively. "Get the job over and done with right now, while I wash the dishes."

Sandra glanced at the greasy pan and plates: they would be difficult to wash at the cold water tap in the kitchen; she obediently picked up the pail of napkins and queued for the bathroom.

Half a dozen V.A.D.s arrived to see Hilary, announcing their approach with a rowdy chorus of 'Good King Wenceslas.' They were on a tour of the camp to look up all their friends, and took her off with them.

Outside in the corridor there were joyful comings and goings as friend greeted friend. Even some of the flat occupants who resented Sandra's high-handedness and Melly's disturbing presence popped their heads into the room and called 'Merry Christmas!'.

Mr. Bridger and two of his clerks came, bringing a small tin of jam for Sandra, and a pair of yellow bootees he had got someone to knit for Melly. A gang of young policemen with whom Sandra had been billeted in the Gloucester Hotel arrived with a great bundle of kindling for the fire, and invited her to join them to visit other friends. She got them to peg out the washed nappies while she brushed her hair; then went off with them

When Pamela was alone she tidied the room and was wiping the window-panes with a damp cloth when yet another visitor knocked on the open door.

"Good morning Miss Doran.. Pamela.." Mr. Gasson stood hesitantly on the threshold. "I just thought I would look in to wish you the compliments of the season, a Happy Christmas to you!"

He refused the chair, choosing to stand with one hand on the door. "I was wondering how you were getting on in these.. unusual circumstances."

He was not wearing his glasses, and she noticed for the first time that his eyes were hazel. "I broke the darned things.. trying to clean them," he explained. She hid a smile, because the whole office used to joke about his habit of continually cleaning his glasses: everyone thought he extended the operation to give himself time to think what to say next. "They were sent into town three weeks ago to be repaired. It's very trying without them, but never mind.. I'm sure you have your own problems, in a room with a little baby: does she disturb you much at night?"

"Not every night now, thank goodness. Either she's improving, or else we're getting used to it; a bit of both, I suppose." They had never had so long a conversation before, and she found herself stammering. He had little to say, yet seemed reluctant to leave, clearing his throat and staring down at the bare floor.

"Are you all right for cash?" he suddenly jerked out. "It's a long time since we had a little handout. I wouldn't like to think.. well, would you accept a small present from me.. a Christmas present?" He took a ten yen note from his jacket pocket and thrust it at her.

"Oh really, Mr. Gasson, I couldn't.." She was touched to the heart at the offer, yet her purse was empty, and would remain so until the next issue of cigarettes which she could sell for profit.

"For Christmas," he repeated, sidling round the door, "and it's Guy, you know.." He was gone before she could protest further.

She felt quite tearful as she put the note safely away, grateful beyond words and still astonished at Mr. Gasson's generosity: now she would be able to buy eggs at next week's canteen!

Jenny flew in soon after; she looked very festive in a red cotton skirt and white blouse, her hair tied back in a short pony tail with a matching red ribbon. "It's a bit off the hem of the skirt!" she explained. "All alone? Merry Christmas! Just dropped in to give you a present." She held out a small bottle of tomato ketchup.

"Something for Melly, too," she added, dropping a brightly-coloured woollen ball into the cot.

"How can you possibly spare food, Jenny?" Pamela shook her shoulders in a gesture of helplessness. "With your large family.. and I've nothing for you."

"Didn't expect you to. My parents decided about the present, you helped us so much with the costumes for the Nativity Play, I shall go mad if the Japs never let us do it - I've never been on the stage before." At the door she paused then added "You wouldn't care to come to Mass in the grotto with me, would you?"

She had intended to go with Hilary and Sandra to the United Church service on the Indian Quarters green; it seemed a less inviting prospect without them; she found herself saying to Jenny "Yes, please, I'd like to come."

The Roman Catholics had chosen to have a separate service in the grotto, a small clearing near the large accommodation blocks, surrounded on three sides by massive rocks, with a sandy floor strewn with stones and scrub bushes. At one end a flat slab of concrete had been wedged into a cleft in the rock to serve as an altar, beneath which a somewhat battered doll lay in an old rattan vegetable basket.

Jenny held Pamela's arm and led her into the congregation of over one hundred men, women and children - including Jenny's parents and brothers, who nodded beaming welcomes. Father Heyer, the elder of the two American priests, appeared on the scene bearing a load of evergreens (strictly against Japanese rules, since they deemed that all trees and bushes were the property of the Emperor of Japan). As he arranged the branches round the base of the altar, four altar boys came forward in their usual camp garments of khaki shorts and T shirts. The priest pulled on his chasuble and proceeded to serve the Mass.

There were no seats; the congregation either stood, or knelt on the uneven ground although the children sat down cross-legged during the sermon. Pamela was surprised that most of the Mass was said in English instead of Latin - a fact which made her feel less of an outsider.

Almost every one present filed down before the altar to receive Holy Communion, their serious, serene faces as they returned gave her some unidentifiable pang: she had not once communicated in her own church in Stanley - and very rarely since her parents had left for England.

When at the end the familiar carols were sung, she felt moved beyond words; the air was like wine, the sun shone brightly in a sky of cloudless blue, and she was left with a conviction that, whatever its hardships in Stanley, life was good.

The communal Christmas meal was served at noon to the appreciative queues. Of course there were no communal dining rooms so as usual every one ate in their rooms; and of course there was no turkey, no sprouts or stuffing, no ham, roast potatoes or gravy; and no Christmas pudding or wine; but there was a satisfying rich meat stew, with carrots and sweet potatoes as well as rice.

In each block later that day private parties continued until lights out. It was only at bedtime when quietness descended that there was time to brood on absent family and friends. Pamela wondered about her parents in England, vulnerable to German bombs; about Roddy, confirmed now to have been a passenger on the 'Lisbon Maru' although his fate was unknown: about Keith in the Kowloon camp who, despite his own needs still occasionally sent her five yen; about Belle and the children - safe in Australia, but surely forever anxious for Keith and the rest of the family. She could hear Hilary trying to stifle her sobs - a nightly agony since the sinking of the Japanese ship, and thanked God that time had taken the edge off her own anxieties for Lawrence, who had now receded into the shadowy past in the same way as had Danny Russell.

SPRING/SUMMER

Hilary managed to live with her torment about Roddy by keeping so busy by day that at night she was drooping with tiredness and slept through most of Melly's disturbances. She sought the hardest work at the hospital - sheet and blanket washing, which had to be done by hand in luke-warm water in tin baths in the hospital yard. She took up German, and joined the chorus of a musical show under rehearsal. As soon as the weather was warm enough she went to the beach whenever the Japanese allowed swimming. Every time she returned to Room 19 she held her breath, bracing herself for news of Roddy, the bad news which was all she could expect.

One morning she blacked out as she was wringing a heavy blanket, and came to in the arms of Ben, one of the policemen who did heavy work and stretcher bearing at the hospital. He cradled her and soothed her while his colleague Micky ran for the doctor in the nearby ward. She wept because she was so weak, and because she felt such comfort from the encircling arms and they weren't Roddy's.

She spent a week in hospital when it was found she had an overactive thyroid - a latent condition exacerbated by overwork and poor diet. She felt thoroughly spoilt, sleeping on a real bed and having a glass of fresh milk every day. Friends who came to visit her seldom came empty-handed, producing a small slice of bread made with ground rice-flour, or an ounce of sugar in a paper twist, or a few bright nasturtiums. She saw Ben every day as he went about his chores, sweeping and mopping the stone floors and cleaning the windows. One afternoon during visiting hours he appeared at her bedside with Micky who handed her three red tomatoes the size of marbles. "Home grown," he said proudly.

"From the seeds of tinned tomatoes," beamed Ben. "Really too small to pick, but we wanted you to try them - now."

They were sweet and delicious. "You should have eaten them yourselves." - She felt guilty because both men had large frames on which the flesh hung in wrinkles.
"There'll be plenty more," Micky assured her. "When you've recovered come and help us pick them."

The day she was discharged, Ben insisted on taking her home and carrying her little case.
"Are you coming back to work here?" he asked as, naked to the waist and barefoot, he padded alongside her.
"I've asked to, but Matron won't have me until the doctor gives the O.K., and even then, no more blanket washing thank goodness - I'll be on the wards."
"Sure you'll be strong enough for that?" He glanced obliquely at her thin brown legs.
"I'm always like this," she grinned. "Wiry, that's me."
All the same, she had to stop and sit down on the steps leading to the Married Quarters. Ben sat companionably beside her until she felt able to continue. "Take care of yourself now," he said at the door of Room 19, handing over the suitcase, He bit his lower lip in embarrassment when she thanked him, seemed about to say something, then changed his mind, gave her an elaborate salute and sidled away.
"Welcome home!" Pamela called from the floor where she was holding Melly erect. "We were going to come and fetch you, but Melly suddenly started walking! Come on, Melly, show Auntie Hil!"
Pamela nudged the child forward while Sandra, a yard away, dropped on to her haunches and held out her arms calling "Come to Mummy, Melly!"
Melly tottered forward and collapsed with a giggle just before she reached her mother.
"She really can do it," Pamela declared. "She's walked four steps TWICE this afternoon. It's lovely to have you back, Hil, are you feeling really fit now?"
"As a fiddle," she declared, but already the deep depression was returning at the sight of the pail of napkins and the atmosphere of child-domination in the room.
In the hospital she had lived on a different plane, meeting so many other patients, and feeding very well because smaller units like the hospital were able to produce more appetising meals than the big blocks; she had been able to calm her fears for Roddy there. Now she was back to the same old irritations, made even worse because Melly was cutting back teeth. There was nothing to rub on the swollen gums, and no sedatives to calm her. Night after night Sandra and Pamela took turns to carry her about the small room. Hilary's conscience didn't trouble her sufficiently to impel her to take a shift, but the added burden of disturbed nights - gnawing hunger - hit her as badly as it did the other two girls.
All the Red Cross food was gone, and it was some months since Sandra had

received a parcel from Miles' firm, indicating that even the benefactors in town were suffering hardships.

She no longer had energy to make the tiring walk to the beach and back; some one else had taken over her part in the musical while she was in hospital; the German classes had lost their appeal; Matron considered she should not work at the hospital for another month. Bored, one evening she sought out Micky and Ben in their garden on the craggy hillside behind the hospital. Among rocky outcrops and scrub they had gouged out a plot about eight feet square and planted every inch with something edible - Chinese cabbage, carrots, spinach, lettuces, tomatoes.

The orderly rows of green shoots sparked some enthusiasm in her troubled mind; they represented so much thought and hard work and dedicated care: she felt the urge to be part of the project. Soon she joined them in the daily tending, weeding between the crops while the men did the watering, making many journeys to the hospital to collect water in old tins. She had never gardened before and found it enthralling, watching each day for the appearance of new shoots.

"You should have your own garden," Ben said one day. "Mick and I will get the ground ready for you."

They cleared a rectangular plot about six feet wide and three feet long and Hilary spent some precious yen in the camp canteen to buy a bottlecapful each of lettuce and carrot seeds. Pamela caught her enthusiasm and she too put her spare hours into garden work. Tiny lettuces were the first fruits, picked and eaten as soon as each had a few small leaves because of the risk of their being harvested by conscienceless internees. Tips from more experienced gardeners resulted in Ben and Micky providing manure from their own waste matter; in due course the effects showed in the dramatic growth and strength of the plants - and they diffidently offered manure for the girls' plot. The offer was accepted. "After all," as Hilary said, "all the vegetables we used to eat prewar were grown in the New Territories and we know human manure was always used there."

The gardening brought Hilary and Pamela, Ben and Micky together as a casual foursome, sometimes going for walks, or swimming, and attending concerts and talks. It became a reciprocal acquaintanceship, the men carrying the water up the hill for both gardens, and gathering twigs for the fire on which the girls cooked their produce. When Hilary found bugs breeding between the canvas and wooden stays of her bed, the two men carried all three beds and Melly's cot down into the courtyard and scrubbed every inch of them, deftly executing fleeing bugs between finger and thumb.

Sandra also had her assistants, having gradually acquired a retinue of young men who were forever calling on her, taking her turn in queues, and bringing her presents ranging from a tiny folding stool to a cooked sweet potato filched from the kitchen.

The value of such friendships to morale was inestimable, for this second year of internment was even harder to bear than the first: in addition to deprivation and near-starvation, there was a new fear in the camp - that of air raids. The first Allied air raid on the colony had been reported in November 1942 although the area attacked had been too far from Stanley to be visible or audible there. Since then Allied planes were occasionally spotted high up in the sky, and faint bombing heard. Now almost every week the Japanese blew the whistle indicating an air raid alarm which they called 'kyushu', when internees had to run to the nearest cover; sometimes the alarm period lasted for hours and people would be marooned wherever they'd happened to be at the time it started. No one ever considered that the bombs would be dropped in the camp but it was a very small area and accidents could happen, and there were no real shelters.

Clothes became more of a problem; already much-washed, they were rapidly disintegrating. The men's khaki shorts became off-white. Women's patched dresses were converted into skirts and worn with skimpy suntops made out of remnants, exposing a bare mid-riff. There was nothing to allay the summer heat - no iced drinks, no ceiling fans, no nets over their beds to ward off the mosquitoes which found their way into camp despite the sanitary squad's constant efforts to obliterate possible spawning areas.

It was difficult to sleep at night on sheets damp with sweat, even with all windows and doors open. Cold baths were out of the question because the baths were regularly used for storing water now that the stopcocks were only turned on every third day because of the seasonal water shortage.

The only respite from the heat was swimming, but the price was too high for many people - the hot afternoon sun on bare heads on the beach, the tough climb up from the bay afterwards; and the risk of air raids in an area where there was no cover whatsoever.

Suddenly, in May, repatriation news was in the air again; there was even a guarded official notice about it.

"Imagine,being back in civilisation again!" drooled Sandra. "New toothbrushes! S.T.'s! Shoes! Melly might even have her first birthday in freedom!"

"Don't expect miracles," Hilary warned. "It'll take longer than three weeks to organise such an exodus. I'm still going to keep the garden going, anyway."

Euphoria permeated the whole camp. Women who had kept their hair cropped short bemoaned the fact that it would not be long enough for a perm when they were released. Men with shaggy beards because of lack of razor blades and shaving soap loped round the camp on bare horny feet, anticipating an end to these peripheral trials of internment. Alas, within a few days the men's hopes were dashed: this scheme was to apply only to women and children.

"At least we men will get SOME benefit," was the philosophical comment of Guy Gasson, now a frequent visitor to Room 19. "We'll be able to spread ourselves when you ladies have gone, and we should get better meals if the Japanese keep on sending the same amount of food as they do now."

Now every day that dawned was theoretically the one on which the date of departure would be announced, but when that day came, it brought only dismay and disappointment to the majority of women: this repatriation would not take place until September and was for Canadian nationals only.. a mere hundred or so internees, including Rosemary and her mother.

Despondency lasted for weeks; the British women could only accept the situation by believing that the ship which was to repatriate the Canadians would bring shipments of Red Cross food.. and would in due course return to take away the rest of the female internees.

Additional food was desperately needed, the daily rations rarely contained any meat and very few vitamins; more and more people developed sores which would not heal, failing eye-sight, and drop-foot. Grassy areas in the camp formerly used for recreation were now converted into communally-farmed vegetable gardens whose produce helped to supplement the inadequate diet.

Into these difficult days crept disturbing news of another kind: several high-ranking Government servants in Stanley were arrested by the Japanese and taken to the adjacent gaol. Rumour had it that they were connected with the use of a radio and in passing messages out of the camp. Not only relatives and friends of those detained watched daily for their return: throughout the camp there was a growing uneasiness about what the future held.

Melly was walking sturdily by her first birthday. Pamela had made her a frilly dress and knickers from part of Sandra's sheet and she looked a picture of charm, her hair a light thatch of feathery auburn curls, her tiny feet encased in khaki cloth shoes fashioned out of bits of the ubiquitous khaki jerkins.

Room 19 was crowded with well-wishers for her party. Rosemary had brought a little cake made of rice flour and wong tong; some one else brought savoury biscuits made of rice flour mixed with carrot tops. A surprise visitor was Mr. Bridger, who produced the small tin of condensed milk he'd saved from his Red Cross parcel. This being a Stanley party, guests had brought their own cups or mugs for the watery tea which was all that could be provided.

All the toddlers wanted to play with Melly's presents - mainly home-made soft toys stuffed with scraps of material; the exception was a small wooden elephant, roughly carved by one of Sandra's men friends from a piece of old wood. These children had never seen or held such a thing, they were intrigued with it and fought with each other to handle it. In the excitement, one small hand hurled the elephant across the room; it hit Melly above her right eye and she screamed as a spurt of blood spread over her face. Rosemary who was nearest pulled Melly on to her lap to comfort her; Sandra darted forward and pulled the child into her arms, and Hilary dabbed at the wound with the corner of a dampened towel. The boy who had caused the damage was removed, howling, by his embarrassed mother, who slapped him all the way out into the corridor.

"It's only a minor cut," Hilary assured Sandra. "But better take her to the hospital for a dab of antiseptic."

"I'll take her!" Rosemary made to take the child from Sandra and reached for the pram handle.

"No you won't, she's my child!" Sandra pushed Rosemary aside and put Melly carefully in the pram. "You come with me, Pam."

There was after all no need for stitches; the only damage seemed to be Rosemary's *amour propre:* when Sandra and Pamela returned with Melly from the hospital, she was washing nappies in complete silence.

That evening after Melly had settled in her cot, Sandra announced she was going for a stroll. "I feel like some social life of my own, it's been such an exhausting day." She cocked her head at Pamela and Hilary. "Are either of you in for the next hour? Grand! Melly's bound to sleep after all that's happened today. See you later."

She was gone before Hilary's sarcastic ".. Two seconds before curfew, I bet!"

"Rosie's going to miss Melly terribly when she leaves," Pamela said. "She was really put out today at not being allowed to go to the hospital: no singing while she was doing the washing, was there?"

"I don't blame her for sulking. Anyway, we shall miss Rosie much more than she will miss Melly," yawned Hilary. "At least, Madam will miss her: I'm not going on the baby-sitting roster, I can tell you."

There was an air raid alarm early the next morning, inhibiting movement within the camp.

"Damned nuisance," muttered Sandra; it was half past ten and still every one was marooned in their quarters. "The way things are going, Rosemary won't get here until after her chow."

"If she comes at all," said Hilary. "You might have put her off yesterday, not letting her go to the hospital with you."

"She did look a bit peeved," Sandra admitted, "but nothing would stop her from looking after Melly, she loves doing it; it's a kind of therapy - you yourself said that."

All the same, she apologised to Rosemary as soon as she appeared when the alarm was over, explaining "I was in a bit of a state at the time."

"Weren't we all?" Pamela gave a quick laugh in an attempt to cover up the awkwardness. "What an aim that awful boy had!"

Rosemary made no comment, but plonked Melly into the pram and edged it out of the room.

"Wait for me," called Hilary, "I'm going visiting as far as Bungalow C."

Rosemary's glum face cleared. Prancing down the road with Hilary at her side, she felt on top of the world again. She had lain awake for hours last night crying, convinced that Sandra no longer wanted her as a nursemaid. There was nowhere she could go to hide her misery. Her mother had tried to comfort her, reminding her that she would soon be saying goodbye to Melly when the repatriation ship arrived.

"I can't bear to think of leaving her, ever," she had sobbed.

But today, everything was fine again, Sandra apologising, and Hilary, whom she admired so much, walking along beside her. So many people smiled at Melly and enquired about the mercurichromed splash on her forehead; stopped to talk and earned beaming smiles from Melly.

The way to Bungalow C was through the tiny cemetery. There had been a time when she'd first come to Stanley when she had avoided the cemetery, knowing that the victims of the holocaust she'd witnessed at St. Stephens were buried there. But Hilary had made her go and explained that there was nothing frightening about the lovingly tended communal grave, across which the words 'Greater love hath no man than this..' were picked out in tiny gravel chips... not the spilled blood and broken bodies of her tortured memory. In the same way, it was Hilary who had insisted on taking her to concerts at St. Stephens, gradually helping her to see the main hall no longer as the scene of horror when it had served as a hospital ward, but as it had now become - a school venue on weekdays, an entertainment hall most evenings, and a church hall on Sundays.

Melly was getting restive in the pram, so they stopped outside the upper gate of the cemetery and let her toddle round on the grass while they sat on the low wall, enjoying the shade of the gently swaying pine trees.

"You've done a marvellous job, looking after Melly," said Hilary. "I would have gone mad in that room without you to help. You ought to go in for nursery governess work when you get back to Canada."

"Will you give me a reference?" giggled Rosemary. "Why not?" Hilary was perfectly serious.

Melly stooped down to examine an ant's progress with bewitching concentration. "I'm just dreading losing her. " Rosemary's voice trembled. "She means so much to me."

"One day you'll marry and have your own babies to look after: lucky babies they'll be, too, having you for a Mum."

"I feel terrible, Hil." Rosemary swallowed a sob. "I've forgotten Johnny! I can't remember what he looked like, and I lost all my photos in.. you know. I couldn't have really loved him, to have forgotten so soon, could I? I feel so guilty!"

"It's much the same with me, and I knew Roddy much longer than you knew your Johnny.. there's this feeling of unreality, I'm sure it's the same for everyone here, so cut off from real life. Look!" She jumped up suddenly, "There's a funeral party coming through the lower gate - we'd best move."

Father Messell, the younger of the two American Catholic priests, in white soutane, was leading a small procession; the two-wheeled stretcher with coffin pushed by two men wearing only shorts, was followed by a straggle of mourners.

They lifted Melly back into the pram and left the cemetery. Hilary branched off to her friends' billet, Rosemary manoeuvred the pram along the narrow path past the bungalows, where internees disported themselves outside on the grass. She envied them their comparatively luxurious billets, away from the busy and noisy main blocks teeming with people; envied them too their panoramic views of the shimmering sea below, and the shoulders of distant hills of all hues behind.

As she approached St. Stephens, two of her V.A.D. friends appeared and stopped to talk. She proudly took Melly out of the pram to give a demonstration of her walking prowess. After they had left, Melly insisted on helping to push the pram herself. Rosemary didn't mind that this was a very slow process - there was no hurry on this beautiful June afternoon.

She heard the distant droning of planes when she was halfway between St. Stephens and the Science Block. Suddenly there was great activity on the road twenty feet below; Japanese sentries clattered along, waving arms and rifles and shouting 'Kyushu'; internees all round hurried obediently to the nearest cover. Planting Melly quickly back in the pram, she paused uncertainly, undecided which way to run. Behind her she could hear hoarse shouting and the approach of thudding feet, then priest and funeral mourners emerged from the path she had left, running with the empty stretcher trolly, and chased by a yelling and gesticulating soldier.

"Run!" urged the priest as he panted towards Rosemary. "To the Science Block."

The noise of the planes grew, but even louder were the guttural shouts from the pursuing soldier who was brandishing his rifle and gaining on the fleeing party.

Melly was wide-eyed, screeching with fright and clutching the sides of the pram as it lurched along on the uneven ground. The soldier caught up with them just as they reached the door of the Science Block. Still shouting, he reversed his rifle and beat the priest's slender shoulders with the butt, while the others in the group watched in horror; the priest simply put his hands together, closed his eyes and murmured prayers.

"NO, NO, NO!" screamed Rosemary. Memories so long shut out surged into her mind; the soldier's frenzied shouts re-echoed the triumphant cries of the invaders of the hospital, and all that followed after. She was in the blood-stained hall again, stumbling over bayonetted bodies; dragged away by ruthless soldiers. This time she had to escape, and she had to save Melly, whose hysterical cries were attracting the venemous glares of the soldier. While every one else stayed motionless as the priest continued to bow his head each time the rifle butt smote his shoulders, she suddenly dashed away with the pram towards the hillside path leading down to the road; ran with superhuman energy when she heard the soldier shouting and stampeding after her. Her heart was pounding so loudly she could scarcely breathe; her legs began to buckle; she could run no more, she was done for - but perhaps she could save Melly. With a last burst of strength she thrust the pram forward, and sank to the ground as it tipped over the edge of the hillside.

All night Sandra ranted, refusing to go to hospital for care, refusing tablets to induce sleep. Mrs. Burwood and two of the St. John's ladies offered to stay in the room overnight but Sandra pushed them away, repeating endlessly "Melly's dead! Rosemary killed her!"

Mrs. Burwood quietly set her bed up in the corridor outside; several times Hilary and Pamela called for her help, grappling with Sandra when she fought to leave the room, declaring her intention of finding and attacking Rosemary.

Now, in the morning, she was sitting on her hands on the bed, muttering in a tired husky voice "She's wicked, she's wicked! She didn't want to go to Canada and leave Melly behind, so she killed her. She killed my child!" Her voice soared to a scream.

As soon as curfew was lifted, the St. John's ladies returned. "You two girls go out for a while and have a break," whispered Mrs. Burford to Pamela and Hilary, who were drooping with misery and weariness. "We'll stay here as long as you need us."

Some of Hilary's friends were hovering outside the door and they took her off with them.

"I want to go to the hospital," she managed to articulate between stiff lips. "I have to see Rosemary."

They tried everything to dissuade her.

- "She won't know you.. it will be distressing."

- "Her mind's gone completely, it won't do any good.."

"I have to see her," Hilary insisted.

At the hospital, a tiny store room on the ground floor had been hastily converted into accommodation for Rosemary and her mother and a mental nurse.

Rosemary's face was calm and untroubled, her eyes blank; she cuddled a tightly rolled towel in her arms, called it 'Melly' and crooned her favourite songs. She looked up and smiled sweetly when Hilary was shown in, then looked down tenderly at the towel and said "Melly's all right, you see. I took great care of her."

Jenny, lurking in the corridor, waylaid Pamela as she left Room 19.

"Come and see Father Messell," she urged. "He asked after you." It was Father Messell who, despite one beating and the wild-eyed guard, had sped down the path to where Melly had been tossed out of the pram, gathered up her crumpled body and ran with it to the hospital.

Jenny held Pamela's hand and led her out of the Married Quarters. Pamela couldn't look at any of the passers-by, ready to cry again at the first glance of sympathy.

"Father Messell wanted to come over, but he's too diffident to intrude unless asked," Jenny explained, on the way to the American Block where she and her family were billeted, and where the two American priests lived in a tiny amah's room. They passed Father Heyer in the alleyway leading to his room. He was planing the edges of an old drawer, and looked up and gave Pamela a compassionate smile when Jenny introduced her.

Father Messell was pale and stooping as a result of yesterday's beating. There was no space in the priests' room for visitors, for it contained rough double bunks, one chair and a small chest of drawers piled with boxes and miscellaneous oddments. Two drawers were missing from the chest, but the space was stacked with books.

"Too hot to sit outside I guess," murmured the priest and Jenny left him and Pamela sitting on the stone stairs.

"Why.. why.. why?" Pamela wept.

"Maybe God wanted the baby now. You girls had her for a whole year, to love and cherish."

"Sandra can't bear it - "

"You must help her."

"She won't let us."

"Yes she will.. keep trying."

"She wants to kill Rosemary. She keeps saying it, I'm so frightened.."

"No one can hurt Rosemary now. We must pray for her, and for her poor mother."

"But why did the guard chase after and terrify her? It was his fault."

"He was simply doing his duty, getting all internees under cover during raids; he was answerable to his superiors; he was scared of being caught disobeying orders - that was why he lambasted me."

In his gentle voice, he continued to talk and calm Pamela, neither of them appearing to notice the coming and going of residents who stepped carefully past them.

"Come and talk some more, any time," he said. "And I think I have a little book which might help you, I'll get it for you now." They went to the amah's room, where Father Heyer now had the drawer balanced across the chair, and was arranging inside it the remnants of a child's white satin dress, crimping it carefully and securing the folds with pins; upended against the door was the bottom of a second drawer, its edges neatly planed. With a great sob Pamela realised she was looking at Melly's coffin.

Late that afternoon, she stood round the tiny grave beneath the pines, tears blurring the scene around her. The Catholic children's choir sang 'Yes, Heaven is the prize, my soul, just think of this!' The Church of England padre conducted the service; Father Messell was there too. It seemed that every one but Sandra was weeping; she stood, stony-faced and still, supported by Pamela on one side and Mrs. Burford on the other; she gave one anguished strangled cry when it was time to leave the grave to be filled in.

When the girls returned to their room, everything connected with Melly had been removed by concerned friends. Now Sandra's tears came again, and long, shuddering sobs.

Well into the night Pamela and Hilary patiently soothed and comforted her, their tears mingling with hers.

"No need for you to cry," she whispered brokenly to Pamela. "You've nothing to reproach yourself for.. you always did all you could for Melly, but... I never loved her enough."

AUGUST

Despite overwhelming kindness from friends and neighbours, Pamela and Hilary bore the brunt of Sandra's despair. She had to be reminded to wash herself; for weeks refused to brush or wash her hair and wouldn't allow any one else to do so. Unwanted but persistent and patient visits by the Protestant padre who had buried Melly eventually restored some of Sandra's self-respect. The first sign of recovery was when she demanded that Pamela cut her hair: "As short as possible - it will be easier to wash then." Pamela immediately got out her scissors in case Sandra changed her mind, and Hilary ran to queue for hot water and returned half an hour later with just enough to fill a third of the wash-basin. This was a 'dry' day when no water flowed from the taps. No one had shampoo now - only rough yellow washing soap with a high soda content. Rinsing was sketchy since each internee was only allowed to use five souptinfuls of cold water from the store in the bath, but the whole operation brought immense relief to Hilary and Pamela, even though the shorn hair emphasised Sandra's ravaged face.

She lived mainly on cigarettes, many supplied by sympathetic friends; when there were long gaps between deliveries to the canteen, she was presented with substitutes made from crushed pine needles and sweet potato leaves; there were times when even these were not available, and then her brittle mood worsened, and Pamela and Hilary took it in turns to get respite from the room, to ensure she was never left alone.

"What's the matter?" she demanded when their strategy became too obvious. "D'you think I'll commit hari-kari if you're not around to nanny me? No fear of that! I've always been good at looking after No. 1 - haven't you noticed?"

At first she dismissed the boy-friends who tried to interest her in swimming and concerts; she clung to Pamela and Hilary, with whom she had no need to keep up a front. The mixture of Pamela's constant sympathy and Hilary's bracing homilies sustained her, but even they could seldom persuade her to walk beyond the Married Quarters. They dared not press her too much, recognising her dread of meeting Rosemary, even though this was highly unlikely since Rosemary was only occasionally taken out of her room to exercise round the hospital precinct.

At the end of September the fat grey 'Teia Maru' steamed into the Bay and carried off the Canadian internees, including Rosemary and her mother. The British women who watched the ship leave were not too despondent, for they were confident that it would deposit the Canadians in Goa, there pick up ex-Japanese internees from Canada and take them to Japan, and then return for THEM.

Now Sandra became more settled, she began to mix again with her boy-friends, and Hilary and Pamela were able to lead lives of their own once more.

One afternoon Guy Gasson called on Pamela asking for help to mend a tear in his jacket. When the job was completed he thanked her in his usual formal way, then added "Do you feel like a walk?"

"That's just what I do feel like." Pamela put away the precious needle. "Mustn't be away long, though Sandra will be back soon."

"I so admire the support you and Miss Bately give Mrs. Lamb," Guy said as they ambled along. They avoided the cemetery, which Pamela could not yet face without tears.

"What else can we do?" she shrugged. "We have to keep her going until the ship comes back."

"It will be a sad day for us men when you ladies go, happy though we will be for you." Guy led her up the rocky path beyond the hospital. Below, the sea hissed and tugged at the rocks. "Do you mind if we sit here a while - it's so pleasant."

They found precarious rock seats above the path. Pamela watched the sun glinting on the curling waves and felt a kind of balm.

"I was wondering.." Guy cleared his throat and started again, staring at the ground. "You'll soon be leaving here, otherwise I would not dream of approaching you in this way so.. so abruptly. You know of course that I'm some years older than you are - almost 18 in fact, but would you consider me as a suitor.. after the war, when life is normal again?"

She heard the waves thud against the rocks below four times in the silence that followed, while she mustered her tumultuous thoughts. Unbelieving, alarmed, her mind shouted 'You're too old, almost as old as my father! You're a good kind friend, but that's all.' Yet her eyes were filling with tears of weakness, after the ordeal of the past months, grateful that someone cared for her and wanted her.

"Would you, Pamela?" Guy was repeating, pressing her hand between his.

Gently she withdrew her hand because three little boys suddenly slid down the hillside above them; glad of the interruption, she tried to think of the right words when the children slithered away. "You've taken me by surprise, Guy. I value your friendship so much, but, well, I never dreamt you felt like this."

"Think it over." He patted her hand. "It's quite wrong of me to expect an answer right away. It has only been since the prospect of your leaving has crystallised that I realised how much your company had come to mean to me. I could give you security, you know. You realise that our Government salaries are accumulating for us, and of course you will qualify for a marriage gratuity; I shall have a good pension when I retire in seven years' time."

She tried to form words of protest, feeling unable to let him think for another moment that she could consider marrying him, but he shook his head and gently put one hand across her mouth. "Not yet, my dear. Please think about it first, I beg of you."

There was no one she dared consult. This was no time to have a serious discussion with Sandra, and although she valued Hilary's directness and wisdom, and Jenny's honesty and friendship, she could not bring herself to talk to them about Guy because she felt so sorry for him, and to discuss him would be to betray him.

It was Jenny, quite unconsciously, who helped. "Father Messell asked me yesterday how you were getting on; why don't you go to see him again?"

She called on him that evening. Together they walked up and down the periphery of the American Block while she explained her problem.

"He sounds a very good man, Pamela, and he sure would look after you!" the priest said. "There's much to be said for choosing a partner who has had the same camp experience as yourself. You don't love him, you say; but emotional, passionate love isn't always that necessary in a good marriage; genuine love, caring for the person and wholly concerned with his well-being is the most important. He's C. of E., is he?"

"I suppose so, we've never discussed religion, we've only spoken about everyday things. He's really just a close friend, or has become so since we've been in Stanley. Before that he was just my boss, I hardly knew him as a person."

"I'd guess you still don't know him very well! And you don't have any romantic feeling for him?"

"None at all, " she found herself herself saying firmly.

"You feel sorry for him? Then don't promise to marry him!"

It was a comfort to have confirmation of her instinctive feelings, and the next day she found the words to tell Guy that she must refuse his proposal.

"Then we'll say no more about it," he said cheerfully, "but my offer still stands, remember, if you should change your mind."

It took her quite a while to shake off a feeling of awkwardness and guilt whenever she passed him or noticed him at concerts, and she was surprised to discover that she missed his company, his quiet considered manner was so different from the perpetual clowning and teasing of Ben and Micky, who never seemed to be serious - until one afternoon when all four were lolling in the cemetery beneath the trees, chatting and joking - and she noticed Ben's hand close over Hilary's.

That evening there was a musical recital by Betty Drown, the versatile pianist who gave weekly concerts which had developed into an hour of magic nostalgia for her listeners. Most of the audience sat on the floor, crammed closely together; others were packed on the low window-sills, some with their eyes closed, shutting out present surroundings and dreaming of other days when they had heard these same tunes. The two girls and the policemen arrived too late to find four spaces together. Someone squeezed up to make a little room on the nearest windowsill and here Hilary and Ben somehow wriggled in. Micky tried to propel Pamela forward to force space for them in the front but, reluctant to sit so close to him, she resisted and hung back, preferring to stand against the open door.

The atmosphere was comforting and hopeful. When Betty played a rollicking 'In eleven more months and ten more days we'll be out of the calaboose', the accompanying chorus almost drowned the piano. Immediately after, the delicate notes of 'Clair de Lune' had everyone silent again. Looking across the hall, Pamela was shocked to see that Ben had his arms tightly round Hilary, whose head was resting on his shoulder. As always, the recital ended with the camp song 'We're going to SAIL AWAY, SAIL AWAY, We know internment here will end some day..' leaving everyone in an optimistic mood. Afterwards, Pamela and Hilary and the two policemen wandered round the periphery of the Married Quarters together. When the men waved goodbye at curfew time to return to their billets at the hospital, Pamela was relieved to see no further sign of the closeness she had observed between Ben and Hilary, and decided the two had simply been carried away with the romantic music.

She was taken unawares that night when she and Hilary were undressing while Sandra was in the bathroom, and Hilary said tentatively "Pam, I want your advice. Ben keeps asking me out on my own and I'm afraid he might be getting serious. For weeks I've been saying it's no good, him and me, because of Roddy.. but I don't know what to do."

Pamela took a long time to pull her jumper completely over her head, trying to control the dismay she knew showed on her face.

"How do you really feel about Ben?" she asked at last.

"I'm beginning to get fond of him," said Hilary slowly. "It's lovely to be fussed over again, and to have a shoulder to lean on.. and perhaps there's no Roddy. More and more I feel now he must have been lost on that ship, it's more than a year, and no news.."

"Heaps and heaps of people have had no news, and all their men can't be dead!" Pamela shouted the words in an effort to convince herself.

"I know, I know. But how many more years are we going to be stuck in here, just waiting to get on with our lives?"

"Do you mean," - Pamela picked her words carefully. "Do you mean you're trying to decide whether to.. to assume that Rod is gone, so that you can start courting Ben? Oh Hil, but if he's alive and waiting for you..."

"That sounds dreadful!" Hilary's voice was thick with emotion. "You're right, though. Put like that, of course I mustn't even begin to think about starting anything with Ben."

Pamela put an arm round Hilary's bony shoulders and went on "I'm trying to look at the whole thing as if Roddy isn't my brother, but, well, the answer comes up the same. And I can't help thinking that if you were really falling for Ben as his own person, and not as a sort of comforter, you wouldn't have needed to ask my opinion at all."

SEPTEMBER

When an ambitious ballet went into rehearsal, Hilary joined the cast, glad of a new interest to fill the gaps in her life now she had limited the time she spent with Ben and Micky.

"Why don't you join too?" she urged Pamela and Sandra. "We have a grand time at the rehearsals, and the dancing is going to be fantastic."

"Not me," shrugged Pamela. "I'm no dancer."

"Dancing? What kind of dancing?" Faint interest flickered across Sandra's face.

"Mainly eastern, they're still working on the choreography. Come along to the next rehearsal tomorrow and see!"

The ballet soon became the pivot of Sandra's life. She threw herself wholeheartedly into rehearsals, began to eat again, and was quickly promoted from a modest role in the chorus with Hilary to that of one of the principal dancers. The ballet was billed as a farewell show by the women and children, and generated great enthusiasm. Any one seen with a garment which attracted the wardrobe mistress's eye was coaxed into lending it.

On the day of the dress rehearsal the Japanese announced that the jailed civil servants arrested two months earlier had been executed. The numbing notice forbade church services or other gatherings to mourn the victims.

Having adapted to internment and settled into a toleration of the circumstances until it should be over, the realisation was now forced upon the internees that sinister dangers surrounded them. No one knew who would next be arrested and executed, for it was obvious that an underground network of contact was in operation within the barbed wire.

At first there was talk that the ballet should be postponed or cancelled as a mark of respect, but the final decision was to proceed as scheduled - if there was ever a time to boost camp morale, this was it.

Like all Stanley shows, it was performed on three consecutive evenings, and proved a stupendous success. For two hours the rich music, the professional dancing and the ingenious costumes transported the rapturous audience from the dreary unhappy camp into the court of Esther.

"I don't know where you got all that energy from, leaping about three nights in a row," Pamela marvelled when Sandra and Hilary came home after the final performance.

"Sheer adrenaline," said Hilary. "I'm glad it's over, though - I'm beat."

"I could do it all over again!" Sandra pirouetted about the room, humming snatches of the impressive music. Thoroughly worked up, she talked about the show far into the night, but the next morning stayed in bed, silent and withdrawn.

"It's half past ten," Hilary reminded her. "Aren't you getting up today?"

"Nothing to get up for," Sandra snapped. Pamela collected her food for her and watched anxiously as she picked at half of it and left the rest. Friends who called on her were rudely turned away; once more Pamela felt chained to the room.

"Don't fuss over her so," Hilary whispered as they washed the dishes in the kitchen. "It would do her good to make the effort - she'd have to get up and look after herself if you weren't there to do it."

"I'm afraid of her getting like she was before," Pamela fretted, "I couldn't stand all that again."

Her worst fears were realised. That night Sandra pulled her bed alongside Pamela's and clung to her in paroxysms of weeping for Melly. She spent the next three days huddled in bed, refusing to see any visitors. Hilary lost all patience with her, and Pamela became desperate and called a doctor; he prescribed a precious sedative but she would not take it; suggested a stay in hospital which she also refused. The C. of E. padre came and Father Messell came, but she would not listen to either of them.

One afternoon Mr. Bridger arrived while she was dozing. Pamela spoke to him in the corridor.

"We've been anxious about her since we heard what was happening," he whispered. "My colleagues and I clubbed together to get her a present to try to cheer her up. Can I wait until she wakes?"

"You can.. but be prepared for the screaming when she sees I've let someone in."

He sat patiently on the edge of Pamela's bed while she sewed busily in the chair until Sandra's eyes opened. He forestalled the panic by raising his hand and saying apologetically "I'm only here for a moment, Mrs. Lamb, to give you something."

Pulling herself up in the bed, Sandra watched guardedly as he took from his jacket pocket an unwrapped manicure set, the outside of the container covered in shimmering silver linked scales; the tiny instruments within gleamed silver, with shining ivory handles.

"This is for me?"

"For you, from the firm."

"But.. such an expensive thing.."

"No matter. Miles would have wanted you to have it."

"It's so beautiful!" She ran her fingers over the undulating scales, savouring the luxury of gazing on something new and clean and exquisite amid the make-do of camp life. Whoever had sold it to the men would have demanded a great price. She stammered "I just don't know how I can thank you, Mr. Bridger.."

"Why not come up to the bungalow with me for a cup of tea, and thank the others as well, if you're free now?"

That was the beginning of Sandra's true recovery. Every afternoon John Bridger called for her and took her for a walk, ending with tea at his bungalow. Before long, he and his friends had taught her to play bridge which soon became an obsession with her.

"I wish John lived in our block," she told Pamela one evening as the girls were sitting cross-legged by the fireplace where Hilary reheated some of the rice they had saved from the 5 o'clock meal: a little food last thing at night helped them to get off to sleep; there could be no comforting hot drink then, for the boiler had to shut down at curfew time. "John's an expert cook; I had a delicious snack with his gang this afternoon. He does wonders with ground rice flour; we could all mess together if he lived near enough."

"Sounds as though you don't appreciate our cooking," growled Hilary. "Ask John for some tips, then you can try them out here." This was her snide way of reminding Sandra it was time she took a turn in the evening cooking, with its tiresome struggle to keep the fire sufficiently fuelled without using up all the twigs and grasses before the food was hot enough.

Some internees had acquired tiny electric hot-plates, but electricity cuts were now so frequent that more and more people were using twig fires for private cooking. This meant that fuel was harder than ever to come by, any available branches or twigs being grabbed by the earliest scavengers every day, and all burnable objects in the billets long having gone up in smoke. Some one then realised that the parquet flooring in the more modern quarters was easily removeable in tiny sections; the floor base being tarred, a layer of tar also adhered to the underside of the wood, so these sections burned very well indeed. Those in such quarters now had a wonderful commodity beneath their very feet; they could burn what they needed, and sell off some to those living in stone-floored billets.

In Room 19 the girls started using their blocks sparingly, starting with those beneath Pamela's bed. Many friends and acquaintances, and ultimately complete strangers, called to buy; they could have sold the entire stock within a week, but Hilary insisted on caution. "Let's only sell enough each week to get money for the canteen - we don't know how long this firewood has got to last us."

"What about cigarettes?" said Sandra. "With this bonanza, we could afford for me to have your two shares instead of selling them. Cigarettes are as important to me as food."

"It's time you started cutting down on your smoking, not stepping it up," snapped Hilary. "More food and less cigarettes would be better for you."

"I'm the judge of that!" Sandra stared at her boldly. "Anyway, it's only until the ship comes."

NOVEMBER

It was two months since the 'Teia Maru' had left ample time for her to have returned to Hong Kong for the Stanley women and children. There was even talk of another 'farewell' concert, but before that could be done a new notice headed 'Repatriation' appeared. Once again there were tears of disappointment - the scheme had been altered; instead of repatriation of all women and children, only a total of 800 internees were to be selected, made up of children and their mothers, and sick and elderly of both sexes; no date was given.

Pamela and Hilary had to face the fact that they did not qualify, but Sandra's bereavement gave her a place on the list. "So we'll get some consolation out of it," commented Hilary, grinning at Pamela's reproachful expression. "Come on, admit life will be a great deal easier in this room when she's gone."

Pamela studiously ignored Hilary's remark, saying "We'd better start going easy on using the floor boards." Already one third of the flooring in the room had gone, leaving an ugly tarry scar with an uneven surface which it was impossible to sweep clean. "We don't know how long what's left has to last us."

Sandra came home that evening with John Bridger's pyjama jacket rolled up under her arm. "Can you lend me your needle, Pam, and spare me a length of thread? I want to get all John's mending up to date before the ship comes." Pamela offered to do the job for her but Sandra refused: "I know I'm terrible at sewing, but I'm trying to become more versatile. John's teaching me to cook, too."

"Better late than never," snorted Hilary.

One morning two weeks later, an elderly couple came to the door of Room 19 asking to buy half a dozen floor boards.

"We don't really want to sell at the moment," Hilary explained. "Two of us here aren't on the list to go, we'll need all we have left."

The couple pleaded; although both due for repatriation, the wife explained that her husband's stomach could no longer tolerate the camp meals unless they were re-boiled; her unspoken fear was clear - he would not survive until the ship arrived unless his meals could be made more disgestible. The girls had a hurried consultation, then agreed to sell four boards.

"We should start under your bed now, Sandra," said Hilary, getting down on her hands and knees. "Come on, give a hand with your bits and pieces."

Sandra, seated on the window-sill, didn't move, but her hand flew to her mouth. Hilary heaved out bundles and bags, then exclaimed "Oh, we've already started taking from under here - when did we do that?"

"I didn't think we had," Pamela began, then saw Sandra's red face.

"Give these people their boards." Sandra's face was muffled in embarrassment, "and I'll tell you what happened."

She had started secretly selling the flooring beneath her bed three weeks ago, using the money to buy extra black market cigarettes for herself and John Bridger, and had now cleared the entire area hidden by her possessions. To Pamela and Hilary's angry reproaches she repeated tearfully "You just don't understand what I've been through."

"We've done our damnedest to help you!" Hilary was white with anger, "but all we get is this cheating. Well, let's have no more joint messing from now on; Sandra can look after herself, or get this John Bridger to look after her."

Sandra shed tears of contrition, begged for forgiveness and promised to sell her next ration of cigarettes to provide money for the kitty. Pamela accepted the gabbled apologies - the last thing she wanted was to break up the little côterie in the room which represented home: much as she suffered from the constant squabbles and irritations, the three girls were like a family unit which she could not bear to see broken.

Hilary took longer to be won round, but eventually a truce of sorts was achieved; Sandra even brought tiny offerings of cooked food from the bungalow, proud of John Bridger's expertise.

"He must spend more time cooking than playing bridge," said Pamela, sighing over a delicious piece of cake. One afternoon, she discovered that he had even more interests: she was ambling along the coast path past the hospital with Jenny when she noticed a couple sitting in a clearing below the path; they had their arms round each other and their faces were not visible, but Sandra's newly sprouting red curls were unmistakable, and the black hair against them could only be John's.

"Gee, and he's a married man, isn't he?" hissed Jenny.

"Oh, it's nothing - just camp companionship." Pamela's words concealed her concern. It was not unusual for internees whose spouses were not in the camp to team up with someone of the opposite sex, the men doing the queuing for meals and foraging for fuel, the women cooking, mending and washing the clothes; mutual shouldering of the trials of Stanley often made the difference between survival and non-survival. A few frail and lone internees had lost the will to live and just drifted into the grave. That there were not a great many more deaths was due in part to the healthy position of the camp, and also to the patience and diligence of the medical staff who had to dredge up the energy to keep going at their jobs.

Nevertheless, Pamela's concern grew as Sandra spent more and more time away from Room 19, sometimes not even appearing for the five o'clock meal, and arriving just at curfew time. There came an evening when she didn't return at all. Pamela spent a sleepless night, convinced that Sandra had left the bungalow after evening curfew and been caught by the guards; several internees had recently been arrested for this reason, kept at Japanese Headquarters all night and only released after severe lectures and dire cautions.

"Of course I didn't get caught!" Sandra laughed when she turned up the next morning and Pamela poured out her fears. "We'd forgotten the time and John wouldn't let me leave after curfew in case the guards saw me."

"Lucky for us all there wasn't a roll call last night," said Hilary. "We'd all have been in trouble if so ."

"I knew there wouldn't be - it's only two days since the last one. John said it would be O.K."

After Sandra had left the room, Hilary echoed sarcastically "John says! If I hear that once more I shall scream! You know what's going on between those two, don't you?"

"It's just.. companionship."

"Rubbish! They're having an affair."

"We don't know that -"

"Oh Pam, be your age! They've both been used to the married state.. they have the same needs."

"But a man in Mr. Bridger's position wouldn't.. and anyway, how could they, with all the people living in the bungalow?"

"Surely it hasn't escaped your notice that at least a dozen babies have been born in Stanley in the last twelve months? There are secluded hidey holes on the hillside; there are bath-rooms, and I know three married couples living in one room who by mutual arrangement each get an hour's privacy. And look at the number of people in our block who sleep up on the roof in hot weather! You really are a little innocent; it's time you grew up. You spend too much time with young Jenny and her pals."

"Jenny makes me laugh. We're good for each other. I tell her off when she's too flippant about serious matters, and she tells me off when I'm too much of a wet blanket with my cautiousness: surely you at least approve of that?"

"Granted, but you should be more outgoing. Apart from the people you meet at these Catholic socials she drags you to, the only men you really associate with now Guy's stopped calling are Ben and Micky."

"I can't fall in love to order!"

"You should be playing the field. Goodness knows how much longer we'll be marooned here - we could both be as old as Methuselah by the time we get out."

Pamela was silent. She recognised Hilary's bitterness against Sandra as resentment that she had deprived herself of a satisfying friendship with Ben out of loyalty to Roddy.

With growing dismay she observed the escalation of Sandra's attachment to John Bridger. He seldom called at Room 19 these days. "He has these terrible ulcers on his legs," Sandra explained. "He can't walk far."

("Too ashamed to show his face in here, that's why he doesn't come," growled Hilary afterwards.)

The following week, an air raid alarm just before night curfew gave Sandra the excuse to spend another night at the bungalow.

"You'd better stop this," Hilary told her coldly when she re-appeared the next morning, just in time for a snap roll call. "I've had enough of it."

"We can't help being anxious, in case you're being beaten up," Pamela added quickly in an attempt to dilute the attack. "When they signalled the roll call this morning, it was really nerve-wracking."

"I didn't find it nerve-wracking," Hilary broke in icily. "I find it disgusting, you spending all that time with a married man. Why don't you move in with him completely? It would be much more convenient for you both, wouldn't it?"

"Mind your own bloody business!" Sandra's face was scarlet.

"It's our business too! Pam and I will be quizzed by the Japs if you're missing from our line. I can't imagine how you can justify what you're doing: don't you ever think of any one but yourself? What about John Bridger's wife and kids in Australia?"

"That's exactly it - they're in Australia. He needs care and comfort here, now, and I can give it to him!"

"I don't like sharing a room with a tart!" Hilary yelled.

"I'll move out then!"

"I wish you would - the sooner the better!"

Before the day was over Sandra had gone, her possessions borne away with John Bridger's assistance.

"It's all your fault!" Pamela accused Hilary that evening. "You forced a confrontation."

"Maybe I did - but she would have gone to John eventually."

"You pushed her. She needed us - "

"Not me!" Hilary's voice was scornful. "Oh, she needed you all right before she had John; she's made use of you for years, leaning on you for help with her kid."

"I wanted to help; I loved Melly!"

"She didn't though - Melly was just a nuisance to her. She didn't care two hoots about her husband either - only married him to escape from her parents. You know that as well as I do, so don't pretend to be so shocked. She's a spoilt selfish devil, and we're well rid of her."

"Stop it, stop it, stop it!" Pamela rolled on to her bed, pressing her hands to her ears.

They barely spoke again that night; in the morning Hilary tried to defuse the situation by acting normally.

"We'd best do a clear-up," she said, "I expect we'll be getting someone else in the room before long."

"But we can't have any one else - Sandra will come back." Pamela's voice sounded more uncertain than her words. "The bungalow people won't want an extra person, it's crowded enough as it is, they'll complain to the Billeting Officer. I'm sure she'll want to come back here when she realises how stupid she's been. Give her a chance, Hilary!"

"It's not up to me." Hilary shrugged. "The story's all round the water queue this morning - too many people heard the row in here yesterday. When the Billeting Officer hears, he'll either tell her to come back or he'll put some one else in here, and if she DOES come back, I'm off to St. Stephen's."

Distraught, Pamela made for the bungalow immediately after the meal. She found Sandra in an alcove at one end of the entrance hall: a space about three feet long and six feet wide beneath a small circular window, shielded from the public by half a torn sheet draped over a headhigh line of odds and ends of string knotted together. There was just room for two camp beds wedged side by side; John sat on the nearest one while Sandra tightened the bandage on his ulcerated leg.

"I'm sorry to barge in." Her mission was so important that Pamela disregarded Sandra's hostile look. "Can I see you outside just for a minute?"

"You can say anything you want to say to both of us," Sandra snapped.

"Please.." Pamela's voice quavered as she appealed to John.

"You girls can talk here," said John, patting Sandra's shoulder placatingly as he got off the bed. "I'll be in the kitchen."

"Two minutes!" Sandra faced Pamela with a look of hatred.

"Don't stay here!" Pamela begged. "You can't, it's not a proper room, not like ours; they'll be billeting someone else with us if you don't come back right away. I know awful things were said yesterday, in the heat of the moment, but.."

"I'm never coming back," Sandra interrupted.

"Hilary has offered to move to St. Stephens." In her desperation, Pamela had no compunction in twisting the truth.

"To hell with Hilary! To hell with you! You two have done nothing but criticise me and I've had enough of it. I'm going to be happy in Stanley from now on, so don't waste your time." She turned her back on Pamela, who grasped her arm and gabbled "I know you're looking after John, but you could still do that if you were living with us; you could visit him every day; that way, people wouldn't think.. you know.." "I don't care a damn what people think."

"But his wife and children -"

"I'm helping them by keeping him well and happy." Defeated, Pamela could only sob brokenly. "Sorry this is upsetting you so much." Sandra's voice softened a little. "John and I need each other. I can't expect you to understand, because you haven't been married; and you've never been really roused sexually, have you? When that happens to you, you'll understand."

There was a new occupant in Room 19 when Pamela returned - Mrs. Garrett, white-haired and in her early seventies; she had obviously been obese in pre-camp days and was still quite well-built but from her neck and arms drooped loose bags of flesh. She had somehow managed to bring a good wardrobe of clothes into Stanley and was always well-dressed except that her frocks were far too big for her. She oozed charm at first - until her will was crossed, when she became haughty and demanding. She expected the girls to collect her water and her meals, complaining if they didn't queue early enough to be the first ones served. It soon transpired that she was a reject and had changed billet several times, always at the urgent request of her former room-mates who could no longer stand her autocratic ways. Her overpowering presence should have driven Pamela and Hilary closer together, but it had the opposite effect: both girls still in a highly emotional state, felt further pressured by Mrs. Garrett. Pamela continued to agonise over Sandra and John's situation and could not forgive Hilary for precipitating it. Hilary, feeling unjustly accused, could not tolerate Pamela's tight-lipped disapproval; she also nursed a secret anxiety - increasing attacks of dizziness which she feared heralded a return of her thyroid trouble.

A week after Mrs. Garrett's arrival Hilary went to see the Billeting Officer and obtained permission to move to St. Stephen's to join the V.A.D.s.

"I don't like leaving you," she told Pamela sadly, "but we're not doing each other any good, are we? Remember though, I'm still your friend - you know where I am if you want me."

PART 9

December 1943 - March 1944

DECEMBER

No matter how carefully he timed it, Danny could never avoid the distressing scene outside the Convent. The only sure way would be to arrive late and find Celeste waiting for him; then SHE would be the one having to look on while the beggars lining the pavement begged and whined and died. That she had at last found the confidence to leave her home every day to teach at the Convent was a small miracle; the scars of her experiences in Hong Kong were still there, but teaching was helping to divert her mind. Much as it revolted him to walk among the starving and deprived as he chaperoned Celeste to and from the Convent, he knew this was a small price to pay for the return of her tranquillity.

Three times a day, one of the Irish Sisters and a Chinese Novice came out of the Convent, bent double over the weight of a huge cauldron of fish soup. This was why the crowds congregated here, always hoping to be among the beneficiaries before the supply ran out. Some of them were too weak to hold a bowl themselves; he had seen the Sister holding their containers for them, apparently undeterred by their stench, their seeping sores and pus-filled scabs; sometimes bones poked through holes in their tattered rags. More distressing still were the children, their hair matted with sores, their eyes puzzled and hopeless as they put out skinny arms and whimpered for cumshaw.

This was the legacy of the Far Eastern war for Macau, its economy formerly dependent on import/export trade and tourism. The godowns were now empty of food stocks and other essentials, for the Japanese blockade had put a stop to sea trade. Unemployment was rampant. The poorer classes, most of whom lived from hand to mouth, were virtually beggars now. The better-off were able to live frugally on their savings; the Portuguese residents helped by occasional allowances from Lisbon or other overseas contacts. Danny's hotel engagements became less frequent as the blockade tightened and money became scarcer than ever. He feared the time was coming when he would be signed off completely, and have no income to offer to the communal kitty in the villa.

Standing on the opposite side of the road to the Convent, he waited until Celeste appeared at the top of the steps outside the main door. She could not walk unaided down steps because she had lost so much weight that the leg iron no longer fitted properly. She leaned against the door, shading her eyes against the sun, looking excessively thin in a black skirt and cardigan, her narrow shoulders slightly hunched, her hair cut in a short bob.

Plunging across the road, Danny forged his way through the scrabbling dregs of humanity, holding his breath and trying to ignore the whining voices and the hands pulling at his clothes. As he was helping Celeste down the steps, a municipal cart pulled by two coolies drew up. The coolies surveyed the crowds on the pavement, poked gingerly at several recumbent bodies, lifted up three of them and heaved them on to the open cart.

The putrid smell lingered in the road for some distance on the slow walk home. "I wonder how long it will be before cholera or typhoid breaks out," mused Danny.

In pre-war days regular injections had always been able to prevent a serious epidemic; now Macau was as short of medical supplies as of everything else.

"We must hope and pray for the best. Maybe the war will be over soon." Celeste was always optimistic.

"Not for another year at least." Even reading between the lines of the fanciful Japanese news reports, it was obvious that the Allies were nowhere near defeating the Axis, despite the naval reverses in the Coral Sea admitted by the Japanese some months ago.

They were passing through the main shopping area - no longer bustling and overcrowded as it used to be.

On either side of the road, deep rain-carrying gutters were clogged with smelly refuse. Above them stood rows of two-storeyed tenements, the upper floors supported by columns and overhanging the pavement. Washing extended on bamboo poles protruded from windows and verandahs. The ground floors had been shops, but now very few functioned as such, the rest serving as accommodation for refugees. The plaster on the columns was scarred and gouged, and pasted here and there were flapping garish advertisements in huge Chinese characters. Bunches of electricity cables hung from one floor to another even looped across the lanes which intersected the main thoroughfare.

They walked in the middle of the road to avoid the smells from the gullies. Despite poverty, coolies still squatted in little groups, playing with their flimsy oblong cards, enjoying gambling on an infinitesimally modest scale and smoking evil-smelling, flimsy home-made cigarettes.

The passing traffic consisted mainly of rickshaws, bicycles and hand-drawn carts. Only officials could afford to run cars now. Grunting coolies thrust by with gross loads suspended from bamboo poles bent into a curve across their shoulders. Starving refugees wandered from side to side, scavenging anything on the ground - a broken-off cabbage stalk or stinking fishtail, or the bottom half of a match box, or a rusty nail: everything had a use for those who had nothing.

Celeste's arm suddenly tightened on Danny's. A posse of Japanese Kempetai was approaching. Smartly uniformed, eyes alert, faces expressionless, the men walked liked puppets, their presence removing as if by a magic hand the people in their path. If he had been alone, Danny on principle would not have moved from his route, but he was conscious of the tension in Celeste's grip, so guided her towards the edge of the gutter until the posse had passed.

The Japanese, still officially observing Macau's neutrality in the war, had no real right to patrol the streets as if they owned the territory; but there was no one strong enough to dispute their intimidating presence - it was obvious that the smallest Japanese force could take the colony over if Tokyo so decreed.

How Danny hated this twilight life, with no regular job, little food, and the misery of living in a house where his mother's relatives resented him. His cousin Marie struggled to hide her pain that her husband was presumed lost on the 'Lisbon Maru', while Danny, who could well have been on that ship, walked free and alive. At family evening prayers, he was continually reminded of his situation for Marie's parents prayed especially for their prisoner-of-war sons known to be in Japan, especially now that the Americans were bombing there.

"I have something very special to tell you," Celeste said, stepping aside to avoid two ragged toddlers who were running backwards in front of her with their palms outstretched. "I meant to wait until I got home, to tell Mother and Father first, but I can't keep it in a moment longer: I shall be joining the Sisters soon!"

"You mean.. you'll enter the Convent?"

"With God's grace, early next year, Mother said; maybe at Easter!"

"Are you sure, quite sure, this is what you really want to do?"

"Of course Danny!" She gave him her broadest smile. "You know that!"

"Yes, but.."

She shook her head to silence him and he respected her wish, thankfully realising that if she was ready to become a nun, her mind had at last put away the shaming memory of the rape in Hong Kong.

Yet he mourned her renunciation of what he considered normal life; if she were not his direct cousin, he would make her marry him - she was everything a woman should be, and he knew she adored him whole-heartedly.

They passed a long rice queue where the poor and servants of the rich stood side by side. Near the front there was pushing and complaining, but further back the waiters were patient and orderly, stoically accepting that the supply of rice might have run out by the time they reached the front: then they would leave a member of the family to begin the queue for the next issue.

"This is why I want to be a nun!" Celeste spread a hand towards the queue. "I just want to pray and pray for no one to be hungry or cold or alone, and for the war to end."

Playing at a few dances in the hotel over Christmas earned Danny a little money but it didn't go far. Fullscale Christmas presents were out of the question, even small gifts costly. The only special food in the villa on Christmas Day was the addition of a tiny chicken to the usual stew. After the New Year's Eve Ball he had no further hotel engagements in view, and fretted because he could not contribute to the family expenses.

The Bellarios depended heavily on a periodic remittance from Marcus in America to supplement the allowance from Lisbon, and for some months nothing had arrived from America. Money was needed to provide Celeste with her postulant's outfit so her parents decided to sell some of their possessions and wondered how to go about it.

"I know someone to ask." Danny leapt at the chance to be of service to a household where he felt a parasite. He sought out Lexie, whom he suspected had a finger in every lucrative pie in Macau. Yes, for a tiny commission on every sale concluded, Lexie would introduce him to a Eurasian, half-Chinese, half-Irish - Mr. King, with whom he could deal.

At half past eight one evening Danny sidled into the appointed rendezvous, a small teahouse in a side street, carrying inside his coat an antique carriage clock. The few customers were all Chinese. As previously instructed, he made for the table nearest the kitchen which was occupied by a figure holding the menu up to his face.

"Good eefening Mr. Russell!" The menu was lowered, and Danny found himself facing a well-built Chinese in his mid-thirties, wearing a traditional long Chinese gown. If this was the half Irishman, the only legacy from Ireland was the colour of his eyes, a sparkling blue. "I understand you wish to conduct some business with me?"

"Perhaps, Mr. King." Danny kept the clock out of sight, knowing the advantage that lack of eagerness for a deal might bring.

"You wish sell some item? Jewellery? Gold?"

"Oh no, nothing like that." Danny's spirits dropped as he sensed the other man's disappointment. "Something quite valuable, though - an antique carriage clock from Europe. Would that interest you?"

"Carriage clock.. carriage clock.. Not much business in large items. Gold rings, stones, can carry easy, yes, but clocks.."

Not attempting to cover up his disappointment, fully aware of the workings of the oriental mind, Danny rose from the chair and put out his free hand. "Then I won't bother you any longer, Mr. King. I am sorry to have wasted your time."

"But the tea I order just arriving!" beamed Mr. King. "You must take a cup with me."

"Well," Danny pretended to hesitate, then said "Thank you very much" and sat down again as the tea was poured.

"While tea cool," said Mr. King, "tell me about the clock; is possible I might know a frien' who might know some person who is interested."

Danny produced the clock, pointing out its inlaid marble surround and the 'Made in Switzerland' inscription on the back.

"Not so old," said Mr. King deprecatingly as he examined it minutely. "Good clock, but not so antique. 1885 I think."

This being the date Mr. Bellario had quoted, Danny realised he was in the presence of an expert.

"Clocks not very popular, now wartime." Mr. King bent his head to listen to the tick. "Glass cracked, too. I think not worth much, maybe fifty patacas."

"You're joking of course!" Danny laughed engagingly. "More like five hundred." "Now you make joke," smiled Mr. King blandly. "I think maybe my frien' pay ah.. one hundred twenty."

They settled on two hundred, from which Mr. King deducted his ten per cent commission, and Danny went home with the balance well-pleased. The family seemed delighted with the one hundred and forty he gave them; ten patacas had to go to Lexie for his commission, and Danny secretly kept thirty for his private fund for his mother's medication.

Thereafter, the family regularly handed him a succession of heirlooms for which Mr. King paid reasonable sums. The secret fund, hidden beneath a floorboard under his bed, grew quite sizeable.

One afternoon, coming out of the pharmacy with his mother's tablets, he was approached by a be-spectacled Chinese youth in a European suit. "You see this watch, Mr. Russell?" The youth pulled back the sleeve of his jacket to reveal Danny's grandfather's watch which he had recently sold to King. Danny gazed at it intently, not anxious to reveal recognition to this stranger.

"My father buy from Johnny King, pay big price," said the youth. "Johnny buy from you, you pay him commission, you pay Lexie Savora commission; better, next time you want to sell, you tell me - my father give you better price than Johnny King and charge only five per cent commission - and you no pay Lexie anything!"

Attractive though the proposition sounded, Danny prevaricated. He didn't know this father and son, so had no guarantee that they were reliable dealers. Also, he felt wary of them as they seemed to know so much about him and his affairs.

"I may not have anything else to sell, Mr..?"

"Rene Chang. My father K.T., K.T. Chang. We live in house on terrace above your villa. Very easy to arrange meeting."

"The red brick house with the stone lions on the gates?"

"Ah, you know it, Mr. Russell? So we can do some business, huh?"

Again Danny had an uncomfortable feeling of having been under observation. "I must think about it, when.. if I wish to sell anything else."

"You can leave message for me at the pharmacy." Rene gave a confident nod. "My father K.T. owns it."

"Don't forget your violin!" his mother called from her bed as he blew her a kiss from the door.

"I almost did! What would I do without you, mumma?" He darted back into the room and picked up the case.

"Soon you will find out, Danny," she said, and he hugged her fiercely with his free arm. She was as frail as a Christmas tree ornament; she needed good food and he was determined to get it.

The violin he left in his own sleeping quarters. It had been agreed with the rest of the family not to tell his mother of the sale of more valuables, so as not to add practical anxieties to the burden of her illness: she had grieved enough over the sale of the carriage clock, She was allowed to assume that his evening meetings with the black market negotiators were engagements to play at the hotel.

He would have preferred meetings in daylight, for marauding robbers were becoming increasingly active as the need for food became more desperate. Only two weeks ago a Russian woman had been stabbed to death near her own home, and her fingers chopped off when her rings could not be removed by the robbers. He was still dealing with Johnny King, who chose a different rendezvous for each transaction. "Is best for both, Mr. Russell," Johnny explained. "Bad men watch all time. If we always go same place, same time, soon they find out, then they try to rob us."

The appointed place tonight was particularly insalubrious: a tiny room containing two tables, reached through what in better times had been a garage beneath a down-at-heel block of tenements. King sat at one table; the other was occupied by roughly-dressed Chinese who were smoking and playing mah-jong. It was only when one of the players looked up and swiftly surveyed the room that Danny suspected they were all King's henchmen.

He wanted the business concluded quickly to escape from this sinister place, but Johnny seemed in no hurry. He fingered the ivory figurine Danny produced very carefully before making a ludicrously low offer. When Danny protested he spread his hands in a helpless gesture. "You know, Mr. Russell, not much money in Macau right now."

"I also know that things like this don't stay in Macau." smiled Danny. "Who would want them here?"

"You must be very careful, Mr. Russell." It was the hint of warning in Johnny's voice, lightly spoken yet somehow steely, which decided Danny this would be his final transaction with the man. He made as if to leave, but allowed himself to be cajoled to stay and discuss the price further, eventually agreeing on a figure one hundred patacas above Johnny's original offer.

"One thing more," Johnny paused as he was handing over the notes. "Because ah, bad business lately, I must raise my commission next time to fifteen percent. Most other dealers - twenty per cent, but I.. only fifteen per cent."

It was good to be looked upon as a benefactor in the house, and to know that the meals, without his contribution, would be even more inadequate than they were. The rice was poor quality and gritty; vegetables consisted mainly of stringy wild mushrooms, bamboo shoots fibrous and tough, and potatoes - when at all available - the size of marbles. The red meat his mother so badly needed was rarely available even at exorbitant black market prices, being snapped up by the best hotels. Sometimes, scouring all shops and black market sources, he managed to buy a small tin of corned beef with his self-awarded commission; this food he had to hide from the rest of the family, putting slices of the life-sustaining beef into his mother's sandwiches.

The next time Celeste's father asked him to negotiate a sale, he contacted Rene Chang through the pharmacy. Within twenty-four hours a very successful deal was made on a bench overlooking the Grand Praya, and the price Chang paid for the small cloisonne vase was more than Danny had expected. Before long he was arranging regular sales of items for recommended friends of the Bellarios, and his savings soared.

"I not see you long time!" Johnny stood in front of him and barred the way forward one afternoon. "I hope you and your family keeping well?"

"Very well, thanks, Mr. King. You too, I trust?"

"Yes, yes, thank you, Mr. Russell. You know.. ah, business very good again. Last time we make deal, prices very bad, very bad. Now much better. Maybe you like to show me some more good thing some time soon?"

"Maybe." Danny shrugged his shoulders with a gesture of regret. "But just now, no one I know seems to want to sell. Shall I contact you at the Swan Tea House if anything crops up?" He made to pass on.

"Crops up?" queried Johnny, holding Danny's arm.

"If any one brings me something they want to sell, I mean."

"Ah yes, Mr. Russell. 'Crops up'.. very strange words, huh? You working now?"

"Sometimes." The lie came easily.

"You still play in hotel?"

"Now and again." This lie was easier - the hotel might call on him one evening.

"Good pay, yes?"

"Good enough," he smiled, shaking Johnny's hand and moving determinedly on.

For two weeks after that encounter he felt too uneasy to undertake more sales, explaining to the Bellarios that the market had gone quiet. They were disappointed, having come to rely on the proceeds of the sales, especially as their friends for whom Danny also negotiated usually gave the family a percentage in gratitude. In truth, he would like to abandon the business altogether. What had begun as a thrilling money-making venture had gradually become sinister; and he had saved enough to keep his mother in medical supplies and extra food for some months.

FEBRUARY

Celeste was counting the days until her entry into the Convent. Her trousseau was ready. It was difficult to persuade her to eat a proper meal; she wanted to be generous and give her portion to those at the table with large appetites. She was blissfully happy these days, especially as she had made a new friend at the Convent, a Chinese student of about eighteen who had recently enrolled to improve her English.

"She did her studies at school in Canton," Celeste explained to Danny. "Her name is Cherry Hau. She goes from class to class, just for English lessons. She wants to learn to play the piano as well - I'm teaching her."

It was now Lent. Celeste's time of leaving the Convent each afternoon became irregular for she liked to stay after teaching hours for Lenten devotions in the chapel. Cherry stayed too, so when she volunteered to bring Celeste home each day, the offer was accepted.

Danny was introduced to her one afternoon when she arrived with Celeste. She was short and rounded, with dimpled cheeks and languorous brown eyes. Her permed hair tumbled about her shoulders. The Convent uniform - a navy blue sailor suit with broad white collar - looked incongruous on her fulsome chest. She laughed a lot, talked excitedly, and aroused in Danny feelings which he had not experienced for a very long time. She reminded him of some of the girls he had known in Manila, yet without their hardness and sophistication. After he had returned to Hong Kong, there had been Portuguese and Eurasian girl-friends - fun to take to the movies and exciting to kiss when this was permitted; but since the attack on Hong Kong there had been no room in this hard, grim life for any romance.

Now, more often than not he strolled towards the Convent in the afternoon and joined the two girls on their way to the villa after which Danny would walk Cherry to her flat in a quiet part of the town. When she met him for their first date he was disturbed and thrilled at the sight of her tight-fitting cheong sam in cornflower-blue linen. She wore golden dragon earrings, and had made up her face.

"You do not recognise me, no?" she laughed as he stared, fascinated.

"I don't think the Sisters at the Convent would," he said cautiously.

They left the cobbled streets behind and ambled up the broken steps leading to the ruins of the Sao Paola Cathedral, the single relic an elaborate stone façade with cherubs and saints carved in its many niches. Behind lay waste land which had once been the nave of the Cathedral. Bees hummed and crickets chirupped among the burgeoning bushes. Exalted to be with someone so glamorous who so obviously enjoyed his company, for the first time in Macau he was aware of the city's attractions. The view from the Cathedral plateau across tenement roofs to the sea and the islands beyond was beautiful, especially as the sun was setting in a painted sky. Cherry chattered inconsequentially about the irritations of the war, the dreadful meals at the Convent, and the shortage of shampoo for washing her hair.

"It always looks shining and lovely," Danny daringly fingered the dancing tendrils across her forehead.

"My amah is always brushing, brushing, brushing." Cherry moved away from his hand. "She is so fussy. She said she got to come with me this afternoon. I say no can, Mr. Danny Russell is gentleman."

"I should hope so!" He could not hide his pleasure at the realisation that this casual remark somehow advanced their acquaintanceship.

Using some of his treasured hoard of money, he took her to the cinema the following week. This time Cherry's amah appeared, following the couple at a short distance. "I say, she can come with me tonight because dark when we come back," Cherry explained.

"Is she coming in with us?"

"Oh no, she go see friend, then wait outside cinema until film finish."

'Alexander's Rag-time Band' had been shown so often in the past two years - few English language films had happened to be in Macao on the outbreak of the Far Eastern war - that it broke down several times. During these delays, Danny became increasingly aware of the voluptuous presence at his side. With great self-control he reminded himself that his companion was a young Catholic student, not in the same category as the blasé singers and dancers in the hotel in Manila who had tempted him beyond his strength.

Tonight she was wearing a black shiny cheong sam shot through with golden flowers. Tentatively he took her hand and held it. She allowed it to remain in his for five seconds then withdrew it, but that brief cool touch sent his senses reeling.

They began meeting several evenings a week, sometimes in one of the small tea-houses which managed to keep going, sometimes in the cinema. The little amah was always somewhere around, which meant that hand-holding had to be surreptitious.

These outings ate into his savings, and the time was coming when he would need to replenish them. When he called at the hotel in the hope of getting another engagement, Lexie said "You seem very rich these days, Danny. I often see you out with your new girl-friend. It's a long time since I had a cut from business with you and Johnny King.. I hope you haven't been doing any deals with him behind my back."

"As if I would!" He laughed, but his heart thudded uncomfortably.

"Anything worthwhile coming up for sale soon?"

"Nothing I've heard of. I think my people keep hoping things will improve and they won't need to part with anything else."

In fact, he was constantly being badgered by the Bellarios to organise more sales for themselves and their friends. When he could resist them no longer, he arranged another meeting with Rene Chang; the chosen venue was the Protestant Cemetery at night. Doubly apprehensive now that Lexie as well as Johnny seemed suspicious, he decided to take all the items at once, to conclude one bulk deal instead of risking several meetings. The pickings on the collection of silver necklaces, wedding rings and bracelets should be good.

In the unlit cemetery, the shadowy tomb stones looked like silent watchers. In his nervousness he didn't haggle too long over prices, and was astonished at Rene's generous offers; Rene too seemed to be in a hurry and it crossed Danny's mind that he was pleased with the deal and wished to conclude it before Danny realised he had underestimated the value of his items.

"I don't expect to have anything else for a very long time." Danny pocketed the notes carefully. "Maybe nothing more at all."

"So, if no more, never mind," Rene shrugged. "If more, send me message."

By agreement they left the cemetery separately, Danny taking the steps down to the road at a quick pace. At this hour the road was deserted except for the street sleepers, packaged like parcels in rattan matting and sheets of newspaper. In the tenements above naked bulbs shone in curtainless rooms; he could see people eating, working, playing mah jong: could hear the clack of the tiles, shrill conversation, laughter, dogs barking, and Chinese music on stringed instruments.

Rain had been threatening all day. Now it came suddenly, dropping like steel needles. As he started to run, the street sleepers yelled irritation at having to rouse and move further beneath the verandahs. In the commotion Danny didn't realise he was being followed until he was seized from behind, his arms pinioned by many hands, and pushed to the ground. The suddenness of the attack took his breath away. Resistance brought vicious kicks. Anonymous Chinese faces glared into his, rough voices in Cantonese demanding all his money. When he tried to protect the wad of notes in an inside pocket, a knife was held at his throat. Convinced this was the final moment in life, he gave up the struggle and called on God. The money was grabbed, his face and stomach kicked to render him dazed and incapable of movement while the gang made its escape.

"I'm still alive!" was his first coherent thought as he crawled, sodden and bleeding, towards the gutter which was gurgling with rain water. No one had come to his aid during the attack; now, cautiously, a few figures emerged from beneath the verandahs and stared down at him. In the distance he heard police whistles, and soon two Macanese policemen arrived. He couldn't talk, his face and jaw swollen and stiff; his hair was matted with blood. He was taken to the hospital, where one of the nurses recognised him and promised to notify his family. After his wounds were dressed the nurse gave him an injection and sat beside him holding his hand as the drug began to take effect. He was floating and it was heavenly, but he knew there was something wrong, something he should be worrying about; he tried to think what it was as the floating sensation engulfed him completely.

Slowly recuperating in the hospital, there was nothing to do but anguish endlessly over the loss of the money - other people's money. It had been impossible to keep the incident from his mother; she was too ill to visit him but sent him loving notes which could not disguise her distress. Celeste came to see him the day before she was to enter the Convent, but this only added to his deep sadness.

He was hurt that no word came from Cherry. Celeste said she had left the school. The letters he sent to her flat were returned unopened and her name on the outside crossed out. The suspicion crept into his mind that she had been used by Johnny King to try to discover if he was involved in clandestine trading elsewhere. He remembered passing Rene Chang one evening when taking Cherry to the cinema. Rene had not spoken to him, just raised a finger in acknowledgment. That tiny movement would have been enough for a briefed Cherry to suspect his connection with Danny, for King undoubtedly knew the identity of all his competitors.

He was even more unhappy when he went home. The Bellarios could not hide their distress at the losses to themselves and more especially, to their friends. His mother tried to console him: "It was not your fault the money was stolen, Danny. But you must promise me you will have nothing more to do with those dealers! You could have been killed! However bad things are, somehow we will manage to exist without this dangerous business. You should never have been put in this position... the family should not have asked you to do this.."

The emotional outburst had taken all her strength. She flopped back in the bed and tears ran down her cheeks. "You will never be safe in Macau now, Danny. Those thieves will watch out for you again. You must go away."

This fear had lurked in his mind ever since he had regained consciousness.. fear not only of thieves but of the sinister possibility that the robbery had been organised by Johnny King. "But where could I go?" he asked hopelessly.

"Back to Hong Kong! You have your British passport.You can request the Japanese to intern you; you would be safer there."

Danny thought her idea completely mad: who would deliberately seek internment, loss of liberty? Terrible tales had leaked back to Macau of hardships in the Hong Kong camps; besides, there was always the risk of being sent to Japan, and perhaps drowned on the way.

"You know I would never leave you, Mumma." He hugged her close. "Never!"

"I would be happier, knowing you are away from the dangers here; leave as soon as I am gone, please!"

"Don't talk like that!" he begged, but she persisted with her request and exacted a promise from him that he would try to get to Hong Kong after her death.

Meanwhile a further trial had to be faced. He learned that the Bellarios were endeavouring to recompense their friends for their lost valuables, by handing over to them a percentage of the Lisbon allowances. His conscience told him he must give the family what remained of his private savings. The hoard had to be explained; his mumbled confession of the commission he had awarded himself left him feeling forever damned in the family's eyes, even though his grandfather was adamant that his mother should not know about it.

He had never felt so abysmally wretched. He could see his mother's days were numbered. Celeste, his dearest friend, had gone from him. He felt panic every time he left the villa, the more so when he heard that Rene Chang had been attacked and both arms broken. Then a kind of fatalism overtook him; he felt doomed, and decided to throw caution to the winds and spend what life he had left in making money to liquidate the moral debt to the family. He haunted the hotels again, but none could afford to employ him now.

Spring was approaching; food shortages were even more acute; the municipal carts busier than ever picking up corpses in the streets. The identified dead whose relatives could afford funerals were trundled to the cemetery in rough, tar-painted coffins on four-wheeled trolleys. The mourners were so transparently thin and listless that it was obvious they would themselves be victims before long.

He missed Celeste's company painfully. They had often sat on the stone parapet beside the Rua Praya and watched the fishing sampans poling into the harbour. Now there was nothing to do but stroll moodily along on his own, envying groups and couples who, chattering and laughing, passed by. With the burdens on his mind, he wondered if he would ever laugh again.

One evening he noticed a number of people were standing beneath the steep escarpment on which one of the larger hotels stood. Approaching them, he realised why they were lingering there: they were listening to the just audible strains of the dance band playing in the hotel, for its French windows were thrown open. He stood to listen himself, saw the loiterers' reluctance to move on, and others take their place when they did and an idea was born in his mind; of course, it was unheard of, for a European or Eurasian to play music in the streets for money; the very term 'street musician' was derogatory - but the circumstances of life in Macau were so unusual - could never have been imagined before the war.

He thought the matter over that night and the next day. In the evening, wearing his navy blue trousers and a white shirt, with a blue scarf tied loosely at the neck, he decided on a pitch on the Praya Grande well away from the hotels, took out his violin and began to tune up. The notes sounded thin and tentative in the open air. He tried to ignore the curious stares of passersby, and, heart beating furiously, began to play. When the first coins were dropped in the open violin case, his throat constricted for a moment: this was begging, wasn't it? No, not if he gave value for money! Gradually, his old confidence returned; the music took him over; he played powerfully, with closed eyes, and when he opened them, a dozen people - Portuguese, Chinese, Eurasian, Japanese, were hovering nearby - and the violin case was gleaming with coins of all sizes as well as some notes.

He was too apprehensive of his family's reaction to reveal the source of this new income when he handed his takings to them, but within a few days he was recognised and the family informed. The younger members were horrified and ashamed, the older members more understanding.

"Danny, there is no need for that," his grandfather muttered. "We admire you for your determination to help, but whatever would your dear mother say?"

"I'll tell her," said Danny simply. "She will understand."

She did. She told him he should use his talents in whatever way he could, but he could see the pain in her eyes. Some evenings he did well, at other times he knew the feeling of rejection when his best efforts brought little money and many sniggers. After one exceptionally good night he could not wait to get home to show his mother his bulging wallet, but his smile faded when he saw the change in her as she lay pressed back against her pillow. She wrapped thin fingers round his hand with the wallet. "Keep it for your steamer ticket to Hong Kong, Danny darling.. remember your promise! I know you will! You have made me so proud.. always."

The priest was called. The family gathered round for the Last Rites, The house was full of sympathetic people as neighbours too came to condole, but he had never felt so alone.

PART 10

1944

MAY

For some weeks after Sandra and Hilary left Room 19 Pamela had wallowed in unmitigated misery. Jenny tried to help by pressing her to join in the activities of the highly-organised Catholic community, but she was too apathetic to accept. Her loneliness became so acute that she was tempted to re-establish her friendship with Guy Gasson, holding back only because she realised this would be unfair unless she was prepared to further the relationship. Her rejection by both Sandra and Hilary had shattered her self-esteem, she felt chary of making other friends in case the same thing happened. Thrown entirely on her own resources, she slowly re-thought her life.

When volunteers were sought to augment the staff in the hospital office, she jumped at the chance of a new interest, for her sewing jobs had become mere chores without Hilary and Sandra to chat to while she worked. Mrs. Garrett was poor company, always complaining and demanding, and the school teacher Avis Minter, who had taken Hilary's place in the room, was a constant trial because she suffered from severe asthma. The hospital office proved a haven, and she quickly slipped back into typing and clerical work. The two ancient typewriters were in need of overhaul, the ribbons worn pale, but there was a feeling of normalcy, dealing with paper and carbons as in pre-war days which helped to restore her equilibrium.

The hospital job soon became much more than a personal therapy - it was an education. She heard the first cries of new-born babies; admired the doctors' ingenious improvisations necessitated by lack of medical equipment: admired too the nurses, always immaculately dressed in their white uniforms and veils, giving no hint of the grossly congested conditions of their dormitories. She saw surgeons who had spent the morning in the operating theatre, sitting on benches in the hospital office tucking into the same meagre lunch as every one else. She watched the life-blood of a new mother gushing along the gutter outside the theatre as she haemorrhaged to death; saw a gaunt-faced husband regularly bring the best of his own daily rations to his terminally-ill wife.

She discovered that Hilary no longer worked in the hospital because of ill-health, and one day went to St. Stephen's to see her. Hilary was propped up in bed chatting to some V.A.D.s. She looked very pale but her eyes were bright and she welcomed Pamela warmly, assuring her "Nothing wrong with me that rest and repatriation won't cure; I kept getting a recurrence of those dizzy spells, it's the old thyroid again."

"Meanwhile, she's living the life of Riley, being waited on hand and foot," laughed one of the girls who brought two mugs of pale tea and handed one to Hilary and one to Pamela.

"How's the garden going?" - Hilary chatted as though they had never quarrelled. "Sorry I had to abandon it when I moved, but I just didn't have the energy to walk that far."

"Micky and Ben run it now." Pamela didn't add that she too had abandoned the garden because Hilary's departure had taken the pleasure out of every aspect of camp life. Sitting on the floor, discussing current rumours, she felt the beginnings of a return of the old relationship.

"And how's old Grumbling Garnett? Still as bossy as ever?" asked Hilary when Pamela got up to leave.

"I think she's mellowing a bit."

"Like us all?" Hilary suggested lightly, taking Pamela's hand and squeezing it. "When I'm up and about again, I'll call on you and we can have a good natter - right?"

"I'll look forward to that!", Pamela turned at the door to wave goodbye and bumped into a tall fair bronzed young man whose eyes looked past her and focussed on Hilary.

"Oh-oh, that man's here again," sang out two voices in unison.

"Third time today," some one added.

"How is my girl now?" The newcomer made straight for Hilary's bed, bent down and kissed her.

Weeks later she met the pair out walking arm-in-arm, and was shocked at the apparent closeness of their relationship. Dismayed and disapproving, she was unable to return Hilary's smile, and walked by stony-faced. She learned that his name was Stefan, a Belgian bank clerk with a promising future; soon there were rumours of an engagement. Brooding about this, she gave in to Jenny's invitations to Catholic activities as a means of channelling her thoughts elsewhere; soon she was making toys for the forthcoming Christmas Party organised by Father Heyer, creating soft animals out of threadbare garments and basic dolls' houses out of the brown Red Cross cartons. These interests brought her new friends from among her co-workers, mainly young people of various nationalities. She began to toy with the idea of converting to Catholicism, seeing the influence of their religion on her new companions, and in the care and concern shown to her in her most despondent moments; she felt an outsider and wished she wasn't, yet shrank from obeisance to a church whose temporal head was what her father had always referred to as 'a foreign Pope in a foreign country'; shrank too, from the repercussions which conversion would evoke in her family when they knew.

"It has to be your decision, Pamela," Father Messler said when she confided her fears and anxieties. "You're an adult, you have the right to choose."

There were many aspects of Catholicism which bothered her, until Father Messler showed her an extract from the writings of St. Thomas More:-

'Let us have done with theological refinement. A man is not lost because he cannot tell whether the Spirit has one principle or two. Has he the fruits of the Spirit? That is the question. Is he patient, good, gentle, modest, temperate, chaste? Inquire if you will but do not define.'

Confession, which had originally seemed a daunting hurdle, proved surmountable under Father Hessler's gentle guidance. She recalled asking her childhood Catholic friend Philip what he told the priest in the confessional. He'd said 'Told lies, hit my sister, pinched a bloke's pencil, cheeked my Mum.. that sort of thing,' None of those peccadillos applied to her, and at first she wondered what she could find to confess: was astonished, after reading through the pages in the prayer book on 'examination of conscience' to discover a long list of sins which DID apply to her.. uncharitable thoughts, envy, pride, sloth.

When she decided to attend Mass for the first time she risked offending Jenny by insisting on going unaccompanied; she wanted to find her own way in this experience, without someone at her elbow, watching her reactions. It was a Low Mass; she found the quietness and intensity of the Consecration inspiring, and envied the look of earnest devotion on the faces of the communicants as they walked back from the altar. By Easter she was one of them.

Hers was a fragile faith. She doubted if she would ever acquire Jenny's easy familiarity with the Almighty, Jesus and Mary, but she achieved a measure of tranquillity. Instead of anguishing about Roddy, Hilary and Sandra, she learned to pray for them. Even the irritations of Mrs. Garrett and Avis Minter could be turned to good purpose by enduring them with toleration rather than showing exasperation.

Yet the comforts of her new-found religion failed her when first she awoke on her 25th birthday and stared disconsolately at the pencilled calendar on the wall: 1942, 1943, all crossed through, and 1944 crossed out up to today, 28th May: how many more birthdays was she destined to spend in Stanley? She recalled last year's birthday; Hilary and Sandra had arranged a surprise party, with Melly staggering uncertainly from one person to another; she thrust the memory away, it was too poignant to be borne.

On her bed two feet away from Pamela's, Mrs. Garrett yawned and sighed. The frilly neck of her floral nightgown contrasted grotesquely with the uncurtained room, untidy with jackets and bags hanging on bent nails, its floor black and ridged now that all the floorboards had been sold.

Against the window a dipalidated bed was held level by the substitution of concrete blocks for two missing legs; here lay Avis Minter, flat on her stomach, her long dark hair straggling over her slender shoulders. She was a school teacher in her mid-thirties and, like Mrs. Garrett, a reject, her original room-mates driven to distraction by her tortured breathing.

"Congée up!" came a call from the courtyard,

"Whose turn to collect?" yawned Avis.

"Yours," said Mrs. Garrett, who always knew.

Avis got up, pulled a dress over her underwear and padded barefoot to the corridor with three dishes. Congée was an additional meal recently introduced to bridge the long gap between 5 p.m. supper and 11 a.m. lunch - a proportion of the rice ration being boiled in sea water to a porridge-like consistency, and delivered to the corridors in a zinc bath. Even eaten without milk, sugar or wong tong, it was greatly relished as a stimulating start to the day.

Sitting on her bed, slowly spooning up the mush, Pamela could not help feeling sorry for herself; no one in the room knew about the birthday, no one cared.

She wished now she had woken earlier and gone to the short Mass said every morning; it would have been possible, because this was her day off from the hospital office.

She said her morning prayers when it was her turn for the bathroom, too self-conscious yet to make the sign of the cross in front of Mrs. Garrett and Avis.

This being a 'dry' day with no water running in the taps, she scooped part of her day's ration from the store of water in the bath and poured it into the wash basin for a sketchy toilet. When she pulled the plug out of the basin, the used water drained into a kerosene tin beneath, which, when completely filled, was poured into the cistern to flush the lavatory.

Clothes washing had to be left until a water supply day - unless one was prepared to go to the narrow concrete nullah which carried stream water down the hillside near the hospital, finally emptying into the sea just below the barbed wire fence above the rocks. This she decided to do this morning - it would take her mind off the empty birthday. Back in the room she collected her dirty clothes and wrapped them up in her only sheet.

"Washing day, Pamela?" - Mrs. Garrett could always be depended upon to state the obvious.

"Better the day, better the deed," Pamela managed to control her irritation, putting a precious sliver of hard yellow soap into the pocket of her shorts.

"Oh, while you're at it, would you mind.." began Mrs. Garrett, but Pamela slipped quickly through the door, basely dodging the inevitable request to wash Mrs. Barrett's smalls as well as her own.

It was always a relief to leave the bustling blocks, past the courtyard where chattering women stood over a table formed by an old door lying across rough trestles, where they chopped chives and taro - the main ingredients of the next meal.

She walked slowly towards the hospital (no one hurried anywhere these days, conserving such little energy as the poor rations generated.) The distant view was soothing and beautiful. On the right, the dark green mountain of Stanley Fort soared up against the brilliant blue sky; on the left a succession of hills paled one behind the other, fissured with shadowed valleys. Ahead, a tiny islet a few hundred yards beyond the rocks outside the hospital looked like a pale green cake edged with icing as small waves frothed against its coast. Familiarity with these scenes never diminished their splendour, but re-stirred the ache for a time when they could be enjoyed without the privations and uncertainties that bedevilled every day in the camp. Now the scene was already spoilt by passing internees: a middle-aged bearded man, bare torso and limbs healthily tanned, but whose every rib was outlined, and whose stomach bulged with a hugh hernia beneath his shorts; a group of spindly-legged teenage girls who had long outgrown their skimpy skirts.

There were so many people doing their laundry in the nullah that Pamela settled herself on the spiky grass above to await a vacancy. Clasping her bent legs with her hands, she gazed out to sea and tried to imagine a life other than this. The scheduled repatriation of 800 women and children and sick had never happened, so hope for a ship for herself and other fit women was an impossible dream, just as impossible as awaking one morning and finding not the alien Mrs. Garrett and Avis, but Sandra, Hilary and Melly.

Two women were moving away from the nullah, and she quickly slithered down the bank to take their place. It was difficult to crouch at an angle of 45°, with soft mud oozing between her bare toes, as she held each garment in turn beneath the trickle of water and soaped and rubbed it.

"When we're back in town," announced one perspiring mother who was attending very sketchily to the family laundry, "I'm going to pay my wash amah twice as much as I used to - it's real hard work, this! - Oh damn!" She had dropped her soap in the nullah and it slipped beyond her reach; women further down tried unsuccessfully to grab it as it slid irrevocably beneath the barbed wire.

Meanwhile, rumours both feasible and far-fetched were cheerfully bandied: the war in Europe was declared to be almost over (because even the Japanese newspapers reported that Allied troops had secured a toehold in Italy); the Russians had annihilated the Germans (because the sketch maps in the newspapers revealed that the Russians were beginning to halt the assault on their country); the U.S. Navy was back in the Pacific in strength and sending the Japanese fleet to the bottom (because the newspapers boasted daily sinkings of U.S. ships). Best of all was the theory that every one in camp would be repatriated within the month, and Red Cross parcels would arrive next week.

"I just hope they contain soap if they do come," was the soap loser's rueful reaction. Issues of soap, and other precious commodities such as salt, sugar and cooking oil, were made rarely and unpredictably and in tiny quantities: you never counted on them - simply felt grateful when they arrived.

"I'll tell you something that's 100% authentic," said a young woman who had just joined the washers. "The Japs brought a new fellow into camp this morning."

"An internee, d'you mean?"

"Uh-uh. He's billetted in the block next to mine - Indian Quarters. Quite young, I think - I only saw his back view."

"Might be one of those men who've been in the gaol.." It was known that several British arrested at the same time as the group who had been executed last year were serving terms of imprisonment.

"Shouldn't think he came from the prison." said the young woman, "he had a violin with him."

"Your friend Jenny left a message for you," said Avis when Pamela returned to the room having hung her washing on the line in the courtyard, within sight of the window so she could watch that no one appropriated any of it. "She says to meet her outside her block at 3, to take a pancake to someone; does that sound right?"

"Understood." Pamela had recently been roped in to Father Heyer's scheme to supply extra sustenance to the sick and elderly. He provided dried egg yolk, bought with the proceeds from selling to rich internees the food parcels he sometimes received from Chinese priests in town; the patient provided a small amount of his uncooked rice ration which the appointed helper ground, mixed with water and egg yolk, fried in whatever pan or tin was available wiped round with an oily rag, and delivered.

"We're to do the pancake later on," said Jenny when Pamela met her at 3 p.m. "First, I want to show you something." She led the way to her family's room and threw open the door with a flourish.

"Happy Birthday Pamela!" shouted a dozen voices.

Smiling at her were Jenny's parents and the boys, the two priests and some of her new Catholic friends. A cake made of rice flour was produced, and a home-made birthday card from her co-workers which they had all signed. She was so touched that her voice shook when she thanked them.

"But how did you know?" she asked Jenny as, later in the afternoon, they went to the Indian Quarters with the pancake for Tom McTavish, an old marine engineer recovering from malaria.

"I remembered from last year it was some time in May, and I noticed last time I was in your room that the 28th was ringed every year on your calendar."

"Well, I couldn't have had a better birthday," Pamela beamed. "And I was feeling so miserable this morning."

Tom, bent and shaky, was embarrassingly grateful for the food, and his three elderly room-mates openly envious as he tucked into it. They made much of the honour of being visited by 'two charming young ladies' and would have kept them there talking longer, had not the Indian Quarters' supper been signalled. While Tom chased the remains of the pancake round the plate for which the girls were waiting, the other men went to join the food queue. The girls stood on the verandah and watched the growing line of internees snaking across the green towards the kitchen.

There was a depressing sameness about the adults' attire, the men barefoot and wearing just shorts, the women with bra tops or brief blouses over faded skirts or shorts. Children darting among the queue wore minimal cut-down garments. Amid such drab uniformity, a newcomer stood out, a slight figure wearing long dark trousers, a white shirt with long sleeves, and black shoes.

"Who can he be?" Jenny nudged her. "I've never seen him before!"

Ever since the gossip at the nullah in the morning, Pamela had wondered about the new arrival with the violin: it couldn't be Danny Russell, who would either be in the military camp or with his Portuguese relations... yet now she could see him there was no mistake. She said slowly "I think he's Daniel Russell, a musician. I used to see him playing the violin in the hotel bands."

"Dishy, isn't he? I wonder where he's been all this time?"

Pamela wondered too, but reminded herself that this should not be her concern; the brief affair seven years ago seemed make-believe now, and he had been out of her life for so long that the adults they had both become were complete strangers. She insisted on leaving the Indian Quarters by the short cut behind the blocks to avoid walking past Danny, even though this involved an exhausting scramble up a stony and almost vertical slope.

"Do you know, Daniel Russell has been at Mass the last two mornings," Jenny reported. "I told Father Messler about him being a violinist, and he said I should invite him to our social on Sunday and maybe get him to play for us. So I did, and he's going to come, but he doesn't feel like playing his violin yet; poor guy, his mother died last month. Father is going to say Mass for the repose of her soul next Sunday."

Pamela made polite comment then changed the subject, anxious not to say anything which might reveal her former close relationship with Danny. That evening she bumped into him; he stared at her for several seconds before recognising her, then cried "Pamela! Pamela Doran.. is it still Doran?"

"Doran it is," she said, her hand tingling in his firm grasp.

"It's great to see you safe and sound!" Danny was still shaking her hand vehemently.

She noticed that his impressive clothes were in reality carefully repaired in many places, and his shoes worn down at the heels. "I've just heard about your mother," she said. "I'm so sorry."

He dropped her hand and his face worked. "She had been ill for so long; now she's at rest. Tell me about your family - I'm all out of touch, I've been in Macao until a week ago; did your brother come through the fighting O.K.? I met him during the thick of it, you know."

"He survived the fighting, but we haven't had any news since he left for Japan and the ship was torpedoed."

"The 'Lisbon Maru'? Two of my Bellario cousins were on board, we heard Jack had been saved and is now in Japan; but Ricky and Marie's husband were lost.. I'm sure you would have been notified if Roddy didn't make it.. I sure hope he did. What about your married sister and her husband?"

Chatting about her family members again, after months of isolation from any one who had known them, warmed her heart. He told her about his mother's last illness, and of conditions in Macau.

"It must have been very bad if you chose to come here," Pamela smiled; his hollowed cheeks and serious eyes gave him an attractive maturity.

"At least you get food given you here, without having to forage for it. Look Pamela, I'll have to be going, I'm due to meet someone before curfew."

Taken aback by this sudden abruptness, she put a hand on his arm and said "Tell me about Celeste first - is she in Macau too?"

"Yes, she's a postulant in the Convent there." He was fidgetting with the winder of his watch.

"So she really is going to be a nun? Sandra couldn't believe she meant it when she told her in the Jockey Club Hospital that Christmas: you know Sandra is here?"

"I guessed she was."

"And that her husband was killed during the fighting? Then she had a baby girl in camp, but poor little Melly died when she was only a year old."

"I am so sorry to hear all that, what a lot of tragedy for her." He was edging away. "I must say good night now; it's been really nice meeting you again."

His blatant lack of interest after the initial welcome astonished her; she could only assume that what she had taken for spontaneous pleasure at seeing her was nothing more than his habitual politeness. Nothing could be clearer from his final remark than that he had no intention of continuing the conversation. He hadn't even asked for her camp address. What surprised her even more was the realisation that she was hurt.

She met his astonished stare at Mass the following Sunday as she walked back from the altar after receiving Holy Communion. He waylaid her outside. "You didn't tell me you had become a Catholic, Pamela! I was so surprised!" His face was alight with interest again. "How long have you been one of us?"

"Two months," she said, consciously withdrawn to avoid another snub.

"Congratulations! I must try to get a letter through to Celeste, she will be so thrilled."

They were at the turning to the Indian Quarters. "Will you be at the social this afternoon?" he asked as he left her. "I've been invited by Jenny some one."

"I can't come, I'm afraid." She didn't add that she had offered to work the Sunday afternoon shift in the hospital office specifically to avoid meeting him at the social.

SUMMER

The daily rations continued to diminish in quality and quantity. The morning meal usually took the form of fish or melon, and rice of such poor quality that cooking it turned it into mush. Meat was a great rarity, and when it did appear it was in such small quantities that you were lucky if you had one good mouthful of it in your ladle of stew. The delicious extras - eggs, bananas, wong tong, egg yolk and peanuts, were only available to those with money. Reasoning that the menacing presence of Allied navies in the Pacific restricted shipments of food to Hong Kong didn't help allay hunger. The little private gardens were taken over and worked as communal plots to supplement the daily rations; the growing produce was often raided at night by the boldest of the hungry who risked the wrath of fellow internees and arrest by the Japanese for being abroad during curfew hours.

Under such starvation conditions, the black market flourished as never before. Any saleable possession was handed to an internee dealer who negotiated with the Formosan guards over the barbed wire at night. The guards found buyers in the city in return for Yen which, less their commission, they eventually passed to the dealer, who took his cut before giving the original vendor the proceeds. People with gold fillings in their teeth could suddenly become millionaires if they were prepared to have the gold removed by the camp dentist and sell it. Those who made more Yen than they needed lent some to the penniless in return for promissory notes, to be repaid after the war. Pamela parted with her watch and ate well for several weeks afterwards. She hesitated to borrow money: despite Guy Gasson's conviction that they would receive back pay after the war, she dared not incur huge debts which could swallow up this hoped-for nest egg.

The water shortage became so acute that now the taps were turned on only every fifth day; the bathful of water had to even more carefully eked out. There was not enough used water to flush the lavatories adequately; when complaints about this were made to the Japanese, the answer was "You dig latrines.. trenches outside every block."

While the trenches were being dug - no mean task on poor rations - protests on hygienic grounds mounted at the prospects of using them. The Japanese, always sensitive about hygiene, relented and allowed teams of men, under supervision, to collect sea water for flushing purposes. Twice daily, the water squad could be seen staggering back into camp under the weight of leaking containers of every description.

All these hardships were suddenly thrown into perspective the day the news broke that the Allies had made a landing in France. At first the Japanese newspaper highlighted the Germans' success in containing the invaders, but as the little maps accompanying the reports showed advance upon advance, it became clear that the Allies really were pushing back into Europe: so at last there was a glimmer of hope of liberation in the Far East; the dream of repatriation was shattered forever, but it was replaced by the dream of ultimate release.

"You hardly ever come swimming these days," Jenny complained as she and Pamela walked back from St. Stephen's after delivering a pancake to another of Father Heyer's beneficiaries. "Why don't you, Pam?"

"Too lazy - call it old age; it's such a slog, climbing up that hill from the beach."

"You can take it slowly - everyone does. Do come with us tomorrow afternoon, you're off duty aren't you?"

"I am, but I've got a German class." This was one of Pamela's new interests, deliberately fostered since Jenny was completely taken up with Danny in organising a church concert.

"The lesson isn't until four is it? You could be back by then. It's such fun, Danny is marvellous with the kids we're trying to teach to swim."

"I told you." Pamela's voice was a little edgy. "I can't take that hill, especially if I need to hurry." She had had no further conversation with Danny since that first Sunday, although their paths frequently crossed and they exchanged polite greetings.

"He's great company," Jenny rattled on. "He kept us all in stitches last evening, doing impersonations. You know, I could really fall for him."

"I thought you already had!"

"I mean, really seriously, Pam!" Jenny gave her a fond push. " I never get the chance to talk to him on his own, though, there's always the gang in his block he's so friendly with; or else he's surrounded by all those little fiends he's teaching to sing for the show."

Squatting on the concrete floor of an old garage trying to learn German verbs was not an inviting prospect as Pamela sprawled across her bed after her morning shift at the hospital. When one of Jenny's brothers knocked on the door to say Jenny had a tummy upset and wanted Pamela to take her place on the beach with the children, she found herself agreeing, despite a secret vow not to seek Danny's company again.

She had never before seen him bare to the waist. Like all internees, of necessity he swam in shorts. His dark skin was no longer so very different from her own - over two years of life in the open air had given everyone a deep tan.

At first in the water Pamela knew acute embarrassment as her T shirt clung revealingly to her bosom. This had not bothered her when swimming with other girls; now, feeling Danny's eyes on her, she quickly turned away.

"You watch the girls, Pam, while I give the boys a session" Danny called after her. She attempted to teach the little girls to float until Danny summoned her. "Edward's going to swim to you, Pam! Come on, Edward, you can do it! I'll give you a push, and you swim towards Miss Doran. Just keep going, we won't let you sink."

Pamela reached out and seized the flaying arms just as Edward's agonised eyes were about to disappear beneath the water. Panting and spluttering he yelled "I swam! I swam!"

"One up and three to go!" Danny jerked a thumb in the air. "Jolly good, Pam, huh?"

"Marvellous!" Now she was enjoying herself immensely. This was one place in Stanley where internment could be temporarily forgotten - especially after the swimming, sitting on the sand, feeling the hot sun drying her clothes. It could be any pre-war Sunday afternoon, with the prospect of a good dinner the amah would be cooking, and maybe a trip to the cinema later.. almost any afternoon, except for the disturbing presence at her side - Danny sitting with his arms clasped round his knees. She badly wanted to forego the German lesson, to protract the afternoon, but sternly reminded herself that her company today had been thrust upon Danny, not chosen; also she had told him firmly on the way to the beach that she would have to leave at half past three. She stood up and brushed the sand off her clothes.

"You're not going already?" He leaned back on his elbows and squinted up at her.

" 'Fraid so. My lessons's at 4."

"But it's too early to take the kids home."

"You don't have to leave," she pointed out.

"Surely you're not going to abandon me to the mercy of all these children? Please don't go yet, Pam."

She sat down slowly, searching for the right words, then said "I thought.. I thought you were avoiding me."

"I thought you would prefer it that way." He looked down and sifted sand through his fingers. "You know.. after what happened before."

"We were youngsters then. We're different people now."

"I don't think you are any different, except.." He stopped suddenly, looked down again and went on "We can be friends, can't we?"

"We'd better be!" Pamela gave an exaggerated laugh to hide her embarrassment. "Because Jenny is enlisting me to help with the show you're so busy with."

"You do the costumes, don't you, for the R.C. plays?"

"Ever since Father Heyer discovered I could thread a needle!"

"I remember a beautiful dress you designed for yourself, pale green, with dark green bits.. piping wasn't it called?"

She remembered it too: remembered wearing it one afternoon when they were sauntering along the narrow road round the Peak and he first ventured to put an arm about her shoulders.

"Oh-oh, looks like a fight's developing down there!" He said, leaping up and running to the water's edge to separate two small boys who were punching each other.. all in fun, as Pamela could see: this was another of his strange changes of mood when he seemed to regret having spoken to her. He quickly organised a game of football, using a clump of seaweed as the ball - much to the amusement of the Japanese corporal on his perch above the beach from which he supervised the swimmers and blew his whistle every time any of them swam beyond the confines of the bay.

"You haven't seen Danny's act yet to decide the kids' costumes," Jenny reminded Pamela. "They're rehearsing in the hall after school this afternoon, can you come?"

This was official business, so Pamela had no choice. As they entered the hall, she was instantly reminded of childhood days, for the line of children was singing 'Felix keeps on walking' while Danny strutted backwards and forwards, urging them to imitate him. He caught her eye and grinned at the look of recognition on her face.

"Isn't he grand?" whispered Jenny. "A real professional."

At the end of the rehearsal, he sat on the edge of the stage and mopped his wet face and hair.

"Looks like hot work Danny." Jenny sat down beside him. "We think it's a wonderful act, don't we Pam?"

"I'm just hoping you don't expect me to dress them all up as cats," Pamela laughed.

"Just give them tails, that's all they need," Danny said. "If they do their parts properly, the way I intend them to, the audience will believe they ARE cats, whatever they're wearing."

"But where am I going to find eight tails?" groaned Pamela.

"Tell Father Heyer what you need, he'll produce something suitable." Jenny leant over and straightened Danny's shirt which had stuck to his damp back.

"Thanks, pal," he smiled, giving her arm a squeeze.

"Swimming tomorrow afternoon?" Jenny asked, an invitation in her glowing face.

"Maybe; it depends on what else I may have to do." He hesitated, then went on "I'm doing a little trading for Les Hinger. You girls don't have any jewellery or trinkets you want to sell, do you?"

CHRISTMAS

"Not many here, Sister." Viola led the blond toddler towards the little knot of children waiting with the nun in the shade of the atap-roofed shelter in the centre of the compound.

"Four only - Morag will make five," smiled Sister Marta, taking the child's hand, "but perhaps more will follow when they wake up."

A siesta was essential on steaming Banka Island which straddled the equator. Even their Japanese captors allowed a break in the workload delegated to the prisoners.

Sister Marta, her once flowing white habit reduced to a mere respectable covering since she had donated all excess material to needy women to make underwear, knelt down on the dry earth in front of the children. "Let us begin: one, two, t'ree," she counted in heavy Dutch accents, raising her bony right hand. " 'Sleep, Holy Babe..' "

Viola trudged back to her hut, her bare feet well hardened to the sunbaked sandy ground. A Japanese guard outside the administration hut beside the barbed-wire camp gate meandered curiously over to the shelter. She was not sure if he had noticed her, but to be on the safe side she turned round and bowed towards him: experience had taught the prisoners the expediency of obeying the rigid camp rules. Even the simple act of bowing hurt her chest and back. It was the same for all the women, suffering from the effects of dragging fallen logs and branches from the nearby jungle to chop into manageable firewood for cooking; of humping containers of water from a stream half a mile away - the only water supply;

hacking at the soil within the compound to grow vegetables so necessary to supplement the poor rations.

"All prisoners work. No work, no food," the Camp Commandant had decreed. "Only sick wimmins no work."

In fact, not one of the women was fit. They were all half-starved, debilitated; some swollen with beriberi, others subject to malaria and infections from gashes and sores resulting from their manual chores. Even the few like Viola a little stronger than the rest felt their powers of concentration diminishing. Inertia was endemic in this low-lying camp to which they had been moved four months earlier - their third move since capture.

Now an undiagnosed fever was claiming fresh victims every day. The sick hut was overcrowded; many other patients had to be nursed in their sleeping huts, adding to the risk of infecting their neighbours. The two previous Christmases had been determinedly made memorable by concerts and parties, but this year, 1944, no one had the heart or strength to plan much. Even the band of Dutch nuns was too depleted by deaths and weakness to set up the usual Nativity play; Sister Marta's lone attempt to rehearse a children's choir was all that could be managed.

Viola half-thought of touring the huts to try to entice more children along, but resignedly abandoned the idea because she had a more important commitment before her daily duty as latrine pit cleaner. For the past months she had been giving English lessons to fourteen year-old Dorina Terwisga, daughter of a Dutch father and Malayan mother. Mrs. Terwisga dabbled in the Black Market and was rich by camp standards; she paid Viola well to make and mend her clothes and Dorina's. She had recently died and in her last days begged Viola to continue to teach Dorina. Never very enthusiastic about the discipline of the lessons, Dorina hated them more than ever after her mother died; sullen and numb with desolation, she had to be coaxed and sometimes bullied, but Viola felt honour bound to persevere.

It was now three days since Dorina had last appeared for a lesson. To let things slide any longer would be the beginning of the end, so instead of hunting for choir members, Viola went in search of Dorina. She found her sitting cross-legged on the ground outside the shaded back wall of the Dutch hut, giggling with a little côterie of older teenagers, British and Dutch. Two were smoking camp-rolled cigarettes.

"Time for your lesson," said Viola lightly.

"I am busy." Dorina looked up, but the small brown eyes slid towards her companions, and her lips twitched to hide a smile.

"You can spare half an hour if I can - surely?"

"I am busy," Dorina repeated, hunching her bare brown shoulders.

"You don't look very busy." Viola had long since stopped treating her with kid gloves. "Still, it IS Christmas Eve, I suppose we can have a break today and tomorrow - but I'll see you the day after."

She turned away quickly, pretending not to hear the barely-suppressed comments about her bossiness. This kind of rebuff was frequent; she tolerated it because she recognised that the stimulation of teaching was an essential part of her own survival.

Dorina's close companionship with the older girls was a new development; up to now, her friends had been children of her own age. It was common knowledge that the teenage girls in the camp were a great problem in the camp; they were bored, resentful of the manual work they had to do while coping with camp hardships, and their developing bodies were deprived of the food they needed for proper growth; they were also without male companions of the same age, who had been removed to the men's camp. Mothers feared that their daughters' bold audacity might attract the attention of the younger Japanese guards.

Viola glanced back at the gang. Heads dark and fair were close together. There were squeals of laughter, followed by irate shouts from inside the hut demanding peace and quiet during siesta. Why shouldn't they get what fun they could out of this dreadful existence? Maybe she should leave Dorina to her own devices after all. The Catholic nuns in the Dutch hut would keep an eye on her, even though she had been brought up in the Dutch Reformed Church and her mother a pagan.

At least Dorina's defection today gave Viola a little time to herself. She could hear the patient voice of Sister Marta coaxing the youngters through 'While shepherds watch their flocks..' as she stepped out of the searing heat into the shadow of her hut.

"No pupil today?"

Pat, the Scottish nurse she had befriended on the raft from the 'Liang So', was stretched out on her bedspace (called a bali-bali), a 2ft width of the wooden platform built on either side of the narrow hut with its earthen floor and atap roof.

"She chickened out." Viola reached above her own bedspace to the high, rough shelf above it and took down a rolled bundle of sewing. "At least it will give me a chance to get on with Morag's dress.. oh., look who's coming."

A Japanese guard loped through the doorless entrance, and the resting women kept their eyes closed to avoid having to get up and bow.

"Mrs. Ten Yen!" shouted the guard, signalling to Viola. "You come H.Q. now!"

"So much for my free time." Viola tossed her sewing back on the shelf.

These summonses were frequent and their timing unpredictable. She had taken on the task of camp liaison oficer between the British and the Japanese early on, when a volunteer was demanded. She'd learned a smattering of Japanese in Singapore when Raoul, always realist, was taking lessons. Since internment, she had assiduously extended her knowledge through conversation with the guards, who were amused at her surname which they always pronounced 'Ten Yen'. Despite unpopularity in certain quarters where she was considered to be currying favour with the enemy, there were sometimes advantages - the ocasional gift of bananas, or an egg - for which Viola rated criticism a small price. There was sometimes another price to pay: when, as representative, she had to bear the brunt of humiliating lectures and anger because of the alleged misbehaviour of one or other of the 'proudful wimmin' as the Japanese Commandant, Colonel Hindo, termed his prisoners.

"Speedo," the guard urged. Viola obeyed, but with deliberate dignified tread. She made a deep bow to Colonel Hindo as she entered the tiny office in the raised wooden hut.

"Good afternoon, Mrs. Tennien. You are well I hope?"

The courtesies were always observed and gave no indication of the nature of the summons.

"Yes, thank you, Colonel."

"Many wimmin sick in the hospital hut, yes?"

"Very many, Colonel, and many more are ill in their own huts because there is no space in the hospital for them. If we could build an extra hut.."

He held up his right hand with its first two fingers missing - the reason he was not with a fighting corps. "Soon all wimmen strong again. I have good news. Red Cross parcels coming, more medicine, more food."

"That is good news, Colonel Hindo! May I tell the women this."

"Yes, yes," he nodded benevolently.

"May I tell them, please, when to expect the parcels?"

"Soon. When transport can bring them."

She dared to ask delicately: "Every one is so hungry.. do you think it will be very soon, Colonel?"

"No more questions Mrs. Tennien!" He thumped the table so heavily that its legs wobbled. "Japanese give orders to wimmen, wimmen not ask questions. Now go please!"

As she walked down the wooden steps she passed the representative of the Dutch women, an anxious middle aged housewife, urged on by a following guard. Elga cast an agonised questioning look at Viola, clearly seeking a clue for the summons. Viola gave her widest smile and surreptitiously extended one thumb.

The news roused even the most apathetic women, who pressed Viola for more details.

"He didn't say when, and he didn't say how many parcels," she explained patiently.

"Sounds like the same old rumour," sneered the chief pessimist. "I'll believe it when I see the stuff."

"It must be true," Pat reasoned. "Hindo would lose too much face if it wasn't."

Siesta time was over now; the bell in the compound clanged for the resumption of camp chores. Viola bound a ragged bandana tightly over her hair and with Rhoda, a small Australian in her early thirties, set off for their task of emptying the outdoor pits which served as toilets, the user crouching precariously on bamboo slats across the pit. There being no drainage system, effluent (heaving with maggots) had to be scooped up with part of a coconut shell into buckets which were then carried outside the camp gates and dumped. Viola found the best way to tackle this task was to fix her mind on some happy memory of prewar days and relive it, but Rhoda's extrovert comments continually disturbed her train of thought.

"Heave ho, my hearties!" Rhoda sang as she staggered away with the first load. "Pity we don't get paid one Yen for every bucketful of this liquid gold. My old Mum always said I'd end up having to take a manual job if I didn't work hard at school; if only she could see me now!"

"And if Raoul could see me..." Viola thought with a catch in her heart. She couldn't assume that he was still alive, and even if he was there was the fear that he too was a prisoner of the Japanese undergoing even worse conditions than hers.

Nothing could kill the smell of festering faeces which clung to the girls' bodies and clothes when the work was over, despite a sluicing in the jungle stream. The half-mile trudge through thick undergrowth, wearing uncomfortable wooden trompers while shrubs and branches tore at face and limbs was well worth while; they might not smell fresh and clean, but they felt it and looked it, and the banks either side of the stream were ablaze with gaudy and sweet smelling flowers - the only view of beauty, apart from the dramatic sunsets.

It was six o'clock when they returned to the camp.

"Ne'ly chowtime, Vi'la!" Morag greeted her, struggling through the hut entrance with a tiny table made of slats of thin wood roughly nailed together.

"Good girl!" Viola allowed the child painstakingly to manoeuvre the table hard up against the outer wall of the hut for extra support.

"Now table cloth!" Morag trotted back to the hut while Viola bent over the chatty where Pat was stirring the yam stew and fanning the smoky little fire, and said "Smells good: what's the secret today?"

"A tomato from Mrs. Van Tink - quite a big one in exchange for weeding her plot. She picked several this morning; we were born with the wrong nationality if you ask me."

Morag returned with the square of limp material which served as a cloth, and tried to smooth it over the uneven surface of the table top. Viola brought out three miniature stools made of stout branches across which was sewn a loose piece of cloth like a roller towel, and set them round the table.

"Now dishes!" chanted Morag, echoing the routine Pat and Viola had established to make the pathetic meals as eventful as possible. The dishes were halves of coconut shells; Pat, eyes reddenned with smoke from the fire, shared out the food with another coconut shell. "Grace," she announced firmly as the child bent towards her helping. "Thank God for this meal, Amen."

" 'Men," added Morag dutifully, reaching for her first handful of food; there were no spoons.

"Amen," repeated Viola, grimacing to herself: internment had given her a kind of religion, whereby she thanked the deity when graces were bestowed, and doubted when disaster struck. It was Pat who persisted in teaching Morag prayers, and Viola who insisted on certain standards like that of learning to eat at a table with a cloth on it, instead of sitting on the bali bali, or squatting on the ground with the dish in her lap, as did the majority of the internees.

"Slowly!" Viola ordered as Morag started to wolf her food. "Your tummy doesn't like too much food in it at once."

"But I do!" Morag smiled disarmingly, but she waited for ten seconds before scooping up the last of the meal with her fingers. "No more?"

"No more," said Pat, showing her the empty cooking tin, "but tomorrow is Christmas, and you'll have CHRISTMAS PUDDING.. it's like cake. Go to sleep early tonight, and when you wake up it will be Christmas."

"Go to bed now," said Morag eagerly, and for once there was no difficulty in getting her settled for the night.

Just as the women were whispering goodnight to each other and climbing on to their straw mats, Morag woke up. "Kismus!" she said happily, scrambling off the mat.

"Not yet - it's not morning! You've only been asleep a little while." Viola lifted the child back on to the bed and patted her down.

"Kismus!" Morag's elfin face, framed with cropped white hair, turned her heart over.

"Tomorrow. It's not tomorrow yet."

"Cake tomorrow, Vi'la?"

"If you're good, and go to sleep right away."

The blue eyes were promptly shut, but the lips smiled. Viola bent forward, moved to hug this miraculous reminder of Raoul - the unexpected fruit of that last hectic week in Singapore - but contented herself with a gentle stroke on the child's head. Because so often the women were ill, laid low with dysentery, enteritis, beri beri or sheer exhaustion, those with young children had become a côterie, looking after each other's offspring in time of need. In the last year, several young mothers had died, too weary to struggle against continuing ill-health. It was for this reason that Viola had taught Morag to call her by her Christian name; she rationed her outward loving, so there would be less for Morag to miss if she were to fall victim to any of the dread illnesses which swathed through the camps.

She never ceased to marvel that the embryonic Morag had survived all her traumas of shipwreck and becoming a prisoner of the Japanese; days and nights of uncertainty and hunger and discomfort; herded into old buildings with concrete floors for beds; transported in battered ferries to camps where the women learned to live communally and evolved some kind of life within the limits allowed them. Because menstruation ceased for the majority of the women prisoners, she had not realised she was pregnant for five months - just before Girlie, the anonymous baby rescued from the sea, had died from dehydration. She and Raoul had decided long ago that they would postpone parenthood until the Far East was in a more settled state: it seemed ironic that she should bear a child in the worst conditions of all.

By ten o'clock there was silence in the hut. Outside, monkeys chattered in the trees and birds shrieked, but the women were used this noise and slept through it. Viola took her sewing and crept towards the kerosene lamp hanging from the roof. The women were instructed to ensure that it remained on all night: the watcher must not be encumbered with covers to keep off the marauding night mosquitoes, she must be on her feet and alert at all times, and to ensure compliance Japanese patrols appeared at various times during the night.

Tonight Viola had the prized slot - the first hour's shift, much preferable to being shaken awake to take one's turn in the small hours. She intended to use the time completing her sewing, but had to be prepared to hide the work if the soldiers appeared. A nearby creak alerted her, but to her relief this only signalled the arrival of Pat, who whispered "I'll take over now if you like. You sit down and finish the dress. I'll stand up ."

Viola squeezed Pat's hand in gratitude, then sat on the edge of the nearest bali bali - very carefully so as not to disturb its occupant, and continued her work.

"Seemed strange, having no carols this evening," Pat said.

"You know, after I was fifteen I rejected the religious side of Christmas." Viola bit off the cotton because the owner of the only pair of scissors was asleep. "I'm still not sure I believe in God, but the one thing that gives me a glimpse of faith is Morag, seeing her develop in such a deprived babyhood. Yet even that doesn't really make sense: look at little Girlie.. and all the children we've watched die here."

"We're all born to die," Pat said. "If God kept us all alive, we'd be falling over each other on earth, toothless and gibbering."

They grinned at each other in the shadowy light. Viola held up the sun dress, made of different oddments of material sewn together.

"You should patent that idea after the war," Pat whispered. "The Jig Saw dress.

It would be a great fashion hit - with dressmakers too, because they could use up all their remnants."

Viola remembered her own childhood dresses in Hong Kong, exquisitely made by Chinese tailors in voiles and silks, with intricate smocking at the yoke and on the sleeves; Morag's dress was a travesty of those lovely clothes.

The sound of approaching heavy footsteps automatically brought her to her feet. Two fully-armed Japanese guards appeared through the hut opening and slouched along the gangway between the bali balis. They inspected the lamp and grunted approval. One smiled and said in Japanese "Very hot tonight."

Viola replied in the same language: "You must be very uncomfortable in your uniforms."

One decided to try out his English. "C'ismas tomollow. Plenty food for wimmin."

"I hope so," said Pat, adding sotto voce "We can sure do with it."

"What wimmin say?" demanded the English speaker sharply, pointing to Pat.

"She say, Japanese very kind to send extra food at Christmas," Viola said with a huge smile - but once the soldiers had left the hut she puffed a great sigh of relief.

Sorry," muttered Pat. "I almost put you in it then."

There was no let up in the daily routine on Christmas morning: the usual tenko parade, with the guards complaining because gaps in the ranks due to illness threw their counting system into chaos; the collection of rations, then preparing and cooking them; the struggle to chop firewood for the brickbuilt cooker; the weary trail to the stream for water.

The handful of comparatively healthy nuns and missionaries held a brief Christmas service beneath the small shelter in the compound, but few other women attended; so many were ill or exhausted, others had completely lost heart, and some had lost faith. The little choir which followed attracted more spectators. Women sitting outside their huts peeling vegetables or mending clothes left their work and drifted over to stand, wet-eyed, as the youngsters' off key voices trailed behind Sister Marta's firm contralto.

"Wot flox?" Morag demanded afterwards as Viola led her back to the hut; she could hardly keep still, proudly twirling round in her new dress to watch the skirt flying out.

"A flock is a lot of sheep."

"Wot sheep?"

Viola sighed at the limitations of the camp, the only world Morag knew. She drew an outline of a sheep in the air and promised "I'll show you a drawing next time I get some paper."

"When, when, Vi'la?"
"I don't know, so it will be a surprise, won't it?" Writing paper, like all material things in the camp, was a rarity. When native cigarettes could be bought on the black market, the blank inside of the packet provided a tiny sheet of writing paper which was much prized. Locally-made pads of thick grainy paper on which pencil marks barely showed could sometimes be bought from an old Indonesian man who was occasionally allowed to wheel his cart of miscellaneous goodies to the gate; such luxuries were only affordable by the moneyed Dutch; the British preferred to spend their meagre means on tinned meat when available, or bright cotton material for skirts, even though the first wash reduced the pattern to a hotchpotch of all the colours.

At least today's rations were augmented by a small issue of pork which gave some flavour to the usual vegetable stew, but the real highlight was the so-called 'Christmas pudding' organised days ahead, with every one contributing some ingredients - a handful of currants, half a banana, a few peanuts or a spoonful of wong tong, cocoa, and some ground rice flour.
Siesta time found the women groaning with the discomfort of unaccustomed full stomachs as they lounged in their huts, reminiscing about pre-war Christmases. The nostalgic pleasure of recall helped allay the absence of their husbands and fiancés.
They were suddenly interrupted by raucous shouts from the compound.
"It's still siesta time!" came indignant protests as Viola went out to investigate.
"Letters for wimmins," called the nearest guard. "Leader wimmins to go Commandant to get."

Letters - the first ever to arrive during the three years of incarceration! Siesta was forgotten, the hut leaders mobbed when they returned bearing not only letters but also a few parcels wrapped in native newspaper.
There was nothing for Viola; all the mail had come from the same source, the men's camp some five miles away. The lucky recipients sat on their beds and wept over the stilted messages on the field post cards, while children whooped over small rough-hewn wooden toys carved by their fathers.
As she wistfully watched her neighbour read and re-read the card from her husband, Viola couldn't help saying: "If only I knew where Raoul was!"
"It doesn't help much, having Ted so near," said the woman in an effort to console. "He might as well be a thousand miles away instead of five, for all the good it does us."
The Japanese had consistently refused any contact between the camps; even when working parties of the men passed the women's camp, the women were prevented from standing near the wire to watch them.

For once Viola almost welcomed the latrine chore that day. Hard physical labour helped divert her mind from Raoul. The job completed, it took all her willpower to face the long walk to the stream to clean up. Rarely had she felt so drained and despondent as she trudged back to the camp - for once several yards behind Rhoda. She wondered if she was about to fall ill, and her heart fluttered in panic, then she told herself that this must not happen, she had to survive for Morag's sake, for Raoul's sake.

"Look Vi'la, look!" Morag greeted her excitedly, holding up a small wooden shape. "A sheep, a sheep!"

It could have been any animal, with its misshapen legs, jutting head, crooked body and stump of a tail, but to Morag it obviously fitted Viola's description of a sheep.

"Dorina brought it as a present for Morag," Pat explained. "Her father sent her a wooden plate as well, so she wants Morag to have the.. the sheep."

Viola so seldom cried, but now she held Morag tightly, and cried for herself, for Morag - and for the first sign of humanity in the bereft adolescent.

PART 11

1945

JANUARY

It had been a very lean Christmas, the contents of the Canadian Red Cross parcels long since exhausted. The daily rations of rice and spinach, occasionally augmented with a tiny amount of fish, were depressing and inadequate. The much-envied internees who received food parcels from friends in the city felt the pinch too, as the gaps between deliveries grew longer, and the parcels smaller.

Hunger gnawed especially in the long cold evenings; so many people no longer had the energy to make the uphill walk to St. Stephen's Hall for entertainments.

There was to be a concert this evening. Pamela decided against going and was sitting on her bed with her feet huddled in her blanket when Jenny called in: "Coming to St. Stephen's, Pam? (Good evening Mrs. Garrett, Good evening Miss Minter)."

"I just can't be bothered."

"Do come, lazybones! Logan is going to sing, let's go and give him some support."

Jenny could talk of little else these days but Logan Barry, a young Scot whose light baritone voice had recently been revealed in a talent contest.

"If you're there that's all the support he will need," Pamela grinned. He and Jenny were to be seen walking with linked arms every day. Jenny blushed and sat down on the floor beside Pamela's bed. "We're going to be engaged in June," she whispered.

"Why June?"

"Daddy said we had to wait until we'd known each other for a year."

"Did any one ever tell you girls that it is bad manners to whisper in company?" demanded Mrs. Garrett.

After a year of the old lady's company Pamela was well-used to such interjections and criticisms, and simply ignored them. "Will it be a year come June? I hadn't realised you'd known him so long," she whispered back.

"Well, I first NOTICED him last June.. oh Pam, you're just as bad as Daddy! Are you sure you don't want to come tonight? - Danny's playing too, you know."

"So?" Pamela's challenging look threw Jenny into confusion. "Sorry," she muttered.

There was nothing Pamela would have liked more than to go to the concert that evening. This was the time when couples or good friends meandered round the camp together, or sat chatting; it was the time when she felt most the loss of Hilary and Sandra's friendship, and the sadness on Roddy's behalf of Hilary's defection to another man. There was no one in her circle of friends who could fill the void of the old friendships with the exception of Jenny, and even she had little time for Pamela since Logan's appearance.

Daniel Russell came into quite a different category. He was the only man in camp she found attractive, but the same barriers which had ruined her relationship with him in 1937 still existed, forcing her to act warily in his presence; rationing acceptances of his invitations to walks and socials. No matter how often she argued with herself that internment with so many Eurasians had partially eroded the race divisions; that in any case there could be no harm in allowing herself to drift into the companionship she needed, she could never forget her months of misery following the breakup with Danny long ago, and its effect on him.

Jenny had once remarked on Pamela's obvious avoidance of Danny, and received a curt reply: how could she explain the root of the problem to Jenny, a Eurasian herself?

"Are you leaving soon?" Mrs. Garrett addressed Jenny autocratically. "If not, please close the door!"

Pamela suddenly made up her mind. "I'll come with you, Jen," she said and reached for her broken-down shoes - the weather was too cold for bare feet tonight.

Sitting cross-legged on the floor in the hall, shoulders rounded because she lacked the energy to sit upright, she spotted Hilary and Stefan sitting close together. Conscious of her own isolation, she began to feel some understanding for Hilary, bereft of news of Roddy and uncertain of his survival: no wonder she had sought comfort elsewhere; but she could find no compassion in her heart for Sandra, who was sitting on a window-sill with John Bridger.. someone else's husband.

Jenny wriggled with excitement while Logan was singing, "Wasn't he grand?" she sighed when he had finished.

Danny came on next. He began with a soulful 'O Sole Mio', then plunged into a spirited version of 'The Man on the Flying Trapeze', singing one verse in a falsetto voice which convulsed the audience. His was the final act, and his antics sent the audience home with smiles and light hearts.

When Logan joined the two girls outside the hall, it was easy for Pamela to drift away on her own in the darkness. She was buttoning up her coat against the night air when Danny caught her up. "Hi Pam, wait for me! I'll see you home."

She fell easily into step with him. "I enjoyed your act, especially the last piece."

"It was fun to do," he said. "Pam, I was surprised not to see you at second Mass last Sunday, you're usually there."

"I've started going to early Mass." Since he had joined the church choir she had found his positive presence too disturbing to her concentration on the service.

"Can't stand my singing, is that it?" he grinned.

He walked with her to the entrance to the Married Quarters, and they stood chatting about the latest rumours: the continuing progress of the Allies in Europe;

the footholds the Americans had established in the Philippines. "The Yanks will be here before we know it," Danny declared. "It won't be long now! By the way, anything more to sell? The people in town are desperate to get rid of Japanese Yen, they know it will be worthless here when the war's over."

Every one talked with confidence about a speedy end to the war in Europe; and after that, the Allies would be able to concentrate their power on the defeat of Japan, its fleet already surely weakened by the depredations of the United States fleet, and its cities pounded nightly by Allied bombers.

"There's my gold revolving pencil." This was the remaining half of a set presented to her by the staff at H & S in Ipswich as a farewell present; she had already sold the fountain pen. "And when the weather gets a bit warmer, this thick coat can go."

"You keep your coat, Pam." He patted her shoulder. "If things get that bad I'll sell mine and we'll share the proceeds. I'll make enquiries about a market for the pencil when I see my contact tonight."

"Be careful, Danny," she ventured.

"You bet! It's worth a small risk to get decent food." He had recently taken to calling on her to give her tiny amounts of black market luxuries - a slice of salty bacon, a newspaper poke of white sugar, once a cube of cheese. Welcome though these gifts were, they embarrassed her because of the tenuousness of their relationship, also, each visit evoked acid comments from Mrs. Garrett who stated loudly that all black market agents were taking advantage of internees' hunger by charging excessively for their goods, and she usually added pointedly "especially the Eurasian dealers."

She didn't see him the next morning after all, because from nine o'clock onwards Allied planes filled the skies. Internees watched in delight, they had never seen so many planes before and wondered if invasion was imminent.

Between the air raid alarms which confined them to wherever they happened to be, people scurried to attend to their chores. Meal times had to be adjusted as some cooks could not get to the kitchens, nor internees to the food queues, the Japanese guards more adamant than ever that everyone stay under cover while planes were about.

Distant explosions sounded throughout the day. People crowded round windows and open doorways trying to glimpse the planes as wave after wave of heavy aircraft roared high overhead. Ack-ack fire rattled from the outskirts of the camp. It was evening before the alarms petered out and people were able to meet their friends in other blocks to discuss the excitement and implications of the day's raids. Experts estimated that some 300 Allied planes had taken part, pin-pointed the targets, and calculated possible dates for invasion of the colony.

Danny just had time before curfew to call on Pamela to say he hadn't yet been able to find his Black Market contact, but hoped to do so that night.

"Why not wait a few days, in case we get more raids tonight?" Pamela found herself pleading. "You take such dreadful chances.. what if one of those guards had turned round suddenly last night and caught you putting your tongue out at them?"

"None of them did," Danny laughed.

No planes were heard that night but the next morning they returned just after 8 o'clock, glinting in the brilliant sunshine. Again chores and meals were disrupted, and normal life impossible.

Between raids, Pamela ran to the hospital for her afternoon shift, keeping a wary eye on a Japanese machine gun erected on the roof of the Gaol one hundred yards away. Another raid began as she reached the office. Graceful formations of Flying Fortresses showed silver against the blue sky; small puffs of ack-ack fire ballooned around them, but the planes continued in faultless formation, swelling the hearts of the spectators with pride and comfort.

Suddenly the picture changed. The wing tips of two planes touched, one immediately fell out of the sky with flames pouring from its tail and plunged out of sight behind the hills. The other plane faltered in the air long enough to allow two figures to bale out. One parachute with its tiny burden was seen to float downwards; the other was fouled by the falling plane and crashed on the hills. For a time a piece of one wing lingered in the sky, turning over and over in slow descent, in dreadful confirmation of the disaster.

Now there was horror among the watchers instead of excitement: apprehension instead of exhilaration as the raids continued.

All day the pounding of heavy bombs could be heard, and above the hills rose a pall of dense smoke, proof that the city had been severely attacked. Late in the afternoon a group of planes suddenly swooped low over the camp, dropping small bombs in the bay near the Gaol. The ack-ack guns on the prison roof barked incessantly, and camp guards fired their revolvers and rifles at the planes every time they came over. Two bombs landed on the rocks so near the hospital that many of its windows were shattered. Pamela cowered beneath her desk with two patients who had been discharged that afternoon and were waiting to return to their billets.

The din was deafening and continuous; at five o'clock one tremendous explosion rocked the whole camp.

"That one can't be far away," muttered one of the doctors watching from the hospital office, but with guards around, waving rifles and revolvers, no one dared venture out to investigate.

A great plume of dark smoke rose above the cemetery.

"They must have hit Jap HQ," some one hazarded, a guess strengthened by the sight of one of the Japanese Supervisors racing towards the hospital.

"Some persons in bungalow hurt," he panted. "One is on point of death. Bring doctors."

"HQ bungalow?" asked the nearest doctor, pulling on his jacket.

"Not Japanese... internee bungalow."

'Which one?" Pamela wanted to shout, thinking of Sandra, but the Supervisor was already rushing away with two doctors and a nurse, followed by two men pushing the mobile stretcher.

Another figure could be seen hurtling towards the hospital: a middle-aged missionary, normally the calmest of people; he burst through the office door, shouting hoarsely "Half the people in Bungalow J are dead: we need doctors, and shovels, and people to dig."

Pamela's heart lunged: Bungalow J was very near Sandra's billet. The moment the 'all clear' was signalled and general movement throughout the camp permitted, she made for the disaster area. The stricken bungalow was out of bounds to all except rescue workers so she had to take a roundabout route; on the way she heard horrifying rumours that some internees were trapped in a flattened garage.

Sandra's bungalow was crowded out with shocked and crying survivors of the bombing next door. Sandra was sitting on the bed with John's arm round her. Her face was white and tear-stained.

"I was so worried about you!" Pamela hugged her in relief; they had not spoken to each other for over a year, but the rift seemed unimportant now.

"We're O.K." Sandra said shakily, squeezing Pamela's hand. "I was so terrified, though.. All those people killed in that split second! We knew them all well, we're such buddies up here, and now so many are dead. I just can't believe it! And we could ALL have been killed." She started to cry.

"You're safe now," John comforted her. "Let's see what we can do to help these others.. we'll have to make room for some of them to sleep here."

With so much activity in the bungalow Pamela felt in the way. "I have to go," she said. "It's getting on for curfew."

"Then come again," begged Sandra through her tears. "Promise you'll come again! I've missed you so much."

The sudden deaths nearby two hours ago had completely altered Pamela's perceptions; perhaps it was time to tolerate Sandra's affair with John, and try to repair the broken friendship which had hurt her so much. "I will," she said, "and what's wrong with you two calling on me sometime?"

Walking briskly back towards her quarters, she heard her name called urgently, and Danny emerged from the gathering darkness.

"At last! I've been looking everywhere for you!" He took her hands and grasped them tightly. "You O.K.? I've been back and forth to the hospital and your room; no one knew where you were."

"I went to see Sandra," she explained.

"I've been to help dig those poor devils out of the garage." His clothes were spattered with earth and dust, his hands dirty and scratched. "Some of the others were lying on the lawn as if asleep.. no injuries, the blast killed them. My God, Pamela, I've been terrified for you all day through the raids! Down in the Indian Quarters we couldn't see what was going on in the rest of the camp. We could hear bombs crashing down near the hospital." He gave her a sudden hug and she found herself crying against his jacket, overcome as much by his tender concern as by the events of the nerve-wracking day. "I've wanted to do this for so long," he whispered, holding her tighter.

"And I've wanted you to, Danny."

"You never let me know!"

"I didn't know how you felt; sometimes you were distant, sometimes friendly -"

"Same here, I was uncertain of my welcome. Mother of God, I was sure it was going to be the end of us all this afternoon, and you were the only person I thought about." He bent forward suddenly and kissed her. She wanted to cling to him, to stay in his comforting arms, but the old caution made her gently pull away.

"Everyone's looking at us," She wiped her sleeve across her wet face.

"Who cares? Anyway, every one's far more concerned about what happened this afternoon to bother about us."

Her heart was singing, but this situation was too new and too sudden; her self-confidence faltered - suppose this was just was just a spontaneous reaction to the frightening events of the day? Gently, she disengaged herself from his detaining arms and insisted they walk on with decorum.

"Do you think.." She tried to speak normally, but her teeth were chattering. "Do you think we'll keep on getting raids like this now?"

"I wouldn't be surprised. There's got to be an invasion here sometime, like in the Philippines." His hand sought hers again. "But don't you worry, Pam. I'll look after you."

- "Lucky thing, Hilary! Wish I was going!"

- "Don't you dare come back empty-handed.. bound to be marvellous eats."

"I'll do my best." Hilary hobbled down the stairs in borrowed white high-heeled shoes as her colleagues waved her on her way to the wedding of Berta van Torton, whose father was Stefan's boss. Already the unfamiliar shoes were hurting her feet which were unaccustomed to such high fashion. Her stockings had long since disintegrated and no one had any to lend, so her bare heels and toes were rubbing painfully against the leather.

Apart from the cracked mirror in her small compact there was no looking-glass where she could view her borrowed finery, but the flowing peach georgette dress felt satisfyingly feminine after the old shorts and skirts she usually wore. Of course, before the war every woman wore a hat at a wedding, but this was out of the question in Stanley, although she knew Sandra Lamb had with her in camp her wedding hat - but Sandra was the one person out of the 2,500 internees whom she would not ask to lend anything.

The combined contributions of her fellow nurses had produced enough rouge, lipstick and powder to make up her face. Every one she passed as she picked her way down the uneven slope from St. Stephen's to the Dutch Block smiled and called out admiring comments - even people she barely knew. All the men gave cheery wolfwhistles.

The ceremony was held in the small hall adjoining the Dutch Block. It was already crowded with guests, mainly Dutch resplendent in their pre-war best clothes which they had somehow been able to bring into Stanley. Stefan was already there, standing beside the bridegroom and looking magnificent - and completely unfamiliar in a light grey sharkskin suit, white shirt and blue tie; a bright nasturtium glowed in his buttonhole.

There were sighs of delight when Berta entered on her father's arm; she was a shy girl in her late twenties, transformed into a beauty by a white satin dress with flowing full-length skirt, a short veil and white satin shoes. Her posy of nasturtiums was like a flaming torch against her dress. No outfit as exquisite as this had been seen in camp before. Clearly it had been obtained through powerful contacts with Third Nationals in town. Although her year-long friendship with Stefan had given Hilary an idea of how much better equipped the Dutch were in camp compared to the British, she had not until this moment realised the full extent of their advantages. Only the Dutch community could have furnished the two blond bridesmaids with frilly pink voile dresses, and crowns of artificial flowers. Besides all this, Hilary felt self-conscious in her borrowed dress and ill-fitting shoes, but Stefan, glancing back and meeting her eyes, gave her a wink of admiration.

After the ceremony she followed the party to the Dutch Block for the reception. Strains of the Wedding March could be heard as every one surged along the corridor and up the stairs to the room occupied by the bride's family. Inside, she saw Danny Russell playing his violin, accompanied by the camp ukelele expert. Neighbouring rooms off the corridor were wide open to accommodate the overflow of guests. Even the verandah in the Van Tortons' room was jammed with people, the bride proudly pointing out what she called the 'honeymoon suite' at one end - a six foot high cubby hole formed against one corner of the verandah with suitcases piled on the third side, a curtain across the top, and another curtain across the front entrance.

Liberal supplies of home-brewed beer were distributed during the speeches; tongues quickly loosened with the unaccustomed alcohol.

"You two will be the next happy couple, I suppose?" laughed the groom, raising his glass to Hilary and Stefan.

"With luck!" Stefan's hand caressed Hilary's back and she shivered with excitement. In recent weeks, since the bombing of Bungalow J, they had discussed their future endlessly - like every one else in the camp, more conscious of their mortality now. Alas, there seemed no way round his firm's strict ruling of no marriage before the age of twenty-eight years.

Amidst introductions to Stefan's boss and banter from his colleagues, Hilary ate everything which came her way - sweet biscuits, orange quarters, sweets, peanuts, corned beef sandwiches made with real bread, and a hunk of delicious dark rich wedding cake complete with a thin ridge of white icing. Munching happily, with Stefan at her side, she was astonished to see Pamela come in and shake hands with the newly-weds.

"Hullo Hilary!" Pamela made her way through the mêlée; she had been a little more friendly since the big air raid; now she beamed when Hilary introduced her to Stefan.

"Isn't this cake absolutely out of this world?" Hilary smiled back, eager to try to reinstate the old relationship.

"Bliss! I'm so glad I was invited - because of Danny playing, you know." Pamela nodded towards the band. She too appeared to be wearing borrowed clothes - white sling-back shoes and a blue satin dress too small for her which strained over her curves. Later, somehow a tiny area was cleared in the middle of the room and couples began to dance, relishing the opportunity, for dancing was officially banned by the Japanese.

Stefan held Hilary tightly as they slowly gyrated in the same small circle. "You look gorgeous," he whispered, kissing her nearest ear.

Embarrassed, she said "My feet are killing me."

"I could take your mind off your poor feet, if you would only give me the chance." There was a devilish twinkle in his eyes. "Have you seen the little love nest on the verandah?"

"Is that all the Dutch Committee can manage?" she giggled.

Now only the ukelele player strummed because Danny was dancing with Pamela. Watching them so happily engrossed with each other, Hilary recognised the reason for Pamela's well-being. "Oh Lord," she thought, "Not again." But this time she was not tempted to interfere: Pamela's business, like her own, was a personal matter.

The music stopped; she noticed that Danny's arm was still round Pamela as they went over to the table for drinks.

"You are with Bexton, Miss Bately?" Mr. Van Torton planted himself between Hilary and Stefan as they edged off the dance space. He had obviously been a very large man who not even the luxuries of the Dutch community had been able to maintain at his pre-war weight; his jowls were lined and drooping, and there were tucks in the waistband and breadth of his trousers.

"Yes," she nodded, "I joined in 1938."

"So you would have known Mr. Frame, who retired in 1940?" suggested Mrs. Yan Torton who had joined her husband.

"I've SEEN him - he was the No.1, so I didn't come across him much. I was in the Shipping Department on the second floor."

Some one called Stefan away and she was left to face the interrogation alone.

"I believe your parents were in the service of the Government?" Mrs. Van Torton's eyes were fixed on Hilary's feet; she was standing on one leg because she'd lifted her left foot from her shoe to ease the painful rub against her heel.

"They were, they've retired now. In England," she answered shortly, having now realised that this was an inquisition such as she had undergone years ago from Ian's boss.

"You will rejoin your parents in England, after the war?" smiled Mr. Van Torton.

The question, with its implication of no post-war involvement with Stefan, took her by surprise. While she hesitated, he materialised with another drink in his hand. "More for anyone else?" he asked, his speech slightly slurred.

"I've had enough thanks." Hilary would like to have added "So have you," for even the two glasses she had drunk to his five had made her feel woozy.

The Van Tortons were now shaking the hands of departing guests. The honeymooners had vanished from sight into their hideout on the verandah. Stefan wanted to dance again, his steps more jerky, his arms more tightly round her; he kept pressing wet kisses into her neck. The delicious sensations this caused were more overpowering than her embarrassment at such a public display of affection.

"Let's go." Stefan suddenly; with his arm round her for support as much as in affection, he led her over to the Van Tortons to pay his respects, then directed her along the corridor and down the stairs, where he stumbled.

"Careful," giggled Hilary. "What's the hurry?"

"You'll see," he mumbled. "We're going to my room."

"But I've got to leave, it's almost curfew.."

"Not yet. This way!" He shouldered her past the open front door and along to the ground floor room he shared with three colleagues. "The others are still upstairs.. just started another round of drinks. No one's in here."

He pushed open the door and propelled her inside; closed the door with one foot and enveloped her roughly in his arms, smothering her with kisses. "You never looked so desirable before," he muttered. "I've wanted you for so long.. can't wait a moment longer."

Aroused by his hungry approach and too confused with the unaccustomed alcohol, Hilary allowed herself to be pulled on to the bed beside him. There was not much room, nor did it seem to matter that there was no lock to the door and any one might walk in at any moment and see them together - she with her dress bunched up to her waist, and Stefan in his wedding suit minus his trousers. All that mattered was the compelling consummation which she had resisted for so many months.

No one disturbed them; they clung together in befuddled bliss until the curfew bell sounded. Only then, when the delicious relief was past and the danger of discovery over and they were hastily reclothing themselves, did Hilary face the reality of what had happened. They had broken a commandment, the worst sin. She could become pregnant: Stefan would have to marry her right away if so, even if he had to lose his job. Agonising over all this in bed that night, sober and frightened, she made herself face a more terrible fact: it should have been Roddy, not Stefan, it should have been Roddy.

-"The Russians are fifty miles from Berlin."
-"We're going to get mail - some one saw a pile of post cards up at HQ."
-"Germany's on the point of capitulation."
-"Red Cross parcels are due any day now - it's almost official."

The happy rumours flying round the camp meant nothing to Hilary now, her mind wholly occupied with her own personal turmoil.

"Are you still worrying?" Stefan went to fondle her neck as they sat on the hillside.

"Of course I am." She had to will herself not to move away from his gentle hand.

"I have told you one thousand times, you don't have to worry. If there is to be a child, then we will marry sooner instead of later, and that's fine as far as I'm concerned. They won't sack me, I'm sure." His words were firm and brave but he could not altogether hide the anxiety in his eyes.

"You can't really be sure of that."

"Well," he shrugged his shoulders, "Mine isn't the only firm in Hong Kong. Do relax darling. Don't spoil what happened by being so unhappy when it was so marvellous."

How could she say what was in her heart, that she was full of guilty regrets about Roddy? Every day she prayed for a period. She hated herself for flinching from making a clean break with Stefan while there was still the risk of a baby. It was a relief that he did not press for more love-making - further proof that he was as anxious as she was about her possible condition.

She longed for a confidante. The other nurses were all good friends, but with none of them had she ever found the rapport she had once shared with Pamela.

Despite the thawing in Pamela's disapproval at the Dutch wedding, Hilary was not sufficiently confident of her reception to approach her now she needed her; in any case, what right had she to burden her with a matter which could only cause her more pain on Roddy's behalf?

Almost every day now there were air raid alarms. Seldom were planes seen, but the lesson of that terrifying day in January had been well learned; people no longer dared linger far from their own quarters at any time of day. This at least made it easier for Hilary to limit her time with Stefan. Every day that passed increased her fear; she lost her appetite and didn't want to get out of bed. Stefan often brought her tempting titbits which she couldn't face.

"Matron's getting concerned about me," she told him shakily as he knelt on the floor beside her bed, smoothing her creased forehead. "She thinks I should see the doctor."

"Perhaps you should." He looked away with a small sigh. "How long is it now?"

"Thirty-eight days.. but I'm often a bit late."

"Then what are we worrying about my darling child?"

She turned away, tears spilling out of her eyes. He put his arms round her and she clung to him for reassurance, and because the attraction was still there, despite memories of Roddy. She was confused and desperate.

"I think you are starving yourself," Stefan told her gently. "I want you to try to eat, just a bite or two, of everything I bring you; and at least one spoonful of your ration meals. If there is to be a baby you must think of his health too."

She considered this after he had left. If she was to escape the escalating solicitude of her colleagues, and Matron's insistence that she see a doctor, she would have to try to pull herself together.

"You must get out of this room: no wonder you are so pale, lounging on your bed all day!" He chivvied her constantly, taking her for slow walks, when the sight of a mother with a whining toddler sent a frisson of fear around her heart.

With the turmoil in her mind, news in early March of the actual arrival of Red Cross parcels made little difference to her. When these were distributed and there was wholesale disappointment as they proved to be the the remains of the 1942 consignment and only amounted to one parcel per person, Hilary looked on apathetically, thinking that even twenty parcels each would not ease her personal problem.

Still the escalating rumours could not touch her, even when substantiated by guarded reports in the Japanese newspaper: American forces entering Manila: a conference in Yalta between Churchill, Roosevelt and Stalin which the camp politicians interpreted as a discussion about the future of Europe when the war was won, and ipso facto, Hitler must almost be beaten!

Taking her turn in the open kitchen serving St. Stephen's, she chopped smelly chives and rank damp lettuce, continually swallowing her bile against the malodorous fish soup bubbling in the boiler nearby. She could take no interest when her fellow workers chattered excitedly about the thousands of Allied bombers said to be pounding Germany into submission.

The prospect of a baby she didn't want was overwhelming enough; almost as daunting was the continuing necessity to allow Stefan to think she wanted to marry him, when she knew she would leave him if she should not be pregnant: she would jettison him as she had jettisoned Ian. What was the matter with her? She had always considered herself level-headed and independent; with what confidence and superiority had she criticised Pamela's life in the past!

Stefan's concern only added to her distress. Despite the restrictions caused by air raid alarms, he contrived to call on her directly after Roll Call each morning before his stint on the log-chopping squad. On Easter Sunday, he astounded her by producing a red foil covered Easter Egg in a somewhat battered coloured cardboard box, explaining it had been stored in a godown in town since before the war, and obtained after long drawn-out negotiations across the barbed wire at night.

"I didn't think it would make you cry, darling," he joked as the ready tears ran down Hilary's cheeks. She shared the faintly musty chocolate with her roommates, enduring their admiring comments. - "Wish some one could find me an Easter egg!" -"Some folk have all the luck!"

Later in the morning she accompanied the girls to the Easter Service in the Hall it was another way of avoiding Stefan who, though nominally a Lutheran, was not a churchgoer at all. Even the joyful hymns failed to lift her heavy heart. Looking round at the sunburnt men, women and children in their pathetic camp clothes as they joined in the full-throated alleluias, she felt alone and helpless. The heat among such a press of people was suddenly overbearing; she felt sick, and a great ache gripped her stomach; the whole hall swam as she collapsed on the floor.

"Are you all right now darling?" It was an hour later; she lay weakly on her bed and Stefan was bending over her.

"Perfectly all right, it was only a faint."

"She went out cold for five minutes," someone supplied. "At least she didn't hurt herself falling - we were all so tightly packed."

"No wonder she passed out, it was breathless in there."

Momentarily left alone, Hilary took Stefan's hand, pressed it hard and whispered urgently "I'm really all right, everything's all right."

"You mean..."

"Yes.. it was a false alarm."

His relief had to be controlled because of the company on the other side of the room, but he hugged her so tightly that she had to squeal in protest.

Four days later she waylaid Pamela in the canteen queue. "Have you a spare half hour today Pam? - Something I want to tell you."

Pamela looked somewhat wary, enumerating her various commitments - she'd be freer tomorrow.

"Please try to make it today," said Hilary in a voice that shook, and Pamela immediately agreed.

They met on a bald bank outside St Stephen's kitchen.

"Stefan and I have broken up," Hilary began, and told Pamela all that had happened. "I feel so dreadful, Pam. I've done to Stefan exactly what I did to Ian, and he's so damned decent about it! I told him I was fond of him but I loved Roddy. He said" - here she wept a little - "he said he'd wait for me until the war's over and we know about Roddy. Oh Pam, I can't tell you how ghastly I've felt these last five weeks! I just yearned to have someone to tell, to help. You know, I'm very fond of Stefan and I really thought I was in love with him until after we'd slept together.. then I thought of dear Rod and how careful we'd always been not to get carried away when we were together.. and I knew then that I'd wait forever for Rod, but if there was going to be a baby, what else could I have done but marry Stefan? I've messed up everything."

"Don't worry about it any more." Pamela patted her arm. I'm sure Roddy's still alive, so let's go on praying, and believing it."

"I'm not much of a prayer-person, but I've sent up a lot these past weeks, I can tell you. I heard you'd become an R.C. Do you get a lot of comfort out of it?"

"I do." Pamela looked quite shy. "I felt very isolated after.. after all the changes in the room, but now I feel more at home with myself; and I don't feel alone any more."

"I'm not surprised - you seem to spend a great deal of time with Danny."

"Quite a lot, but it's different this time, Hil we're just very good friends."

"Don't kid me it's all platonic!"

"Well, not exactly.. but it's not a serious, passionate thing. We're comfortable together, we each need the companionship."

"And in the future?" Hilary couldn't help asking.

"I just don't know. There are so many imponderables. The race thing, for a start. I no longer feel it's the great barrier it was when we first went out together, but my parents would and I know they'd be horrified if I were to marry Danny."

"Marry him? Has he asked you to marry him?"

"We've discussed it in an abstract kind of way." Pamela wrinkled her forehead. "He knows I'd have to go Home and see my parents first, I wouldn't dare to take such a step without telling them - and he's convinced that means I'll never marry him. I THINK I want to, but that might be because of the circumstances here, when it's so marvellous to have some one to lean on, a companion, someone to care for and someone to care for me."

"Cautious as ever, aren't you Pam? I wish I'd used some of your caution a few weeks ago.. would have saved myself a hell of a lot of misery."

"There's something else," Pamela went on carefully. "Danny needs to be given confidence in himself, and I long to give it to him. He told me (and he didn't have to) that he's illegitimate! He didn't find out until just before he went to Manila - that's why he didn't try to contact me when he came back to Hong Kong and I was no longer under my parents' ban of not seeing him. He felt.. sort of stained. He's had a pretty bad time."

"He never seemed to lack girl-friends whenever I saw him around in Hong Kong."

"He told me all about them too, and lots of other things he needn't have. He's such a sincere, humble person. He knows it will take him a long time to get on his feet again when we get out of here; he hopes to get his old job back, but if not he'll have to look for something else and find somewhere to live. His salary will only be about half of what I earn, so if we DO have a future together, it's a very long way off."

"I shouldn't say this." Hilary spoke very slowly. "After all, I can't run my own affairs efficiently, but.. what you've just told me doesn't sound like a recipe for success and happiness. Won't it bother him that you'll always be the major wage earner?"

"Everything bothers him." Pamela's brows were tightly knit now. "It's all so complicated that we decided just to make the best of being friends now. After all, we may not all get out of here alive."

This last thought was very much in everyone's minds. With the certainty of an early Allied victory in Europe - so obvious that even the Japanese newspapers carried reports of impending German capitulation - an Allied invasion in the Far East was more than a possibility.

The camp guards were jittery and ebullient. The Black Market was operating even more feverishly as more and more people in the city were clamouring to exchange their Yen for material goods. A proportion of the rice ration was roasted and some stored in every block so that it could be chewed without cooking if a time came when it was impossible to leave one's billet.

"Stefan thinks there will be an invasion next full moon," Hilary ended. "He wants us to stay friends so he can take care of me if the worst happens here, but I have to make a clean break now, it's only fair."

She missed him during the ensuing weeks, missed his cheerful personality, his terrible heavy-humoured jokes, his endless supply of rumours, and his practical assistance in collecting fuel for the private cooking in the girls' room. Also, she missed the comfort of his presence at a time when the future looked bleaker than ever. No one doubted now that an Allied attack on Hong Kong would precipitate the massacre of all internees. The empty trenches around the blocks were a constant reminder of their ultimate purpose.

There were several premature marriages, the parties deciding to make the best of what life there was left. This meant one of each couple cramming his or her bed into the room the spouse already occupied with several others.

Hitler was defeated! He was dead, so was Mussolini! The Japanese newspapers carried full reports. Over the years, many of the stories in these newspapers were laughed at and disbelieved, notably when the Imperial Japanese Navy was said to have sunk many more American ships than that navy possessed. This time there could be no doubt. The camp cheered and gave thanks for Europe's release from subjugation.

Hilary was trying to mend a tear in the canvas of her bed when she heard a commotion outside the room.

"Whatever's the matter?" some one was demanding when Pamela appeared, almost falling into the room and stumbling over to Hilary, waving a piece of paper.

"A card from my parents!" she gasped. "Roddy's alive, look!"

The much-travelled post card trembled in Hilary's hands as she read:

'Mother and I both well. Heard from Rod in Cherry Blossom land. Belle and children O.K. in Melbourne, they had card from Keith in Kowloon. Chin up.'

Later, in bed that night, Hilary's euphoria slowly evaporated when she calculated that the year-old post card only proved that Roddy had been alive in

1943. Anything could have happened to him in the last two years; and even if he was alive now, anything could happen to him in the fraught future in Japan which was now under constant ferocious attack from Allied planes.

MAY

Looking at Sandra across the bridge table - simply a square of tired grey wood balanced on top of a Mimi Lau - John Bridger again felt a surge of affection and compassion. The incipient curls in her close-cropped hair softened the pointed face and protruding cheek-bones. Her almost non-existent bosom was covered with a narrow blue sun-top made from a section of one of his disintegrated shirts. Her dark blue shorts had similar origins: the legs of his trousers when they had been converted into shorts for him. In repose, as she studied her well worn cards, she was really beautiful, with no hint of the petulance and self-centredness he had so despised when she had first come to work for him.

"Your bid," his right-hand neighbour, perched on a low camp-made stool, reminded him.

"Three clubs," he said, and met Sandra's surprised stare.

"Where were you this afternoon?" she demanded later as she squatted beside the chatty and fried a sliced onion. He had taught her all about cooking ("I used to be a boy scout") and she had come to take a great pride in her culinary efforts. "No wonder we went down so badly - your calling was atrocious."

"You must make allowances for my advancing years, my dear," he smiled. "Is it time to lay up?"

This meant placing their spoons and old enamel plates on their respective beds, for it was not their turn to use the bridge table for this meal. A shout from the kitchen announced it was ready. John went off with the plates, on each of which was placed a helping of rice and a ladle of watery stew whose main content was soya bean. Without the addition of their onion the meal would have been almost tasteless.

John's sloping garden plot on the hillside beneath the bungalow was too small to be taken over communally; here he grew in tiny quantities spinach, tomatoes and onions, and was experimenting with peanut plants nurtured from peanuts from the canteen. Most buyers ground their nuts into a rich and gritty butter, but John had insisted on planting a few in the hope of a good yield - for which he was still waiting. His friends joked "Do you reckon your nuts will be ready before we're released?" Every few days he carefully scraped the soil away from the roots and inspected the soft cream-coloured skin which would one day harden into shell.

After the meal Sandra took the empty dishes to the kitchen to wash.
"Did you hear that?" asked a resident who was waving her plate about to dry it. "Some one just called through the window that repatriation is on again - for all the women and children."
"I'll believe that when pigs fly," her companion sneered.
"It's said to be God's truth this time."
"Like that tale last month, when someone swore we'd be told the Japs would march us off somewhere the next day because of expected invasion: pull the other one, do!"

Recounting all this to John, Sandra said "Where do these fables start, I wonder?"
"They're not all fables," said John slowly. "I heard the repatriation one at this morning's meeting." He and several business colleagues had started having discussions about their future in Hong Kong after the war. "The theory is that now there are no German subs lurking around the oceans, safe passage could be better guaranteed. There's a strong feeling repatriation is on the cards."
"I wouldn't go!"
"You were always frantic to get away when that list was first published."
"That was years ago; I was ill then."
"If you're given the chance I think you should take it, San. We just don't know how things will end here; it could be very grim."
"All the more reason for me to stay here to look after you. Let's not talk about it any more." She replaced the plates and spoons on top of the piled suitcases.
John knew better than to pursue the subject at this point. "Concert this evening?" he asked.
"Far too hot. I'd rather sit outside and enjoy the sunset: O.K.?"
"O.K.," he smiled, masking his inner disquiet.

One of the advantages of living in the bungalows instead of a large block of flats was the air of peace and tranquillity, especially in the evenings when chores were over and everyone in relaxed mood. An added bonus was that there were no children in John's bungalow, one of the many reasons why he had taken Sandra in after Melly's death, when she could not bear the sight of sound of small children. He'd been appalled at first when she arrived to stay, but was too concerned for her distraught state of mind to turn her away. He'd disregarded the protests of the other occupants of the crowded billet; their appeals to the billeting authority were unsuccessful - they were asked to try to be tolerant of the unwanted arrival because of her recent tragedy. Sandra had cared for him so devotedly, daily dressing the suppurating sores on his ulcerated legs, that she earned grudging respect from the neighbours. It took him months to calm her shattered nerves, to convince her that she had some personal worth, and that some one really cared about her.

When his legs improved and he was able to walk normally again, he taught her to garden as well as to cook. Everything, in his book, had to be done methodically and thoroughly. She took to saluting smartly when she felt she was being given too many orders, grimacing in a cheeky way that made his heart leap, immensely grateful now that she had thrown in her lot with him.

The communal cooking was done by the bungalow residents in pairs on a roster. When it was their turn, he marvelled at the way Sandra tackled the task: washing and chopping rank-smelling lettuce or slimy carrots; even a tired and tough conger eel failed to daunt her as she hacked it into slices before tossing it into the stew.

Now, almost two years after she had moved in, she fitted easily into the mixed côterie of seventeen men and ten women. She had even developed a social conscience and joined a roster to do the laundry for the elderly men and women in the bungalow.

The last thing he had expected, when he first offered his condolences on Melly's death, was that he would gradually drift into an affair with her. What had started as genuine concern for a colleague's widow, slowly developed into a tenderness, quickly fanned by Sandra's physical attraction to him. In satisfying this, he found he had a powerful need of her.

His conscience often troubled him, but it was easy to accept Sandra's blunt "If some one doesn't look after you, you won't survive for your family." There was always the implicit understanding that this was no long-term commitment: easy to accept up to the end of 1944 when release seemed far in the undefined future - the two post cards he'd received from Phyllis in Melbourne seemed to have come from another world. But now, with the war in Europe over and news of constant heavy raids over Japan, he thought uneasily about his future. This was brought home the more by rumours of contingency plans being formulated in the camp to cope with an invasion of Hong Kong. Against cross-fire between the invaders and defenders, internees could do nothing but stay indoors and live on carefully hoarded but limited emergency food. A more frightening possibility - a furious Japanese army seeking revenge on defenceless internees - loomed; he had been perfectly honest when he'd told Sandra he wanted her out of Stanley for her own safety, but it was true that her departure would begin to solve his major personal problem.

Sitting on the grass outside the bungalow that evening with their backs against the warm wall, they watched the glorious sunset of incandescent colours.

"Much better than a third-rate concert," said Sandra, leaning against him contentedly. "So peaceful."

His mind still full of the physical dangers the future might hold, he said carefully "Won't always be like this, San. I know you don't want to talk about these things, but I must say this: I don't want you here for the invasion."

"You really want me out of your way, don't you?" Her voice was very low.

"Out of DANGER!" he emphasised.

"But you're trying to ease me out of your life."

"That isn't the reason I want you on that ship, but we shall have to face a parting some time."

"Not now, not now, while everything's so awful and uncertain; not now, John."

With a suppressed sigh, he cuddled and comforted her. He knew he was greatly indebted to her - she had helped him as much as he had helped her; she'd nursed him back to good health and put meaning and sparkle into his bleak camp life. Without her, he doubted if he could have survived. He could not abandon her yet.

His dilemma was exacerbated when the Japanese suddenly sent into Stanley the contents of internees' safe deposit boxes which had been stored in the city banks. John received a large envelope containing insurance policies, his birth and marriage certificates, and photographs of his wedding and a family group taken the last year they had all been together - photographs which he had hastily added to the deposit box when the Japanese first landed on the island.

Because there was never any privacy, Sandra was sitting near him when he took out the papers and photographs. He examined them for a long time, then laid them on his knees and put his head in his hands. He was looking into the past, seeing the prim young girl he had married while on leave in England; remembering her timidity when first plunged into life in Hong Kong, the birth of the two children who had turned them into a family; teaching them to swim on golden beaches, taking them to school for the first time; remembering the pain of parting with Phyllis and the children on the dockside when they were evacuated to Australia to a future none of them could imagine: and the last glimpse of Phyllis' taut face from a high deck, tight with fear of what might lie ahead for those left behind in Hong Kong.

His thoughts came back to Sandra. Slowly he looked up, but she was no longer there. She reappeared in time for the meal, smiling jauntily. He suggested a walk after they had eaten and they set out on the usual circuit of the camp periphery. Conversation was jerky.

"Where did you go this afternoon?" he asked at length.

"Called on Pam. She's still having a difficult time with that old dragon in her room. Danny was there to, old Garrett is so rude to him, but he just smiles politely."

"Is Pamela really serious about him?"

"Don't know," she shrugged. "I hope not - but I'm not in a position to criticise her, am I?"

Perhaps this was the time to broach what weighed so heavily on his mind. Hesitantly he began "I have been most unfair to you, Sandra."

"I haven't noticed." Her voice was dismissive.

"We just have to talk about this.. let's go somewhere more private."

"If you like." Her tone was discouraging but she followed him off the path, down the rocky bank which provided sheltered nooks.

"Seeing those photos this afternoon," John said slowly as they sat side by side on a rugged rock, "it reminded me of things I've been pushing to the back of my mind for a long time."

"Your family," she said coldly. "You've mentioned your wife and kids many times. You never pretended they didn't exist."

"In my mind, I DID pretend - otherwise how could I have virtually lived with you these past two years? I've done you an appalling disservice, taking your good name and allowing you to waste yourself on some one who had no right to monopolise your attentions."

"You sound like Mr. Bridger-in-the-office!" she snapped, aiming a stone viciously down the hillside.

"I think I should become Mr. Bridger from the office again," he said, trying not to meet her eyes.

"Not yet, John, not yet." Her voice broke. "I need you, you need me."

"But there's no future in it, my dear."

"None of us might have any future beyond Stanley, so why plan so far ahead? Let's go on getting what we can out of life here."

"It's dishonest."

"It always has been, so why make a big thing out of it now? And as to my reputation and yours, the damage has already been done. We can't just rub it out because those photos have made you feel guilty."

She looked so vulnerable, sitting there glaring at him with tears welling in her eyes. He gathered her into his arms and held her tightly. She was warm and vibrant, exciting and seductive: she was far more real than the wife he hadn't seen for five years.

"You see?" she was whispering. "You can't just shrug me off yet. This war might go on for years. There's no point in both of us being miserable alone, when we can enjoy life together."

SUMMER

To onlookers, he and Sandra were as close as ever, but things were no longer the same. Their cautious couplings on the hillside became rare, theoretically because John had to spend more time at planning meetings for post-war Hong Kong. Sandra was as devoted and passionate as before, but he could not miss the new wariness in her eyes - all the harder to bear because the scent of fear was in the camp.

Hunger was more rampant than ever; extras to supplement the miserable basic rations hard to obtain even for the moneyed, for the canteen rarely opened now because most food supplies from town had been diverted into the Black Market.

Japanese working parties could be seen on the nearby hills, building what appeared to be gun emplacements; there were air raid alarms almost every day, yet none one morning when a large plane flew slowly over Stanley and dropped eight bombs. None exploded but billets were damaged and a number of internees injured. This brought back fears that the carnage at the bungalow in January could easily be repeated.

With all these anxieties, news that a general election in England had brought down Winston Churchill did not seem very important; a greater stir was caused when the Japanese suddenly ordered two hundred named internees - technical men, their wives and children - to pack up their all within a few hours and assemble for departure to some unstated destination. Logan was among them. The entire camp watched them leave for the jetty, the children jaunty and excited at the prospect of adventure ahead, the adults outwardly hopeful but inwardly apprehensive.

Later, from the bungalow, John and Sandra watched two small barges pull away from the jetty below.

"Those poor people.. they must be jammed in the holds," Sandra shuddered. "It could be us next, being taken goodness knows where."

Next day the Japanese newspaper carried headlines that Russia had declared war on her. This added to the uneasiness in the camp: anything that upset the Japanese was liable to affect their attitude towards the prisoners.

Later that week an Allied plane zoomed suddenly over the camp, homing in on a small Japanese patrol vessel laying a boom in the bay. The plane repeated its run over the camp three times and sank the patrol boat, while the guards fired their rifles over internees' heads into the sky. Here indeed was grim evidence of what the future held for the camp when a full-scale invasion began.

"Don't!" gasped Mrs. Garrett, as Pamela lunged at the darting cockroach with the shoe in her hand. "I can't stand the noise of it being squashed!"

"We've got to kill the damn things." Pamela spoke heatedly because she too loathed the juicy scrunch which would result if she could target her quarry. "We'll have to move everything out and do a thorough clean."

"I can't do that," Mrs. Garrett whined. "Ask your boy-friend to help - he's always round here, he might as well do something useful."

Having maimed the cockroach, Pamela was obliged to put on her shoe and stand firmly on the rotating remains; she would have to ask Danny to dispose of the strongly smelling mess.

Bugs and cockroaches had gradually taken up residence in Stanley. Vigilance was essential as there was no insecticide and no kerosene, but the pests could be partly controlled by scrubbing the beds and turning out cases and cartons of possessions - very hard work in this hot weather for undernourished people.

Danny, when summoned, agreed at once to help. He cheerfully dragged Mrs. Garrett's effects from beneath her bed under her critical supervision: "Careful with that, Daniel, it's fragile!" "No, not on top of that one, put this one at the side!"

Pamela ached with compassion because Mrs. Garrett never made any attempt to hide her disapproval of Danny, yet made use of him whenever it suited her. He was always so eager to please, although perfectly aware of her disapproval. She screamed at him when he disturbed yet another cockroach and killed it.

"Why don't you go downstairs and take a little walk?" he suggested. "I'll call you back as soon as this job is finished."

She refused to go, and Pamela knew why: in her luggage she still had several precious curios, mainly small ivory pieces which she kept wrapped individually in crumbled yellowed tissue paper. Neither Pamela nor Alison was supposed to know about these treasures, but they could not fail to notice them as Mrs. Garrett was always unwrapping them and examining them covertly. Recently, Pamela had urged her to sell some now that all her jewellery had gone to the Black Market, to buy extra food. Despite the old lady's autocratic and suspicious ways, Pamela had found a grudging respect for her attempts to keep up what she called 'appropriate standards.'

"I don't want to part with anything more - the ivories are all I have left from Arthur's collection, all I have to remind me of him." Her house on the Peak, with the memorabilia of her late husband's long business career, had been demolished by Japanese shells; she was fortunate to have survived.

For two consecutive days after the room cleaning the fish sent in with the rations was condemned by the doctors as unfit for human consumption, so the meals consisted simply of rice and watery lettuce stew. By the second day Mrs. Garrett was too weak with hunger to walk downstairs to collect her food from the queue.

"I'll get yours for you," Pamela offered. She knew Alison would not do so - the situation between those two had become worse because of Mrs. Garrett's constant complaints about Alison's asthmatic snorts.

"When I'm on duty I won't be able to collect for you," Pamela reminded the old woman when she handed her her food. "You really ought to look after yourself properly. Surely your husband wouldn't expect you to starve to death, rather than part with some of his treasures?"

It was several days before Mrs. Garrett gave in; her health was failing drastically and she rarely left her room. In the past she had taken her jewellery to a dealer internee who lived in St. Stephen's. "I can't get that far now," she told Pamela as though it was the dealer's fault.

"I'll take them for you," said Pamela, but Mrs. Garrett would not entrust her valuables to any third party. "Ask that Daniel to come and see me. Oh, and make sure Alison's out when he comes, I don't want that one to know my business."

"I don't know why you're so anti-Alison," Pamela sighed. "She's all right, just sick. Are you quite sure you want Danny to try to sell your things, though? You've been rather critical of him in the past."

"All Black Marketeers are crooks," said Mrs. Garrett firmly, "but I might as well deal with one I know."

"It's worth a few thousand," Danny told Pamela delightedly, fingering the small ivory carved ball with smaller balls rotating within. "I can't say how much my contact will be offered for it, but, well, it's just about the most expensive thing I've handled."

There was the usual anxious week of waiting to complete the transaction. The particular guard who was Danny's main contact had to wait until his day off duty when he could go into town and hawk the ivory round his contacts to find a buyer, the buyer having named his offer, the guard when next back on duty in Stanley would contact Danny to find out if the offer was acceptable.

Mrs. Garrett was affronted by the first offer of ten thousand yen.

"I knew you were a crook," she raged at Danny. "I expect to get double that amount! I won't sell at that price. Get my property back and I'll deal with someone else."

"I'll tell him you're not prepared to accept so little," said Danny hastily, while Pamela deeply embarrassed, hovered, by the door in case Alison walked in. "Leave it to me, Mrs. Garrett. I'm sure I can get more for you if you'll wait another few days for your money."

Reluctantly she agreed.

"I hope that old witch isn't taking it out on you," he said to Pamela afterwards. "Ten thousand would keep her in eggs and sugar for several months."

In the end Mrs. Garrett had to accept twelve thousand which she did with very bad grace, wagging her finger at Danny and declaring she would never do business with him again.

"Is it really worth all the risks you take?" Pamela asked him when he related with relish how he had dodged being caught in mid-transaction the previous night by a conscientious Japanese sergeant doing the rounds of the camp boundaries.

"Sure it's worth it! I'm saving for the future as well as keeping us both well now." She knew he earned commission on every one of his sales; now he explained that he was only buying extra food with a small proportion of his earnings, the bulk of which he lent to internees willing to sign cheques for the sterling equivalent, redeemable after the war. Gleefully he revealed that he had already had four hundred pounds in cheques; she was so thrilled for him that she broke a golden rule and kissed him. It had always been Danny who had initiated any romantic approach; now he was instantly stirred, held her tightly to him and protracted the kiss until she was breathless.

"Dearest Pam!" His arms enveloped her again and he covered her face and neck with little kisses; she was laughing until she saw the yearning in his eyes and gently pushed him away. She was remembering Hilary's confession of near disaster, and this tiny incident warned her that Danny needed no encouragement.

She recalled, too, a recent confidence from Jenny:

"I have to be so stern with Logan; he wants to kiss me and all that whenever we're alone. It's lucky we don't have many opportunities else I'd be at Confession every day."

They were to be married as soon as the war was over. Pamela envied their certainty of their future - Logan was under contract as a ship's engineer and his job would continue as before.

"What do you think of this, Pam?" Danny held out a narrow gold ring with tiny twinkling green emeralds. It was exquisite, the sight took her breath away.

"It's beautiful.. indescribably beautiful." In the drab camp, where clothes were faded and rooms stark and only the scenery was beautiful, the emeralds gleamed boldly. "How can any one bear to part with it?"

"Needs must," he shrugged. "It was the lady's engagement ring, she cried when she handed it over, but it should net about five thousand for herself and her kid."

"Don't show me these things," she said, folding his hand over the ring. "It's too upsetting."

"No one can afford to be sentimental if they're starving," he said, pulling a cooked sweet potato out of his pocket and tossing it to her.

"He's coming round."

"Rod, Rod, can you hear me? It's Greg."

He could hear the voices but dismissed them as existing only in his fevered imagination. How could Greg be here with him in the solitary confinement shed, where there wasn't room for even one person to lie down at full stretch on the earthen floor?

"Wake up, man, wake up!"

With a tremendous effort, he raised his bruised eyelids and dimly saw Greg bending over him, and the truth slowly registered in his tired brain: he was no longer crouching in his own excrement, suffering bouts of delirium from dysentery and untreated septic sores, no longer in the windowless punishment shed where he'd been thrown, beaten almost senseless, a week ago for stealing wood from the saw mills where he worked: he was in the sickbay hut on a narrow bed. He had never expected to get out of the hell-hole shed alive; now helpless tears trickled down his cheeks.

"You're O.K. old man," said the Irish orderly, patting his shoulder. "You'll be back with your pals in no time - we need your bed for someone else."

Roddy heard a muttered whisper from Greg: "Oh-oh, here comes Coffin Charlie."

Every one in Ominu Camp knew the diminutive sergeant in charge of the work squads who daily walked through the sick bay deciding which of the patients was now well enough for duty. It was his habit to tap each patient's foot with his short cane, announcing to those too ill to react "No work: you for box."

The rough wooden coffins were stored at the far end of the sick bay in full view of the patients. Roddy, holding his breath to control the shaming tears, kept rigid when his feet were poked.

The sergeant's callous "You next for box" gave him a fierce determination to prove him wrong; he could hear the hated voice again, detailing prisoners outside to chop kindling for the cremation of those who had died during the night. Somehow, later in the day, he managed to leave the sick bay, wobbling on rubbery knees and half-supported by Greg. Flies kept settling on the sores on his shaven head; his vision swam, and his back ached agonisingly, but he had cheated Coffin Charlie.

The following week he was sent to join a working party at a steel foundry. The work was heavy but gave plenty of opportunities for sabotage and stealing - the principal interests of all the prisoners. Pipe-fitting, plate bending and threading, they worked as slowly as they dared; feigning ignorance, they spoiled as much material as they could. Morale was sustained by news of Allied victories. Some items were passed on by a few friendly Japanese workers at the factory, but most was gleaned by the handful of Japanese linguists among the prisoners, who studied old newspapers provided for toilet paper and for patching broken windows and cracks in the accommodation huts.

Air raids were daily and nightly occurrences. When they first saw B29's overhead and heard the bombs detonate and felt their vibration, they cheered lustily in spite the risk of the bombing to themselves. Although they complained when rations were reduced, they also rejoiced because the air attacks were disrupting Japan's infrastructure. Despite frequent stoppages at the factories through electricity breakdowns, the work squads were still marched off every morning, looking like clockwork skeletons. In the evenings there was little energy left for even the simplest of pleasures - a rubber of bridge with camp-made cards, or a game of chess with men carved from stolen off-cuts of wood.

Roddy had long since given up writing imaginary letters to Hilary. Since life had become such a struggle for survival, fantasy had no part in it, for day-dreaming lessened fighting instincts.

The daily hazards were plenty - disease from unhygienic latrines; the sudden aggressive moods of the guards; occasional earthquakes which though mild by Japanese standards, shook the barracks and caused the very ground to tremble.

And now the increasingly heavy air raids! At the factories and foundries, work squads were constantly being herded into huts stronger than the flimsy workshops. The prisoners were surprised to be given any shelter at all, for they had seen what passed for protection for the Japanese civilians - simply holes in the ground covered with sheets of galvanised iron.

Every prisoner went to bed with his personal belongings beside him, ready for a mass escape if the huts were bombed. Sleep was punctured by the drone of heavy bombers, earth-shaking explosions, and the constant flashing of fires and search-lights.

A work party in the nearby docks picked up Allied leaflets to the Japanese which were quickly translated: if Japan did not surrender, Allied forces would completely destroy her cities.

Roddy was at his bench in the foundry one morning when the inevitable alarm sounded. Machines were immediately switched off and the workers ordered into their shelter. As they poured out of the sheds, a thunderous explosion echoed and re-echoed; a great blue flash shot across the horizon, and a small dark cloud began to expand and rise over the distant city. Two guards followed them inside and closed the door. The prisoners were not allowed to speak, although Greg managed to whisper to Roddy: "Can't hear any more bombs."

After an hour in the airless shelter, it was a relief to hear movement outside; the door was opened a crack and a third guard jabbered rapidly to the two inside who immediately left the hut, locking the door behind them.

"What's going on?" The prisoners were mystified and growing agitated, for the noises outside - clattering footsteps, frantic shouts and noisy revving of transport engines - conveyed fear and confusion.

"Just the bastards getting over-excited as usual," said Alec, the oldest of the group, although he was only in his early forties.

"Bit more than that, Dad," a voice said nervously. "We've never been locked in before."

The noises died away in the distance. All the men were streaming with perspiration, two collapsed.

"Let's open up and see what's happening," Alec decided. Three men shouldered the door off its hinges and every one surged out. Blinking furiously in the daylight, they stared towards the city. The cloud was now thousands of feet high shaped like a mushroom. It was black, it was purple, it was grey; at its base a thick layer of smoke was continually curling in and upon itself like some giant evil genie.

No guards were in sight, no Japanese factory supervisors or workers. The sheds were empty.

"What in God's name is going on?" some one asked

"Must be ammo or fuel dumps going up.."

"The whole town must be on fire..." Already they could feel the unnatural heat in the air.

Their uppermost thought was the fear of reprisals from the Japanese. They decided to return to their camp and barricade themselves in. Splitting up into twos and threes, they found energy they hadn't known they possessed to cut across the paddyfields and through woods.

Emerging cautiously on to the main road to approach their camp, the first group stopped short at the sudden view of a packed multitude of people advancing very slowly towards them. Were they refugees from the raid? Or incensed Japanese coming to wreak vengeance on all the Allied prisoners they could find?

The prisoners could scarcely believe what they were seeing. This approaching mass of people was almost silent. The only sounds were the shuffling of their feet, and the creaking of the axles of the handcars some were pushing full of a miscellany of household possessions. Their clothes were torn and dusty; faces and limbs were bright red and bleeding, their expressions blank. They hardly glanced at the prisoners as they trundled past.

At the tail end were people unable to keep up with the rest; some were without hair or eyebrows; some were naked to the chest from which all the skin had been burnt. Several were blind and walked with red raw arms outstretched to keep in touch with the person ahead. All hung their heads in dreadful apathy. A child clung to his mother's shredded kimono, his face livid and raw, and one eyeball was hanging on his cheek.

"Whatever's happened over there, we've got to try to help," Alec said hoarsely. No man thought otherwise; they hurried towards the city, above which the pall of smoke and dust was so widespread that the sun was completely obliterated. The roar of great fires could be heard, and detonations as fresh places ignited; the disintegration of buildings; bent metal groaning; glass shattering. They passed smouldering heaps of wood, tiles and possessions which once were houses; piles of rubble, charred telegraph and power poles leaning drunkenly over the roads.

The heat, the smoke and the crackling of fire intensified. Their eyes began to run, their lungs filled with smoke. They came upon stricken casualties, sitting aimlessly on the ground, grotesquely burned, emitting tiny pleading cries. Some were quite naked, staring numbly at their skinless bodies.

Mesmerised by these appalling sights, the men didn't realise rain was falling until their clothing felt wet; then they shouted out at the grey stains the large spots left on their bare arms and legs, spots that turned red and burned.

"No good staying here," they told each other, choking with smoke, breathless with the growing heat. Most of the Japanese they saw now were either dead, or beyond any help. The black rain was stinging and burning; they didn't understand it, knew it was a phenomenon they had never seen before. By common consent they turned and made for the camp as fast as they could; no one spoke.

Hilary was sitting on her bed cutting her toe-nails with blunt scissors when the news was shouted into the nurses' quarters: "It's over! The war's over! The Japs have surrendered!"

"Heard that before," she said, and went on with her task, but the rumour persisted all day. That night every one was too excited to sleep, discussing over and over again more tales which were circulating: that the Emperor of Japan had broadcast news of the surrender to his people; that the Japanese Camp Commandant had smashed his radio when he heard it; that food ships would sail immediately from the Philippine Islands to bring succour to Stanley.

"We could be on a ship for England this time next week!"

"No more rice!"

"Imagine a real bed with a mattress and a pillow!"

"And a hot bath, with soap, and shampoo!"

"And deodorants, and disposable S.T.'s"

"A new tooth brush!"

"A pink gin - a double!"

It was an overwhelming disappointment when no triumphant announcement came the next morning, but hopes soared again when the time came to assemble for the weekly outside roll call; no agitated sergeant arrived to chivvy them into their orderly rows, no inspection party to receive the obligatory bows about which they had been so severely lectured only two weeks ago. Obviously something was afoot, and the queues for the eleven o'clock meal buzzed with fresh conjecture.

At noon the residents in each block were summoned by their Representative who read a short statement from the Colonial Secretary.. the news every one had been waiting for so long. Hostilities had ceased! "Be cautious and prudent," the statement ended. That meant no exultant cheering, no visible celebrations, no outward demonstrations of victory, because until Allied troops re-occupied the colony, prisoners and internees were still at the mercy of the armed Japanese: who could guess what their reaction might be to a situation in which they had been so humiliated?

"It's finished, we're free," people said over and over again, but it soon transpired they were by no means free. Japanese officers were still nominally in charge of the camp but remained discreetly in their headquarters, their guards remained on duty outside the perimeter of the camp, while British Police internees patrolled the camp itself. Mr. Gimson as Colonial Secretary gave orders, the most important of which was that no internees were to leave Stanley until permission was given.

"We couldn't get into town even if we wanted to, unless we walked," Hilary said as the nurses streamed back to their rooms.

There were parties throughout the camp, using iron rations carefully hoarded against a siege. Hunger was satisfied for the first time for months, even years. Electricity was re-connected after a year without it. Dusty hot plates were pulled out from beneath beds and meals and drinks were heated; the lights were on everywhere as soon as darkness fell.

Debate and conjecture went on all night. How soon would the Allies come? When would husbands and fathers and boy-friends in the Kowloon camps be re-united with their Stanley kith and kin? And when would the men in Japan return to Hong Kong?

Next morning a fire engine clanged into the camp, the drivers two of the technicians who had left Stanley two weeks before; on learning that the war was over, they had returned in the first form of transport they could find, and quickly spread the news that the rest of their party of 200 were safe and well in Kowloon.

In the afternoon a small launch brought three British Officers from the Kowloon camps, with scrappy notes from other prisoners of war to their relatives in Stanley - and an assurance that many more visitors would come as soon as transport could be obtained.

Still the thrills of the day were not over! Early that evening a British plane flew over the camp doing a Victory Roll and dropping leaflets which warned the internees to remain in their camps until the arrival of an envoy to organise supplies of food, clothes and medicines, and to liaise between the Japanese authorities and the British authorities in camp until the Allied Forces appeared.

"Which Allied Forces? British or American?" some one wondered out loud.

"Or Chinese?" Among the rumours had been one that General Chiang Kai Shek was to become Governor of Hong Kong, but no one took it seriously.

With lights everywhere and no curfew, the camp was alive that night with strollers exchanging ideas and rumours. It was while she was outside the Married Quarters, looking for Pamela, that Hilary heard the first whisper about a new kind of bomb. "That's why the Japs gave in," said some one. "There's a notice about it."

She hurried towards the notice-board and wormed her way through the crowd to see it. There she read that Russia's entry into the war against Japan, and the dropping of atomic bombs on two Japanese cities, had brought about the surrender.

"Atomic bombs? Whatever are they?" puzzled voices were asking.

"They're the ultimate in bombs," said an expert. "Let's hope they weren't dropped near our p.o.w. camps there."

Pamela's work at the hospital had become a trial. She longed to be free to range about the camp, watching every new development in these thrilling, unpredictable days, with fresh rumours every hour, and sudden issues of extra food. Chinese fisherfolk in bobbing sampans poled their way to the water's edge, bartering fresh fish and bananas across the barbed wire in exchange for old clothes. Already internees were neglecting to collect their rice and stew, being satiated with much more delectable goodies.

Five days had passed since the declared end of the war, and still no envoy or troops had arrived, nor any message from them. There was a great yearning for some contact with the outside world to dispel the fear that there was some sinister reason why Hong Kong remained isolated and apparently forgotten. When some one reported that a busload of men from the Kowloon camps had arrived in Stanley, Pamela writhed at her desk, wondering if Belle's husband Keith was among them. An hour later, Hilary led Keith into the office. Painfully thin, walking like a matchstick man, his face and limbs burnt darker than his khaki jacket and shorts, he beamed broadly as soon as he saw her.

"Dear old Pam! Why, you look great!" He hugged her and kissed her soundly. Later, in her room they chatted endlessly. Keith produced the few post cards he had received from Belle in Australia, then added slowly "There's another one Belle sent - from England; she and the children went there last year because.. I'm afraid your Mother died, Pam, so Belle was needed to look after your father, he's in very poor health."

Pamela felt she should cry, but it was hard to remember her parents - she had only lived with them for two years out of the last fifteen. What did affect her was the realisation that after Keith had reclaimed his family and taken them to his next posting, someone else would be required to look after her father - herself. Up to today, the barrier to peace of mind had been the knowledge that she must tell her parents she had become a Roman Catholic, and that she intended to marry a Eurasian; now there was an even greater anxiety - that she might find herself with no future at all other than staying in England indefinitely to nurse her father.

She had not as yet mentioned Danny to Keith, putting off the difficult moment. It was a relief when Danny himself turned up at her door just as Keith was due to leave.

"This is my friend Danny Russell," she said. "Danny, meet my brother-in-law, Keith."

"But I know you, don't I?" Keith shook hands heartily. "The best musician in town, if I remember rightly?"

"Nice of you to say so," smiled Danny.

"We're just on our way to the bus," Pamela explained.

"Right - see you about seven this evening?"

"O.K." Pamela could not miss Keith's first surprised reaction. Something had to be said on the way to the camp gates.

"Danny and I are quite close these days," she began.

"I noticed that." He smiled down at her. "Am I allowed to ask how close?"

"We intend to get engaged after I've been Home and told Dad about him... and something else: I've changed my religion, I'm a Catholic now."

Keith stood still for a moment, then squeezed her arm. "Bravo Pam! You've become your own person at last!"

"But I'm just dreading telling Dad all this!"

"You're 26. You have a right to please yourself, for goodness' sake!"

"I'm so afraid he might try to keep me in England to look after him."

"I won't let him. We'll make some arrangements. You must run your own life!"

They had reached the two battered buses which didn't look capable of running through the camp, let alone negotiating the twisting roads back to town.

Keith gave her a brotherly hug. "It's so marvellous to find you so well after all this! I'll get over again if I get the chance before we're shipped off Home. But Pam.. take things easy, won't you? Remember that camp life has been a kind of marking time, not like normal life at all. Give yourself time to take stock before you make any more big decisions, won't you?"

She knew exactly what he meant; it was disappointing to realise that after his initial encouragement, he had reservations about her engagement to Danny.

The two buses could only carry so many passengers, so a different batch of men from the Kowloon camps visited Stanley each day. It was astonishing how couples united for the first time in three and a half years accepted the inevitability of parting again when the buses left in the evening. They had been told to remain in their respective camps, so they did, realising that until occupying troops arrived, the camps were the safest places. There was no question of returning to pre-war homes; the men travelling from Kowloon had seen ample evidence of wrecked and looted houses and apartments; had seen too that the starved condition of the Chinese population was even worse than that of the themselves: at least food came regularly into the camps.

Linen Boy came one day, hollow-cheeked and transparently thin in his loose grey cotton tunic and trousers. Now there was no bulging white bundle across his bowed shoulders; instead, he carried a little broken-down rattan basket, from which he took out with great reverence a tiny Union Jack which he held up before the delighted internees. Next, he lifted out a pile of envelopes and handed them round to his old customers who beamed with pleasure at the contents - an embroidered handkerchief - something new, something fresh and clean, something personal: such a generous gesture brought tears to the women's eyes.

"You ask your Danny Russell when he's going to bring my money!" Mrs Garrett's daily request to Pamela was getting on her nerves. A few days before the surrender Pamela had persuaded the old lady to sell the last of her ivories, but when the great news broke she changed her mind and wanted Danny to return the ivory; he insisted the deal was too far advanced to be halted.

"Don't forget," Mrs. Garrett called as Pamela made for the door. "Make sure you ask him about it right away."

"I will," muttered Pamela wearily. She found Danny sawing logs outside the Indian Quarters' kitchen. His brown bare torso glistened with perspiration as he strained at the blunt saw, his muscles flexing. His face was serious and intent on the job, his hair flopping across his forehead with every movement. He stopped when he saw her. "Morning Pam!"

"Morning! I won't stay, I'm late already for the office, but Mrs. G.'s nagging me again, I promised I'd ask you about her money."

"I'm sorry she's bothering you. I'll call on her later this morning. See you this afternoon - if the Fleet doesn't get here first!"

Thrilling as these days were, anxiety was mounting at the non-arrival of the promised envoy, or of any Allied Forces: supposing the Japanese had refused to sign the Peace Treaty? Could it all be a ploy on the part of Japan to secure a lull in the fighting - and then start up again? What hope would there be for internees and prisoners under those circumstances?

A disquieting rumour was circulating, too: that some American officers had been hiding on a tiny island off Hong Kong studying tides and weather, and sending radio reports back to base in anticipation of an Allied attack on the colony with 2,000 planes, beginning that very week. Of course it wouldn't happen now that the war was over.. but WAS it really over?

At the end of her morning stint at the hospital, Pamela returned to her room and found Mrs. Garrett sitting on her bed crying despairingly. "He's a thief, that Russell boy," she sobbed. "I'm sure you're in it too, Pamela Doran - you persuaded me to go on selling my ivories!" Her words became mangled with emotion.

Pamela looked enquiringly at Alison who mouthed "He says the guard who took the ivory for valuation has gone.. disappeared. So - no yen."

"I was afraid this might happen when the war stopped so suddenly," Danny told Pamela later that afternoon. There was no point in reporting the matter to Japanese Headquarters because officially Black Market operations were not recognised.

"She's going to report you to the camp committee," Pamela fretted. "She'll make a lot of trouble for you."

"I'm sorry for the old girl, but it's not as serious as it could have been if it had happened a month ago when food was short: she won't starve now. Anyway, I'll help her a bit - I'll give her two thousand yen as a goodwill gesture."

In the end he had to give her five thousand before she would drop her threat to report him, and Pamela's heart ached for his glumness at such a drain on his savings.

The rest of the technicians' group were suddenly brought back to Stanley. Jenny, her face alight, called on Pamela with Logan in tow.

"They've had a dreadful time - haven't you Logan?" Jenny's eyes never left his.

"Pretty grim," he agreed.

"They had to live in broken-down barracks, and only had watery stew and rice to eat, didn't you Logan?"

Before he could do more than nod Jenny rushed on "Then they had to cut up barbed wire with awful pliers."

"Do you want me to tell Pam, or do you want to?" he laughingly reproached her.

"Oh, it's so heavenly to have you back, Logan, telling me off all the time!" Jenny had never looked happier as they walked off arm in arm, blissfully unworried about the vacuum in the colony which was causing such concern to so many others in the camp.

At last, Mr. Gimson took matters into his own hands, requested transport from the Japanese Camp Commandant and took a small staff into town to set up an interim administration.

"Very brave of them," John told Sandra. "Anything could happen, with the Japs still nominally in charge, and no peace treaty signed yet."

Sandra had watched him grow further away from her in the past week. He no longer reached for her hand when they lay side by side in their beds at night. She saw his increasing involvement with his office colleagues. His most respectable trousers and shirt lay folded ready for wearing when he should be allowed to leave Stanley. She wept inwardly knowing she was losing him.

It had been all very well to maintain that she would worry about the future when it came: now it was upon her she could not bear to let him leave her and return to his family. She had told him this so often in the last few days that she began to hate the sound of her own voice. He had stopped reasoning with her, just looked sad and guilty, and it tore at her heart the more because she knew only too well that she had initiated their affair.

Ah Ling arrived on the ration truck one morning, holding up a piece of cardboard with "SANDRA LAMB" printed on it in uneven capitals. Looking ten years older, her lined face was wreathed in smiles disclosing gaps between her teeth where the gold ones had been removed and sold for yen to buy food. Her first question when she was taken to Sandra was "Where baby? Where baby?" Sandra told her, and stood stony-faced while Ah Ling sobbed loud and long, then said that Ming too was dead - shot by the Japanese for looting when he was actually burying some of Miles' silverware in the garden to prevent looters making off with it.

The dustbins were crammed with fish bones, banana skins and empty food tins. The twice daily stew contained real meat sent in from the freezer storage godowns.

The daily visitors from the Kowloon camps arrived with their pockets bulging with paper twists of peanuts, white sugar, tea and coffee. From what source? 'Liberated' was the usual laughing reply.

Yet none of these luxuries could dispel the anxiety at the lack of direct contact with the free world. There was a feeling of unreality, suspension, of living in no-man's land. An ancient wireless sent in to the camp supplied periodic news bulletins; reception was poor and the news disturbing, telling of delays in the signing of the Peace Treaty, of problems in organising envoys to get to the various camps, and there had been two separate incidents of Allied planes flying over Japan being fired on by the Japanese.

In this uneasy atmosphere, more officials essential to the running of the colony were sent into town to work. Mr. Gasson called on Pamela to tell her he was due to join the temporary administration the next day. "You are likely to be called in before long," he said, "so have your things ready packed."

"Lucky old you!" was Hilary's envious comment when Pamela told her about this. "I wish some one would send for me." She had drooped noticeably since news trickled through of the cataclysmic effects of the two atomic bombs dropped on Japan which had triggered off the surrender. Apart from a vague statement that prisoners of war would be flown out of Japan as soon as feasible, the only hard news was that supplies of medicine and food had been parachuted into the camps, bringing vigorous waves and cheers from the men most of whom appeared to be almost naked.

"Conditions there must be dreadful if they've no clothes," Hilary wept to Keith when he visited Stanley a second time.

"I expect they were wearing fandushis," he said cheerfully. "We were all issued with them, they look like napkins, and we wore them to save our decent clothes for the cold weather."

But none of the excitements of these days could prevent Hilary from sliding further into depression. When a list was put out of those due to be sent to England on the first available ship, her name was on it.

"But I can't leave Hong Kong until I know about Rod," she sobbed. "If he's alive he'll come here to look for me, I couldn't bear not to be here."

"Everything's hypothetical, remember," Pamela soothed. "Sure there's a list - but no ship yet, and by the time there is, I'm certain we'll have had news from Rod."

She wasn't certain at all. The casualties as a result of the atomic bombs were still not known, but it was obvious they were unparalleled in human history and misery.

"A PLANE WILL DROP SUPPLIES INTO THE CAMP TOMORROW."

Stanley was electrified by this notice, but the next day was stormy; rain cascaded down and the sky was overhung with thick cloud. No one could imagine a plane appearing in such weather - but it came, it came! - a huge shining American plane, flying very low, so slowly and carefully. Great oblong packs were pushed out and floated down on different coloured parachutes - green, scarlet and white. Spectators moaned and sighed at the sheer beauty of those glorious splodges of colour swaying this way and that until they settled on the open ground between the quarters. There were screams of sheer exuberance every time the plane turned, made another measured approach and dropped more packs. Here at last was tangible proof that Stanley was not forgotten.

After the final drop the plane flew over the camp once more, at such low altitude that it seemed it must hit the roofs. There were beams of delight at the sight of two large men leaning out of the side of the plane, smiling and waving - men who were free, men who had probably had a bath that morning, and eaten eggs and bacon for breakfast! The fourteen packs proved to contain small supplies of medicines, cigarettes, food, toiletries and stationery - little enough among so many, but sufficient to lift morale sky-high.

The next morning tens of planes repeatedly zoomed over Stanley, dropping cartons of cigarettes. Spectators on the rooftops peering out to sea could glimpse the Fleet advancing majestically towards Lye Mun Pass, then disappearing from view as it approached the harbour.

Convinced that Naval officials would soon arrive in the camp, every one made hectic preparations to look their best. Flags of all nations represented in Stanley were hurriedly attached to poles already erected on the grassy space outside Mr. Gimson's room in the Married Quarters. In the midst of all this, Pamela was told to prepare to leave for town that afternoon to work for Mr. Gasson. As she could hardly wear her old khaki shorts for this occasion, she had already borrowed Hilary's floral skirt with which she wore her least-faded T shirt.

"I just wish I had some decent clothes," she said to Danny, when at four o'clock he carried her camp bed and belongings to the gates to await the promised transport.

"You look great." Danny squeezed her hand.

"I don't feel great, and my shoes are murdering my feet!" They were the brown suedes she had worn during the fighting and all she possessed; the heels were badly angled, the soles holed and the toes scuffed; many soakings had caused the suede to shrink and her bare heels and toes were already pinched and rubbed.

A dusty car appeared on the road and slowed down at the gates, but it was not the expected transport; the occupants were senior members of the Secretariat one of whom called out "Admiral Harcourt will be here in a few minutes, tell everybody to assemble!"

Every internee within earshot shouted the magic words "Admiral Harcourt's coming!". People who didn't know they could run sped from all corners of the camp, congregating outside the Married Quarters.

Pamela was torn between keeping watch for the transport into town, and witnessing the official relief of Stanley.

"Come on," urged Danny. "Leave your stuff here! No transport is going to get through with the Navy on its way, is it?"

With one anxious backward look at her worldly possessions abandoned by the roadside, Pamela allowed Danny to hurry her up the road to the join the crowds on the grass. A great cheer echoed at the first glimpse of the line of naval vehicles flying the R.N. flag. Marines arrived first, large blooming men with cheeks so pink that they appeared to be wearing makeup, the pinkness emphasised by their their glaring white starched uniforms. They sat upright in an open top green vehicle such as had never been seen in Hong Kong before. Two large shiny cars followed, one carrying Admiral Harcourt and his retinue and the other Mr. Gimson and other Government officials. Some one started to sing 'God Save The King' then every voice joined in. Tears coursed down many cheeks. The Union Jack was hoisted, then the flags of the other nations. A lone bugler sounded the Last Post, and some 2,000 voices, husky with emotion, sang 'Oh God Our Help In Ages Past'.

"Three cheers for His Majesty the King!" called the Admiral. The response was deafening and echoed round the hills while the Admiral made a brief speech, ending with his regret that he could not remain longer in Stanley as he had other urgent commitments.. a reminder that Hong Kong was not the only place to be relieved.

"So this is really the end," Danny gave Pamela a quick hug. "I'm beginning to believe it at last."

"I keep expecting to wake up! Look Danny, I must get back to the gates quickly, I dare not risk missing the van or whatever it is." She pulled away from him and struggled through the crowds which were in no hurry to disperse until the departure of the Admiral and his retinue.

"I'm losing you," he said flatly as he caught her up. "You won't need me in your new life now the war is over."

"Don't be so silly! Of course I'm thrilled to be called in to work, but we'll be able to see each other, and I'll write when I can."

"Make sure you do! I'll get into town as soon as I can wangle it."

By now a dozen other men and women summoned to the town were waiting at the gates; among them were Lois and Norah from the Secretariat staff.

"So glad you're coming too!" Pamela beamed at them. "I'd been feeling a little apprehensive."

"I won't wait," Danny muttered with a scowl, and walked swiftly away.

Pamela started to run after him but the others called her back because the transport was arriving - a decrepit orange bus, half of its windows glass-less, and some of the centre floor boards missing.

She quickly forgot Danny's miserable face as the bus left the camp and swayed and bumped over unmaintained roads, in many places overgrown by unrestrained bushes and plants. When it went across puddles, water sprayed up on to the passengers through the gaps in the floor. Now and again they passed a tiny group of Chinese outside pathetic homes made of old doors and wooden crates; despite their extreme poverty, these people grinned and shouted a welcome and waved enthusiastically.

"Look at THAT!" Pamela, with the rest of the passengers, shrieked at the first glimpse of the harbour which was dominated by three British men-of-war, fully lit in the dusk.

"Pinch me!" demanded Lois. "Go on, pinch me, someone!"

Norah obliged, and Lois sighed blissfully "It's true! The Fleet really IS in."

Once in the environs of the city they were shocked into silence by the obvious neglect and poverty. The streets were dirty and almost deserted, the small number of Chinese about contrasting shockingly with the jostling crowds of pre-war days. Every one looked pinched and skeletal. The tram lines were empty and rusted, the only transport cars and trucks flying the R.N. flag.

They were to work and live in the French Mission building near the Colonial Secretariat which had been badly bomb-damaged. Walking through the huge ornate doors, across the mosaic tiled floor round the little square of garden beside which Pamela had four years earlier received a blessing from an unknown priest, she found it hard to recapture her thoughts that day when fearing extinction from enemy fire. Now ex-internees in their threadbare summer clothes were hurrying in and out of the ground floor rooms, up and down the wide staircase to the upper floors; telephones were shrilling, people calling, typewriters clattering, even though it was seven o'clock at night.

"Ah girls, you've arrived: good!" Mr. Gasson appeared from one of the rooms carrying a sheaf of papers. "Plenty of work for you to do tomorrow."

The girls were directed to a room on the top storey with a polished floor instead of the bare tarred ridges in the rooms in Stanley; there were real beds with ample bedding; there were chairs, a wardrobe and a dressing table with mirror. This was the first time Pamela had seen her full reflection since the surrender in 1941. She stared at this unknown self, with skin burnt brown, and skinny arms and legs. Her face seemed to have become longer, with hollowed cheeks and slight furrows across her forehead. She grimaced at her cropped hair, kept that way for coolness and because it was more hygienic, then sank blissfully into an old armchair, revelling in its softness, and eased off her crippling shoes.

Lois lent her slippers to wear to dinner, which was served in a ground-floor room - an introduction to civilisation. There was a table, with a white laundered cloth; there were flowers in a vase; there were Chinese serving boys; there were enough chairs to seat all the diners, and a folded serviette at every place.

And the food! Creamed tomato soup, with croutons floating on top; hamburgers with mashed potato, beans and eggplant; to follow, pineapple enclosed in pastry, and coffee with milk AND sugar. Even the luxuries sent to Stanley during the past two weeks paled into significance - and smokers shook their heads in disbelief as cigarettes were proffered and lit for them by the table boys.

One of the clerks ran into the room carrying a portable radio, announcing "We've just heard there's going to be a local broadcast to the world." He put the set on the table and twiddled the knobs; after much noisy oscillation a thick American voice boomed: 'This is George Moorad representing the Columbia Broadcasting System and the London Daily Mail, speaking from a jubilant, liberated and rather chaotic Hong Kong. Royal Marines from a British Task Force have been ashore since early afternoon.'

As the slow, level voice described the joyful welcome the Fleet received, Pamela kept reminding herself that this was history which she herself had witnessed, and now was being relayed all over the world: perhaps her father and sister in England were listening! 'You can spot a Hong Kong internee a block away,' Moorad continued. 'His gaunt legs and arms show up too clearly his tropical shorts and summer shirts. Many are prematurely white, with deep sunken eyes'.

"Do we really look like that?" demanded Lois indignantly.

Tired though she was, Pamela found it difficult to sleep that night, as the events of the day kept surging into her mind. A shrill bugle call from the nearby Naval Yard penetrated her fitful dreams and she found she had to take her turn in the bathroom queue. There was real soap but alas no hot water. The utility companies were doing their best to assemble their surviving staff but were hampered by years of neglect and lack of essential equipment for repairs.

Breakfast brought another taste of Heaven: real porridge with tinned milk and white sugar. ("There's two months' ration sitting in that bowl," some one remarked.) There was also tinned fruit; a fried corned beef cake and potatoes, bread and tinned butter and marmalade.

"I don't think I can stand up, let alone work, after all that," groaned Pamela, but within five minutes she was caught up in the frantic activity of the office. The girls were constantly in demand by any one who wanted a memo or letter typed; they also had to answer the two telephones which rang incessantly, involving tiring journeys up and down the stairs and in and out of the offices to find the persons required. Above all this clatter was the continual roar of planes, so near and noisy that they always sounded about to crash.

"Sorry you girls have to work so hard," Mr. Gasson said when they covered their typewriters at seven o'clock that evening, but they didn't worry about the long working hours, fired with exhilaration at helping to bring life to the new administration. Every day brought fresh arrivals summoned from Stanley to help turn the wheels of some other public service or business. Every one was given a small amount of Yen as a salary advance - not enough to buy the clothes; they badly needed, but sufficient to pay for beers, cigarettes and ice-creams from the few shops that had opened. The most enterprising was the Asia Company which had regularly supplied groceries to the girls in the Kennedy Close flat.

Now it had converted part of its premises into a mini-restaurant; flags of all nations fluttered round the open door: nostalgic old gramophone records were playing in the background - it soon became a popular meeting point.

SEPTEMBER

There had been blind obedience to the Emperor's order to his men to surrender peacefully. Now the Japanese troops and civilians were behind barbed wire, as much for their own safety against reprisals as for the security of the British and Chinese. Because of rumours that lawless elements from China might filter into Hong Kong to stir up trouble, there was a 9 p.m. curfew.

The Japanese policy of deportation to reduce the number of mouths to be fed had left a great dearth of labour. Food shortages posed serious problems. Hasty exploration revealed that rice stocks in the colony would only last another two weeks. Fuel supplies - wood and coal- were also dangerously low; the hillsides had been denuded by desperate people needing firewood. The present precarious electricity supply was liable to fail, and emergency arrangements were made for warships to provide power until more fuel could be imported.

After five busy says Pamela was given three hours off so hitched a lift to Stanley in a food lorry, wedged between sacks of flour and crates of tinned meat.

The camp had already changed. Every one she met seemed to be chewing something and all the men were smoking. Small naval ships were anchored in the bay and uniformed sailors lounged on the grass surrounded by chattering internees.

First she visited the Indian Quarters, searching for Danny. He was sitting in the shade outside his billet with three teen-age girls, and leapt up the moment he spotted her. Together they called on Hilary and found her lying on her bed, white and ill.

"They say I've got to leave on the hospital ship tomorrow," she wept, "but I can't! I'm only ill because I'm so worried about Rod. I'll be all right as soon as I know HE is, so I just have to stay here until then."

No amount of reasoning and comfort helped; she was still crying when they left. The V.A.D.s' Matron waylaid them outside the block. "Don't worry," she said. "We'll make sure she gets on board, she won't have any choice."

The kindly-meant words gave little comfort to Pamela, who feared the effect of enforced removal on Hilary's distraught mind.

"There's a chance I'll get into town in a couple of days," Danny said as they waited by the lorry while the driver checked the engine. "I've heard a buzz that my bank is trying to start up again, and I'm pretty sure they'll want me in."

"I won't see much of you," Pamela warned. "If your office is anything like mine, you'll be working round the clock."

"Never mind, it will be better than being eight miles away from you. I've missed you so much." In the excitement and bustle of the new life in the city, she had almost forgotten the sensual pleasure of being close to him, the press of his hand on hers, and the kiss he insisted on exacting in front of the lorry driver.

Two days later Danny turned up at the French Mission. "I'm back at the Bank," he announced happily. "Our premises are in a bad state - they were bombed and never got repaired; we're sleeping there as well for the time being. Hey, I've got a message for you from Hilary! She's still in Stanley - kept out of sight when the sick were being taken on board the hospital ship."

"I suppose she knows what she's doing," sighed Pamela. "I just hope her health holds out."

Although the night curfew was still in force, there was time that evening for them to amble into town and have a cool drink in the Asia Cafe. They discussed the current story that all internees and prisoners of war would be shipped out of the colony within the week.

"I'm not going anywhere," Danny maintained. "Where would I go anyway? Better stay here and get a career going again - but I can't bear the thought of you leaving."

"I'll be back before long - remember my job's here." She spoke with a confidence she didn't feel, the spectre of her sick father still hovering.

"You don't have to go if you don't want to, surely!"

"You know very well I have to see my Father," she said reproachfully. "In any case, the powers that be in U.K. have decided we must all be mentally unstable after so many years of internment, and need a break to recover. Do you feel mentally unstable, Danny?" She smiled in an attempt to inject a lighter note into the conversation.

"Only because I might lose you forever if you go to the U.K."

There were daily invitations to visit Naval ships, but Pamela declined, preferring to spend her brief free time with Danny, despite the lauded attractions on the ships. ("Absolutely topping food, NOT corned beef, and NOT rice!" "You've never seen such banquets!" "And the drinks.. wowee!")

The huge grey 'Empress of Australia' arrived, disgorging 3,000 British troops. Looking enormous and intimidating, they filled the streets and wolf-whistled any one in a skirt.

"We girls have been told we can leave on the 'Empress' if we like," Pamela reported to Danny that evening, "but I said I'd stay on here while I'm needed."

"I'll say you're needed. I never needed any one so much as I need you!" Danny's hand tightened on hers meaningly.

"You shouldn't say things like that," she said primly.

"Why not? It's true!"

"We can't really talk like that.. for a long time yet.."

"Oh Pam, Pam," he said despairingly, "You don't understand, do you?"

The next day, as she was tidying her hair in her room after tiffin, a messenger called that there was some one downstairs waiting to see her - "a Naval bod."

"I don't know any one in the Navy," she thought as she went down the stairs, but at the last step her mind added "except Lawrence."

Lawrence it was, devastatingly handsome in white Lieutenant's uniform; he took her hands in his and gripped them firmly.

"Pamela Doran as ever was! How grand to see you again! I met some Government people last night and asked after you - they told me where to find you. Let me look at you!" His eyes, alive with interest, searched her face, and he squeezed her hands again.

She had forgotten his charm, his endearing engrossment with the person of the moment; her heart began to jump.

"I thought you'd been.... lost years ago, every time I heard about an aircraft carrier being sunk," she jerked,

"I've had two ships sunk under me," he smiled, "but I was determined to live to tell the tale - couldn't waste good experiences like that. Can we go somewhere quiet to talk?"

"Now?"

"Why not? It's six years since we met, why make it any longer?"

"But I'm working - and I'm due back in the office in five minutes."

"Who's your boss? I'll have a word with him."

"You can't do that!"

"Anything is possible if you go the right way about it; he'll soon find someone else to do his typing if you're not available. Which is his room?"

While thrilled by his persistence, she couldn't help feeling indignant at this belittling of her job, and stammered "I can't come now, Lawrence. I've shorthand notes to transcribe, and heaps of lists to sort out. I should be free by six though."

He frowned at his watch then said "It will have to be seven. I'll take you to dinner at the Gloucester. In the meantime, dredge up all the facts of your internment, I want to hear every little detail, don't forget!" His smiling eyes swept her face and registered frank appreciation as he walked out of the door adjusting his cap.

For all she achieved in the office that afternoon she might as well have taken it off.

"Feeling under the weather, Pamela?" Mr. Gasson asked when she handed him a letter which would ordinarily have been typed in half the time she'd taken.

"It's the heat," she muttered, wiping her carbon stained fingers on the rag she used as a handkerchief; but she knew it was the magic of Lawrence's appearance which had upset her equilibrium - and it disturbed her.

"I can still get you on the 'Empress' if you'd like to go," he pressed with concern, but she firmly declined. The last thing she wanted to do was leave Hong Kong and the heady excitements - and Lawrence, especially as the alternative would bring nearer the confrontation with her father.

"As long as you're sure you're really fit enough to go on working." He gave a small sigh, and she pushed into the deeper recesses of her mind the suspicion that he still cared for her.

"Some one's taking you out to dinner?" Danny's voice over the phone sounded incredulous.

"Some one in the Navy I used to know years ago," she explained. "He just turned up, out of the blue, this morning."

There was silence at the other end of the line, so she went on "I'll tell you all about it tomorrow."

"If you want to," he said distantly and put the phone down.

As they walked into the hotel Pamela noticed admiring glances at Lawrence from people she knew. The last time they had sat in the Gloucester together she had been the smart one, wearing an immaculately ironed dress and wedge-heeled white shoes, he a cheap civilian suit made by a local tailor; now he was resplendent in his immaculately laundered uniform, and she was still wearing Hilary's skirt which was a little too long for her; the only new item she'd acquired was a pair of white gym shoes.

"This occasion calls for champagne if they can find any," smiled Lawrence,

"Then we'll swop stories."

He told his first; how he'd survived the sinking of the 'Ark Royal' in the Mediterranean; then the more traumatic sinking of the 'Prince of Wales' off Malaya, and rescue by a destroyer which had taken him to Colombo; he'd eventually reached England and taken part in gruelling convoys to Russia. In between all this he'd managed to find time to have a book published about his life in the Navy and was planning another. "That's why I want to hear YOUR story," he ended.

"There's not much to tell, really." Beside his action-filled past, camp life seemed very tame.

"Tell me about the battle first, when the Japs attacked," he prompted. "Where were you when it all started?"

It was difficult to concentrate with his intent gaze on her; his face so close that she was reminded of the gentle kiss in Christchurch Park in Ipswich. Sometimes as he listened, he ran his fingers through his chestnut hair and this reminded her even more of his youthful attraction.

When her halting reminiscences dried up, he said "After all these hardships, is there anything I can get you?"

"Only clothes," she said, "but we've been promised some from the Red Cross any day now. We hate our camp togs."

"You've had a tough time," he nodded, "but believe me, nothing like as tough as the Jews in Belsen."

"Where's that?"

"Belsen, you've never heard of Belsen? Belsen Extermination Camp? Didn't you know that millions of Jews were exterminated in Hitler's camps? You need educating, young lady." He wagged a finger at her. "I prescribe that you see me every evening I'm off duty, and I'll bring you up to date with what's been happening in the outside world while you've been locked up."

Her mind aflutter, she managed to say "I'd like to know all about the outside world.. but I'm not free every evening.."

"Boy friend? Serious? I'm not surprised - you've grown into an attractive wench, so different from the little mouse I first knew at H. & S. Is he from the camp too? Grand - he'll be able to give me another angle: bring him along too if you want to."

She wasn't at all sure that she would.

The new Military Administration arrived and began to take over from Mr. Gimson's Interim Government. These officials brought their own secretaries and clerks, so Mr. Gasson's work gradually ran down. For the first time since leaving Stanley Pamela had a Sunday morning free, and walked slowly up Garden Road to the Catholic Church. It was a strange sensation, going through the gates to the church she had last entered when she was ten years old.

Hesitantly she dipped her finger in the Holy Water font and ventured into what seemed a gloomy cavern in comparison with the bright sunlight outside. Chinese, Portuguese and a handful of Europeans occupied the pews. As her eyes grew used to the muted light, she found the church garish after the stark recreation hall used for Mass in Stanley. Stained glass windows glowed with colour; painted life-size statues on either side of the ornate altar seemed almost an intrusion. The candles had already been lit and their waxy aroma was wafted around by slowly rotating ceiling fans.

She knelt down and closed her eyes to shut out her alien surroundings, and wondered how she could pray with all these visual distractions which reminded her of her misgivings before becoming a Catholic. She kneaded her hands together in agitation and agonised over her problems - then realised she was actually praying, praying for the safety of Roddy and Viola; for help to avoid a stifling future in England looking after her father, and for the ability to sort out her confused feelings... to stop her from thrilling to every attention from Lawrence; from contrasting his initiative and wordliness to Danny's humility and simplicity; to restore the peace of mind she had found in Stanley.

She was thankful that Danny was not kneeling beside her to disturb her prayers: he was spending the weekend with relatives in Kowloon who had just returned from Macau. It was better that she try to sort out her troubled thoughts with single-minded concentration. On either side of her, Chinese matrons fanned themselves continually and jangled their Rosary beads while droning their aves audibly in Cantonese. Half a dozen people stood in line before the Confessional; this triggered off early memories: of her ten-year-old self lurking at the back of the church while Philip queued for Confession, of Celeste Bellario in her long white First Communion dress, of the child Danny coming back from Confession with a serious expression so different from his customary grin... this church wasn't alien after all.

A bell tinkled; an elderly priest in a plum-coloured chasuble emerged from a door at the side of the altar followed by two small boys wearing low-necked white surplices over black full-length gowns; all genuflected and stepped up to the nave.

"In nomine patri et filio et in spiritu sancto" intoned the priest. "Introibo ad altare Dei.." She began to feel at home.

"Where did you meet that guy?" growled Danny the day after he had been introduced to Lawrence.

"In England, when I first started work; then he joined the Navy and came to Hong Kong for a year after you went to Manila, so we met again."

"You seem mighty friendly with him."

"He's interesting. I love hearing all about what's happening in the outside world, and about Ipswich where I used to live and about people we both knew there. He describes things so graphically."

"Are you going to go on seeing him?"

"If he asks us. Don't you see, Danny, he's just as interested to talk to you as he is to me, and he was really intrigued about your life in Macau and wants to know more."

"I've already told him all I can," said Danny shortly. "I thought he was very rude about your appearance - I was amazed you didn't seem to mind." (Lawrence had noticed at once the new skirt and blouse from the Red Cross, and the shampoo and set she'd just had at the hairdresser's. 'Now you look civilised,' he'd commented.)

"I'd have been more annoyed if he hadn't noticed," she tried to laugh Danny out of his sulks.

The 'Empress of Australia' lay in Stanley Bay, dwarfing the Royal Australian Navy mosquito boats transporting internees from the jetty to the liner. The children in every boat continually roared out the Stanley song 'We're going to SAIL AWAY!'. Smoke from the bonfires in the camp consuming rejected belongings disturbed the blue sky. Even Hilary was affected by the universal euphoria, for she had been assured by so many officials that the men imprisoned in Japan would be taken directly to the United Kingdom. Hundreds of men from the Kowloon camps were already on board, waving and whistling from the decks. Not until actually setting foot on the gangway could the Stanley folk believe they were free of internment at last.

Hilary and six V.A.D.s and their Matron were allotted what had once been a luxury stateroom for two on the promenade deck. Three pairs of bunks had been added, but the accommodation remained luxurious to the new occupants.

"Feel this!" One nurse sat on her bunk and bounced. "A mattress! What bliss!"

"And pillows - two each!"

"Sheets, white, starched, ironed sheets!"

"And we've got our own bathroom and shower!"

The joys of the sumptuous dining saloon were even more overwhelming. These passengers had not sat in a chair at a table for a meal for so long that such a simple pleasure delighted them, so did the white damask tablecloths, gleaming cutlery, and hot crusty rolls which they spread with unlimited real butter. Many couldn't manage all the mouth-watering courses that followed, having gorged themselves with too many rolls, but Hilary, her insides knotted with anxiety for Roddy, found it difficult to eat anything at all.

Strolling round the deck afterwards, waiting for the ship to sail, she came across Keith.

"Thought you might be on board!" he greeted her. "Is Pam here too?"

"No, she's staying on to work: I had a note from her yesterday, she says she expects to be on next week's ship - and she's put on two pounds in weight!"

"That's good news! What about you? You don't look as if you've had much extra food since I last saw you."

"Seem to have lost my appetite now there's all this food around," she shrugged.

"You're still fretting, aren't you? Your job is to get yourself as fit as possible! I absolutely order you to start eating properly - Rod won't want to see you looking..."

"Like a scarecrow?" She had been shocked at her appearance in the mirror in the cabin: a gaunt ghost in skimpy flour-bag shorts and a bra suntop made out of a petticoat; huge eyes in a wan face framed with short blond hair bleached white and dry with the constant sun. "Rod probably wouldn't recognise me, and even if he did, he might not like me."

"You're the same person inside." He gave her a re-assuring grin. "But we will all have to get to know our loved ones again when we meet them.. and as for my children, I'm sure even the older two won't remember me, it's been five years!"

When the ship began to move out of the bay, Hilary stood on the deck which was so densely packed that those at the back were sitting on others' shoulders. Strains of the Stanley song competed with 'Show me the way to go Home' and 'Today I feel so happy.'

With so many passengers, even on the second day out Stanley folk were still discovering old friends among the men from the Kowloon camps. Many of the wounded soldiers who had been nursed in the Military Hospital hailed their former nurses with gratitude and exuberance.

Some husbands and wives were united at last, their blissful faces as they held hands and ambled round the deck together brought tears to the eyes of the women whose hoped-for reunions lay in the future - if their men were indeed still alive.

Yet even the most apprehensive could not fail to enjoy this voyage. Every meal was a banquet; there were concerts and film shows. Bales of good secondhand clothes were opened and distributed, the women delighting in brightly coloured dresses and skirts.

But getting Home, that was what really mattered, back to civilisation, family and friends. Mothers with children were determined to put them into school immediately, where they would have full-time education instead of the half-day sessions with few text-books, exercise books, or writing materials.

"I never want to leave England again," many declared. "I'm going to stay there for the rest of my life."

Hilary could think no further than a reunion with Roddy; nothing mattered but that.

On the third morning land was sighted - not Singapore as most travellers expected, but the Philippine Islands, Slowly the liner edged into Manila Bay which was literally a graveyard of half-sunken ships both Japanese and American. Some wrecks were sitting squarely on the seabed, with just masts showing, some baring a rusty bow at a sharp angle; all bore silent witness to the ferocity of the Japanese attack in 1941, and of more recent American counterattack. Even the pier alongside which the 'Empress' berthed was mangled, with twisted stanchions and bent girders.

The reason for calling at Manila was now revealed. Many of the troops aboard were so unfit that they were to spend a week in an American Rest Camp there to recuperate, while all the other passengers remained on the ship until the convalescents returned.

"Cooped up here for a week, in this heat? How can we bear it?" groaned women whose children were already covered with prickly heat. Enviously they watched hundreds of men trooping down the gangway in the early evening; their departure left more room on the decks and in the public rooms, but that was the only advantage to those left behind, bemoaning the enforced delay on the passage Home.

"We've already forgotten to count our blessings," observed the Matron in Hilary's cabin as they tried to sleep that first airless night. "Here we are, with all the luxuries we dreamed of a month ago - and we're still belly-aching!"

"What must it be like in the inside cabins on E deck, when there's not even a breath of air up here with an open porthole?" added Hilary. She was wearing a short vest and pants and had given up trying to sleep; she sat up across her upper bunk, legs dangling, her back against the bulkhead. She must have dropped off eventually because she suddenly jerked awake at the sound of a voice on the tannoy: "...I shall repeat that: would the following ladies please report to the top of the gangway on C deck aft, where their husbands from Japan are waiting for them." A list of seven names followed.

"Whoopee!" By now every one in the cabin was awake, "Let's go and watch!"

"... And also," went on the voice over the tannoy, 'Would Miss Hilary Bately come and meet Roderick Doran?"

Afterwards, she didn't remember leaping off the bunk and stumbling barefoot towards the door; a colleague hauling her back and shoving her arms into someone's dressing-gown: crying and panting along the passageways and down the stairs to C deck; stopping as she neared the gangway, clutching her arms about her in agony in case she didn't recognise him, or, worse still, he didn't recognise her. All she remembered was suddenly glimpsing among the crowd at the gangway the beloved face anxiously scanning every one in sight.

"Here, Rod, here!" She couldn't get through to him, pushed and waved; then her face crumpled as he forged his way towards her, his delighted, unbelieving gaze fixed on her until he reached her. They were both crying and laughing, so was everyone around them. He was almost bald; as thin as she was despite having spent nearly a week in the Rest Camp, and smartly kitted out in new khaki trousers and shirt, brown shoes and socks.

Their unexpected appearance so late at night was soon explained - when the contingent of troops from the 'Empress' arrived in the Rest Camp and it was learned that Hong Kong women were aboard, the understanding authorities provided transport for the men already in the camp whose wives were thought to be aboard to pay an immediate visit.

Hilary and Roddy found a corner on an upper deck, cuddled and talked for the two hours allowed. She confessed her affair with Stefan, and learned a little of the deprived life in Japan and the horror of what Rod had seen of the atomic attack; he could hardly speak about this last experience without shaking. Over and over again he hugged her, saying "Tell me this is true, darling. We're both alive, and we've found each other!"

Parting with him when the transport on the quay hooted impatiently was hard, despite authority's promise that all these men would rejoin the ship before it sailed. It was the longest week of Hilary's life, with far too much time to sit and anguish lest something happened to change the plan.

So few piers were in service that the 'Empress' had to move out into the harbour, tied up to the mast of a sunken ship. The heat was searing, there was no respite from it anywhere - even a cold shower or bath gave no relief because only sea water was available and this left the skin sticky and itchy.

Authority kept its word. One morning the 'Empress' returned to the quay; there, the waiting lorries disgorged Roddy and the other midnight visitors, as well as all the other troop passengers.

"I kept thinking something would go wrong, and you wouldn't get back," Hilary stuttered.

"Nothing could have kept me away - nor ever will again. We'll get married as soon as we possibly can."

"Oh yes, Rod, yes." She had a flashing vision of a wedding from her parents' home in Sidmouth, but he was still talking: "If you don't mind about all the paraphernalia of weddings, we could even get married here."

"On board?" she squeaked.

"I made some enquiries in the Rest Camp," he nodded. "Spoke to the padre, in fact. Marriages can take place while a ship is at sea, the captain can legally perform them if there isn't a chaplain on board. So what do you think, Hil?"

His suggestion had taken her breath away, but she managed to gasp "Oh Rod, yes!"

"No wedding dress, no veil; no bridesmaids, no wedding cake or reception; no honeymoon in Repulse Bay.. O.K.?"

"No nothing - except us," she drooled.

"Half a mo', Miss!" The corporal who had given her a lift into town in the cab of his van which had brought supplies into Stanley leapt out and helped her off. "Here you are." He then climbed on the back wheel hub and brought down the luggage. "Will you be O.K. with that lot now?"

"Yes, thanks so much."

Already a ragged coolie was approaching and pointing to her suitcases. When Sandra asked him in Cantonese to carry them, his grin split his face; it was good to exchange banter with these friendly people again.

Queen's Road was pot-holed, the deep gutters broken; most shops were boarded up. Uniformed servicemen vastly outnumbered civilians; white faces predominated.

Avoiding being shipped away from Stanley on the 'Empress of Australia' had not been too difficult; getting a permit to visit the city for the day was not so easy but she had managed it at last; it was sheer luck that no one in authority saw her boarding the van with her luggage. The final hurdle to achieving her plan was booking into the Gloucester Hotel, and it proved surprisingly difficult, with much pencil-sucking and anxious flipping over of pages and lists on the part of the Eurasian receptionist. Sandra gave the firm's name as surety for the bill and added "You'll see Mr. Bridger is already registered here." Finally convinced, the receptionist told her she would have to share a room with another female, who turned out to be a casual acquaintance from Stanley, a middle-aged Australian news reporter.

The hotel room though shabby was little changed from pre-war days, because the Gloucester had been used as accommodation for Japanese officers. The pre-war Chinese employees were gradually drifting back, but the present chronic shortage of staff meant there was no room service, and Sandra mentally determined to seek out Ah Ling to help - but that could wait: for the moment she had something much more important to do. She straightened her white blouse and pale blue skirt from the Red Cross and combed her tousled hair and touched up cheeks and lips with the remnants of her makeup, then set off for John's office.

The blistered front door proved to be locked. She tried to press the bell button but it remained solid in its circlet of corroded brass: hulloed through the stiff letter-box which gave a view of the dark unlit vestibule. All the ground floor windows were boarded up; so were some on the upper floor, the others were without glass.

She took off one shoe and hammered the door with it.

"Who is it?" John's head appeared through one of the empty window frames on the top floor. "Good God!" His face registered first disbelief and then unmistakable dismay. She had time to prepare herself before he reached the ground floor and opened the door. "What are you doing here? I thought you'd left last week! Come upstairs; lift's not working yet I'm afraid."

She sneezed as she followed him up the echoing stone stairs, and he apologised for the dust. "It's the same everywhere, but better upstairs because there's air through the broken windows."

The main office was in dreadful disarray. Floor boards had been wrenched up and removed, leaving dangerous shards of wood; loose telephone and electric wires sprouted from the damp-darkened walls. At one end festered a a dank heap of torn paper, books, broken spittoons and ashtrays, waste paper baskets, broken bottles and crushed tins.

"We've simply pushed all the rubbish there for the time being," he explained. "Come and sit down in our only chair - such as it is." The rattan seat had a hole in the middle so she sat down carefully. "This is our only desk," he went on, indicating a door balanced across two crazily dented green filing cabinets. "There's not a stick of furniture left in any of the rooms: all looted."

He stood in front of her, leaning against the wall. His hair and face were damp, his clothes dingy and wet with perspiration; his brow creased as he asked "What happened, Sandra? How come you didn't get away on the 'Empress'?

"I decided not to go," she said in a small voice; she had intended to be determined and confident, but was disarmed by his worn appearance.

"That wasn't a good idea, was it?" he said gently.

"I thought it was. You see John" - he was looking at her so compassionately that her voice shook - "You see, after this week without you, I find I can't let go of you after all." Her chin was up in an attempt to keep the tears from spilling down her cheeks.

"My dear girl!" He knelt beside her and took her hands. "This just can't be. We both knew this all along." Now she couldn't stop the tears and his words became jerky and incoherent. "I had no right... can't forgive myself.. you're so young... re-marry, someone more worthy.."

"I don't want any one else." She slumped against him. He put his arms round her and she could feel him trembling. "We have to face it, Sandra, it's over. I can never thank you enough for all you did for me, you kept me alive - "

"For someone else!" she sobbed.

He stood up and regarded her sadly. She forced the sobs back and shouted "I can't accept that we've no future together! I won't accept it without fighting for you. Oh I know in camp I always said I'd let you go back to your family when the war was over, but John darling, I didn't guess then how hopeless I'd feel without you ."

"It's no good, my dearest girl. You make me feel so humble, I shall never forget your caring support; I shall be eternally grateful."

"But not grateful enough," She knew she had finally lost him, but grasped pathetically at what was left. "At least I can be with you until you leave! I'll work for you, there's so much I could do, and you look so tired. I'll get hold of Ah Ling tomorrow, she'll get some coolies to come and clear out this mess for a start."

"I'm afraid I can't ask you to work here, it wouldn't be fair to you."

"To hell with being fair! I choose to work for you, it's my job anyway!"

John shook his head. "I don't want to hurt you any more than I have already, but I must tell you I wrote to my wife last week.. about us, before she could hear it from other people. I've asked her to forgive me; I promised her that the affair was over, and I must keep it that way. Also, Gloria is coming back to work tomorrow so I'll have help. Now I must do the best I can for you. I'll see someone right away about a passage.."

"That won't be necessary," Sandra cut in, standing up and trying to speak naturally although her lips were stiff. "I'm perfectly able to look after myself."

He made to help her down the gloomy staircase but she whipped her arm away from his.

"I'll find someone to give you a lift to Stanley," he began.

"I'm not going back to Stanley! I've booked in at the Gloucester. Oh don't worry, MR. BRIDGER." She spat out his name. "I won't come to your room to try to seduce you again, I won't come within your orbit at all! I'll avoid you like the bloody plague. Go back to your office and write another letter to your wife telling her how noble you're being."

He stood motionless on the landing as she walked proudly down the first flight. When she turned on the lower landing to descend further, he was still there but had slumped against the wall and his hands covered his face. Tears rained down her cheeks but she walked firmly on.

Even though she was now working shorter office hours, Pamela was beginning to wilt, and not only because of the mid-September heat.

"The men from England were right when they said we weren't fit to work," she told Danny as she sank into a chair opposite him in the café after work. "I find it a real struggle to get up these mornings."

"Too many late nights," growled Danny. "What time did Lawrence bring you back last night?"

"Eleven.. just after curfew; we had to drop Sandra off at the hotel first."

"Is she any better?"

"Puts on a good act of being happy, but she's still suffering dreadfully. She's got terrific spunk! Persuaded someone to repair an old car and has made herself an unofficial chauffeur to any worker in the hotel who wants a lift; and she's trying to get herself another billet so as not to be in the same hotel as John, but hasn't managed it yet. I do hope John leaves soon, it will be easier for her to cope then."

"It won't be easier for me to cope when YOU'VE gone, Pam," he said gloomily.

She rapidly changed the subject. "Look, I had a cable from my father today." She pulled the cream form out of her handbag and laid it before him:

'Thankful you and Keith safe stop No news from Roderick stop A home here for you with me stop Come soonest stop Love Dad.'

"He obviously expects me to stay in England forever." she pushed her hands through her hair.

"You're an adult, you don't have to obey his wishes."

"Easy to say that, but he could make it very difficult for me to get away again, especially if Roddy.. if Roddy.."

"Don't talk like that! No news is good news, they say. I've an idea - let's take in a film this evening, there's a musical on at the Queen's."

"Not tonight. A crowd of us from the office are going swimming at nine o'clock to Deep Water Bay, someone managed to get the loan of a van - I was just going to tell you: you're invited too."

"Thanks, but I can't come." His voice was taut, his eyes hurt. She knew why; he'd told her so often in the past two weeks that he wanted her to himself, didn't want to share her with others.

"I do wish you'd join in things more, Danny! I'm longing for a swim tonight, just the thing after such a sticky day, but you make me feel guilty, going off without you."

"No need for you to feel guilty," he shrugged moodily. "It's up to you to enjoy yourself in whatever way you choose."

Touched by the despair in his voice, she covered his hand with hers. "Forget about the swimming," she said. "We'll go to the pictures instead."

The film was a riot of colour and dancing and music; at times she was carried away by it, but whenever Danny's arms tightened about her shoulders her anxieties returned: for the safety of Roddy and Viola; the inevitable confrontation with her father when he learned she had become a Catholic, and the dread of having to play nursemaid to him for the rest of his life.. and worst of all, the subject overshadowing everything else, the subject she had been trying to ignore for a week - Danny. For the first few days following Lawrence's arrival, she'd been dazzled by Lawrence's attentions and mesmerised by his good looks and authority. He had brought a new dimension to her life. He organised launch picnics, evening drives to the beaches, always bringing along colleagues from his ship and throwing out invitations to any girls he met. He distributed copies of his published book freely. It did not take her long to realise that the ambitious young clerk at H. & S. had become arrogant and self-opinionated, and more intent on a brilliant career than on a steady relationship with any one girl. Nevertheless she found his presence stimulating and, with transport at a premium, enjoyed the excursions he arranged. After his exuberance, Danny's company was a relief, but she was greatly disturbed that for those first few days her mind had been full of Lawrence with no room for Danny at all. Could this mean that she didn't really love Danny? Had she subconsciously used him in camp as a sympathetic pair of arms, a shoulder to lean on in her loneliness? And if so, was it right to consider becoming engaged to him?

After the film they walked slowly along the waterfront; it was still a thrill to see Allied warships riding at anchor, dominated by the great dark shapes of the battleships. They stared down at sampans tied up to the rings in the sea wall, and exchanged waves and smiles with the little families on board, squatting in a circle enjoying their evening meal.

"No more news of your ship yet?" Danny asked.

"Just the usual rumour - 'in a few days'." she held back her fervent feeling that the ship could not come soon enough for her; she was weary in body and spirit.

"Can't we get engaged before you leave?" Danny begged earnestly. "I could feel sure then of not losing you.. and it would strengthen your hand against your father if he is as difficult as you fear. Please darling, please!"

"I have to have time on my own to think about the future," she prevaricated. In the nearest sampan a young mother was unselfconsciously breast-feeding a baby, with a child a year older strapped to her back. She thought 'I'm not ready for any of this.'

"I'm so scared you'll never come back," he sighed.

"I'm determined to come back to Hong Kong, whatever my father wants!" Of that, at least, she was sure. "My job is here, after all. But you know, Danny, we could each meet someone else, it is a possibility and we both ought to feel free.."

"Oh Pam, Pam!" His voice was stricken. "Don't even SAY that! I'll wait for you forever! There's no point in my slaving to make a future to offer you if you're not promised to me." He stopped and stared morosely at the slimy green water heaving with flotsam gently against the wall. "I always thought it all too good to be true; you don't love me as I love you."

She didn't know what to say because she couldn't give the denial he needed. "Give me time to think things over," she muttered.

"You weren't like this in camp," he accused. "It's Lawrence, isn't it? You've fallen for him, I could see it right away!"

"I was delighted to see him at first," she admitted, "and he's fun to be with, but there's nothing more. You can see how he plays the field when he comes across anyone who can be of use to him! Look how he spent all last Sunday with Sandra going over her epic journey during the fighting from the Jockey Club to the Military Hospital!"

This cheered him up; he became his old self again, joking about the rats in the office where he was still sleeping: "They've actually eaten the buttons off my shirt, they're so hungry - can't help feeling sorry for the little blighters now we've known what it is to be without food!" They stopped beneath the trees at the top of Battery Path and embraced; she had never known him to be so passionate before; she was trembling when they said goodnight.

"I must love him," she told herself on the way up the stairs. "I wouldn't feel like this if I didn't."

She was flabbergasted to see Sandra waiting outside her room.

"I thought you were never coming Pam!" Sandra's voice was high and plaintive. "The others girls are downstairs in the lounge; they wanted me to wait there for you, but I didn't want to."

"Didn't expect a visitor at this time of night! It's half past ten! Is something wrong?"

Sandra pulled at Pamela's arm as they went into the room. "Let me stay here with you tonight!" She began to cry. "I can't stay in the hotel. I've just heard that John's leaving for Australia tomorrow morning, and I couldn't bear to spend this last night so near him: I'd have to try to see him and talk to him, don't you see?"

Pamela saw with great clarity. There was no spare bed, and the other occupants might object to a lodger, but Sandra's distraught appearance overrode all this. "Of course you can stay; have my bed, I'll sleep on the settee."

It was a dreadful night. The settee was soft enough, but the thick cretonne covering generated great heat. Deep sleep was impossible in any case, with Sandra snuffling, and getting up periodically to lean out of the window smoking. With Lois and Norah also in the room Pamela could offer no words of comfort. She was bleary-eyed when morning came. Sandra was already up and dressed, standing by the window, smoking continuously.

"Come and have breakfast, I'm sure I can arrange it," urged Pamela at eight o'clock.

"No thanks, I'm not hungry. Anyway, I must go now. They're due to leave the hotel in half an hour."

"They?" began Pamela, then stopped suddenly. It was difficult to converse privately in the presence of the other two typists; scenting Sandra's intentions, she conveyed her feelings by shaking her head and pressing Sandra's arm firmly.

"I've got to see him!" Sandra was by now past caring who heard her. Pamela had seen that look so often before, a wilful determination which would brook no interference, whatever the cost.

"We're off to breakfast," muttered Lois, slipping quickly out of the room with Norah.

"Keep a place for Sandra and me," Pamela said, closing the door behind them and smartly turning the key in the lock. Seeing this, Sandra rushed towards the door, shouting "Let me out! I'm going! Let me out!"

"It won't do you any good to see him, only upset you both again," Pamela pleaded earnestly, standing solidly with her back to the door: a scene outside the hotel or on the jetty would be appalling and scandalising.

"That's my business, not yours. Out of my way!" Sandra threw herself at Pamela, trying to move her, scratching and pinching her bare arms. With one hand behind her, Pamela scrabbled frantically at the key, got it out of the lock and gripped it tightly.

"Give it to me! Give it to me, damn you! Trying to do your goody-goody act again, aren't you?" Sandra punched and pummelled, but Pamela kept her hand tightly closed, even when Sandra fastened her teeth over it. With her free hand Pamela fought back, and with her extra height managed to gain ground momentarily to wrench her bleeding wrist away from Sandra's grip.

"I'll kill you for this!" Sandra, attacking again with a fiendish kick at Pamela's back, sent her reeling towards the window. With a lightning movement Pamela tossed the key out then, completely winded, collapsed on to the floor. For a moment she feared Sandra would in her frenzy throw herself out of the window too; instead, she raced over to the door, shook the handle wildly, banged and shouted and screamed, There was no response from outside - every one was at breakfast two floors below. She gave up at last and sank on to her knees with great heaving sobs. "All.. my.. life.." she hiccoughed, "all my life you've criticised me, and preached to me! I hate you, I hate you! You've never really liked me, have you? You just put up with me in your Girl Guide way, and sneered at me ." The sobs took over completely and her words became indistinguishable. She curled up on the floor and moaned like a tortured animal.

Pamela, getting her breath back, slowly sat up nursing her wrist. "I'm so sorry," she offered at a distance, not sure if another attack would be forthcoming. "So very sorry I had to do that."

Sandra turned away from her and moaned again.

"Do forgive me." Pamela moved cautiously nearer. "I really care for you so much, Sandra. It's not true, what you said. You're one of my oldest and dearest friends. I couldn't let you hurt yourself even more."

"I've lost everything," came a muffled broken voice. "Miles, Melly, and now John. I've nothing left at all."

Pamela reached out with her uninjured hand and patted the hunched figure until the tears finally stopped. Utterly defeated, Sandra got up and slouched over to the wash basin and sluiced her face and hands. When she noticed Pamela's bloody wrist she stared at it and cried "God! Did I do that?"

"It's not as bad as it looks," Pamela muttered. "I've got a plaster in the drawer."

"Let me do it." The mad mood gone, Sandra wept her apologies as she covered the angry teeth marks with the plaster. Yes, she admitted in a sad little voice, it would have been a great mistake to have tried to see John again. Of course it was now too late; he would already be on the launch taking him to H.M.S. Vindex in mid-stream. No, she wouldn't have breakfast with Pamela; she would return to her room in the hotel, have coffee then start her morning driving duties.

"Let's go then," said Pamela, taking her arm with a false heartiness to mask the weariness of the bad night and exhausting morning.

"How the bloody hell do we get out of here?" demanded Sandra as they came up against the locked door; they both broke into hysterical laughter mixed with some tears as they hammered for help.

"I'm leaving tomorrow morning!" Pamela couldn't keep the jubilant note out of her voice when she telephoned Danny. "On an aircraft carrier, the 'Skater"; so are most of us from the office; Sandra as well, she's just rung me. I'm finishing work at twelve, can you get the afternoon off?"

At his request, they took a bus to Stanley. The camp seemed very strange, the only occupants a few hundred newcomers of all nationalities. Appetising smells came from the kitchens which no longer sprouted lengthy queues. Everyone wore shoes. No one was working in the gardens or sawing wood.

"You'd hardly believe we really lived here for more than three years, would you?" Danny stared down at the Indian Quarters.

They visited Pamela's old billet. No children played in the porch of Block 3. The first floor landing was bare, with no clue that a mother and child had once lived there behind a patched piece of curtain. Her former room was empty except for a broken spoon and crushed soup tin lying on its side. A kaleidoscope of memories flickered through her mind: Melly taking her first tottering steps; Sandra pirhouetting round the room demonstrating a dance routine in the camp ballet; Hilary standing at the door and declaring she wouldn't share the room with a tart: did all that really happen in this same room?

"Look Pam - at least you've left your mark on the place." Danny was examining the calendar she had pencilled on the wall, the last date crossed out August 29th, the day before she had left the camp.

"What are the rings for?" he wanted to know.

"My birthday; the day Melly died.. and the day I was received into the Catholic Church."

"Why don't we put a ring round today?" Danny pulled her close to him and looked earnestly into her face.

"Let this be the day of our engagement, Pam darling; don't go off and leave me with nothing to count on! I'll be so lonely without you."

She shook her head, wrinkling her forehead. She was tired, her mind still a tangle of anxieties. She took comfort from his enclosing arms, but when she sensed his growing passion she wrenched herself away, muttering "I don't want to stay in here.. it's far too hot.. let's take our favourite walk round the perimeter like we used to every evening."

"If that's what you want, Pam." His face was dejected and he made no attempt to take her arm as they walked towards the cemetery. Here, little had changed, except that no internees sat beneath the shade of the casurina trees, or played bridge beside the massive tombstones of the early settlers.

"Oh Melly!" Pamela sighed as they passed the tiny grave. They sat on the low cemetery wall and gazed out to sea because they had always done so in the days when they dreamed of release.

"Pam, I know you don't want to talk about it," Danny began, "but I must say this. With all my heart, I want to marry you, more than anything else in the world." He kept his hands tightly clasped, he might almost have been praying. "I know damned well we can't think of marriage for years, but if we could only be engaged now, before you leave for England.. I'd be so happy!"

She still wasn't sure that she loved him enough, but she cared about him and worried about him; couldn't bear to see him hurt, longed to take the misery away from his vulnerable face. It would be so easy to agree to his plea: would release her from her uncertainties as well as help to thwart her father's wish to keep her in England.

"Do say yes! Look, I have the ring ready." From his inside pocket he produced a small square black box and snapped the clasp open. "Try it on.," he urged, watching her face.

"It's like the one you sold for some one in camp!" Pamela's eyes rounded as she gazed at the exquisite emeralds. "It IS the same one, isn't it?"

He nodded. "I decided not to sell it, because you admired it so much; so I bought it myself, I did so want you to have it. Last week I managed to get a box for it." He picked the ring off its velvet platform and held it out to her.

"It must have cost you almost all your profits." Her voice was awed.

"It did, but that's only an iota of how much you mean to me, Pam dearest." He took her hesitant left hand and held the ring over her fourth finger. "You will wear it for me, won't you?" How could she refuse?

"If any one had told us three weeks ago in Stanley that we'd be leaving Hong Kong on the 22nd September on an aircraft carrier, we wouldn't have believed them!"

"Or sleeping four deep on sailors' stretchers with fifty other people, and being blasted every morning with 'Wakey Wakey' over the tannoy!"

The ex-internees on H.M.S. Skater accepted their crowded accommodation without complaint: they were going Home at last!

Even in this intriguing new life in the care of the Royal Navy, with constant bells, vertical steel companionways between decks and nowhere comfortable to sit except at the staggered mealtimes, Pamela was missing Danny sorely; she hadn't realised the extent of his moral support and devotion until she was without it. The emerald ring she had accepted with such diffidence was a great comfort and much admired by her fellow-passengers.

"So you've given in at last," was Sandra's comment as she congratulated her. "I'm not a bit surprised. You're both very lucky."

"You'll be lucky one day," Pamela didn't miss the hint of bitterness and wistfulness in Sandra's voice; they had been very close since the fight in the French Mission.

"Perhaps.. after my finances are sorted out and I can escape the parental clutches again," Sandra shrugged. She'd received a cable from her father in Canada saying he would meet her in England and take her home; having no money at present, she could do little else. "It will be good to see the old dears for a while - but not forever."

In point of fact, none of the passengers knew if the 'Skater' was going to take them all the way to the United Kingdom, or drop them off at some port en route, although there were plenty of rumours. They were content to wait and see.

On the fourth morning the sea bristled with tiny islands topped with tropical green trees and bushes. Singapore was soon identified as the carrier dropped speed and manoeuvred carefully into the harbour between countless wrecks.

"You're not going alongside," reported an irritating internee know-all who seemed to have a direct line of communication with the captain. "You're only stopping to take on a few prisoners of war and internees."

Pamela's heart jumped. Of course there wasn't the slightest chance that Viola would be among the new arrivals, but at least she might get news of her. She stood on the Flight Deck, waiting and watching and praying. When a small launch approached she could make out several female figures among the little group sitting on rattan chairs near the bow, but none of them looked like Viola. "Of course she'll have changed in five years," Pamela told herself, keeping her slender hopes alive as long as possible. From her position it was impossible to look down into the launch once it was alongside, so she tore down three companionways to the gangway hatch, but could not get very close because the whole area was roped off and defended by a 'No Admittance' notice. She stood outside the ropes and waited with clenched fists as the first arrivals emerged from the gangway: a bronzed ex-prisoner of war, thin and scabby but beaming in new khaki trousers and shirt; a careworn middle-aged couple looking anxiously back to ensure that their precious luggage was following them; and three youngish women with caved-in faces and shaggy eton crops, all wearing the briefest of shorts and tops. None of them was Viola.

An Army Officer followed the last three ladies and handed over a list to the receiving Naval Officer, said something, and turned to the gangway.

A small girl appeared framed in the hatch, barelegged, with short white hair; she wore miniscule blue shorts and a sleeveless yellow vest and white sandals; her skin was deeply tanned. She was followed by a young Eurasian woman and another Army Officer with slouch hat; he was so tall that he had to bend his head to enter the ship. He whipped off his hat and Pamela recognised him at once - Raoul - Viola's husband: Viola must be coming too! She started forward and came hard up against the ropes. She held up her hand, trying to attract his attention, her eyes fixed on the hatch for Viola.

"Raoul, Raoul!" she shouted. "It's me, Pamela Doran, from Hong Kong. Where's Viola?"

"At last, Pamela!" In one bound Raoul was beside her, shaking both her hands. "I have been meeting every ship from Hong Kong, hoping to find you on board. It is wonderful to see you again!"

"Viola? Where's Viola?"

"I'm afraid.. my beloved Viola didn't survive."

In shock, she could scarcely take in his broken words... shipwrecked out of Singapore... dreadful camps in Sumatra... she died of swamp fever in March...

Not determined, resourceful Viola, stout-hearted and always optimistic! Raoul was still talking, "Thank the Lord she left me something of herself - our daughter, born in Sumatra. Come here Morag and meet your Auntie Pamela."

Viola's daughter, with Raoul's colouring and her mother's candid, laughing eyes, started to hold out her left hand, then hastily pulled it back and held out the right. With brimming eyes Pamela tried to manage a smile as she struggled to accept the fact that Viola was gone. How often in Stanley she had longed to talk to her, ask her advice; had yearned for the time when they could meet again and exchange thoughtful conversations on every subject under the sun.

Raoul introduced Morag's companion Dorina, who had looked after the child when Viola and her best friend died; had brought her to Singapore when the camp was discovered by Allied troops, and hounded the authorities daily until they believed her story that Morag was the child of Viola Tennien who had on her deathbed instructed Dorina to take her to Captain Raoul Tennien.

"Morag and I are waiting until Dorina's father gets here from the Dutch East Indies; then I shall take Morag to my parents' home in Switzerland and give her all the lovely things little girls should have, pretty dresses and dolls." He rubbed his daughter's hair fondly.

"And anuzzer sheep," she said.

"Then you shall have one, love! I am always hearing about this sheep! Dorina gave her one as a present in the camp and it was lost in the excitement when the war ended."

"I'll get you two sheep - and a Noah's Ark to keep them in," Pamela promised. "I'll send them to you Morag."

Raoul hurriedly wrote an address on a page torn from his pocketbook. "That would be most kind, Pamela. Do, do keep in touch - you were Viola's dearest friend. Will you return to Hong Kong?"

"Oh yes, my job's there and.." - she held out her left hand - "so is my fiancé."

He was instantly contrite at not having noticed the engagement ring before. "I was so full of my own affairs! Congratulations! Do I know the so-fortunate fellow?"

Of course he remembered Danny Russell, recalled Viola's mysterious request to write an article about him in the Hong Kong newspaper. He was eager for news of her family, of Hilary and Sandra, but they could only speak briefly because all around them were activities indicating that the ship was preparing to depart - curt instructions over the tannoy; running feet; the throb of engines. She was allowed to stand at the top of the gangway and watch the three visitors walk down towards the launch, then turned away and wept.

She was inconsolable for days afterwards. "At least you've still got Danny," Sandra reminded her with some bitterness, but Danny was too far away to give any comfort. She could take no interest in the activities provided for the passengers: a rather alarming demonstration of fire power, with shattering bangs and angled orange flashes streaking into the sky; film shows and quizzes; and a dance on the illuminated Flight Deck, the officers resplendent in short white jackets, dark cummerbunds and trousers, the Captain with a silky white shirt billowing in the breeze while the ship's band fenced in by ropes and coloured flags played dance tunes completely new to the passengers.

Just before the last dance the Captain announced the 'Skater's' destination - Colombo in Ceylon. "We're due in at seven hundred hours tomorrow, and shall regretfully say farewell to all our charming passengers - 'Skater' has other tasks to perform in the Far East; but you will be well looked after in Colombo until transhipment to the United Kingdom."

"Well looked after" turned out to be an understatement. From the moment they landed on the jetty lined with Red Cross buses, they were treated like Royalty. For the first time since learning of Viola's death, Pamela's heart lifted. It was simply impossible not to be caught up in the atmosphere of excitement and expectation. The rich scent of cinnamon and flowers mingled with the unsavoury smells of rotting fruit and drains as uniformed WRNS and WVS led them into the buses, explaining "We're taking you to Echelon Barracks first for registration and clothing; after that you'll be driven to your accommodation."

It seemed a magical journey after drab and dilapidated Hong Kong: along straight palm-fringed roads, past native stalls displaying pyramids of brightly-coloured tropical fruits; past dazzling white Government buildings and pastel-shaded houses and bungalows shaded with lush greenery. Apart from a preponderance of service personnel, there was no sign of battle.

Echelon proved to be a huge campus teeming with ex prisoners of war and internees, who found they had the title RAPWI. Here their personal details were recorded after which they were ushered into an enormous marquee whose interior was draped with great swathes of red,white and blue bunting.

"Make yourselves comfortable here," they were told, "and we'll call you in alphabetically to kit you out with summer clothes."

They sank gratefully into comfortable armchairs and were plied with tea, cold drinks, cream cakes and biscuits, and handed the ultimate luxury - English newspapers and magazines: yes, they were several months old, but what did that matter to people who hadn't seen any for years?

When it was Pamela's turn to go to the fitting room, she tried on a navy blue linen skirt and pink blouse and was led over to a full-length mirror to view the effect.

"It's lovely!" she said happily, then stared at a small photograph wedged into the top right-hand corner; stared closer, pointed to it and stuttered "It's.. it's.."

"Yes, it's us with our bride and bridegroom!" smiled the Red Cross helper. "They were married on the 'Empress of Australia' last week and were here four days ago being kitted out on their way to the U.K."

"It's my brother Roddy and my friend Hilary!" Pamela shrieked. "He was in Japan and we thought he was dead!"

"Oh my dear!" All the helpers gathered round, mopping Pamela's tears of happiness and hugging her. They had been so thrilled at having a new bride in their midst that they had looked out the best clothes they could find and insisted on taking a photograph of the newlyweds. It was months before Pamela learned the details of the reunion on the 'Empress of Australia' - but for the moment she knew enough to put stars in her eyes.

After the fitting, baths were on offer. Pamela, in common with most of today's arrivals, had not had a bath or shower for more than three years; in Hong Kong the water supply was still meagre, and on the 'Skater' the long queues outside the ablutions had precluded anything more than a hasty wash. Now, chittering and squeaking like schoolgirls, they occupied the line of bathrooms which were separated only by head-level walls, calling out to one another as they exulted in the joy of washing with gifts of scented soap and bath salts. They shampooed their hair, then wrapped themselves in thick white towels a million times removed from the threadbare pieces of towelling which had served them in Stanley. Hair-dos, facials and massages were available, and doctors, dentists and opticians for those in urgent need.

While awaiting instructions for departure to their billets, every one explored the campus, hailing friends and acquaintances in their new finery. Amidst all the joyousness there were sobering scenes: queues of ex prisoners of war who had only just arrived from some jungle camp; they wore only bedraggled shorts; their hair was close cropped, and sores dotted their bony bodies and limbs.

"And we thought we were hard-done-by in Stanley," muttered Sandra. "Look at them.. some haven't any teeth."

Late in the afternoon they were taken to their billets, Sandra in a large group to the WRNS barracks; Pamela and two nurses from the camp hospital to a private residence in a quiet avenue. A tree-shaded drive led to a cream house with broad verandahs, set in a garden bordered with tropical flowers. A middle-aged British couple named West welcomed them as if they were long-lost friends rather than complete strangers.

The luxury of living in a real house, sitting on gracious chairs and sofas, fingering exquisite brocade cushions; admiring shimmering silk curtains, and gleaming mahogany furniture; and the almost sensual pleasure of sleeping in a real bed at night in a place of such tranquillity was almost unbelievable. Once Pamela woke in the night and had to shake herself to confirm that she wasn't dreaming, and that Roddy and Hilary were together at last.

OCTOBER

The Wests' house was not within walking distance of the town centre, but any service vehicle passing could be hailed for a lift, so every morning the three women thumbed their way to Echelon Barracks. The first objective was a visit to the Information Bureau in the hope of news of transhipment. After that they ranged the campus to seek out fellow internees and compared news, and enjoyed the wide range of amenities available - cinemas, reading rooms, and snacks. They often roamed through the city shops and bazaars, continually amazed at the wonderful array of goods on sale, and carefully spending the tiny advance of Rupees the authorities allowed them - very welcome but not enough to buy more clothes to add to the one-of-everything handouts which were slowly becoming tighter as their wearers gained weight. Most evenings ENSA gave shows at different venues, and lorries toured the accommodation billets to pick up their audiences.

"It's Sunday tomorrow, girls," said Mrs. West at breakfast on the fourth day. "I thought I'd mention it in case you've lost count in your hectic life here! If any of you want to go to church, there are a couple quite near."

The Catholic Church was one of them. Pamela walked in ten minutes early and sat near the back. A group of British sailors occupied the front two pews; elsewhere a scattering of European civilians was greatly outnumbered by families of assorted nationalities. All her prayers these days began with heartfelt thanks for release from camp, and for Roddy's reunion with Hilary. Her heart was still heavy at Viola's loss, but at least she could thank God that Raoul and Morag had survived.

The sound of marching feet on the gravel outside intruded and a shouted order, then, khaki caps in hand, a small contingent of soldiers led by a slightly-built officer walked past her down the aisle and filed into the pews behind the sailors.

The fans depending from the high roof did little to dispel the heat. The backs of the soldiers' shirts were dark with perspiration. Despite sitting near the open front entrance, Pamela had to keep pulling her damp blouse away from her sticky back.

At the end of the Mass she stayed sitting in her place until the servicemen made a move. All eyed her curiously as they passed by, one soldier with so much interest that he bumped into the end of her pew; she could not resist a small smile, and caught the eye of the officer in charge who nodded a wry acknowledgment.

When she left the church, both naval and military parties were assembling in their respective groups. Later, they passed her, in marching order, the Army Officer in front swinging his arms enthusiastically, his face pink with exertion.

"We're taking you swimming this afternoon," said Mrs. West at tiffin. "I can lend you swimming suits."

Feeling like film stars, the three girls cavorted on the golden beach pounded by billowing surf beside the Galle Face Hotel; they swam lazily in the warm water, then lounged on the sand beneath great palm trees, enjoying the warm breeze. Afterwards, on the verandah of the hotel they drank iced drinks and ate sandwiches and cakes and gazed at the deep orange sunset which took their breath away.

Pamela sighed at the beauty all around her, senses stirred by the scent of great flowers among the bushes further up the beach, but she felt restless; wanted to get on with her life yet couldn't envisage what that life was going to be.

There were endless invitations to parties run by the services. She went along because every one else did; danced and chatted with friendly servicemen, discouraging the overfresh, drank iced coca-colas in breathless halls. Sometimes she glimpsed Sandra, usually on the arm of a Naval Officer, but never the same one.

"Didn't I see you at Mass last Sunday?" one of her dancing partners asked her. "My buddy bumped into your pew. You're from one of the camps in Hong Kong, aren't you?"

"I am," she smiled.

"The camp.. I suppose I shouldn't ask, but was it ghastly?"

"Not really. It was almost a relief to get to Stanley at first, after the fighting was over and realising I was still alive. After that, it was frightening sometimes, but mostly rather boring."

"You were starved, though, weren't you?"

"We were always hungry, and short of everything you can think of. The worst thing was the uncertainty, never knowing when it was going to end, and whether we'd still be alive when it did."

It was only that night, in bed, thinking over the day, that she realised the uncertainty still existed. She had survived the war and internment; she was engaged; she no longer lacked for food; she knew she would shortly be on her way to England to be united with all her family, and Danny was waiting for her in Hong Kong: why then, this restless, discontented feeling?

It was a week since she had arrived in Colombo and the answer at the Information Bureau was still "No ship yet." As she turned away with the nurses, Dora and Lynn, her attention was caught by a large new poster on the wall advertising a boxing match and showing head and shoulder pictures of the combatants hunched over their boxing gloves. One of the faces looked vaguely familiar; a second look confirmed that this was none other than the officer in charge of the Sunday church party. His name was at the foot of the poster - Phil Tait. Her eyes widened; she blinked, then read the name again - definitely Phil Tait. Could this be the child Philip she had known? If so, she wouldn't have recognised him - but he had been an enthusiastic boxer even then, hadn't he? And the officer she'd noticed last Sunday had fair hair and freckles like Philip.. At once she wanted to track him down and introduce herself, but how embarrassing if this was another Phil Tait!

She couldn't help saying to Dora "I think I know one of those boxers - anyway he has the same name - but I haven't seen him since we were both ten years old."

"What fun! Why not contact him and ask?"

"I'd look such a fool if I'm wrong, and he'd think I was being pushy. Actually I saw him in church last Sunday and he obviously didn't recognise ME." (Yet, she suddenly remembered, the Tait family was Catholic, like this Phil Tait.)

"Go on Pamela, it's worth a try," Lynn urged.

"I'll think about it," she said.

She had still not made up her mind when that evening, just after dinner, a jeep drew up in the drive. The moment the Singhalese servant opened the door Sandra's voice could be heard calling for Pamela.

She burst into the lounge, shouting, "Pam, I've got a fantastic surprise for you; guess who I've found? PHILIP! OUR PHILIP! He's waiting outside; come quickly!"

There were two uniformed figures leaning against the jeep. They straightened up as Pamela and Sandra came out and the shorter of the two held out his hand to Pamela.

"It's good to meet you again," he said warmly. "It crossed my mind you might be Pamela when I saw you last Sunday, as I hadn't seen you there before the repat ships started coming... then I decided it couldn't be you as you weren't R.C."

"She is now!" Sandra interrupted. "Just imagine, Pam! He looked through all the lists of arrivals from Hong Kong,but it only gave initials and surnames and he couldn't remember our surnames! Just like old Philip to forget - as hopeless as ever."

It transpired that Sandra too had recognised Philip's name on the boxing posters proliferating the barracks; had immediately made enquiries and finally contacted Philip on the telephone.

"I didn't hold out much hope of seeing any old friends from Hong Kong," Philip explained. "You might all have left there years ago, or got yourselves married."

"I did, but I'm widowed," Sandra put in quickly.

"And you Pam?"

"I'm engaged." She noticed there were still freckles on the backs of his hands.

"To Danny, Danny Russell who played the violin," sang Sandra. "You remember him, don't you? He did Felix the Cat at my party, and you walked all the way up the Peak to come to it!"

"I certainly do remember Danny - and that party! Well I'm jiggered!" laughed Philip. "Look we've so much to talk about: let's get ourselves to a cool bar and have drinks."

In an open air café they talked the evening away. Philip's father had died within three months of leaving Hong Kong, and his mother remarried. He had served apprenticeship as an engineer, joined the R.E.s on the outbreak of war, fought in France and survived Dunkirk; then he saw action in Burma and had now been a year in Ceylon. One sister was married with two children, the other single and serving with the ATS.

"Are you married?" demanded Sandra.

"Not me! Had two close shaves, though - almost got engaged but each time the girl threw me over to marry a type with more stripes than I had."

It was only after they had been talking for some time that Pamela could accept the slim young man opposite her for the grown-up Philip. Thoroughly relaxed, one leg crossed over the other, his arms laid along the sides of the rattan chair, he answered Sandra's quickly-fired questions laconically. Gordon wanted to know about life in Stanley; before long conversation developed into an exchange between Sandra and Gordon. Philip was silent and Pamela decided he simply wasn't very interested, but when the time came to leave he turned to her and asked "And Danny, was he in Stanley as well?"

She thought he hadn't been listening. "Only the last year or so. He fought with the Volunteers during our war. Afterwards he went to Macao with his family but then his mother - remember she was my music teacher?"

("Mine too!" Sandra interposed.)

"She died, and she'd made Danny promise to get into Stanley - his father was English so he had a British passport... she thought he'd be better off than in Macao where they had to forage for all their food; at least in camp we were always sent SOME food."

"But we were always hungry," added Sandra fervently.

"We must try to make all that up to you," smiled Gordon, waving to the Boy to bring the chit. "How about having a slap-up meal with us at the Galle Face tomorrow evening?"

"Absolutely super!" Sandra said at the same moment as Philip waved a deprecating hand: "Not me, alas, it's my last night of training."

"You could come along and just have a light meal," Sandra cajoled.
"Sorry, I'm under manager's orders.. Can't even have a fag tonight," he smiled.

There was no telephone in the Wests' house but there was one in Sandra's billet. Meeting at Echelon the next day Sandra told Pamela that Gordon had phoned to invite four or five other girls to enlarge the party at the Galle Face that evening as he would be bringing more colleagues. Pamela was rapidly going off the idea; meeting Philip to talk over old times was one thing, but wholesale socialising with a group of strangers quite another. She invited Dora and Lynn but decided she herself would not go along.

The Wests had an engagement so after dinner she sat alone on the patio overlooking the back garden; owls hooted, bats swooped, and fireflies glowed among the buses; the richly scented air made her pleasantly drowsy.

She was suddenly disturbed by car wheels crunching on the drive; the door bell rang twice before the sleepy Boy responded, then Philip was announced.

"Come to take you to the hotel," he said, explaining he had suddenly decided to join the party after dinner for dancing, and finding she was not there, left at once to fetch her. Pamela's heart jerked alarmingly. Warning bells were sounding in her ears as she admitted to herself that she had only declined the dinner date because Philip had said he wouldn't be there.

She started to make feeble excuses. "It's too late.. I'm tired.." but he would brook no refusal.

"I'm under orders to return to the hotel with a dancing partner," he said, leading her out of the house.

"I thought you were in purdah with your training," was all she could think to say as she got into the jeep. "So I am - up to a point - but this evening was too inviting to miss." He started the engine. "Pam, there's something I'd like to ask you before we join the others. Tell me to shut up if I embarrass you, but I'm so intrigued to find you are now R.C.! When did you make the change?"

"In the camp."

"Ah, because of your fiancé, of course."

"No, before Danny came, actually." She told him how she had found comfort in the church after Melly's death, but said nothing of the rifts in friendship that followed.

"The Church is a great help, but it puts terrible restraints on one's personal life." He sighed wryly. "I drifted away in my teens.. couldn't face Confession - I was afraid of shocking the priest! But the war brought me back, I guess I needed all the help I could call upon when things got sticky."

He guided her into the brightly lit hotel. The party was on the dance floor - except for Gordon who leapt up from his chair when they arrived. While Philip ordered drinks, Gordon put in a claim for the second dance with Pamela, taking it for granted that Philip would have the first.

It didn't work out that way. When Pamela had drained her lemonade Philip nodded to her and Gordon. "Go ahead and join the fray, you two: I'm in no hurry to get in a lather." Pamela was astonished and affronted, since he had chosen to bring her to the hotel, then remembered he'd said he'd been ordered to bring a dancing partner, so that was what she was, just an extra dancer.

When the dance was over Gordon and Pamela drifted back to the table where Sandra was telling grossly exaggerated tales of childhood in Hong Kong involving Philip's shortcomings. He didn't appear to mind, a smile on his face as he sat back in his chair steepling his fingers.

The band started to play again.

"I'm dancing with Phil this time," announced Sandra, grabbing his arm. Pamela was quickly appropriated by Gordon again and whisked round the floor. Mechanically she parried with his light-hearted banter, while she was acutely conscious of a pang of pain at the sight of Philip and Sandra circling the floor together. The pain only subsided when the music stopped and every one flopped into their chairs again. More drinks were ordered, chatter and laughter erupted all round her, but she sat silent and inwardly bewildered, trying to analyse her feelings.

"May I have this dance Pam?" Philip was leaning forward and speaking to her across two people.

"Oh yes!" She wished she hadn't sounded so fervent, but she knew that if he had danced with anyone else next she would have burst into tears.

"My favourite tune," Philip said as they danced to 'In the Mood.' He held her lightly and hummed to the music in the tuneless voice which he'd always been teased about at school. Even this slight contact confirmed what she had come to suspect: she was falling in love with him, with the boy she had always cared for and the man he had become. She wanted to be with him anywhere but on a crowded dance floor.

"Are you always this quiet when you're dancing?" He smiled at her serious face. "I know I'm no Fred Astaire, but does it take so much concentration to follow me?"

Unable to explain her tumultuous feelings she stammered "I'm out of practice. We weren't allowed to dance in the camp."

"We must make up for lost time while you're in Colombo, mustn't we?"

"That would be nice," she croaked.

She had to dance with several other partners before Philip asked her again. This time, walking into his arms felt like coming home.

She hardly slept that night. It was no good reminding herself that she couldn't possibly fall in love with Philip because she was engaged to Danny; no good telling herself firmly that she was simply being nostalgic about childhood memories. She knew without doubt that the chemistry between herself and Philip bore no relation to the affection she had for Danny. For the first time, she glimpsed what Sandra had meant years ago when she'd said "You've never been really roused, have you?"

Next morning the visit to Echelon bore fruit: all the ex-passengers of the 'Skater' were down to leave in three days' time on the 'Lowland Monarch'.

"What a shame!" was Sandra's instant reaction. "I'm really enjoying myself here, with Philip and his friends. Are you going to the fight tonight?"

"No fear." She couldn't bear the thought of seeing Philip taking punishment. Yet, when the time came she couldn't keep away: it seemed less agonising to be present and see what was happening to him, rather than not being there and imagining worse.

She had once seen him box as a child, and had cringed then for his safety. Now, she watched with her heart in her mouth, feeling every punch on his slender body, praying for the bell to ring between rounds, entirely oblivious to the baying of the partisan spectators.

Towards the end of the fifth round a cut appeared above Philip's right eye, and his gloves gleamed red every time he tried to stop the blood obscuring his sight; this allowed his opponent to get past his guard and hammer his face freely. Philip staggered backward against the ropes and the other man closed in for the kill. Pamela didn't realise she was standing up shouting "No, no!" until Sandra pulled her back to her seat. At that moment the blessed bell sounded and Philip's seconds led him to his corner. By now his face was covered with blood and the fight was stopped. Pamela gazed fearfully at his corner where he was obscured by seconds working speedily with towels and sticking plaster. Soon he was on his feet, smiling and waving to well-wishers.

"See, he's not too bad at all," Sandra nudged Pamela. "Why ever did you get in such a tizz? I bet he'll be as good as new at the swimming picnic tomorrow afternoon." "I might not come," she muttered.

Her heart told her she loved Philip as she had never loved Danny; her head told her that she had briefly imagined herself in love with Lawrence only a month ago - could not the same thing be happening here? And even if she did love Philip, there was no sign of reciprocated feeling. If only she had Viola to consult!

Constant heavy rain the next day cancelled the swimming party "but we'll see the boys at the NAAFI dance this evening," Sandra reported when the girls met at Echelon. "Philip can't come though, he's on late duty."

Pamela didn't want to go dancing with all these cheerful strangers, yet to beg off when Philip was absent might be misconstrued.. no, she honestly corrected her thoughts, correctly construed as an indication of her interest in Philip, an interest she dared not reveal. She had to attend, though, because this Saturday night dance was open to all troops, and Mrs. West took it for granted all three girls would be going. "A van will call at about 8.40," she said at tiffin. "I'm going too, they need all the women they can get, even old biddies like me, to provide partners for the boys."

It proved more enjoyable than she'd anticipated. Philip's friends were there, so were about 300 other servicemen, all pressing for partners. All wanted to talk throughout every dance, shouting to make themselves heard above the din of voices, music and shuffling feet. Huge flags hung round the walls and from the rafters. Some of Pamela's partners were ex prisoners from the Siam railway; two weeks of good feeding in Colombo had filled out the hollows in their faces and bodies, but their broken teeth, bruised nails and scraggy tufts of hair between bald patches evidenced their recent ordeal.

Gordon managed to waylay Pamela outside the hall after the last dance. "Don't wait for the van, we'll take you and the nurses back," he said. "Sandra's already in the jeep."

On the homeward journey another swimming date was made for the next afternoon. In the exhilaration of the evening Pamela's problems had been pushed to the back of her mind; now she faced them again. "Don't think I can come, thanks," she said; it would be too painful to see Philip again. "There's too much to do to get ready for that ship on Monday."

"What is there to do?" jeered Sandra. "Pack two suitcases, that's all! You're just being cautious old Pam again, aren't you? The boys will get us back early enough to pack, won't you?"

"Easily," grinned Gordon, "but of course, if Pam really doesn't want our company.."

She gave a shrug of surrender.

She woke early the next morning, her thoughts still anguished. In a borrowed dressing gown she stood on the balcony drinking in the magic scene before her; the sun glinting on broad green banyan leaves, bright flowers be-jewelling the garden. Cicadas shrilled, and in the distance, a nasal song interspersed with the twang of a native stringed instrument. She rested her arms along the cool steel balustrade and asked herself again 'What would Viola do if she were me?' Her own instinct was to do absolutely nothing, to distrust her emotions, to try to act normally and allow events to shape themselves; but Viola had acted differently, hadn't she, when she flew off to Chungking when Raoul was injured? 'But Viola knew Raoul wanted her,' she remembered. 'I'm just an old childhood friend to Philip.' Yet, hadn't he made a special trip to seek her out and take her to the Galle Face the other evening? Viola, she felt sure, would make something of that, she would make things happen and hang the consequences. Perhaps she should show her feelings towards Philip.. and it had to be done today, before she left Colombo.

She got ready for church as quietly as possible, for being Sunday only the servants were up and about. As she emerged from the drive on to the pavement, a faint toot made her turn round - and there was Philip sitting in his jeep a few yards back. He ran the vehicle very gently towards her.

"Good morning," he smiled. "Going my way - to Mass?"

"Yes, I am." Taken unawares, she struggled for words as she climbed up beside him. "Where are all your men?"

"They're down for late Mass. I'm not in charge today, and the bloke who is doesn't like getting up early! I hear you had a busy time of it last night."

"It was quite an experience - my feet are still aching. And it was so hot, I'm sure I lost pounds in weight." The stereotyped words revealed nothing of the thumping of her heart at the realisation that he had actually been waiting specifically to take her to Church.

She couldn't help asking "How did you know I'd be going to early Mass today?"

"You did last week, and in my long experience I've noticed that in this respect R.C.s are creatures of habit, so I took a chance; if you hadn't appeared in time for the first Mass, I'd have called for you just before the second."

She digested this casually imparted information, in silence for so long that he added "You don't mind being given a lift, do you? I mean, your fiancé wouldn't object?"

"Oh no, Danny isn't like that.. it's a very elastic engagement because his future is so uncertain. It's.. it's very kind of you to call for me."

He was concentrating on parking outside the church and didn't speak again until they were strolling towards the entrance. "I was hoping," he said slowly, "that we could have a chat together, just you and I, about old times.. before you disappear into the blue tomorrow.

She dared not let herself read into his words what she hoped lay there, and deliberately misconstrued them. "You'll be at the beach this afternoon, won't you?" she said carefully. "We can talk then."

"I think that might be rather boring for the others, don't you? They must be tired of hearing about our childhood by now. Besides, Sandra did most of the talking the other evening: I want to hear more about you, and your family."

He wasn't looking at her, his gaze directed at a line of ants crawling across the mosaic floor of the church porch. "Would the elastic stretch far enough to permit you to come for a drive if I call for you at, say, half past ten?"

Once free of the streets congested with cyclists, elderly cars crazily driven, bullock carts and bowling rickshaws, they sped along straight roads, past stilt fishermen perched in the shallows of tiny bays; slender rubber trees, whitewashed coolie quarters roofed with corrugated iron; Tamil women in bright saris husking rice, grinding millet and scraping coconuts. All the time they exchanged memories, triggering off yet more memories. They stopped at Mount Lavinia Hotel for tiffin, watching great ocean rollers dashing on the magnificent beach below.

"We'd better not eat too much if we're to swim when we get back." Pamela was studying the enticing menu ruefully.

"I was wondering.." Philip was playing the piano on the tablecloth with his left hand. "Are you mad keen to swim with the others this afternoon? I mean, we could stay here instead.. but only if you'd prefer it."

Her heart somersaulted; this was her chance to be positive, to risk showing her feelings. "I... would... prefer... it." She had a mad desire to cover his restless fingers with her hand. "I'd like that very much."

"That makes two of us. Now we can order a decent meal! Sort out what you'd like while I find a phone and let the lads know not to expect us this afternoon."

When he returned to the table she could no longer hide her delight and pleasure.

"Had to leave a message with the exchange in the Mess," he said, "Every one was out. Made up your mind what you're eating yet?"

"I'd like the set meal, please." It was difficult to articulate those words, because what she wanted to say was quite different: 'I want to tell you I love you, and I think I shall die if you don't tell me that you love me.'

Philip said "A curry for me - you get such smashing etceteras with it." For a slightly built person, he tackled an enormous meal, then leaned back in his chair and asked her permission to smoke. He fished an open packet of Camels from his pocket and she watched mesmerised as his face was illuminated when he put a match to the cigarette. He glanced up and intercepted her steady gaze. "Sure you won't have one too? You look rather wistful."

"No thanks." She tried to compose her features, now anxious lest she had revealed too much.

"You know Pam, that's one of the things I remember most about you, you were perpetually anxious about something; and for some reason, you always worried about ME! Quite bossy about it, too: had I remembered to do my homework, or brought the right books to school? And I've never forgotten the time I turned up for the Art exam with an indelible pencil, and you broke your drawing pencil in half and sharpened the other end to lend me. I depended so much on you - I missed you when I went to school in England and had to depend on myself."

"I haven't anyone to nanny now," she smiled.

"What about Danny - or doesn't he need nannying?"

"Oh no, he's very organised. He has his future all mapped out."

Philip fiddled with his watch strap, then said "Mind if I ask you something very personal?"

Her heart leapt again, then she quickly reminded herself that he had preceded the mundane question about her change of religion with just such words. "No, go ahead," she said as calmly as she could.

"How long have you and Danny been engaged?"

"Since the war ended.. about six weeks." She dared to add "Why?"

"Just curious." He blew a smoke ring and changed the subject. "What shall we do this afternoon? We could drive up to Kandy.. only thing is we'd need to turn round and come back almost at once, it's a long way; or we could.."

She cut in boldly "Can't we just stay here? It's so beautiful and relaxing."

"Suits me. Won't be able to swim though - we haven't brought our togs."

They meandered round the hotel gardens, among arches covered with bougainvillaea and clumps of huge white lilies before sitting in the shade of magnolia trees in comfortable rattan loungers. They discussed their respective careers.

"I've got another three months before I'm demobbed," Philip concluded. "I'll be in U.K. in January." He seemed completely undecided about his future. "Something will occur to me when the time comes," he smiled.

"You ought to make some plans," Pamela remonstrated. "I can't talk though - I'm no good at making decisions, I've usually had them made for me."

"You mean you're a good little girl who does as she's told," he laughed. "Yes, you always were. Sandra was the rebel - and still is from what I've seen of her this past week."

Pamela nodded. "We've had terrific rows during the past years but we've both survived them. I admire her strength of character." She sketched the tale of Sandra's escape from the Jockey Club during the war. "And she was pregnant at the time!"

"I'm greatly impressed. And what did you do during the war Pam?"

"Damn all," she shrugged. "Just tootled back and forth between the tunnel below Government House and my digs in town; and typed whatever was put in front of me - nothing I can boast about to my grandchildren, if any."

"You and Danny planning a big family?"

"I don't know, we've never discussed it." She flamed with embarrassment and guilt, knowing now she had no future at all with Danny Russell.

He glanced at his watch. "It's half four. If we leave soon we can link up with the swimming party when they end up at the beach restaurant for tea.. or we can stay on here and take in the Tea Dance. What's your preference?"

She looked down to try to hide the turmoil she felt must show in her face. With all her heart she wanted to stay with him and dance with him, but feared that once in his arms she would be unable to conceal her feelings.

"You really are bad at making decisions," he drawled, "so I'll decide for you - we'll stay here and dance."

It was just as she had feared - and hoped; when his arms went round her she knew she belonged with him and no other. In between dances they sat out on the terrace eating wafer thin sandwiches and sipping iced tea.

"We go quite well together, don't we?" smiled Philip; strands of his blond hair had been blown adrift by the ceiling fans above the dance floor, making him look even more endearing.

"I've never felt so.. comfortable dancing with any one before," she said with honest fervency, then blushed and tried to modify the declaration by rushing on "I've had some terrifying partners in pre-war dances! There was one who used to swoop all over the place, with me hanging on for dear life - he thought he was the cat's whiskers."

"Was it a tango? I'm not up to that I'm afraid."

"No, it wasn't a tango." The words didn't matter, it was simply important to keep on talking, to say anything to stop her from showing her surging feelings. "It was just.. a dance.. and I wasn't long out from England and such an amateur! Sandra's a super dancer, isn't she? She used to dance in the shows in camp; she could be a professional if she wanted to, I expect you've noticed."

"I don't really want to talk about Sandra." He took her hand and held it tightly. "I'd far rather talk about you."

All day she had been afraid to believe the signs; now she bit her lip and shivered a little.

He bent his head nearer, his expression very serious. "I don't usually say this to engaged young ladies, but it so happens that I'm in love with you Pamela, damn it."

"And I love you," she whispered. "I've known for days but I didn't know what to do. I never dreamed you.. felt the same."

Regardless of other guests at the surrounding tables he bent forward and kissed her gently. "I've been longing to do this," he murmured into her hair, "but I couldn't see how it could be accomplished, with you wearing Danny's engagement ring."

"I can't wear it any more." She pulled it from her finger and slipped it into her handbag. "I can't possibly marry him now, even if.."

"Even if what?" He held her left hand and caressed her fingers.

"Even if.. you're not serious."

"I'm bloody serious, my love. I want us to be engaged right away, before you leave tomorrow; and to get married as soon as I've got myself settled in some job after demob. I'm sorry for Danny Russell, but you're MY girl."

"Oh Philip, Philip!" She had no other words to describe her happiness and love.

They spent the rest of evening sitting on the warm sand holding hands and marvelling at this miraculous meeting in Colombo. When other loungers moved away, Philip gathered her into his arms and kissed her again and again, with mounting passion. It hadn't been difficult to resist Danny in such a mood, but it took every ounce of her will-power to break away from Philip.

"You're right.. time to call a halt. I do apologise." He lit a cigarette.

"No need to apologise," she said shakily; she couldn't bear to see him looking abashed. "Don't think I didn't like it but.. you know what I mean."

He nodded wryly. "Just as well you're leaving tomorrow - at least we'll escape from 'occasions of sin.' When I was a kid I always used to wonder what that meant when I read the prompt list of sins in my prayer book before Confession! Dearest, I think we should be on our way back - we've a lot of business to sort out before we say goodbye, but first I must make sure I haven't rushed you into all this.. I haven't asked you yet if you will marry me. Will you?"

"Oh please, yes!"

He pulled her up off the sand and exacted another long kiss before they walked to the jeep. On the drive back he said "I should tell you that I'm a very bad financial risk. I'm overdrawn at the Bank and I'll be unemployed in four months' time. I've no idea what or where my next job will be. Can you accept that - take me blind?"

"Of course!" She was dizzy with darting thoughts: she would resign her job; she would never return to Hong Kong. "I'll get a marriage gratuity from the Government," she remembered, "and my pay for the internment years."

"You'll be worth marrying for that alone," he grinned.

She told him her fears of becoming permanent nursemaid to her father. Philip brushed this aside. "Between your brother and sister and ourselves, arrangements can be made for your father. He's had his life, it's our turn now. You'll be doing your bit if you stay with him until we're married."

"I could get a job locally for a while." Nothing seemed impossible with Philip at her side, not even the dreadful task of writing to Danny and returning his ring.

"Do it tonight," Philip urged gently. "He must know as soon as possible, but I think we shall have to keep our engagement secret until the letter is posted."

She nodded, but wondered how she could disguise her happiness from her friends, especially after the last lingering kiss in the jeep outside the Wests' house.

When she went indoors Mr. West shot out of the lounge. “Here you are, Pamela!” The relief on his face was plain. “You’ve had us all worried. My wife is at a neighbour’s house, phoning round to try to find you.”

Before she could reply Lynn thundered down the stairs in her night-gown. “Where have you been Pam? We’re all frantic, wondering what had happened to you.”

“I went with Philip to Mount Lavinia for the day.” She kept her ringless left hand covered as she went upstairs.

“And half the night too. You might have told us!”

“We didn’t know we were going to be away all day at first.. and Philip phoned his Mess from the hotel and left a message.”

“None of the boys got the message; in the end we assumed you were with Philip, but nobody knew for certain..”

“Hurry up and do your packing,” Dora urged. “It’s eleven o’clock and the van’s coming for us at seven tomorrow morning.”

“It won’t take me long.” She was in another stratosphere, aware only of her own emotions. “I have to write a letter first.”

“Write a letter?” chorussed the two nurses incredulously. “At this time of night?” They stared in bewilderment as she sat down to do so.

He was waiting on the jetty which was crowded with ex passengers from the ‘Skater’ when she arrived with Lynn and Dora. Then she hadn’t dreamed it, yesterday had really happened! She handed him the package to post to Danny.

“I’ve got something for you.” He pressed a tiny box into her hand. “Wear it when you’re ready to,” he whispered. “Sorry there wasn’t much choice - I had to knock up a jeweller this morning. I hope it fits; if not you can have it altered.”

Standing side by side, decorum had to be observed - they were simply old friends who had had an unexpected reunion in Colombo. Only a slight wink from Philip when their eyes met confirmed what had passed between them the previous day. She intercepted a shrewd exchange of looks between Lynn and Dora and tried to hide a smile.

“Hullo Phil!” Sandra was pushing her way through to them. “Grand of you to come to see us off! We missed you at the beach yesterday - what happened?”

“Otherwise engaged,” Philip smiled, and Pamela wanted to giggle. They could only squeeze each other’s hands tightly as a last goodbye because Sandra stayed chattering until the moment of embarkation on the launches.

The busy harbour had no interest for Pamela now; only the receding figure on the jetty mattered. She was in a daze when she clambered up the gangway to the black-hulled ‘Lowland Monarch’. Her life had been turned completely round in the last twenty-four hours. Where most of the passengers explored the ship after they had been shown their accommodations, she could only sit on her bunk in the four-berth cabin and dwell on what had happened to her. Had it not been for the little package in her bag she might again have wondered if she was dreaming. The ring was very modest compared with Danny's, it was of slender silver with a tiny diamond either side of a larger one. She tried it on; it was slightly loose, but if she continued to put on weight it would soon fit snugly. Hearing footsteps in the corridor she quickly pushed the ring and box into her bag.

"Here you are!" Sandra appeared. "Some one said this was your number. Not bad in here, but come and see my cabin, it's super and there are only two berths in it!"

"In a minute." She couldn't bear to keep her secret from her closest friend for any longer. "Look," she said, holding out her left hand.

"What at?"

"My ring finger; I'm not wearing Danny's ring."

"Don't say you've lost it! That gorgeous ring!"

"No, I haven't lost it. I've sent it back to Danny because.. I've changed my mind. I'm going to marry Philip instead."

For a full minute Sandra looked at her in silence, then stuttered "So that's what was going on yesterday! You can't do this to Danny! You've only known Philip, grown-up Philip, for ten days! You can't ditch Danny just like that, it's cruel, it's wicked."

"I know it's dreadful of me, and I'm most terribly sorry." After all the emotion of the past two days, tears came quickly. "But I'm in love with Philip, I can't do anything else but marry him."

"Then you couldn't have been sincere when you took Danny's ring!" Sandra stood back as if she couldn't bear to be too near. "No one could change their mind so quickly.. you must have known in Hong Kong you'd never marry him.."

"He kept on begging for an engagement," Pamela mumbled miserably. "He wanted to be sure I'd come back. I had to give in."

"You wanted a prop, you mean!" Sandra went on mercilessly. "You told me you were scared stiff your father would make you stay in England forever, so you used the engagement as a prop to give you the courage to stand up to him. My God, all these years I've thought of you as goody-goody-two-shoes, and myself as the one who breaks all the rules! I've put up with your endless lectures! You've looked down on me for my faults and I've always accepted that you were the good one. But not any more! This will ruin Danny for life; you know better than any one his sensitivities about being Eurasian, he'll think that's why you changed your mind and it will destroy his confidence for ever. He'll never forgive you, and neither will I!"

She stormed out of the cabin, banging the door closed behind her. Pamela slumped back on the bed, shaken and weeping. So much of what Sandra had said was true.. she should have resisted Danny's pleas for an engagement; in her guilt-ridden state, she could believe Sandra was right in maintaining she had used the engagement as ammunition against future arguments with her father.

The ship began to throb with life. She got up, washed her face and went on deck. Steely sun dappled the water: glared on the buildings surrounding the harbour and paled their bright colours. Somewhere, in that slowly receding city, was Philip, promised to her for the rest of time - a prospect which diminished the ugly scene with Sandra. She edged through the crowds towards the rail and, with her companions, waved to every one on the ships they were passing to the accompaniment of a cacophony of hooters and whistles - and a shower of coal smuts.

She glimpsed Sandra at the stern, standing with her back against the rail, in rapt conversation with several ship's officers, and felt sad that their long friendship had ended like this - yet she couldn't blame her.

She intended to go to bed immediately after dinner, but decided to take a turn round the deck first.

"Pam, can I have a word?" Suddenly Sandra was at her elbow.

Pamela nodded, not taking her eyes off the scudding sea, and bracing herself for another onslaught.

"Look, I'm so sorry. I shouldn't have said what I did."

"Most of it was true."

"Even then.. you took me by surprise, the words just came out. It's dreadfully sad for Danny. I've thought of nothing else but you two and Philip these last few hours, and I realise you of all people wouldn't lightly change your mind, not my cautious old Pamela."

"Thanks" was all she could manage in gratitude.

"This means you're giving up your job I suppose? Not going back to Hong Kong?"

"I'll go where Philip is," she nodded.

"Starting all over again, really. I'll have to do the same, I suppose." Sandra sighed deeply. "I'm getting used to having lost John, but I just can't imagine what the future holds for me."

"Funny, when we were in camp, we talked endlessly about what we'd do when we got out - have lots to eat, comfortable beds, and things like that." Pamela moved closer and their hands were touching on the rail. "But I don't think we ever really thought about the future in practical, realistic terms; release just seemed a great goal, and when achieved, everything would be all right. We forgot we'd have to take decisions, and run our own lives again, didn't we?"

THE END